The
Resurrection
of
Joan Ashby

The
Resurrection
of
Joan Ashby

A Novel

CHERISE WOLAS

FLATIRON
BOOKS
NEW YORK

THE RESURRECTION OF JOAN ASHBY. Copyright © 2017 by Cherise Wolas. All rights reserved. Printed in the United States of America. For information, address Flatiron Books, 175 Fifth Avenue, New York, N.Y. 10010.

www.flatironbooks.com

The Library of Congress Cataloging-in-Publication Data is available upon request.

ISBN 978-1-250-08143-8 (hardcover)
ISBN 978-1-250-16658-6 (international, sold outside the U.S., subject to rights availability)
ISBN 978-1-250-08144-5 (e-book)

Our books may be purchased in bulk for promotional, educational, or business use. Please contact your local bookseller or the Macmillan Corporate and Premium Sales Department at 1-800-221-7945, extension 5442, or by e-mail at MacmillanSpecialMarkets@macmillan.com.

First Edition: August 2017

10 9 8 7 6 5 4 3 2 1

For Peshka Rudolph,
who would have been a writer had the world been different,
who told me I was one, when I was just a child.

And for Michael,
everything else.

It does not matter what you choose—be a farmer, businessman, artist, what you will—but know your aim, and live for that one thing. We have only one life. The secret of success is concentration; wherever there has been a great life, or a great work, that has gone before. Taste everything a little, look at everything a little; but live for one thing. Anything is possible to a [woman] who knows [her] end and moves straight for it, and for it alone. I will show you what I mean.

If she has made blunders in the past, if she has weighted herself with a burden which she must bear to the end, she must but bear the burden bravely, and labor on. . . . If she does all this,—if she waits patiently, if she is never cast down, never despairs, never forgets her end, moves straight towards it, bending men and things most unlikely to her purpose,—she must succeed at last.

—Olive Schreiner,
Story of an African Farm

If I told you the whole story it would never end. . . . What's happened to me has happened to a thousand woman.

—Ferderico Garcia Lorca,
Doña Rosita la Soltera: The Language of Flowers

(RE)INTRODUCING JOAN ASHBY

Joan Ashby is one of our most astonishing writers, a master of words whose profound characters slip free of the page and enter the world, breathing and enduring, finding pain or solace, even happiness, seeking a way forward, or a way out, their lives keenly and deeply observed. From the muscular to the sublime, her language renders precisely the shadowy contradictions she finds in human behavior, capturing, distilling, and purifying the complex, ambiguous, often porous lives her people navigate. Through the powerful lens of her work, readers discover the secret hearts of their own temperaments.

Enthralling, riveting, often shocking, her stories are as undeniable as her talent. She has said that reaching the marrow of her people, their quintessential facets, requires her own fortitude, an ability to simultaneously engage and detach, to be passionate yet impassive, and sometimes even remote.

We have been allowed to explore the notebooks she once religiously maintained and still possesses. Labeled *Favorite Words, Books I Am Reading, Quotes Never to Forget, Stories,* and *How to Do It,* they are fascinating reading, for in them the young writer announces, if only to herself, who she is, who she intends to be, what she intends to accomplish in her life.

In the notebook titled *How to Do It,* thirteen-year-old Joan Ashby articulates nine revealing precepts she was determined to follow in order to become a writer:

1. Do not waste time
2. Ignore Eleanor when she tells me I need friends[1]
3. Read great literature every day
4. Write every day
5. Rewrite every day
6. Avoid crushes and love

---

1   Eleanor Ashby, Joan Ashby's mother.

7. Do not entertain any offer of marriage

8. Never ever have children

9. Never allow anyone to get in my way

Eight years after penning these precepts, she burst onto the literary scene with her brilliant collection about incest, murder, insanity, suicide, abandonment, and the theft of lives. She was just twenty-one, the year was 1985, and *Other Small Spaces* was an extraordinary accomplishment. An instant sensation among reviewers, critics, and loyalists of literary fiction, it was a surprise entry on the *New York Times* hardcover best-seller list, where it held for two weeks. The subject matter was disturbing, but the book's unique heralding quality deeply touched readers whose adoration of the work turned rabid and created word-of-mouth interest beyond its initial fan base. Several months later, when this unsettling debut by such a young writer was crowned with the National Book Award, the anointment generated unprecedented attention and controversy. As a result, an enormous domestic audience searched it out, and when the collection was translated into thirty-five languages, its audience became universal. Amidst such excitement and furor, the book reappeared on the bestseller list and remained there for a year, the rare story collection to attain such status. Soon, Joan Ashby was a writer known throughout most of the world.

In 1989, four years after the publication of *Other Small Spaces*, Ashby continued her tremendous success with the compelling and complex *Fictional Family Life*, a collection of superbly interlocked stories with a sixteen-year-old boy at its center.

Fictional Family Life spectacularly demonstrated Ashby's vast range, and the world again responded. At twenty-five, she had a second acclaimed collection. When the book was shortlisted for the Pulitzer Prize, it catapulted to bestselling status and remained on the *New York Times* list for its own remarkable year.

It has been nearly three decades since Joan Ashby published anything new, and in our desire to introduce, or reintroduce, Joan Ashby, we are reprinting excerpts from both of her collections.[2]

We start with "The Last Resort," and "Bettina's Children," the stories that bookend *Other Small Spaces*.

---

2   Reprinted with the permission of the publisher, Storr & Storr.

THE LAST RESORT

For a month, Owl Man has been saying he will let me out of here if I am honest. Again and again, he says to me, "Just once, I want you to do what I've asked. Wake up and write down the thoughts that first assail you."

"Owl Man, *assail* is a glorious word," I say to him five mornings a week when I am hauled in here at ten sharp by colossal black-as-night guards dressed all in white, my scrawny biceps in their paws, my paper-slippered feet dragging behind me. It's a lesson in geometry, the way they gently unhinge my angles and joints until I am seated in the brown leather chair that faces its mate, where Owl Man sits. The guards always wait until I swallow my pills, and when they leave us, Owl Man says, "Let's tackle these easy subjects again. What's your name?"

"Guess," is my regular opener.

"Can you tell me where are you?"

"The Last Resort."

Sometimes when I say that, Owl Man smiles.

Today it's the same routine: Released from my barred and locked room by Jim I and Jim II—my names for them, though the tags on their broad chests say Terrence and Golly V., one American, one clearly Indian-from-India—I'm dragged down a bunch of hallways to Owl Man's office. Then it's me in my seat, the cone of water in my hand, the pills down my gullet, the guard's usual question: "You okay here, Doc, we can stay outside, be available to you?" Terrence does all the talking for he and Golly V., and despite my sustained fury, I think it's sort of nice how Terrence has Golly V. under his wing, the same way the pills are winging their way into my bloodstream.

This morning, after Owl Man shuts the door, but before he begins the usual grilling, I jump in and say, "Got something for you, Dr. Samuel Swann," and it's fun watching his head rear back because I've used his real name.

In the beginning, my hands were shackled, bound together with those plastic handcuffs, but today I've been delivered with my hands belonging to me. I hold them up now, say, "No weapons, just something I've got for you, something that will make you sing and set me free."

Slowly, so slowly, I reach down into the crevice between breasts once lovingly admired and pull out a sheaf of pages. Already the handwriting looks foreign, shaky and disturbed, not at all the beautiful penmanship that used to win me gold stickers in childhood.

"You want to know the thoughts that assail me when I first wake? Well, here you go. Ten pages of my true beliefs," and I drop into Owl Man's flushed palm the whole of my life.

He asks me something real then, his voice nearly tender. "May I read these pages aloud? So we both can hear what you have to say?"

My head is doing the weird pill dance, swinging back and forth like a dying flower in a strong wind, the petals about to fall to earth, to be trampled and turned into crap that sticks, with other crap, to the bottoms of soles. Amidst all the head-bobbing, I say, "Here's my offer. You find the relevant parts and read them out loud, or I shut this down. I don't want to hear all of it again, not from start to finish. I've lived it once, would rather not return for another visit."

"Which would you prefer?"

"I don't know Swann, you're the doctor. I'm fairly certain that in my real life I own a lovely apartment and have two cats who adore me, and once, not even that long ago, I used to have friends, and a serious profession, and I went to movies, and thought about going to the ballet and the opera, and I took hot baths, and never worried about offing myself, and I had a man who loved me and knew how to make me yell out in delight. So, what will it take to get me out of here and back home? What's going to have the most ameliorative effect?"

"Ameliorative effect," Owl Man says. "I like that."

"Me too," I say, in a calm voice that surprises us both.

Owl Man begins to read and I am convinced, first, that I am a wizard with words, how I make them arch like green leaves over tiny beauteous flowers, and send them soaring like silvered planes that leave behind fairy dust in the blue firmament, that I am a remarkable talent. Second, that I am shocked by the person I have become. I do not recall writing, just this morning, about my desire to kill everyone I have ever known. All the throat-slitting, the fish-gutting, the stranglings I intend to inflict on the people I thought I still loved.

Swann's harmonious tone stays even, but I feel a million insects shivering up through my insides, taking up residence in the thin layer of skin that no longer protects me well from the world. When he comes to a stop and looks at me, I pretend I am lamb-calm, whistling through the wind.

"So the gist is, you would like a clean slate, live in a world where you can start fresh, become someone else, have no ties to the past, eliminate everyone currently entwined in your life."

I don't answer, just study his hanging diplomas in their fake wooden frames, think about the havoc I would wreak in a second on the supposedly innocent, how I would demonstrate to every one of them, in slow and painful ways, the taint lodged so deep in their hearts—

BETTINA'S CHILDREN

When Bettina was twelve years old and already half an orphan, her great-aunt—the aunt of her still-living father—gave her a series of books that told the story of Nurse Claire Peters. These books were not picture books; nonetheless Bettina could picture Claire, bright in her white uniform, beautiful despite the small white cap atop her lush blond hair, walking hushed hospital corridors, entering room after room, moving from bed to bed, her cool hands bringing relief, her changeling voice flowing from blue to violet to purple to the prettiest of greens, different colors for different maladies, the right ones always returning her sick and sometimes crotchety patients to vibrant life.

In Bettina's mind, Claire's lips were always shimmering in Claire's favorite pink lipstick, and Claire's eyes, observant and alert, the color of purified honey, were opened so wide that she always saw the truth of it all: what people were like when death was upon them. She held their hands then, to bring them forward to the light.

It took Bettina nearly that entire year to read the twenty-book series straight through, wishing with juvenile hope that her curly brown hair would turn as golden and straight as Claire's, that one day her own lips, thinner than she would have wished, but prettily bowed, would look nice in some similar shimmering pink shade, and when Bettina stacked all the books in her closet, she had decided she would become a nurse.

In nursing school, Bettina found peace with her own uninteresting looks, turning herself outward, focusing quietly, privately, on her natural healing talents; she was often several diagnostic steps ahead of the doctors to whom she was to defer. In the books, Claire never aged or thought about romance, despite being surrounded by handsome doctors, but in her own daily chores as a nurse, Bettina found true love.

At odd times in the staff's cafeteria, she would see one of the emergency room doctors, the tall ascetic one, but otherwise their paths did not cross: Bettina worked up on a general floor, and he down below, where the world washed ashore its human traumas.

One day, that emergency room doctor bought her a tea, a few days later a lunch. Standing in the cafeteria line next to Bettina, he looked down upon her from his great height and said, "I'm Jeffrey Caslon," and Bettina nodded and slid her tray up to the cashier, and he said, "Oh, no, I'm paying. After all, this is our first date." She had not realized it was any such thing.

Some weeks later, on a crisp and starry night, Dr. Caslon led Bettina outside, kissed her with a fervency she returned, and, at his request, Bettina transferred to the emergency room, aligning their shifts. She had not thought she would like her new assignment, but she relished its feral nature, the way the maimed, the shot, the stabbed, and those mysteriously sick arrived in the impure hours past midnight. Six months later, they had a small wedding in the chapel on the hospital grounds. A few months after that, their life then combined into Jeffrey's spartan bachelor flat, he inherited a substantial sum from an old great-aunt of his own.

When Jeffrey said to Bettina, "Would you consider moving to Africa? Do our part to make the world a bit better?" they were in the emergency room, facing each other across the body of a middle-aged man who, in death, exhibited the true dourness that had infected his soul.

Bettina needed no time to consider. She would be Claire Peters on a grander stage, with money in her pocket, love in her heart, her portable nursing skills freely available to those whose locus of birth created lives rife with disease, with too little to eat, with water that was unclean.

Soon, the Caslons were in a remote part of Nigeria. Jeffrey spread his inheritance around, hiring locals to build them a house, and the clinic they named the Caslon Clinic. They received the first shipments of medical equipment brought, on its last leg, in a rickety plane that landed on a dusty strip beyond the village, used as a playground by the native children for their made-up games.

The Caslons were a great draw; their pale skin, their small features, the certainty they exuded, the smiles they bestowed, all of it warmed the villagers.

When the clinic was upright, secured by a front and back door, a roof that could withstand heat and wind, the freshly married couple got to work. The equipment intrigued the villagers, but intermittent electricity made the plugged-in machines of little use to doctor and nurse. At least the village streets were designated by names, unpronounceable at first, but which gave Jeffrey and especially Bettina the feeling that life, despite how it seemed, was not completely freeform. Neither imagined returning home after the locals befriended them, passed their days hanging out on the clinic's stairs, on its porch that the Caslons furnished with abandoned chairs.

The Caslons received care packages of food from home which they shared; serious about abandoning all they had once known, their own prior creature comforts, to prove that people could band together and make something better and finer, although impossible to refine. A year into their life in the Nigerian village, Bettina got pregnant the first time, and then again the next year, and the year after that. She was heeding the Nigerian way.

In the right time, each time, Bettina gave birth to three bouncing babies, two boys and a girl. Children who laughed a lot and smiled early and seemed very intelligent and were healthy, so healthy, until they gained their footing and ran with their friends, mingling in the sweetness of childhood with the ebony-bright village children who laughed without knowing the desperate futures only they faced, or so the Caslons believed with a kind purity in their hearts.

Then once, twice, three times, Bettina and Jeffrey peered into dug-out holes, innards tossed up into mounds just beyond, laying each small wrapped body Bettina had birthed, deep down, to avert the scavenging animals capable of digging to China to get what they were after. Each time, Bettina fell to her knees, shocked by what she now shared with the village women; that there was nothing to keep her, any of them, safe. The Caslons were the same as the people they aided, adding their own blood to the heated red dirt.

Neither was religious, and they refused the crosses the Nigerians, thinking they were offering what was right, carved for them. Instead, they asked for wooden placards upon which Jeffrey and Bettina wrote the names of their dead children—Marcus Caslon, Julius Caslon, Cleopatra Caslon—their birthdays, their death days, marking their entombments in an earth that rarely felt the rain, that the wind blew away in devilish swirls of dust.

A month after their last and final child, called Cleo for short, was laid to rest at the age of three, the same tender age as the others, Bettina stood at the graves of her flesh and blood, and the hot, hard sun seemed ludicrous; death deserved darkness for more than a few hours. She wanted nothing to do with what Jeffrey was offering—a try for a fourth. What was the point of the inevitable prolonged suffering parents and child would endure? Marcus, Julius, and Cleo all set afire by temperatures that traveled up to one hundred and eight, that could not be reduced or assuaged. Three times, sitting by the bedsides of her loves, the fruits of her labor, Bettina had watched the skin peel free from their bones in strips as translucent as butterfly wings.

Jeffrey, brave and stoic, sure their sacrifices were part of his mandate, would not hear of leaving it all behind, this godforsaken country, as Bettina was then calling it, these people who demanded too much. When the rickety plane carrying Bettina was airborne, its small windows blinded by the light, Jeffrey wondered if, from up there, she was looking down, could see his hand raised, the tears on his cheeks.

She did not return to the American city of her birth, where her father had raised her, such as he could, where Jeffrey had plucked a young nurse filled with belief from obscurity, leading her into adventure, then into something else that Bettina knew should not be identified. She never sent a card or picked up the phone to call Jeffrey's parents, his sisters, to say there had been a rift in their marriage, that he remained in the world she had fled from. Instead, Bettina chose a big eastern city where winters were racked with high drifts of dirty snow. Her impressive nursing skills, her experience with diseases most of the doctors had only read about in medical books, allowed her to orchestrate her future: a hospital where she was given free rein over the toughest pediatric unit, with skeletal children who would never enjoy a day at the beach, or play with their older siblings, or fall into or out of crushing love. She cared for their deflated sacks of skin and fat, untested muscles long gone, bound up in heavy blankets, tiny tubes inserted into their tiny veins, watched over by their parents, huddled and grieving, sitting close by, holding tender sets of fingers.

It was too late to save these parents from suffering as she had, though Bettina never kept them at arm's distance. She embraced the parents, she cried too when tears swamped their eyes, and she did what she could to make her sullen, saddened babies, her toddlers with a couple of front teeth peeking through swollen gums, comfortable.

Nigeria had taught Bettina to recognize the irrefutable line, how once it was crossed, it marked the end of time. In the large eastern hospital, when she saw the line crossed, when the parents had gone to the family room for a few hours of desperate sleep, Bettina sent her little foregone loves on to whatever world lay beyond. She emphatically did not view her actions as murder; she was no killer, but a loving nurse whose own maternal history had changed her initial reason for being: when there was nothing left to do, she heeded her training and made the suffering stop.

When they came for her—

Fictional Family Life, Ashby's immensely praised second collection, is a razor-sharp look at family life, focused around a teenaged boy who may, or may not, have tried to kill himself. That unclear violent act is dissected by two sets of narrators: Simon Tabor's family members, and the doctors and nurses who put him back together again. While the truths and lies of real life are debated, broken Simon Tabor remains in his hospital bed, in an inexplicable coma, and in that netherworld, he creates his own alter ego, a boy his own age, also named Simon Tabor, who is stuck in *his* room, creating *his* alter egos—boys who live the fantastical lives both Simon Tabors wished for themselves.

The following excerpt is from "I Speak," the only story in the collection in which the real Simon Tabor speaks for himself:

This is the only time you will hear my voice, the only time I will speak to you directly. Right now, I am on a table in an operating room and the doctor and nurses are racing around, working hard to repair the damage I have done to myself.

This isn't one of *those* stories—about a near-death experience that changes one's life, or a revelation about what happens when a person dies for some minutes and is revived. I haven't died and I won't. I am completely aware of everything going on around me, how, in their gowns and masks, the medical staff look like superheroes protecting their real identities.

Dr. Miner has just said, "Scalpel," and is now slicing into my skin, a zzzziiiippppp through the various levels of dermis, then a sucking sound, my blood spurting all over, and he says in this tight voice, "Clamps, now," and then he's clamping off various of my blood vessels that are dancing like beheaded snakes. Even with all the activity, my hearing is so stupendous I can tell Judith, RN, is sorting through the plates and screws, and Louise, RN, through the pins, trying to find all the right-sized pieces of hardware Dr. Miner will soon insert into my body.

Hours from now, when Dr. Miner finishes stitching me physically back together, I plan to slip into an unexplained coma, and stay there for a good long time. I am looking forward to it. I think it will be fun, and restful, and give me time to think.

Plus, in the five hours I've already been in this operating room, I've discovered my own superhero power: I have the ability to know what's going on in the private lives of these people caring for me.

Like Dr. Miner, for example, he's setting my shattered left femur now, will do the right femur next, and while he's focused precisely on what he's doing, another part of his brain is back home, where just hours ago the woman he loves told him that she doesn't love him, that he is lousy in bed, and that she has been sleeping around. He doesn't want her to pack and leave him, but what else is a real man supposed to demand? I agree—the traitor has to go, who needs to love someone frightful like that?—but I can tell Dr. Miner is weak and this betrayal will affect him for the rest of his life.

And the anesthesiologist monitoring my pulse, calibrating my state of unconsciousness, she's debating telling her husband she wants a boob job, to reduce, not to inflate, and she knows he'll put up a fight, the way he loves doing all manner of things to them, stuff she can't stand, and I can see in my mind the things her husband likes to do. I think the anesthesiologist might be kind of squeamish, because it all looks cool to me.

And Dr. Miner's right-hand nurse, Judith Sonnen, she's handing Dr. Miner a plate to screw into my femur, and she's got a prayer running through her head in a gobbledygook language, praying not for me but for her own strength. Born Esther Sonnenberg, her parents turned into evangelical Baptists when she was a kid and changed everyone's names, and Judith Sonnen thinks she may want to be the Jew she was born to be, reclaim her name at birth.

You can see, right, why I might not want to give up this power I've developed out of the blue.

Eventually, I'll be wheeled into a hospital room, already deep in my coma. Here's the warning. When I'm in my coma, you will hear theories about why I did what I did, posited by those who love me and will rarely leave my bedside: my parents, Renata and Harry, my sisters, Phoebe and Rachel, our occasional housekeeper, Consuela, and my dog, Scooter, as well as theories tossed about by Dr. Miner and the nurses, Judith and Louise, who feel a sort of love for me too, because they have seen inside my body, are invested in my slow progress back toward life.

But don't believe any of them because they will all be wrong.

I was not depressed, psychotic, delusional, did not think I was Christ, or some disciple, or a prophet whose name I can't pronounce. The blood tests will prove I wasn't on drugs. I will, however, be on great painkillers for close to a year.

I have already conjured up my alter ego to entertain me during the silent months to come. His name is also Simon Tabor, and he'll tell you about his life, and about the alter egos he—or rather I—create. Four boys, the same age as us, who live the kinds of lives we

want to live. Both of us Simon Tabors stuck in rooms for very different reasons, yet sharing the same desire to experience other lives.

The bottom line is that my plan to fly did not go as expected. A
lapse in judgment, I agree, and a question to be resolved another day.
I'll have plenty of time to figure it out, but here is Dr. Miner leaning
over me—

It is impossible to overestimate the titanic interest that attended Ashby's
every move during those years when her collections dominated. In an era
that pre-dates our current obsession with celebrity, her stunning success at
such an early age, which also included receipt of a PEN/Malamud, and a
Guggenheim, made her a phenomenon, one of the first literary celebrities
on a modern-day scale. For a time, until she disappeared into small-town
life, photographers often followed her—to the Korean grocery, the Laundromat, on her walks through the city.

Equally amazing is that *Other Small Spaces* and *Fictional Family Life* are
now in their twenty-fifth and twenty-third printings respectively.

In William Linder's first *Wall Street Journal* interview with Ashby, when
she returned from the *Other Small Spaces* book tour, her remarks display
an innocence at odds with the splendidly dark nature of her writing.

"I took a temporary leave from Gravida Publishing, locked up my apartment, and was sent to Columbus, Fargo, Salt Lake City, Nashville, Austin,
Seattle, Los Angeles, San Francisco, Boston, Chicago, and Newport, Rhode
Island.[3] I was raised in a smallish suburb of Chicago, so before going on
this tour, I had only seen that Midwestern city and, of course, New York,
where I live. Seeing America as a new author was an incredible experience.
I read to eager audiences, signed stacks of my books, was interviewed in
hotel lobbies, in white-linen restaurants, in diner booths with gummy
tabletops. I was photographed in local libraries and bookstores and, for
some unclear reason, photographers posed me outside, on the shores of
Lady Bird Lake, on a Newport dock in front of gleaming yachts, with my
toes in the sand and the Pacific Ocean behind me, the camera clicking
away. *Young writer musing* is how I imagined those pictures, all pride and

---

3   When *Other Small Spaces* was published, Ashby, who graduated early from high school
and completed college and graduate school in four years, was a fiction editor in New York
at Gravida Publishing, now subsumed within Annabelle Iger Books, a subsidiary of Hargreen
House.

intention, eyes lowered against the sunshiny rays, the wind whipping my long hair around my throat until I was sure I would choke."

The New York Review of Books conducted an in-depth interview with Ashby that coincided with the publication of *Fictional Family Life*. Much was written about her following *Other Small Spaces*, but in the *NYRB* interview, for the first time she disclosed certain salient facts about her upbringing that helped explain her authorial precociousness, as well as the characters she wrote about, the fine line of their actions.

"I was an early reader, maybe because I was an only child, literally made by people not at all interested in me. It seemed to me that I had crashed through some kind of atmospheric orbit, landed on a planet where I defi- nitely did not belong, and was not wanted, left huddling out in the cold, beyond the tight parental circle of two. Whether that circle was forged before I came along, or as a result of my presence, I've never known. What I did know was that they had no idea what to do with me, and I was left to my own devices.

"Most children in such underloving circumstances would act out, or de- mand their rightful attention, but I was made differently: I interpreted my familial outsider status as an invisible cloak granting me freedom, allowing me entry into a forbidden world where I could hear what was unspoken in the silent spaces and watch the misalignment between people's words and their deeds. I was seven when I crossed over, began stealing what I saw and heard, grafting my thefts onto people I imagined, whose stories I started writing down. My characters became *my people*, their worlds, *my worlds*, and it made me feel whole, happy, and safe. Books gave me succor and my parents' disinterest set me loose as a writer.

"If I had felt a natural kinship with my parents, who knows what I might have found myself writing about, or whether my work would have been of any interest to others. But my parents are who they are, and my upbringing was what it was, and I, through acclimation and natural constitution, was solitary and watchful.

"The concept of love completely mystified me—it still mystifies me— but I have always seen the darkest emotions with absolute clarity, the depths to which people can so easily descend. I gleaned all that in childhood, saw how the theory played out in my own family. It was a short step to believing we all possess the innate power to inflict great damage, even to kill, with the right convergence of events."

Ashby acknowledged that her parents did not intend to read her collections. "They have no interest in my work, are completely indifferent to
me and my career. When I was ten, I handed my mother a story I horribly
called 'The Meaning of Love.' With that title, no doubt she hoped to read
something that might convince her I would end up a *normal* girl. But the
story was about the opposite of love, and she quailed in the face of those
I gleefully murdered, her only comment: 'I don't understand what goes on
in your head, Joan.' She never again asked to read anything that came from
my pen. My father never asked once.

"Their disinterest was my great luck as a writer. I have never felt compelled to harness myself because I have not been burdened by what they
might think. My characters fall apart, immolate, decimate, grapple with
the sinister impulses in their natures, injure themselves and others, kill too,
and I am free from parental approbation. It is a way of writing that I highly
recommend."

When Linder interviewed Ashby again, after the *Fictional Family Life*
tour, she had this to say: "My publisher sent me around the United States
for the second time, which I loved, and also to London, Paris, Rome, Zurich
and Geneva, West Berlin, Cairo, and Istanbul. Switzerland struck me as
odd, but apparently the precise Swiss secretly enjoy reading about lives
that are not neat at all. West Berlin was distressing, knowing what was on
the other side of the Wall. Cairo and Istanbul seemed like random choices
until I was told that *FFL* was a runaway bestseller in Egypt and Turkey, something I could not have imagined. Of course, I never imagined that either of
my books would experience the great success that they have.

"But to answer your question, Mr. Linder, traveling for *Fictional Family
Life* was something else entirely. This was my first time abroad, and being
feted in those international cities was exciting. However, there were
palpable differences between the two tours, because with *FFL*, suddenly I was
no longer a debut writer, introduced instead, and uncomfortably, as the
young and revered Joan Ashby, my name enunciated worshipfully, as if it
were suddenly coated in a gorgeous veneer that should have taken centuries
to develop. And everyone made clear to me—my agent, Patricia Volkmann,
and my publisher, Storr & Storr, the foreign publishers of both my collections,
writers I met, journalists who interviewed me, critics who have written
about my books—that my first novel is eagerly expected. Of course I feel

the pressure. But my own expectations for what I can accomplish likely are grander than theirs, and I feel confident about meeting them."

During the years when her star shone so brightly, some journalists were intent on positioning her as a feminist writer, though she refused such a limiting designation. "On that particular subject, I will say only this: I am a writer."

Indeed, when Ashby wrote about so-called feminine themes, such as love, family, and domesticity, she twisted such themes entirely, reversed them, turned them inside out until they were virtually unrecognizable. In *Other Small Spaces*, her male and female protagonists are children, teenagers, or adults, all ingrained in their lives, and, to various extents, flawed, hurt, suffering, vengeful, angry, kind, thoughtful, sometimes brutal with others and gentle with themselves, or vice versa. The scenes might be domesticated, but she was not writing merely, or solely, about domestic arrangements. With extraordinary beauty and burly power, she wrote about people of both sexes clawing their way out of stifling, smothering, or shrinking worlds, some believing wholeheartedly in living what Ashby called *an out-there life*, meaning a specifically determined life that did not conform to modern-day expectations. Other writers took Ashby up as a cudgel, as proof that being female did not lessen the impact of the work.

She also claimed male territory as her own, especially in *Fictional Family Life*, where she wrote deeply about Simon Tabor's multiple versions of himself, and the adolescent boy's self-imagined cast of make-believe fathers. In writing those daring and unpredictable fathers, juxtaposed also against Simon Tabor's real father, a self-destructing stockbroker who finds personal redemption as an insurance broker in the Bakersfield desert, she displayed her dazzling virtuosity, somehow both luminous and formidable.

Ashby writes for the sake of the work, although, when pressed, she did not apologize for seeking her own lasting place in the world of letters. In a 1988 interview with *Esquire*, she said, "It's not actually possible to write for an audience. Or at least I can't. I write for myself and hope others may find themselves in my work. It takes a lifetime to attain a writerly expansiveness, and finding an audience is the least of it. Of course, when I'm honing a story for the thousandth time, I admit my desire for that audience may have become conscious. I labor to be in charge of my own material, and if that hard work allows me to sit at the table with other serious, great writers of this and past generations, I don't shy away from that. Why would I? I write for myself, but I seek to be read, for the work to be deeply felt."

The Linder interviews and the *Esquire* interview are also interesting because Ashby limited the questions she was willing to answer to her childhood, her life as a young writer, her literary dreams. She never discussed her current personal life. As a result, many of her fans were shocked to learn she had married just before the international tour for *Fictional Family Life* commenced.

In early June 1989, under the bright lights of television cameras, Ashby read to a sold-out, standing-room-only crowd at Barnard College. Afterward, many female members of the audience inundated her with questions about her recent marriage, expressing their dismay. We note that the following transcription of Ashby's remarks are set out here for the first time. The program that aired on PBS did not include these revelations.

"Sometimes I worry, too, that what I have done will end up disappointing myself. Beware of friends encouraging you to take a break from your writing, telling you to have a little fun and celebrate your success, if only for a long weekend. Beware, because your life may move in ways you didn't expect, or want, suddenly hallmarked by the seemingly traditional. In other words, beware of finding yourself living an unintended life.

"I don't normally divulge the personal, but it seems right to share how I ended up here. A road trip a couple of years ago with friends, fellow—or rather female—editors at the publishing house where I used to work. They chose Annapolis because the Naval Academy was there; all those strong and handsome men excited them. I wasn't interested, I had my focus. But there we were on the July Fourth weekend, in a bar on the waterfront promenade. My friends let themselves be swept away, but I held on to my place at that bar, thinking I'd stay and observe and slip back to the motel, make a few notes for the future. Then a man introduced himself to me and his extravagantly long hair was eccentric among all those shorn skulls of the naval cadets.

"If I had figured out immediately the kind of man he was, things might now be different. I believed then, as I still do, that my writing benefits from my perceptual abilities and my observational skills. So I absorbed this man's long hair, his long fingers, his long eyelashes, his romantic brown eyes, and I wondered what a painter or a sculptor, some kind of artist anyway, was doing in this naval bar. He struck me as likely leading a peripatetic life, attributing his unsteady schedule to a muse. But my snap denouncement of him was completely wrong. He was at John Hopkins, a doctor in the midst of a fellowship, specializing in rare eye surgeries, enraptured by his ability to help people see their worlds again. He was home for a visit with his vice admiral father, at the bar taking a breather from the old man who was still angry that his son had refused the navy.

"Groan now, because I know you will. He bought me a drink and said that when he completed his studies he was moving to a small town that had a world-class research hospital and lab where he would work on his theories for revolutionizing neuro-ocular surgery. What I heard in all that was *small town*, and I could not imagine anyone wanting to live in such a place. Two drinks in, I stupidly agreed to see him the next day. That turned into two more days spent together. I could see he was infatuated, but the notion did not fill me with unalloyed pleasure. I was not looking for love. Love was more than simply inconvenient; its consumptive nature always a threat to serious women. I had seen too often what happened to serious women in love, their sudden, unnatural lightheartedness, their new wardrobe of happiness their prior selves would never have worn, the loss of their forward momentum. I wanted no such conversion, no vulnerability to needless distraction. Since childhood, I had kept my literary ambitions at the fore of my mind.

"On the trip back to New York, I refuted my friends' belief that love had found me. 'He's a doctor who looks like a disheveled artist and neither he, nor any man, figures into my plans for my future,' I told them, in those or similar words, and I meant it.

"I held my ground against his romantic campaign of phone calls and handwritten love letters for a while, and then I agreed to see him again, on my own territory. [Much laughter here.]

"Come on, most of you probably would have done the same thing! I didn't anticipate our coordinated humor, or our perfect balance in those other meaningful ways. After that, every third weekend, he took the train to New York or I took the train to Baltimore. I had assumed I would live happily alone, passionately consumed by the lives of my imagined humans, but for the first time, I found my thoughts synced to those of another. I had never before experienced that with anyone. Being cherished took me longer to acknowledge and accept. He makes me kinder, more generous, when I step out into the world, and there is a gorgeousness in seeing oneself in the loving reflected glow of a worthy other.

"When I finally settled into the seriousness between us, the palpable love, it struck me as rather marvelous. Obviously, I put up serious barriers—my work comes first, no children, we'll consider a dog—but he wasn't put off, not even during this insane year with the publication of *Fictional Family Life* and my constant absences.

"What I also discovered is that I'm having no problems writing what will follow *Fictional Family Life*, thrilled that the work contains no words about either of us at all. [Much laughter here.]

"You laugh, but I'm incredibly relieved. The idea of mining material straight from my own life is abhorrent to me. I have no desire to write self-indulgently. I say this with appropriate trepidation, but I think love might make me a better writer, a writer able to delve even more deeply into what makes people human, because I am now experiencing the full range of emotions. If nothing else, discovering I have a speed, other than breakneck, has been revelatory.

"We've bought a small house in a place that calls itself a town but is no bigger than a village.[4] I've been living there for exactly two weeks, most of my time spent in a spare bedroom that is now my study, continuing to work on my first novel. And no, I won't tell you what it's called or what it's about."

The novel Joan Ashby was working on in her Rhome study in 1989 remains a mystery, for she has not published anything since *Fictional Family Life*. The Barnard event would be the last time Ashby read or spoke publicly, and thereafter she ceased granting interviews of any kind. On that evening, twenty-eight years ago, Ashby was wholly unaware that she, newly married, was pregnant.

(Continued after the break)

---

4   In *Ashby Close Up*, an unauthorized 2000 biography, Geoffrey Collins wrote: "When Ashby returned from her successful European tour for *Fictional Family Life*, it was not to her Lower East Side apartment. Instead, she and her new husband settled in Rhome, in northern Virginia. Title records show Ashby purchased the thirteen-hundred-square-foot house situated on four private acres in her name alone."

Part I

ANOTHER STORY IS WRITTEN

Ēka aura kahānī likh di

1

Joan Ashby was frank with Martin Manning right from the start: "There are two things you should know about me. Number one: My writing will always come first. Number two: Children are not on the table. I possess no need, primal or otherwise, for motherhood."

Martin had grinned, looked beneath the checked tablecloth—"In case those imps you don't want are hiding"—then checked what remained in her wineglass. "I'm flattered," he said, "but isn't this sort of discussion premature?"

She had vigorously shaken her head. "Truth is never premature. I don't want to mislead you."

When it was no longer too early for that sort of discussion, when they had acknowledged the seriousness of their love, when Joan had reiterated those two truths about herself twice more—in Battery Park, staring out at the Statue of Liberty, all green and distant, the waves churning in a spring wind, and on a bench in Central Park, reading the Sunday paper, both of them sweating in the humid hundred-degree heat—Martin never hesitated, always answered the same way.

Once, he raised her concerns himself. With both hands over his heart, Martin declared, "My own life plans don't require a version of myself writ small. I don't need anything more, except for whatever time you give me. We're everything together, as special as any couple could be." She laughed because he understood, because he was lovely, because she never intended to be the recipient of such romanticism, but she thought he had the equation wrong: the specialness each possessed had nothing to do with them as a couple.

On a wintery Sunday morning they made a definitive pact: if they moved forward together into the future, they would not sideline their lives with procreation. Joan asked Martin to swear to it as they lay in her bed in her East Village apartment, then made him sit up and raise his right hand and repeat it again. When he said, "I promise. No children," snow began falling, hushing the city, and they stayed beneath the covers the whole of the day. By nightfall, when Martin was tossing his things into his weekend bag, the snow had ceased, but outside it was still silent, not a car or a taxi or a bus tracking through the white drifts that had accumulated. Joan's block, crusty and exhausted, had turned into a winter wonderland.

From her living-room windows, four floors above the ground, Joan watched Martin inching across the coated street in his loafers, his footsteps the first to mar the pristine. He was heading uptown to Penn Station for the 6:05 back to Baltimore. He hurtled over a curbside snowbank, landed on the sidewalk, and stopped. He found her at the window, waved madly, then turned the corner and was out of sight. Fifteen minutes later, Joan was in her flannel pajamas at the nicked wooden dining table long used as a desk, reading the proofs of *Fictional Family Life*, its publication imminent. She looked at the vase Martin had brought her, filled not with hothouse winter flowers, but with the red licorice vines he had learned she liked, the treat she indulged in judiciously, when the work was going well. She proofread late into the night, aware she was smiling, and that she had never worked with such a look on her face. A month after that, Dr. Martin Manning asked Joan Ashby to marry him.

Their wedding was modest. The ceremony, eloquent and stirring, unfolded in a small Manhattan park, with rows of red and yellow tulips in the beds, their petals flaring and open. Joan's dress, long and white, was unadorned, simple, her slender neck, her shoulders, all bare in the early spring sun, her black hair in a braid peppered with tiny white flowers. Martin wore a smart black suit and a serious tie.

There was no family in attendance. Martin's father, whom Joan met only once after they were engaged, had been interred in the Columbarium of the US Naval Academy in Annapolis on a rainy day three months before. And when Joan reluctantly phoned her parents to invite them, upending their pattern of brief every-other-month calls, her mother said, "*Impossible, mais nous vous souhaitons bonne chance.*" Impossible, but we wish you good luck. Eleanor Ashby was not French, and had never been to France, but she fluently—though rarely—spoke the oft-proclaimed language of her true soul, had insisted on Joan's fluency in it as well. For Joan, it was debatable whether Eleanor Ashby actually had a soul, but the French *bonne chance* indicated that her mother was attempting to be kind. Her use of the formal *vous*, rather than the intimate *tu*, an apparent denial of their mother-daughter relationship, did undercut that kindness, but it was better than Joan had expected. "*Merci, maman*," Joan said, relieved she would not have to see them.

The guests were not evenly divided; the groom's far outnumbered the bride's. All of Martin's college and medical-school pals made the trek from whichever states had become home, and ten of his new colleagues from Rhome carpooled together from the campus twenty miles outside of town that housed the hospital and the lab. But Annabelle Iger was there, Joan's former colleague at Gravida Publishing and the closest she had ever come to a best friend, along with the few other friends Joan had managed to make, and keep, during the years before her literary career exploded.

After she and Martin said their vows and slipped the wedding bands on each other's fingers and engaged in their first marital kiss, the small party whooped and clapped. Annabelle Iger said afterward to them both, "Your love makes me desire love in my bones, but only for the short term." Martin said, "Go find my friend Max. He's funny and smart and he thinks as you do," and Joan whispered to Iger, "He has good lips, too." At a nearby French bistro slightly down at the heel, the wedding party drank and feasted and danced until nearly four in the morning.

In the afternoon they woke and Martin said, "Wife," and Joan said, "Husband," such a strange word in her mouth, a word she never expected to apply to a man in her bed, or out of it. She wondered what else it meant, besides spouse, mate, to use sparingly or economically, to conserve. Then they tangled their limbs together again.

The following evening, Martin put Joan's suitcase into the trunk of an idling cab, before he too left the city, headed back to Rhome, to their newly purchased house, to his practice and research, while his bride flew away, for the foreign leg of the *Fictional Family Life* book tour. Her apartment had been emptied out, the landlord given notice of her permanent departure, and when she returned to the States, it would not be to JFK or LaGuardia, but to an airport near Washington, DC.

Then Joan was flying across the ocean, sitting on trains, unpacking in glamorous foreign hotel rooms, reading to large and small gatherings, signing books, afterward spending the evenings with bookstore owners, critics, reviewers, emissaries of her overseas publishers, fellow writers, listening to trenchant debates about which new novels thrilled, which writers had been wrongfully blessed and did not deserve the worshipful, florid praise, whose work was unjustly overlooked, the glare eventually finding Joan again, a press of queries about what made her write, why she wrote what she wrote, when her first novel would be published.

Every day she composed a special postcard for Martin and sent it on its way, a pretty stamp in the corner from the country she was in. When they managed to talk on the phone, he said, "It's great getting mail in our new mailbox. I read your postcards and kiss your signature, then tack up each card on the kitchen wall." When she came home to Rhome, Martin had made a collage of all of her words.

It was two months since they married, three weeks since she had set-tled in Rhome, and Joan's tall, handsome husband was kneeling down, as he had not kneeled when he proposed, and the hands his colleagues called *miraculous* were pressed against her flat belly.

Joan placed her own hands on his head, in a kind of benediction, feeling the silk of his brown hair with fingers that were naked except for the slim platinum wedding band on the fourth. The ring was still an unfamiliar weight, a sight that surprised her several times a day when she looked up from the page rolled into her typewriter and caught its silvery flash.

Her new husband was on his knees on the painted wooden floor in her new study in their new house. The floor was maple, but the stain had taken on a curious orange tinge, and when Joan was finally there, her boxes unpacked, her last appearance in front of a huge crowd at Barnard a memory that still made her tingle, the laughter that rose up when she said Martin did not want children either, only wanted to know if they might one day get a dog, the two of them had painted the floor white. Three separate coats on three successive Saturdays until the floor in her study gleamed.

Martin was kneeling and the heat from his hands passed through her thin sweater, branding her skin, and Joan found herself praying, not to God, or a god, for religion had not been part of her upbringing, but she was invoking her own personal kind of prayer, the soothing she had taught herself in childhood, reciting favorite words—*horological, malevolent, splattering, spackled, fossicking, bedlamite, shambles, oblate, coruscating, shambolic, furbelowed, aperçu*—this silent recitation, word after word, a beseeching, a cry for remembrance, for benevolence, for fairness. One by one, the words clicked through her mind, and then Martin looked up at her and he smiled and Joan saw his smile and felt a rip of fear, her eyes retreating from the beatific look on his face, landing on a corner of the room where she saw they had missed a place, a strip of wood not quite as brightly white as the rest.

"Joan," he said, gripping her belly, as if his long surgeon fingers might cradle the infinitesimal and unwanted that her body was harboring. There was a gauzy shimmer across his brown eyes. She had never seen him shed a tear, not even at his father's funeral, but the threat was there now, and another favorite word passed through her mind, *trembling*, because there were trembling teardrops poised behind Martin's long lashes, ready to fall, and this time she could not look away, could only stare back at him as her body tightened, turned rigid, her heart all at once shocked into pounding, white noise filling her ears, her mind still reciting words—*chaotic, barbate, insufflation, prodrome, otiose, misprision*—but still she heard him say, "I've never been so happy."

She watched him rise from the floor. He was speaking again. "We've got to celebrate. I'll go out and get some champagne and something sparkling and nonalcoholic for you."

And then he was out of her study, his tread heavy on the maple floors as he walked through the rest of their small house, the rattle of his keys as he plucked them from the bowl on the shelf next to the back door, the door slamming, his old Toyota revving up.

The shock did not relax its grip on her. She stood rooted to the white wooden floor, stunned that Martin did not remember their pact, the oath he took twice that snowy day not six months before, that his instinct was not hers, to do away with it completely, right from the start. A quick operation, she barely anaesthetized, her womb left clean and uninhabited, barer even than the bare rooms in this new house of theirs.

She thought of the story in *Other Small Spaces* that had become a revolutionary call among a small contingent of Joan's most fervent female fans, the opening paragraphs flowing right through her:

It felt right to Elizabeth that her hand should be freed of that finger with the rings that pronounced her his property. The stump had stopped bleeding, but there was so much more blood than she expected, a spreading pool across the new kitchen floor, just beginning to stagnate.

Surely her blood would stain the white tiles, the white grout, but perhaps that was as it should be, an indelible reminder of her suffering. She bent to stare into the bloody pool, surprised at its deep hue, a rich, heavy burgundy, like the wines Stuart preferred, not the happy red that pebbled her fingertips from a paper cut at the office or a paring knife nick when she chopped vegetables for dinner. She wondered how difficult it would be to clean and nearly opened the cabinet for the cleaning stuff, but what was the rush, she wondered. She would leave it for another day.

She stood up and felt her bones knitting back into place, as they never had to do before he took to pummeling her. On the new kitchen counter, called Centaur Granite, lay the offending digit. It was rosy when she first cut it off, but it was paler now, a fine sort of blue. Like a work of art, really, a sculpture on a pedestal in a cool downtown gallery, with a placard beneath it that would read Drained of Life.

But the finger glittered because of the engagement ring she had been so excited to own, to wear, a rare and perfect four-carat diamond that sparkled in the sun and had no inclusions, no spots, no clouds, no cavities, nothing to disfigure the view, the opposite of her own pocked eyesight when she had looked at Stuart's smooth exterior, that handsome face, and said, "Yes, Stuart, I say yes," having no idea of the violence he could not contain. And nestled next to the diamond ring, curled up tight around it like a sleeping snake, was the golden wedding band that had always been too tight.

She could not imagine Stuart's face when he returned and saw the bloody floor, her dead finger on the counter in a position of accusation and blame. How strange all that sawing had not damaged its fine tapered shape, had not chipped the polish on the nail. Even now, the shade was still pretty, a pale pink color called Princess Fairy Tale—

Joan thought it might not be too late to slip off her own wedding band, tell Martin their young marriage was at an end, that the only conception she was interested in was what she birthed on the page.

Their house was in a new development, some of the roads still waiting to be paved, the market ten miles away, the wine and liquor store next door. Perhaps there was an hour before Martin returned, and imagining him back in the house, beaming, popping corks, making toasts, set Joan panting, her mouth open like the dog they should have gotten immediately. She felt faint, her vision blurring in the middle, as if her blue irises were turning black, a shade dropping over them. She made it into her chair before her legs gave way, dropped her head between her knees, and waited.

When her eyesight cleared, and her heart was only galloping, she sat up and looked at the shelves Martin had hung, stocked with copies of her two award-winning, best-selling books, all the different covers, the titles in myriad languages, proof that she had readers around the globe. She looked at the goose-necked lamp they'd found at a yard sale when she joined him in Rhome; at the old battered wooden dining-room table brought from New York, on which she had written her stories; at her solid typewriter atop, an Olivetti Praxis she loved; at the four hundred pages of her first novel she was calling *The Sympathetic Executioners*. She wished she could unravel time to the moment before she accepted Martin's offer of a drink in that Annapolis bar.

She looked down at the narrow wedding band on her finger, the inscription—*MM loves JA*—hidden underneath, and thought it would be easy enough to place it in Martin's hand, to separate their belongings, to let him buy the house, or perhaps she would simply give it to him, deed it over as a kind of consolation prize for the end of their marriage. She would return to New York. She had some money now, would not be stuck in the sooty East Village with its pungent streets, its buildings marked with aggressive graffiti. It would take less than a week to pack up and arrange for the movers. While she searched for a new place to live in the city, she could stay with Iger, a senior editor now at Gravida and the new owner of a two-bedroom apartment on the Upper East Side. Joan could accomplish everything, she thought, without losing too much time, without being away from the book for too long. Too much was happening in the lives of Silas and Abe, her young killers for hire, the sympathetic executioners, for her to break stride.

The blare of the ice-cream truck's tune shattered her hectic silence, the song growing louder as the truck journeyed through the unfinished neighborhood, a man yelling, "Wait, wait! You've got two little customers coming!" making Joan think of the lonely, stilted childhoods she and Martin had both endured. His mother dead when both he and she were too young, left with his stern father, ever the navy vice admiral who never wrapped his son in a hug, did not put a warm hand on his head or his shoulder; and Joan's life, unwanted in her parents' house, lost and alone unless she was reading or writing her stories up in her bedroom, or tucked away in the town library doing one or the other. How her parents had stared, as if her connection to them, her very existence, was an unsolvable puzzle. She instantly could see her father at the end of his working day, nearly motionless in his chair, the news on the television, a crossword in his lap, a glass of neat bourbon by his side, head turned away from his wife, from Joan's mother, who stood on the other side of the living room, phone against her well-tended wash-and-set, her lipsticked mouth wide in pretend surprise as she listened to friends' secrets, to gossip making the rounds. The furtiveness between the people Joan called Mother and Father, when her mother hung up the phone and sashayed over to sit on her father's lap, a soldered circle of two Joan observed from the fringes, seated at the top of the staircase when she, no matter her age, was done with her reading and writing for the day. How they inclined their heads toward each other in those long minutes in the living room, and later at the kitchen table, telling each other about their days, neither ever asking Joan a question about anything. She remembered those awful dinners of her mother's calf's liver, and her father, so pale and bloodless, tearing into the flesh, his knife and fork scraping across the plate.

Martin was not pale and bloodless, she thought, sitting in her

Rhome study. He was brilliant, as passionate about his work as she was about hers. He was strong and engaging, good and handsome, always looking as if he were fresh from a sunny day at the beach or from a whirlwind run down the slopes, burnished from the inside out. His days were spent on the campus, in the laboratory, or in the hospital's operating rooms, but when he emerged he liked music and conversation and an abundance of others, as she did not. Her ability to sometimes be charming made people mistake her for a social creature when she preferred the turning of her own thoughts. She had learned to enjoy the parties they went to by considering them experiential interludes, potential fodder for her work one day.

People sought out Dr. Martin Manning, wanted to be in his presence, thought of him as their best friend. And he *was* a good friend, caring, considerate, kind, taking under his wing the newly minted doctors doing their rotations. Children flocked to him too. In New York, on his weekends there with her, she had seen infants and toddlers smiling up at him, waving to him from their strollers, as the two of them walked past, she evading the fat wheels of the buggies, he leaning down with a quick hello, saying, "Nice hat, buddy, you going fishing?" or "You're wearing such a pretty dress, I wish I had a camera right this minute." He had told Joan more than once that when he was a boy he wished for the impossible—for siblings and cousins to play with at the holidays, for holidays at all, celebrated with laughter and noise. His parents, like Joan's, had been only children.

How did she miss so completely that Martin might want people who belonged to him through bonds more durable than friendship, that being a surrogate big brother to scared medical residents might not suffice, that waving to the children of others would not heal the hole in his heart? He had vowed to her they would not reproduce. Perhaps he had been honest when he swore to it, perhaps not. Regardless, Joan had proof that he wanted a child, he wanted this child.

She looked at the clock on her desk. An old-fashioned thing that had belonged to Martin's father, one of the few items Martin kept when he sold everything in the Annapolis house, sold the house itself. It was bulky like Martin's father. The hands sluggish, as Martin's father had not been, its tick-tock loud when Joan's writing was difficult, otherwise she didn't hear the noise at all. She was surprised Martin had held on to it once she heard how fearfully he watched that clock when he was growing up, counting down the hours, then half hours, then minutes, then seconds, until his father was home from the academy. Before dinner, he pushed Martin out of the house, into the backyard, yelling out the navy calisthenics Martin was to do: "Get down, boy, give me forty push-ups." And after they had eaten their dinners in silence, Martin watched the clock again. It was always ten minutes after Martin cleaned up the kitchen that his father demanded to see his finished homework, a red pen clutched between the vice admiral's thick fingers.

Looking at the second hand's slow sweep, Joan couldn't figure out how many minutes had passed since Martin's departure in pursuit of libations for an illusory celebration.

The day before, her knowledge of the clock's history did not alter the tick-tocking of their glorious future ahead. But now she felt as Martin must have felt waiting for the hands to reach the dreaded hour. Out of time. The expanse of their expected life together seemed suddenly reduced to nothing.

If she had this baby, it meant a second baby, Joan understood that now; the only discussion would be one of timing. Martin would want to create a foundation of family, Manning children who would be their responsibility to nurture through the years, though Martin would view them as a gift. Manning children who would grow up and have their own children, and their children would have children, and on and on, until no one would be left on their own. The opposite of how Joan lived her life, the opposite of what she required for her work. She knew that other women managed both, had for centuries. But most of those women desired motherhood and they came to it, Joan imagined, with a set of beliefs about what it would be like, a faith even, in their maternal abilities, their qualifications. Their faith and belief in the worthiness of motherhood providing them with answers, with succor and calm, about navigating it all. She was not like those women; she did not want motherhood, had no underlying faith in her ability to negotiate the enormity of the obligation, had no interest in the supposed majesty of the experience. She had always felt differently, had never yearned for marriage or for a child, had never played make-believe house, had never played with the doll she received on her fifth birthday, so lifelike with its soft skin, its gurgles and giggles and cries when its middle was squeezed hard. She had no answers because those domesticated questions had never interested her, and her only belief was knowing, as her mother used to say regardless of the situation at hand, she was not cut from the right cloth. And she hadn't wanted to be.

If Joan extinguished the thing inside, she would have to leave Martin, or he would have to leave her. The joy that lit up his features, that timbred his voice when she told him the horrendous news, belied their vow, was clear evidence that such a break would be required. Dilation and curettage, grinding away at the cells rapidly multiplying inside of her, that soon enough would form into a face, a heart, two tiny feet, would puncture their happiness if she made such a drastic choice.

She could be fine without Martin. She would holster her love for him and rely, as she always had, on the exceptional traits mined during her unloving childhood. Those traits—detachment and heightened abilities to perceive and observe—had guided her through those awful years, had turned her into the writer she was. Without Martin's love, her current engagement with the world would fade, but living at a remove had served her work well, and she was fierce enough to adapt. Returning to her original life, the one she had planned on, would not be a problem, but when she looked down, her own palms were curved protectively around her belly. Instantly, she clasped them together.

She sighed. It was true that she was infinitely happier with Martin than she had been before, without him. But was holding on to this love worth suffering the mammoth changes that would upend her life if she nurtured this microscopic speck through all the following months, ate right, did not drink, thought good thoughts—which could not include hoping she miscarried—and brought forth into the world a baby that would be theirs forever? Was she actually considering freeing Martin from his vow? Having this thing?

What would it look like if she did, hypothetically? What did people typically worry about in such a situation? The sanity of the mother, the fitness of the father, the health of the fetus, the amount of money in the bank, the grandparents and what they would want to be called—stupid names like Marmie and Pappy—postpartum depression, C-sections versus natural births, genetic defects, ancestry, history, time.

What would she worry about? The regularity of her routine, her writing hours, her reading hours, how seldom she allowed herself to be pulled off course. Her ability to be as present in this world as she was in those she invented, among characters more real to her than most of the people she knew, than the people she used to know or observe in New York, strangers she now analyzed in the bookstores, in the library, at the market, on the streets, and in the restaurants of Rhome.

If she went through with this, hypothetically, she would have to be present for the baby, could not do what her own mother and father had done to her, what Martin's father had done to him. There could be no coldness, no isolation, no distance, no disaffection, no paltry pretend-love. The baby would have a right to a joyous childhood, which meant she—they—would have to give it that joyous childhood. She would have to find within herself additional love and patience, admirable traits she doubted she possessed in sufficient quantity, flawed as she was, consumed with her imagined human beings, the often grievous or heartrending situations she wrote them into and out of. She would have to willingly give all of herself, or at least most of herself. And the sacrifice new parents so loudly and proudly proclaimed themselves willing to make, willing, they said, to lay down their lives for the good of their offspring . . . could Joan do that, sacrifice herself, if such was required? These days, for years really, in service to her work, she sacrificed others, but never herself.

Only the day before, her future had been so clear, but it was suddenly impossible to see into the distance, all because an accidental breach had left her undefended.

She swiveled in the chair and stared out the large window that faced her desk. The undulations of their vast acreage, humps of dirt that rose and fell over the four solid acres, rolled out into the distance; she could not see to the end of their property. She and Martin weren't gardeners, and who knew if they had green thumbs, but she could imagine the dirt gone, the land vibrantly green, an emerald carpet of soft grass, a swing set, a sandbox, a jungle gym. The kid could have a playground all its own, they had that much land. But wouldn't playing in a public park be better for it? Wasn't engagement with others a socializing force?—what Joan had avoided as a child by never leaving her desk or walking out of the public library she had visited most days after school. Being unloved had turned her into a writer, and her writerly way of living, alone most of the time, had not harmed her at all, or not much. Until this stealthy attack by Martin's swimmers, look at all she had accomplished so far.

Her sudden laugh was hollow and high, collapsing quickly, then trying to rise back up through her throat, tearing at her vocal cords, some inhuman wail wanting to be released, that she forced back down. How ridiculous, planning a termination and the resumption of her solitary life one minute, and in the next, designing a personal, private playground for an undesired child.

She closed her eyes and thought it was a perfect time to cry. She had not cried past the age of seven, when she found a pen and a notebook and began conjuring up her own people, people she could control and direct, living the complicated lives she chose for them, the good and the bad they were forced to endure.

When she opened her eyes, the late-afternoon sun had shifted, throwing her typewriter into a cone of warm light. The platinum band on her finger sparkled. If she were writing this as a story, if Joan were one of her own characters, would she see the movement of the sun, the gleam of the ring, as an omen or a blessing, something to be heeded or ignored? Her characters often suffered the sudden fall through a floor they had mistakenly believed was solid, a demarcation point between *then* and *now*, a point from which they could not retreat, when the *before* of their lives changed in an instant. She had written their devastations, then watched their brave resolutions to see it through, to welcome the *after*, regardless of what actions they ultimately took. She had never imagined it happening to her, or that it would feel this way, as if there were no ground at all to stand on, nothing within sight, the sky so far away.

This could be one of her own stories—a woman facing what was, for her, the unthinkable, and her love over the moon because of the news. What would she have the character do? After the anguish of discovering, too soon, her good husband's fallibility, would that woman pull herself out of the abyss, open her heart more, not abandon love, or eliminate the fledgling life within; would she welcome the quickening, become a wondrous pregnant woman, a loving mother, bask in the adoration of that flawed husband, their home a place where the good outweighed the bad, where eventual childhood hurts were magic-wanded away? That character might, Joan thought—and in the process discover her untapped abilities to live a full life, in real life, outside the pages of the stories she wrote, the novel-in-progress she was working on. That character would never abandon her own work, her reason for living, would remain a serious writer no matter what life threw at her, would finish her first novel, and the novel after that one, and the one after that, and all the novels that would follow, as she wrote and loved her unexpected child, and the second one too, through the run of delightful years. Of course, the woman's story would need some tragedy, some arc of calamity and catastrophe and misfortune and heartbreak, but this was not the time to ponder that. She knew she could write such a story, but could she write herself into it, become *that* eponymous Joan?

She heard Martin's car rumble into the driveway, the engine's long whistle of relief when it found itself at rest, and Joan thought, *I guess I'm going to try.*

"Joan Ashby Manning, where are you?" Martin called out, and immediately she wondered why she agreed to take his last name, even if its use was limited to their personal life, the name on their joint checking and savings accounts.

She heard him rattling paper bags in the kitchen; noise traveled fast in a house so small and contained, three bedrooms and two baths. Just right, really, for an incipient family. They had not yet figured out what to do with that third room, which echoed in its emptiness.

From her desk, she heard the pop of a cork, the whoosh of liquid poured into a glass, then the crinkle of foil pulled free from the bottle of sparkling apple cider, what all newly pregnant women seemed to drink, the faux elixir of celebration.

Joan looked at the hard-written pages of *The Sympathetic Executioners* and wondered whether it would be possible to finish the book in time.

"I'm still in here, Martin, but I'm coming," she called out.

She joined him in the kitchen. The sparkling apple cider in the fluted glass he handed her looked like a test tube of urine, but it was frothy, its bubbles fizzy, with a surprising, delicate sweetness she held for long seconds on her tongue. They walked out the back door and stood together on their land. When he reached for her hand, she allowed it, felt the way his swallowed hers whole.

"Thank you," Martin said. "I know what this means."

She was still down in the abyss, unable to see the treacherous path she would need to climb, to find traction again beneath her feet, and so Joan said nothing, remained silent, practiced what she thought *Joan* would do—stay quiet, keep her own counsel, figure things out.

Every so often, Martin thanked her again, and again, and again, always in a whisper of words, until the light bled out of the sky, the blue turning a sad, desolate gray. At the back door, before Joan followed Martin inside, she looked up once more, tried thinking of the sky as something more, as the heavens, the place where wishes were sent, where they were granted, but it looked only like an old rag wrung completely dry.

2

Even to herself, Joan Ashby could not deny the truth: she *was* a pregnant goddess. Hormonal forces had turned her naturally good health into something patent and extraordinary. Her skin glistened, the whites of her eyes radiated, and her long hair, always a waterfall of black curls, was growing at a breathtaking rate, had already reached the small of her back, a perpetual tickle against her naked skin when she slept. Her eyelashes had become palm fronds over her bright-blue eyes, which had also altered, the color exotically deepening, eyes that startled her when she looked up while brushing her teeth. She had always been objective about her beauty, but even she was surprised when she glimpsed herself in a mirror; she *was* a goddess, and in the bath, a new nightly routine, she felt like a mermaid.

She often silently thanked the baby for being more thoughtful than she had expected it to be. She had feared it would punish her, for not wanting it, but she suffered no morning sickness or exhaustion, and as it grew, it kept itself nicely contained, swelling her gracefully, not wrenching Joan's natural physical delicacy into something cumbersome and ungainly.

The friendly people of Rhome frequently stopped her on the street, telling her she was a gorgeous mother-to-be, sometimes asking, sometimes not, before reaching out and rubbing her belly, every one of them saying, "For good luck," though whether she was to bring them good luck, or they her, she didn't know. At night, after her bath, when Martin wanted to do the same thing, she often said, "Please don't. I've been rubbed so many times today, I feel like a Buddha."

She was not the only pregnant woman in tiny Rhome. There were six others, but she was the town's first star. The celebrated writer from New York, with the dashing husband who was a neuro-ocular surgeon, who'd purchased a house out in the new development that was not formally named but some had taken to calling Peachtree, which made no sense to Joan. There were no peach trees in their neighbor- hood, no trees at all, not yet, no grass or gardens, just neighbors set far apart who waved to one another as they backed out of freshly graded driveways.

Small-town life had its benefits; she was not pursued like a fox by hounds, as she had been back in New York, her banal errands there somehow worthy of recording, a constant irritation because everyone shopped at the market, read the paper at the Laundromat, bought fresh fruit from the greengrocer. In Rhome, however, she wasn't completely anonymous. The Tell-Tale and the Inveterate Reader, the town's two bookstores, one on either end of the pretty main street, imaginatively named Strada di Felicità, had been artistically displaying her books in their windows for months, and the books had been flying off the shelves, so people recognized her from her photographs on the back flaps, from newspaper articles about her in the *New York Times* and *Washington Post* that featured a picture, but they approached her diffidently, politely, with charitable words, asking that she inscribe the title pages of her books, wanting to know, after rubbing her belly, when the baby was due, if she had any favorite names in mind, if she and the doctor were having an easy time settling in. Joan smiled graciously at the gentle intrusions, introduced herself properly, learned names and professions, engaged in a different version of life's chitchat than perhaps the locals were used to; she tended to dig quickly past the superficial, asking pointed, gritty questions. But she could see they liked her, and she felt welcomed, even if it was the baby that served as the icebreaker, the pregnancy making her seem less formidable, easier to approach.

Only once did a man tail her, when she was five months pregnant and taking a break late in the day from the novel, the new paragraphs still in her mind:

The magazine was glossy and expensively produced, printed in Englewood, New Jersey, and each month, there were twenty pages of classifieds under a single heading: Kind Killers Wanted. Each ad a heartfelt request seeking the services of executioners. The one that caught Silas and Abe's attention read:

WANTED—CARING FATHER KILLER: My father once was a delightful man, a high school principal, who was fair and firm. He would be appalled if he knew how he groaned every hour of every day, if he knew the thick auburn hair that was his secret pride had thinned down to strands, exposing a skull tender as an egg. I can tell that he knows he has veered far from his course, that he has lost the thread of his life. He used to sling words with aplomb, but his eyes now reflect an awareness that he is regressing to an infantile state. He should not suffer this way. Please respond if interested. Will pay going rate.

The man tailing Joan froze in his spot on the sidewalk when Joan wandered into a store, then followed in her wake when she resumed her stroll. She turned to look back at him and white stars exploded in the air, the flash of the man's camera, a photographer stalking her, and Odile, who owned the Tell-Tale, flew out the front door of her shop and gave him hell. When the man yielded instantly, throwing his hands protectively around his camera and running fast down the street, Joan knew he wasn't a regular among the mob that used to trail her in New York—none of them would have given up so easily. But Odile didn't stop yelling until he disappeared around the corner.

There were requests that she give readings at the bookstores, at the library, that she jump into the town-run book group held monthly at the Rhome Community Center and lead all of Rhome's serious readers. She made a list of recommended books for the group's leader, an elderly chatterbox named Renee, who said, "I'd be happy to step aside, absolutely happy, happy to do that, thrilled to be one of your followers. I'll make sure we have fresh-baked cookies and real lemonade at the center for book group. What's your favorite? Oatmeal? Chocolate chip? Butter? Just tell me, and I'll make sure all is in order. We'll get you a comfortable chair too, not one of the metal ones the rest of us use."

But Joan declined everything that would have swallowed her time, kept her from working on *The Sympathetic Executioners*, the status of which her agent, Volkmann, was checking on regularly: "You've disappeared from the civilized world, so we have to make sure your voice rings out from that hinterland you've gone to, and is especially loud and clear. So write fast, Joan, write very, very fast."

Martin, too, frequently asked how the book was coming along, usually when she was in her nightly bath, when she needed absolute quiet to let her brain think on its own, to let the baby roll around without being slapped down. Each time, when he said, "Can I read something?" his smile and eagerness left their imprints behind, papering over her peace. *Other Small Spaces* was already hugely out in the world and she had been finishing the last of the connected stories that became *Fictional Family Life* when their courtship began. During their weekend visits with each other, she had seriously assessed the impact of burgeoning love on her work, whether love altered the time she spent at her desk in her East Village apartment, or at the Friedheim Music Library at Johns Hopkins when she was with Martin in Baltimore. But her output had not slacked off. She had written most of *The Sympathetic Executioners* with him in her life, experiencing his magnanimous nature, his respect for her creative intensity, when she returned to him spacy and otherworldly at night. Not once had he ever presumed to ask to read her pages, and if he had, she would have debated whether the relationship could survive. Now, when she was pregnant with his child, he was turning into a man claiming such a right. She knew he did not mean it that way, but more than once, after such a request, she had the desire to take her belly and what it contained, and walk out the door. "Maybe soon," she would say, not meaning it at all.

Several times a week, Joan was at the community center, in her maternity bathing suit, swimming slow laps. The other pregnant Rhome women swam too, breast-stroking up and down the lanes, keeping their heads dry, talking about their sex lives now that they were ballooning, about their food cravings. The only thing Joan craved was the buoyancy of water. On Mondays, Wednesdays, and Fridays, at noon, she pinned up her abundantly long hair, pulled down the swim cap, and swam the crawl with her head underwater.

Augusta, Carla, Dawn, Emily, Meg, and Teresa were the "Pregnant Six," as they had taken to calling themselves, childhood friends who had gone away separately to university or college, then traveled, before returning home for good. In the locker room afterward, when they talked, Joan was surprised that seeing the world had not altered their desires, their plans, did not convince them to settle down somewhere more interesting—any large city really—to participate in the bigger life she so recently left.

The women huddled around her, wanting to know whether New York was as dangerous as they heard on the news. When they told her of the countries they visited after receiving their degrees, they called that time "our youth," and it was the usual trio: France, England, Italy.

Where had Joan been, they wanted to know. She did not mention all the countries she visited while touring for *Fictional Family Life*, and said instead, "So no one's been to India? That's the country I want to see. Ever since I was a kid." She and Martin had not taken a honeymoon, would not do so now that she was pregnant, but it was to India that Joan wanted them to go. It didn't matter much that Martin waffled about it, said he had no interest, did not want to be immersed in the dirt and the poverty, who knew when they would take a trip anywhere with life already altered.

The Pregnant Six felt as Martin did about India, and Joan did not explain her fascination with the country. She wasn't sure if they were readers or not—none of them spoke to her in the star terms the other Rhome locals did, did not mention that they knew she was a writer—and so she did not say India beckoned loudly because of the books she had read in her childhood, by E. M. Forster, R. K. Narayan, Mulk Raj Anand, Raja Rao, and others, all describing ways of being, of seeing, landscapes alien and wild, completely different from what she had seen from the windows of her parents' house—other similar houses with backyards and front yards, identical trees and flowers planted in the same neat arrangements. Even in spring and fall, when the flowers were blooming, the world around her had been soaked in sepia, but in the Indian stories she read, flora and fauna teemed and seethed, and hard lives were fully, vibrantly lived out in the streets; everyone had a story to tell, their own or somebody else's. Those small and poor Indian towns in the books had been immensely more interesting to Joan than where she was growing up. The books had been a touchstone, as both reader and writer.

The questions Joan asked of the Pregnant Six in their post-swim conversations, when everyone's skin reeked with heavy-duty chlorine, allowed her to glimpse beneath their placid surfaces, their constant giggles, the way they brushed stray hairs off one another's faces, complimented a pedicure color. They were not unsubstantial women. Carla owned Craftables on Laurel Place, just off Strada di Felicità. Joan had wandered in and immediately out, the place a warren of cubbyholes filled with colorful skeins of knitting yarn and embroidery thread. Needlepoint samplers hung from fishing lines. There were trays of beads and amulets, and silk cords on which those beads and amulets were to be strung, in every shade of the rainbow, each color bunched together, thick as horses' tails, hanging on hooks. Carla also ran a knitting group at the store, and an embroidery group, and three times a year she brought in artists who created original drawings on needlepoint canvases for her customers. "It's commissioned self-art, really, if that's a real thing. Because the customer only has a picture on mesh until she needlepoints it herself." Joan had seen the prices on those original samples; Carla charged upward of five hundred dollars. An excellent business apparently for Rhome, shilling out the goods for pursuits unfathomable to Joan, but she had dashed down a few notes later, about a town buried beneath an avalanche of yarn, the people unaware of the disaster because they never walked out their front doors, too busy knitting and needling their lives away.

Dawn owned Boulangerie de Rhome, next to the Inveterate Reader. After college, she had taken a thirty-two-week intensive pastry-arts program in France, and opened the store immediately upon her return, with funding from her father. "I paid him back years ago with interest," she told Joan, holding her hand up for slaps from all the others. She was up at four each morning, working in the kitchen behind the shop, turning out all kinds of French breads—Pain a l'Ail, Pain au Froment, Pain aux Noix, Pain au Beurre, Pain Beignet—as well as the recognizable baguettes, and Joan's favorite that she bought each week, Pain Bâtard, bread that came out of the oven lopsided, in odd shapes, were mistakes. There were cast-iron French bistro tables in the shop and cooling cases filled with neat rows of delectable petit fours, tarts and tortes and éclairs, custards and curds and ganaches. Martin had already deemed Boulangerie de Rhome off-limits for himself. He had not, he said, known he had such a sweet tooth.

Meg and Teresa's vocations were more ordinary; both were teachers, Meg of sixth graders at Rhome Elementary, Teresa of physics at Rhome High.

Augusta and Emily were lawyers in practice together. "We focus," Emily said, "on family and matrimonial law, including adoptions and divorces, as well as real estate, trusts, wills, and the execution of estates." It sounded to Joan as if they were the town's grim reapers, covering everything from cradle to grave. She wondered how a town Rhome's size generated sufficient legal matters to keep them both employed; its population was somewhere around seven thousand. Did that many houses change hands? she wondered. Were there so many people needing to bequeath vast estates? And although the six were proof that the town had no issue with fertility, she wondered about the number of adoptions they facilitated. She had not seen, as she did in New York, the Russian and Chinese children pushed around in strollers by parents who clearly did not share ethnicity with their bundles of joy. But apparently the town brought most of its legal work to Augusta and Emily, because sometimes one or the other was too busy to make it to the pool at noon.

If Joan had not inquired, she would have learned only that the Pregnant Six had all married boys they knew, but had not dated, back in junior high—two Bills, one Jim, one Dave, one Kevin, and one Steve—and were proud of their expanding bellies, their bounteous breasts, Augusta especially, who said, "This is the first time in my life I've worn a bra." When they spoke about their stores, their teaching responsibilities, their practices, their accomplishments, they were individual, stand-alone women. But when they massed together, as they always did in the locker room, they colonized, insect-like, the group emitting a high drone. Perhaps it was the similarity of their haircuts, blunt and bobbed, in various versions of butterscotch, that gave them the appearance of a hive. When Joan joined them there, the last usually to leave the pool, they were buzzing about, like a collective on a mission to haul back crumbs to those left behind. And yet, when her entry split them apart, they resumed talking in normal voices, laughing about how many times a night they rose to pee, bemoaning, with pride, the loss of their figures, the weight they had gained, quick to share tips and advice, including Joan in those sessions.

"Joan's the lucky one," they said. "At your age, you won't lose your figure at all, and whatever changes will spring back fast. We'll have to work harder." Before this accident of life, Joan never imagined worrying about her figure having to spring back. And she wondered why the Pregnant Six seemed intent on stressing their ages. Perhaps by small-town standards they were old for first-time motherhood, all of them thirty, treating her as if she were a member of a different generation, though she was not that much younger than any of them. If the baby came late, she would be twenty-six when she gave birth.

The Pregnant Six liked talking about how their priorities would change. It was husband, then work, then themselves, but soon it would be baby, then husband, then work. They set themselves up as the wise ones, with inside knowledge, though all of them were novices at pregnancy, at eventually being mothers. During those locker-room cabals, Joan silently bucked at their certainty about how they would conduct their new lives, pronouncements solid as stone. Joan thought there was something between her own mother's disinterest and this hovering the Pregnant Six were already embracing. It should not be impossible, she thought, to keep her different aims and goals separated, to move back and forth between simultaneous worlds, to live her various lives as they unfolded in parallel universes.

With so many expecting in Rhome, the community center decided a prenatal yoga class was a good idea, to be held twice a week at one in the afternoon, a lunchtime retreat for the women in the midst of their busy days. Teresa had been consulted about the chosen hour; she sat on the community center board and thought yoga after swimming would make a nice combination. Joan did not hear about the new yoga class until they were all in the locker room after swimming one day, and the Pregnant Six stripped off their wet suits and pulled on loose track pants or shorts, bra tops and T-shirts, then clamored around Joan, who was still in her own dripping suit, and said she had to attend, smiling and encouraging, reaching out to touch a sodden curl, telling her they would have fun.

"It won't be the same without you," they cried out. "You've got to come, at least once." She had never been invited into a group, a clique really, and it was entirely because of the baby.

Her instinct was to decline, but one Friday, in her sixth month, after her swim spent pondering the family of tombstone carvers who had appeared in the novel—a mother and father and three daughters given free rein to choose the gravestones, to decide on the embellishments and the epitaphs of those eliminated by the sympathetic executioners—Joan found herself in a small mirrored room, standing on a mat, listening to a broad-shouldered woman telling them about prenatal yoga. The woman's hair was a brazen red, a fakery that failed to impart the youth she must have been after.

"Hi, everyone. I'm Lannie. By your wet heads, I'm guessing you've been swimming, which is good cardiovascular exercise, but yoga will help you stay limber, improve your balance and circulation, keep your muscles toned, and teach you to breathe right and relax, which will come in handy for the physical demands of labor, birth, and motherhood. I'm going to show you several poses, but we're going to start with *ujjayi*, a special breathing technique which will prime you for childbirth. *Ujjayi* will let you fight the urge to tighten up when you're in pain or afraid during labor. You'll take in air slowly through your nose until your lungs are completely filled, then exhale completely, until your stomach compresses."

There were laughs and the Pregnant Six grabbed at their bellies.

"Yes, of course," Lannie said, "but you'll still be able to feel it from the inside. Now watch me."

She inhaled until her large nose narrowed and her chest rose up like a bulwark, then there was a whoosh of an exhale that went on forever, which Joan found loud and annoying.

"Got it, everyone?" and the Pregnant Six yelled, "Got it."

They were their own cheerleading squad, and despite their inclusion of her, Joan felt distaste, remembering the horde of girls at her high school, she younger than everyone in her grade by several years, fourteen when she was a senior, and those girls, in short swingy cheerskirts and crop-tops, roamed the hallways, making what they believed were pithy, hurtful remarks in superior voices that made some kids cry. About Joan they once said, "There's the girl who sure loves her pens. Wonder what she does with them alone in her bed." An unclever comment that had failed to land, proving to Joan, again, how easily people cracked away at others' humanity, the pain they inflicted comforting something inside of themselves. She couldn't help wondering what the Pregnant Six said about her when she was not among them, when they were massed and crooning together.

They practiced *ujjayi* breathing, their exhalations out of sync, until Lannie said, "Okay. Good enough for the first time. We're ready now for our first *asana. Virabhadrasana I*, a standing posture, the first of the three warrior poses.

"Yogis are known for their nonviolent ways, but the *Bhagavad Gita*, the most respected of all the yoga texts, is actually a dialogue between two famous and feared warriors that takes place on a battlefield between two great armies spoiling for a fight. What is commemorated in this pose is the *spiritual warrior* who bravely battles against the universal enemy, *avidya*, which is self-ignorance, the ultimate source of all our suffering. What you all want to work at battling in yourselves."

It was obvious to Joan that Lannie had memorized her yoga patter, but into *Virabhadrasana I* Joan went. Then *Virabhadrasana II* and *III*, *Tree, Downward Dog, Cat-Cow*, and good old-fashioned squats, out of place when Lannie was talking on about the meditative benefits of yoga, silencing their inner dialogues, and learning just to be.

Joan found she was curiously limber and graceful doing the poses, that she enjoyed heeding the instructions, ceding control for the hour, focused not on her novel's unfolding story, as she did when she swam, but on the mystical way she was contorting her body, watching herself in the mirror transitioning easily from one pose to the next, despite her belly, and the sloshing, along with a kick or two, from inside. When she looked at the others, she was surprised by their precious way of holding themselves, mincing through the poses, hands rarely straying from their cargo, as if they were vessels for the world's next great philosophers.

"Time for *Baddha konasana*, sometimes known as cobbler's or tailor's pose," Lannie said. "Drag your mats to the wall. Backs up tight and straight against it, put your soles together and let your knees fall apart—

"*Meg, you're not grounded. Get grounded.* Yes, spread those ass cheeks apart so you're stable."

At last, they were told to lie on their sides on the mats. "Time for a pregnancy-modified *Shavasna*, corpse pose. Get comfortable. Eyes closed. Arms and legs relaxed. Palms facing upward. Now, *inhale.* Pull that breath into your lungs. Now, *exhale.* Force all that air out of you. Now, everyone, tense your entire body gently. Hold it. Hold it. Hold it. Now, let go. I'm going to shut off the lights and you can stay as long as you want."

When Joan opened her eyes in the darkened room, she was alone, her mat the only one left on the floor. The clock above the door read 3:05; the class had been over for more than an hour. She felt happy, hazily happy, a feeling that lasted as she drove home, and through two more hours of writing, and through dinner with Martin, laughing when he told her about the day's mishaps made by the residents assigned to him, listening carefully to him describe the initial steps for a radical surgery he was conceiving that might be able to restore sight in a permanent way for certain ocular diseases. Through it all, she honestly felt the glow of pregnancy; she had not felt it, not truly, before.

In bed that night, lying on her side with her back to Martin, straddling the body pillow as if it were a horse, she said, "I liked the yoga a lot. I'm going to do the classes with Lannie, but after the baby comes, I'm going to find a real yoga teacher and real yoga classes, even if I have to drive to another town."

Martin yawned and said, "Sounds good. Whatever you want to do sounds good to me," and then he was lightly snoring.

Joan thought about her old neighborhood in New York, the yoga studio she had often passed. Not once had she thought of opening its door, going in, checking it out. She felt her heart softening toward the baby a bit more; the way it was offering her something new in exchange for room and board.

3

Silas and Abe were left in a wicker basket at a firehouse, to the right of the red bay doors, found by the captain, who looked beneath the tattered blanket and discovered twins, nametags pinned to their onesies. A cooler bag was next to the basket, diapers on top, nursing bottles below. When the captain pulled out a bottle, it was full. All the bottles were full, each one labeled *Fresh Breast Milk* in fluorescent pink ink, and dated; the one in his hand dated that day.

The captain carried the basket and bag into the house, and his husky men, who threw themselves into fires, cooed over the babies, made goo-goo faces and trilling sounds, changed them and fed them while he called Children's Services.

The woman from the authority arrived and said, "At least they're infants. That's the key. They'll be placed in a heartbeat."

The captain said, "Please make sure they're kept together. Hard enough start to life, without them having to go it alone. They'll always be looking for each other, if you don't do the right thing."

It wasn't what the woman wanted; separating them would make her job easier, but the captain made her swear, and she, a failed mother herself, agreed.

During the following years, as infants, toddlers, young boys, then teens, Silas and Abe moved across the Midwest, from Kansas to Iowa to Indiana, coming to rest in Illinois. Their various foster parents, four sets in total, all of good cheer, made sure the boys had plenty to eat, warm comforters on their beds, books to read and television to watch, basketball hoops for H-O-R-S-E, and the benefits of fine public-school educations. And they were good boys—both blond, sunny, and light—handsome boys popular at the schools they attended, and with the girls who sidled up. Sweet and shy girls liked them too, not just the fast ones whose hips molded early into sensuous curves, whose breasts jiggled inside red or black bras.

For the past five years, Silas and Abe had lived in a three-story house in Chicago. Of all the houses they'd lived in, this one felt most like home. Their foster parents were an accountant and his piano-teacher wife. Short people from hardy stock, although the hardy stock was unclear because both wore thick glasses, were blind without them. The boys called them Frederick and Shirley, but when talking about their days at school, about their nightly and future dreams, sometimes their minds slipped, and to themselves, they replaced Frederick with *Dad*, Shirley with *Mom*. That was how close the twins felt to them.

On their eighteenth birthday, they crashed down the stairs for Shirley's annual birthday-king breakfast—pancakes, waffles, omelets, thirty strips of bacon, and fresh-squeezed orange juice. Bottles of boysenberry syrup and maple and a jar of Marshmallow Fluff on the dining-room table, along with an enormous sheet cake sprouting twin sets of eighteen candles. Streamers decorated the room, and from the ceiling, a homemade sign read: HAPPY BIRTHDAY! YOUR FUTURE AWAITS!

When the platters were emptied, the orange juice finished, the cake plates smeared in frosting, Shirley shooed them into the living room. Silas and Abe resisted. They had been raised well by all their fosters, to bring their manners with them wherever they were, to help out. "We'll clean up," the boys said, and Shirley shook her head. "Not necessary. We have a gift for each of you, the kind of gift that gives and gives."

Under the arch that led into the living room, they slipped off their shoes, Shirley's rule: No shoes on the carpeting. But she surprised them. "Not necessary this time. Tie those tennis shoes back up right now. Keep 'em on, you're going to need them. Now go and sit on the couch."

The boys retied their laces and tiptoed over the carpet, looking at each other sideways, acknowledging silently the freakishness of being allowed to do the forbidden. They sat on the couch, just inches apart, and in came Frederick and Shirley, both barefooted, each wrestling a large present in their arms. They placed the wrapped packages just beyond Silas and Abe's tennis-shoed feet.

Shirley sat down at the baby grand and played the birthday song. Frederick clapped his hands and sang along. Then Shirley twirled around on the bench and said, "Ready? All right, go! Rip those bows right off, tear through the paper. We're not saving any of it this time."

The boys looked at each other again. What was meant by all these new instructions, the breaking of her inviolable rules? Shirley had a trunk in the basement filled with used wrapping paper, ironed precisely, and bows, second-, third-, and fourth-hand, that she kept in plastic bags.

They shrugged and did as instructed.

When the wrapping paper was off, standing before them were brand-new rolling suitcases, the fabric in army green. The suitcases were nice, but not what the twins had been hoping for, which was one of two things: to be adopted by the Jacksons or given a used car they could share.

"Thank you very much," they each said.

"That's just the first gift," Frederick said.

"Yes, like we said, this is a gift that will keep on giving," Shirley said. "Go on, boys, unzip the suitcases."

Inside the bags, each found new T-shirts, socks, underpants, jeans, and pajamas, and at the bottom, underneath the everyday attire, the boys pulled out black suits, crisp white shirts flat in their store packaging, marked 13 ½-inch neck, one tie each, in the same design, Silas's in red, Abe's in blue. The boys were confused. Shirley had recently taken them shopping for the summer clothes folded away upstairs in their shared room. They had not worn suits to their high school graduation and wondered why they would be given them now, when summer was just starting, when they would be lifeguarding at the public pool, in swim trunks and flip-flops all day long. They were looking forward to marking themselves with zinc oxide. Their faces in tribal patterns.

"Thank you, Frederick," said Silas.

"Thank you, Shirley," said Abe.

"You've been so generous to us," Silas said.

"Why suits?" asked Abe.

The Jacksons did not answer, but Frederick said, "Now put every-thing back in and zip up the suitcases." Which the boys did.

"Now roll them over here, to the front door," Shirley instructed, and the boys obeyed.

When the twins were at the front door, with their suitcases beside them, and Frederick and Shirley facing them, like short tackling blocks, Frederick said, "Put out your hands for the last birthday gift."

Two white envelopes. They peeked inside; a wad of crisp bills, marked by Shirley's iron.

"That, boys, is a thousand dollars each," Frederick said, and Shirley reached between them and opened the front door. The boys turned their heads and looked outside. The four of them stood there in silence, staring through the open door, down the walk lined in daisies, to the street, where cars were neatly parked. A little girl on a yellow bike rode past and beeped her horn.

"It's the way it works," Frederick said at last. "We really are sorry."

"Wait, what?" Silas said.

"What works what way?" Abe asked, his eyes wide, never moving off Frederick's face.

Then Shirley said, "You've been selected, so there's no reason to delay the inevitable. Anyway, we need your room for the next set of needy kids."

Over the years, the Jacksons had said the twins would never have to go, would not be fostered out at eighteen, would stay with them for as long as was right, through college and graduate school. Silas was interested in architecture, Abe in medicine. There had been talk, when they were younger, that the Jacksons would make sure that by the time the twins walked out the open front door, they would be set up for life. What Shirley said made no sense to them, but clearly some-thing had happened, or gone wrong, to change the minds of their surrogate parents.

Silas and Abe protested, then yelled, then grabbed on to the frame of the front door, but Frederick and Shirley, short as they were, were much stronger than they looked, stronger than the boys expected, all that hardy stock, and they found themselves outside the Jacksons' home, outside of *their* home, they thought, the handles of their rolling luggage gripped tight in their fists.

Silas did not look back, but Abe did, and he saw the front door slam, heard the lock turn.

It was a shock they could not process, standing halfway down the flowery path. Everything they owned, collected, cared for, was on shelves and in drawers, in the closet, up in their room. Silas had a prized baseball he caught at a Chicago Cubs game, and a mitt he was still oiling, yearbooks signed by all the girls, and Abe thought of his microscope, a present from the Jacksons last Christmas, and the books he had acquired so far in the Netter Collection: tomes on anatomy, biochemistry, cardiology, and epidemiology. He had planned to use his lifeguard earnings to purchase, at the end of summer, the volumes on anesthesiology, infectious diseases, and pathology. There were also the two dirty magazines his friend Tad had given him, tucked under Abe's mattress, naked pictures of gorgeous girls with their beavers fully exposed. Silas had lost his cherry, but Abe had not.

"What are they talking about? Selected for what?" Silas said. He was the tough twin, but tears were spilling out of his eyes, down his cheeks. He was cross-legged on the sidewalk, his face hidden behind his hands.

All their life, until this moment, Silas had been their leader, the more dominant twin, the one who made the plans, who led the way, but it was Abe who said, "Pull yourself together, Silas, we've got to do something. We've got to find a place where we can think. A place that has a phone. There's the minimart three blocks down, let's go there. We'll get Yoo-hoos and sit on the curb and figure out what to do. We'll call Frederick and Shirley. Maybe this is all just a joke. An initiation of sorts."

When Silas did not move, Abe laid his hand on his brother's shoulder and softly patted until Silas nodded, and rose, and followed Abe.

Thirty minutes after their kingly breakfast celebrating their eighteenth birthdays, they were rolling their luggage down the street, the wheels loud in the noon quiet of the summer Sunday.

On the corner of Unsworth Avenue and Third was the Exxon station and the minimart behind it. A man in a mechanic's jumpsuit was pumping gas for a pretty woman in a white Mercedes. "You Silas and Abe Canwell?" Abe nodded for them both. "You're expected. Go on into the market. Ask for Milt. He'll give you what you need."

Joan finished reading the opening pages of *The Sympathetic Executioners* and dropped them to the floor. She was stretched out on the living-room couch because she no longer fit at her desk. The couch, a hand-me-down from a colleague of Martin's who had moved on to another hospital five hundred miles away, was ugly, tight checks in blue and green, but it was deep and comfortable and supported Joan firmly. Physically, she was as comfortable as she could be these days, but her heart felt squeezed tight, and it wasn't the baby agitating her.

She had finished writing the novel by her own deadline, two weeks in advance of her estimated due date, the necessary time to catch her breath, before making final edits, bundling it up, and sending it off to Volkmann. She had imagined a third book tour, wondered what she and Martin would do when it was time for her to leave Rhome, leave the baby behind, and travel again. She had wondered how old the baby would be when that happened, and if she would feel torn away and unmoored, or find herself stepping lightly and fast.

For the last seven days, she had not peeked at all at the manuscript; instead she kept herself out of the house. Mornings she spent at Dawn's Boulangerie, though Dawn was not there, eating warm Pain Bâtard with butter and raspberry jam, drinking mugs of decaffeinated Earl Grey, and making lists of unusable baby names, like Plutarch, Reimann, and Winchester; Esmeralda, Clothilde, and Aine—names that would encourage targeted bullying, a few impossible to pronounce. She read them to Martin at night, to hear him laugh. After, she swam in the overheated community pool, catching glimpses of the cold weather through the large windows and the clear retractable roof. Gloomy skies every day, rain, sleet, one brief snowstorm that left no evidence behind. The yoga class had ended, but she slid into the warm water with pleasure, with relief at being weightless, thinking the baby must feel as she did, floating in its pool of amniotic fluid.

She swam alone, sometimes floating on her back, until the baby rolled over, rolling her over. The Pregnant Six no longer swam, were no longer pregnant. They were *nesting*, they all said to Joan, when she had driven from one house to the next, delivering identical baby gifts to them all. Each had gone into labor on a separate day, six days in a row, and now their babies, every one had given birth to a girl, consumed them. Watching breasts pulled out at feeding time, listening to the baby talk that came from the new mothers' mouths, Joan promised herself she would feed her child in private, talk to it in her regular voice, in full sentences that did not rise up at the end, as if everything in an infant's nascent life was already an existential question.

Head underwater, swimming back and forth, she spent the seven days considering the theme of her book: *The traumatic experience of a child also symbolizes the eternal verities of the human condition.*

As a teenager, she had read all of the short stories by the Indian writer Mulk Raj Anand, but only after *Fictional Family Life* was published had she come upon an old interview with Anand in which he discussed some of what Joan's own writing was after. With this first novel, she had sought to wrangle with the concept obliquely, had researched Stockholm syndrome, and the statistics about how many vulnerable people could be persuaded to resist their own morality, how likely people were to be hypnotized. She had been interested in exploring what happened to children abandoned at birth, who were later dropped into a strange alternative world. What happened especially when those children had been well tended by caring foster parents—would the tragedy of their unwanted births and abandonment wipe out the interim temporary love, make them amenable to killing? If they were led in that direction, given the tools and a code to live by, a rationalization tucked into their skin that allowed them to consider the work noble, would they become euthanasiasts for hire? She had liked the underground group of foster parents analyzing the children they sheltered, searching out those with the requisite aptitudes. She had wanted to see what happened with Silas and Abe, if they naturally took to the work because they unconsciously tapped into the early realities of their existence.

Now, on the couch, the rain sheeting down, their four acres a muddy field, Joan was debating her authorial choices. She'd deliberately begun the book on their eighteenth birthdays, with just a quick summation of their fostered years. She had wanted to get to the crux, to the meat, was most interested in writing about what happened next, the path they were led to discover, whether they had the strength and rectitude to resist, or whether they would give in, welcome the lives chosen for them, the work they were told they were suited to do.

Had she made a mistake? Should she have begun further back in time, written in depth about Silas and Abe's entry into the world, the parents who had made them, the nature of that relationship, whether it was abusive or simply bad luck, two kids finding themselves parents too early in their lives.

The questions she had not had to answer by starting the book where she did raced through her brain: Who had abandoned the infants at the firehouse—the mother, the father, the two of them skulking before dawn to leave the basket at the door? Was the mother all on her own, living in a falling-down shack, pumping her milk to fill those bottles she inked with a pink marker? Or were the parents still a team, with regular jobs and tax returns, but the prospect of raising two at once, and identical, was overwhelming, far beyond what had been anticipated?

Had she made a grave error by not exploring the twins' early years, the balance of power between Silas and Abe, how it might have teetered, before settling?

Perhaps it was the hormones, her brain no longer wholly her own, her intelligence usurped by the baby, but the dismay did not lift away.

She read on:

Then Silas and Abe were through the double glass doors. A fat man with stringy black hair and a silver ring through his nose was manning the minimart's cash register.

"Come closer, young gentlemen. I'm Milt. No last name needed and absolutely no reason at all to be frightened. I get that it's a scary time for you, but all will be explained, all will be okay."

It was Abe who bravely approached the counter when Milt held out a rolled-up magazine. Abe took it and stepped back and Silas leaned over his shoulder. The magazine fanned out and revealed no name on the cover, no sharply photographed picture. The back and front were completely blank, shiny though, and solidly black, the paper of good quality, heavyweight.

"You can read the articles later, a fascinating bunch this time around," Milt said. "Lots to learn in there. But for now, I want you to read the classifieds, really read them carefully, then come back in and talk to me, tell me which one grabs your guts first. Only then will I explain what's going on, the presents you were given, the reason for the suits, the shirts, the ties. In those classifieds, young gentlemen, is your future. Anyone need something to drink before taking the first step?"

Abe stepped forward again and nodded. "I'd like a chocolate Yoo-hoo, Milt," then turned to his brother and said, "Silas, what do you want?"

In later chapters, they learned to pick locks, to move stealthily, to disguise themselves utterly, to kill gently with their bare hands and not leave a mark. The code the twins would live by was drilled into them: *Only by knowing the truth of a person can I guarantee that those I free from pain are dispatched with pure beating hearts, belonging to both killer and victim.* Their preparation included boning up on their subjects. They were handed large blue three-ring notebooks that contained the voluminous histories of their targets, everything about their lives, their loves, the people they had cared for or hurt.

Joan liked the shocking intimacy of the twins befriending those marked for death, the murders paid for in advance by thoughtful family members who wanted their loved ones no longer to suffer from brain tumors and cancers and cirrhosis and Alzheimer's and Parkinson's and systemic organ failure and any other disease that broke down the flesh or the mind.

Their first target, an elderly lady named Ginny Sauvage, pink-fleshed and white-haired in her retirement community bed, looked innocent in old age, held out her hands when the twins introduced themselves, after slipping past the guards, evading the nurses roaming the floor. But with those hands, now crippled and clawed, Ginny Sauvage had once beaten every one of her children.

Now that Ginny Sauvage had been found, her location determined, her mobility assessed, the twins made their way out of the retirement community and waited at the leafy entrance for their ride.

Abe said, "She was a brute, Silas, you've got to remember that, when we return to do the job. I've found what I need, something black in my pulse, and I'll teach you how to find it in yourself, how to feel it moving through you, the way you can harness it, and let it do the work for you."

Hours later, when Joan finished reading, the manuscript pages were out of order, no longer neatly sequential, but it didn't matter. It seemed to her there was something all wrong about the book. Was it too dark and deadly? Did it suffer from the lack of that unwritten familial history and backstory? Whatever it was, she had not found her way in.

She huffed into a seated position, then up off the couch, and made her slow way down the hall, into her study. She dropped the manuscript on her desk, turned away, then turned back. One by one, Joan dropped the four shelved dictionaries onto the five-hundred-page manuscript, listening to the booms of those tomes, feeling the reverberations in her body, until her work was completely hidden from view.

She thought about calling Volkmann, asking her to read it, as a reader, not as an agent ready to deliver the anticipated book to an eager publisher, having Martin read it as well.

In the novels of others, Joan always flipped first to the acknowledgments page, read the names of those who had provided the author with *immeasurable help, essential help, critical help, guidance, love, good meals, a place to write looking at the ocean, a lake, a pond, a sand dune.* There were no acknowledgments listed in Joan's collections; she had not sought input from others, had relied on her own instincts to determine when the work was complete, exactly as she wanted it to be, had fought against the editors assigned her and won. She had not felt anyone deserved to be thanked.

She would not alter her methods now, she decided, she would stay true to herself. She would not give *The Sympathetic Executioners* to Volkmann or to Martin, their thoughts and impressions were irrelevant. She knew how she felt about the book. Intended to further the tremendous trajectory of her literary career, it would not have that effect; she would not be turning it in.

There was a niggling thought that Joan erased in an instant. The baby inside of her had done nothing wrong, had not leached away something vital in her, had not thinned her out as a writer. For a brief moment, the tumult lifted; that she did not apportion blame to the baby, that she considered the faults of the book all her own, seemed as good a start to motherhood as any.

In the nursery, she turned on the light, a small chandelier she and Martin found at another weekend yard sale. At night, when it was lit, the teardrop crystals threw magical floating shadows at the walls, dappled the ceiling. The room was now painted a pale yellow, the color of buttercups, a neutral color because Martin did not want to learn ahead of time whether it was a boy or a girl. It had been furnished for weeks. Crib against the far wall, with colorful mobiles hanging above, changing table across the way. A large bookcase against the long wall, already filled with thick books, none meant for children.

She sat down heavily in the recliner, put her feet up on the ottoman, and opened to where she'd left off the previous afternoon in Anthony Trollope's *Can You Forgive Her?* She had been reading aloud to the baby for months, had already read it *Anna Karenina*, Wilkie Collins's *The Woman in White*, the stories in the Portable Faulkner. She had thrown out all of Hemingway. The words he used to depict his narrow range of characters, his adoration of machismo, felt wrong on her tongue, too salty and hard-bitten, and if the baby was a boy she did not want him to turn out that way, that view of women congealed in his brain. She had replaced Hemingway with Jane Austen.

Joan hoped the baby would sense from the womb that she was treating it like a whole person, that by initiating it early into a life of books, she might create an embryonic connection between them, smoothing away any jagged edges in advance of their introduction to each other, or at least make the initial introduction smoother than it might otherwise be.

She still could not imagine holding a baby, her baby, in her arms. When the no-longer Pregnant Six had offered, lifting their babies into the air, ready to hand them over, Joan had demurred, rubbed her nose, and said, "I think I've got a touch of a cold." The bonding she knew she would have to do, it could only occur with her own.

"Okay, we're picking up near the top of page 376, in the Penguin Classics edition—

She gave him her hand, and muttered some word which was inaudible even to him; she gave him her hand, and immediately endeavoured to resume it, but he held it clenched within his own, and she felt that she was his prisoner. He was standing close to her now, and she could not escape from him. She was trembling with fear lest worse might betide her even than this. She had promised to marry him, and now she was covered with dismay as she felt rather than thought how very far she was from loving the man to whom she had given this promise.

'Alice,' he said, 'I am a man once again. It is only now that I can tell you what I have suffered during these last few years.' He still held her hand, but he had not as yet attempted any closer embrace. She knew that she was standing away from him awk- wardly, almost showing her repugnance to him; but it was altogether beyond her power to assume an attitude of ordinary ease. 'Alice,' he continued, 'I feel that I am a strong man again, armed to meet the world at all points. Will you not let me thank you for what you have done for me?'

She must speak to him! Though the doing so should be ever so painful to her, she must say some word to him which should have in it a sound of kindness. After all, it was his undoubted right to come to her, and the footing on which he assumed to stand was simply that which she herself had given to him. It was not his fault if at this moment he inspired her with disgust rather than with love.

Joan read to the baby until she had finished the chapter called *Passion Versus Prudence*.

The day before her water broke, before she knew that day would be remembered that way, Joan trashed *The Sympathetic Executioners*. She ripped up the pages until her hands were worn out, crumpled up the rest into loose, crinkly balls, stuffed it all into a trash bag, stuffed the trash bag into the garbage can at the side of the house. She would never revisit

the work, had no need or desire to keep the book, not even for poster-
ity, not even as proof that she had gone beyond the short-story form for
which she was so praised. She would have to start all over again, a new
novel from scratch.

Martin had not noticed when the typing stopped a few weeks before, had not been aware that she'd finished the book, had not noticed
when the manuscript was no longer visible on her desk. He was out early
in the mornings and home late. Major eye surgeries to perform every
day, research that filled up the breaks. She knew he wasn't aware that
he had stopped asking to read the pages in progress, unwittingly giving
her space and peace. Of course, it was no longer relevant.

She could not sleep that night, thinking of the loss of all that
excruciating effort that had been so pleasurable. At midnight, when she
still hadn't found a spot in the bed that suited both she and the baby,
she gave up. Martin was sleeping deeply, his arms and legs starfished,
the way the newborn daughters of the no-longer Pregnant Six sprawled
in their cribs. She could not recall ever seeing Martin in such a position.
He looked boyish and she felt far away from anything girlish.

She did not flip on the light switch in the nursery. She walked across
the cool wood floor and stood at a window. The sky was black, no
moon or stars. She could see nothing outside, and it was as if nothing
existed beyond the house in which a despondent, frightened woman
was wide-awake and a contented man asleep. She had failed Silas and
Abe. She had failed herself. She was not in the place she wanted to be,
with a finished first novel that would pre-date the child.

When she lifted her nose off the cold glass and stepped back from
the window, the low hallway light reflected her faint outline, and she
locked on her eyes. She tried to catch herself blinking, but couldn't.
She wondered how she would handle it all, how she would be as a
mother, when she would again have blocks of time for herself. The
baby would keep her from immediately starting something new.

She looked out into the void, into the invisible distance. She would
have to develop the narrative of real life, but already she missed her
submergence in those other worlds, within the only narratives that
had ever mattered to her, with her very own people, the fallow time
worth nothing at all.

4

Joan was propped up in the hospital bed, feeding their newborn son. Martin was on the bed with the two of them, his thumb and index a circle around both tiny ankles, above the tiny blue booties. The baby slipped off her breast and Martin took the infant into his arms.

Childbirth, and seeing the baby for the first time, and feeling his heart beating against hers, the suction between his slimy, steaming skin and her own, which had been mottled and wet, did not miraculously change Joan's worldview, as the no-longer Pregnant Six said it would. She did not suddenly feel it was her responsibility to solve war, genocide, disease, famine, hunger, low literacy rates, drug overdoses, the overcrowding of prisons. But she felt love, more than she thought she would, even though she was still not prepared, as other new parents seemed to be, to lay down her life for him, or for anyone.

She did not glow immediately after, but the baby did, not wizened at all, not old-man wrinkled. He did not emerge splotchy and crying. Instead, a light shone from his eyes, which he instantly opened, and when she looked down upon him, his eyes caught hers and did not let go, the two of them staring directly at each other, a kindling of sorts, until he fluttered to sleep.

And he was beautiful, a beautiful baby with blue eyes that matched her own, and a full head of downy dark-brown hair like Martin's, curls at the ends, for which she was responsible. He was good, too, rarely crying in these first few days, and when he did, it was as soft as a kitten's, and lasted for barely a minute. And he ate well. She had heard stories from two of the no-longer Pregnant Six about their own infants who hadn't figured it out, who didn't take to the breast, no matter how often an engorged nipple was stuffed into their mouths, who had lost a few precious ounces of birth weight before the mothers had resorted to formula.

The lactation specialist who came into Joan's room with pamphlets said it had been a long time since she had seen an infant latch on so easily, as Joan's did with her, that really, for now, there was no instruction she needed to give. And Joan felt a sense of pride, that at the start, she managed to do something right. She had not cursed it while it was baking inside of her, and he had emerged unscathed, with all his fingers and toes, with lungs that rose and fell, with a rosy mouth, with perfect lashes and brows, and the tiniest little bud between his legs that made both she and Martin laugh.

Martin cradled the baby against his chest and said, "We really should figure out what we're going to call him." On the table next to her hospital bed was the baby name book Martin had packed into her bag at the last minute, after she left a puddle in the kitchen, before he helped her out the back door, into the Toyota, racing out of Peachtree, down, through, and out of Rhome proper, to the campus where Martin spent most of his hours, Rhome General ablaze at four in the morning.

Joan picked up the book and let the pages fly. Then she closed her eyes, opened randomly, put her finger on the print, and looked down.

"Daniel," she said. "A Hebrew name. The biblical prophet and writer of the Book of Daniel was a teenager when taken to Babylon after the destruction of Jerusalem in 607 BC."

"We're not Jewish," Martin said.

"We're not anything, so does it really matter? What do you think of the name?"

"Daniel Manning," Martin said. "I like it, it's strong, the two names work well together."

They looked at each other and Martin said, "So is that this little guy's name? Daniel?"

"Yes," Joan said. "I think it is."

If Martin wanted to look up the name's other meaning, the book was right there beside her. She did not know why, not exactly, not in thoughts she could have articulated, but it seemed right to her that Daniel meant "God is my judge."

5

Joan saw their reflections in the glass doors, mother in the hospital-required wheelchair, blanket-wrapped baby in her arms, father standing behind, the bizarre manifestation of an instantaneous miracle, all at once a family. Then they were through the doors, and the baby was in the infant seat hooked into the back of Martin's Toyota, and Joan felt the frigid clouds on her skin, and they were on their way home.

Within hours, the snow began falling. They moved Daniel's crib into their room, and during the nights, while Martin slept, Joan lifted the baby out and breast-fed him, marveling at his perfect weight in her arms, his sated burps smelling richly of her own milk. In the mornings, at the living-room windows, she gazed out at the frozen range of white with peaks, summits, and ridges, and each time Joan bent down to kiss Daniel's soft forehead, he was already looking up at her, his eyes studying her face, never once looking away.

It took no time for her to fall deeply in love with her unexpected child, with the rigors and rituals of unwanted motherhood, with having Martin home, so naturally fathering, doing all that he could, cleaning the kitchen, changing the diapers, singing to their infant son in his crib. They were dreamily nesting, just like the no-longer Pregnant Six had engaged in, and Joan found it utterly satisfying, thought then she might be capable of having more than one dream, might possibly thrive in the pursuit of both.

She was not writing at all, did not expect to sit at her desk in these early days, but *happiness, pleasure, elation, sweetness, treat, treasure,* and *gratefulness* were added to her list of favorite words. Daniel was so good, easy to satisfy, to fill up, to put to sleep, and she knew it was only luck that had created this angelic child.

And then Martin returned to the hospital and the lab, a husband around only at dawn and at night when the stars were their brightest, and caring for a baby with only two hands, no matter his goodness, was like boxing up the Sahara with a spoon. Showers, if at all, happened in the late afternoon; she subsisted on crackers and cheese, relied on Martin to market, the hamburger meat, the steaks, the fish he bought sliding into the freezer and never considered again. She kept up with the laundry, but otherwise the house was a mess, and still she resisted Martin's suggestion of a nanny to help out.

"I'm wary of having another body around the house all day long," she said. Martin insisted, striking where she was weakest. "A nanny could let you get back to work."

Eight weeks in, Joan stepped into her study for the first time since giving birth. Illuminated by the cold winter light, the room was a frozen preserve. The typewriter on her desk, lifeless and cold, the dictionaries she hadn't reshelved still sat there, hulking books she barely remembered paging through with delight, finding words she once lovingly, ecstatically, used in her writing. When Martin returned home that night, she agreed.

A week later, Joan opened the front door to a tall young woman wearing a high-collared, long-sleeved dress in bright tropical colors, magenta and teal and cobalt blue and orange. Flower earrings budded from her earlobes, and her hair, the color of wet sand, was pulled back tight in a ponytail. It was barely thirty degrees outside, high drifts of snow in front of all the houses, small paths from front doors to road, but the young woman wore no coat, no hat, no gloves, and did not seem at all cold.

"I'm Fancy," and she shook Joan's hand with a hidden might. "Sorry," she said when she saw Joan's face. "I think I've gotten rather too vigorous. I joined the gym at the community center, been working out with weights every day since landing here in Rhome."

At the kitchen table, she tightened her tight ponytail, and said, "So I'm Canadian, grew up on Lake Ontario, the eldest of seven brothers and sisters. There comes a time when all chicks must leave the nest, and when my time came, I grabbed my best girlfriend, Trudy, her family lives down the block from mine back home, and we jumped on a bus and kept traveling until we stopped in Rhome. Strada di Felicità is just so pretty, and it seemed to me like this would be an interesting place to live, the way the town is a bunch of circles, getting larger and larger and larger, all the lovely stores, the lovely houses, so I turned to Trudy and said, 'This is the place, you game?' and she said she was, so we got off the bus and got down to business. We've got an apartment over Rudolph's Delicatessen on Tennessee Place. Such good food there, I must say. And I loved learning that the Italian man who founded Rhome thought every town should have a Street of Happiness running through it. I figured I could be happy in a place with a Strada di Felicità. And it's true, we are, the two of us, and we just love the busyness of the town, how there's always people out and about."

Joan thought Fancy's Canadian hometown must be minute indeed, because Rhome was charming, but sleepy, even with the hopefully named street.

"When I saw your advertisement for a nanny at the community center, I thought, 'Fancy, that's the job for you.' And now looking at you, such a pretty mother, I know I made the right decision to call. I'm nearly twenty, the oldest in my family by five years, so I've got tons of experience taking care of little ones. I practically raised my siblings myself. And this might be important to you, to gauge my seriousness, so I'll tell you now that I have no interest myself in men or romance. I leave all that to Trudy. Do you mind if I make us some tea? That's a nice kettle you've got on the stove. Just point me to the cabinet with the cups."

Joan did not laugh although she wanted to, listening to this Fancy, this odd young woman with her whirlwind of words, and instead said, "The cups are in that cabinet," pointing to the cabinet next to the sink, "and there are all kinds of teas in the drawer next to the fridge. Choose whatever you'd like."

Fancy was up and out of the kitchen chair, smoothing down her tropical dress, opening the cabinet, taking down two cups and saucers. "Nice, bone china," she said. "My family's never had much, but we always drink our tea from bone china, keeps it hot and makes one feel regal." Then she was opening the drawer and inspecting the boxes of teas. "Orange Pekoe okay with you?" and when the kettle whistled, Fancy brewed them tea strong as coffee, telling Joan, "This is what our queen, the queen of England, drinks, tea just this black."

Steam swirled up from their cups and Joan said, "Isn't Canada an independent country now? I didn't think the Queen still ruled there."

"Well, it's a little hard to pin our independence down to just one date. Some say it happened in 1867, but the truth is, it wasn't official until 1931, and it's only eight years ago that it was finalized, with the Canada Act of 1982. But the queen is still the official head of state, and she is our monarch. All Canadian children learn to speak the queen's English, and we are taught our table manners by imagining we are dining with her, that she is sitting just across the table from us. For instance, did you know that the proper way, the queen's way, of consuming soup is by sending the spoon through the liquid, away from yourself?"

"I don't think I did," said Joan, unable to picture the way her spoon moved through soup when she ate it.

Joan sipped her tea and Fancy drank hers down in two large gulps. "Nice, isn't it, when tea is sharp and powerful?" and Joan said that it was and then led Fancy out of the kitchen, down the short hallway, and into the baby's room, where Daniel was asleep in his crib.

Fancy took long strides across the room, leaned over the crib, her head falling forward, as if loose from her neck, and said, "He's a beautiful cherub and sleeping so well. What time did he go down for his nap?"

"Thirty minutes ago," Joan said. "He should wake in an hour."

Fancy straightened, and Joan thought she must be close to six feet, a good six inches taller than Joan, just a couple of inches shorter than Martin. A basketball player in flowers.

"I'm so glad you've got him on a schedule," Fancy said. "Too many mothers today think naptime is catch as catch can, which is nonsense in my book. A child on a sleep schedule is a happy child indeed."

Fancy stepped back nearly to the doorway and Joan watched her take in all of the room, her eyes moving from painted blank walls to bookcase to closet to changing table and back to the walls. Joan was waiting for the day when Daniel crayoned pictures and she framed them and hung them up.

"This is a lovely nursery," Fancy said. "I'm so pleased you chose yellow for the walls. Did you know that the yellow wavelength is relatively long and its stimulus is emotional, so it's the strongest color, psychologically? A yellow like this lifts spirits and self-esteem. It is the color of confidence and optimism. Living within it will help the cherub's emotional strength, his friendliness, his creativity. If you had chosen a brighter yellow, it could have caused his self-esteem to plummet, given rise in him to fear and anxiety, irrationality, emotional fragility, depression, anxiety, and a propensity for suicide. Or maybe in you, considering how much time you probably spend in here with him."

"Yellow can do all of that?" Joan asked. She had not considered the psychological ramifications when she and Martin chose the paint at Olinsky's Paint & Hardware in town, she had simply liked the shade.

"Definitely. Just think of that phrase, 'He's got a yellow streak,'" Fancy said. Joan thought that had to do with cowardice, rather than suicide, but who knew, perhaps cowardice could lead to suicide.

"Do you mind?" Fancy said, opening the closet door. Then she was murmuring to herself, "Nice sheets all lined up, nice clothes all hung up. Nice spare comforter for the crib. I'll show you how fast I am," and instantly Fancy was lifting the sleeping Daniel from the crib, cradling him in one long floral arm, stripping the mattress, remaking it, yanking the sheet tight as the navy vice admiral used to make Martin do, fluffing the small comforter, and in two minutes flat, Daniel, still asleep, was laid back down.

She was, Joan thought, a wacky kind of Mary Poppins. She hated that movie as a child, all that officiousness, as if children could not know their own minds, when Joan herself certainly did, but watching Fancy, Joan's perspective altered.

Fancy ran her fingers over the colorful mobiles hanging above the crib, checking for dust, Joan thought.

"I hope you won't be offended, but you could use my help. I can nanny and clean, and neither will take away from the other. And I was thinking, if you hired me, I could cook sometimes, if you'd let me. You have a very nice kitchen, and Trudy and I, our kitchen is just a pass-through sort of thing, not enough counter space to make anything real, and I miss cooking, which is a conundrum, I will say, since I swore I would never cook anything ever again once I hightailed it from home. All those mouths to feed morning, noon, and night."

She *was* a Mary Poppins, an original kind of fairy godmother in action, now at the bookcase, checking out the novels on the shelves that Joan read to Daniel while she nursed, as he nodded off for a nap.

She was reading him the second of Trollope's Palliser novels, *Phineas Finn*. Since he had manifested as a real baby, sometimes Joan bent to convention and read him silly children's books, about dogs and spots and hills and pails, which were stacked in the case as well.

"That's quite a variety of books you've got there," Fancy said, then continued on without taking a breath. "This is what I would suggest. I'll be here by seven every morning. And if you trust me, you can give me a key. And if you want, or need me, I'm happy to sleep in here, with the little darling, stay over, take the night feedings to give you some solid sleep. I'll just need a camp bed I can fold up and put away, or a mattress I can blow up, and a light blanket, nothing more. Otherwise, I'll be out of your hair when the little one is down for the night."

Fancy was offering to nanny and cook and clean and was willing to take the hateful night feedings, and Joan hired her on the spot.

"How wonderful. I can start tomorrow, if that's good for you. And apologies, I forgot to ask you, what do you call the cherub?"

"Daniel," Joan said. "Yes, please start tomorrow. Is there a list of things you'll need?"

"I'll get the lay of the land in the morning, and if it's easier for you, we'll make the list together, and I'll shop for whatever we need. I don't have a car, but I'm licensed to drive, so if you've got a car, I can use that."

"I do. It's in the garage. Should we talk about what you'll be paid?" Joan asked.

"Whatever you think is right," Fancy replied, and just like that Joan had an extra set of fast-moving hands helping her again.

Fancy was a miracle of competencies, a helpmate in motion, the way she danced around the kitchen, bathing slippery Daniel in the sink, bundling him up in a snowsuit, covering him with blankets, pushing him in the carriage over the Mannings' land, up and down the snowy hillocks all the way to the property lines.

"Come spring, I'll help you plant grass, if you want, and flowers, too, you've got so much space out there, you can't even see your neighbors. Once the snow melts, it would be a shame to leave it unloved." Fancy made the offer each time she came in with the baby hocked over her shoulder, Daniel blowing spit bubbles, his eyes dancing around.

Fancy sang to Daniel when she put him down for his naps, baked cakes and chickens while Joan napped too, or closed herself up in her study and sat at her desk, her hands folded in her lap, the Olivetti's plug pulled from the socket, coiled on the white painted floor.

Martin liked Fancy too, calling out, "Hello, all my good people," on the rare evenings he was home early. "It's so great walking into the house," he told Joan, and it was true, Fancy kept everything under control. The kitchen was always fragrant, something delicious cooking in the oven, a cake frosted on the kitchen counter, and the baby on the table, cooing in his portable bassinet.

On those early evenings of Martin's, he stayed in the kitchen, making himself a drink, talking to Fancy, playing with Daniel. When Joan grew tired of trying to remember how writing was once as natural to her as breathing, the typewriter still unplugged, no paper rolled in, she listened to the laughter, to the baby's happy gurgles, to Fancy's funny voice going on, and Martin jumping in, talking about this and that and nothing at all, until she gave into the delight, rose from her chair, and joined them all in the kitchen.

6

It was Fancy's fourth month with them when Joan plugged in her typewriter, rolled a piece of paper onto the platen, put her hands on the keys, and wrote a first sentence, then a second, then the typewriter keys were quietly rat-a-tat-tatting, sounding to her like a symphony, her heart beating to the rhythm, her breath falling in line with the tune.

Each word she put down shined, imbued with love for her son and for her husband, and with appreciation for this nanny they hired who already felt like a member of the family Joan never wanted. But the words belonged to her alone, and for the first time since becoming a mother, Joan found herself on the firm ground she inherently recognized. She was, she realized, out of the abyss.

During every one of Daniel's naps, she secreted herself in her study, calming Fancy when she worried that Joan was wearing herself out, was planning on weaning the baby too quickly.

At first, she was writing about a quirky young woman like Fancy, but within days Fancy disappeared, and Joan was writing about babies. Unusual babies, rare and wondrous, odd and strange, philosophical babies who could opine about almost anything. Her creations had turquoise hair, or ears meant for elephants, or toes and fingers fused together that did not alarm but instead allowed for happy paddling in baths and ponds, or hearts that beat outside of their chests marking their levels of happiness, or an ability to speak multiple languages immediately after letting out their first cry. Their traits, their characteristics, were elegant and weird, and varied from story to story.

The babies in "The First Play Date" compared their experiences while they had been inside, discussing whether the wombs they had chosen to inhabit had been cramped or roomy, whether the water had been too cold or just right, about the one-eyed sharks some saw coming at them nightly, while others said they never saw such a thing, just used the time to practice their acrobatics.

In "Our Needs, Our Dreams," babies in a hospital nursery fervently discussed the difficulties they were having managing their miasmic ids, their enormous desires to come first, to always be heard, to be fed at the first pang of hunger, wishing someone, their parents or the nurses, understood their incomprehensible babble, for they had so many nightly dreams that needed immediate telling.

In "Twins," a solitary baby in his crib stared up at the fluffy white clouds he could see from his window and soliloquized about how it felt watching his twin die in their mother's womb, when just moments before they had been playing a chatty patty-cake together, how awful it had been barreling down through the tunnel alone, leaving her behind, a pale specter beginning to disintegrate.

In "Role Reversal," the babies effected a cataclysmic shift that turned mothers into fathers and fathers into mothers, and in "The Miniature Caretakers," the babies wound up nursing and feeding and rocking and singing to the adults meant to care for them.

In every one of the stories, Joan's creatures unspooled odd familial tales. She called them her Rare Baby stories, but they weren't written for children.

She was surprised by the new lightheartedness in her writing. So much of her earlier work was about the damaging events that bowled her people over, and she had thought Daniel's birth would intensify her dark view of the world, that she would envision tragedies that would take Daniel away, but she found she did not fear for his safety at all, had faith in her newfound abilities, and in Fancy's and Martin's, to protect him.

Despite the disturbing qualities of her fictional babies, they were additional proof that motherhood was continuing to soften her. She had feared the opposite would occur, that she would become rigid and unyielding, as her mother had been. Instead, because of her own child, her writing was veering in a new direction; it was an unanticipated surprise.

Joan wrote five, then eight, then ten, then fourteen of the Rare Baby stories, and there were so many more bouncing around inside of her brain, in her heart.

"Tell me about them," Martin said. But the work was too new, and strangely personal, and Joan gave him no details; she did, however, tell him the truth: "Their sole purpose is just to get me working again, amidst the glorious mess of my reconfigured life," and he laughed the way she had hoped he would.

When Daniel was fussy at naptime, he settled when Joan leaned into his crib, stroked his face, and said, "It's time for a Rare Baby story." She took the recliner, and Fancy, hunched down on the short stool, reached through the wooden bars to hold Daniel's hand, her small hazel eyes already focused at some distant point, her mouth, with the gap between her front teeth, already opened, breathing excitedly about what was to come. One afternoon, Joan said to them, "This is the beginning of a story called 'Speaking in Tongues.'"

Since nearly the beginning of time, there were four inalienable truths about the Eves.

The first truth was that every single member of the family was female. There were no grandfathers, fathers, uncles, brothers, or nephews; there never had been. Each woman, on her own, without the need for any man, gave birth to a single child, and it was always a girl. It was Eve lore that their pure matriarchal line was a result of DNA, or caused by an undiscovered aquatic element, or was passed down in dreams from Eve to Eve, generation after generation.

The second truth was that the Eves had a specific, hallowed mission, every single one a musical thanatologist, playing harps or violins or cellos or flutes or lutes or using their lush a cappella voices as prescriptions rather than performance. Musically ushering the dying into the next world, or providing a quiet space for those facing eternity to reflect, ponder, rest, and muse on the meaning of life and death. Some of the dying were recipients of a single musical vigil, their time so near and at hand; others were treated to several, over weeks or months, calibrated to diagnoses, blood pressures, the insistence of diseases, the contraction of organs, the shifting of breaths, before they were claimed. Patients called the Eves angels of mercy, protectors of souls, but they were merely women curiously suited to the work, able to provide profound human connection with their invulnerable flesh, the way suffering flowed right through them without creasing their hearts.

The third truth was that every single Eve came out of the womb with identical features: long brown hair that fell to the waist, brown eyes that watched everything, and seashell ears that heard the slightest of sounds.

The fourth truth was that all Eves spoke early, by their eighth month. Training to become a musical thanatologist took a very long time, involved classes in music theory, in appreciation, in instrument and voice preparation, in rehearsal time, classes too in the workings of the body, in anthropology, in the history of death, potential sources of an afterlife. Over the eons, evolution unique to the Eves had shaved away the extra sixteen months normal children required to find their tongues, their voices, their words, their speech. Any Eve who did not begin speaking in that special eighth month faced an uncertain future, potential banishment from the clan, relegated to an unhappy life among boys and men whose harsh voices could force birds from the sky, turn soft rain into a killing machine, cause floods, famine, disease.

The Eves began with Ruth and wound through thousands of years down to Esther, who birthed Bessie, who birthed Annette, who birthed Willa. Of course, Willa looked exactly like her mother, like all her forebears, but she had sailed past her eighth month of life and had not said a word. Now that her first birthday had come and gone, fear was often in Annette's heart.

Willa was a good baby otherwise, a calm and still child, but she made no sound, not even a peep, and even when she cried, which was rare, she made no noise, her tears falling silently until they dried up and disappeared, leaving her long eyelashes beaded together, and the faintest silvery trail down her pink cheeks, grains of salt that some- times her mother licked off.

It was lunchtime on a Tuesday, and Annette was expected at two at one of the hospices on her regular route, a request for a violin vigil, made by the man himself. When he called, he said, "I'm 110, so there's no time like the present. To be bathed in the sweetness of the violin in the hands of a master like yourself must be one of the loveliest ways to go. I have come to terms with it all and I am ready to close my eyes for the last time, to be taken away by the melody of a *nigun,* the *Baal Shem* specifically." A *nigun* was the most taxing of soulful and religious Jewish songs, calling upon Annette's deep improvisational abilities, but the man's choice of the *Baal Shem* meant she had centuries of that *nigun* to follow, its overarching form structured by so many other violinists who had come before her, reflecting the mystical joy of intense prayer.

As she fed Willa the mashed peas she adored, one spoonful at a time, the *Baal Shem* was soaring through Annette and droplets collected in the corner of her eyes. Any crying by a thanatologist had to occur in advance, but certainly outside the walls of the hospice.

Another spoonful of the green mash and when the food slid in, Willa closed her perfect little cherry-red mouth and swayed with happiness. The kitchen clock never made any noise, but suddenly Annette heard the ticking, turned to look, watched as the second hand stopped sweeping, then moved forward again, one noisy click at a time. She felt her heart flutter, watched the spoon flip over in her hand, a dollop of green landing on the black and white tiled floor. Her head whipped back to her lovely little daughter, and she screamed.

Willa's unspoiled face had altered entirely, was suddenly abstract. There was her original mouth, the cherry-red one, so pert and lovely, but right next to it, as well-shaped as the first, was a second mouth, the deep purple of an overripe plum.

And then Willa spoke for the first time. From the cherry-red mouth came the words, "I love you, Mommy," and simultaneously, from the plum mouth, came the words, "You are a witch with a black heart, Mommy, I know what you really think about when you play your music, send those people to death"—

and Fancy inhaled so sharply that Daniel turned his head at the sound and let out a funny little laugh.

There was a timelessness for Joan in the act of creating these stories, a harkening back to when she was a young girl and beginning to write. After the failure of *The Sympathetic Executioners*, it was a relief to write without thoughts of publication, awards, and best-seller lists. The writing was pure again, the way it had been with both collections. And by reading aloud parts of the Rare Baby stories to Daniel and Fancy, she experienced the youthful pleasure denied her as a child, all that intense longing for a different mother who would have sat on Joan's bed and read Joan's stories aloud, exclaiming over what her child had produced. In the nursery, Joan's good voice floated, and the words of her strange stories rode the quiet air, and something way deep down inside of her was soothed, a release of the anger and hatred she had long carried about her mother, Eleanor Ashby, the force that colored Joan's earliest memories.

Each time she sat down to work on these stories, she knew they had something specific to tell her, perhaps about how she would be as a mother to Daniel as he grew up, encouraging his creativity, making true the positive effects of the buttercup-yellow paint. She sensed they were not meant to be heard by any others, not to be read by anyone else either.

At least once a weekend, Martin said, "How's the work coming? When can I read them? When are you going to send them to Volkmann?" He asked these questions, one or all of them, again and again, opening the door to her study while she was working, throwing her a kiss when he finished his querying, until shivers ran through Joan when she heard the knob turning, making her breath catch in her throat.

Each time, she said, "Soon, maybe," the way she had when he wanted to read pages from *The Sympathetic Executioners,* then said, "Martin, I need a little more time, then I'll be out."

Her husband, brash and brave in the operating room, in his focused research for groundbreaking ocular surgeries, seemed truculent in those freighted moments, before she responded, petulant even, and she felt incapable of explaining—had no desire to explain—the intrusiveness of his endless questions.

One day when they were alone in the living room, Fancy with Daniel in his room, Joan said, "Does it work for you that when you want to talk about your successes or failures in surgery, whether the research is going well or not, I listen, but otherwise I don't try to burrow into your world, just give you space to move and roam and be on your own, with your thoughts, hopes, and beliefs?"

"You're wonderful that way," he said, failing to make the leap he should have been able to make, to see that he was trying to burrow into her world, a place where he did not belong, and the single unspoken sentence jammed in her mind: *You've got to leave me alone.*

For a man so attentive to his patients, aware of their fears and their foibles, how had he forgotten this about her, her need to keep her work to herself? At the very least, when he was home, why didn't he notice that Fancy never, ever, knocked at the study when Joan was inside? If she thought a sign on the door would do the trick, she would have hoisted that sign right up, written in big black words: MARTIN—DO NOT DISTURB ME, but even that, she knew, would not keep him out. Sometimes she thought the only way to silence his voice, extinguish his interest, would be to stone him to death.

Breast-feeding ended, and bottles began, then rolling over and baby food, then gummed toes, solid food, first steps, and when Joan was not with Daniel or working on her Rare Baby stories while he napped, she and Fancy planted infant red maples, elms, and Cleveland pears around the property's entire perimeter, a weeping willow tree not far from the house. They hoed and raked the ground, eliminated the weeds, prepared the soil, tilled and fertilized it, then planted Kentucky bluegrass, tall fescue, fine fescue, Bermuda grass, Zoysia grass, and perennial rye, and took turns watering every morning and afternoon from spring to late fall. On weekends, Martin pitched in, allowing Daniel to think he was helping, his small hands gripping the hose just behind his father's big ones.

In their second year of planting, when the grass was finally fully established, Joan and Fancy figured out how to lay down sprinklers, and turned them on. "The water's going to be cold," Joan warned Daniel, but he ran laughing through the arcing sprays. "Look, Daniel," she said, and he stopped and looked at all the rainbows dancing around their backyard.

Joan and Fancy devised the shapes and boundaries of all the various gardens, marked them with sticks and flags, then got down to work, troweling, fertilizing, and planting lilac bushes, bougainvillea, hyacinth, phlox and poppies, tulips, wild violets, and gerbera daisies, everything in various hues of lavenders and pinks and purples and scarlets and burgundies and white, a field of lavender too. Their first vegetable garden was seeded with carrots, cucumbers, radishes, domestic toma-toes, beans, and lettuce, the vegetable world that thrived regardless of the gardener's abilities. Near the house, they built the playground Joan had imagined while weighing Daniel's early extermination. He now had a large sandbox to play in, and a swing set, and a bright-red jungle gym that took Martin three days of hard labor to put together.

In their third year of planting and gardening, all the flowers came up, a riot of blooms. Joan and Fancy took Daniel with them to the lumberyard, bought planks of wood and panes of wavy old glass and the building specifications for a gardening shed. They sawed and hammered, figured out how to make window frames, how to install the glass, and the shed rose up behind the weeping willow tree that was still so small, Daniel shimmying up its baby trunk yelling, "Look at me," all of twelve inches above the ground. When Fancy went home to Canada for a family visit, Joan painted the shed green by herself and stored all the gardening equipment within. By then, they had a potting table, ceramic planting pots stacked up like mismatched wedding-cake tiers, a large assortment of dinged and muddy trowels, rakes and hand mowers, bags of rich dirt for settling cuttings of delicate flowers into the pots until the new baby plants were sturdy enough for life outdoors. Sometimes, Joan escaped to the shed for an hour of quiet with a glass of wine, lowering a window for an illicit cigarette, briefly longing for the time when she had not created a different story for herself, longing too, for other ideas to flow through her mind, something beyond her rare babies.

Daniel was nearing four when Martin began flying to England, Germany, Croatia, and Russia, requested by private hospitals to operate on their citizens. Against the odds, he was having great success with his newly devised surgery, returning sight to people who lived in an underworld of barely recognized shapes, or no shapes at all.

Joan was on the bed watching Martin pack for his tenth trip abroad—lucky scrub caps, the funny clogs he wore during his long surgical days, his toothbrush, toothpaste, razor, a T-shirt and pajama bottoms, two suits, shirts, ties, his shiny leather loafers, a winter sweater, jeans, and snow boots all went into his travel bag.

He turned to her suddenly. "Come on, Joan. You've let me read a page here and there, but why can't I read the Rare Baby stories from start to finish? I've got all these hours on planes and it would be great to read something other than medical journals and the newspaper."

Three and a half years writing those stories and they still felt like a secret to Joan. She had all the audience she needed in Daniel and Fancy. She touched her belly and wondered if she would read them aloud to the new baby. There was always going to be a second child, and soon there would be.

She watched Martin's mouth moving. He was still talking, inveigling her to let him read the work, but Joan was thinking of something else entirely, of how the news she was pregnant again had spurred a sort of silent trade-off: Martin no longer opened her study door without knocking, did not enter unless invited.

She tuned back in when his mouth clamped shut, his face clouded with hurt, and she thought she ought to give him the benefit of the doubt. She climbed off their bed, went into her study, gathered up five of the stories, and handed them over. She watched as he placed them neatly inside his briefcase.

A week later, back home, unpacking his bag, he pulled out her stories, all marked up, and her heart was once again beating too fast. She felt churlish, though, and remonstrated, when he pulled out a wrapped package and gave it to her. He had brought her a present, but when she opened it, there was a frightening device in her hand, antique and rusted, and Martin said, "That's a scleral depressor from the early twentieth century. I found it in a store in Cologne. Isn't it great?"

He turned it over in her hand. "You insert the tip between the globe and the orbit, the space occupied by the probe displaces the retina inward and creates an elevation. It helps locate and diagnose lesions that may otherwise go undetected, like retinal holes, tears, or vitreoretinal adhesions. It's used to assess patients who present with complaints of flashers and floaters, or who are at risk for peripheral retinal anomalies, such as high myopes or those with a history of blunt trauma."

He returned the depressor to its velvet-lined box. "I saw it and thought since I'm traveling to so many places, I should keep a lookout for these kinds of things, start a collection of old tools of the trade."

She felt the ghosts of eyes touched by that tool, the coldness of the metal still singed her palm.

Then he said, "Come on. Let's take Daniel for a walk."

It was Sunday and they were Fancy-free. Daniel was in his room, on his bed, the novel she was reading to him—*The Happy Island* by Dawn Powell—on his lap, and he was pretending to read.

"Mommy, listen to me," and he read, "*Everyone who knew James knew of his Evalyn, and that a visit from the Inspector General could not cast a town into greater confusion,*" and Joan was shocked. She recognized the sentence from the book, and he read on, "*No one found her agreeable. Desperately James told stories about her to make her appear interesting, but she only emerged a more intolerable figure than before.*"

She called out for Martin, and when he stood at Daniel's door, she said, "He's reading already! Whole sentences without sounding out the words. Just like I did, but I was older, five, when it happened."

Martin kneeled before Daniel. "Are you reading now, my man?" and Daniel nodded and began telling his father about the bachelors of New York City, and Martin looked up at Joan.

When everyone was zipped into their winter coats and out the front door, Martin whispered, "Maybe we should make sure he reads age-appropriate books." That wasn't going to happen on Joan's watch, but the battle could wait for another day.

They walked the wide streets of their development, the paving all complete, young trees bare-limbed in the cold, and were quiet for a while.

"So about your stories. I loved them all, but especially 'Otis Bleu Sings.' The way that baby could belt out an opera without any teeth in his mouth."

Daniel twisted around in his stroller and called out, "Mommy already read me that story."

They made rights and lefts through the neighborhood and all the while Martin was telling her his thoughts about the stories, the emotions he experienced while reading her work, then asking her questions. "How do you develop these characters? How does your brain hit upon these creations? What makes you think as you do? Are the stories based at all on Daniel, on the things he does? Are you imagining the new baby inside of you when you write?"

It was perhaps the hundredth time Martin quizzed her this way, wanting to dive into the depths of her mind, to know exactly how she put things into place, now asking specifically how she came up with the traits of her rare babies, their names, their family configurations, the outrageous things they did and said. This obsession he had to expose her processes, to aerate the pure elements of her work, he seemed to want her fully oxidized. She did not bask in his interest, as genuine and real as it was. Instead, she felt as if she were standing back at the abyss, and if he did not stop, if she could not stop him, she would fall into the darkness for good.

In the kitchen, after their walk, Joan told Martin he was in charge of dinner and closed herself up in her study. She sat at her desk and wished she were configured like other women who welcomed such keen attention, or at least like other writer-mothers who seemed to connect everything together, who handled with relish the confusion of it all, combining writing with motherhood, everything out in the open. There was a heroic disorder to their lives, but she could not abide it. This coalescing amalgamation of the disparate parts of her life—writer, wife, mother, pregnant woman again—was not what she had ever wanted. She had a baby, was going to have another, was writing about babies, had a husband who wanted to know everything about what their baby did in his absences, about how the baby inside was treating her, what her rare babies were up to, and how they had come to be. She was consumed by domesticity: the normality of her flesh-and-blood family juxtaposed against her manifested world, which was mystical, numinous, sometimes supernaturally odd, filled with erudite babies illuminating what others could not see.

She put her shaking hands on her typewriter, watched them settle, all the while feeling the impulse to walk out, to disappear, as she had considered doing when she told Martin she was pregnant the first time, their incongruent stances about the life she was carrying rocking her entirely, an earthquake upending the life she had anticipated for herself.

Her soul, she realized, was in disarray, and this second pregnancy was not helping. It was not at all like the first. She had morning sickness day and night. She was not miraculously glowing. A second baby would intensify the disorder she needed, somehow, to compart-mentalize.

Over the next several days, she read through all fifty of her Rare Baby stories. They were beautiful, the writing strong and densely molded, but she did not want to publish such a collection, did not want to be yoked forever to these creatures who had been intended only to help her maneuver through that first vital metamorphosis.

She would not read them aloud to the new baby, when it finally arrived. She could not indulge in this exercise any longer. If she did, she would slip entirely away, become irreal, an outline when she was made more solidly than that. It was the first Joan Ashby, the realest Joan Ashby, the one who was neither wife nor mother, that she was in immediate danger of losing. She had to eliminate the concentric circles that dominated her life, otherwise she would not be able to carry on building the family they were building, would want only to cut the bonds that tied her down.

With Daniel, she had imagined herself as a character who would hang on to the love she had been given and love her unwanted baby, and she had done that exceedingly well. She would do it again when the new baby arrived. But before that happened, she needed to reframe her existence, fracture her life, bifurcate Joan Manning, wife and mother, from Joan Ashby, the writer, erect boundaries to prevent any accidental bleeding between the two.

Volkmann called only twice a year now to confirm Joan had received her royalty statements and checks. She no longer asked about Joan's plans for her first novel, assumed Joan had ceased writing entirely, consumed with something like the joys of motherhood, and Joan allowed her that belief. The same was true with Annabelle Iger, who called every couple of months, saying, "Haven't you had enough of this pastoral existence, all this mothering and wifedom? Aren't you sick of love and diapers? Start writing again before it's too late." She and Iger talked of so many things, their editing days together, the men Iger was toying with, the plays Iger saw, the dance clubs Iger still frequented, but Joan never mentioned *The Sympathetic Executioners* or the Rare Baby stories to her either.

She was again at a critical juncture, and this time, she needed to maintain the divide, husband and children out in the real world, but on her own, the writing she did would be truly private, consecrated, known only to her. No more reading her work to Daniel and Fancy. The new baby's arrival would eliminate her study, soon to be transformed into another nursery.

She watched the reddened sun pale and set, and she pictured a castle with a tower that soared into the sky, a moat that rendered it inviolable, an imaginary place where she would write for the next years, without Martin knowing. She would throw him off her scent, lie and tell him she was taking a break, void entirely his inquisitions. She did not want to hear him talking about her work, suggesting, pontificating, analyzing. On the walk, the names of her characters had been far too familiar in his mouth. He had her and Daniel and the child to come; that would have to be sufficient.

In that high tower, that place of pure self, she might find her way to that first novel, at last write a book worthy of the reputation she had developed. She only wanted what belonged to her—what she created, her characters, her people, those with whom she spent the clearest hours of her days. It was, she thought, the way to make that truest part of herself whole once again. And if she protected her most essential qualities, the core of Joan Ashby, she could continue to give the rest of her heart to Martin, to Daniel, to the baby inside.

She thought about Fancy. She could trust Fancy to keep her secret when Joan returned to her work, after the early months with the new one.

She looked at Martin's father's clock on her desk. It had taken only thirty minutes to arrive at her plans for the future. Joan opened the study door and headed toward the living room, where her family was gathered. She could hear the roll of dice, the movement of plastic pieces, Martin and Daniel laughing, accusing each other of cheating, and she was aware how those voices both attracted and repelled her.

7

The delivery-room music was raucous in her thirty-second laboring hour. The baby was ten days late, and at the twentieth-fifth hour, she had still been ticking off appropriate words: *troublesome, exasperating, perverse, contrary, recalcitrant, obstreperous, disobliging,* and then the few *u* words she could recall: *unaccommodating, unhelpful, uncooperative, unwanted.* Wait, she'd thought, when *unwanted* spiked, an articulated word she hoped only she heard. And then: *entirely true, entirely not true, this time, last time, true and not true.* She was sidetracked, the dictionary in her brain slipping away when a nurse increased the sweet epidural drip, and the music changed nature entirely. There had been Beethoven, Bach, and Mozart sailing through the delivery room, she was not an expert in classical music, but they were easily recognizable; now electric guitars were wailing, drumbeats pounding away, licks and harsh syncopations, and Joan's voice croaked when she yelled, "Please! Change the station." Nothing changed and she couldn't tell if the music and her yelling were only inside her own head. *Please,* she prayed then, though the years had not changed her position about God, or gods, and she had already run through the panoply of words she used to invoke, could remember.

Daniel's birth had been rapid, like a rocket, he set a record, leaving Joan with most of her self-respect intact, but not this time, this one already determining the time line of life. Her sweat, rivers of it, started out sweet, had gone sour, then yeasty, and now there was a meaty scent she was inhaling. She felt like a sick and cowering dog.

The bright lights all at once dimmed—why hadn't they been lowered from the start, hadn't they asked for a calm, quiet, melodic delivery?—and then Martin was soothing her forehead, whispering into her ear, "It will be okay."

A contraption rose over her belly, gloved hands draping reams of thick plastic over it, cutting off everything below from her view. She was in parts, leaving those on the other side to contend with what was beneath her curved flesh. Scrub caps darted around, white, pink, and yellow disks rising and falling, rapid voices chasing each others' tight tails, words like *maternal tachycardia, fetal distress, spinal block, catheter, IV lines*, and Joan felt something sting her hand. Out of the cyclone came her doctor's quiet voice, "Scalpel. Starting Pfannenstiel incision."

How wonderful now that everything was silent, the pain and fear gone, just the slow, slow beating of her own heart, her mind in a white haze that transformed into bleedingly bright primary colors. She remembered the pictures of a C-section that she had seen in one of Martin's medical books, the scalpel so sharp against the thin skin that the underlying yellow fat layer burst, revealing the shiny, tough, fibrous fascia, over the abdominal muscles. A scalpel nicking an opening in that tough lower layer, then pulled apart, revealing the filmy, flimsy layer, the peritoneum, the actual lining of the abdominal cavity; it, too, was opened, with sharp, thin scissors. Then a small cut through her retroperitoneal. She heard "Retractor," and pictured her bladder pulled down toward her feet, away from the rest of the surgery, sparing it injury. A final incision across the lower portion of her womb, her uterus easily tilted up and laid on her belly, revealing the baby only to the doctor and nurses busy working. There were pictures of it all in Martin's book and a sentence that read: *Pulling gently on the head will allow the rest of the delivery.* She heard "Clamping umbilical cord," and then she heard no more.

She woke in a hospital room and wondered why she was there, wondered when someone would come to explain why she felt nothing below her waist, nothing at all. She knew she should be afraid, but something in her bloodstream was lifting her up, up, up, out of the bed, and she was floating just below the ceiling. Looking down, she was at the old dining-room table she used as a desk, the wood floor of her East Village apartment sloped under her feet, pages crawling with words flying through the air, stacking up next to the typewriter, there was a title on the tip of her tongue, that slid right off, and she, too, slid away.

She woke again, and knew she was in her hospital room, that there was, or had been, a baby. Martin was on the bed, carefully balanced, tenderly looking at her. She heard him say, "That was all unexpected," then ask how she was feeling, but she couldn't respond, couldn't keep her eyes open, they were like windows slamming shut, and her last thought, It's *all* unexpected, reverberated then faded away.

She woke again and Martin was in the armchair next to the bed, the baby hidden in a blue blanket. So the operation had been successful, the baby alive. "He emerged with bravado and his eyes clenched tight. He has all of his parts," Martin said, and Joan wanted to say, "Turn down the painkillers, I can't stay awake," but she was gone before the words left her mouth.

She was awake and alone in her hospital room. She felt wrecked and sore and the clock hands were elongated snails inching around the black markings of the day, but perhaps it was night, and late, because she couldn't hear the nurses laughing at their station, couldn't hear the shush of their foam-soled shoes.

She woke and knew it was morning from the slant of the sun lighting up her hands, the veins standing out, needles inserted and taped down, and then the heavy door pushed open, and there was Martin, smiling and cradling the new baby, sitting down on the bed, transferring the infant into her arms. "Your first glimpse of your mommy," Martin said, and Joan saw a cap of jet-black hair, skin white as alabaster, the combination giving him the look of a baby ghoul or a vampire, something medieval, potentially poisonous. But everything was where it belonged. "He's beautiful, isn't he," Martin said, and Joan thought the pain meds were affecting her sight, for the baby looked so white, as if he were bloodless, when Daniel had been golden and rosy.

You've been in and out," Martin said as he untied her hospital gown, pushed it down past her breasts. She hadn't said a word yet, her throat still clenched tight, but he understood she wanted the baby's flesh on hers. She had been right, with Daniel, about the essentialness of that first connection, not wasting it on anyone else's baby. She was overheating, but the infant was cool and dry, not damp and sticky as Daniel had been, and even though they were skin-to-skin, the way this one looked up at her, she thought she had to be wrong, that it wasn't an arrogant stare, a smirk on his pale lips. He blinked, then turned his head away, already his own person.

She tried feeding him. He latched on. She felt the suction between his pursed mouth and her nipple, but suckling did not interest him, he was content to lie there, just like that, before tucking back into himself. Four times she tried, before Martin paged their ob-gyn.

Dr. Hinton lifted the baby from Joan's arms and said that because of the C-section and the meds coursing through her, he hadn't been allowed to suck after being liberated from her womb. Dr. Hinton actually said, *When he was born*, and Joan revised his words because *liberated from her womb* expressed the gravitas she thought this birth deserved. "The suck reflex is strongest then, right after birth. Delayed gratification sometimes makes it more difficult later on. But it's only the third day." Joan hadn't realized she had been out for so long. The doctor stroked the baby's lips. "To evoke and test the rooting reflex," he said, and the baby pulled the doctor's pinky into his mouth. "He's gone into full reflex, pulling my finger in, wrapping the lateral sides of his tongue around it, creating a medial trough, starting the peristaltic motion from front to back toward the soft palate and pharynx. Nothing's wrong with the short frenulum, because his tongue's moving forward easily. His airway is all clear, no mucous. So everything looks fine. He's got a powerful suck, see how he's moving his whole head, his face wrinkling and dimpling?" Joan and Martin nodded. "I'll send in the lactation specialist. She'll be able to help."

But the baby had made his decision. He would not partake in such intimate nurturing, was disinterested in receiving nourishment direct from Joan's body. At her request, his bassinet was moved out of the nursery and into her hospital room. On a frequent schedule, the nurses had her pump, then returned with bottles of her milk wrapped in white cloths, as if mother and son were about to embark together on a fine dining experience. But he did not want Joan as the source of his sustenance, his tongue touched the plastic nipple, held on, sucked once, then he turned away, closing his eyes as if to say, *I've made it clear, haven't I, that I don't want what comes from her?* He was fed bottles of formula instead. Her milk was donated to a baby down the hall whose mother could not nurse at all.

At least Joan could keep him tightly grooved to her body, and she held their new child for hours, letting him go only when he was solidly asleep. It had been so different with Daniel, the way love had bubbled up, until the stream was an ocean, too large to ever spring a leak. Every day in the hospital, Joan waited for this new one to grab hold of her heart, to adhere to her beat, but a cool river ran between them that neither seemed capable of fording.

She and Martin had learned its sex ahead of time, no need for mystery with the second. And they had chosen a name. But only sometimes did Joan remember that fact, to use it when she spoke to him quietly. His birth certificate read Eric, Norse for *ever or eternal ruler*. Neither she nor Martin had any connection to that Nordic world, but it sounded strong, as strong as *Daniel Manning*. Just days old, and it seemed to Joan that Eric was indeed already ruling over his world. The kisses she gave him often felt premeditated.

Years later, Joan would wonder if she had already known everything, about him, but not just about him, about all that was to come, seeing the future while still in her hospital bed, clutching the baby to her heart, hoping the separation between them would close and heal, looking into his unfathomable eyes.

Perhaps it was the epidural she had been given, with its local anesthetic and narcotics, or the general anesthesia during the C-section, or the painkillers she was swallowing every four hours, but future events tumbled through her mind during those days and nights in the hospital, whipping past her eyes so quickly they could not be called visions, a kaleidoscope of images, mere flashes immediately forgotten. Through the years, certain situations would feel familiar, the feelings too, that sense of recollection, a déjà vu she could not place, not remembering that her mind once overflowed with an abundance of vital information. There would be no sense of that déjà vu, however, when the family she had never wanted twisted down into unknown depths, into a different kind of abyss, from which a roaring animal would race, up through dank tunnels, to tear into tender flesh. None of *that* was captured in those frenzied images. Did a broken heart reveal itself in X-rays, or was an autopsy required to see the fracture lines running through the four chambers, where ventricles and atria had shattered?

But in those earliest days, when nurses flitted in and out, checking her incision, rubbing her down with lotion to abate the itching, forcing her to cough, and to take short walks, as she tried mothering Eric, what Joan saw clearly were the vast, indecipherable truths written across his eyes, keenly felt the way he demanded and rejected her attention.

Her heart had opened wide for Daniel, with an unexpected and boundless adoration for her firstborn, but she knew instantly that Eric would not hold the same sacrosanct place, that he would never want what she could offer. And although her immediate reflex was to deny the notion of unequal maternal love, she realized that motherhood might also include what falls away.

THE ALTERATION OF PLANS

Yōjanā'ōṁ me badlav

8

On a hot windy day that tore the clouds apart, Joan and Martin brought Eric home. The pink roses out front had died while she and the baby were in the hospital, and carrying him up the brick walk, through that dead arbor, seemed like a funeral procession.

Framed by the opened front door, Daniel clutched Fancy's hand, still dressed in his camp clothes, his face peeking out from behind her wide flowered skirt.

He had a sweet, confused look on his face, a tremulousness about what was happening. He looked at his mother's belly, no longer as enormous as it had been when he felt a leg, a hand, the kicks, squealing when the skin rippled, like waves on a lake, when the baby somersaulted around. Joan and Martin and Fancy had each explained the concept, that what was inside of Joan would eventually come out, that Daniel would have a brother, and now the baby was here, at the doorstep, about to enter their home, changing the nature of their threesome, their foursome, forever.

Fancy's face was all lit up, her big front teeth shining, that gap between them like a secret.

Joan settled on the couch, and Fancy said, "A cause for celebration. Mr. Martin bought a nice bottle for a toast, and there's ale in the fridge for your milk." Fancy did not know yet that Joan's milk was of no use.

Daniel clung to Fancy's hand until she said, "Master Daniel, climb up and take your first look." When Fancy was nervous, formal appellations preceded their names.

He let Fancy go, kicked off his small tennis shoes, and climbed up on the couch.

"So Daniel, this is Eric," Martin said, and Daniel stared up at his father, then back to the baby.

"Can I?" he said, and Joan said, "Of course," and when Daniel gently touched the baby's face, his confusion fell away.

"He's so soft." Joan laughed. "Just like you, my love, when you were his age. The way you still are."

Daniel looked out the window at his playground. "When can I show him the sandbox and the swings and the jungle gym? When can he hang from his knees, like me?" Martin lifted Daniel into his lap. "A few years, buddy. Then he'll want to do everything with you."

The next day, Daniel insisted on feeding his baby brother, this infant he was already imagining as his friend, eager, even, to boss around; not knowing that someday Eric would neither heed nor follow, would leave Daniel in a silent, stormy race for dominance that Eric would know nothing about.

It was difficult to pry Daniel away from the baby. His new life in kindergarten could not compare. He did not want to leave with Fancy each morning, came running in at noon, insisting on knowing everything that happened in his absence before he would agree to eat his lunch. "Tell me the whole story of this morning," he would say to Joan, "and don't leave anything out." And she described it all—the feedings, the diaper changes, the naps, the drools, the songs Fancy had sung, what part Joan was up to in the book she was reading to Eric. During her late, heavily pregnant months, Daniel's favorite bedtime tale was hearing how Joan read to him when he was a tadpole, making her recite the names of those books he heard from inside her belly.

When Eric had been home for several weeks, Daniel said, "Mom, I'm going to make a list and you have to read those books again to Eric. I'll listen too, if I have time."

His seriousness made her realize she had not read to Eric in utero, as she had with him, and that whatever Eric heard during those nine pregnant months when she read to Daniel tucked up in his bed, was unintentional, secondhand, an afterthought.

Daniel included the Palliser and Trollope series; Balzac's *Lost Illusions*; Maugham's *The Painted Veil*; all the Dawn Powells, and so many more, but her Rare Baby stories weren't on his meticulous list.

Those stories were in the past and she wasn't going to read them to Eric, but Daniel had heard them until he was four and, childishly, Joan wanted to know why he had left them off.

One afternoon, when Joan was in the recliner, Eric in her arms sucking hard at a bottle, Daniel ran in. "Where are you?" he demanded. "We're starting the chapter called 'The Two Dukes' in Trollope's *Phineas Redux*." "I remember that chapter, it's a good one," he said, and Joan thought he had to be pretending, wanting to impress her, as he liked to do, by demonstrating his smarts. He often joined her in the nursery, sitting on the stool while she read to Eric, frequently telling her he remembered that scene or that character, when so-and-so did this or that, but it was always a recollection after the fact. Still, if Daniel was telling the truth, then he remembered everything, which had to include her Rare Baby stories, and Joan wondered why he never mentioned them.

The weekend after they celebrated Eric's first birthday, Joan was on her knees in one of the gardens, her hands thrust deep into the rich earth, packing in mail-order tulip bulbs, thinking about whether she owed her parents a note. They had sent an unexpected birthday card to Eric, with a wrinkled twenty-dollar bill inside. The card had been devoid of preprinted sweetness, just Eleanor Ashby's truncated *"Good Luck"* in English, rather than in the professed French of her soul. And Joan couldn't figure out whether her mother meant the sentiment sarcastically. And if she did, whether it was directed at Joan, or at one-year-old Eric, who was another grandson her parents had no interest in meeting. But all that internal debating ceased when Fancy ran toward her, calling out, "You've got to come quick. Nothing's wrong, but hurry."

Daniel was in the baby's blue-walled nursery, the color suggested by Fancy. "Blue is the color of the mind," she had told Joan and Martin. "Blue is soothing and will foster the new one's intelligence, communication skills, serenity, logic, coolness, reflection, and calm. Pick a strong blue to stimulate clear though. The flip side of blue, or choosing the wrong blue, is a child who is cold, aloof, lacks emotions, or is unfriendly." Martin had laughed, but Joan thought the buttercup yellow they had chosen for Daniel's room was, perhaps, responsible for his wonderfully balanced nature, his early ability to read, his voracious love of books, his easy laughter, his ease falling instantly to sleep at bedtime; and at Olinsky's Paint & Hardware, Joan and Martin had selected Imperial Blue, like the velvety background of a star-laden night.

Daniel had dragged the nursing recliner over to the crib, in which Eric sat holding the stuffed giraffe Fancy had given him as a birthday present. His brown eyes were so round as he stared at his big brother. Daniel was holding the blank notebook he'd asked Joan for a week earlier. From where she stood, she could see that at least two pages were covered in words he had written himself.

Joan put a finger to her lips and Fancy nodded, the two of them staring into the room through the jamb of the open door.

"Henry is a very small squirrel with ocean-blue eyes. His fur is gray and so is his bushy tail. He lives in a park that has lots of trees. One of those trees is a weeping willow and that is his home, in a hole in that tree, where he lives all alone. Sometimes that makes him very, very sad. Sometimes he cries at night when he remembers he once had a mother and a father and a baby brother, all of them gone one day, leaving him behind. He gets mad, too, when he remembers they didn't even leave him a note, just left him to try and do his best by himself. On his sixth birthday, he woke up wondering how to make the day special, when he wouldn't have any presents or balloons. He scrambled out of his hole, his bushy tail waving, and he looked all around the park. In the pond in the middle, he saw a baby duck swimming around, and he ran straight there. The duck was so little with feathers that looked like snow. 'Hi, Duck,' Henry said. 'It's my birthday and I want to know if you want to play with me.' Duck said, 'Okay. Come swimming with me.' Henry said, 'I don't know how to swim. But wait. I've got a great tail, and my feet are sort of like flippers, and maybe they'll keep me from sinking. So here I go.' And then Henry was in the pond with the duck and they splashed and played together for hours.

"The End," Daniel said, and it was silent in the nursery for two or three seconds, and then Eric began to laugh his baby laugh, a gurgle more than anything else, but the sound he was making, the emotion he was conveying, was obvious, and Daniel said, "I don't see what's so funny. It's a good story."

Joan and Fancy smiled at each other and tiptoed down the hall into the kitchen. It was a Saturday, Martin was at the hospital making rounds, and Fancy pulled out a bowl and cans of tuna fish, then opened the fridge for the mayonnaise. "Daniel's five years and seven months old and *he's* writing. How about you?" Fancy said.

"How about me, what?" said Joan.

"You know," Fancy said, and Joan did know.

The month Eric was due, Joan had done what she intended, told Martin she was taking a break from writing. "You know me," she had said to him, "I need a room with a door to work and my study is the baby's nursery now." Martin had nodded. "Whatever you want to do. Whatever makes you happy." It was so easy to get the lie past him, that would permit her to write without his knowledge, to keep him and their family far away from the precious part of herself. Still, she had been surprised he did not question her ability to cut herself off from her work, for whatever period of time, and disappointed to know he wouldn't think of scaling the stone walls of her imaginary castle. Where did he store all the knowledge he had gleaned about her during their eight years together, or had he cleared his mind entirely, simplified his life, patients and research coming first, good and loving fathering in the off hours. Regardless, the lie was not supposed to come true, and more than a year had passed since Joan had written a word, those rare babies still figuring into her dreams. She had no satisfactory answer to Fancy's unstated question, and it caused the usual sharp pain in her heart. For the past year, she had kept small notebooks and pens in her nightstand, in the nursery dresser, in her bag, but the pages remained blank, all that hostile white space, and she wondered if it was her fault, that the small notebooks made her think of journals, of diaries, repositories of dated lies and half-truths.

"I've seen Daniel so intent at his desk, but I didn't know he was writing a story," Joan said to Fancy instead. To celebrate his coming advancement into first grade, Joan and Martin had bought him a small white desk. Daniel had known what he wanted. "Something," he said, "that makes everything I do look good."

"First one I've heard," Fancy said. "But that cherub's got a first-rate imagination, just like yours. See how well the yellow walls worked out."

Joan wanted to tell Daniel she heard him reading his story to Eric, praise and encourage him, express her thrill that he was her miraculous son, a writer just like she was. She nearly said something, until she thought back to the Joan in the story she was actually living, and knew *that* Joan would not interfere prematurely in the creative life of her firstborn.

"Daniel wrote a story," Joan told Martin in bed that night. She felt the mattress depressing as his long body rolled over, felt his breath on her cheek. She stared up at the white ceiling. Why hadn't they painted their bedroom a color specially chosen to increase or decrease the particular characteristics of its inhabitants, as they had done with the rooms their children lived in? Fancy had never presumed to suggest they paint their room, but what did she make of their white box? What did white signify, aside from purity, cleanliness, simplicity? Hostility, Joan thought, considering the pages of those notebooks stashed and unmarked. But why not white, and why bother now, when no paint color in their bedroom could alter their own long-formed personalities.

"I know," Martin said. "He's been showing them to me."

"*Them?*" Joan said, and sat up. "He's written more than the one Fancy and I overheard today?"

"Maybe three or four," Martin said. "He finds me and hands me a story and waits until I read it, then wants to talk about it with me, asks me what I think. I've told him he's inherited your talent."

Joan twisted her hair up in a bun, found a pin on the nightstand, and stabbed it in. "Why wouldn't he bring *me* his stories instead of you?"

Martin pulled Joan back down. "Maybe it's a father-son thing, who knows." She let him stroke her face, her neck, but when he reached to kiss her, she said, "I'm wiped. I've got to sleep."

But he was asleep before her, and in the dark, the moon through the open drapes highlighted the whiteness of their room. Joan thought of Daniel writing away and debated how long the duration could be, without writing, before a writer was no longer considered a writer.

It took Daniel several months before he told Joan he was writing stories. She didn't ask why he had chosen his father first, kept all that to herself, just said, "I think that's absolutely wonderful, I can't wait to read them," and Daniel dashed away into his room and came back with three one-pagers. Then the stories grew longer, to two pages, then three, then more, and Daniel brought Joan every new one first, and every single one featured Henry the Squirrel.

She marveled how Daniel made him a Cub Scout, an animal tracker, a hiker, a surfer, a sailor, a long-distance swimmer making his way from Miami to Cuba, finding the particulars of the ocean's currents from the set of encyclopedias kept on the bottom shelf of the living-room bookcase. Daniel put Henry into risky situations, ascribed to him a catalogue of fears, and then forced the squirrel to use his wily imagination to overcome the challenges he faced. What would Henry do now that he was stranded at the Everest base camp; how might he tame the shark following him in the ocean; how could he pull a teenager drowning in a pool to safety?

In the stories Joan wrote when she was Daniel's age, she had murdered her characters, while Daniel had his one character facing down dangers and searching for answers. The genesis of the stories was clear to her: because Daniel felt loved and safe within his family, he could imagine himself taking risks, venturing out onto figurative limbs. He was lucky, Joan thought. She had only felt loved and safe within the worlds she created.

Joan encouraged his writing, praised him honestly, offered him help when he said a passage wasn't coming out right. He would return to her again, saying, "I think I got it now," and Joan would find he had not changed a word, or he had changed words, but not as she suggested. At first she was taken aback, reacting, she realized, as a writer, as her own editor, as the editor she had been for other novelists at Gravida, and not as a mother of a little boy finding his own storytelling path. The way Daniel threw away her suggestions—her editorial advice actually—stung, but she had done the same thing with her own editors. When Malcolm West was assigned to *Other Small Spaces*, he was just a few years older than Joan, his youth and inexperience turning him dictatorial, forcing her to attend their meetings with a false piety, calling him a few days later to report that her attempts to execute his suggestions had all failed. My fault, not yours, she always said, and her first collection was published as she wanted, unspoiled by a heavy hand. With *Fictional Family Life*, a senior editor named Philip Krauss took Joan under his wing, her accolades making her worthy of his attention, but even against him Joan had won every battle.

When she stopped feeling hurt, she applauded Daniel for his resolve, his firmness, his inability to be swayed by the suggestions of another. To keep him excited about what he was doing, she bound every one of his stories, even those that were a single paragraph, between cardboard covers that she ornately decorated and titled, with *By Daniel Manning* in huge letters on the front cover.

Still, it was disquieting, disconcerting, to be reading her child's stories about achievement, when she was not writing a thing, other than lists of errands, of things either she or Fancy should buy at the market, of calls she was to make to set up playdates with the mothers of the boys in Daniel's first-grade class, with the daughters belonging to Augusta, Carla, Dawn, Emily, Meg, and Teresa, the former Pregnant Six, who each now had birthed three to Joan's two, dental appointments for her and Martin, pediatrician appointments for the boys, the phone company when the telephone line fizzed and died.

When she buried *The Sympathetic Executioners*, she did not blame Daniel, then kicking around inside of her. She had been right—it wasn't Daniel who had thinned her out, any fetus would have caused the same harm. She knew now how children were—how Daniel was—their smiles, their kisses, their tears, all the precocious methods they employed to ensure their futures mattered, came first. Would she be writing now if Daniel weren't beautiful, loving, inquisitive, creative, good at tangling his arms around her neck, whispering, "I love you, Mommy"? At this age, as unconditional as a cat or a dog.

Glimpsing her typewriter on the shelf in Eric's nursery, it seemed long ago that the room was her study. Somehow Eric, who could not move around furniture, alter the position of his mobiles, change the location of the books on the shelves, had made it his own. Would she end up writing about Eric one day, about a child in his infancy who already knew his own future?

No, no more rare babies.

She would do right by her real ones, but they weren't entitled to populate whatever she might write in the future. The millions of ideas she used to have each day had disappeared. Where had they all gone?

On Fancy's first day back with the Mannings after her father's funeral in Canada, she joined Joan and Daniel in the kitchen for breakfast and said, "He was such a good man. He couldn't do everything he wanted for us, but his heart was in the right place. It was a lovely ceremony. There's nothing like the sound of dirt hitting the top of a coffin. Makes me ache, but it's the ring of time, calling a tired soul back to the earth. The cemetery was so pretty, bushes and flowers everywhere, and I spent an hour walking around, reading what people had etched onto grave-stones, so much love for those buried in the ground."

Martin was home early, not at the hospital late, not in some distant country, and when he walked in the door, Fancy said, "We're having steaks and baked potatoes."

An hour later, Eric was in his high chair, already fed, with a plastic bowl of cereal to play with, and everyone took their seats as Martin came in bearing a bottle of red wine. "Fancy, let's toast your father," he said, and Fancy brushed a tear from her eye.

The bottle was opened, wineglasses filled, and Martin lifted his glass. "I never met your father, but you're a treasure, and he must have been one too." Fancy said, "He was. Thank you. This means so much to me."

"Fancy," Daniel said then, "what happened after they buried your father in the ground? After the dirt hit the coffin? Did flowers grow fast?"

Fancy ruffled his hair and said, "So here's what happened. Down in the ground my father went, the coffin this big old pine thing, huge because my dad was seven feet tall, where I get my own height from.

There were prayers and poems and people sniffled and cried, and when it was over, my mom said, 'Fancy, are you coming home now, we've got lots of people coming to mourn.' And I said, 'Not yet, I've got to go to Dad's favorite place,' and my mom understood, and off I went to the bridge, where he used to cast his fishing line on Sunday mornings at dawn, and I stood there, and the hours passed, and the sun grew hotter, and I waited and waited, and then all of a sudden, one fish, then a second, then a third, came flying out of the river, arcing over me, their fins flat out, their gills flapping, until they landed back in the water and swam away."

Daniel's eyes were huge, and he said, "That's a great story, Fancy."

And Martin said, "It is. That kind of stellar experience, being a part of an experience cherished by another, is what I see when I operate on people's eyes, their profound and genuine dreams, the wishes they have for their lives, if their sight is returned."

Daniel stared at his father, then said to Joan, "Does everyone in the whole world tell stories?" There was a fillip of concern in his voice, a fear perhaps tied to Fancy's father's grave, the sound of dirt hitting the coffin.

"Lots of people do. A story requires two things: a great story to tell and the bravery to tell it," Joan said.

Daniel cut into his meat, sawed a bit off, put it in his mouth, chewed, nodded, then said, "Oh."

"*You* are brave enough," Joan said, wanting to allay his concern, but she sensed that Daniel feared something that might be more awful than death or looking into the depths of someone's eyes: that perhaps the world was overrun by storytellers better than he.

"Book, book, book," Eric yelled, and Joan heard Daniel yell back, "Get away, that's mine. Don't be a pest." Since turning eight, Daniel was not only writing, but also climbing what he called his *ladder to literature*, a plain metal ladder he dragged in from the garage, warned about using without the steadying hand of either Joan or Fancy.

That first time he climbed up, Joan found his perfect little toes gripped around the top rung like pale commas, his hands pulling down big, heavy books. "Mom, I want to read the good stuff on my own," he said, and she understood, she had been just like him at the same age.

Tolstoy's *War and Peace*, Solzhenitsyn's *Cancer Ward*, Kozinski's *The Painted Bird*, he read each of those books and dozens more, drawn to the Russians, to a Romanian, to love and war and infidelity, to the Soviet police state and terminal illness, to tales of cruel acts and heroic escapes. The suggestion Martin had once made—that Daniel read books geared for children his own age—had been roundly rejected by Joan, a child-rearing debate she had won. "It just makes me sort of sad," Martin had said. "I don't want him losing his innocence so soon."

"That ship seems to have sailed," Joan replied, and Daniel read whatever he wanted.

Once, *The Happy Hooker* was among the books he pulled down. "Mom," he yelled out, and when Joan came into the living room, Daniel was staring at the cover, the salacious book a dead golden bird in her son's small, outstretched hands, and she was disturbed to find herself thinking of the way the hooker had screwed her brother-in-law, then allowed herself to be penetrated by the stubby red penis of the brother-in-law's German shepherd.

"Can I read this one too?" he asked, and Joan said, "Of course, but only when your baby teeth are so long gone you will have no memory of them, and you live on your own, far away from Daddy and me." Clutching the sex book against his chest, Daniel said, "But why would I ever live far away from you and Daddy?" She gathered him up into a tight hug and gently removed the book from his grip. That night she handed it back to Martin to hide well.

One afternoon, when she was feeding Eric in the kitchen, Daniel pulled up a chair and said, "I think we should talk about the books I'm reading," and in the late afternoons, when he was home from school, and Eric was napping, and Fancy was in the kitchen preparing dinner, Joan and Daniel sat in the living room, or ran across the grass, up and over the knoll, to their special glen where they stretched out on a blanket and talked about what he was reading, what he liked or disliked, if anything had scared him. Sometimes they brought their books and mother and son read silently side by side, lifting their heads occasionally to determine the shifting shapes of the clouds.

From the start, Daniel did a curious thing each time he finished a book. Before returning it to its place on the living-room shelves, he crossed out Joan's name on the flyleaf and wrote in his own. When she asked him why, he said, "I'm taking possession, Mom," and she laughed because even at such a young age he needed to leave a piece of himself behind, in the work of others, with his own work. Exactly like her, or rather, exactly like the way she had been.

9

From his birth, Eric was like that nursery rhyme: when he was good, he was very, very good, and when he was bad, he was horrid. All that was missing was the little curl right in the middle of his forehead. His hair was as black as Joan's, but the same texture as Martin's, straight as a pasture of reeds, not a curl to be found.

When the daughters of the former Pregnant Six came over for playdates with Daniel, it was Eric who absorbed their attention, whom they insisted on mothering, ordering Daniel around in supercilious tones—"Bring me his blanket," or "He needs a new bottle, make sure you warm it up right"—while Eric cooed in their arms, wrapped long blond or brunette or pale red hair around his chubby fingers. He was angelic with the girls, never screamed when he was their make-believe baby. But with his own mother he screamed, jags that lasted for hours when he wasn't hungry, or thirsty, or wet, or dirty, or ill, or hurting, or teething, and Joan couldn't figure out if it was because the world seemed to him a frightening place, or if it was simpler than that—mere frustration that he could not yet make himself under-stood. When he would finally lock his lips together, the silence itself rang, as if a bomb had decimated all the sounds in the world, leaving nothing behind.

Daniel was usually a good sport and played the game of happy family while Joan and some combination of Augusta, Carla, Dawn, Emily, Meg, and Teresa watched a version of the future unfold. But sometimes, when he grew tired of heeding commands, he disappeared, and Joan would find him in his room, at his white desk, a notebook in front of him, a pen in his hand. During one of those afternoons, he started a story about Henry refusing the kind offer of another squirrel family to join them. *"Come be with us," the mother squirrel said. She was fat and round and her fur was brown. "No, I'm not interested in having*

any brothers and sisters, not anymore. Being on my own is much better."
Joan silently agreed.

When the weather was nice, the women sat outside at Joan's old writing desk. Purchased in a secondhand store for twenty-five dollars when she was eighteen and new to New York, there was no longer room for it in the house, but she had not wanted to set it out on the curb, dumped into a garbage truck. It hurt her to use the table this way, on which she had written so much, now stained from sweating glasses of iced tea and wine and gin and tonics and soda cans, but at least she could sit at it, her bare toes kicking at the cool grass she and Fancy had planted. Listening to the women's delight with how their eldest daughters so naturally cared for Eric, Joan would wish just one little girl would refuse to hold him, would say she had different dreams for herself, did not want to waste her time learning how to mother, that it was a skill she would have no use for. But such was unlikely, for as smart as Augusta, Carla, Dawn, Emily, Meg, and Teresa were, they were vocal about their maternal fulfillment, their satisfaction in having children, "Even better than we imagined it would be," they frequently said, in earshot of their daughters. "Don't you think so, Joan?" they asked her, and although Joan smiled, never did she nod her assent.

Once, her life had been completely fulfilled by a different kind of striving, that did not involve watching children interact and hearing ecstatic mothers describe their crushes with motherhood.

It always came as a shock to her then, that she was no different from any of them: a formerly famous writer now a stay-at-home mother, taking a yoga class two towns over twice a week, reading to Daniel, listening to his stories, trying to find a way in with Eric, a four-day weekend twice a year with Annabelle Iger in New York, happily hearing her rail against marriage, against children. Joan's failure to produce the first novel demonstrated, Iger said, the norm's destructive, debilitating effects. The way Iger held Martin wholly responsible would give Joan a sense of malevolent glee.

One cold afternoon, when the daughters of Augusta, Teresa, and Dawn were playing their usual game with Eric and Daniel in the nursery, and the women were in Joan's kitchen, cups filled with hot coffee, plates filling up with slices of Reine de Saba, the chocolate almond cake Dawn was testing on them before offering it at Boulangerie de Rhome, the news of the day was that, in Vermont, a social worker was shot to death with a rifle by a mother fearing she would lose custody of her children. Meg and Teresa pressed their hands to their mouths, as Dawn said, "I'd do the same thing, shoot anyone who tried to take my kids from me." Joan nearly said aloud what she was thinking: she loved Daniel, she did love Eric, but sequential hours at a desk of her own, in a room of her own, with the ideas, or at least one idea, flowing, having a brief respite from custody, from mothering, from Daniel's after-school questions about everything, from Eric's screams, would not be half-bad.

At two, Eric's first word was not *Mommy, Daddy, Daniel, Fancy, grass, bath,* or *candy,* or any variation thereof, but *no*. And it was not a general *no*. It took Joan and Fancy several days to understand what Eric was trying to refuse, and even Daniel, who could decipher Eric's grunts and waving hands easily, was confused.

No meant no more reading to Eric at bedtime, no more big books, no more children's books, no reading at all, refusing that which was essential to Joan. However, if promised a red lollipop, he would listen to a story of Daniel's. He seemed to like the little gray squirrel, but the lollipop had to be in sight at all times, otherwise he stuffed his little fingers into his little ears and turned his face to the starry blue wall.

If the color blue, among other things, encouraged efficiency and communication, then Eric excelled at combining those two traits, efficiently communicating his needs and his wants without linguistic prowess.

No more reading came first, then *No diaper*. "No diaper," Eric said to Joan when she was changing him one morning. "No diaper," he said to Fancy that same day, when she was doing the same thing. He tugged at the diaper, pushed it down, figured out how to get one leg free, then the other, then ran through the house naked from the waist down, his chunky little ass so low to the ground.

"He's done with diapers," Daniel said to Joan.

"I get that, love, but he's only two. Barely potty-trained. He's not ready to make that decision for himself," and Joan diapered Eric again.

"No diaper," Eric yelled in the middle of the night, abandoning sleeping straight through, a trick only recently mastered, until his demand was honored. It was three in the morning, and everyone was gathered around his crib. Martin said, "He knows his own mind. So let's try underpants. Maybe he's telling us he knows more than we do."

Apparently he did, and Joan thought his name was proving itself—he was ruling his own world, setting the guidelines by which he was willing to live. Superheroes ran across his bottom from then on. Somehow, he had trained himself.

The week Eric left diapers behind, Daniel said, "How old was I when I stopped wearing diapers?" Joan thought, then said, "Almost three. Right, Fancy?" And Fancy nodded. "So does that mean Eric is smarter than me?" The corners of his mouth turned down, his eyes, too, were drooping like some old hunting dog, like the oldest hunting dog in the world. "Of course not," Joan said. "Everyone lives their life on a different schedule. Eric is early in this area, you were right on time."

Eric was, however, very slow to talk. He gathered up one word at a time, then ran with that word as if it were a kite on the end of a long rope. At three, his favorite word was *sandbox*. Led to the sandbox, he would spend happy hours alone building battlements, bridges made of fallen branches and twigs, forts with his own shirt and pants, holes filled with water from the hose that he figured out how to uncoil and turn on. Usually, he did not destroy what he created.

If blue fostered intelligence, then Joan had her doubts, both about the efficacy of colors employed this way, and about Eric. At four, his mouth was a receptacle for items other than food—bobby pins, pennies, paperclips, buttons, crayons, the sundered hoof of Fancy's stuffed giraffe. At four and a half, he began eating sand, clumps of dirt, chewy leaves, flowers plucked from the gardens, his baby teeth masticating it all. At nearly five, he was also sucking on pebbles, mashing pen caps of cheap ballpoints down, like some steel-toothed machine, until he bit through the plastic. It was as if his refusal to breastfeed had man-

ifested into an unquenchable oral fixation. Martin issued his professional determination that it was a phase he would outgrow.

But when Fancy found a sliver of bark between his front teeth, his
tongue green from leaves, teeth marks scratching the surface of a rock he
had in his pocket, she brought her concerns to Joan, and Joan couldn't
keep herself from yelling at Eric. "Why are you eating all this crazy
stuff?" and Eric, calm with that irritating half-smile on his lips, said,
"I just like how it feels in my mouth." She left Fancy with Eric outside
on the swings and went inside, to a living-room shelf where she found
Martin's *Diseases and Disorders* and searched its pages for a disorder
that might explain why he was stuffing strange things down his gullet,
if it indicated some kind of mental disturbance, and there it was:

*Pica (/'paɪkə/ py-kə): the persistent eating of nonnutritive substances
like paper, clay, metal, chalk, soil, glass, sand, ice, starch. Probably a behavior pattern driven by multiple factors. Some recent evidence supports
including pica with the obsessive-compulsive spectrum of disorders. There
are several theoretical approaches that attempt to explain the etiology:*

*Nutritional theories attribute pica to specific deficiencies of minerals,
such as iron and zinc.*

*The sensory and psychological theories center on the finding that
many patients with pica say that they just enjoy the taste, texture, and
smell of the item they are eating.*

*A neuropsychiatric theory is supported by evidence that certain
brain lesions in laboratory animals have been associated with abnormal eating behaviors, and it is postulated that pica might be associated
with certain patterns of brain disorder in humans.*

*Psychosocial theories surrounding pica have described an associa-
tion with family stress.*

*Addiction or addictive behavior has also been suggested as one
possible explanation for pica behavior in some patients.*

*Treatment: Education about nutrition. Psychological counseling.
Behavioral interventions for children with developmental disabilities.
Closer supervision of children during play. Child-proof homes and play
environments.*

Eric didn't seem to have developmental difficulties, or an obsessive-
compulsive disorder, the sandbox was regularly raked, there was no
lead paint in the house, none, as far as she knew, in the dirt. He was

the youngest member of a loving family, and chewed a children's mul-tivitamin every single day. What stress could he have?

That night, Joan showed Martin the pica entry and said, "I think our youngest son might be suffering from this."

They had a heart-to-heart with Eric in the living room. Martin on the couch, Eric on the ottoman, Joan in the comfortable armchair some distance away. Triangles were the only thing she remembered from junior high geometry, and if a line were drawn from Martin to Eric, Eric to Joan, Joan to Martin, they were the three points of an obtuse triangle, and she, way out there, was the longest side, the point at the end of ninety degrees.

"Eric, do you feel compelled—is something making you eat dirt, sand, pebbles, leaves, twigs, sticks, stones, grass, and anything else that people don't usually eat? Something inside that's telling you to eat those things? Voices, or just a hunger you can't explain to yourself?" Martin asked.

"No," Eric said.

"No what?" Martin asked.

"I don't hear voices and I eat real food when I'm hungry." It wasn't an explanation, but it was something.

"Will you stop eating dirt, sand, pebbles, leaves, twigs, sticks, stones, grass, and anything else you know doesn't belong in your mouth?" Joan was impressed Martin could reel everything off twice in the same order, although surely he did the same thing, with medical terms, in the operating room.

"Yes," Eric said. "It's just for fun anyway."

"Will you promise not to have that kind of fun anymore?" Martin asked.

"Yes. No more fun," he said. "Can I go?"

Martin nodded and Eric ran from the room, his bare feet stomping on the hardwood floor. He had Martin's loud walk.

"Pica crisis averted," Martin said. "Next."

And it was true, the crisis disappeared or never truly existed; still, it seemed strange to Joan that Eric would have eaten any of those things in the first place, and she wondered what went on his head.

10

A fair came to Rhome the first weekend of August, setting up in a huge field where the hay had been sickle-mowed, leaving behind a flat, golden carpet. The field was ten miles past the Mannings' neighborhood, now called Peachtree by almost everyone. It was hot and sunny, the cloudless sky a rich blue. All of Rhome seemed to have turned out, as well as a good part of the populations of the towns on either side of it, for the fair was bustling when Joan and Martin and the boys arrived. White and beige tents dotted the landscape and booths had been set up and were doing a brisk business selling local produce, home-made jams and preserves, cheeses made from cows and goats and sheep from the nearby farms, wine bottled from Rappahannock County and Shenandoah Valley grapes. For the kids, there were Italian ices and sno-cones to lick, cotton candy to pull apart, and rides—a Ferris wheel, a merry-go-round, a small roller coaster, a riding ring where old horses were taking the youngest for slow rides, round and round. The aroma of barbecue was in the air.

Joan assessed the crowd, lighting upon the most interesting: young men turning white T-shirts into art, pinching the material tight and rubber-banding each section until they looked like porcupines being dipped into huge steaming vats of colored dyes; the young woman with a bird's nest of purple hair sitting at a potter's wheel, slamming down hunks of clay, her hands moving nearly as fast as the wheel, cups, vases, plates, bowls, trays, appearing like magic; the elderly man in a worn blue linen suit, a jaunty straw boater on his head, a smeared palette tight in his hand, painting a mammoth canvas of people on a beach staring out at an ocean where a sailboat bobbed in the distance, though he himself was standing in a mowed field; the handsome young man at an old-fashioned school desk, a manual typewriter in front of him, a stack of paper to the side. He had long pony-tailed hair and round wire glasses perched on the bridge of his nose, and his sign read: $5 GET YOUR OWN PERSONAL SHORT STORY. Joan absorbed these people and something clicked inside of her.

Daniel brought her back, tugging at her hand, saying, "I want to go exploring. I'll take Eric with me, but I've got so much to see and you and Daddy are walking too slow." He was a serious, responsible boy.

"He'll pull you every which way," Joan warned Daniel, wanting him to take Eric, thinking a good mother would let her older son run free, not obligate him to watch over his younger brother.

Martin touched her shoulder. "Let them go," he said, and she wondered why he would think she wouldn't.

Martin handed Daniel ten single dollar bills. "For whatever you guys want," he said. "Meet us at five at the entrance, okay? There's a lot of people here and it would be tough to have to search for you."

Daniel held up his wrist, showed his father his watch, the birthday present he had chosen for himself last year. He was obsessed with time lately: how much time had elapsed between one event and another, how much time had gone by since the beginning of the world, since he had written his last Henry story, since he had given Joan a story to read, since he began reading the latest big book he was reading, how little time was left before he was late to a friend's house, before he started fifth grade, before his tenth birthday in late December, before he was all grown up.

On the way home, the boys bounced off the backseat, chattering about the rides they had ridden, everything they had eaten, the new tie-dye T-shirts they were wearing, the clay vase painted yellow and white that Joan was holding in her lap, bought from the girl with the bird's-nest hair. Bounding into the house, the boys said they were full, they did not want dinner, and did not argue when Joan said, "Baths! Alone or together, whatever you want, but you both need to wash your hair." Wonderfully worn out, they were asleep long before their usual, well-guarded bedtimes.

Joan fixed salads with tomatoes and cucumbers from their own garden. She held up a bottle of wine, and Martin shook his head, "Work," he said. She opened the bottle anyway, poured herself a glass, and they ate at the kitchen table, the windows all thrown open. The sun was just setting, it was nearing eight, and Martin was on his way back to the hospital. "I may sleep there tonight," he said, which he sometimes did when he was worried about a patient who was not doing well. He kept a clean suit, shirt, and tie in his office. He never told her the names of his patients, gave her only brief précis of who they were. This one that he was worried about was Japanese, a grandfather, father, husband, a lover of the tea ceremony, and Joan had named him Mr. Kobayashi.

Martin grabbed a couple of apples from the bowl on the counter, kissed the top of Joan's head, and shut the back door quietly. She heard his new car rev up, a Mercedes, all black. Years of driving secondhand Toyotas, he adored his car like a mistress, teaching the boys how to wash and wax on a couple of weekends. He had gotten the top-of-the-line sound system installed. Once he was beyond Rhome, he had twenty miles of pure highway, always racing beyond the speed limit, blasting the music, the windows down, screaming the lyrics.

The kitchen was clean and Joan was back at the table, her type-writer, silently retrieved from Eric's closet just minutes earlier, plugged in for the first time in five years. She had dusted it off, checked that the cartridge still had ink, which it did. She had found reams of paper in that closet too, had taken one. Ripping off the wrapping around five hundred sheets of virgin paper had felt like love to her, overwhelming, never-going-to-happen-again love. She was thrilled Martin had gone back to the hospital to watch over Mr. Kobayashi. The idea had come to her in one fell swoop during the afternoon, because of the fair, and she had to start to get it down.

There was a potential novel there, she knew. She felt its commanding logic, both internal and external, powerful enough to keep her tethered to home, to silence the fears that she would never write again, eliminate the horrid daydream in which she sometimes indulged, about simply walking away from this alternative life she was living, filled with its soft poetry and hard tediousness, its spectacular, love-ridden times measured against meaningless hours and days and weeks and months, a life where her past accomplishments were long forgotten, where she was called, most often, Joan Manning, leaving her tongue-tied and wishing she could say, "I'm not Joan Manning, I'm Joan Ashby, the writer." That indulgent daydream about leaving all this behind. Leaving the children, Martin, the house that was too small, the great stretch of land that was, like the house, in her name alone, where she used to think she would set up a writers' colony. Leaving it all behind and never returning, stepping back into her original skin, where she was only, foremost, supremely, the writer Joan Ashby, no longer tied to the person she still mostly loved, the children they had made together that she loved with unequal force.

She thought about the boys in their beds, before their existences entirely fell away, their breathing no longer her concern. There was only the hum of the overhead light and the refrigerator, and then only the words in her head rushing onto the page.

We were young, and some of us were beautiful, and others of us were brilliant, and a few of us were both. Citizenship demanded only an ability to create, to use our minds and hands and bodies in unforeseen ways. We believed we knew more than those who had tried before us. Their experiment had failed, but their hard lessons would serve as our guide. Passionate, arrogant, certain we would not falter, or deceive, or betray ourselves, that we would not blacken our lives with whitewashed expectations, our presence here, in this arcadia, proved we had slipped the ropes and chains of expected, normal life. We considered everything. Except everything. By its very nature, everything resists corralling; it is far too expansive. You think you've avoided every last trap, but what you hadn't considered, what you never could plan for, it is that which trips you up.

11

Joan had never liked fairs, had only occasionally pushed through the crowded blocks of the Feast of San Gennaro in Little Italy when she lived in New York, down the avenues closed to traffic for the street fairs that sprung up in spring and summer there. But it was the fair here, in the place she referred to as home, regardless of how it actually felt to her, with its tie-dye artists, potter, painter, writer, that cast a spell, shifted the gears in her brain, charged up her heart, unleashed her soul. She felt the bonds loosening, her tortured body stretching, already picturing herself walking free and unfettered. There was a future out there, only a spot on the horizon, and years away, but she could see it there in the distance, with her naked eyes.

It was past midnight when she stepped outside. In one hand she held the piece of paper with the single paragraph it took her twenty-four attempts to get right, and a glass of wine in the other. Her old desk was still pitched in the grass, and she set down the paper and glass, sat down on the wooden bench they had found somewhere, a yard sale, or the thrift shop, and she looked up, searching for the man in the moon.

The last time she felt this flame she was writing the Rare Baby stories, and before that *The Sympathetic Executioners*, no matter its failure, and before that, her celebrated collections. Five long years of a depleted brain, worried, then certain, that the precious part of herself had been destroyed. Fiction was what she read in books written by others, borrowed from the Rhome Library, purchased from Odile at the Tell-Tale, from Sessa at the Inveterate Reader, sent to her by Iger in the form of Gravida's prepublication copies, where Annabelle was now the senior vice president and associate publisher. Joan had not written a single line in these last years, not even an entry in those small notebooks she once stashed in various places, all discovered and used for other purposes a long time ago.

But now there was most of August to endure, before Eric started kindergarten and Daniel fifth grade. A sprawling month before Eric was gone from nine until noon, and Daniel gone until three. She could not bear the thought of delaying, of shuffling through the rest of the summer while the story was fresh in her mind. She could make notes, write longhand, but it would not be the same, she had not written that way since she was a girl. She needed quiet, emptiness, the compression of her fingertips on the keys, her Olivetti pulsing to her internal beat.

Martin never came home in the middle of any day, but she needed the boys, and Fancy, out of the house on a predetermined schedule, for a dedicated number of hours Monday through Friday.

Fancy was wonderful with them, taking them to the park to play, for bike rides along the river path that fronted the Potomac, within riding distance of the house, special trips for miniature golf or bowling and pizza one town away, but the time frame was not at all firm, sometimes it lasted for a morning or an afternoon, other times barely half an hour. And if Fancy dropped Daniel and Eric off at the homes of their friends, between the delivering and the fetching, she always ended up back at the house for the duration, busying herself in the kitchen, preparing fabulous dishes, but it was the only room in the house with a table on which a person could spread out and work.

Joan might steal time during their out-of-house adventures, but there was no certainty to it, and to truly get under way she needed what she used to have: hours that piled up in a freewheeling way, not writing in some truncated fashion. She needed to feel secure in her ability to get lost in this new dazzling world she was conceiving, and that would not happen if she had an ear cocked for a car that sounded like hers, Fancy at the wheel, the garage door opening, then the back door, suddenly accosted, waylaid by children with questions. She did not want to race around the kitchen, yanking the cord from the wall, stashing the typewriter, pen, pad, the pages she planned to write beyond that initial paragraph, the notes she would soon make, the first edited pages that would accrue, into a box in the hall closet, to be hidden beneath a pile of old jackets she had failed, since spring, to drop into the Goodwill bin in the supermarket parking lot.

It was too late to sign the boys up for day camp, and even if it wasn't,

Daniel would not willingly go. He could be found most of the time this summer past the knoll, down in the grassy glen on their land, where the two of them still sometimes had their informal chats about the books he read. He was never without the book he was currently reading and his notebook filled with drafts of new squirrel stories. Weekends were not the issue; by now, Joan was well versed in how those formerly empty hours, during which she once always worked, filled up with the needs and wants of others.

A shooting star punctured the night sky and Joan ran through a list of what she would give to have all the days available to her again. Martin did his best to be home on the weekends, to schedule tricky surgeries on Thursdays, rather than Fridays, planning his travel so that when the children woke on Saturday mornings, he was there at the breakfast table as often as he was able. When he was home, the children ran to him, jumped on his back, wanted him to play catch, kick around a soccer ball. He was a genuinely fine and good father, invested too, just not around consistently, or all that much. At the start of the summer, there had been an article in the *New York Times* about one of the new surgeries he was perfecting, toric IOL implantation in patients with *mild* or *forme fruste keratoconus*, and since then he was busy presenting his findings at hospitals in New York, New Jersey, Connecticut, and DC. When he was home, though, by noon on the weekends he set up the Slip 'N Slide she had bought at Walmart, rolling out the long plastic sheet down from the top of knoll, then spraying it with water from the hose. Joan always joined them out there, on a towel at the crest of the small hill, yelling, "Go Daniel. Go Eric," as the boys threw themselves on the wet plastic, their faces lit up, their smiles so huge. She had the sense, those weekends, that she was storing up memories that one day, if she needed them, she could flip through like photographs: a hot sun, a cool ride across bright-green grass, the paintbrushed colors of the flower gardens in the distance, the boys not waiting for their own turns but chasing each other down the wet runway until they careened into each other on the plastic, sending up rainbows of water, she and Martin laughing and cheering. She loved watching their trunks sliding down their pale backsides from the friction of skin on water on plastic, the way they both hauled them back up, as if she and

Martin had not seen them naked from birth. Several times, watching Joan and Martin in their bathing suits sliding down the plastic through the cold water, like the children they had never been, the boys screamed in delight. They still had fun when it was just Joan who readied the Slip 'N Slide, but they didn't scream the same way, as if letting free everything they carried inside. The proportions were off, they were growing older, and Martin was a necessary ballast, the one who was not tarred with the eternal tag of *Mother*.

The breeze blew through the red maples, the elms, and Cleveland pear trees she and Fancy had planted nine years before. The maples were nearly fourteen feet high, the elms fifteen, the pear trees thirteen, their spreads now impressive, no longer the stick figures they had been. In the spring, the dense profusion of white pear flowers and maple buds was beautiful. Now everything was green, the pear leaves glossily green, but a little worn out from the heat. A week straight in the nineties. But the night breeze was cooling things down, and Joan went inside.

It was past one, and she was too wound up to sleep. She poured herself more wine and remembered when Daniel was four and a half, and she and the Pregnant Six signed the children up for swim lessons at the community center. Back in the pool they had once swum in together, seven mothers standing in the water, holding six girls and one boy in brightly colored suits, colorful water wings wrapped around their tender, unformed biceps. Such trust in Daniel's heart as she pulled him through the water. He had cinched his head back like a turtle, his eyes squinting against the splash of the water.

"I used to swim here every day," she had whispered into his ear. "When you were inside of me. We swam together before you could breathe air, both of us in the pool. Actually, you swam in two pools, in this one, and in here," she said, pointing at her stomach.

"So do I already know how to swim and I just forgot?" he had wanted to know.

In the second lesson, he gathered his courage, as the little girls did not, striking out on his own across the length of the shallow end, his feet kicking hard, his clear water wings flapping, his brown curls flattened against his small wet skull. He had looked like a lacewing, those slender, delicate insects with large and clear membranous wings that had discovered the roses she and Fancy planted at the front of the house, feeding, they learned, on the aphids that had taken up residence, distorting the flowers, leaving behind pale green secretions like mini-honeydews in a patch. Daniel could destroy nothing, that grin on his face, looking as if he could lift himself out of the water and fly away, so pleased with himself when his fingers grasped the concrete ledge on the other side.

Joan finished her wine and went inside. She brushed her teeth and washed her face. She was tan from the summer, her cheeks pinkly glowing from the day. She found the jar in the medicine cabinet and moisturized as she did not always remember to do. Clean T-shirt and pajama bottoms, she climbed into the empty bed, and the memory of those swim classes with Daniel gave rise to a viable plan.

She was dreaming that she was in a field, grass, enormous sunflowers, hundreds of beautiful people stretched out, languorous and laughing, on blankets and sheets, dancing to the sound of chimes and tam-bourines and acoustic guitars, others were handing out tiaras and crowns, crystal glasses filled with blushing wine that sparkled in the sun. They were young and old, and those like her, neither young nor old, in ball gowns, dashikis, loincloths, bathing suits, fringed jackets, and naked bodies too, in all shades, a thousand languages being spoken all at once, a chorus of sounds lifting up into the atmosphere. Hanging down from the clouds in the sky were paintings of stars, the moon, the sun. Wild horses ran in the distance, sinews caught in the sun. Over the glorious cacophony, the stampede of those hooves was fading away, the horses disappearing, racing down into a canyon she could not see.

A noise woke her. She leaned over to Martin's empty side of the bed, her eyes were barely open, she was the tiniest bit bleary from the wine. She tried reading the hands on his dead father's clock. It was four, or maybe five, in the morning, the hour and minute hands were too similar to discern which. The creak of wood under bare feet, nearing their bedroom, then Martin was slipping into the bed behind her, naked, running his hands under her T-shirt, cool against her warm skin, pulling down her pajama pants. He was deep inside of her when he whispered, "Do you ever think of having another child?" She did not turn her head when she said, "I never thought of having the ones we did."

12

Martin was gone before she woke on Monday morning, a note left for her on his pillow. *I loved you this morning*, in his doctor's scrawl. He used to leave notes for her all of the time, now less often, but as typically cryptic as this one. Did he mean that this morning when he came in, he felt love for her, as perhaps he had not felt earlier in the day, or that he loved her this morning as he always did, or that, this morning, they had made love. She blew out her breath and stuck the note in a box she had kept for years, a big blue box with a black ribbon in which something she could not recall had been given. It was filled with all of Martin's notes and letters since his first letter to her after that holiday weekend when they met in Annapolis. Only some of them were love letters.

The children were still asleep, Fancy's summer hours started at ten. Joan made a fresh pot of coffee, called the Rhome Community Center, and was informed that a children's introductory swim class was starting on Wednesday, an August special, a one-hour class held five days a week until Labor Day.

"Yes," the woman said, "your older child can swim then too, we only cordon off a section of the pool for the class, the rest is open to everyone. And we've got floats, inner tubes, noodles, and after the class, the teacher sets up fun relay races for everyone who wants to join."

It was nearly an Olympic-sized pool, the retractable roof open during the hot summer months, lounge chairs for the towel-wrapped kids to rest on, a snack shop that sold milkshakes, sodas, juices, and sandwiches, and Joan thought she might count on three hours alone in the house, every single weekday. She would set the hours for Fancy, tell her to take the kids to the pool from noon until three. One hundred and eighty jeweled minutes each day that she would not waste.

She signed Eric up for the class, and when Fancy arrived, Joan drove to the new Target outside of Rhome, bought everyone new bathing suits and huge beach towels, caps and goggles for the boys, fins and a snorkel for Daniel. She wanted to make it special for him, so that he did not feel banished, did not imagine himself unfairly lumped in with younger children. He was sensitive these days, and until he saw all the kids at the pool, he would not take anyone's word for it. There would be lots, of course; the pool was a huge draw in the summer for families all over Rhome.

"Who wants to go to the pool at the community center every single day for the rest of the month?" Joan said when Fancy and the boys were just back from the park, flushed and sweaty from running around in the heat. There were cheers and she added to the excitement by tossing two of the new towels onto the kitchen table, saying, "Choose your favorite," then, before the boys could tussle, handing around the presents she had hastily wrapped, no neat corners, no hidden tape, bows that drooped just a little.

Eric immediately pulled the red swim cap onto his head, the goggles over his eyes. Daniel stuck the snorkel in his mouth and ran his hands down the kitchen walls, saying, "Look at this neat coral, and those fishes, do you see those fishes, Eric, glowing like they've got lightbulbs inside?" Eric lifted up his goggles and said, "I don't see anything at all. It's got to be real, Daniel, to be seen."

She handed Fancy her gift, a swimsuit in the florals she was still wearing, the modest cut something she might find comfortable, suitable. There had always been something Mennonite in how Fancy dressed, covered from shoulders to calves. Joan used to wonder what Fancy was hiding beneath all that fabric, but she was always sunny and cheery, open about everything—her plans when she was not at the Mannings, the young men Trudy fell in and out of love with—she could not be hiding scars on her body, self-inflicted or otherwise, and if she was, then she was the most talented of liars.

Fancy lifted away the silver tissue paper Joan had found in a drawer. "Thank you so much, I just love it," and Joan was glad she had selected well, Fancy's smile could not be faked.

"You don't want to take Eric for his lessons yourself?" Fancy asked. "You had such a hoot doing it with Daniel."

"I thought you might like to do it this time. It really is a lot of fun."

She hoped Fancy understood what Joan was after. But so much time had passed since Joan read the Rare Baby stories aloud to Daniel and Fancy, since Fancy had tried to ask when Joan would return to her writing, that it was just as likely Fancy connected up nothing at all. But she could not tell Fancy directly, to do so seemed a betrayal of Martin, even of the kids. She was entitled to keep them in the dark, it was her work after all, to be done in the secret part of her life, but it seemed wrong that someone else should know what she was planning, when they would not.

Fancy reported that Eric loved the pool, was not scared under-water, held his breath until she feared he was drowning, and liked smacking into the other kids in the class, and Daniel swam real laps, back and forth so many times she lost count, and after the swim class, the teacher taught him to do those kick turns, but he would not participate in the relay races, though Fancy said he seemed like a very fast swimmer to her. He insisted that after Eric's lesson they come home. "I am engaged in serious endeavors and have little time to waste," is what he had said to Fancy. He had written by then perhaps thirty of his squirrel stories.

So it was not perfect. Barely two hours, not three, those days in the house by herself, at the kitchen table, the typewriter blazing away, but it sufficed. At least, she was moving again, headed in the direction of her original life.

It was the year President Clinton was tried by the Senate on impeach-ment charges and was acquitted. The United States Coast Guard intercepted a ship with over 9,500 pounds of cocaine aboard, headed for Houston, Texas, one of the largest drug busts in American history. A West African immigrant named Amadou Diallo was shot dead by plainclothes cops in New York, inflaming race relations in the city. White supremacist John William King was found guilty of kidnapping and killing African American James Byrd Jr., by dragging him behind a truck for two miles. In a military court, a US Marine Corps captain, with the same last name as Joan, Richard J. Ashby, was acquitted of the charge of reckless flying that resulted in the death of twenty skiers in the Italian Alps, when his low-flying jet hit a gondola cable. The Supreme Court upheld the murder convictions of Timothy McVeigh in the Oklahoma City bombing. LEGOLAND California, the only LEGOLAND outside of Europe, opened in Carlsbad. *Shakespeare in Love* won the Oscar for Best Picture. A Michigan jury found Dr. Jack Kevorkian guilty of second-degree murder for administering a lethal injection to a terminally ill man. For the first time, the Dow Jones Industrial Average closed above the 10,000 mark. In Laramie, Wyoming, Russell Henderson pleaded guilty to kidnapping and felony murder, to avoid a possible death penalty conviction for the hate-crime killing of Matthew Shepard. The World Trade Organization ruled in favor of the United States in its long-running trade dispute with the European Union over bananas. The personal fortune of Bill Gates was estimated at exceeding $100 billion. President Clinton was cited for contempt of court for giving "intentionally false statements" in a sexual harassment civil lawsuit. Two Littleton, Colorado, teenagers, Eric Harris and Dylan Klebold, opened fire on their teachers and classmates, killing twelve students and one teacher and then themselves. The shooting sparked a media debate on school bullying, gun control, and violence. Norman J. Sirnic and Karen Sirnic were murdered by serial killer Angel Maturino Resendiz in Weimar, Texas. The House of Representatives released the Cox Report which detailed the People's Republic of China's nuclear espionage against the United States over the prior two decades. The Colombian government announced it would include the estimated value of the country's illegal drug crops, exceeding half a billion dollars, in its gross national product. Texas governor George W. Bush announced he would seek the Republican Party nomination for president of the United States. Benjamin Nathaniel Smith began a three-day killing spree targeting racial and ethnic minorities in Illinois and Indiana. US Army Pfc. Barry Winchell was bludgeoned in his sleep at Fort Campbell, Kentucky, by fellow soldiers, he died the next day of his injuries. Off the coast of Martha's Vineyard, a plane piloted by John F. Kennedy Jr. crashed, killing him, his wife, and her sister. The Woodstock '99 festival was held in New York. Lance Armstrong won his first Tour de France. The last Checker Taxi Cab was retired in New York City and sold at auction for $135,000. NASA intentionally crashed the *Lunar Prospector* spacecraft into the moon, ending its mission to detect frozen water on the lunar surface. EgyptAir Flight 990, traveling from New York City to Cairo, crashed off the coast of Nantucket, Massachusetts, killing all 217 aboard. The NTSB later reported that the co-pilot, Gameel Al-Batouti, deliberately crashed the plane, a claim disputed by Egyptian authorities. The Recording Industry Association of America filed a lawsuit against Napster, alleging copyright infringement. At the end of the year, the United States turned over complete administration of the Panama Canal to the Panamanian government, as stipulated in the Torrijos-Carter Treaties of 1977.

Turbulence, dissension, horrific killings and murders, hate and racism and cruelty, the very rich and the very poor, the political with its unlimited ramifications for the personal lives of so many, a world long awry and inching ever closer to an undefined point of no return. Joan kept up with it all, but found herself on the other side.

She was no longer writing about tragedies that blew apart people's lives, but about something else entirely: how dreams could keep hope alive and fresh. Dreams dreamt by her array of imaginary characters who were instantly more real and alive to her than anyone else she knew in Rhome.

Strangers all, they would ford oceans, fly through the skies, pack up old cars and painted RVs, all drawn to a new community in a sparsely populated town in a small unnamed American state. Painters, sculptors, ceramicists, writers, poets, musicians, songwriters, filmmakers, photographers, collagists, doll makers, vintners, and the predictable pot growers who followed the artists—successful artists from the old enclaves of Cologne, Berlin, Paris, London, and Santa Fe, tired of the existing tenets that codified what art could be, and those who had never been artists but had always desired to execute their mindful dreams—would all travel until they reached a narrow, single-lane freshly paved blacktop that sailed up and around purpled hills, and then dropped into a pastoral valley spread out below. They would find themselves in verdant meadows, with dandelion fields, through which brooks with cold, clear water ran, surrounded by bouldering mountains. Near the atmospheric energy vortices, the artists would build a contemporary version of the Old West, reimagined as an artists' mecca.

Buildings would rise, one-room cabins with uneven porches, tree houses with running water, modernized tepees raised above the flood line, rooming houses built with soda cans, using for insulation old rubber gathered from the side of a main highway thirty miles away, blown off the sixteen-wheelers that flew through. Meetings would be held to resolve issues rapidly so that their mecca would run well. Her key characters—Bash, Lila, Minu, Zena, Bernard, and Anton— would create their art and couple in ways that expanded the meaning of *honing the work.*

By the end of the year, Joan had written fifty tight pages, and she had reams of notes and research. When she wasn't working, everything was hidden in that box in the front hall closet under the old jackets she had held on to. Her secret was still her secret. She was writing up in her castle, in the tower she had constructed for herself, away from prying eyes and Martin's need to expose the complicated mechanics of her mind. She was happy, in that unique, specific way that only came to her when she was at work. Her brain was never at rest. The lives of her characters, their motivations, the art they created, the fights they had, the words they spoke, ran through her daily domesticated routine, her dreams when she slept, in the yoga class she still went to twice a week, when the grueling hour was complete and she was in *Shavasna.* She bought another notebook, kept it in her pocket, along with a pen, jotted down abbreviated notes only she could interpret when she made breakfast, bagged Daniel's school lunch, drove the boys to school, went to the market, made dinner when Fancy was not around. She was thinking of calling it *Words of New Beginnings.*

13

"*Zǎoshang hǎo. Wǒ de hǎo er zi.*" It was Martin, calling the boys on their first day of school. It was just eight on the warm fourth day of September, but Daniel had been dressed since six, in a new pair of jeans and a striped dress shirt, a junior version of what his father wore most days, wanting to look like the seventh grader he was about to become in an hour, and Eric, heading into second grade, which he said he already hated, was in his favorite blue shorts, favorite yellow shirt, his banged-up tennis shoes without any socks, which he hated as well.

She heard Martin's Chinese greeting on the speakerphone, which she clicked off when both boys had phones to their ears, wanting to hear his every word.

Over the past few years, Martin had become their famous father. Articles about him and his innovative surgeries first appeared in medical journals, and then in major newspapers, and the boys collected copies of every one. Martin did not seem bowled over by the attention— he told the boys he was a doctor, not a celebrity, and the exposure was good only if it served the higher purpose of increasing funding for his research. Joan mostly believed him. She knew firsthand how fame held momentary appeal, the warmth of its bright and special spotlight, how that spotlight could overheat, melt a person down if they weren't solid, mature, and grounded. But Martin possessed that triad of traits, neither preened about nor discounted his good fortune. In the spring, a reporter from *Time* magazine had spent several days in Rhome interviewing Martin, shadowing him on hospital rounds, observing a few of his surgeries, talking to the doctors and nurses he worked with, to patients who had given permission, to the boys, asking if they had any interest in following their father into medicine, to Joan, about what life was like with a surgeon whose skills were demanded around the world. She couldn't help wondering how that article would read when it was published, whether she would be allowed her own name finally, or, as in all the previous articles, identified only as *the wife*. She tried not to let it, but it pricked a bit, the way she had been rendered anonymous.

From the hall, Joan could see Daniel at the kitchen table and Eric kneeling on the living-room couch, heard their responses to their father's long-distance questions. Martin was good at calling them frequently when he was away, opening the conversation with greetings in the language of the country he was in.

"Yes, I have my new backpack already, and my lunch, and my newest Henry story because my homeroom teacher, Miss Nilson, called saying everyone had to bring in something to share about ourselves," Daniel said.

"And I made my own peanut butter and peach jam sandwich," Eric said loudly. "And Mom said it was okay if I took two bags of Fritos, if I took an orange too, and ate it. And I will."

Martin was in Beijing, for the third time. On his first trip there, he performed intracapsular cataract surgeries on the eyes of seven old Chinese men. On his second, a dozen orbital surgeries on the eyes of six middle-aged Chinese women suffering from anopthalmia, enucleation, and evisceration. This time he was there to operate on the eyes of several young Chinese boys suffering from dacryostenosis; overflowing and unstoppable tears caused by infections; abnormal growths; injuries of the facial bones or surrounding tissues; and underdeveloped puncta. He planned to probe and irrigate, passing a small metal instrument through the nasolacrimal ducts, but had brought stents he would insert to open up those ducts if the simpler operation failed. He had flown out on the eve of Labor Day weekend and wouldn't be back until Friday.

"Are your patients nice?" Daniel asked, and a moment later Eric yelled out, "Mom, they're the same ages as us." The Beijing-Rhome conversation continued while Joan ran the cereal bowls and spoons under the faucet, put away the milk.

The morning also marked the start of her third year owning the length of each school day, and she felt like a horse on a lead, pawing the ground, eager to be let loose, to run straight back into her artists' mecca, to return to the arcadian place she was creating in that small town in an unnamed American state, to rejoin Bash, Lila, Minu, Zena,

Bernard, and Anton. She had been on a roll, five hundred pages into the first draft, and then Joan's summer writing plans turned to dust.

"Trudy's left Rhome," Fancy told Joan when she brought the boys home from their last day of school. "She went back to Canada, and I think I should go back too. Right away, if I can. I love all of you so much, and I know I'll be leaving you in a lurch, but I feel lost without her." Joan saw there would be no convincing Fancy to stay, so what else could she say but, "I'll write you an outstanding recommendation, crafted to highlight all of your numerous talents, just write down where I should send it." When Martin came home and heard the news, he left the kitchen and returned with an envelope for Fancy. "A thank-you, but not enough for all you've done for us." There were hugs and kisses, and the boys walked with her to her car, and stood on the sidewalk holding her hands, not wanting to let her go, both of them crying. Then Fancy drove out of their lives.

Ice-cream sundaes followed her sudden departure and, later, Joan said to Martin, "I've always wondered if Fancy and Trudy were just friends, like Fancy always said, or if there's always been something more between them." They had come to know Trudy at the holiday parties and summer blow-outs in the backyard Martin liked them to throw, and which Joan had become very good at organizing with Fancy's help. Trudy was small next to tall Fancy, mousy when Fancy was brave, quiet when Fancy could talk and talk and talk, but every once in a while, Joan caught a look passing between them, or Trudy gazing at Fancy, or Fancy gazing at Trudy, and she would wonder and wish that Fancy felt free enough to live her life completely. "Definitely, they're together. They'll buy a little house in that little town they're from, on the edge of Lake Ontario, and be happy the rest of their days." He shut off the bedroom lights, and in the dark, Joan hoped that was true, as true as the hole Fancy was leaving in their lives, as true as Fancy's plans extinguishing Joan's own summer hope. Later, when they discussed hiring another nanny, Joan looked ahead to the fall, to writing each day in an emptied house, and said, "No one could ever replace Fancy, so let's not bother."

But she wasn't prepared for Fancy leaving, had no summer plans in place for the boys. Had she known, and over their complaints, she would have sent Eric to day camp, Daniel to sleepaway. Instead, they spent the sunny days at the community center pool. Daniel took lessons with the swim coach, wanting, he said, to try out for the school team in the fall. As a seventh grader he could do that. Eric ran around with the other kids, cannonballing into the water, despite threats of expulsion never carried out by the lifeguards. Some mornings Martin gave Joan a break and took Eric with him to the hospital, where he played on his father's office computer, then dropped him in the early afternoon at the pool. She and the boys saw a lot of Augusta, Carla, Dawn, Emily, Meg, and Teresa there, with all of their children. The six women could field a swim team of their own, eighteen children in total. During the school year, their paths no longer crossed, all those playdates fallen away as their eldest daughters and Daniel found other friends whom they preferred, who were not of the opposite sex. It was nice they could reunite for occasional picnics in the park, barbecues at someone's house, the children playing tag and hide-and-seek, the men, sometimes even Martin, drinking beers from the bottle.

And it had been the summer of the big challenge; Daniel's idea, a serious competition between eldest son and mother, and it took all the love in her heart not to groan. She wasn't sure when it had begun, but Daniel wanted to beat her at anything, at everything—if he could cut up a tomato quicker, or bike faster on the Potomac walk, or say more *d* words in a minute than she could. His desire to constantly test himself against her was fascinating, tiring, at odds with her own nature—never had she competed in her life. A week into the vacation, he came up with a challenge she actually liked—who could read the most novels over the summer. She agreed instantly and suggested there be a prize for the winner.

"Yes, yes, yes," he said. "And I know what I want. A typewriter." He was uninterested in what Joan might want if she beat him; he thoroughly expected to win.

"Wouldn't you rather we got a computer for home, and you can use that for your writing?" Martin asked, and Daniel said, "Dad, a real writer writes on a real typewriter, a manual one." Eric, who desperately wanted a computer, had yelled, "No, get a computer, not a stupid typewriter!"

One night in bed, Martin said to her, "If Daniel does win the contest, how about giving him your old typewriter? It's just gathering dust. I know he said he wanted a manual, but he could adapt. Kind of like passing down history, a hand-off from one generation to the next."

She was stunned, relieved that the room was dark, that he could not see her face. Of course he didn't know she was using her typewriter regularly, had been until the start of the summer, would again when the summer concluded. His suggestion that she relinquish it, even to the son she adored, framing it in generational terms, the passing of the writer's baton, the assumption he was making that she had abandoned her writing life, would never write again, she felt punched in the stomach. She hadn't been able to clear her mind, to think of anything to say that would not reveal what she had no intention of revealing, and then Martin said, "Probably not a good idea. He'll want something of his own." And she had managed to open her mouth, to say only, "You're right."

Sometimes Joan read quickly, sometimes leisurely, uncertain whether to let Daniel win, then decided she would, that teaching him to lose graciously was less important than the confidence that would come with achieving his goal. She stopped reading after the twenty-ninth novel, allowed him to reach thirty.

Finding a working manual typewriter had not been easy. Martin found one in mint condition, bought it from a Johns Hopkins friend whose letter-writing mother had just died. The woman had kept it oiled and working like new, stockpiled for years the ribbons it required. It sat now on Daniel's white desk. The story he was taking to share with his new classmates had been written on that manual typewriter, his first time using it, that uncertain typing, those *clunk, clunk, clunk*s without any rhythm. Every time Joan heard him plucking away, she felt proud, then bereft that she had not written a word during those long and hot three months.

"So what did Dad say to you guys in Chinese?" she asked when they were in the station wagon heading down the hill, at last off to the first day of school.

"He said, 'Good morning, my good sons,'" they said at the same time.

"Jinx," Eric yelled, and Daniel said, "Don't be dumb."

She was at the kitchen table by ten, a mug of fresh coffee in hand, her typewriter still in the front closet box, the pages of *Words of New Beginnings* in front of her. She needed to submerge herself in her own words before she could pick up where she had left off. She began at the beginning.

We were young, and some of us were beautiful, and others of us were brilliant, and a few of us were both. Citizenship demanded only an ability to create, to use our minds and hands and bodies in unforeseen ways—

Joan looked up. The image of herself in her study nearly thirteen years earlier was so clear in her mind. The analysis she had undertaken about having the baby she did not want, the choice she had made after imagining the situation as if she were a character in a story she was writing, about opening her heart, the run of delightful years. She remembered thinking the story would need some tragic arc, and she felt that sense of recollection, of déjà vu, she'd sometimes felt since Eric's birth, and she wondered when that calamity, catastrophe, misfortune, and heartbreak might hit.

There had been, thus far, a run of mostly delightful years, even when her life seemed a mirage—sometimes lovely, sometimes not. She might be keeping an enormous secret from Martin, but they were generally happy, still having plentiful sex, the boys were healthy, usually good-spirited, sort of well adjusted, chock-full of their own wonderful idiosyncrasies. Despite her frustration about being pulled away from her work, they had spent a great summer together. Now she was about to return to the book she wanted to be writing, thirty-six school weeks ahead of her when the hours from ten until nearly three were in her possession, and she felt a pinch of fear that things could not last.

She was waiting for them when school let out, leaning up against the station wagon. The school had a single red door, beyond which were open-air walkways that fanned out in three directions, leading to the elementary school, the middle school, and the high school, all with separate classrooms, cafeterias, auditoriums, and playgrounds. The door was deceptive, a whole town of children and teachers was right behind it.

Eric ran out first, then raced down the steps to Joan. She ran her fingers through his hair, said, "Sweetie, how was the first day?" and Eric began talking, and she was listening, but then she saw Daniel, trailing behind a group of laughing kids. His head was down, and he was dragging his feet. Eric held on to her hand as she started toward Daniel, but Daniel ducked around her, opened the wagon's back door, slid into the backseat, and slammed the heavy door closed. Eric whined, "Daniel," and Daniel opened the door again, and Eric jumped in.

Joan started the car, but kept the parking brake engaged. "How was your day?" she asked Daniel. Since kindergarten, he had always leaned over the rim of the front seat to kiss her, and say, "It was good, I missed you, I'll tell you all about it." Today, Daniel didn't lean over and kiss her, did not answer her question, just stared out the window looking forlorn. On the way home, Eric told them a long story about the games he had played at recess, that tetherball was his favorite, that he was the day's champion, gave them a blow-by-blow account of a game he had played with some other little boy, filling up all the space in the car.

At bedtime, she knocked at Daniel's open door. "Can I come in?" He shrugged, and she decided to ignore it.

"How is your new teacher? Do you like Miss Nilson?"

He shrugged again.

"Is she nice?"

"Yes."

The story he had taken to school was on his desk, and Joan said, "Did you enjoy seeing your friends from last year?"

"I guess. I only know Trevor in my class."

Daniel's sometime best friend, whom Joan didn't much like. He was a fair-weather kind of pal. The two were best friends one day, not talking the next.

"Are you okay with not knowing anyone else yet?"

"I guess."

"Was it interesting to see what the others shared about themselves?"

"Kind of."

This was not like Daniel, these shrugs, this yanking of words from
his mouth.

"What kind of things did the other kids share?"

"Pictures of their vacations. One girl went waterskiing. Someone
climbed a big mountain. Pictures of their families. A boy named Francis
has eight brothers and sisters. A girl named Tammy brought her
hamster named Giant. He was really cute."

This was the Daniel she knew, talking with his own free will, and
he continued on, identifying what all twenty children had brought in
as evidence of what they thought expressed them best, of who they
were, at this particular moment in time.

When he said nothing about his story, when he picked up from the
nightstand the book he was reading, *Oswald's Tale* by Norman Mailer,
she sat down on his bed. "How did you share Henry with the class?"

"Miss Nilson had me come up to the front and read it."

"Did you like doing that?"

Daniel nodded.

"Did the class enjoy it?"

Daniel nodded again.

"Mom," he said, "did you used to be a writer?"

She inhaled sharply, unsure where this was coming from.

"Yes," she said. Short, simple, sweet.

"Are you still a writer?"

What was this about?

"I am," she said. "Once a writer, always a writer." Though not too
long ago she had debated that exact thesis.

"I've never seen you writing. Are you writing something now?"

Christ, Joan thought.

"Do you remember me reading you stories that I called the Rare
Baby stories? You were really little then."

Daniel nodded.

"Well, those are stories I wrote."

"I don't think I knew that when I was a baby. I really liked them,
I remember that."

Joan smiled. "I'm glad. I loved writing them."

"Did you have books published?"

Once, when she was pregnant with Eric, Martin had explained to Daniel that his mother was a writer. Joan had been in the kitchen, standing over a pot of boiling macaroni, shaking out the powdery contents of a silver pouch that turned into a sticky bright-orange cheese, knowing Fancy would never have made such an unhealthy dinner, and through the cutaway above the sink, she could see Martin and Daniel on the old plaid couch. "Your mother has prodigious talent," Martin said to their son, and Joan had stopped stirring. Martin's choice of that adjective, the way he elongated it, had made her question whether her work— with its alarming interpretations of life—had unsettled him years ago, still bothered him, despite what he had expressed to her. Why hadn't he chosen as a way to describe her talent *great, terrific, wonderful, amazing, super,* rather than the inexplicable *prodigious* which made it sound as if she had contracted a horrendous disease and might soon die.

Looking at her son looking at her, Joan realized she had forgotten that scene entirely, and she was certain that Daniel had too. She had never spoken to him about her life before motherhood and Martin thought she was no longer writing, so where was he getting his information from?

"Yes," she said. "I published two collections of stories. One is called *Other Small Spaces* and the other is called *Fictional Family Life.*"

Deliberately, she did not tell him he could read them if he wanted to, that there were a dozen copies of each book in English, and more in all different languages, in a box on the top shelf in the closet in his parents' bedroom, that there was probably a copy of each on the living-room bookshelves. It wasn't only that many of her stories were disturbing, Daniel had read tough material since he was young, but she wanted his picture of his life, of their family, to be pure, unsullied by the way his mother once thought, sometimes still did, if she was honest.

He didn't say anything for a few moments. Didn't ask what the titles of her books meant or if he could read them. When another long moment passed, she hoped he wouldn't recall the other question he asked her.

"Are you writing now?" And there it was.

It was scary how fast the brain could process various rationales for not answering a question one did not want to answer. Daniel was competitive and she did not want him competing in this way, over writing, his versus hers. Martin did not know, and so Daniel could not know that she was writing, a novel, a second novel actually, because a child should never have to keep a parent's secret. Something had happened at school that day to make him ask her these questions, but what that could be, or how it tied in with Henry the Squirrel, for she was certain that it did, she couldn't figure out.

"No," she said instantly, and did not take a breath, did not want Daniel to ask another searching question, wanted him only to feel good about himself. "I'm so proud of you, love. Proud of you for reading your terrific story to your new classmates."

She kissed his forehead and said, "Don't stay up too late reading. It's only the second day of school tomorrow."

She checked in on Eric again, but he was fast asleep, covers thrown off, thumb in his mouth. His oral fixation had calmed in the last years. No more greenery and pebbles, but now sometimes he sucked his thumb when he had not done so as an infant. Were his baby teeth at risk of becoming buckteeth, if he kept it up? He'd only lost one so far. Well, she thought, they'll all fall out eventually anyway.

She poured herself a glass of wine and went outside. The moon was full, an eerie white. That déjà vu she had felt earlier in the day, the thought that tragedy was required in the story of a woman who had a delightful run of years as the mother of an unwanted baby, was it just a foreshadowing of the uncomfortable questions Daniel asked her that night, or were the questions not that important, and it was his shrugs and monosyllabic answers that were portents of what everyone said were the brutal teen years? How she would miss her wonderful boy, the son she felt closest to, the son whom she tried never to favor over his younger brother, but did, if only in her own heart, because of a crimson kinship thicker than blood, beyond DNA. Their hearts had meshed from the beginning, and then there was their shared adoration of reading, their love of writing. How she would hate it if that time were already here.

Daniel was still quiet at breakfast on Wednesday morning, but he ate the scrambled eggs she made and three pieces of toast, and teased Eric until Eric laughed, and Joan thought whatever had been going on with him had passed. She waved as they walked together through the red school door, wondered if they had a ritual for parting, if Daniel messed Eric's hair, or Eric reached out a hand to touch his older brother one last time until the end of the day.

At the kitchen table, she continued reading *Words*. She had warned herself against editing, but the instinct was too ingrained, and she covered the typed pages in thunderous black ink, and the pad next to her filled up with notes. Finally, she read a page straight through.

He thinks how far he has come from his childhood in Goa when he knew only bare feet and the beach and the Arabian Sea, and nearly nothing about how huge the world could be. He has made this good life possible for his family, teaching himself both English and Italian, finding this job in the Tuscan countryside, as the marchesa's majordomo at her fine hotel, that once was an enormous farmhouse, and was still surrounded by its fertile lands. His long days are spent translating the marchesa's directives, to his mother and two sisters who prepare traditional Italian fare for the biking groups who come for riding and good wine, and to his father and brother who tend to the olive orchards and the livestock. They are now all asleep over the barn, in the large apartment that has been their home these past six years.

The guests are at the long-planked table in the garden, their dishes scraped clean, though the briny smell of the fish dinner lingers. The wine bottles are nearly depleted, and a married man, whose wife is sleeping upstairs, is feeding an olive to a young woman here on her own. Bash hears him say to her, "Your voice makes me think of ecstatic sex in gorgeous rooms. I long to experience that with you. I want to do wonderful things to you, and for you, for a lifetime. Whatever you want to say to me, I will listen."

It is late, past midnight, and Bash watches those two, and the other guests, their smiles and laughter caught in candlelight. He uncorks another bottle for their pleasure, lights a few more of the citronella candles to keep the bugs away.

Tomorrow, he will hide among them, gathered on the graveled walk of the hotel, suitcases beside them, headed to the airport, leaving Italy behind. He has saved enough to disappear like this, to fly across the

sky, to take the large highways and the small roads to the place he read
about, that rural valley where others are gathering, where he might
finally make good on his long-cherished dream to cease taking orders,
to turn those words in another direction, to grab hold of them for
himself, to write the book he's long had in his mind.

A honking horn returned her suddenly to the kitchen, to the ticking clock on the wall showing her she was out of time. Then she was
shoving her work back into the box hidden in the closet, covering it
with the old coats, grabbing her car keys and racing down the hill to
pick the boys up. Daniel wasn't smiling when he walked out of school,
but in the car, he sort of leaned over the seat and gave her a quick kiss
on her cheek. She was delighted, and relieved, and she called over her
shoulder, "Who wants to go out for pizza tonight?"

Thursday afternoon, she put away early her pen, her pad of notes, the
draft-in-progress of the novel. She was averaging about fifty-five pages
a day, reading it through and marking it up. At this rate, it would take
her all of the following week too before she was ready to start writing
again.

She looked at the long supermarket list and missed Fancy, and
wondered if she had made a mistake in not hiring another nanny. She
had been spoiled by Fancy, often not seeing the inside of a supermarket
for weeks at a time. It was all up to her now, and Martin was coming
home the next day from China and the fridge was mostly empty, and
the weekend weather forecast said it would be nice, and Martin would
want to grill both evenings. Daniel would take himself to the glen and
read while his father was basting and flipping the meat, calling out,
"Rare, medium rare, medium, well done," in a kind of singing rhyme,
and Eric would stand next to his father, his ready helper, the extra set
of tongs in his hand, waiting for a chance to show Martin he knew
what he was doing.

She tossed into the grocery cart breakfast and school lunch staples,
along with meats for grilling, gallons of ice cream, and in the pharmacy
aisle, a box of baby aspirin. It was September after all, school was back
in session, and it never took any time before one or both of the boys

had the sniffles, a sore throat, a slight fever, and in Eric's case, the dramatic moans of a child who wanted to stay home from school.

The boys were on the sidewalk when she pulled up to the school. Eric was jumping from square to square and Daniel had a book raised to his eyes. She honked and they piled in and were off, Eric jabbering about his day, about the boys he played with at recess, the math teacher he liked, and that everyone in his class had to take a test on Monday.

"The Q test," he said, and Joan glanced at him in the rearview mirror. "Do you mean an IQ test?" He nodded.

"I took that test," Daniel said. "Was I in second grade like Eric when I took it, Mom?"

She nodded and said, "I think you were."

She had missed the notice the school must have sent. She carried in the mail each day from their mailbox, but had not opened a single piece, just sat down at the kitchen table and went back to work. She would have to search the pile for the notice, see if there were special instructions about it. She couldn't remember if there had been any when Daniel took that test.

They pulled into the garage, and Joan said, "I'll pay you both two bucks to unload the groceries and put them away."

Daniel snorted, and Eric, looking up at his big brother, snorted too.

"Five," Daniel said, and Eric said, "Five," and Joan laughed and said, "Fine."

Joan woke Friday morning to Daniel yelling, "Mom, Mom, MOM, MOM!" and she threw off the light duvet, yanked the door open, and ran out, and there was Daniel showing her the empty bottle he found behind the living-room couch.

The kitchen clock read 6:30 and Daniel was crying. Eric was on the couch kicking his feet.

She had left the boxed and sealed bottle of baby aspirin bought at the market the previous day on the kitchen counter. She had forgotten to put it away.

"Goddammit," she yelled, ignoring Daniel's shock that she was swearing, thinking of all the crap Eric used to put in his mouth, that conversation Martin had with him when Joan feared he was suffering from pica, and now Eric, seven and old enough to know better, had torn open the box, peeled off the plastic safety wrap, opened the childproof bottle, stabbed through the silver shield, and eaten all two-hundred and fifty peach-colored baby aspirin tablets.

"What the hell were you doing?" Joan yelled at Eric, but it was Daniel who answered, still crying, saying, "Mom, I'm so, so sorry." Eric looked at her calmly and said, "I was watching cartoons." As if that answered the question, made sense.

"Daniel, call Trevor, ask if his mother can pick you up. Tell her you'll be outside at eight forty. Watch your brother until I throw on some clothes. Make sure you eat breakfast when we're gone. Make yourself lunch."

Gastric lavage, that's what Eric endured, a flexible tube inserted into his mouth, down his esophagus, coming to rest in his stomach. Saline flowed through the tube, then up it all came, hundreds of dissolved aspirins, regurgitated, the cornflakes, milk, and sugar he'd also consumed at dawn, the process repeated twice until nothing was left inside.

His big brown eyes gleamed black when he said, "Mom, what's the big deal? They tasted like candy. Plus, I got out of going to school today."

Martin did not experience the fear, or the panic, or the guilt Joan felt. And after the fact, the way Eric told the story, it was almost funny, showing his father Friday night, just home from China, how he had munched the aspirin as if they were SweetTarts, how long the tube had been that went down his throat.

This, she thought, is what I've been worrying about all week, the arc of tragedy I was waiting for.

She had spent all summer encouraging both children to heed their own paths, to not blindly follow another child's wrongdoing, to not jump off a figurative cliff just because one of their friends did, and, well, Eric apparently was following his own path, a child who did not think ahead, who was immune to consequences. He did not have pica, there was no definitional *phagia* for the mass consumption of baby aspirin, but listening to Eric bragging to his father about his bravery, that the gastric lavage had not scared him at all, that he had not cried even a little, Joan shuddered and she felt a chill, and wished he suffered from pica, at least then there would be a logic to it.

That sense of recollection and déjà vu she felt after their first day of school, it wasn't about Daniel and his questions that came out of nowhere about her life as a writer, but how she had felt when Eric refused to nurse, squirmed in her arms, chose *no* as his first word, refused books, then diapers. From his entry into the world, Eric dictated the progression of his life. Punching against parental boundaries and limits was to be expected, in teenagers, but a seven-year-old evincing so early a predilection for risky behavior? Was she reading Eric accurately—that he was thrilled by the events he created?

She was at fault for leaving the aspirin out, but she would not allow herself to feel guilty about her work. The last four days spent engrossed in her pages could not have undone all she did over the summer. For three months, she had been fully present, both sons had known she was right there with them, thinking of nothing else, most of the time, but them. Yes, she was back to work, but they didn't know that—she had been there at breakfast, at school drop-offs and pick-ups, at after-school snack time, at dinner, at bath time, at bedtime. Had Eric sensed her waning attraction for motherhood, her desire to have gorgeous time without them? Why couldn't Eric have devoured all those aspirins during one of the rare times Martin was on duty?

Seeing her husband with their youngest son, not taking him to task the way she thought Martin should, she imagined one of Daniel's contests—which parent knew more about their children? She would win, hands down. Did Martin know that Eric was a boy who loved to take shortcuts, to simplify, to make things easy; that he preferred his room sparse and bare, could not abide Daniel's room, with its towers of books, his collection of bound Henry stories that Joan was still making for him, his swim goggles and swim cap and baseball glove never put away, his swimsuits hanging from the knob of the closet door; that Eric liked puzzles, and building intricate LEGO constructions that he immediately dissasembled after showing Joan and Daniel his creations, all the pieces back in their plastic containers, neatly tucked under his bed; that he preferred to be on his own, could keep himself entertained, liked only math in school, doodled numbers that he could not explain to Joan, had no interest in athletics as Daniel did; that he spoke in full, well-made sentences and talked softly until he yelled; that once, he said he wished his name were Thomas; that he could be stingy with his hugs and his kisses, but every so often, he would seek Joan out and hug her so tight, she felt the air emptying out of her lungs; that an interest in reading had never kicked in, but he still allowed Daniel, every once in a while, to read him a Henry story at bedtime, leaning against Joan, allowing her arms around him, while Daniel sat at the bottom of the bed and read them the squirrel's newest adventure, until Eric pushed free, and said, "Enough cuddling for one day. Enough reading." No, Martin did not know these things, and despite never having wanted motherhood, despite the 250 aspirin Eric had ingested, she knew she was a goddamn great mother.

Eric had milked the escapade for sympathy, asking for ice cream for dinner, saying that his throat hurt, which it probably did, which she hoped it actually did, and Martin, yawning from jet lag, had spooned the ice cream into a big bowl.

"I don't blame you at all," Martin said later that night, after the boys were in bed.

And Joan thought, You'd better not.

Her husband was asleep in seconds, and Joan left their bed, threw on a light sweater, retrieved from the front closet another chunk of *Words*. She went out into the backyard and got to work at her old desk, wishing she were back in her old East Village apartment, when the table was still untarnished, and she was solely herself, a woman apart, a writer at work.

14

Way before dawn on Monday, Daniel tiptoed out of his bedroom, past his brother's room, into the living room, where he slipped a book of short stories free from its place on the shelves, tiptoed back to his room, hid that book in his backpack, slept for another hour, got up, got dressed, ate breakfast, and waved to his mother when she drove away from school. At nine, when the bell rang, when Daniel was supposed to be in homeroom with Miss Nilson, he was in the library, sitting behind the last stacks, opening his backpack, pulling out that book, and opening it to the first story called "Deep in the Valley."

He read the first paragraph:

She rents the motel room for a few days. The clerk at the desk, a boy, is nice enough. He smiles but does not make dumb polite chatter. He does not ask to see her driver's license. She is used to showing her license because she looks so young, older than a teenager, but not quite a woman. She knows she looks perpetually suspended, otherworldly, not fully grown, though she's thirty-three. She signs the receipt in her cramped handwriting. The clerk's silence seems right to her. She is near now. Probably no one ought to talk to her.

He read the second paragraph:

The room is sort of okay, beiges and pinks, with a flat king bed. It is a motel, but the mini-bar is stocked. There is a binder filled with information about tourist attractions, a Bible in one nightstand on sticky floral contact paper, a local phone book in the other. Neither is quite the Book of Life she thinks, and unpacks her bag. She walks down the quiet hall to fill the plastic ice bucket, hears the hum of the ice machine, aware that the hall is not fresh, the paint faded, stale smells of fear and desolation, but she has lived in much worse. She has lived in places she tries to forget. She plunges her hands into the ice when memories of those places squiggle her brain.

He read the third paragraph:

She knows where she is going because there is nowhere else to go, nothing else to try, no other beliefs to believe. She no longer imagines that she can be like everyone else, that she can live her life as they do. She is thinking clearly now—about how she has always been inside a box. Inside a little box that has no floors, no doors, no windows, only walls that are closing in on her, relentlessly pressing toward the center, where she stands, where she has long stood. It won't be long before she is sealed up for good, and no one will ever know she was once here.

Unlike Daniel, who inhaled and read on and remained in the library where he was not supposed to be, Eric was where he was supposed to be, at his desk, in his classroom, with his teacher, Mr. John, at the blackboard, on which was written in large chalky letters, IQ TEST DAY.

Mr. John explained they would each be administered the Wechsler Preschool and Primary Scale of Intelligence, a sixty-five-minute test that would generate a Full Scale IQ representing each child's general intellectual ability. It would also provide primary index scores in verbal comprehension, perceptual reasoning, working memory, and processing speed, that represented each child's abilities in discrete cognitive domains.

None of what Mr. John said made any sense to Eric, or to his classmates, and everyone rolled their eyes at everyone else, but they cheered when Mr. John said they could draw or read or do whatever they wanted, quietly, very quietly, until it was their turn and their name was called.

At twenty minutes after ten, the school secretary walked Eric to the auditorium, where a long desk and two chairs were set up beneath one of the basketball hoops. A nice lady sat down and told him to sit down. She asked him lots of questions: about the meanings of words, and about similar words. She had him solve lots of puzzles: for the words she was looking for, for what was missing from pictures, for what symbols went together, for what shapes went together, for what word or symbol or shape he would choose to fill in various blanks. She had him put red-and-white blocks together making patterns he liked, and while he did that, she read him a long line of numbers he had to try to remember so he could repeat them, and he did that easily, reeling them right off, forward and backward. Everything she had him do he thought was great fun and very easy. "Good job," she said. "You're all done."

The school secretary led him back to Mr. John's class, and the whole way, he thought if school was like that test, he wouldn't hate school as much as he did.

By eleven thirty, he was out on the playground, playing dodgeball because the line for tetherball, which he preferred, was too long.

From nine forty until two forty, Joan sat at the kitchen table reading and editing and making notes on and about *Words*.

At three, she was parked outside of the school, waiting for her children to emerge, which they did five minutes later.

By three thirty, they were home, and the boys were eating a snack.

At four, Martin came home early from the hospital, still jet-lagged from China, feeling that his presence had been missed, that he needed to be around much more, that Eric required a watchful eye, despite his being good all weekend.

At four fifteen, Martin was in the backyard, and the three Manning men were tossing a football around, or rather Martin and Daniel were tossing a football around, and Eric was complaining that he did not want to play, that football was stupid, and why couldn't they get a computer.

At five, Joan forced Eric to take a bath and wash his hair.

At six, the family ate in the backyard, fish that Martin had barbecued and no one particularly liked.

At six thirty, Joan brought out bowls, spoons, the gallon of Mint Chocolate Chip, the squeeze bottle of chocolate syrup.

At seven, Daniel went into the house, went into his room, pulled the book from his backpack, moved quickly down the hallway, looked out the living-room windows where he saw his parents had not moved from the table. Eric was in their father's lap, their mother was lifting a glass to her mouth.

He slipped the collection, called *Other Small Spaces*, back into its place on the bookshelves. His mother's name had not been written on the flyleaf because her name was printed on the title page, and on the spine, and in raised letters on the front cover that he could run his fingertips over.

He did not write his own name on the flyleaf as he always did. He didn't want to, not since the first day of school when Miss Nilson altered his world.

On that first day, he'd read his story aloud, and Miss Nilson asked him to stay past the bell, and she said, *"You must feel like the luckiest boy to have such a talented writer for a mother. I've read her books and all of her other published stories. You must be so proud, knowing that your mother's work has been read by so many, that she has received such big prizes for her writing. I can only imagine your family's dinner conversations. And look, you're following in her footsteps."*

He had not known about any of that. He had not known his mother was a writer, was famous, that he was not the only writer in his house.

And that night, when he questioned his mother, she admitted she had published two books, but she had said nothing, nothing at all, about winning prizes and awards, and said *no* when he asked if she was writing now.

When she left his room, he tried not to blame her, but he did, and it was all desperate anger inside him. And he had thought how Eric always said, "You're my best friend, Daniel," and sometimes Trevor was Daniel's, or at least he would say that when they were getting along, but really, his best friend had always been his mother, so how come, when he asked her those questions, she hadn't been able to read his heart, or feel his pain, or know his mind was filled with confused thoughts jumping around like rabbits.

And it was then, right then, he instantly understood what he had read in the big books he loved, that when people were hurt down to their bones, it was because they had been betrayed, and *he* had been betrayed, and betrayal felt like *this*. The very fact of her had stamped out what made him special, crushed his secret desire to be a famous writer.

And all this past week, he felt rooted to the ground, clenching his hands in fists, saying to himself, "She's a mother, just a mother, that's all she is."

But this morning, hiding in the library reading "Deep in the Valley," he had realized three things: that her talent was unique, that he could never hope to match it, and that he would never get over it. The fury he felt toward her was blinding and white-hot, because she had destroyed him, completely and absolutely. Why that should be so, he could not explain to himself. He hadn't been able to read another story, had slammed the book shut, and stayed in the library the rest of the day, his face in his hands.

He looked once more at his mother's book on the shelf, then turned away, went back outside, sat at the table, and pretended he did not hate her.

At eight, Eric went to bed.

At nine, Daniel went to bed.

At ten, Martin went to bed too.

Joan did not go to bed. Since Friday night, she had been taking advantage of Martin's jet lag, continuing to make her slow way through *Words*. She had one hundred and fifteen pages to go, and a lot of work to do to bring what she had written thus far into being, the ways in which she thought her characters, and their stories, needed to move forward, the new chapters she was keen to write. She still was not certain whether she would start anew, or wind back to the start and first revise all of those pages. But she was working with pleasure, with relief that Eric's mishap with the aspirin had not harmed him, and that Daniel, while still quieter than usual, had smiled a few times at dinner, even as she sometimes caught him studying her. He hadn't kissed her goodnight, but he hadn't kissed Martin either. She was eager for the next day, for Martin to brush the top of her hair with his lips and leave by the back door, to drop the kids off at school, to return to the novel she could feel in her marrow had the poetic heft, the depth, all the sinews and tissues, to be extraordinarily fine.

At two in the morning, Joan slid naked into their bed. She was no longer angry with Martin, about his comment that he did not blame her for Eric eating all of that aspirin, the bottle left out on the counter. He had meant to assuage, even if his words had had the opposite effect. She settled against him, and he moaned softly, and then his right arm, his right hand, fell across her left thigh, and she, too, went to sleep.

On Tuesday morning, the world blew up.

15

There was shock and horror and fear. In the future, the events of Tuesday would be labeled with a shorthand name summing up the crashing planes, the burning fuel, the people jumping from the tall buildings, the passengers wrangling with terrorists before dying in a Pennsylvania field, part of the Pentagon sheared away, all the deaths, the family traumas, the country's trauma, the loss of innocence and invulnerability, the guilt eating away at survivors, the degrees of separation between those who had been spared and those who had not, the recollections of where everyone was when it all happened. There would be nonfiction accounts, political and religious analyses and screeds, wars begun as a result, fighting, supposedly, to regain balance, to right the wrongs, leaving behind more body counts of the dead, the dying, and the maimed. Fiction, too, would be written, novels and short stories that had at their bloody center that Tuesday morning and its aftermath. But right then, on that beautiful blue September morning, everything just halted. There was no school for the rest of the week. Martin's surgeries were rescheduled, except for the emergencies, the hospital with all of its patients a soundless tomb. The streets of Rhome were empty, as if its population had also been incinerated in an instant. Everyone stayed inside, huddling and crying with their families, with their aging parents, with their young children, with their girl-friends or boyfriends, with their spouses they were considering divorcing, with their cats and their dogs and their birds and their hamsters. Televisions remained on permanently, the voices of newscasters and journalists around the globe settling into every corner of every house. At the end of that long and incomprehensible week, the mayor of Rhome, along with a priest, a minister, a rabbi, and a

Buddhist monk—like the start of a bad joke—presided over a candlelight vigil on Strada di Felicità. Thousands of Rhome residents emerged from their homes for the first time in days and listened to their wise, empty words. For a long time, nothing would be as it was.

16

The reverberations continued, but life resumed, and three weeks later, a letter came in the mail from the Rhome Elementary School principal stating that, unless the Mannings objected, Eric would be transferred from his second-grade class with Mr. John to the third-grade class presided over by Mr. Nevins. His score on the Wechsler Preschool and Primary Scale of Intelligence had been off the charts. The principal had written: *Eric is supremely gifted and would benefit greatly by moving up a grade. We considered moving him up two grades, but the age gap would be too great. To hold him back from moving ahead, however, would be a travesty.*

At the kitchen table, Eric's head pinged back and forth, from mother to father and back again, as Joan and Martin debated whether such a move was a good thing for him or not.

"What do you think," Joan said to Eric as Daniel stomped into the kitchen, dragged a chair out from the table, and sat down hard.

"I don't know," Eric said.

"I don't understand. I bring home all A's because I work hard, but no one's moving me up a grade. And Eric, he never opens a book, doesn't read a thing, barely does his stupid homework, unless you force him to. He only likes LEGOs and numbers and Dad's office computer, and now supposedly he's some kind of genius?"

"I'll still hate school, even if they put me in third grade. Does that make you feel better, Daniel?" Eric asked.

It did not.

"So, Eric's a genius, and Dad has a surgery named after him now, and you, Mom—" Daniel pushed his chair from the table and stormed away, slamming the door to his bedroom.

In mid-October, when the leaves on the trees were hinting at fall, pale reds, oranges, and golds shimmering among the green, the typewriter was humming, a fresh page rolled in, Joan's fingers poised above the keyboard. This was her first day back. Since that Tuesday morning, in the harsh light of what had occurred, she had questioned writing about a blissful arcadia, about artists and their dreams, their desires to create eminent lives, filled up with as much virtuosity and brilliance as their talent and personalities permitted. But weren't people ultimately and irrevocably lost if they abandoned those dreams, ceased trying to create a rich alternative world, for themselves and for others? Wasn't the beauty of art found in the uncovering and discovering, in being taken, or led, to the line, the step, the curve, the color, the note, the word? Wasn't the ability to start anew, again and again, the very definition of human endeavor? *Words of New Beginnings* was about all of that, and about what was good in the world, about collaboration, and collective creativity, about individuals striving for something grand, about finding ways to protect themselves and one another as they pursued what their souls commanded. She pressed down on the keys and saw the black words stamping into the white. She already knew what she was going to write.

Anton is all tender veins, fresh blood, a smacked and small beating heart, and she must help that little heart to grow, cannot do a thing that might break it in half, or into tiny pieces, or into any pieces at all. Lila feels how she holds his heart in her hands and must safeguard it, an obligation she understands she has taken on, has made herself responsible for him, and although he does not realize it, he is counting on her to shepherd him into the next stage of his life. He has taken the first steps, Anton is here after all, in this place they all now call home.

Joan leaned back and thought the act of writing had never felt as exquisitely important, so much like prayer.

17

Eric moved into Mr. Nevin's third grade, and other than playing with different kids at recess, it made no difference to him, except that his father bought him a computer and set it up in his room. He spent hours figuring out how the thing worked, how he could make it work in different ways, and one Saturday morning, he said, "Mom, will you take me to the library?" Surprised that this second child of hers was finally expressing an interest in reading, Joan said, "Sure. We'll go right now." On the drive over, she asked what kind of books he was looking for, and Eric said, "Coding," and Joan had no idea what he was talking about.

Daniel made the swim team, the only seventh grader to do so. When the swim season officially started, and the team began attending meets, his events would be the 100-meter individual medley, swimming butterfly, backstroke, breaststroke, and freestyle, and the fifty-yard freestyle. Joan bought him special shampoo and soap to wash away the chlorine, but it stuck to his skin, the scent entering rooms before he did. He did his homework with his usual attention and continued to get top grades. He still read big novels that he took off the living-room shelves or checked out of the library, but he didn't often want to talk to Joan about what he was reading. And gradually Joan became aware that she no longer heard the plunking of the manual typewriter keys in his room, that he did not mention the squirrel at all.

It was the day after Christmas. The house was quiet, their land brown beneath the cold sun, and Joan and Martin were in the living room, the coffee in their mugs cooling, reading the *New York Times*. Eric had disappeared into his room, reading the books they had given him for Christmas, six coding books recommended by one of Martin's

Johns Hopkins friends, who'd been told that their seven-year-old was fixated on computers and had been reading serious books intended for those already in the computer science field. Though he had never opened a children's book willingly, Eric read perfectly well when consumed by the subject, and when Joan finally returned the oft-renewed library books, the pages had been frayed. Daniel was at the community center, as he usually was, in the pool with the swim team.

Joan put down the paper and said, "Something's wrong with Daniel. He's stopped writing about Henry."

Martin rubbed his eyes. "He'll start up again, if that's what he wants to do."

"I don't think he will. He's doubting himself for some reason."

"Isn't experiencing doubt part of growing up?" Martin said. "A useful way to test your limits and surpass them?"

"True, but give me one example where we wouldn't try to shore up our sons' doubts, would just allow doubt to hang in the air, pretend not to notice the struggle."

When Martin could not, Joan said, "You don't have a lot of experience with doubt. But I do. When the writers I edited faltered, I kept them from falling down. In my own work, there were many times I had to push through. We—I—have to do that for Daniel. I think he's giving up on something vital, that thing that makes him who he is, and he's too young to know he will suffer in the future from the actions he's taking now. We need to help him."

Martin shook his head. "Sometimes a forceful push can have the opposite effect. Maybe he's just taking a break. He's certainly found a new area of interest with swimming. And anyway, isn't writing something he can choose to do or not?"

"Daniel's compelled to write, he has been since he was little, just like I am—" she said, feeling heat in her face, on her chest, wondering if Martin noticed the slip. "If the compulsion has disappeared so quickly, something's wrong."

Martin hadn't noticed her slip, and it struck Joan again, as it had occasionally over the past several years, that he had never questioned her, or worried, when she said she stopped writing. That to him, her writing was something far in the past, as if she had never been a writer at all.

"Maybe, but let's not say anything right now. Let's give it time.

Everyone's still reeling, no one feels sure about the world anymore. Why should an eleven-year-old be any different?"

"Twelve in four days," she said.

"Right, but in four days he won't suddenly process what's happened any better."

Joan wasn't interested in hashing it out, in revealing the existence of *Words*, so she allowed Martin the last word and they went back to reading the paper. For the rest of the day, she debated about whether she ought to press Daniel. If he had stopped writing, there was something that needed to be aired out and discussed.

In bed that night, she thought how Daniel seemed happy enough, with the swim team, with keeping track of his times, with his books, and his friends, blushing a little when he talked about a girl in his class. In the morning, when no clear answer had revealed itself, Joan decided to default to Martin's suggestion for just a little while, to see whether Daniel started plunking away again.

In early February, she leaned against Daniel's door. "So, I was just wondering what new adventure you're considering for Henry." Daniel looked up from his desk and shrugged. "I'm not." She saw the hemming in his eyes, there was something he wanted to say, but he shrugged again, swallowed once, twice, then said, "Mom, I'm too busy with everything else. I have a history quiz tomorrow and I have to study. Okay?"

She wanted badly to push, to make Daniel speak, but instead she said, "Let me know if you want me to test you, or you get hungry and want a snack."

Daniel nodded and dropped his head back down into his history notes.

Perhaps Martin was right. Her son, always an open book, always talking to her about whatever was going on in his life, was closing his covers, with secret thoughts of his own, and perhaps she needed to wait for him to reach out to her, to bring up whatever was on his mind.

For a long time, she thought Daniel would, when he had been thirteen, fourteen, fifteen, and came to find her out in the gardens, hoeing or raking or reseeding or deadheading the flowers, the gardens still her creative outlet when the family was around and she could not write. He would join her, help out for a while, and she would wait for him to say something, that he missed writing, mention the name of his squirrel, but he did not. He talked of other things: school, friends, the girl he did have a crush on, the swim team, filling Joan in, disclosing details, still as close, even if he had cut one of the ties that bound them together.

She left it in the past, tried not to think of Daniel the writer, until the fall of his senior year, when he was studying for the SATs, filling out college applications. He said he wanted to major in business, to make money, to be rich, to be powerful. Such a completely different future from the one she had thought, hoped, believed he should pursue. It wasn't so much that she had an expectation of who and what Daniel would become, but an assumption, and that assumption had not included him tossing away the talents and promise of his childhood, allowing them to flag, wear out, and die.

It was late October when she found Daniel boxing up his stories, most of them between the sparkling covers she had made.

"I need more room on my shelves," he said, and she saw the huge hole where they had always been.

She watched him place the last few into the overfilled box. "Those bring back such wonderful memories, you writing and reading them to me, or me reading them to you."

He nodded. There was a pause, and then he said, "Me too."

"How many did you write before retiring him?"

Retiring seemed a better choice than *failing, abruptly stopping, giving up without explanation.* She knew exactly how many he had written.

Daniel nodded again. "Ninety-nine."

He was right.

She wanted to say, *Don't you feel you shortchanged yourself by not writing that hundredth story?*—perhaps if he had written the hundredth, he might have continued—but she said instead, "What an accomplishment."

Daniel put a hand on the top book, ran his fingers down the cover, said, "Thanks," then bent into the mouth of his closet. Out flew tennis shoes, flip-flops, hiking boots, snow boots, and the dress shoes he had worn only once, in July, to a girl's Sweet Sixteen, a very mature sixteen-year-old who had not wanted an all-girl celebration. Those shoes probably no longer fit him. When he had carved out space, made an empty cave, he pushed the heavy box to the back of his closet until it hit the wall.

He stood up and looked at her. "I have one more application to finish, the one I really want. The undergraduate business program at Wharton, at UPenn."

All summer and now into the fall, he had been talking about how that school, with its courses in finance, analytics, innovation, and entrepreneurship, was the place for him to go.

"That's great, love. If you need any help, want me to read over your essays, you know I will." She had helped him do that for all the other colleges he was applying to.

She left him organizing his shoes in neat rows, wondering if she had done the right thing four years ago, or whether she had made a serious mistake. If the loss of the squirrel would mark Daniel, had already marked him, in some way, for life. There was an enormity to it that Martin had discounted, that Daniel had seemed not to consider at all.

She closed the door to her and Martin's room and sat on the bed. A golden light came through the windows, its undertone slightly blued. The chill and cold would soon settle in. Most of the trees on their property had already shed their leaves, just a faint red haze still remained on the maples.

She, who'd last cried at the age of seven, who did not cry the day she realized she would have to have a baby, nearly cried. Daniel once cared about how commas, and colons, and semicolons affected the meaning of a sentence, linguistic tools now reduced to separators of information on applications, in essays in which he articulated his dreams, the adventures he said he wanted to experience in his own life, so distinct from what he used to have Henry experience, undertake. Daniel's were so *safe*.

She wasn't aware her hand was pressed against her throat until she saw herself in the large bathroom mirror. She and Martin had recently been to a party where a palm reader in a turban had read the palms of all the partygoers sloshed on margaritas. The woman, Madame Something-or-Other, had read Joan's, identifying the health line (very good and not crossing the life line, so she should not expect ill health, inherited illnesses, digestive problems, or a lack of stamina, good information to have); the sun line (long and vertical, denoting many blessings); the hard worker's line (curving toward Joan's thumb, a truth she already knew about herself); the heart line (a curved line some distance from her fingers that revealed her generous, sensual, and loving nature, not true as a young writer, now mostly true as a wife and mother); the head line (touching both sides of her palm, indicating a focused individual, although Madame said it also suggested some-one self-centered, which Joan took to mean her work on *Words*); the life line (mostly long, but there were two breaks, suggesting more than one change of direction in life, easy enough to interpret); and the fate line (a double line foretelling two careers, again easy enough to interpret).

But now that palm, with all of its positive affirmations, was clutched around her own neck. It seemed improbable that one could strangle themselves in this way, the autonomic nervous system would kick in, the implement meant to bring death would fall away, the lungs pulling in air, but there was a residual red hand print against her throat, any harder and she might have been able to see all of those lines in a map across that fragile skin.

She leaned in close and appraised herself. Forty-two now, in that vast middle section of life, past the chronological bloom of youth. In terms of her writing, it didn't much matter, the nature of her stories had saved her from being viewed as an ingénue. But she was vain enough that looking a full decade younger than she was, satisfied, even delighted. Her hair remained black and lustrous, loose curls still poured down her back, trimmed since she was pregnant with Daniel, of course, but she had never hacked it off, as the Pregnant Six had, going shorter and shorter each year, until their butterscotch bobs had lightened into short bright blond hair tight against the shapes of their heads. Joan's haircutter knew not to take more than an inch at each four-month visit. The eyes Daniel inherited from her were as blue as ever, the finest fan of crows' feet at the corners, one light line running across her forehead when she was stressed. Her body slender as it had been at twenty-five, lithe and toned from her ritualized two days of yoga every week, though no longer on the weekdays—devoted as religiously as possible to the novel—but a sacred hour each Saturday and Sunday. Those weekend mornings, over in Starborough, she was a purely physical being, torqueing and twisting herself in and out of the poses she had come to know so well, while the Manning men bonded at the Rhome Diner over pancakes and waffles and bacon, talking men-talk, whatever that might be, when one was twelve, the other sixteen, the father forty-nine.

She was seven years and eight hundred pages into the third draft of the novel, but was not yet at the finish line. Some writers knew where they were going from the start, tacked up graphs and flow charts, plot points on notecards, but Joan had never written that way, could not write like that, her characters needed room to breathe, to find their own ways, as she did. She wasn't sure if she had a hundred pages to go or more. She kept herself from thinking about the book's future, about her future when she completed it, she was still at the stage where the only thing that mattered were the words on the page.

Perhaps she was projecting, perhaps the loss she felt for Daniel was misplaced, that the loss she was mourning was her own, that she was this age and still had not completed *Words of New Beginnings*, still had not published that first novel now no longer eagerly expected. She hadn't heard from Volkmann in years, other than a card at the holidays, a dashed note along with the statements identifying the number of copies of her collections sold that year, the Storr & Storr checks written out to *Joan Ashby* tucked inside. She knew very well that the book represented her own new beginning, whenever that day might finally arrive. That was her focus; she could not worry about Daniel. He was old enough to know his own mind. If he had decided he was not a writer, then he wasn't, and she would have to respect that.

CREATED BY THE GODS

Dēvatā'ōṁ kē dvārā nirmit

18

If it was true that infants were born with all knowledge and talent, it seemed to Joan there were three potential roads thereafter: the knowledge solidified, intensified, the budding talents flourished, turned tenacious and lasting, as her own had; or all that knowledge, all that childhood talent lacked the tenacity to remain everlasting, like with Daniel, at least with the writing—what he might do in the future was a complete unknown—or the knowledge and talent was hidden by obstreperousness and emerged later to stunning effect, like what happened with Eric.

At the start of the new year, the small Manning house began filling up with strange boys who played no games, no pranks, and told no jokes, but the snacks and cold drinks Joan set out in the kitchen for them vanished without a trace, without her ever seeing them come and go, and they left behind no crumbs, no used napkins, no empty cans. Eric never cared much about having friends, but now he was somehow the leader of these boys, ghostly boys who were pale-faced and jean-clad, but did not look scary or rabid, did not wear solid black or trench coats, did not listen to heavy metal or any music at all, but along with Eric, they spent evenings after school and every weekend at the Mannings', searching for some Holy Grail, following a mosaic trail only they could see. She thought they were older by more than the year that separated Eric from his eighth-grade classmates, and she was right, his troop of quiet and intense and intensely quiet followers were all juniors at Rhome High.

"Computers, Mom," Eric said. "We're teaching ourselves to code. Well, really, I'm teaching them because I've been teaching myself."

His having friends was a change, good or bad Joan wasn't sure, but he was becoming social in a way he had not been before, even if he lacked the easy charm Daniel inherited from Martin, their shared ability to make friends quickly, adored equally by old women and children. Joan took to throwing open the front door when she saw the ghostly boys coming up the snowy path, welcoming them in dulcet, happy tones. Even then, they merely nodded, avoiding her eyes, shy maybe, but several bent at the waist, a half-bow in her honor, as if they were at a cotillion. She laughed when she told Martin about it later.

In February, Eric began campaigning to attend, for ten weeks, a summer computer camp for advanced children that specialized in coding and programming and development, held at a college a hundred miles away.

"Well, he's advanced," Martin said to Joan. "Or at least that IQ test said he was, though his grades don't really reflect he has any smarts at all." And Joan said, "He's never once wanted to go to camp. What if we send him and he calls crying the first day, the second, after the first week?"

They took their concerns to Eric, who said, "I will never call and beg to come home. This camp is different than those places you wanted to send me. I won't have to do things I don't want to do, like swim races in a lake, or ride horses, or make lanyards, or sing songs around some stupid campfire. This camp is critical for me. For my personal growth. There's no computer science teacher at school and I've learned everything I can learn on my own, and the camp has all these PhDs as counselors. If you let me go, I promise I'll work harder and get better grades next year."

When did he learn the term *PhD*, Joan and Martin wondered, and when Joan said, "Eric, it's only February, you can start working hard at your schoolwork *now*, get good grades *this* year," Eric said, "Sure, sure. That's what I meant."

Joan and Martin traded looks, and Eric saw the looks that they traded, and he said, "Just wait, I'll show you," and he loped out of the living room, down the hall to his bedroom, and then loped back, never much of an athlete, handing the camp's brochures to his parents.

"I wrote away for this stuff before Christmas," he said proudly, head held high. He certainly knew how to take care of those things that mattered to him.

The camp was incredibly expensive, the cost greater than a semester's tuition at the undergraduate Wharton program Daniel was hoping to be accepted into. But Joan didn't care. A dozen PhDs were indeed listed as counselors in the brochures, their full bios and CVs, the schools they had attended, the breakthroughs they had made in their fields, the professorships they held at major universities—MIT, Harvard, Yale, Princeton—during the school year. In capitalized and bold letters, the brochure stated ONLY THIRTY STUDENTS WILL BE ACCEPTED. An application was required, including an essay written by the aspiring computer whiz. And that's what the application said: *An essay of no less than 1,000 words written by the computer whiz.*

Joan read through the brochure, as Martin was doing, and all she could think about was that this child of theirs who now, more than ever, required a keen, watchful eye, who still had the tendency to put foreign objects into his mouth, to suck on a nickel when he was at his computer, who said, "The nickel keeps my attention from wandering," whose attention never did seem to wander as long as he was engaged in what he loved, regardless of the nickel, whose clothes were often grimy, reused for days after his quick five-minute morning shower until Joan said, "No more. New rule. Fresh underwear, fresh jeans, fresh shirt every single day," and Eric humphed and said, "Mom, I always put on fresh underpants," though it was clear he didn't care much if he was perceived as a slob, this son who had made friends with a number of equally odd boys, this son would be those PhDs' responsibility for ten glorious weeks.

"Absolutely, you'll go, if you're accepted," Joan said a few days later, not having meant to say *absolutely*, wanting Eric to understand life did not always come through as one might expect. But she didn't backtrack, after all she and Martin were agreed, and she was elated.

"I'll be reading your essay, so make sure you do a really great job on it. And don't—Eric, are you listening? Don't wait until the last minute to write it. I want to see a draft in two weeks." She wanted him to be admitted, to go there, to be gone for all of the summer.

Whoops and catcalls, then promises of how good he would be, the studying he would do. "I'll go and write the essay right this minute, right now, see I'm going, I'm going, I'm gone," and his door banged shut. Joan crossed her fingers for luck and believed only some of it. He would, however, begin writing that essay at once.

Two days later, Eric handed Joan a thousand convoluted words about how computing and coding did not level the playing field, but instead lifted everyone up. She read the essay through, and then read it again, not completely understanding her son's thesis, wishing he had inherited an iota of her literary talent. But he lacked her fluidity with words, the fluidity she had passed down, in large measure, to Daniel. Eric's essay had no chance of opening the vaunted doors to the camp. She debated for a minute, then sat down at the kitchen table and rewrote it until it made sense and read well enough to warrant his admission to the camp, but not so well that it would raise suspicion.

When the acceptance arrived, she wasn't sure who felt the greater thrill.

In March, Martin was away all of the month. Norway, Sweden, Finland, Estonia, Latvia, across the Baltic Sea to Denmark, across the North Sea to the United Kingdom, then home. Daniel kept track of his father's travels, stuck tacks into the map of Europe he hung on a bedroom wall for his AP European history class.

Martin called home at the beginning of his stay in each country and said to the boys:

"*Din far her å si jeg elsker deg,*" in Norwegian;

"*Du är både utestående pojkar oavsett, vad din mamma säger,*" in Swedish;

"*Et tiedä kylmä ennen kuin olet, missä minä olen,*" in Finnish;

"*Julge olla, olla õnnelik, ei lase elu jama sa up,*" in Estonian;

"*Jūs, iespējams, nav pietiekami daudz jēgas, lai saprastu, cik laimīgs jūs dzīvot, kur mēs,*" in Latvian;

"*En fiasko, men alle de andre har været mirakler for videnskab,*" in Danish;

"*Hello, mates,*" when he landed in the UK.

Daniel kept a log of Martin's greetings:

Norwegian: *Your father here saying I love you.*

Swedish: *You are both outstanding boys, regardless of what your mother says.*

Finnish: *You do not know cold until you are where I am.*

General: *Tell your mother that I'm just leaving the three countries where all those mysteries I've been reading are set. No wonder the detectives are so morose, having to search for the killers in all of this snow.*

Estonian: *Be brave, be happy, don't let life mess you up.*

Latvian: *You probably do not have enough sense to understand how lucky you are to live where we do.*

Danish: *One failure, but all the others have been miracles of science.*

Successful surgeries in all of those places, except Latvia. In Riga, Martin had not been able to save a young mother's sight. "Advanced diabetic retinopathy. Abnormal new blood vessels growing right in the center of Valija's eyes. I tried laser photocoagulation to control the leakage, and a vitrectomy to remove blood from the vitreous fluid of the eye, but sometimes there is no magic to be made. Such a shame, her little girl will have to learn to do for her mother." Daniel had no interest in medicine as a potential profession, but he liked hearing the procedural steps, the gory details.

In April, Daniel opened the envelope from the Wharton program at UPenn, and he ran to Joan, hugged her hard, said, "Best day ever of my life," and though she was excited for him because he wanted this, it was, she knew, the wrong place for him, a whole curriculum for which he was not suited. He did not have that hardened glossy shellac, that abundance of blustering ego the big financial suits wore like armor. He was still her sweet, sensitive boy, meant for a life of words, big problems solved by fiction. The books he had read as a child, was still reading, were largely responsible for the young man he was becoming. Despite the swim team, where he was now on varsity, a top swimmer in the state; despite the dates he had taken Tammy on, the girl he first met in seventh grade, the owner, still, of hamsters; despite the AP classes he had taken and was taking; despite how hard he worked to polish off each semester with a report card of solid A's; despite how much he had studied for the standardized tests and scored well, that was the truth of him: a boy with big dreams who had to work hard to see them realized.

When she tried to imagine Daniel in a suit with a serious tie, lace-up shoes on his feet, sitting around a large lacquered conference-room table, debating the terms of some corporate deal in financial-speak, she could see nothing at all, not even the room.

Martin did not share her concerns; he was delighted the books Daniel read in such quantity had not made him a dreamer, that Daniel had serious aspirations for his future that involved the making of serious money, facing people head-on across that conference-room table, rather than staring down into their eyes as Martin did, until he gave them back their sight and they all walked out the door, rarely returning to show Martin what they had done with the gift he had given them.

Joan had not known Martin felt this way, and before she could say, "Wait, slow down, when did you stop loving the work you do?" Martin said, "Our son aspires to be a great white shark," and Joan thought there was no great white shark hidden beneath Daniel's thin skin. If anything, he might be a dwarf lanternshark, a little-known species of dogfish shark that measured, at most, 8.3 inches long, the shark Daniel once had the squirrel wrestle, Henry thinking the whole time how big and brave he was, how steadfast and true, taking down the impossible, when his nemesis had been less than the length of a school ruler. Daniel was five feet ten inches now, and still growing, and he read the business section of the *New York Times* every day, a subscription of his own that he asked for as one of his seventeenth-birthday presents. The paper had long been delivered to Joan and Martin, but only from Friday through Sunday.

"I need to know what's going on in the business world every single day," he had said. Once, he had cared about what would happen to Countess Ellen Olenska in Edith Wharton's *Age of Innocence*.

On the last day of April, the wind blowing since Fool's Day—keeping away the bees and the wasps, tossing around the hummingbirds, ripping the pear tree buds from the branches before they could flower, until the greening grass looked ice-dusted—finally ceased. The kitchen windows were open, a slight perfume from the flowers unfurling their colors. All the Mannings were around the kitchen table eating dinner, an occurrence that was happening less and less often.

"So what do you want for your big birthday, Dad?" Daniel asked.

Martin's birthday, his fiftieth, was not until the end of June, but Daniel was the son who planned ahead, who stored up thoughtful gifts to bestow upon his family members. Eric rarely remembered to write out even a homemade card.

"To renovate the whole house as soon as school ends, after your graduation," Martin said, and Joan's mouth dropped.

She was thinking of a trip somewhere to celebrate, to India, if she could convince Martin that vacations on Caribbean islands should be a thing of the past, that this birthday required an adventure, a challenge, an unexpressed opportunity for her finally, all these years later, to go where *she* wanted to go, even if it was his birthday. And if that was refused, which was likely, then a week in New York. Iger could set them up with reservations at the chic restaurants she still went to, arrange tickets for them to the off-Broadway shows she thought worth seeing. A lot of time away together, or a little, either way, they could use it.

But this—she was not expecting this. Not at all. Not ever, and not this coming summer when she was hoping to finish *Words*. Not this summer when both boys, at last, for the first time, would be gone: Eric at the computer camp, and Daniel, after graduation, knocking around the country with two friends, setting up their tents in national parks from coast to coast, home in time for Joan to pack him up, for the Mannings to take a road trip to deliver him to the University of Pennsylvania for swim team tryouts before school began.

Joan had been dreaming of an entirely empty house, counting on those summer months. Her own future was beginning to feel tantalizingly near. She had written another hundred pages, five new first-draft chapters, and she was getting close, she could feel it in her spine, in the electricity that sparked her fingers when she touched the finished pages, when the vibration of the typewriter keys entered her being as new words and sentences and paragraphs found their way onto paper. She was writing voluptuously.

Eric's brows met in the middle. "What happens to my room, to my computer?" he said, and Daniel said, "I don't get it, a new house when I'm leaving?"

"Eric, we'll make sure everything is protected, and Daniel, this is always your home. It's where you grew up, the place you can always come back to. It will just look entirely different. And there would be so much space. Space we've never had," was what Martin said.

To Joan, he said, "I've really thought it through and I think it's the perfect time. I've already talked to an architect. Actually, I've done more than that. Come with me."

They left their half-eaten dinners on the table and followed him into the living room. He pulled a long tube from a cabinet, uncorked it, tapped out what was inside—a set of architectural plans. Three that fit on top of each other: Floor plans, section plans, exterior elevations. He spread them out on the floor.

"So this is what I'm thinking," he said. "This is what I want as my birthday present."

The plans showed a soaring structure of angles and space and voluminous rooms with huge windows that would flood the whitewashed place with light, bring the seasons inside, unlike the small windows the house currently sported, that palled the interior in the deadness of winter. The square footage of the new space would more than quadruple their small house, everything still on one floor. She saw perfectly planned rooms identified by names that did not adequately encapsulate what she was looking at: a massive kitchen, a formal dining room, a sky-lighted living room, a study, den, and library, each with built-in floor-to-ceiling bookcases surrounding the large floor-to-ceiling windows, the boys' new large bedrooms had their own bathrooms, and Joan and Martin's bedroom would be a real master, no longer the same size as their children's, three times as large as the other large bedrooms, a huge space of their own, with an en suite bathroom, two sinks, separated shower and tub, and an interior room that housed matching walk-in closets.

Martin could not often still surprise her, but he had.

"What do you think?" he said to Joan.

She had never thought about a new house, did not need a new house, a new house would get in the way of her plans. She had bought this house and the land when Martin was still paying for his medical school education, but since then, he had taken excellent financial care of them all, the continued earnings from her books were in her own separate account, and although she selfishly wanted to douse his wish entirely, what else could she do but take a seat on the floor, put a finger on two of the walls of the proposed master bedroom overlooking their expansive property, the flower and vegetable gardens, the red maples, the elms, the pear trees, and in the distance, the knoll and the glen, and say, "Would it be possible to make those walls glass? Sliding glass doors, wall-to-wall glass?"

"Why not?" Martin said, smiling at her, grabbing her hand.

"And look at this, everyone," he said, pointing to a spot on the plans. "This is the knoll where we used to put the Slip 'N Slide, and this is the glen where you guys used to read books, and this is what I was thinking, we put a pool in the glen at the same time we renovate the house. You can swim again, Joan, if you want to, and Daniel, you'll always have a place to swim when you come home. Maybe we'll make it a saltwater pool. We can keep it heated year-round, swim when it's snowing. How great would that be?"

If this was a midlife crisis, it was better than those the Pregnant Six said their own husbands were experiencing—the growing of mustaches, of beards, the suddenly popular Caesar haircut, so awful with the hair brushed forward, short bangs fringing wide foreheads, ears pierced and strung with small silvery hoops, the purchases of the muscle cars of their youth, the motorcycles they had coveted but never owned. She hadn't heard who might have stepped beyond their marital bonds, perhaps dallied with some nubile young woman two decades south of their ages, but that was typically part of the crisis. Martin had a new acquaintance at the hospital, a plastic surgeon named Larry Sumner, whose second wife was that nubile young thing, Miranda of the golden skin. Larry had left DC for Rhome, opened a new practice after his divorce, brought Miranda with him to the small and charming town. Miranda herself was not small, but very, very tall, some kind of graphic designer, and gorgeous.

Joan looked at Martin. Still so handsome, his dark hair just silvering along the edges, in good shape though he did nothing physical on any kind of consistent basis. All those nurses at the hospital, the women passengers on the planes that took him to all those countries where he shared his surgical expertise, operating on people in need, the flight attendants in their tight uniforms serving him his meals, bringing him drinks, though he said he never drank on the plane—how could he not indulge every so often as he told his tales of medical glory to his female seatmates and the women paid to be kind, attentive, adoring to first-class passengers like Martin—the chipper, shiny girls checking him in at the hotels he stayed at, asking whether he was alone, asking perhaps if he might want company for dinner, all the women fans garnered during his many recent appearances on live news programs in New York, discussing neuro-ocular medical breakthroughs, a result of the published article about him in *Time*. She had not, until this moment, considered the sheer number of women who might eagerly desire to be with him—his good looks, his good brain, his specialized fame potent allures. She had not, until that moment, considered how much time Martin had at his disposal for extramarital flings.

He and the boys were talking, their heads bowed over the architectural plans, and she thought again about how even *Time* had kept her the nameless wife. The young magazine journalist had been lazy, or perhaps held some antiquated notion that a woman, no matter her own accomplishments, was only a support in the background, for he had failed entirely to learn who she was. Hundreds of articles had been written about her and her prizewinning collections, including two in *Time* itself, and if the journalist had only lightly scratched the surface, he would have been inundated with material. She had not needed personal approbation in an article focused on Martin's work, but in *Time* she was not even a cipher, just a ghost, and for a day or two it had annoyed her. A worse outcome would have been if she were identified as the once very famous writer who was now the longtime wife of the increasingly famous doctor. She would have loathed that. Better to be the ghost.

Martin caught her eyes, and she thought how disappointed all those women must be when their attempts to interest him in a covert drink, meal, or seduction failed. Joan knew his attention would never wander, for she possessed what Martin did not: detachment. The years had weakened it, but the remnants still clinging to her insides allowed her to do her work in private, as a secret. Perhaps that's why she did not worry about what Martin did in his downtime in those exotic countries, or when he was in New York on his own, or stayed overnight at Rhome General: she could keep a secret and he never could.

If this house was what Martin wanted, so be it. She could not manufacture righteous indignation about the way his desire would skew her own private plans when he worked so hard and had accomplished so much in his professional life. She paid no attention to their bank accounts, to their 401(k)s, to the investment accounts he maintained in his and Joan's names, to the college funds he had set up for the boys. She briefly glanced at the totals on their joint tax returns, then signed. He was entitled to this upheaval if the finished product would give him pleasure. But she knew she would be the one marshaling it through.

She felt for a moment that she were eighteen years in the past, working so arduously on *The Sympathetic Executioners*, wanting to finish that first novel before Daniel came along and stole her time, wanting her first novel to predate the first child. She had failed then, but she would not fail this time. The boys would be gone this summer, and she would figure out how to keep writing regardless of the sudden construction, would finish the novel before their return.

She would not—not yet—imagine that September might include excitement beyond Eric's final year of middle school, beyond Daniel turning into a college freshman, the building of the new house, that the school year would bring her a transition of her own.

And it was true, aside from her suggestion that their bedroom be enclosed in glass walls, it was the house she would have built, resituated to take maximum advantage of the land, to do justice to the gardens lushly blooming from early spring, the vistas brought inside, made a part of the structure. It was the house she would have designed, had Martin asked her in advance, brought her into his plans.

She wrote vigorously until early May and then resumed all of her motherly duties. Shopping for graduation presents for Daniel, and the clothes and toiletries and the millions of other small things that Eric needed for computer camp, that Daniel required for his cross-country trip, helping them both pack for their time away, beginning to pack what Daniel would take to college. After Daniel's graduation, that awkward party thrown by the Pregnant Six, which the Mannings attended: "The kids have known each other practically since birth, they ought to be sent off together," Carla, Dawn, and Teresa had said. The three Manning men spent a weekend ferrying furniture and everything else the boys and Joan and Martin did not require for the coming months into a rented storage unit outside of town. Until they left, Daniel and Eric wanted to sleep in sleeping bags out on the grass, if the warm temperatures held.

On the morning of the boys' departures, Joan's car was out front, packed up with Eric's suitcases, a box of computer stuff he had been working on, a bag of his favorite candy, a couple of nickels within; and Daniel's backpacks were at the front door, ready to be thrown into the backseat of Martin's car, later hefted through forests, carried along trails. He had packed light, taking only one book about the founding of the Federal Reserve Bank. He told Joan he would tear out the chapters as he finished them. "People always leave books behind when they camp, so I'm sure I'll find others." It was the first time Joan knew him to choose nonfiction over a great big novel.

"Everyone, out into the backyard," Martin commanded, checking his watch, and they left the breakfast dishes on the table, and filed out the back door. The sun was high, the day warm, the sky a blue sheet, except for one puffy, square white cloud in the distance, like the insistent base of an exclamation point.

Through the side gate came a large bald man wearing aviator glasses and swinging two sledgehammers, one in each fist.

"This is Gus, our contractor extraordinaire," Martin said, introducing Joan and their sons. Then he nodded at Gus, and Gus laughed, and said, "Your dad wanted to give you guys a treat," and he handed each boy a sledgehammer, and pointed to the wall that divided their rooms.

Daniel and Eric both turned to their father, and Martin said, "Go for it," and they yelled, "Cool!" and struck the first blows at their old house, smashing holes where their heads used to rest on pillows on their beds.

Gus's men trooped in then, and the family went back into the house. Daniel picked up his backpacks, then the four of them were down the walk, to the cars parked at the curb.

The boys looked at each other, grasped hands in a familiar way, as if walking through the red school door for so many years had taught them a code for brotherly love, no matter their differences, a secret way to say goodbye.

Daniel grabbed Eric into a rough hug, said, "Take care, buddy. Don't be too weird at camp and try to come back as the brother I love." Eric nodded until Daniel let him go.

"Mom," Daniel said, pulling Joan close. He whispered into her ear, "I'll be fine. I'll be great. After all you've made me who I am. A kid who can take care of himself, who can figure shit out." He kissed her cheek and stepped back.

He shook Martin's hand gravely, the kind of parting Daniel thought this deserved. It would be his first time away from home for such a long period, practice before the real thing.

Eric threw himself into his father's arms, said, "I love you, Dad," then did the same thing to Joan.

"Honey, I'm the one taking you. Plenty of time to tell me how I'm a superlative mother, how we're superlative parents letting you go to this camp."

The summer was hot and dry and the grass, unchecked, grew high, covering their land in a dazzle of green light. Gus had promised that, absent any bad weather, the house would be finished by early August, an abbreviated construction schedule costing them a premium. Each night, when Martin came home from the hospital, he said, "Did you listen to the weather report, see any clouds?" and Joan would say, "I did. The weather is complying," and, indeed, Martin's prayers that it remain rainless were answered.

They were nomads, Joan thought, she and Martin moving ever forward in their house while the rooms in which she had raised her unexpected, unwanted family collapsed behind them. Later, they would wonder why they had not moved into Rhome's only hotel at the far end of Strada di Felicità, lived dust-free at night.

Two weeks into the renovation, she and Martin were living in the kitchen, their bed was in there, and the television on top of the fridge, and out in the front hallway, their clothes hung on rolling racks, and in the front closet was the box securing Joan's typewriter, pads and pens, and the thick draft of *Words* still hidden beneath those old coats. She would need somewhere to hide everything once the kitchen and front hallway came down, and, for a while, that box that contained her lifeblood was tucked in the trunk of her car.

She worked wherever and whenever she could in the house, if the noise was not too loud, and when it was, she edited chapters in a carrel at the Rhome library. But her presence was needed at home, on-site, in the zones of construction. She could not be absent for long, could steal only a few hours each day. She came to know Gus and his team very well, and then Tony, the swimming-pool builder, and his team.

Slowly, their new house began rising phoenixlike from the ashes. It was fascinating walking through the new cool and bare rooms, family life absent from the air. Family drained away the mystery of life, slowed, then stilled, its otherwise intrinsic thump-thump, and the cave—the cage—in which they dwelled, might change form as children grew, wriggling first fingers and toes, then gaining inches, saplings that might bear weight or give in to a hard wind. But in this new house, these new rooms, everything seemed possible once again, as possible as what Bash, Lila, Minu, Zena, Bernard, and Anton were creating in their arcadia, in the pages of *Words of New Beginnings*.

Only much later when the house was furnished, when other things had happened, would Joan realize what had always been absent from those lovely and detailed architectural plans. There were the boys' new bedrooms, large and light, and bathrooms they could roam around in; and the new master bedroom that was breathtaking with its windowed walls where she could lie in bed in the early morning and feel the weather, its enormous bathroom where she could take her nightly bath; the new den with comfortable, deep couches, and a flat-screen for watching old movies, and Martin's cherished turntable at last having a place, the shelves of his vinyl records, the speakers in the walls; the new study with its long marble desk and new ergonomic chair, its sleek new computer not to be commandeered by Eric, and with the artifacts and relics of Martin's profession that he had found in dusty and disquieting antique stores on all his trips operating abroad that she hoped he would not put back on display, but did; the new library with its walls filled up with all of the books she had read from childhood on—books Daniel read growing up—and Martin's medical reference guides, textbooks, and journals, comfortable armchairs to rest in, to read in, to dream in; the new living room with its skylights that brought down the stars on their heads, with its long white womanly soft sofas, redolent of pleasure; the new dining room with its long gleaming table; and the neat square arch that led into the enormous kitchen with the massive limestone center island that was quarried in Croatia and required six burly men and a small hydraulic crane to install. The rooms were all gorgeous and inviting, but not a single room, Joan would discover, belonged only to her.

She would realize this when the gale of Eric emptied her head, turned her book into something remote, years of work hard to recall. An illogic to it all, about what was happening. It was then, too, that she considered Eric's name, its Norse meaning—eternal ruler—that *ick* at the end.

And Joan would wonder if it was true, that the good child rarely came out on top, and the child problematic since birth, slightly troubled in a way hard to identify, whose undeniable genius swelled in his teens, would win, taking up all the air in whatever room he happened to be in, in the house as a whole, in her every thought, setting she and Martin at odds, another triangle, this time a scalene, all its sides and angles different.

Joan would think back to that day in her old study, when she debated the thing her body first held. Had she done away with it from the start, there would have been no second child, this son blasting everything in his path, but neither would she have had Daniel. She tried holding on to that.

She would remember those parents who claimed they would give their lives to secure the life of their child, how she had scoffed, rejecting it outright. But there was a place that lurked beyond thought, beyond the notion of the now and the real, beyond personal and private dreams. She would wonder if that was what motherhood meant, the way a child could affect the way she breathed, her heart pumping hard, not with love, or maybe some love, but not only love, just the need for life to tick on, instant after instant after instant. Moments that strung out into days and weeks, then months and years, reduced from secret writer to some kind of crazy den mother, then a mother viewed as crazy, all those adolescent denials of Eric's, before she was eventually proven right. All those years of knowing that at any time, an instant could fail, a person could crack that instant in half, into atomic, then subatomic pieces, and she would still need to be here, in her place. She had given life to them both, she could not allow one to die on her watch.

But before any of that, there was this:

Daniel sent postcards to Joan, so many that one arrived every single day, telling her what life was like on the road, the nature of highways, of truck-stop diners, the smell of the trees when he was in his tent alone at night, the creaking of branches under the waning moon, the crackle of lightning at dawn, the books he found at the campsites.

I'm reading Faulkner again. Someone left behind that Portable version. I swear it's the same one you used to read to me. Did you ever read the introduction? Reading about his mythical kingdom is so cool, and it says when he started writing he wasn't writing for other people, just telling stories to himself, like a lonely child in his imaginary world.

She thought then that Daniel wasn't totally lost to himself, if he was still contemplating the nature of writing, showing her they were still united, a team.

Eric sent a total of one letter, a list of everything he was learning, that neither she nor Martin understood.

Dear Mom and Dad,
The people are nice, the food is good, the counselors are AMAZING. Yes, Mom, we take showers every day. This is what I've learned so far.
Programming - Basic, ML, C, LISP, Fortran, Logo, Pascal, CP/M
Computer theory
Utilities
Peripherals
Machine language
Assembly language
Scripting

Coding
Problem-solving
Software architecture
Graphics
Spreadsheets
Databases
Software operations
Apps
*I am working on writing my own program. The counselors all
say it's a great idea.*

It was clear Eric was deliriously happy, and at the end of the letter
he wrote, "I really don't need school anymore," which made them
laugh.

Joan marshaled Gus and his men, and Tony and his men, and when
the lap pool was finished, a long sweep of darkened concrete filled with
saltwater that turned a deep purple in the sun, she planted maiden
grass seeds all around it, just beyond the apron of blue flagstone tiles
that surrounded it, tiles that led up from the pool in the glen, past the
knoll, through the gardens, to the house of nearly all windows, and
another set of tiles that marched from their glass master bedroom
through the gardens, and down to the pool.

When Martin was free, he and Joan drove into DC, flew for a fast
weekend to New York, looking for furniture, a trip so short and directed,
she didn't bother to call Iger. They found what they liked, put the orders
in, Joan gasping at the figures.

"We're fine," Martin said. "Plus, this is the house we'll really live in
for the rest of our days."

It was a thought Joan liked very much when Martin said it, instantly
imagining herself leaving it for a book tour, leaving it for readings, for
panel discussions, for literary conferences, perhaps this time she
would agree to participate in those conferences she had refused in the
aftermath of her first, then second, collection. She would enjoy being
one of the touted writers brought in to talk about her work, lending
an ear, perhaps some basic advice, to the young writers so eager to
become her, to enter the exalted group to which she had belonged from

the start, but would make herself known again with *Words*. But how lovely it would be, Joan thought, to return to this sensational house when she had her fill of the outside literary world, was content with her place in it, needed the peace, the quiet, the silence to work on the next novel she would write. When she came back home to this home.

The workmen disappeared after the first week of August, their work completed, the house empty except for the furniture she and Martin retrieved from the storage unit, which would be tossed when the new arrived.

On the tenth of August, sitting again at their old kitchen table, the typewriter singing, Joan made the last minor edits to the final few pages of *Words of New Beginnings*.

The nine hundred–page book was finished. The long-expected first novel she would be proud to publish, that would recall the astonishing nature of her work, cement her reputation—a legacy now, rather than a trajectory, but the book would reconfigure that legacy into a trajectory. She knew it with absolute and immodest certainty.

Joan cracked open a bottle of champagne, meandered through the seven thousand feet of bright space, walked out onto their land, following the blue flagstone tiles as if she were playing a child's game, through the bougainvillea she and Fancy had planted, the flowers climbing the wooden trellises they had built together, and the lilacs and hyacinth that were hanging on at the end of summer, and the pink and purple of the phlox and poppies and tulips, the wild violets, the lilac bushes, and field of lavender, the scarlet gerbera daisies, past the wooden benches arranged over the years throughout, where sometimes she and Martin sat and had a drink, past the vegetable plots that were dying, because they had mostly eaten out during the construction, so little picked the harvest.

She was swigging from the bottle as she went, the bubbles tickling her tongue, amazed by her accomplishment, amazed that motherhood, in the end, had not stifled her creativity, or her ambition, that she had managed to carve out a writing schedule to which she had mostly adhered these last nine years.

She would let the novel marinate until Eric was back in school, Daniel ensconced at college, then she would read *Words* through once more. The heavy lifting was done, but one more searching go-through was how she liked to work. Then she would tell Martin about it, call Volkmann, get on with her own life.

Back in the kitchen, with its clean cabinets, its shiny new appliances, the long limestone island so cool to the touch, she ran her fingers over its white swirls, its pale-green comets, took another swallow from the bottle, and set it down. On the bottom of the title page, she wrote in pen, *Final Draft: August 10, 2007.* She turned the book facedown, picked up the last few pages to read once more.

For ten solid days and nights in their arcadia, rain pelted the meadows and dandelion fields, bled the purpled hills gray, the mountain peaks were lost to the mist, the slow-moving brooks became torrents that rushed and screamed, the energy vortices were extinguished, sopping wet, blown out.

Everyone huddled in their one-room cabins, in their tree houses, in their modernized tepees, in the rooming houses they shared, in their painting and sculpting and pottery studios, their rehearsal rooms, their writers' alcoves, their music spaces, that they had built together when Devata was founded.

Five years of golden mystical weather disappeared with a thunderclap, the slap of first rain. But even though the muddied streets emptied, and the land's energy locked itself away, no one stopped working, no one flagged, or took a break, or slept.

Through the lightning, the thunder, the teeming drops big as cats and dogs, everyone carried on, refreshing themselves with bread the bakers baked, with wine from the grapes the vintners nurtured, then stamped into juice, then bottled and let ripen, with cheese from the cows and goats farmers herded and milked, the milk curded, salted, and cured, getting naked for a quarter of an hour with another, to replenish their creative stores.

Anton and Lila finished the final strokes on the triptych they had jointly conceived, a rash of colors unknown to man, ground from the random stones and rocks found around Devata. Lila had been careful with Anton's tender heart; it had flourished, grown huge, turned a bright, bright red. She had been carrying their baby from the moment they each laid a stroke on the canvases, the third canvas, that first stroke, one they had done together.

Bernard penciled in the final notes of his symphony, a scaffolding of birdsong, its undernotes turned electric and ethereal, that made people believe, when they heard bits and pieces floating from his windows, that if Devata was not heaven, which they thought it might be, then surely a real heaven existed, for the sounds Bernard created were impossible to attain without a belief in something even greater than their own personal talents.

Zena danced like a dervish in the rehearsal space she shared with Minu, whirling and twirling, *adagio, allegro, bravura.* Whipping *fouetté* turns, *arabesques, grand jetés, tour jetés*, and *coupé jetés en tourant.* There were strings of fast *cabrioles*, as Zena beat her legs in the air, one of Bernard's birds gone mad, reaching perfect height and precision, and *pas de bourrée courus*, as she breathlessly glided *en pointe* across the varnished floor. She was wearing a delicate ballerina creation, as pale as the underside of a loving cloud, which clung to her body, made her a sculpture in motion. Minu, her lover, who would dance this dance with Zena, for all of Devata, who had helped to choreograph it from its inception, caught, on her camera, frame after frame of Zena moving through space, through the past, the present, and the future.

Bash, who still thought of Goa, still pictured the Italian marchesa in his mind, could easily conjure the faces of his family, hearts plucked free from their chests when they realized he had disappeared, had escaped in the van to the airport, along with the guests who had biked the Tuscan countryside for a week, or two, or three, whom Bash's family had fed and watered with wine, he had learned a crucial lesson in Devata these years. He was free, unfettered, and it was what he had always known, he had a single life, built one word at a time, until the edifice sparkled, was strong enough to withstand doubt and old memories of hunger and fear and hurt and violence. He had written a glorious novel about his childhood in India, about the little boy who once splashed in the Arabian Sea, who found a seashell on a rock, put it to his ear, and heard the world. On the tenth night of the storm, Bash wrote *The End* at the bottom of the page marked -800-.

Before dawn on the eleventh day, every Devatan gathered in its center, in the rain. They held hands, turned their faces to the sky, let the water flood their skin, slide into their joints, their muscles, their bones. It felt as if they were waterlogging their own souls, their fervent spirits.

At first no one comprehended the sudden silence, but then they did, they understood, saw that the rain had stopped all at once.

In that sudden silence, the sounds they used to know returned. They heard the trees swaying in the faint breeze, the birds flapping their wings, their own breaths rushing in and out.

The mist dissipated, the hills regained their natural hue, the mountains reared up. The sun peered out from behind them, then climbed and climbed and climbed, a molten monolith, golden again and hot, spreading its rays across Devata, across all of their upturned faces, across all of the earth.

Joan felt her own breath perfectly syncopating, a lightness in her head that was not from the bubbly drink, so different, a miracle of expression, of grace, of epic achievement.

She, who had never believed in God, or in gods, who had felt writing was prayer, and that spirituality could be found in words, she thought she now might believe. Her people did. They had named their arcadia Dēvatā'ōṁ kī bhūmi, Hindi for *Land of the Gods*, shortened to Devata; or rather *Joan* had named her conjured arcadia in that small unnamed American state Dēvatā'ōṁ kī bhūmi. She had made gods of Bash, Lila, Minu, Zena, Bernard, and Anton, jointly controlling their own metamorphoses, the manifestations of their ripening talents, seeing beyond the horizon, seeing that the horizon no longer separated life from heaven.

She placed those last pages carefully down on the stone island and ran outside, ran across their land, through the high carpet of unmowed grass, sharp ends catching at her feet, through the gardens, then over the knoll, and down into the glen. She was crystalline ecstasy. Surrounded and protected by the tall trees she had planted, had nursed and encouraged. She called out her name, called out *Joan Ashby*, for that's who she was, had always been. She flung off her summer dress and stood naked for a long time, feeling the sun heating her skin, feeling grounded to the earth, even as she was flying high. Then, as balletic and graceful as Zena would have been, Joan arched herself out into space, and plunged, for the first time, into the new pool.

19

At noon, on the eleventh of August, Joan was at the post office, a heavy package in her arms. Addressed to the United States Copyright Office, the package contained a copy of *Words of New Beginnings* and the copyright registration form she had filled out. The form had been so nondescript that she had signed her name with an absurd flourish. Storr & Storr had copyrighted her collections in the normal course, but it seemed right that she herself put this administrative exclamation mark to the long years spent writing the novel that neither publisher nor agent knew about yet. An insignificant but personal way to cap the achievement.

When it was Joan's turn, she stepped up to the counter and smiled at the large man behind it, but his small red lips did not rise up in return. She placed the package on the counter, watched him drop it onto the scale, weigh it, tap in the zip code, tell her the amount she owed. She reached for her wallet, thinking that such a historic moment demanded something more momentous than this prosaic exchange.

Her cash disappeared into the register and she accepted her change and receipt. With more grace than he seemed likely to have, the man pivoted neatly and threw the proof of her accomplishment into the mail bin with a practiced underhand toss.

"Next," he called out, and she stood there until he held up his hand to the customer behind her, and said, "Lady, you need something else? You need stamps?" She shook her head and relinquished her spot.

Walking out into the sunshine, Joan thought that certain moments in life just had to be perfect the way they were.

Twenty minutes later, she was driving out of Rhome, headed to the computer camp at the college a hundred miles away to retrieve Eric. Later in the afternoon, Martin would collect Daniel from the house of one of his friends with whom he had camped out across the country.

At four, as planned, Joan, with Eric, and Martin, with Daniel, met on their street. They wanted to unveil the new house together, to say a few words, but the boys bolted from the cars, raced up the walk, turned the handles of the new double-height frosted-glass front doors, and stepped inside.

"Hello, hello, hello," they called out into the sharp whitewashed spaces, their own echoes welcoming them home. Then they yelled out their names, imprinting themselves on the fresh wood and plaster and paint and pale hardwood floors, alerting the house to their existences.

The family ate at the old kitchen table, wandered the house, swam in the saltwater pool, finished packing Daniel for college in short increments. He suddenly did not want to leave. "I want to stay forever," he said, following it up with, "I'm just kidding," but there was an undercurrent of truth.

They were all out by the pool when Daniel said again that he wanted to stay in the new house, stay with them all, and Joan said, "We don't want to interfere with the fun you'll have, but come home every month for a weekend. If you want to. We'll all be waiting for you at the train station. Come and stay in your great new room, the new beds will be in soon. And you can swim in the pool, we'll get you a timer so you can track your times, and you and Dad and Eric can watch movies on the flat-screen that will be in the den, and it will be great."

Across the prone bodies of his father and brother, Daniel smiled at Joan, then came to her side and flopped down. Looking at him, she thought she ought to start swimming again seriously, was about to say she would follow his example, but then he picked up her hand and held on for a long, long time.

Eric was a motormouth since computer camp, wanted everyone to listen to the endless details of the beta program he had built there, which none of them understood, asking Joan and Martin over and over, "When does school begin again for me? When does Daniel leave? When can I talk to you both?" "Later," they kept telling him, "once Daniel's at college, we'll focus entirely on you."

Then Daniel was at school, in his dorm room, grinning away, telling his family he was fine, that they could leave, that he wanted them to leave.

"Please go already," he said, and he walked them down the hall, past girls and boys as young and fresh-faced as he, all at the university early for team tryouts in their various sports, their families unpacking bags and boxes, and when Joan and Martin and Eric were back in the car, Daniel said, "I'll call you after I race, tell you if I made the team or not, and thanks for the new cell phone."

He turned on his heel, waved at them without looking back, then jogged to the front door of his dorm and disappeared inside. Joan watched him the whole time.

They had stayed in a Best Western the previous night and now had a four-hundred-mile trip back to Rhome. Martin turned on the engine, then turned to Joan. "I didn't expect to feel like this." When she looked at her husband, his cheeks were wet, tears falling from his eyes. She leaned over and kissed him and said, "I know."

Martin reversed out of the parking space, put the car into drive, and slowly headed toward the gates that led beyond the campus, into the busy streets of Philadelphia.

At the first red light, both Joan and Martin looked back, one last glimpse at where their eldest son would be living for the next year.

When the light turned, Martin accelerated and Eric said, "So this is what I want to tell you guys. I'm not going back to school."

20

The computer camp PhDs had attested to Eric's skills: an extraordinary anomaly; unlimited gifts; a certifiable genius with a rare talent; his computer program revolutionary. Traditional schooling, they said, would do nothing for him.

"I told you," Eric said.

"Absolutely not," Joan said. "No way are you dropping out of school at thirteen."

Over her protests, Martin reached out to additional experts who reviewed the developmental program Eric had designed at camp.

"I don't know many kids interested in overhauling an industry, most of them just want to design games or apps," an MIT professor named Marecks said. Levinol, the chair of the graduate computer science program at Harvard, said, "It will make him a fortune. If he were my kid, and God I wish he was, I'd let him go his own way. Screw school. It's not the place for him. Let him do what he's doing. Won't cost you a thing to have him working at home. Maybe a couple more computers, but that's no big deal. There's a tangible, realistic company to be built on this program, he's found a niche no one else has yet. Its uses are potentially limitless."

And just like that Eric's formal schooling ended. Their original small house had become a fraternity for those ghostly boys; the new house was headquarters for a whole different crew—three, five, then ten boys, all eighteen years old, followed Eric from computer camp to Rhome, as if he were the Pied Piper. They had no place to stay, no money with which to find a place to stay; like Eric, their minds were filled up with ones and zeroes. They were cockroaches or termites, Joan thought, the way they spread themselves over the thousands of new square feet, using Eric's room, Daniel's, the study, the den, the library, chargers plugged into every outlet, the dining-room table stacked with dozens of computers. Cords slinking through every room had to be avoided.

Daniel was speechless when Martin told him what Eric was doing, what he was being allowed to do.

"I don't know what to say," he said, and hung up.

Joan did not know what to say either, and Martin was encouraging the Pied Piper's people to stay, making trips to the supermarket to keep the fridge stocked, to keep them fed while they worked, but Joan refused to give up on reversing this course, she had not yet conceded defeat in this war she and Martin were having. They debated on long-distance phone calls when he was away on his surgical trips, Joan far out on their land, cell phone hard to her head. When Martin was home, they could not have such strident conversations anywhere in the house. Despite the frenetic activity, Eric's immersion in his plans and his deadlines, he was alert to danger, to any discussion that might forcibly stop him in his tracks. When they returned from a dinner out, he could read on their faces what they had talked about. He knew Martin was his champion, and that Joan was not.

For a while, she wondered if she would champion Daniel, if he were the head of this enterprise taking shape. But what did the answer matter, he wasn't.

An incontrovertible fact was the relentless work ethic Eric was demonstrating, never before given to anything other than building forts in the sandbox, or LEGO structures in his room, or playing on Martin's office computer, and then the one they had given him. An asinine present for being declared gifted. They had been idiots caving into that early desire. That computer turning Eric's head so completely, resulting in computer camp, giving rise to this program of his that seemed like the Second Coming. When Joan asked Eric to explain it, he said, "With this program, I'm going to solve the problems hotels have, Mom," and let fly a complicated explication of logarithms and so many other things Joan did not understand at all, including his interest in hotel administration. What she did understand was that the computer, the computer camp, and Eric's incomprehensible program were responsible for the dormitory they were now running, for the fear she knew she was right to feel, and that what she had planned for herself would be delayed.

Was she being selfish, self-centered, as that fortune-teller had said when reading one line of Joan's palm? Well, she had never denied that fault in herself, the selfishness writers required, the reason behind her desire never to marry, to never bear children. Now she was *the* chaperone for Eric and his cronies pursuing something she could not fathom.

She tried sticking to her schedule for *Words*, a simple read-through of her work, hewing to it as tightly as she could, images of being ensconced in her prior, original life so vibrant and bright, then dimming, the colors blending together into the color of dirt. But accomplishing anything was nearly impossible when she was forced into the role of den mother watching over this funky group, thinking of the lawsuits and liability if any of these kids on their property tripped and broke a leg, an arm, a back, drank themselves blind or into oblivion, popped pills, snorted drugs, smoked pot. She had found a coffee can filled with the butts of joints hidden in the lilac bushes, and then another, and another, and emptied orange pill containers, the labels pulled off, and emptied bottles of vodka, gin, and brandy in the outside trash cans, trying to figure out whether she and Martin were drinking more than they usually did—it was possible, she was distraught every night—or whether those bottles were being filched from the pantry by pale, soft hands. She had no problem picturing all of their bodies reduced to simmering, stinking liquids.

She stood once, twice, ten times, in the circular entry and admonished them all, at the top of her lungs, to absolutely no effect. Blank faces turned toward her, as if her words made no sense. The coffee cans filled up, the empty orange prescription bottles appeared, the bottles of alcohol disappeared, even when she hid them away in places she considered cunning. She couldn't control what this new team of ghostly young people popped or drank or inhaled, but she could try to control what went into Eric's mouth, that mouth that had given her so much trouble since it first left her womb. She saw how Eric did not eat, his eyes often glassy, manic energy wiring him up. He and his team were working eighteen, twenty hours a day, flopping on the floors from exhaustion, sweatshirts under their heads, waking early to do it all again, but it didn't account for what she was seeing in him.

"He's doing drugs, or smoking pot, or drinking, I'm sure of it," Joan said to Martin. It was ten at night, the group was meeting in the living room, still empty of furniture, discussing the company shortly to be formed, and she and Martin were on the grass on top of the knoll. Joan looked toward the lit house, then down into the glen, to the lap pool black in the moonless night.

"I think it's just adrenaline," Martin said.

"Then you're not seeing things clearly. I'm the one here all of the time, watching over them, watching Eric marching around like the king of a fiefdom. He's a child, a boy, with so much, too much, riding on his thin shoulders, and I'm telling you he's on drugs."

"If he is, and I'm not agreeing that he is, he'll outgrow it. He's testing the boundaries. If I could have gotten away with it in the vice admiral's house, I would have spread my wings too. What's a little pot smoking when measured against his achievements so far? And, you've got to admit, nothing seems to be hindering him. He's sure the newest version of the program will be ready to submit to the incubator contest by the deadline. If they win, we're talking millions, Joan."

"Martin, who cares about the money?"

"I do," Martin said. "And Eric sure as hell does. He talks of nothing else but winning, about all the great things that will happen as a result. It's what he wants, Joan."

On a chilly October afternoon, there were two lawyers and an accountant in the living room who specialized in guiding start-up technology companies. Eric's team on the floor at their feet, eleven pairs of legs crossed, twenty-two sets of eyes, half behind black-rimmed glasses, staring up at the men from Washington, DC, dressed in expensive suits. Eric was naming his company Solve=MC2. The lawyers were discussing its incorporation, the apportionment of stock options, how salaries would be set if they won the incubator funding. At the moment, everyone was working for free.

Joan listened for a while and then took herself to the master bedroom, sat cross-legged on the bed, closed her eyes, and sent up pleas that Eric not win that prize. She wanted him to fail, for the house to empty out, his team to hitch themselves to someone else destined for greatness. She would handle his upset, his rejection, the depression sure to smack him down for a while. But he was young, he would rally, he would return to school, remember these months as a fugue state. He would do what teenagers did, finish middle school and high school, go to college, date, laugh, move at a more natural pace, find himself before he took on the world.

In late November, when Eric should have been studying for a science test or wishing the pretty girls on the Rhome High tennis team would notice him, his computer program was awarded the grand prize in the incubator contest, three million dollars to be transferred into the accounts of his new company, his team yelling and high-fiving one another, fielding calls immediately after from other early venture funding outfits interested in knowing what his program was about.

Joan watched them pile out the front door for whatever celebration was planned. She felt the dread she used to feel as a child in her parents' house, the sick feeling she had watching them, that there was a story she was to understand, but could not. Martin was as delirious as the Solve=MC2 team, insisting on their own celebration, opening a bottle of wine. Joan refused the glass he offered her.

"How do you not see that this is the worst thing that could have happened to him?" And she walked away from her husband, bundled up in a coat, and marched out to the knoll, where she sat watching her angry breath disappear in the cold air.

Later, Joan sat on the old plaid couch in the library, trying to enjoy the room she had rarely entered since the end of summer, pretending she was not waiting up for her suddenly successful son, revisiting the fight she and Martin had about the news, when she walked away from his thrill, his delight in their son's accomplishments.

It was past midnight when a glass shattered in the kitchen. She ran and found Eric, drunk and befuddled at the fridge, unsure which way to move, the bottle of vodka from the freezer clutched to his chest, his bare feet covered in shards that glittered in the glow from the outdoor lights Joan had left on.

She flicked on the kitchen light and broke the spell. She had hoped the team's celebration would have been pizza and sodas. Their leader, after all, was only thirteen; no restaurant or bar would serve him. But age no longer mattered in this world of dizzying success, she saw that now, none of the regular limits of life would apply to him.

"Stay right where you are," she said, and grabbed the vodka bottle from him, dumped it out into the sink, then handed him the broom and dustpan.

"Clean it up, then clean yourself up, and go to bed. In your bedroom."

He threw down the broom and dustpan, leapt over the broken glass, ran for the front door, grabbed his coat and his shoes, and disappeared into the night.

In the bright kitchen, with the dark night reaching right through the huge windows, she debated getting the car and picking him up on the side of the road. But it was a small town, too late for anyplace still to be open, its crime rate was low, and she, exhausted and furious, let him go.

She shook Martin awake until he sat up. "Are we really going to allow this to continue?"

"What?"

"This insanity. Your son came home stinking drunk and was after more. He ran out the front door five minutes ago."

"He'll come back," Martin said. "Everything he needs for the company is here. Listen, Joan, there's no turning this train around. He's got three million bucks now, and there's going to be more. It's going to get worse before they all find some balance. I've got a surgery at six, I've got to get to sleep." He snapped off the bedside light she had turned on.

Joan swept the kitchen floor clean of the glass, then paced the house until six in the morning, knowing Martin was right. It was no longer relevant what she had wanted in September, last week, yesterday after-noon, for Eric, or for herself. She wore the permanent and indelible identity of *Mother*, and regardless how it had come about, she was incapable of pretending she didn't see how things were going, how they would continue to go, how rapid the changes Eric had undergone, a few short months from obsessed teen to juvenile businessman, thinking he was mature, entitled to live as he wanted. She saw what would happen—the way he would argue with her in the future, whether he was thirteen, fourteen, fifteen, sixteen, ill prepared to live somewhere other than under their roof. His brain, despite its bundle of exceptional neurons, was still developing. He might be managing a company, coffers soon to be filled with all of those dollars, but his decision-making was that of a child, would continue to wring her out. There was no way to tell how long it would take until Eric actually fit the role he had assumed.

In the library, she kneeled down at one of the new cabinets, opened the door, extricated her manuscript from its hiding place at the very back, and went out into the new garage. Large enough to hold four cars, though they had only the two. They had made it a well-lit and organized space, shelves with plastic containers marked for clarity—*Daniel's school projects*; *Eric's school projects*; *Halloween costumes*; *Stuffed animals*; *Toys*; *Puzzles*; *LEGOs*.

On the bottom shelf were six large brown boxes, all labeled *Joan Ashby* in black marker. The boxes held copies of her story collections and all the foreign editions that used to be in their old bedroom closet, the hundred or more composition notebooks she filled up from the time she was seven. Those boxes were proof of how miraculous her life had once been, before the life she had never wanted to experience came to pass.

When Martin was courting her, he told Joan that myopia was the most widespread human eye disease in the world, and she had been surprised to learn that a narrowed vision of the world was an actual medical condition. In the cold garage, with the early morning light sneaking in under the electric door, Eric still not home, she understood that the man she had married, who treated actual myopia, was suffering from a figurative version. One of the country's premier doctors in his particular healing arts, this top-notch neuro-ocular surgeon flown everywhere to perform what only he could do, was refusing to see beneath their son's complicated surface, refusing to recognize their son's race toward the ledge of a cliff.

She ripped open the sixth *Joan Ashby* box. She pulled out hundreds of rubber-banded pictures of people caught in the act of living their lives, all those thrown-away photographs purchased by a stranger, by Joan, for a dollar a bundle at a junk shop in New York. Then she pulled out several dozen folders in various colors, red, yellow, blue, green, purple, each one protecting a story she had written long ago, finished but never published, or never finished for one reason or another. All of her Rare Baby stories were there too, each one in an orange folder, titles across the front, fifty orange folders in all.

She carefully put *Words of New Beginnings* at the bottom, then placed all the folders on top of it, the pictures on top of the folders.

On a hook were rolls of tape, and she took one down, found the end, listened to the tape cry as she pulled it free, then sealed that last box back up.

Joan yanked her hair out of its braid, rubbed her head hard until her black curls were flying through the air, rubbed harder and harder, trying to sink her nails into her skull, to reach the tough dura mater just beneath the skull, hoping to find some other viable solution, some other way to handle all of the next years, a way that would not, did not, involve her.

She felt wetness on her scalp, beneath all of that hair. She had drawn blood. She knew her Latin: Dura mater: *tough mother*. There was no protective covering in the brain that meant tough father. That sacrifice parents made, she guessed this was it, and she, the sacrificing, sacrificial lamb.

THE SEVEN-YEAR CYCLE

Saat barshiye ghatnakaram

21

In mid-December, Joan won a small battle with Eric. The house would be cleared of his Solve=MC2 staff, the computers put away, the electrical cords rolled up, the rooms restored to their intended uses, while Daniel was home for the holiday week.

Daniel had refused Joan's entreaties during the semester to return for a weekend, saying, "I don't want to get in the way of what Eric's doing." Meant to sound selfless, his words blistered with jealousy, the sibling rivalry that until now had flared only once, when Eric was deemed gifted, skipped from second to third grade. Joan had been an outsider in her own family, but an only child who had not experienced sibling rivalry. As a young writer, she had gained fame and success quickly, had risen to the top immediately, and it was only lately, in these months of upheaval, that she felt a tinge of envy when reading laudatory reviews about the novels or story collections of others. But she had her published collections to gird her up, *Words of New Beginnings* at the bottom of a box. She had a life to remember, a way to view herself as other than what she had become. Daniel did not. He was still nearly transparent, striving to figure himself out, unformed as he was supposed to be at this age, a phase Eric was avoiding entirely, his genius coloring in all the blank spaces. Eric lacked many of the skills and talents people required to get along, to get through life, but his genius was all that he needed. That's what was being proven within the walls of their new house.

She knew Daniel's first time home would not be what he rightfully anticipated—college freshman fawned over as the conquering hero, the family eager for every detail about how his first semester had gone, the classes he was taking, how well he had done on his exams, the swim races he had medaled in, the friends he had made. But at least the house could be cleared of the evidence that Daniel's place as the eldest no longer meant much of anything, that Eric's pursuits had reformulated their positions, had altered entirely the concept of family life.

From September through December, both boys had been cloistered, at school and at home, but there the similarity ended. While Daniel was trudging to his classes and doing whatever it was that freshmen did during all those other hours, his younger brother was in the second stage of development for his computer program, managing a team of people, not viewed as the teenager he was, but as a force, the head of a viable company, his age no deterrent to those taking their marching orders from him, or to the investors who wanted to be in early, on the ground floor.

"Hey," Daniel said to Eric when he came in the front doors with Joan and Martin.

"Daniel," Eric called out and flung himself at his brother.

Daniel allowed himself to be hugged for a few seconds, then stepped back, and said, "I'm going to swim, is that okay?" Joan and Martin nodded.

"Can I come too?" Eric asked, sounding like the eager younger brother he actually was.

Daniel shook his head. "Training, buddy. I've got a big meet in January as soon as I get back to school. Now's not the time for me to be fooling around."

Despite the snow that was falling, that continued to fall through his ten days at home, that included his eighteenth birthday, which he adamantly refused to celebrate in any way, Daniel spent as many hours as he could swimming in the heated saltwater pool. Joan felt his despair each time he was too worn out to keep racing against himself, came back into the house wrapped in a towel, dusted in snow, showered and dressed, and found himself with his brother. Joan could see his mental calculations, comparing himself to Eric, and Eric, oblivious as he had always been, nattering on to Daniel about what had happened already with Solve, what would happen in the coming months, the additional two million dollars in investments they had received after winning the incubator prize, never once contemplating that Daniel was not as delighted for him as he was for himself.

Joan found Daniel wherever he was, sitting quietly with him at the limestone island in the kitchen, insisting they go for a drive, or walk in the cold along the Potomac, or have lunch out in Rhome, engaging him in as much conversation as he could stand, asking for more information than she needed about his classes, his roommate and teammates, his professors, the girls he was interested in, the books he was reading beyond the curriculum of his courses.

Three days in, he allowed Joan to crack him open, and then they talked as they used to talk when he was a boy, about his life and his dreams. Regardless of Eric, he still intended to pursue a degree in business.

She heard him when he said, "I get that Eric has this inexplicable talent, but I'm just as smart in other ways, right? Plus, I have what he doesn't have, good instincts about people, I'm sociable and he's really not. Actually, Mom, I see myself as a dealmaker," and Joan understood that he was speaking rhetorically, or, if not rhetorically, he wasn't interested in what she might have to say, was determined to heed no one's advice but his own. She knew he would ignore her, and so she said nothing, but she wanted to shake him awake, thoroughly discourage him, yell, "Daniel, you don't belong in that world, you never have. It's your brother's world now, so find something else, pursue a different avenue!" But she knew she shouldn't, and so she didn't.

She tried hard to imagine Daniel as a dealmaker wielding power, though not the creator. For a boy who once invented a remarkable character, whose imagination allowed him to create all kinds of adventures for the squirrel, his interests then so boundless, Joan could not see him as he saw himself, she did not think that handling the concretized dreams of others would suffice. It was not, she thought, a good fit. He would be better off finding a way to create something of his own, on a smaller scale, and outside the business world, something he could hold in his hands and say, "I made this. This is mine."

She took him back to the Rhome train station just after the New Year, and she felt his pain and her own. She would miss him dearly, even his false brave face. He boarded and found a seat, found her on the platform and they smiled at each other until the train began to move. She waved and he waved back, and she watched him until he was gone, and then she watched the train gliding by, until the last car was out of view. She did not move as the snow fell harder, as the flakes that landed on her cheeks stuck. Only when the cold seeped into her boots did she return to the car and turn on the heat. She did not want to go back to the house; already she felt the loss of his presence, the quasi-normalcy he had brought with him. She wondered how long it would take for that feeling to dissipate, she hoped there would be a few more days before the swarm descended again.

The house was lit up when she reached it, a beacon on a dark day, the clouds so heavy, the snow falling with specific intent. Through the wide front windows, she saw that in the hour she had been gone, Solve=MC2 had set up shop again, and she exhaled in the car. When she walked in, every room crackled with brainwaves and activity, and Martin, leaning against a wall, watching those hunched at their computers around the long dining table, was smiling, with that delight on his face, a look she had grown to detest, and Joan was instantly angry with him all over again.

"Daniel get off okay?" he asked.

"Yep. I'm going to take a bath," Joan said, and kept moving. She detoured into the kitchen, took a bottle of wine from the fridge, a glass from a cabinet. When she came back into the hall, Martin was no longer there. She didn't care where he was.

As she passed all their large and lovely rooms, with the new furniture delivered the day before Christmas—comfortable couches in the living room and den, deep armchairs in the library, the black marble desk in the study—every piece of furniture for the Manning family was inhabited by a Solve minion. She thought how these kids would enjoy it all before she had much of a chance.

She walked into their huge white bathroom, poured wine into the glass, turned on the bathtub faucets, and listened to the roar of the water. Neither she nor Martin had ever locked doors against each other, but now she stepped forward and did so. She did not want him joining her, talking about the ten days of togetherness, about the boys, about all the exciting things in the future. She wanted to drink her wine and soak in the deep tub, in water that was a degree or two below uninhabitable. Since life had turned upside down, she made her nightly bath almost too hot, a failing attempt to detoxify the anger that built up inside of her from hour to hour and day to day and week to week.

She had done everything she could think of to extricate herself from this untenable situation.

She had tried to secure office space for Solve, but under the corporate documents only Eric had the authority to sign contracts. And even if he were willing to move his company elsewhere, which he was not, no landlord was willing to rent to a kid. She told the landlords she and Martin would be guarantors, but they all said, "Sorry, Mrs. Manning, it's not an issue of the rent being paid. We understand the company has money. We're just not interested in having a bunch of teenagers as tenants."

She had hired a kind of babysitter, someone else in the house from morning until night, a trial run for two days, and had endured Eric's rage.

"It's Solve's offices, Mom. Don't you get that? There's secret proprietary intellectual property in the house. We can't work if we're worried some stranger is going to steal what we're killing ourselves for."

"This is our home, Eric. There has to be another way," she had said, to no effect.

The book she was reading for the second time since September was on the bench next to the tub. From the start, it reverberated with nuance for her, the subtext of the writer's personal life, the way Joan was feeling toward Martin.

She had researched the author—a British novelist and short-story writer still alive and writing, a failed fifteen-year first marriage behind her, a second marriage well past its third decade. In the midst of her arguments with Martin about Eric dropping out of school, about the boarding house they were running, Joan debated whether she would consider *their* marriage a failure if she ended it right then, if they crashed and burned a few months shy of their nineteenth wedding anniversary. Couples divorced when they could not weather joint tragedy like the death of a child, but how about when they disagreed over a child's success? She disagreed entirely with Martin, but divorcing him would not solve anything. At least now, sometimes Martin was around, even if his oversight consisted only of waving Eric and the Solve team on. If she were to divorce him, with his travel schedule, she would end up with primary custody. She only had to look ahead to his next months of travel, planned long in advance, to know that it was true: overseas trips to South American countries, Japan, return trips to the British Isles, to Russia and China, the list went on and on of places where he was going to perform his surgeries, leaving Joan to hold down the fort. A spy in her own house.

In her research, Joan had also discovered the endless feud between the writer and her older sister, a writer of equal stature, the winner of a major literary prize. The siblings had waged their battles through "a lifetime of enmity," the younger avoiding the prize won by the older, citing its negative impact on the winners. Watching Daniel trying to tamp down his jealousy about his brother's exploits, she had seen the beginning of that sibling enmity, a valid sibling rivalry, the oddity of the much younger brother pulling so far ahead of the elder in the race toward success, a race not intended to be run for years. Daniel would endure additional pain if he tried to conquer a world even tangentially related to Eric's.

Joan turned the knob and the hot water gushed like a waterfall, and she considered how she would handle each of the boys.

With Daniel, she would continue to let him know that her mothering would never end, that she would always be there for him, at the other end of a phone, in person, when he needed her. She knew this trip had set the routine; he would not be coming home regularly. Maybe his winter and spring breaks, a few weeks in the summer, if she were lucky, otherwise he would avoid Rhome as long as Eric was here, doing what he was doing. She would call him more than she knew she should, but if home only meant her calls, then at least Daniel would hear the voice of home several times a week. She knew too that they had established a tacit understanding while he had been home, that they would talk only of things of interest to them both, novels they were reading, movies they had seen, Daniel's amusing assessments of the young women he had been out with. Eric would not be part of their discussions, and neither would feel guilty pretending he did not exist. Daniel required her love and the certainty that she would not let him down, that Eric might well conquer the world but that Daniel's place in their family would not disappear in the rush over his brother.

With Eric, she had no choice but to watch him and watch over him, as Martin would not. Just as he had not needed her for sustenance at birth, and had resented her intrusions when he was a toddler, a young child, they would both have to find ways to deal with it again. There had been only a few short years when she found her thorny child more pleasurable; now she was in the role foisted upon her that she resented, that he resented, to protect him from himself, from his success.

She tried to read, but it was impossible. She stayed in the tub until the water drained completely, until she was shivering from the cool of the porcelain after the reckless heat. She was dreading walking out into the house.

She pulled on yoga pants and a sweater and looked at the shoebox on the floor of her closet. She and Martin had gone to Delaware in July, a beach weekend to belatedly celebrate his fiftieth while the boys were gone, while the construction was under way. They were happy together then, just six months ago, and she had been giddy because *Words* was going well and the end was in sight.

She lifted the shoebox lid. Nestled on top of the tissue paper were golden sandals intricately beaded with gold, copper, platinum, and clear crystals. She bought them because they made her think of all the Indian writers she read when she was a girl, because she could imagine wearing them down to the Ganges after *Words* was published. She looked at the sandals and vowed she would not wear them until she was actually in India, even if she did not get there until she was an old, old woman. She stuck the top back on and toed the box out of sight.

The arc of tragedy Joan had always known her story would require, it must be this tortured irony. That Eric's meteoric success meant her own veritable jailing, the imprisonment of her book in the dark, the loss of the life she had intended to return to, now so far out of sight. A caretaker for this second son who had never fully conquered her heart.

She stepped into snow boots and slid open the glass door of their bedroom. Their land was a white field out into the distance. She lifted her face to the sky, felt the heavy snow settle on her hair, cling to her eyelashes. When would Eric be prepared to fend for himself, leave home, take himself away? At eighteen, nineteen, or older than that? She hoped he would be in one piece when that day finally arrived. She hoped she would be as well.

22

The Seven Seas.

The Seven-year Itch.

The supposed seven years of economic cycles.

The number seven in numerology—a magical force for the activation of imagination, and the manifestation of results in one's life through conscious thought and awareness.

The number seven in dreams—signifying inner self and rebirth, health and spiritual growth, the need for enlightenment, the good to come, that a person is on a divine path right for them, that obstacles have been overcome, that fruition of one's wishes and true desires is near.

The seven essential chakras that align with the body—root, sacral, solar plexus, heart, throat, third eye, crown—one chakra dominates each seven-year cycle, according to the Vedic Treaties Chakravidya.

The seven-year cycle of life—1–7, 14–21, 21–28, etc.—and its attendant focus. "The seven-year cycle from 49–56 is a good time to take stock of your life: what you have accomplished and learned from your experiences, which will help you raise your state of consciousness. A raised state of consciousness is what you take with you when you return to the world of the spirit. This is a good time to consolidate your life and gain true lasting value from the time and energy you have invested."

Each year of a person's life has seven distinct cycles: first, a period of opportunity; second, good for travel; third, requires the exercise of discrimination and good judgment; fourth, the mental and spiritual nature is awakened; fifth, great success is achieved in personal affairs; sixth, rest, relaxation, and amusement; seventh, the most critical, when elements no longer needed in one's development fall away to make room for new and better elements.

Joan looked all of that up.

She also noted that for seven years, during each seven-day week, each of her days had but two bright spots: her hour of yoga each morning and her hour of conversation with Daniel each afternoon. She calculated it: seven years equaled 2,555 days. Of those 2,555 days, she took approximately 2,500 yoga classes (excepting Thanksgiving, Christmas, New Year's, or being sick with a cold or the flu). Of the 2,555 conversations with Daniel, in 2,525, Eric was never mentioned, but in thirty of them, at the tail end of the seven-year cycle, he was. She felt lost during those seven years, and doubted herself as a mother during those 2,555 days, but her instincts about both of her sons turned out to be right.

Daniel's seven-year cycle spanned college, a very short-lived career out west in venture capital, and then his position as a monthly columnist for *Think Inc*. For the last four years, if he chose to, he could hold up those articles and say, "I've made these. These are mine." Although he didn't say that at all. Still, Joan was convinced that his ninety-nine stories, shipped to Silicon Valley, then back to Rhome, then to his DC apartment, were responsible for how well he was doing in the world, finding where he belonged; being a dealmaker was never going to work.

The end of Eric's seven-year cycle was marked by his landing $400 million in venture funding for Solve and moving to New York, buying an apartment in a luxury building in the East Village, where Joan had lived and written her books when it was tenement walk-ups and railroad flats. His forty employees set up Solve's new offices in an old factory in Tribeca. Seven days of blissful silence in the Rhome house that December, and then, a few weeks before the end of the year, he called

Joan from a rehab center in Oregon. She had flown there immediately, was with him in group meetings led by counselors, chairs in a circle, the afflicted slouching, their spines collapsed, hands gripping their pale, tortured faces, parents, like Joan, and other loved ones, ramrod straight, their feet hard on the floor, their eyes flickering everywhere, unsure where to land.

On a bench in the Oregon fog, Eric told Joan that the connection he made between his accomplishments and his willingness to put himself far out into space was an explanation, but not a rationale, for his reckless behavior.

"I'm sorry," he said to her, words he had refused to say as a child.

The overdose had been drastic, but it could have been tragic, had she not sacrificed herself, stayed home as he built Solve, said to him again and again, "Whatever you're doing to yourself, you need to stop." She had seen what was coming. He hadn't suffered from pica as a child, but he had been addicted nonetheless, eating all that grass and dirt, chewing on all those stones, and one of the theories about pica had stated it demonstrated a tendency toward addiction. She had not been wrong in her assessment of him. Her diatribes must have gotten through, because he was getting help, but she could easily imagine him decrepit and wasted, friendless and homeless, rotting his insides with alcohol, puncturing his skin with needles, his teeth nubbed and yellowed, his laughter unhinged. He swore there had been no needles, mostly pills, a lot of pills, and a lot of alcohol, a good amount of weed.

When he said, "You're off the hook, Mom," guilt had heaved up within her because despite all she had done, he must have felt the equivocal nature of their relationship over his lifetime, sensed her resentment toward him in the last seven years. She had not always hidden it well. What else could she have done when his genius wouldn't be ignored, his ascendency an uncontrollable force, and she powerless to counteract what Martin enabled. As devastated as she was, each time Eric said "You're not to blame," the guilt eased the littlest bit. She stayed in Oregon for a month, called Daniel each day when she returned to the hotel, breaking their pact, talking about Eric.

After ten weeks at the Oregon rehab, Eric was taking a sabbatical, thinking about what kind of life he wanted to live in the future. While Solve ran in his absence, he had taken himself far away. Of all the places her brilliant, wealthy, younger son could have gone, he chose India, the place she had never been to but considered her own. He sent her emails that said, "You and Dad should come visit."

Being married for so long to a doctor, she knew it was a fallacy that every seven years a person becomes entirely new at the cellular level. Each type of cell has its own life-span—months, days, weeks—dying and being replaced all of the time, except for brain cells, which must endure for a lifetime, and are never replaced when they die. But Joan did not care, she liked the idea that every cell in her body was fresh and new, because she had survived those seven unbearable years.

23

There was the cyclonic aftermath of Eric: the brutal discussions and arguments she and Martin had about him, his overdose, her time with him in Oregon watching him shake and shiver while Martin performed surgeries in Hungarian villages without cell service. She and Martin were barely talking when Joan finally pulled *Words* from the box in late February. And then, having endured so much, she could not turn past the title page, fearful that the gorgeous book she had written would not be as she remembered.

Sammy Treeling, the boy who held her hand at naptime in kindergarten, who peed during piano hour in first grade, his puddle soaking the flipped ends of Joan's flowered dress, who gave her a candy necklace in second grade and bit off a bunch with his buckteeth, saved her. They had never seen each other again after Sammy's family moved away, but he popped into her mind like a gift and she had typed his name into the computer in the study, shocked when his obituary appeared. In the ground, or his ashes thrown to the wind, or dissolved in some body of water two years before. The undisclosed cause of his death like a story untold. He left behind a wife and three daughters and his position as chief of oncology at an Arizona hospital, and she saw pictures of his family at one of their daughters' weddings. When she figured out the dates, she realized he was dead within a year of that happy day. Joan hoped that his ending was unforeseen, that he died in an instant, that he was not ailing when the family posed for that picture.

She had thought about what she wanted her own obituary to say. The personal in a penultimate paragraph, the lede that a substantial writer was dead, followed by a lengthy list of her works: the miraculous and long-lived story collections, *Words of New Beginnings*, the other inchoate novels waiting for her to mix and deliver, a list of the awards and prizes her achievements had earned. Why not gild her death notice? She would only ever have one.

Standing at the tall study windows, she had stared out at the frozen white landscape, the trees wearing icicles, thinking no one knew when they would cease to exist. She sent out prayers then for Sammy and his wife and his daughters, for Eric's continued recovery, for Daniel's contentment, for Martin, and for herself and the novel waiting to be freed, the other work she would one day leave behind. An hour later, she set the title page of *Words* aside. A hard eye over the next months on the book she spent nine years writing. In the end, euphoric that the novel's power and prescience had not been diluted, the story not made redundant by its seven years in the box, she made no changes at all.

All of that is the past, Joan thinks, now that it is late spring, Memorial Day weekend. On Tuesday, she will call Volkmann, tell her about *Words*, send her the book. There, on the limestone island, is the copy for Volkmann, and in a box tied with a red ribbon, the copy she will give Martin tonight at the dinner she planned, reservations at eight. He will have questions when she tells him about the book's existence: when did she write it, why did she keep it a secret, why didn't she send it to Volkmann immediately when she finished. Those questions, and more, each resisting the simple answers he prefers, each answer containing a universe of truths, like a pea, next to another pea, next to another pea, in a pod.

She will not blame Martin, though she will want to, and has in the past. There is nothing now to gain by stating explicitly she wrote secretly because he had invaded her privacy, because her daily life had been a thick vine wrapped around her neck, that she had not sent the book to Volkmann because one of them needed to be the responsible, stalwart parent. It hadn't worked perfectly, but at least Eric made it through the worst, is safe.

She will not describe again to Martin how punishing these past seven years have been, how angry she still is that she shouldered the bulk of the emotional burden, that he refused to give credence to her warnings. She has yelled enough about all of that.

She will say to Martin that it seems the right time for her to return to the life she had when they met: Eric may be only five months past his attempted self-destruction, but based on his emails from India, it seems as if he has found a better path for himself, even if it is not a path Martin likes; and Daniel, he's happy working on some mysterious project he refuses to discuss, but tired perhaps, something she hears in the tone of his voice; and Martin himself is reducing his surgical travels, finding new interests—the cycling, the cooking—so it's her turn now.

She will keep to herself her own astonishment that the memories of these seven years are beginning to fade, that the human mind can cauterize the misery, allow a strong woman to pick back up where she was, to recover her inherent power, unleash her personal intention, grab at what she wants, now that she is again free.

24

Barefoot on their front walk, amidst all the blooms, Joan watches Martin as he drives past and waves to her, his sleek black bike attached to the trunk of his sleek black car. He gives a last honk, then crests the hill, and disappears from her sight.

He is headed out again to cycle with the men of Men on Bicycles, his new pals who throw their middle-aged fists into the air to prove they are still adventurous and dynamic, eons away from loosening their hold on the spoils and mercies of life, insisting that they, and their cycling, be viewed with appropriate gravity. They biked seventy-five miles yesterday in the holiday heat. Their goal this Memorial Day Monday is eighty miles. He has told her he might not be home until dark.

It is only seven, already sunny, sure to be hot. She walks through the gardens, headed down to the lap pool in the glen. She pulls off her shirt, steps out of her shorts, and dives in. Easy music on her waterproofed iPod for her first warm-up laps, sunlight glittering when she breaks through the water. The next song is raucous and pounding, and she thinks of Martin in his car, the windows rolled down, his own music at a shattering decibel, the hour drive to meet his cohorts, anticipating the challenge of the steep hills MOB is going to climb today. Then she is slicing through the water, feeling herself moving at an inhuman speed, wondering whether, from above, it might look as if she is merely ambling along.

She tries losing herself in the physical exertion, in the music, but she keeps thinking how Martin did not ask the hard questions she was expecting last night at dinner, after he heard her confession; how he did not interpret her secrecy in writing the book as nefarious, did not ask her to explain how she engaged in such a substantial undertaking for nine years without breathing a word. She would have absolutely asked him those questions, and more, if the situation had been reversed, would have wondered what it said about their marriage if she found he had kept such a secret from her. Instead, he ordered a very fine Malbec from the sommelier, and after asking, "Did you really write the novel on your antiquated typewriter?" said he thought the gardening shed was a perfect office for her, that he was going to buy her a new laptop and printer, and get her one of those small speakers she could plug in, listen to music when she wanted.

She swims for nearly an hour, then stretches out on a chaise. The stalks of maiden grass she planted when the pool was built have grown tall, stand proud and silvery in the morning sun, making the glen feel enchanted, as if this is a place where fairies or sprites might reside once again. She revels in the heat, in her nakedness, in the future that awaits, but when she closes her eyes, she sees herself last night in the restaurant, setting down the red-bowed box in front of Martin, hears again what he said: "I'm here for you. I'll do anything you need me to do." And Joan remembers what she thought, her instantaneous and unspoken response: *Where were you the last seven years? I don't need you now, not for this, this is mine.*

25

She is dreaming about a middle-aged man who never married, whose last sexual congress was back when he still had hair. He is ferrying his elderly mother somewhere, and although he is a good driver, he can see his speed worries her, the way she braces herself against the door, communicating her displeasure, her wish that he slow down. She fiddles with the air vents because the car is too cold for her taste. Little puffs of exasperation from her tight mouth, her tics and sighs impossible to ignore, but he refuses to look over. He is thinking pills or poison most likely; he doesn't want blood, and as much as he wants her gone, he does not need her to struggle. Disposing of her body will be the tricky part, and his daydream, on this quiet back road, is interrupted by a brace of luxury cars, empty and parked in a field. Where are the people who drove all the way out here? Then he sees, up ahead, a flock of cyclists in their bright electric plumage. He passes carefully as his shrunken mother says, "Look at all those stupid peacocks," and he instantly wants her buried in unyielding ground, not even a tombstone atop her grave, and he, free of his filial obligations, astride one of those bikes, his stomach toned, his legs ropy with muscles, wearing the tight shorts and the helmet, joined in fraternal goodwill, connected by the shared act of biking in unison, flying over the road with men he could call his friends. When the cyclists fade from his rearview mirror, he thinks that out here, still far from town, from civilization, this might be the place to do the deed, wonders whether he would be able to handle the sloppy, guilty aftermath, if, by any chance, there might be a shovel in the trunk of his car.

When Joan wakes, the sensation of hatred so close to the skin is still running through her. She understands the bike riders, considering what Martin is doing, but the matricide makes no sense.

She presses a finger to her thigh, sees redness on top of her tan, and wishes she didn't always forget to apply sunscreen before she swims. She wraps herself in the towel, gathers her clothes and her iPod, and walks up from the glen to the top of the knoll. She can smell the lilacs and the field of lavender from here. In early spring, without a word passing between them, Martin assumed Joan's long-standing role as gardener, mulching, pruning, planting, fertilizing, and the flowers have risen up, undulant fields of intense colors. Her plots of staid vegetables are still in place, but Martin has expanded upon them, researching the unfamiliar, purchasing the seeds, planting them, tending to the shoots, yanking out encroaching weeds, feeding them his own mixture for their growth. The Ronde de Nice zucchinis, currant tomatoes, golden beets, Rat Tail radishes, and all the other difficult vegetables he is nurturing are growing with great success. Here is the other new plot he planted—fennel, chives, lime-basil, cilantro, and lemongrass—herbs he uses in the experimental meals he had been cooking for them since the start of the year. Had she known he had culinary talents, she would have put him to work after Fancy left, when making dinners for growing boys and sometimes a hungry husband had been a nightly chore she bore alone. She inhales the tangy aroma of the cilantro, crushes a blade of the lime-basil, breathes in its tart smell. Had Martin sensed the coming changes months ago, before she told him about the book last night?

A ladybug lands on her finger, and she carries it with her through the gardens, until it flies away.

The weeping willow is forty yards ahead and behind it is the gardening shed she intends to turn into her writing studio. When she stepped in there yesterday, the windows of wavy old glass reduced the sun's glare, turned the light serene, transformed the gardens she built into pointillist paintings. She had thought of Fancy, the letters they traded for a few months after her departure, but they lost touch long ago, and she has no idea if Fancy and Trudy gave in to their love, raised children together, if their experiences have been easier than her own. Tomorrow, she's going to move all the instruments of gardening labor into the garage.

Up the bluestone tile path to the patio, with its outdoor table and chairs and Martin's upgraded barbecue, and through the glass doors into the sunny kitchen. She makes a pot of coffee and pulls down her regular mug, finds a folded piece of paper inside. It is a note from Martin, his first in years: *I love you*. She knows he's deluding himself, thinking little will change when she fully resumes her life as Joan Ashby.

She fills the mug with coffee, takes a sip, and wonders what Daniel will say when she tells him about the book. Since Eric's time in rehab, no longer do they ramble for forty-five minutes or an hour, their daily conversations falling away. Now he keeps their conversations short, asks if Eric is still doing all right, if he's enjoying India, adroitly eludes her attempts to find out more about his mysterious project, says that he is finally following his creative heart, which she hopes is true. He came home only twice last year, and has not been here at all this year. Last year, when Eric was still running Solve from the house, Daniel showed up for a weekend in June, surprising her when he asked to read her collections, and then another weekend in November, when he hugged her and said he thought the stories were wonderful. Brief praise, when it had taken him all of the summer and nearly all of the fall to read and respond. But it was a sweet moment, and she had batted away the hurt because she owed Daniel for providing her with rare sweet moments these last years.

She has let things be, simply enjoying the feeling of being carefree, but now she wants to hear what he is up to. She wants to know the details of his mystery project, how exactly he's heeding his creative heart beyond his articles for *Think Inc.*, if he's received emails from Eric about the letters he's writing to the Dalai Lama seeking a personal meeting. She wants mostly to tell Daniel about *Words*.

The ring of the phone startles her, smashing into the eleven o'clock quiet of the kitchen, Martin's new gadget calling out *Daniel Manning, Daniel Manning, Daniel Manning*. She was going to call him when she refilled her mug, but she's so pleased he's phoning.

"Love," Joan says when she answers.

26

When Joan hangs up the phone, her skin feels too tight, as if she might at any moment start shedding like a snake. Rubbing up against any rough surface, a rock, a tree trunk, until the old skin peels away. Snakes are said to be *in the blue* when they are about to shed, and all at once she is feeling that way too, a little blue that Daniel rushed off the phone, did not give her time to ask her questions, to tell him her news. Soon, she will have no further interest in mothering even him, and she would have liked fifteen minutes to talk about the coming changes. She has put in her time and more than paid her dues.

In the study, the ergonomic chair fights her as it always does, resisting her adjustments, her pleas to submit to her will. She used to think Eric's minions had screwed it up, but each time Martin demonstrates how the levers work, raising the height of the chair, firming up the supporting back, everything moves as it should, and he says, "You can tame this baby." Defeated again, she props herself up on one bent leg and thinks she needs a booster seat.

Annabelle Iger has sent her an email.

Joan,

Men: Many, as ever, and delighted that the years are behind me when every boudoir dalliance involved the thought: Do I want a kid or not? I never did, you know, but societal dictums and upbringings are hard to shake.

Home: I bought the apartment next to mine, and the plans for combining the two should be finished in a couple of weeks. Work to start when building permits come through. In six months there will be plenty of space for you to come and stay, a wing, or something of the sort, of your own. You can come for a good long visit or the rest of our lives. Start writing again! Here's hoping you've finally decided that marvelous Martin and married life and children are not worth it. Well, Eric's troubles might have demonstrated that to you already. But how much fun we would have when you weren't working away. Though I know you once were so intense and focused, and could be again, I'd stand over you with a whip, just for the fun of it.

Work: Going well. Having great success with two books written by the same author that I published in tandem in March. *Paradise of Artists* and *The Blissed-Out Retreat*. They remind me of your work. Let me know if I should send copies.

You: What's new?

Xoxox Iger!

She writes down the names of Iger's books, and searches for *Paradise of Artists*. The screen floods with links to hundreds of articles about it, and the companion book, *The Blissed-Out Retreat*, best sellers that have sparked a frenzy of critical analyses.

Good for Iger, Joan thinks.

She opens the *New York Times* review: "These books contain a literary greatness about the pursuit of beautiful art in an ugly world, integrating enormous themes."

From the *Wall Street Journal*: "The author introduces readers to something serious, original, and contemplative about creation, and the creation of lives; just as cutting-edge medicine can introduce into a sickened body new cells able to target the offending disease."

On the NPR Web site: "J. D. Henry has outstripped the feminists who made their reputational bones tearing apart the male-female paradigm of sexual desire and the exertion of control. J. D. Henry has hidden a secret treatise within these elegantly written and compelling books."

An industry has sprung up around them.

The *Rolling Stone* article surmises that the two books contain a history of the sexual and artistic worlds in their current incarnations:

"AIDS and STDs and computer porn and increased violence against women within the larger context of a crumbling economy, a further widening of the gap between those with and those without, a massive increase in the unfettered desire to attain celebrity without commensurate talent, a frustrated mélange of creative impulses lacking sufficient outlets, appropriate forums, satisfactory levels of funding from the NEA and every state arts foundation. Within the artistic storm that looks malevolent to J. D. Henry's characters, to whom he/she has given names conjuring up worlds beyond America, tinged French or maybe Persian, foreign but not foreign, and just American enough, this troop, ranging from their mid-twenties to early forties, repair to an arcadia, intent on finding purity in the works they seek to create, curating their existences as carefully as they do their art—be they canvases, words, music, dance, a small forest of cannabis—through their artistic endeavors, their sexual encounters, and relationships."

Joan's stomach clutches. She searches for biographical information or pictures, but there is nothing in the computerized universe that indicates the author is a real person with a past, a life, parents, a wife or husband or partner, a gym membership.

She looks up from the computer, at Martin's treasures that he set out in the study against her wishes.

There are his presentation boxes, the sun glinting off the polished steel of the instruments displayed within, the caliper gauges and intraocular lens loops, the tonometers and trephines and punches, the spatula picks, and the scleral depressor he bought in Cologne and once put in Joan's hand. She thought she had grown used to them, but today, the antiquated ocular devices of his profession look to Joan like the tools of a serial killer. Ovoid eyes, big as dinosaur eggs, with their removable parts for use in medical school classes, line the bookshelves, sit on the coffee table, glare at her sitting behind the marble desk.

27

Joan scrolls rapidly again through the articles about *Paradise of Artists* and *The Blissed-Out Retreat*, searching now for the quotes she had skipped. She finds one and reads:

> *She had dreamed of this place, all shattered pewter and fluorescent silver, and bold bright greens, the natural world dancing under the sun. She felt at peace, at home as she never had before, her footsteps making no sound as she walked through the meadow to where the others were gathered. Just twenty-five of them, then, on the ground in a circle, talking quietly about the projects they were about to embark upon. One girl, pink-lipped and fair-haired, said, "Dance," and a man with a long ponytail, eyes older than the rest, said, "A symphony of birds," and a young couple, love-struck, held hands, and said, "Three parts of a painting." And Bashi knew only a few of the words she wanted to use, but paragraphs floated like metallic clouds in front of her eyes. "We need a name for our community," someone said, and Bashi, from India, by way of Tuscany, surprised herself when she spoke up and said, "There is a Hindi phrase that means 'Land of the Gods.'"*

She races to the kitchen for the copy of *Words* intended for Volkmann, then back to the study and places it down on the black marble desk. Then she is flipping through the pages, searching her work, finding the paragraph she just read in an article on the screen. Right here, in her own book, is the same paragraph. The only difference between Bashi in J. D. Henry's *Paradise of Artists* and her Bash in *Words of New Beginnings* is a gender reassignment; otherwise, every word choice, every bit of punctuation in the quote is identical to the unpublished page in her hand.

She keeps on, a ravenous comparison between every excerpt from those books quoted in the articles and her own passages about Bash, Lila, Minu, Zena, Bernard, and Anton.

J. D. Henry has kept Joan's work completely intact.

For long minutes, she sits at the edge of the ergonomic chair, her mind whirling, unable to settle. Then—

Who would have done this?

How would anyone have known where to look, when no one has known of the book's existence?

Over the last seven years, only Eric and the Solve kids had been in the house, out to the garage.

Did Eric fire someone, give whoever it was a reason to steal?

Other than the bottles of alcohol that Eric himself stole, nothing has ever gone missing.

Only this, her book.

Her book. Someone with an ax to grind with *her*.

Had one of his team hated her enough to damage her in this astonishing way?

Her fingers are fumbling, but then Eric's mobile number is ringing and ringing, from Rhome to India, and his voicemail never clicks in.

Martin is biking up some hill and out of reach.

She tries all of Iger's numbers, but it's a holiday weekend and likely she's somewhere exotic.

When she tries Daniel again and again, his phone is turned off.

She sits with her breath caught in her chest as the printer whirs into action, those damning articles dropping into the tray.

On the chair in the bedroom are the shorts she wore yesterday afternoon when she and Martin took one of their meandering neighborhood walks, and the shirt Martin wore last night when they had cocktails with Miranda and Larry Sumner, and she pulls on both.

She feels like a sleepwalker, or as if she is underwater, making her way through the house, back to the kitchen, retrieving her car keys from the ceramic pot on the counter. In the garage, she hits the button and sunlight fills the space.

In late February, when she retrieved *Words of New Beginnings*, the box was sealed up, the manuscript hidden at the bottom, nothing seemed tampered with, but she hadn't been looking.

She starts the car and catches her reflection in the rearview mirror. Her tan, the faint sunburn from falling asleep in the glen, all faded into the pallor of death. Her hair is wilder than usual. Piled high for the evening last night, she did not brush it out when she and Martin returned home, simply pulled out the pins, and slept on it. Under each eye, traces of mascara not washed away last night, not dissolved this morning in the pool.

She turns the key again and the engine cries in distress. She remembers then her dream out on the chaise—a son killing his mother.

She looks at her shaking hands gripping the steering wheel, then down at her feet and sees she has forgotten shoes. Last night, she and Miranda sat with their feet in the Sumner pool, Miranda's dozens of golden bracelets tinkling madly as she gestured around the pretty backyard. "I think I'm going to leave Larry soon. Take up the life I'm supposed to be living. I can't keep pretending *this* is what I want. See how everything lines up perfectly, every right angle exact?" The lawn was trim, the flower beds neat, the rocks of the waterfall, square and precise. Only the small figure eight pool lacked right angles. "I despise such perfection. I want mess and craziness. I don't want to have a bedtime. Can you imagine? Larry is in bed, ready to sleep at ten every single night. He wants me next to him. I hate it. I loathe it. I want to stay up all night if I choose to, not lay next to a man already dead to the world."

Last night is ages ago.

Joan runs into the house for her sandals, then back to the car, guns onto the road, hits the crest, flies down the long drop of the hill.

The Inveterate Reader has posted CLOSED FOR HOLIDAY WEEKEND in its window. The Tell-Tale's small parking lot is empty when she drives in, but the sign says they open at one o'clock on all holiday weekends, except Christmas and New Year's.

Finally, someone is at the bookstore doors, unlocking from within. Then Joan is inside, past the shelves with their literary offerings. Handwritten notes by the store staff explaining why they liked this or that book. Kimberly has drawn daisies in a row over her name, Jed's writing is blocky, Rocco's nearly illegible, Sue's letters perfectly formed.

At the table with its sign, RECENT BEST SELLER RELEASES, there is no logical organization, the books are not set out alphabetically, by title or author's last name. Then she spots them. J. D. Henry's books, side by side. A large gold label on each proclaiming its phenomenal status.

Joan is alone in the store, but the checkout girl is readying her register. Ears double pierced, a small crystal stud in the curve of her left nostril, she, too, moves as if she is sleepwalking or underwater like Joan.

A ping and the register opens. Metal-on-metal scraping while the girl wrestles with the cash box until it hooks in. Another ping when she closes the register drawer firmly. Finally, she scans Joan's books through.

"They're really great," the girl says.

Her pale cheeks flush, an upward sweep of pink that colors her pallid, doughy face. If the submerged cheekbones appeared, if the nose developed cartilage, if the eyes opened wider—it is a mutable face, Joan thinks, that could become almost pretty depending on the choices the girl makes in her future. Then she thinks that face will never develop character. Not too long from now, when her belly balloons, the girl will leave behind her double earrings and her nose stud, but will remain behind this cash register, pinging and pinking when she speaks shyly, nervously, to paying customers.

"I don't need a bag," Joan says, when she is allowed to pay, and grabs the books, leaves behind the girl, the store, the glass doors, until she is out on the hot macadam of the empty parking lot, and then back in her car. She turns on the engine just long enough to lower the windows, puts down the visor to block the sun.

She flips through the pages of *Paradise of Artists*, looking for the author photo, the biographical data about J. D. Henry.

There is nothing, just a statement that J. D. Henry is also the author of *The Blissed-Out Retreat*.

She looks for the acknowledgments page.

Three quotes attributed to Lewis Carroll and his two companion books: *Alice's Adventures in Wonderland* and *Through the Looking-Glass*. Snippets from a master of literary nonsense, another writer's work appropriated in place of the personalized acknowledgments Joan has never believed in. She reads them. Then reads them again.

J. D. Henry's choice of Carroll quotes are ridiculous explanations for such a horrendous action.

An explanatory message for aberrant behavior:

> "No, no! The adventures first, explanations take such a dreadful time."

A circuitous statement which confounds the notion of oneself, Carroll's double negatives winding the self into origami:

> "Be what you would seem to be—or, if you'd like it put more simply—never imagine yourself not to be otherwise than what it might appear to others that what you were or might have been was not otherwise than what you had been would have appeared to them to be otherwise."

Lastly, an apology that negates itself by containing a grandiose rationale:

> "Do you think I've gone round the bend?" "I'm afraid so. You're mad, bonkers, completely off your head. But I'll tell you a secret. All the best people are."

At the back of *The Blissed-Out Retreat,* the same three Lewis Carroll quotes.

28

The knowledge is right there inside of Joan, but refuses to coalesce.

She is studying the author's name on the covers. Staring at *J. D. Henry*. And slowly, so slowly, like an anagram clarifying itself, the quixotic pseudonym is revealed.

The surname of Henry is an homage to the squirrel Daniel wrote about as a child.

J stands for Joan.

D, of course, for Daniel.

Her son has stolen her book and masked his identity with a name only she would decipher.

How did Daniel know about *Words*?

How and when did he find it in its hiding place in her sixth *Ashby* box?

How did he go about selling the books to Iger, who has known Daniel since birth, has known the course of his life?

She is trying to puzzle it through.

If Daniel had called Iger, Iger would have called Joan to say she didn't know Daniel was writing fiction. She would have called Joan after reading manuscripts that made her think of Joan's work, would have asked if the manuscripts *were* Joan's.

Joan can hear Iger's voice, asking and answering her own rhetorical questions:

How long have we been friends? For decades.

And how many times have I asked why you stopped writing? Ever since you published Fictional Family Life, *and not once have you ever given me a straight answer.*

And what do I always say to you every single time we talk, every single time you visit me in New York? Get rid of the wonderful husband,

abandon those talented sons, you've done the domestic, now do what-
ever you have to do, but please, before you're dead, start writing again.

Okay, so let me see if I understand. You used Daniel as your stand-in
because you wanted to change agents, wanted to publish with someone
other than Storr & Storr.

But, Joan, why the pseudonym, why didn't you just call me directly?

Iger doesn't know. She believes what Joan wanted her to believe—
that Joan stopped writing decades ago. She doesn't know about *The
Sympathetic Executioners* or the Rare Baby stories. Iger knows nothing
about the work Joan created in her private castle before the jailing she
experienced in that seven-year cycle. Iger would think that J. D. Henry
was influenced by Joan Ashby, but nothing more than that.

This is all Daniel, Iger as his unwitting accomplice.

How could Joan have misread Daniel's secretiveness, think he had
a mystery he was not ready to share. He did, though, didn't he? His
oblique glances in November, after telling her how much he liked
her collections, he was gauging how she might react to his seizure of
her unpublished work, his arrogation of her ambition.

The truncated phone calls ever since, his secret altering the tone of
his voice. She had thought he was tired, perhaps pessimistic about the
events at *Think Inc.*, discovering that the world was not as he hoped,
but what she heard had nothing to do with that, it foretold something
else entirely.

Still, it is impossible to believe Daniel would have done this to
her. Not this son, who has always been so close, so good, loving, and
true. Not this son, with his natural sensitivities, his deep well of empathy, his kindness to others, thoughtful, as Eric has never been. Not
this son, with whom she shared 2,555 conversations over those seven
years, the voice she needed each day, for however long he could give
her, a buoyancy in the midst of insanity.

And his reasons?

She has no idea what Daniel's reasons could be.

What reasons could there be?

Her brain begins skidding.

J. D. Henry is her son, her golden son.

Joan looks at her hands, riveted together. Has she not been through enough? Jailed by one son she has blamed for her lost time, but this is so much worse. This son is a thief. The thief of her words, robber of her dreams, stealer of her love, and the time lost to the mothering maw, once that tiny thing lodged in her womb that she had not wanted at all. She is thinking these thoughts, acknowledging what she knows must be true, still, it does not seem real.

Where does this monumental transgression of Daniel's leave her, when *Words of New Beginnings*, the book so long labored over, is meant to be the door through which she walks to regain entry to the one world where she most naturally belongs?

The choices are all untenable, differing only by degree, the exposure Daniel will suffer, that she will suffer. Eric too, maybe. Her history as a writer out there for all to see, in the midst of a bizarre familial controversy. Her maternal qualifications on trial, judged for her inability to control this son's egregious, grievous, thieving impulse, judged for not being able to keep Eric on the straight and narrow.

But it is this son, Daniel, who elected to steal the part she so carefully preserved all these years. His actions a symbolic feasting on mother's milk. Eric cost her seven sacrificial years, but Daniel, he has obliterated her entirely.

Opposing plans crowd her mind. Stay and confront. Confront and flee. Flee then confront. There are even more possibilities lurking. Which one she executes will depend, she realizes, on how she decides to define herself. Joan thinks then that writers have infinite choices and mothers nearly no choice at all.

29

Screaming is not something Joan can do, has never been able to do, not even with Eric. She had yelled, but not screamed, an emotional coloratura once saved for her work, but she wants to scream, to rend her clothing, to hire her own sympathetic executioners, Silas and Abe, to gun down her son.

Eight long hours since she arrived home from the bookstore, spent on a stool at the limestone island, going through J. D. Henry's books, her novel cleaved in half, her heart ripped from her chest, pulsing madly in her hand. She has not tasted a single drop of the bottle of wine she has emptied, pulled free from the tightly sealed case with fingers that seemed to have grown talons.

Daniel has annihilated her life. Not just her future life as Joan Ashby again, but her past life, all her past choices. She is a statue at the limestone island, waiting for Martin to return.

The night sky has swallowed the sunset when at last he comes in, sweaty and dirty and happy, saying, "We ended up doing ninety miles, and I was close to the front of the pack the whole time."

He looks at Joan, at the empty bottle next to her drained glass, then back to her face. "What," he says. "What's happened? What's wrong?"

She hands him the articles about J. D. Henry's books, the quoted excerpts ringed in fluorescent yellow. Then her own loose pages with mad yellow circles around the matching paragraphs. Then the books themselves, the first pages bleeding yellow until she had given up.

"Okay—" he says. "You're scaring me. What is all this?"

She gestures at the stack piled up in his hands and Martin nods and sits on a stool and begins to read.

Joan retrieves another wineglass, opens another bottle of wine, pours Martin a glass, fills hers back up. She tries to slow her drinking as Martin makes his way through it all. Then he drains his glass and pours himself another.

"More?" he asks her.

"Yes," she says. No matter how much she drinks, the adrenaline of rage is keeping her sober.

Three hours later, Martin knows everything Joan knows: the swim, the dream, the brief conversation with Daniel, Iger's email, Joan's research, her race to the bookstore, sitting here at the island since then, trying to understand what has happened.

Martin wants to storm DC, burst into their son's apartment, force him to explain himself, then smash him, and throttle him, and threaten him with prosecution.

When he quiets, Joan says, "No. No rampage to Washington. I don't know what I'm going to do yet, but I have to handle this my own way."

It takes another hour before Martin concedes, and another thirty minutes before he drags Joan away from the island, from all that evidence of betrayal, forces her arms above her head, takes off her clothes.

When he has tucked her into bed, and is beside her, Martin says, "I'll reschedule my surgeries in the morning."

Joan says nothing until he reaches for her, tries to swaddle her in an embrace.

She steels him away. "No. Go. Don't reschedule anything."

In the morning, when he is gone, Joan finds a wrapped box on the marble desk in the study. Inside is the laptop Martin said he wanted to buy for her, to celebrate her resuming her writing life. She looks at it and wonders what use she has for it now. An invisible being is choking her to death, her lungs straining and straining, and when she pulls in mouthfuls of air, it is the air of a different world, where never again will she draw a nearly contented, nearly happy breath. It is an alarming, discordant world in which Daniel's true self has been revealed, impossible for her to digest.

She has the stamped copyright registration that proves *Words of New Beginnings* is hers, the attached title page shows *Final Draft: August 10, 2007,* proving her son's sedition, his duplicity. But she was wrong—the laptop will be useful, she needs at her fingertips, with a click of a key, an electronic version of her novel.

Her own words, written so long ago, disappear from her mind as soon as they appear on the screen. It's been seven years since she wrote anything beyond a few scribbled notes she didn't hang on to, and as she funnels words, sentences, paragraphs, pages, and chapters into the computer, the dexterity in her fingers returns, she is a typing zealot, maniac, fiend, making her way through the original typed pages, following the rhythm of the book's hard-fought sentences, recalling the stubbornness of her characters who once itched and moaned and sometimes rolled away from her, until she listened to them, let them drag her into the intentional lives they envisioned for themselves.

She retypes *Words* from beginning to end, acutely aware that Daniel did just this with her manuscript, before he sliced her book down the middle, substituted his encrypted name for hers.

At seven every morning and again at midnight, Martin asks what she thinks her next step will be, and Joan always says the same thing: "I don't know. I haven't thought that far yet."

When she finishes, when she has turned all of *Words* into a digital manuscript, Martin is in an icy operating room at Rhome General giving sight back to a partially blinded young man. For the first time, she uses the laptop for a different reason, books herself on a flight that leaves the next day.

She picks up the phone and calls their doctor. "It's an emergency," she tells the receptionist. "I need whatever vaccinations are required for travel to India."

She is at the FedEx in Rhome thirty minutes later, sending off a package. She is in Dr. Abrams's office thirty minutes after that. A cut-and-dry doctor, he never inquires about the personal, except as medically relevant. He does not ask why Joan needed an emergency appointment for vaccinations for a trip to India that surely would have been planned in advance.

"No need to fear measles, mumps, rubella, chickenpox, diphtheria, pertussis, or polio," he says. "Your last boosters will protect you against those diseases. Hepatitis A and typhoid, that's what you need to worry about."

She tightens up when the needle slides into the skin at the back of her arm. There is an ache at the injection site before she feels the medicine fan out through her body.

When she says, "I already feel it," Dr. Abrams says, "Joan, that's impossible. Pull up your other sleeve, better if the injections aren't in the same arm."

She refuses the typhoid pills intended to further protect her against that disease.

"You can't eat lukewarm food, or eat where only locals eat, and you absolutely can't drink anything that does not come in a sealed bottle. Pay attention, Joan. Getting sick there is a serious thing," Dr. Abrams warns.

"I'll be careful," she says. A million vaccinations will not cure the illness festering within her that Daniel has caused. At reception, she writes out a check for her copay.

It is hard to pack her suitcase with both arms bruised and sore from the shots. But then it is done, and she packs up her carryall—the laptop, notebooks, pens, a ream of paper, her travel itinerary, boarding pass, passport, books she can't imagine reading, snacks she can't imagine eating on the plane, her makeup bag, and a pair of pajamas in case her suitcase is lost. It is late afternoon when Martin finds her in the bedroom.

"I canceled my last surgery," he says as he walks through the open doors of their bedroom, then sees her suitcase on the floor, the carryall on the bed.

"Where are you going?"

"India," and she watches Martin clamp his long surgeon's fingers together.

"India?"

"Yes."

"Now?"

"Tomorrow morning."

"Aren't we going to discuss this?"

"I know what I'm doing," she says. "Or at least this feels like what I need to do this minute."

"Let me help you. Let's work through this catastrophe as a team, the way we always do."

"We weren't a team with Eric, and with this, I just can't," she says.

"I'll get a ticket. Right now. We'll go together."

"No, I don't want that. I'm sorry."

He has always wanted her to explain things about herself, when she thinks he ought to know. How does he not understand her need to be in a place utterly foreign, where the old happy memories of she and Daniel will not tag along, where she can more easily imagine her own son dead.

"How long?"

"Three weeks."

"Are you leaving me?"

"Martin," she says, thinking of all she has sacrificed for this marriage, years that affected her as they did not affect Martin, his life continuing apace.

What can she say, when all she can picture is herself at her old desk in the room that had been her study, her mind racing through lists of words, as her new husband instantly abandoned the vow he had made, that there would be no children, that he understood her work would always come first. The underpinnings on which she had agreed to marry him kicked out from beneath her at the very start, forcing her to find ways to live an unwanted life.

She turns away and zips the carryall, ripping up the silence. She hears him in the hallway, the study door click into place.

She strips and pulls on her swimsuit.

Out through the glass door of their glass bedroom wall, down the bluestone tiles, all the way to the glen. She will miss *this*, she thinks.

Then she is in the water, demonically swimming laps, until her heart feels ready to explode.

The dawn sun is starting to climb when Martin stops at the curb, releases the trunk, and pulls out Joan's rolling black bag, a red ribbon knotted around the handle. It is the ribbon she used to tie up *Words* in its box when she gave the book to Martin at the restaurant. Eight days ago. She has no idea if he has started reading, but it's irrelevant now, the book no longer belongs to her.

She checks for her passport and boarding pass, shows Martin she has it all. Even in their early days when they barely knew each other, even through everything with Eric, and even though they said little to each other last night, and have been silent on the drive from Rhome to the airport, they still kiss each other well. Wordless statements being made on each side. What she means by her kiss, how Martin interprets her kiss, what his kiss means, she doesn't know, and he probably doesn't know either.

Then she is through the pneumatic doors, in the early morning bustle of Washington Dulles International Airport.

When she looks back, Martin is pulling out into traffic.

She checks her bag through, finds her gate with its long line of linked plastic bucket seats. She has work to do before this first leg of her trip, her flight to Delhi. She powers up her laptop, connects to the airport's free Internet service, and addresses an email to Iger.

Dear Iger,

There is a problem regarding Paradise of Artists and The Blissed-Out Retreat, the two books you published by J. D. Henry. In 1999, I began writing the first novel everyone assumed I would never write. I apologize for keeping you in the dark, but I did not want to discuss what I was working on, not even with you. I finished Words of New Beginnings in 2007, just weeks before life drastically altered when Eric dropped out of school. J. D. Henry's books were not written by him; they are my book chopped in half. J. D. Henry is Daniel. I cannot explain why my son has done what he has done, and I cannot bring myself to seek out his motiva-tions. I have spent the last several days typing the book into my computer and I am attaching it here. By FedEx, I have sent you the original, along with the filed copyright information. You will see that aside from one gender alteration, he stole my novel in its entirety. Once you have confirmed that for yourself, we can discuss what to do. Of course, I will need copies of the contract between Annabelle Iger Books and J. D. Henry. The matter of what you paid to him, and hence what he owes me, I will resolve with him directly. With respect to royalties and all other remuneration, contractual changes will be necessary to reflect that I am the author. I want all of this kept confidential, even within your own imprint. No one is to know. I am going to be out of the country for some period of time, but I will arrange to get original signatures to you in whatever way you desire.

The box pops up telling Joan the email has been sent, and she wonders how long it will take Daniel to learn his treason has been discovered.

To Martin she writes, Martin, then she lifts her hands from the keyboard. She realizes Martin might not know whether she is leaving him or not. He could interpret in any number of ways her silence yesterday, her arduous swim, the quiet dinner they ate at the limestone island, the old movie they did not really watch in the den, her perfunctory kiss when they climbed into bed, her lack of response to his quiet *Sleep well* when he turned out the light, when she made it obvious during the ride to the airport that she wasn't interested in what he wanted to say. Whatever she writes will not satisfy, but she has no comfort to give. Whatever configuration of the Manning family might remain will have to function without her, and she is not taking bets when she herself does not know what might be ahead.

Thank you for understanding is what she decides to write, then Love, Joan, and sends that email off.

Squawky announcements judder the air. People scurry through the terminal, wheeling their bags, harried already.

She remembers the story Eric told her when he said he was going to Dharamshala, about a woman who had a private audience with the Dalai Lama, and how the Dalai Lama guided her out of her morass, helped her to rid herself of her anger so she could close the chapter on her dead father's abuse. She was now mediating restorative justice between criminals and their victims' families. Listening to Eric, Joan had thought the concept so noble, had said, "How wonderful," and had meant it. She thinks now that the concept is ridiculous and useless; there is nothing Daniel could do to restore justice to her. How did she, with her pride in her observational skills, not notice a fatal rip in his character? How did she not understand how he thinks, when the number of words spoken between them over all of these years is incalculable?

He has made meaningless the life Joan has led, the sacrifices she has made, and now there is nothing left—not the book that would jump-start her silenced career, not the son she discovered she could love so completely, who had saved her from the other one.

If she gives him up permanently, will the loss feel similar to what she felt when she decided to have him, when she determined that, to save herself, she had to lock the writer away in a castle that no Manning mortal could enter, when she sacrificed herself these years for Eric and tried not to think of her work ready to go and hidden away.

In the slippery plastic seat, Joan watches the travelers and thinks that right at this moment Daniel is unaware he has already been exposed. Whatever Daniel obtained by stealing her work, it is destroyed as thoroughly as her own dream for her future. He is her bomber, and whether his actions were expedient or malevolent, she may never know.

She thinks about the guidance Eric hungers for, the numerous letters he has written to the Dalai Lama.

Joan has never imagined writing such a letter, never expected to have a reason to seek such illumination, but she is in need of rescue, in need of clarification and wisdom and guidance, about how she might continue on. She knows what people would expect her to say—how does she carry on as a mother and a wife, but she has played those roles to the best of her ability, and where is she? She wants the Dalai Lama to tell her how she can carry on, as a writer. She wants the guidance she gave to Bash, Lila, Minu, Zena, Bernard, and Anton, as they pursued the dreams closest to their hearts, despite the doubts they felt from inside, sometimes from without, the stern voices of people from their pasts.

She is in a rush now, opening her laptop, pulling up a blank document.

Dear Dalai Lama, she types.

Dear Dalai Lama does not look right on the page.

Do people address this exalted man, encourager of love and healing, good thoughts and kindness, as just Dalai Lama? She searches for an answer and the Protocol School of Washington informs her that the correct form of address is *Your Holiness*.

It is strange to see *Your Holiness* appear on the screen, as if she is addressing a god she has never been sure, has never needed to be sure, exists.

> Your Holiness:
> My name is Joan Ashby. I am a writer—

She writes until a loudspeaker voice says, "Dearest passengers, our wondrous flight to Delhi will soon board and we would be eternally pleased if all of you would be kind enough to prepare by gathering your belongings and making a neat and lovely line."

Inside the carpeted bay leading from airport to plane, the civilized line dissolves with a boarding delay. Information filters backwards about the cause: an obstinate passenger, an old man, is gripping his wheeled walker, refusing to release it, insisting on rolling to his seat on his own. The voices at the front grow louder, and the trapped mass goes quiet when a male flight attendant says, "Sir. Please. Listen to me. The walker won't fit in the aisle. No matter what you do, you won't be able to wheel your own way. Do you understand? We will get you into your seat another way."

People shift from one foot to another, move bags from one shoulder to the other, stare at the advertisements on the rounded walls, avoid one another's eyes, and then the flight attendant's voice rings out again, louder this time. "I do understand, sir. But do you?"

The old man must understand, must relinquish control of his mobility device, must place himself into the unknown hands of others, because there is a swell of movement, and the throng separates, people shifting into place, smiling carefully at those around them, re-forming into a neat line that moves sluggishly onward, heading into the plane.

Joan is two people away from stepping on board. The attendants are checking boarding passes, directing passengers to the various aisles.

A calm flyer under normal conditions, Joan flinches at the sight of the plane's wide hatch, like the open jaws of a behemoth creature prepared to swallow her whole. One person ahead of her before Joan

must step into the jaws of the beast. She has a collapsing fear, a premo-
nition that she ought to run back the way she came, until she is out
again in the hubbub of the airport.

There is movement behind her, a jostling against her spine, and she
takes a step, and then another one, and she holds up her boarding pass,
and then she is inside, and the aisles appear in front of her, long
stretches of rows, each three seats across, all the way to the tail of the
plane, which is too far away to see. She is in a flux of people, tightly
squeezed, but the proximity of all these strangers calms her fear.

Joan looks behind her.

The jaws have turned back into a hatch door, the behemoth is just
a plane, and this is a trip she must take.

There is no reversing through the tunnel.

She does not mind all the bodies angling and stretching, the
mass of hands avidly forcing bags into the overhead bins. People are
scooting down into their seats, arranging their small spaces into
semblances of home, kicking off shoes, settling blankets over laps,
setting out treats in seat pockets, tucking magazines and newspapers
at their sides.

As she inches down her aisle on the far side of the plane, she hears
opera, then something orchestral, then a woman's heartsick voice
wailing; rapid bits of music spiraling out from buds in countless ears,
a curious soundtrack that accompanies Joan's steps, the music changing
form and construction, rising and falling, seeming to track the journey
she is about to make, that she has already begun to take.

Past first class, past business class, she reaches the last curtain that
marks entry into economy, where the cheap seats are. The line slows
again. The overhead bins are already filled with the bags of those flying
in a more comfortable way.

She should have flown first class. Business class at least.

Why did she not think that fleeing home because two sons have
stolen her life in different ways earned her some comfort, a deeply
reclining leather chair, a footstool that would cradle her feet, as much
gratis alcohol as she desires? Martin always flies first class when he is off
to save sight and souls. This is her own soul she is going to try to save
and she could have used the legroom.

She checks the aisle numbers and here is her seat, located halfway between the restrooms at the front of economy and those in the tail.

The first two seats in her row are already occupied.

In the aisle seat is a solid, middle-aged Indian man who looks like he could be a champion weight lifter. His head, a gleaming brown dome. His suit is linen, his striped tie a broad knot at his throat; he is impeccably dressed for a fifteen-hour flight.

The middle seat holds an old woman, teeny, not much bigger than a doll. She is creased and wrinkled and rheumy-eyed. Her eyes, though, beneath their cloudy scrim, sparkle like emeralds. And she is bright. She is very bright. Her cheeks rouged a happy pink. Her sweater a hot pink, the vibrant color masking the heavy load on her sloped, thin shoulders.

She looks up at Joan and smiles. "Hello, darling. Are you here, next to me?" pointing to the seat next to the window.

"Yes. So sorry," Joan says.

The big man steps out into the aisle, one hand in the pocket of his crisp vanilla suit, the matching elbow crooked. He is dressed to promenade a lady in the park, but the idea of a courtly Indian gentleman vanishes when he plows backward, forcing the people behind him to make way. There is audible displeasure, but when he glances back at the muttering, the noise evaporates.

The old woman must make her way now. Seated, her feet don't touch the cabin floor. One foot locates it, plants itself shakily, then she shifts forward, until her other foot finds its way. She warily lifts her body until she is standing, tottering really, and she smiles up at Joan, as if Joan's face might provide her with the necessary strength to carry on, then she takes a cautious sideways step, then another, again and again, until she has cleared the outside armrest, and Joan can squeeze past, move into the row, settle into her seat.

Already she is dreading the future hour when she will need to use the restroom, require them both to give way once again.

The flight attendants roam the aisles, checking seat belts, slamming closed the overhead bins, forcing everyone's eyes forward for the speech about emergency maneuvers in the event of a crash on land or at sea.

Joan listens for a minute and turns away. No one on this plane would survive a crash landing on any surface.

Then the plane is racing down the runway, the scream of rushing air, the nose lifting up, vibrating seconds of suspended uncertainty.

They are aloft.

Part II

TRUTH IS BEAUTIFUL; SO ARE LIES

Ralph Waldo Emerson, bastardized

Satya sundara hai; jhūṭh bhi vaisa hi hai

30

. . . I've considered how best to start, and I think it is like this:

I, Daniel Manning, am the commoner in a family renowned for its brilliance: mother, father, much younger brother, all masters of their particular universes.

My mother's fame and glory blazes as bright as ever, though she ceased writing long ago, had, as I believed, given it all up. Manning, my father's name—my name—is appended to all the miraculous ocular surgeries he has invented. And then there is my brother for whom everything has come so easy. A self-taught wunderkind whose company holds the copyright to the astounding computer program he created at thirteen, that hotels the world over are using to run more efficiently, soon to be implemented by a rash of other industries. He's worth something like a billion now, at twenty-two.

Oh, I was told I was special when I was a child and I believed it, until I absolutely could not. Since then I have feared my own mediocrity, wishing my own innate genius would appear. I have roiled for a long time with anger and frustration and the hot hatred of knowledge that I was not born marked for greatness like the rest of them, the small clan I am tied to for life. No one knows how I really feel, my placid exterior shrouds it all. I think, in that way, I am like my mother. Only recently did I realize that she is a cipher, a chameleon, hiding her secrets away and out of sight.

I did not always feel this way.

For a while, it seemed words would unleash my internal powers. I was five and a half when I began writing a whole lot of little stories about a squirrel I named Henry, and I demonstrated great talent for putting that poor squirrel through his paces, inventing dangerous situations for him to overcome, each story a whole new world I invented from scratch. The writing of those stories meant everything to me, made the earth spin right on its axis, made me feel actual and definite in a way I otherwise did not. This, I knew, was my present, and would be my future.

Although my father talked about reading the dreams of the people he operated on when he was deep inside their eyes, and my mother told me elaborate tales at bedtime about rare babies, critical to my understanding of myself was that my parents may have been story-tellers, but *I* was the writer in my family, the only one who wrote his stories down.

As I look back over those early years, I remember strangers stop-ping my mother on the street, saying a few words, but I was only interested in tugging her away, wanting her all to myself. Even had I overheard what I imagine now were compliments and praise about her work, none of it would have resonated, for my mother never told me about her life before marriage, I was not privy at all to her past. And so, if, as a young child, I had ever known she was a famous writer, that knowledge had long emptied out of my mind by the time I learned the truth about the awesomeness of her achieve-ments, her might and her reach. I was eleven when forced to con-front who my mother really was, and I was devastated, her history wresting away what I had long believed belonged only to me. And then, when I forced myself to read just a single one of her stories, called "Deep in the Valley," its mere existence shattered me completely.

Perhaps if I had come up against Joan Ashby when I was older, I would not have had such a visceral reaction, would not have immediately doubted myself, feared that the *best* I wanted to achieve might be beyond my capabilities, beyond the gift I had then dis-played. I was a competitive boy, and that I was comparing apples and oranges—an eleven-year-old versus an award-winning writer at the height of her powers—was meaningless to me. I raised my boyish defenses, threw overboard my own desires, abandoned Henry the Squirrel to find his own way, and thereafter protected myself from anything Ashby-related.

Treacheries experienced in childhood are among the most difficult to overcome, or to forgive, as are dreams crushed when one is too young. Having to acknowledge your weaknesses can make the best of us fall into a very dark place.

Five years ago, recently graduated from the undergraduate program at the Wharton School of Business, I was nine months into my tenure as an associate at a Silicon Valley venture capital firm, intent on making myself a master of *that* universe. But I hated everything about venture capital. I loathed its abbreviated acronymic language, its locker-room atmosphere, that everything was measured by size: the deals, the bonuses, the cars, the outlandish vacations. I knew early on that either I did not possess whatever was required to succeed there, or I did, but the environment would make it impossible. The equation was already solving itself because I was failing spectacularly.

I lived in a depressing apartment, my room furnished with a cardboard bureau, an air mattress blown up on the floor, a single uncapped bulb overhead. Sometimes I ran into my roommate, a guy named Carlos Wong, who remained during all of those months a pleasant phantom, although we worked for the same company, he a few years ahead of me. At the firm, he was solidly contoured, leap-frogging rapidly over those more senior. The only thing working in my favor was that I was tall, in decent shape from competitive swimming in high school and college, still deft enough with words to talk to girls, get them easily into bed.

When Ashby was forced back into my life, I was twenty-two, and had just finished rambunctiously fucking the girl I was sleeping with. Christina leaned away, grabbed something from her bedside table, said, "Read this," and thrust into my hand an old anthology, *Best American Short Stories of 1984.*

In her few off hours, Christina was trying to expand her education, which had been purely focused on macroeconomics and statistics. She, too, was in venture capital, but she loved it, and she liked me. I liked her, and I liked her apartment, which had lamps and rugs and a good TV and food in the fridge, and a bedroom with a big bed and nice sheets, and a comforter that was not molting, and walls painted a happy shade of yellow, which reminded me of my childhood bedroom, and her bathroom, which she did not have to share, as I did with Carlos Wong, was always spotless and smelled nice.

What I brought to our informal relationship was an understanding of the hours we both kept, my eagerness, if not talent, in all things coitus, and my willingness afterward to read and discuss with her the stories she was making her way through. She was the only person I knew in venture capital reaching for something beyond the requisite business and finance journals.

Unlike Christina, I had always been a voracious reader. My business school education well mixed with liberal arts, and I had surreptitiously minored in English literature, always keeping the venerated Ashby at bay, which had not been easy to do.

In my cubicle at the firm, I kept hidden a thesaurus, although the endless financial documents on which I worked resisted any linguistic zest, and novels that I read in ten-minute increments when I hid in the emergency stairwell and told myself I was only taking a break.

So being ordered in the dead of night by a girl with great breasts to read a story called "An Outlaw Life" did not frighten me. It was the author's name, Joan Ashby, that turned my skin cold, set my heart racing, returned to me the loss of all my childhood dreams.

When I shook my head, Christina said, "What, Daniel?" and then I shook the book, as if eager to comply with her request. She rolled onto her back, a naked carnal display, but I could see nothing, could only feel the old hurts, the old fear coming in waves that intensified, a fear I first recognized at eleven, that Ashby's work contained hidden dangers that would trip me up, plummet me down into some scary, inhospitable landscape, the ground pockmarked and sodden. When I was still a kid, the name *Ashby* would sometimes punch itself unbidden into my brain, and all I could imagine was quicksand, myself being sucked under.

The paperback anthology in my hand turned into a hundred-pound weight, the paragraphs hurtling off the page and smacking me in the face, and I suddenly understood that time had not done its work.

My childhood fragility, the striated pain of that earlier time, which I thought long bulwarked by years of reason and rationality and maturity, had not made me impenetrable and impervious. I instantly felt my thin skin, my hatred about not measuring up, my despair that I could not match her abilities, my sheer ordinariness, everything I felt when I read that other story of hers a decade before.

I realized then that the tumultuous things that happen in childhood are tsunamic experiences that weaken our fleshy armor, leave deep cracks and crevices in their wake, and even when the scars are knitted together, even when there is a tough keloided ridge on top, it takes little effort to rip them wide open, where the pus still pools a hundredth of a millimeter below.

With Christina stroking my leg, urging me to get started, I could not avoid the story, could not avoid what I had always fought against: that Joan Ashby was, is, and will always be my mother, and that she caused me to abandon my dreams.

I focused on the first word and prayed that my courageousness would be rewarded. When I reached the end of the story, there was no reward. Just Ashby, always Ashby, blowing another hole through my impoverished heart.

Reading "An Outlaw Life" that night is marked on my personal time line with a blood-red circle. It marked another massive splintering in my life, but this time I was all grown up, and I could throw those shards skyward, determine what I wanted to do amidst all of the breakage. This is the story that made me rethink everything.

Peck Traynor looked forward to Wednesday nights when she called her sister Margo, telephonically breaching the gulf between New York City and Devils Creek, a little town with innocent fields and crops. Eleven digits, twelve hundred miles of highways, and one swift-moving river separated Peck from her family. Her parents, and her brother, TJ, and Margo and her husband and their children, Bug and Bea, one six, the other four, properly named Beau and Margaret, all lived just miles apart on the vast fertile Traynor land that spread north from the town.

Fifteen years ago, newly quit of Devils Creek, where she was called Thessaly, Peck stood in a courtroom in downtown Manhattan where an old man with tumbled white hair and a gavel said from on high, "Are you sure?" She nodded. She wanted to carry forward some bond to her beginning and when she looked up at the judge, named Sykes, she said,

"Yes, I'm taking my father's middle name as my new first name." The proceedings were intricate, but when she walked out of the courthouse legally renamed, she had forgiven her younger self for the wrong turns she had taken. Had she not veered off course, she would not have found her words, uncovered her voice, flown away to an island in the middle of everything where she could become someone else.

Since then, every Wednesday night, Peck called Margo to hear about the family's week in Devils Creek. When Margo's voice ran down, Peck took over and wondered what Devils Creek residents would make of her tales about the soft-handed college students who signed up for her fall, winter, and spring semester creative writing classes at NYU; classes that inevitably cratered midway because her students, just a decade or so younger than she, misperceived the weight of their worlds, found meaningful that which was not. Unlike her students, the Devils Creek residents were smart and thorny and willfully dedicated, but their world was almanacs, rainfall predictions, growth rates, and Deere equipment, and the concept that one of their own might be a professor and, more important, a highly regarded, semi-famous writer would not compute.

Peck knew that her family, readers all, had never read a single one of her books, not the three story collections, not the two novels. They did not know that her collections had been honored. They did not know her second novel won a major award. They would have been astounded to learn that a hairstylist tied Peck's long brown hair up in an intricate chignon with tendrils trailing her neck, and that another woman turned Peck's pale and pretty blue-eyed face into something golden and fetching, and that a third woman found a long black column for Peck to wear and silver heels to stand in when the press spoke to her before and after the awards ceremony. No one in Devils Creek subscribed to *People* or *Vogue* and so they did not see Peck's photographs on bright shiny paper, the silly phrase *Lit-Beauty* dashed in a tough font below. She had clipped her own images, struck by her slim and bare shoulders and her long curved eyelashes, and taped herself behind books on the shelves in her study. The old saw that the only publicity a woman should ever desire is on the event of her birth, marriage, and death was something the people of Devils Creek would hold true, if they ever considered it, which they did not. The news that a local girl had been nationally feted failed to make the town's single paper, a daily comprised of ten weightless pages, eight of them classifieds. Her family was still unaware of the felicity that attended Peck and her award.

On Wednesday nights, Peck did tell Margo about how her work was going, these days a third novel, but she did not pretend that Margo was actually interested; it was a ten-minute monologue Peck used to untangle recent kinks in her writing, and as a counterbalance to Margo's joy in her children. And although Peck also told her sister about the men she dated and discarded, scores of men since she landed in New York, whatever their names, whatever they looked like, however they spent their days, Peck identified the wrong with each of them, or what should have been present within, but was, instead, absent completely. When she detailed those wrong or absent traits, Margo said Peck was missing something magnificent about what love provided a couple, the truth that children lay bare. "Isn't it enough that I've spotted the problems right up front?" Peck often said, in some form or another, and then listened to Margo sighing her Devils Creek sigh.

She never told Margo about all the men who sprang forward after that ceremonial evening, and then again after the pictures of her were published; that she had acquired an international dating pool if she wanted it. Men from Maine, Nevada, Rhode Island, Texas, New Mexico, and other places, and even from Italy, France, and Spain, sent her post-cards, or wrote her long adverbial letters, all expressing a fervent desire to date or marry her, the most honest writing that they just wanted to bed her, to experience for themselves the wanton woman they assumed was Peck in the stories. It was only a year ago that the award altered the physical mass of correspondence she received, and her postman said, "Listen to me. Too many people know where to find you. You need to erase any reference to your address, set up a post office box, turn in any letters that seem off to the 27th Precinct. Take heed, Peck, about what's in your hands." Peck heeded.

On a heated Wednesday night in early July, Peck called Margo at the usual time. She pressed the phone to her ear, ready for the obligatory dipping-in before settling down to a tell-all when Margo rushed ahead.

"I have to tell you, I'm nearly five months along, but I waited to make sure nothing went wrong this time."

Peck was surprised that Margo had held the secret tight, though it wasn't news that should have startled her—her sister and brother-in-law had been trying for a third child for a while—but something serious unraveled within Peck anyway. With the phone cricked against her chin, Peck rose from the couch and walked into the kitchen as Margo detailed her now-dissipated worries.

When Margo said, "Now that the iffy stage is past, we're teaching Bug and Bea about the new life growing inside of Mommy," Peck retrieved the bottle of Jim Beam from the back of a cabinet. Bourbon was Peck's out-of-bounds drink, the way it released the memories of her wayward youth, her long-ago ability to find trouble even in a place as small as Devils Creek, but Margo's news had already opened that door, and so Peck poured herself a shot and tossed it back.

"Mom and Dad are excited, of course," Margo said, and Peck poured herself another. In the kitchen's low light, the burnished liquid of her past gleamed, waiting to be swallowed down once again.

She tossed the second shot back as Margo said, "I want you to be this baby's godmother, Thessaly." The bourbon burn hit the back of Peck's throat and she coughed.

"Sorry, sorry," Margo said. "My screw-up. I should remember. I *do* remember. I'll never get why you ditched *Thessaly. I* would want to be a Thessaly. I always did want to be *you,* Thessaly."

The rising fumes of the bourbon brought back all those times of mistaken youthful frenzy when Peck was fifteen and up on the Devils Creek cliffs, and the boy, five years older than she, cleverly used his silent mouth, his broad hands. Once, she had thought all of life was there in his arms, with her back pounded into the dust, the distant stars suddenly close and bright, the moon waxing and waning.

"Will you do the honors?" Margo said. "Teach this child everything I can't teach it. Love it as much as I love you?"

On Thursday morning, when she woke, Peck did not remember the end of her conversation with Margo, whether or not she had agreed to shepherd, in some unclear way, her sister's unborn child, but she knew that she had not dreamt while she slept, and she wasn't sure the bourbon was responsible for that intimidating blank. She had not had a dreamless sleep since she was fifteen-year-old Thessaly on Traynor land in Devils Creek, sneaking out most nights and running to the cliffs where she met the boy and got naked, and afterward drank enough bourbon to kill something, although it failed to kill that which it should have. That year, when her body swelled, she began dreaming every night, about many things, and always saw herself writing in notebooks, and on large pieces of paper, sometimes using a pen, sometimes a pencil, once or twice a quill she had only ever seen in movies. The family divided about whether the baby should be kept, given away, or done away with from the start. Her father wanted the baby brought up a Traynor. Her mother wanted Peck to have a chance first at a life of her own. Peck would leave them all downstairs to argue it out and, when she wasn't in school, she cloistered herself in her room, started writing in the diary she mocked when given to her on her twelfth birthday. Nine months later when certain decisions were lost and the diary was all filled up, Peck sweated, pushed, and screamed, and figured out that her stories, about whole lives blown apart on the land, were really about faith eliminated.

In the hospital, Peck saw her daughter for an instant before the baby was delivered to her new life, which Peck hoped would unfold in California or Florida, someplace with an ocean that had endless tides and starfish and shells.

Such thoughts as these, and more, had been brought on by Margo's news, the omen of bourbon, and a night bereft of the dreamy lifeline to her own lost past. Peck rose from her bed, unglued her eyes, and rinsed the cobwebs from her mouth.

In the kitchen, she dropped the half-empty bottle into the trash and started the coffee. When the drops were fat and slow, she thought the time had come to finally take action, to do what she had long desired.

An hour later, she was pointing out to the building's assistant super the walls that sliced apart living room and dining room, and those that enclosed bedroom and study.

"Can you tear all these walls down, Miguel?" she asked.

"If it's possible, of course, I will do it for you, Peck," he said, and she followed him through the apartment, listening as he tapped each wall from top to bottom. The taps sounded hollow to Peck, which she thought was a good thing, that particular structures were not essential.

In her study, Miguel pointed to the filled bookshelves, his hand in front of Peck's own books. "Have you read all of these?" he asked.

"No, not all of them," Peck said, which was a lie, and she looked at her long desk that bisected the room. There was her third novel, in progress, a short stack of pages. A month without the duties of teaching and grading and the stack had grown only incrementally, the work a brutal slogging that rebuffed Peck at every turn. In all her years of writing, now more than eighteen, the last ten as a published author, never had the work eluded her. Never had her teenage years in Devils Creek, the foundation of her work, been so remote. *Vibrant, insistent, and original,* the critics agreed about the stories and novels Peck set in the town where she was born, nothing more than a square and some streets, fields of corn, spring wheat, and sunflowers, flat unyielding plains beyond, and, rearing over the highway, those sandy cliffs rising up, the locus of all her juvenile troubles. Did the loss of her dreams last night, and the grizzled novel in which she could not make headway, signal that she had strip-mined that rich vein, or now stood too distant from those days? Had she lost those tidal feelings that lifted her old recklessness into art? She feared suddenly that she had become staid.

"Are you sure about getting rid of these walls?" Miguel asked. "If you took out your desk and the books, it could be a bedroom, and maybe you will need it. Rosita and I find that a bebé in a crib sleeps better in a room with walls, a door to close."

Peck had not considered that she might need a spare room for someone else one day, that she might again find herself room-turned and swollen, caretaking some other life within. Peck and Miguel stared at each other for a moment, and then Peck said, "No. They need to come down. Do you want some coffee? We can talk about the particulars?"

I read on about how Peck convinced Miguel to demolish all the walls without the requisite permits, for thirty percent more than it would cost if he did the work legally, telling Miguel that, if the work were discovered, she would make sure he was not blamed. Miguel said to Peck, "I've always known you were an outlaw," and when she no longer heard his work boots clumping down the internal stairs, she hoped that was still true, that she was still an outlaw. The work would take Miguel seven weekends, and when he returned on Saturday with his tools to begin, Peck cleared out, wondering where she might go, and surprised herself by spending the day, and the next day, and all the following weekends, in a nearby park, watching children at play. Then I came to this:

On her seventh Sunday in the park, Peck was on an empty park bench up against the filigreed iron fence, shaded by the thick leaves of a maple. In front of her was a boisterous mob of toddlers and older children on the jungle gyms, the swings, the slides, springing up and down on the plastic ponies, their shrill calls, punctuated cries, screams of delight or of ruin entrancing her.

Peck was startled when a stranger's hand came to rest on her forearm. The nails were tough under the cherry-blossom polish, the fingers wind-boughed. The hand belonged to one of the old wheelchair-bound women Peck often saw rolling into the park on her own, still strong, purposeful, alive. Even the runnels carved into her face had resolve. Peck had given her a name, *Sylvie*, and thought she belonged on a Hamptons estate, and not where she most likely lived, at the Home for the Aging, a squat and lifeless brick building a block over.

Sylvie was dressed in unsullied white. Her white canvas shoes resting on the wheelchair ledge were unsoiled. The white bun at her neck, a pearl in the sunshine. She raised her hand from Peck's arm and gestured around the park, as if she were a maestro, and the children her noisy orchestra.

"I've done all of that, dear, and I do not recommend it. I was lucky. Mine turned out exceptionally well, and so I have no complaint. But I maintain that it's not worth the sacrifice. Find love first and only. Keep it small and private. Tend to that love every day and every night. Do not complicate love with children and their endless demands.

"Come to the park to get your fill of their delight. But avoid the abyss. Even perfect children are all just mess and demand and dirty diapers, no matter their age. Sacrifice nothing for another. Give to yourself all that you would otherwise give to a child. Be your own child."

Her pink mouth turned up in a smile, white teeth too bright for her age, and then she engaged her chair and motored out of the park.

For an hour more Peck sat with her hands in her lap.

The scene was the same—children laughing, screaming, crying, ring flying, ladder climbing, pole sliding, skipping from here to there, holding hands, pushing one another down, slapping at will, sharing a treat—but the old woman in white had smudged what Peck had not been aware she was seeing, had not known she was hearing; her impulse to eliminate all the unnecessary walls in her home, the hand on her belly, the confusion of whiplashed anger and happy tears when she heard that Margo was pregnant again, the fact that her own baby, whoever she had turned out to be, wherever she might be living, was celebrating her eighteenth birthday that day.

In the park, the bright colors of the children's clothing, the timbre of their young voices, lowered and darkened.

I reread the sharp words Ashby placed in the mouth of the old woman—about children not being a worthy goal, not worth the trouble or the mess, not even in the long run when they were grown and still loving—and something stormed inside of me and broke loose.

When Peck returned home, her key crunched in the lock, and she stepped into a wide-open vacant womb, bright with the sun that entered the space even as it rounded to seven in the evening. She felt freed, lifted skyward, the unsettled questions about the course of her life left behind. She opened up every window and swayed in the hot drifting current.

On the table at Peck's front door was a package from her father. Inside, an oversized black leather book with *Traynor* embossed in decaying silver leaf that sprinkled over her hands. Devils Creek snow in the late days of a Manhattan August. She paged through old pictures of her father's siblings, their childhood faces not hinting at the angular people they would become. His parents and grandparents had a foot-planted firmness, though they stood tall and narrow on a dirt path, Traynor land rolling behind them. She had never met her father's family. They had all been buried deep in Peck's hometown, sepulchral limestone marking where they rest, sayings that summed them up, before her father married her mother. She wondered why her father had sent this album to her now, tied in somehow with the baby's birthday, but what it meant, what she was supposed to take from it, she did not know.

On the last page of the album, Peck looked at a photograph of her parents kissing, a courtship kiss given and received when life looked like clear sailing, which it mostly was for them. A small envelope was tucked behind their picture, her name dashed across the front in her father's hand, the flaps of his envelope taped down, his words jailed within.

In her outlaw past, Peck acted without thought, but these days, she bided her time, heard words unsaid in shivering silence, sensed what was empty in a choked heart. She could not read her father's words today, words that would remind her of what he wanted her to know: that she ought to try again, find the right man, have another child, remember from whence she came, no matter the name she tossed away, what she left behind, the daughter raised by others.

The clock on the stove read just past four. She plunged her home into darkness and got down to her skin. By the light of the fridge, she poured herself wine, then stood at the windows and stared out at the sky. Despite the unholy hour, the moon was still invested and lively.

She fit herself into the couch's furrow and tipped the wine into her mouth. She heard a ting when the glass rocked on the wood floor, then settled. Down six stories, out on the avenue, the traffic whooshed like the river back home when it was close to cresting its banks.

In the dark, Peck inspected her bared body, the moon's marbling sliding over her breasts and thighs. She imagined her home dark and convoluted again, the absent walls back in place, her nakedness hidden, the moon far away.

One day she would read her father's letter, as a message from the grave or a fortune freed from the cookie. She knew when she did, his hopes for her would no longer matter, his dreams like the walls she had once brought down, that she always would have chosen an outlaw life, would never regret the baby given away.

When I finished the story, Christina had been sleeping for a long time, despite the streetlamp throwing an orange glow through the uncovered window. She lay next to me, but gone was the young shark, replaced by the child Christina must once have been, curled into herself, her sharp knees looking tender and scraped, tucked against her full bouncy chest. I thought how it is only in sleep that our innocent selves are preserved. I felt myself old then, flat on my back, still as a corpse, on the familiar brink of the deep trench filled up with my old childhood anger at Ashby. When I saw I was still clutching the book, I threw it hard against the wall, heard it thud and fall to the floor. Christina did not even turn over.

I don't know how much time passed before I fully unraveled the story, realized that Peck Traynor was Ashby's fictional stand-in, that this was Ashby debating the pros and cons of motherhood, written years before I was born, written before my mother met my father.

When I was little, my mother said *I* had chosen *her*, and I had liked that notion, that somehow, even as a fetus, I already held all the power I would need in my life. And I had grown up being told how much my father wanted me. But right then, I realized never once had my mother said that *she* had wanted me, had waited impatiently for my arrival. And I thought, Why the fuck did I select a mother whose achievements yanked the dream I had been born with—to be a writer—out of my hands?

I looked at the facts: I was not the longed-for first child I had always imagined. I had ruptured Ashby's life, yoked her, prevented her from forging ahead with her own destiny, free of husband, of children, of chains that bound her to the earth. I was the curvature in her spine that spoke of tragedy, the way I had turned her days outward, the fullness of me stagnating her glorious imagination, crud on still water, mucking things up, blanketing that fire in her, goodbye to her work, to her serious future. And those Rare Baby stories of hers that she had read to me, now they made sense. She had written about unparented, unusual creatures because I had not been wanted, had not been rare, was just an average baby then, an average man now.

Still, I understood that she learned to love me, and I did feel that love, and she was good to me, encouraging what *I* had been born with: a love of reading and writing. She talked to me about the books I read, read my squirrel stories aloud. Our happiest times took place in that world we both preferred—of stories and writing, and long, long novels—a world where our being mother and son was irrelevant. It was never the umbilical cord that connected us, but our love of words, that's what we shared during all my growing-up years.

One could say, but you were young, Daniel, give the writing another go, and I did, in college, a million times. I still sometimes fool around here and there. I've got tons of crappy first and second and third paragraphs, some stories I even managed to write all the way through. But every time I try, begin to write something new, remember the power I felt when I was engaged that way as a child, I think of Ashby, of who she is, and my own pursuit seems insipid, fruitless, a tilting at windmills, and I scratch it all out, or hit *Delete, Delete, Delete.*

Christina exhaled a small snore and turned over, and I faced three truths—my mother had not wanted me; she had, unwittingly I'll admit, destroyed my faith in myself when it came to writing fiction; and I would never soar to the grand heights my mother, father, and brother had.

I watched the sky lighten, saw the sun sidle up, and the thought that came to me was a surprise. "An Outlaw Life" was setting me free, giving me the power to make my own fate, to follow, in some way, the tenets Peck Traynor subscribed to, what Ashby herself believed. I could simply discard entirely this useless version of myself.

I rose then and dressed, and even my clothes felt different on my body, seemed meant to be worn by someone else entirely. I said goodbye to Christina, to Carlos Wong, left behind my cardboard furniture, left a resignation note on the desk of a partner to whom I supposedly reported, but had never met, collected my thesaurus and novels, the spare suit, shirt, tie, socks, and underwear folded into a file drawer in my cubicle for deals that required I work through the night. I had banked nine months of substantial pay, pay for the birthing of my own new self. I hopped a plane with two vows in my fist: I would do whatever it took to make a name for myself, and never again would I read another Ashby story.

Recording #2

I see the humor now: that when I hopped that plane four years ago, with those vows clutched in my fist, I was heading *home*, to Rhome, to my mother, who had long ago written "Deep in the Valley," the story that decimated me at eleven, and "An Outlaw Life," the story I thought had set me free at twenty-two; and to my father who would describe the newest surgery he was devising, where his travels would take him next as he healed people's sight the world over; and to my brother who would regale me with the minutiae of his computer program responsible for his fucking success, and watch as he ran Solve=MC2 from the Manning homestead, bossing around his team, strutting like the big man he was, at only seventeen. But home I went, to the renovated house I had so rarely stayed in, and I conquered. Or rather, I stayed as briefly as I could, heeded my father's advice, and used the substantial earnings from my aborted venture capital career to buy an apartment in Washington, DC—aware that I might never again have such a bundle of cash. I moved in and took my Wharton undergrad degree, and the business acumen and glib patter I developed out in the Valley, and talked my way into *Think Inc.*, one of the country's most prestigious financial magazines. I applauded myself for the display of gumption that landed me the job. I could not make my own fortune, but I could write about those who did, and although writing magazine articles was not what I envisioned for myself as a child, I thought I would try to be happy. It was, after all, writing of a sort.

My first published article, "Gold Rush of the Future," was about a young, hard-charging chief executive I nicknamed Golden Boy. He reinvented prospecting for gold in the twenty-first century with an innovative financial mechanism called gold streaming—Wall Street panhandling by purchasing stock in Golden Boy's company, which funded the mining companies: a conglomerated modern-day version of the miners of yore. Golden Boy had the gift, had raised more than a billion dollars during his first swing through the venture capital markets, the hedge funds, and the investment banking firms. He said the accumulation of investment funds was intoxicating, but he most loved the weeks he spent hanging out with the actual prospectors who talked about the sheer exhilaration that accompanied the hunt for gold, the lust and greed that sweetened the entire enterprise. In one of our several telephone interviews, Golden Boy said, "It's an addiction that bit me hard in the ass, my friend, took a solid chunk from most of one cheek," and I felt the cold mine air on my skin, the weight of gold nuggets in my palms, the bump of a bulging wallet in my back pocket.

When I handed in the finished piece to my editors, I did not feel the elation I expected with the imminent publication of my first article, conceived by me, my first byline on top. I realized that Golden Boy reminded me of my brother—the certainty they each had in their synaptic goods, the novel business models they invented, each tearing up their worlds with their genius and their ability to make patent what so few of us can see. People like that always do reach the pinnacle, and both Golden Boy and my brother had. I was not of their ilk, and I realized there were far more people like me than like them, and that those of us who had no extraordinary skills with which to dream big might be very interested in the unconventional ways in which ordinary people catapulted themselves beyond their origins and into the financial stratosphere.

I made a decision then never to write again about venture capitalists, or about the CEOs of major companies, or about people born with a deep and abiding talent they had found and mined well; I held a grudge against anyone who achieved their success by virtue of incomparable intellect, stellar schooling, connections, or the injustice of winning a hereditary lottery. I searched for the average people, the ones who weren't prodigies, weren't members of Mensa, who lacked obvious genius and had no mastermind skills, whose futures had always been of absolutely no interest to anyone, including themselves; rags-to-riches of a sort. I set these stories within a larger milieu, that of the global financial markets, the trends in financing, and the like. It was the kind of column the magazine had never published before, and it became my specialty.

As a result, newly anointed adults, aware that people of all ages were hitting jackpots in unbelievable ways, found in my articles some kind of direction and inspiration. Because of me, *Think Inc.*'s readership soon expanded beyond its stodgy demographics of number-crunching wonks interested generally in how the financial world was going to react to what was coming down the pike, and specifically in the bare bones of how one thing or another would affect investments they had made or might want to make.

I was surprised to find that the actual writing of the articles did not intrigue me as much as interviewing those regular people, rooting through their lives at will, uncovering their tawdry secrets, although never did I expose my subjects' past frailties in print. The secrets belonging to those I wrote about had no personal effect on me, other than empathy, and I found something comforting in the tales of uninspired lives that once ran amok; that even for those who had screwed up terribly there could be magical redemption, and a redemption that included monetary riches. There was, for instance, the rotund and smiling pie maker, sweet as sugar, who took his grandmother's recipe and built an empire of pies. What he hid away was his long prison stint in his youth, twelve years for aggravated assault with a deadly weapon, a juvenile record long sealed, which I got my hands on. In confidence, he told me that dreaming of his grandmother's kitchen, remembering how he helped her make her pies, his hands in the dough, the smell of cherry and lemon and peach baking, had kept him alive, the happy thing he thought about when he was staring at walls and bars, fending off even tougher kids in the prison yard, telling himself that with such delicious things in the world he ought to get his head on straight, come out of prison with his eyes on that gustatory prize. And there were the twins I wrote about—two eight-year-old girls with freckles and pigtails who designed bracelets of neon beads that girls in every first-world country wanted. Their marketing man was their father, whose idea was to donate the first monies received to third-world countries, putting the bracelets on par with other kinds of trinkets that had altruistic appeal to shoppers. The father had lost his job as head of marketing at a multinational when his cocaine and prostitute habits were discovered. Although he was not indicted, did no time in jail, he was summarily fired, divorced, and ruthlessly kept from his children. Destitute and desperate, he returned to his parents' heartland farm, a place he had scrabbled hard to get out of, going cold turkey with the drugs, turning himself into a celibate, finding some peace amidst the squealing pigs. When I wrote about the girls and their beads, the company was a nonprofit; now it's for-profit, and has expanded into all kinds of unisex kid-centric jewelry, and the father, he built a house near his parents' farm, runs the $500 million business from there, only goes into town for groceries and to fill up his old Ford truck.

My point is: I became alert to the secrets all people keep, and when I sensed I was in the presence of a secret, I had to explore it. That is what happened on a June summer weekend sixteen months ago, when I was home for a rare weekend visit in Rhome. It was still early on Sunday, and my father was already at the hospital when I went in search of my mother, and found her in the glen, standing at the lip of the pool, ready to dive in and swim her hour of laps. "Can I borrow your car?" I asked. I wanted to take a memorial drive around Rhome. "Of course, love. Keys are in the bowl. Have fun," she said.

And then I was in the garage, staring at boxes I had never seen before, six large brown boxes in a row, every single one marked *Joan Ashby* in big black letters.

Of course, I knew it was an invasion of her privacy to root around in her things, but my work had inured me to such breaches. The sixth box was the one most securely taped up, and that was the deciding factor, how I knew where to start. I pulled back the tape carefully, opened the flaps, and found myself looking through hundreds of photographs of people I did not recognize. I dug deeper, and pulled out dozens of colored folders, then a huge stack of orange folders marked *Rare Baby Story* with titles next to each one. And then, when I reached the bottom, I came upon an enormous manuscript. I gripped it tight and pulled it free.

The title page read *Words of New Beginnings*. I was sure I was holding another collection of her stories, and I was curious why it wasn't bound and in bookstores, furthering her remarkable reputation. But when I flipped through it, I realized it was a novel, that Joan Ashby had written a novel she finished long ago, on August 10, 2007, precisely, according to the handwritten notation on its title page, and I wondered if the book had been at the bottom of that box ever since, so many years out of sight, out of mind.

Though it changes nothing, I did not read a single word then, but I was overwhelmed by my discovery, gripped by an uncontrollable need to possess it, a desire, perhaps, to punish my mother for having such an enormous secret, for being imbued with genius and wasting it.

I put the manuscript on the front seat of her car, then replaced everything else in the box, exactly as it had been, smoothed the tape back down, hit the garage door opener, and raced down the hill into Rhome, where I paid a small fortune to have a copy run off. In forty-five minutes, I was back at the house, the original manuscript returned to its resting place at the bottom of that sixth *Ashby* box, the old strips of tape replaced with new, the copy in my overnight bag, the overnight bag pushed under the bed in my room, and when I reached the glen, my mother was still swimming.

She rose up out of the water with a happy, brilliant smile, and I searched inside of myself for the guilt I thought I should feel, but didn't. What I felt was a rage I couldn't explain, and the spectacular falsity of my own responding smile. I remember thinking that any minute she would pick up on the strange emanations I had to be sending out, a regular skill of hers, but she didn't.

"I'll dry off and make us some fresh coffee," is what she said to me, "and we can have one of our great chats." I nodded and said, "Terrific."

The subjects of my articles had taught me that there is always a price that must be paid for doing wrong. And I had done wrong: by keeping my mouth shut when I uncovered Ashby's secret, by making a copy of that unpublished novel for myself, knowing that I intended to spirit her secret work away with me when I left Rhome, and so I set my own price, the harshest penance I could think of to cause myself the most harm: reading Ashby's collections from cover to cover.

Later that afternoon, I asked if I could read her books, and when I saw her hesitate, I wanted to say, *Hey, Mom, I already read "Deep in the Valley," which fucked my own dreams entirely, and "An Outlaw Life," so I know you never wanted me, thanks very much, and I know what you've been hiding, so what's the deal with this internal debate*

I see you going through. But then she nodded and led me back out into the garage, opened a different *Ashby* box, and handed over two thick, hardcover books.

That night, on the train back to DC, with her purloined secret and her published collections packed in my duffel, I imagined I was transporting explosives.

I walked into my stifling, airless apartment a few hours later, but I didn't throw open the windows until her secret manuscript was tucked away deep in a drawer, her collections on my nightstand. I didn't actually want them in my sight, but it seemed I owed her that—a display that would explicitly remind me of the wrong I had done.

While the summer lingered on, those two books sat like an over-whelming dare I did not want to face. I forced myself to take their stock each morning, and their voracious strength, so close to my head when I slept, spun a nightmare that made me leap from my bed like clockwork at three a.m., the metronome of *ashbyashbyashby* in my ears, my body slick, my heart thrashing, my mind flailing. I would turn on the light and sew together the images, each remembered frag-ment moving the narrative forward. Then I would retrace it all from the start, as if I could revise my subconscious. A boy, a mother, a two-by-four, a bloody head wound, a cover-up, and a grave. The same dream over and over again.

With autumn came the awful news that in the first quarter of the coming year, *Think Inc.* would be eliminating their traditional monthly print format and transitioning into new media. They wanted me to stay, to succeed in the new environment, but I had to be able to winnow my twenty thousand–word articles down to a few succinct Web-friendly paragraphs. The full text of my articles would be in the semiannual print versions of the magazine available to subscribers who paid for the golden upgrade, but it was mandatory I truncate my work for the new site. I tried desperately to cut and trim my articles, both published and pending, and considered new angles by which I could come at my subjects in an organic way that would work for the Web site, but I wrote long-form and detailed and my attempts at cogent compression were futile.

When I realized I would be remaindered, with some kind of

severance, I carefully considered how I could capitalize on the small name I had made for myself, my own mark on the world, even though that mark disappeared when people trashed an issue of the magazine that contained one of my articles.

I grappled with what to do and decided to write a book investigating the effects the global economy was having on worldwide entrepreneurship. I drafted a seventy-page proposal with clever chapter summaries and polished entertaining briefs about the people I would highlight. I thought: Who wouldn't want to read a book that detailed how the most unlikely among us discovered the idea that made them rich, the steps taken, the sacrifices made, the preposterous results obtained which changed their lives and sometimes the lives of the population at large? I was confident that with such a book under way, I would leave the magazine with a signed publishing contract, become a pundit regularly sought out for Sunday-morning talk shows. I imagined receiving the advance, working from home on the book, traveling to small towns to interview people, eventually being sent out on a book tour, giving speeches at business schools and universities, commanding high rates for my insights.

My editors, enthusiastic about my proposal, championed it to their publishing connections. Although the publishers liked my proposal, and could see a book like mine on their lists, I lacked, they said, brand recognition, notwithstanding that I worked for a national magazine, had a good reputation, and my pieces had won two commendations for journalistic excellence. The advice was to submit the proposal again when I had a larger social media platform that demonstrated I commanded an audience in the millions.

With my proposed future dead in my hands, I was overwhelmed by confusion, unable to figure things out, saw no clear next phase. I wondered then whether my bewilderment stemmed directly from my failure to absolve myself of my sin, not making good on my self-imposed penance to read those damn books.

I decided to spend the whole of the Columbus Day weekend inside, foregoing the moderate fall weather, reading those extolled Ashby collections from cover to cover, whose mere existence I had long despised. I tried convincing myself I would be setting out on a voyage like that undertaken by Christopher Columbus and his crew, but when I woke at dawn on Saturday of his holiday weekend, I felt nothing remotely akin to the Spaniard's yearning to discover the unknown world, his pride in sailing for honor and queen, his elation when the three ships were freed from their moorings. Instead, I felt violently ill, as if I had been seasick for days, and the open ocean ahead of me was no docile thing, but a mad navy sea with gargantuan whitecaps churning in a circle around the globe.

I picked up Ashby's debut collection, *Other Small Spaces,* and I remembered its heft of serious intention, how it felt in my hands when I was eleven. I had not paid any attention to the cover back then, but now I did.

It showed a large keyhole through which one could see a book-lined room. A person of uncertain gender sat in a high-backed chair, hands folded in supplication, face lifted. Its eyes were black dots that suddenly lengthened into rays that bore through the keyhole into mine. It was a daunting cover, and I thought that might be the point: that reading Ashby's work required fearlessness and readers ought to be ready.

I was too wound up to engage the book as I would otherwise normally do—author photo, dedication, acknowledgments, table of contents, if there was one. I felt twitchy paging forward to the first story. Then I was there, opening the door to my own nightmare, to the fears I thought I had put to rest. The title of the first story was "Killing Close Friends," and I was shaken completely. It took enormous will to continue on, to force myself to drop into my mother's world.

Slice the carotid arteries of the self-pleased, so certain their literary pursuits are bound for success; gut the recipients of fellowships and stipends and prizes and contracts; poison those with imitative talent, for they decimate the genuine; smash those who presume that inherited blood fates their work valuable: they are all cockroaches skittering across the shower tiles in the dead of night and ought to be smacked flat with a manuscript that sputtered at liftoff, the match meant for igniting, wet from tears.

Those were Evan's thoughts. The expected *Congratulations!*—or any sentiment of faked delight in Karen's good fortune—was lodged deep in her pharynx, the critical organ for vocalization, digestion, and respiration. Not only could Evan not talk, she felt nauseated, bilious, and vomitous, and she could not breathe. She could not draw a full breath into her lungs, not even a repulsive *cleansing breath*, as Karen said to her now, aflutter, "Take a cleansing breath! I think it's a panic attack, Evan."

The boy's name bestowed upon Evan was of various origins, but she preferred the Celtic translation: *young warrior.* She felt like a warrior, even as she stood sick of stomach, of lungs, of heart, of head, in the kitchen of the apartment she and Karen have shared since college and through their graduate school program nearing its end. She is ready to pick up the long sharp knife Karen was just using to slice into a loaf of French bread, but has put down, to retrieve for her best friend a paper bag into which Evan can inhale and exhale.

Karen paws the kitchen cabinets, rifles through the pantry, searching and searching, while she never stops talking. "You know a panic attack just feels like you can't breathe. But it's not lack of oxygen at all. It's the carbon dioxide concentration in your blood decreasing below the normal level because you're expelling more CO_2 than your body— Oh, here's a bag—"

Karen peels wide the mouth of the brown lunch sack and blows into it, filling it with an abundance of her mediocre air, and hands it to Evan, who starts to fill and conflate the bag herself, her own air livid and wrathful.

"So, as your blood's pH value's been rising," Karen says, "the blood vessels to your brain are constricting. And that means oxygen for your nervous system can't get through."

That she, Evan, is experiencing her first-ever panic attack; that Karen labels her own such attacks as *anxiety* attacks when *the well is dry* and Evan rubs her best friend's hands to arrest the spasms that crick her fingers into claws; that when Karen says, "My well is dry," she means that she and Evan have a deadline for workshop and Karen is without a story to wend and she wants Evan to stop her own work, to open both a bottle of wine and the deep trove of Evan's memories, and give Karen something to drink and something she can use; that Evan always does tap into her magnanimous nature and willingly hands over those true stories at which Karen grinds away until she has a few pages to pass among their fellow writers-in-training who, inevitably, discuss Karen's work too nicely, giving Karen license to monkey around for another day or two before she gives up, turns to Evan again, and claims that her well is, as ever, dry; that Karen, the progeny of writers—a paternal award-winner and a maternal best seller—has caused Evan's first-ever panic attack by waving through the air what Karen says is a contract for her first published collection—*Nearly True* by Karen Sweet—twelve never-workshopped stories, every one of which originated with Evan when Karen's *well was dry*, and who says now to Evan, "You don't mind, do you? After all, I did *write* the stories."

Evan holds the bag to her mouth, breathes in and breathes out, sees flashes of her past, like slides shown for an instant on a white wall in a black room:

The babysitter on her bed, removing Evan's little-girl pajamas, unicorns racing down her legs, across her flat chest, fingers thick as sausages pushed way in, "Ride, little girl, ride. Wait till you see what's next."

Her mother pulling from the garbage half-eaten slices of pizza, rats big as cats leaping out and sinking their fangs into her dirty arm.

Jethro, five men removed from the father she never knew, chasing after her with a belt in his hand, she bouncing off the walls, beaten for saying, "What?" when he asked her a question.

She was named Evan for a reason, every single year of her life proved that again and again, and now another betrayal, by someone she has trusted, a friend she has clung to, for whom she finally opened the trapdoor to her heart. Her life splayed out for all to read under another's name. She wants to pick up the saw-toothed knife and kill Karen. God, if she could catch her breath, Evan would be brave enough to do just that.

Fuck, I thought, furious to be so instantly hooked, wanting to know more about Evan's gruesome memories, her life stories stolen by Karen, the publishing contract Karen is waving around, whether Evan will follow through with her intention when her panic attack passes. I knew that feeling this way was unfair and unwarranted, but whenever I had spared the briefest glance at this book in my hands, and at the other one on my nightstand, I hoped to sigh in relief when at last I began to read. There was no sigh as I lay in my bed, light-headed and suffocating, the dread returning then, viperish and oily, snaking through me. I had to look away from the page, away from Ashby's words that left me exposed, naked, crushed once again.

Then I was in my bathroom, hands leaving sweaty palm prints on the mirror, eyes filled with tears because I knew I had wasted years of my life, had fooled myself into thinking I was fine with where I was in the world. The opening paragraphs of "Killing Close Friends" unnerved me, describing an instant hatred that felt natural and familiar. Faced with enormous betrayal, Evan wanted to slice, gut, poison, and smash this former best friend of hers. I could imagine her gnawing on Karen's bones; an articulation of my own desires back when I was young, when I learned who my mother really was. And I felt mildly insane, fleetingly believing the preposterous—that Ashby had written this story with prophetic knowledge that, far in the future, she would hand over her books and I would read this story and feel certain that it contained a message specifically for me, her son. And I wondered—was I the male version of an Evan or a Karen?

I stood in front of the mirror until my eyes refocused and I saw that my shoulders were hunched up to my ears, my jaw slack.

Slack-jawed, is what I thought, *slack, shocked, shell-shocked.*

The systems of my body chugged back to sudden life, an engine turning over, the tears drying up, the dullness in my eyes receding, a weak light emanating from them once again.

I was exhausted and I had been up for only an hour.

When I returned to my bedroom, I turned the book over and looked at the author's photograph. Even in black and white, she was luminous. Cheekbones high and sharp. Thick lashes framing eyes I knew to be a blistering blue, though they were nearly black in the picture. She was wearing the same special gaze she often wrapped me up in when I was young, our silent mode of communication. Her full mouth was shiny, but I couldn't tell whether she was wearing some heart-dissecting shade.

I looked away from her face and thought I should have listened to her when she suggested I keep writing about the squirrel, and later, when she tried to steer me away from the hard-nosed business world I had mistakenly chosen for myself. Had I not felt toward her an early animosity, a belief that she had been disloyal to me, had committed a perfidy by being a writer herself, and a famed one at that, I might not have refuted and refused. Sitting on my bed, I was sure right then I did not blame her for the dissatisfaction I felt with my life, with the fact that my future was a complete unknown.

I pulled up the blinds, expecting to see a late Indian-summer sky, like the one the day before, but something had changed overnight. The sky was the color of cement, of decay, of the bars of prison cells, and high-speed weather was massing rapidly right outside of my window.

It had remained warm into October, but now I noticed that the gardens in front of the quaint town houses and the refurbished row houses across the street had lost their pep, and the trees that bordered the sidewalk were fraying, their tight leafy summer canopies eaten away. A plinking of light rain all at once, and I interpreted in those slanted drops a harbinger. Rationally, I knew Ashby could not control the natural world, but still I wondered if the escalating weather would end up on her side.

I walked out into the huge main room of my apartment, into my open kitchen, started the coffee, then stood at my wall of windows. Fifty tessellated panes giving onto a view of distant spires and near rooftops, always a monumental draw for me, a way to calm or incite.

The light plinking rain converted into a steady drizzle. Water droplets were dancing on the windshields of the parked cars wedged in, puddling on the sidewalk and road.

I watched a plump girl slowly jog by down below, brushing water from her face. Even three stories up, I could see her ass cheeks crashing beneath her pink sweatpants, as if she had Columbus's ships lashed together in there, and I saw the ship of my own life cruelly buffeted by a storming sea. At the corner, she slowed, tugged her underwear free from her crack, then sped back up. She was trying to better herself, and what was I doing? It was a short drop to the pavement, but if a person flung himself just right, the fall could inflict rupturing damage, broken bones, a smashed skull.

I turned away, filled my cup with hot coffee, and returned to my bed, to resume the weighty obligation to myself that I did not want to be fulfilling.

"Killing Close Friends" was a locomotive on tracks with switch-backs I had not anticipated.

"What are you going to do with that knife, Evan? Kill me? Oh, come on, put it down. You were never going to turn the experiences of your life into stories. You said, 'It would be too hard to put all that pain down on paper,' so why let that pain go to waste, if someone else can gain from it. It's the way of the world, the weak and the strong, those who are battered down, those who do the battering. I'm sorry, but I didn't make things as they are."

The knife was heavy in Evan's hand, its jagged teeth gleaming under the kitchen light. She could imagine herself sinking it deep into Karen's belly, one thrust in, then tearing straight up, through her lungs, her heart, into her throat, silencing her forever. She wanted to see Karen's bright eyes dead, rolled back in her head, limbs twitching, then nothing at all. She wouldn't get away with it, she knew that, the trod-upon never do rise up, the meek never do inherit the Earth. But at least she would have removed one of the monsters roaming the world making it unsafe for the rest.

Evan raised her arm, saw herself as a character in a low-budget horror flick, then put the knife down on the counter and turned away. She could not look at Karen, did not want to see her face anymore. She would tell Karen what she thought of her, then pack up and move out. Someone from workshop would give her their couch for a night or two.

"Good girl," Karen said, and Evan ignored her, pressed her hand onto the French bread, felt the crust snap sharply.

"I can't believe—" Evan began to say, and then it didn't matter. She looked down at her side, at the blade that was through her sweater, her T-shirt, deep inside her flesh, at Karen's hand on the hilt, at Karen's arm, taut with strength, holding the knife steady, pushing in and in and in, at Karen's eyes, so close to Evan's own face, the thrill she saw in them, pupils all dilated, her nose quivering with excitement, her mouth moving, saying words, saying, "Just give in. There's no coming back from this. It will be better wherever you're going," and then Karen jacked the knife upwards and Evan shut her eyes, thought of her name,

THE RESURRECTION OF JOAN ASHBY 273

wondered for a split second if she would finally end up a young warrior in that other world, felt her legs give way, then she was gone.

I thought: *She is a ruthless motherfucker,* unsure whether I was referring to Karen Sweet, or to Ashby. It took me a long time to release my trapped breath while I tried thinking about nothing at all. An empty mind, I decided, was not always a terrible thing.

Then I began "Nina Disappeared."

John met Nina in the Literary Fiction section of their neighborhood bookstore. He saw her neck first, slim as a reed, her head lowered over a book, her hair a golden waterfall. When she straightened and turned, her face dislocated his heart. Pale as an ivory cameo.

He thought of rosebuds when he took her mouth. She had sharp nipples that pricked. Decorative ears that heard words he did not say. She owned an impossibly tiny cunt in which he plunged to glory.

Before she entered his life, John had skated with women along the cool lake of misperception. He had believed that *falling in love* was meant for literal translation—an ecstatic high dive into despair, destruction, dissolution. Nina made him realize he had been all wrong; he felt now that love was a chord that retained a steady hum, not a cliff from which he needed to jump, a crash that left him, always, with bloody wounds. When they were naked in bed, John contemplated the unknowable cosmos, puzzles with missing pieces, trees that stayed evergreen, all of it reviving his belief in true and everlasting love. He said to her, "Move in with me," and she did.

During the first days of summer, before the heat blanched life down to white bone, Nina was swinging in the hammock John had strung up for her. Looking into the distance, she said, "You know, that forest makes me think of desiccated breadcrumbs and witches with surly red eyes." He looked, saw only old ash trees and shade, but nodded anyway.

When she said, "By fall, either we'll marry, which would be good for you, or I'll be dead, which would be bad for me," she didn't blink at all.

John was used to Nina's declamations, the charming way she spoke in either/or and true-or-false constructions, but he could see, in the way she draped a hand around her throat, that the idea she might be dead by the fall surprised her as much as it did him.

When the trees whispered, leaves a bonfire brew, the air still humid and enveloping, one of those two things was, indeed, true.

John went looking for Nina in early November. She said she was off to take her regular walk, but she had been gone for an hour, then two, then three, and John put on his shoes, and followed the path she always took. Down their street, then left, left, left, right, four long streets to the outdoor Olympic-size pool at the community center, where she touched the fence and turned back.

He walked slowly, feeling the autumnal breeze, expecting to see Nina in a second, her face lighting up when she spotted him, running like a gazelle to close the distance between them, wrapping her arms around him, sticking her tongue deep into his mouth.

He turned each corner, walked down each street, and she wasn't there with her smile.

He reached the pool and the gate was open, and he saw Nina's sparkly pink shoes atop the ten-meter diving board, upright at the very edge, as if a sudden wind had lifted her clear out of them.

Then he was running and climbing and crossing the springy plank, cradling her shoes to his chest. And it must have been a trick of the mind, because when he looked down, he saw only that the pool was drained of water.

Standing at the lip, he looked in, and saw what his mind had refused to take in: Nina's body on the chalky bottom.

His single thought: how did she manage to fall so neatly? Her summer dress was gathered nicely around her, her eyes were open and clear, her lips curled in a smile, the rhinestone tiara she put on that morning still perfectly poised on her head. A princess who went for a walk ended up in an infinite nap.

He entered from the shallow end, lifted her pale feet and slid her shoes back on—

It took me fifty minutes to read a story that raced from love to death. Every sentence I read made me wish, again, that I could write as Ashby wrote. I thought of how I had transported my Henry stories from Rhome to Silicon Valley, back to Rhome, and then here, and had never looked through any of them since I abandoned him when I was eleven.

On top of my desk, under the detritus of magazines and un-opened mail, were folders of new stories I tried writing after fleeing venture capital and before being hired by *Think Inc.* Not long before I went home to Rhome that pivotal June weekend and found my mother's secret, I had read a few paragraphs of one, the whole of another, half of a third, the beginnings of two more, thinking they mirrored my life: strong out of the gate, stuck in the rustic middle, failing to find an exit, as if I were nothing more than some cud-chewing cow too dumb to find the pasture with succulent, nourishing grass.

Then rain cracked through my thoughts. The sky was black. The trees were shuddering. Water was sheeting the street, jumping the gutters. Smoke coiling from the town house chimney across the way disappeared instantly into the clouds. Something dropped on the hardwood floor above my head. Some nights, most weekends, I heard something heavy being rolled, pushed, or pulled up there. That morning it sounded like a rolling pin flattening a dense object into submission. It ceased a few minutes later. I had no idea who, or if anyone, lived above me. I never heard footsteps, or traveling sounds, like water in the pipes, a hammer against a wall, television or music too loud. From the turn of the century, until gutted to the studs and refashioned into luxury apartments, this building had been a Catholic girls' school, and I wondered if one of the schoolgirl ghosts had stayed behind, the noises telling me when she was at some hurtful form of play.

One more story, I said to myself, then food, before I pulled out the bottle of good eighty proof. "Away from Home" opened like this:

Robbie thought she would love their Bora Bora honeymoon. She and Luke spent their days on the blinding white sand, their nights in a thatched hut surrounded by azure water, attained only by rowing out from the beach. The days were fine; she was happy in the light. But once Luke was asleep, there was a nightly whir of thousands of tiny wings in the air—she imagined protruding eyes, thin-as-thread legs searching for a way in through the net that hung like a crown over the bed. She could never tell whether she slept, but at sunrise she was strangely alert, listening to Luke's snores and searching for torn-away wings in the fine mesh, but she never found any.

In those solitary dawn hours, Robbie drank cups of strong coffee out on the balcony and watched the fish below in the sea. Childhood visits to an aquarium had terrified her; she had been certain the fish would drown. In this paradise, it disturbed her again, seeing their gills riffling open, their mouths gasping for the sky. She knew now, of course, that fish turned water into oxygen, but the process still struck her as painful.

In the late afternoons, Robbie put on her sunglasses, and Luke laced up his running shoes, and she watched his long legs splash through the white foam at the edge of the water until he was gone. Then she stared at their honeymoon hut out in the water and wondered why her need to live in small spaces had not translated to *that* small island space. The hut was no larger than her current home, than the other minute places she had inhabited.

Luke did not know her reasons for living what he called her nesting-doll life; she had never told him how she fled to New York as instinctively as fish convert one element into another, a critical oxygenation for the still-vital pieces of her that remained glued together, wanting only from that new city a small space in which to live, a place so small that people, love, and words could not be misplaced, would never disappear, where her secrets would always be within reach. She had not moved in with Luke before the wedding, and even while he toasted their future night after tropical night, she wondered if she ever would.

I looked away from the page and wondered whether Robbie's new husband would ever see beneath her surface, understand the mangled, tangled reasons for her anxious self-containment. And whether anyone had ever seen beneath mine.

My family members, with their magical brains that allowed them to fashion complex works of art, impossible surgeries, inventions spun out of gossamer thoughts, could not fathom how I felt, knowing I was not one of the lucky ones, deprived of supernatural gifts to springboard me into their realm of the rarefied, missing the resplendent power to make something lasting. I am certain they never sensed my pain, the jealousy that left tracks across my heart, that scalded the blood in my veins. It is a long-borne burden, knowing what you lack, and I knew what I lacked. My wrath toward them, and toward all those who soared high in their lives and accomplished the unbelievable by creating eternal works, was boundless. And I could not fathom how anyone could put their gifts in a box and walk away. My father was finding new interests, my mother had never published anything after her two collections, my brother was talking about selling his company, while my future was at a standstill, my book proposal dead. Where, I thought, was the lost and found for discarded genius, from which I could select what I desperately wanted and needed?

I swam back into "Away from Home" and learned where Robbie's obsession about living in small spaces had come from. In the house in which she had grown up, there were too many rooms where one could get lost, where a sickened, skeletal mother could die alone in an enormous bed at the end of a long, long hall, and a sister, grieving and despondent at twenty, could find a gun inside an old shoebox inside a rarely used closet and do away with herself, hours passing before anyone noticed she was missing, found only when her blood had turned to sheets of red ice. I read the last paragraphs:

They are tired from the long post-honeymoon flight, and Luke finally agrees to sleep at Robbie's place, saying, "Now that we're married, we're going to combine our lives, clothes, books, and all the rest of our crap, right?" and she closes her eyes to memorize the sweep of his mouth.

When he stirs at dawn, Robbie wills her breath shallow and steady, her eyelids still, her forehead smooth and unwrinkled. He is out of bed quickly, as always, except when they were in Bora Bora. Yellow light from the bathroom cuts the darkness, shower steam blues the air. Robbie rolls over into the imprint Luke left behind, wishing she possessed the exquisite ability of fish to transform the elements in their domain, but she doesn't. She has been too damaged for years. She will kick him out and not return his calls, will sign the divorce papers when they come, will send them back with a note that reads: *Love cannot save a single trapped soul.*

Single trapped souls. I knew I was one of them, and then I was thinking about transformation, about how Ashby's stories were taking up residence inside of me, her fictional worlds somehow truer than real life, a hurricane that turned the familiar upside down in a way that made such sense to me. If I could get my bearings, perhaps there existed a different universe in which I, too, could truly be myself. For months, the physicality of my mother's collections had exceeded their actual dimensions in my life. I had concentrated on my interviews, on drafts of new articles, on the state of my professional life, on the state of the world, taking up with women I knew I would not love, anything to ignore Ashby's work. But when I left my bed, with her book in my hand, I was identifying the myriad themes in *Other Small Spaces*, no longer keeping anything at bay.

I put the book on the coffee table and took stock of my fridge— an unopened half-and-half, jars of peanut butter and jalapeno olives, a stick of picked-at butter, a bent package of moldy bacon, the heel of a loaf of wheat bread, an old container of cream cheese. Not a single breakfast ingredient for a man weighted down by a hard penance.

In my menu drawer was a flyer from a place I'd never tried, called Lucky Star. A deeply cadenced voice answered the phone and took my order, and twenty minutes later, the delivery boy was at my door. His hair was black and brush-cut, his eyes big and round, and his clothes—pressed jeans that sat high on his waist and ended a few inches above his black-laced shoes, his socks bleached white, a collared shirt under a bright-red windbreaker with *Lucky Star* stamped off-kilter across the heart—were too neat for him to have been born here.

When he said, "Hello, sir," I heard the singsong Indian uplift to his words.

"I have performed a magical feat, sir. Nestled your late breakfast or early lunch under my jacket so as to deliver it in perfect condition. Despite what is happening to the world."

I apologized for asking for delivery in such rotten weather. "No problem at all, sir," and he unzipped his windbreaker and handed me a bag that was hot and dry. I paid and then tried to hand him an extra five, but he shook his said. "My father would say that amount is dearly inappropriate. He would say two dollars is sufficient."

I said, "Please take it. It's really awful out there."

He looked at me carefully, then said, "Very true, sir. I will no longer fight you." He pocketed the tip and leaned over the transom, looked around slowly, as if he had no other place to be. "Very nice home, sir. It is warm, yes, and out of the cold and rain. I find it very comforting."

I turned and looked into the immense open space of my apartment, the great room, as the real estate agent had called it when I bought the place, that lately deflated me, made me feel I was back in a shapeless adolescence, without hope for a sharply delineated future.

Light blue walls. Twin blue couches facing each other across the mirrored coffee table reflecting the dark clouds outside. My favorite blue armchair aimed at the far wall, where a red antique Chinese cabinet hid stereo, speakers, and wiring. The flat-screen television above it, flanked by large art photographs, each three feet by two feet, of a busy Istanbul marketplace, and Egyptian pyramids under a hazy, thin white moon, though I could not recall how I came to have those photographs. My desk near the front door, a long slab of wood, my laptop flat as an old vinyl record, a folder containing my rejected book proposal, folders with my failed stories, my tall shelves along the adjacent short wall, the books looking like crammed teeth, the recessed ceiling lights on low, the two standing lamps at either end of the room, the open-plan kitchen, and that entire wall of windows.

"Thanks," I finally said.

"Yes. Very nicely furnished. I feel like I am in the sea. Comforting though, is the word that first comes to mind. A place for the making of a good life, I think."

Such a different assessment from my own, and before I could think of a response, he pointed to *Other Small Spaces* on the coffee table.

"And you are reading, which is good for the brain and the soul. I will not disturb you further, except for you to know this. My name is Kartar. Call me anytime. We always deliver."

"I will," I said.

Kartar smiled and his teeth, so straight and white, looked more adult than the rest of him. I thought he was sixteen or seventeen, still in high school, although he had none of the traits of the native-born, no teenage swagger or hostile vocabulary. His clothing and his calm, rhythmic walk down the hallway to the elevator suggested that he ignored whatever his classmates might have tried to teach him, that he was continuing to walk the path intended for him at birth.

When the elevator door closed, I left the Lucky Star bag on the counter and looked down from the windows. Double-parked on the car-dense street was a little red car with a short man standing valetlike at the passenger door. His stomach, shoulders, and face enveloped by an enormous red umbrella also stamped *Lucky Star*. I could read it clearly from where I stood. I saw Kartar run down the walkway, leap the flowing gutters, throw himself inside. The short man slammed Kartar's door, ran around to the other side, javelined the umbrella into the backseat, and jumped behind the wheel. The engine revved and the car shot forward, skidding on the slick pavement, then correcting. I heard two toots of the horn as the car turned the corner.

I returned to the kitchen, unpacked the containers, flattened the bag, and wrote *Kartar* across the front because he was a memorable kid and I might call Lucky Star in the future.

I sat at the counter, turned on the Weather Channel, and ate the omelet and the strips of crispy bacon, which left behind a pleasant aroma. I perked up when the newscaster said, "Hey, Susanna, it's Saturday, Columbus Day weekend. Most of the country has temperate weather, sunshine, turning leaves, but that's not true here in our nation's capital, so what can you tell us?"

Susanna stood in front of a color-coded map of America. I always liked watching her plushy pink lips, her pointed feline tongue that darted out from behind her blinding smile, her round breasts snuggled so tight beneath her conservative red or navy sweater.

"Well, Jed, there's light precipitation in the surrounding suburbs, but we're facing a rare weather phenomenon, an unprecedented storm, previously untracked, that has taken up residence over the capital. Our meteorologists are hard at work analyzing it, but expect severe atmospheric disturbances, lightning, dangerous gusts, rain, hail, you name it. All you capital folks, you're going to be underwater soon. Stay home, stay dry, and if you have to go out, just a warning, galoshes and umbrellas won't cut it. Hope you're all good swimmers."

So, I thought, my mother could actually alter the weather. I cleaned up after myself, figured noon was a good time for a large scotch, and spread out on a couch with the book open on my chest, the drink at hand. Rain battered away at the thick glass, groans rose from the old casements when the thunder cracked. Despite what Weather Channel Susanna had said, I was sure the rain would stop the next day, and the sun would shine fast, and it seemed to me then that the weather was like life, how it unfolded was impossible to predict. I turned to the next story in Ashby's first collection, titled "Glorious Summer," and buckled back down.

Esme sits quietly on the porch of the summer cottage and listens to the words her heart would say if it could speak. On Friday evenings, when Howard returns for the weekends, says, "Hi all my lovelies. What's new?" Esme's heart betrays her, goes silent when it should scream.

The girls are down at the lake, Howard is due around seven, and this summer feels like all their previous summers, except now that Aster is nearly eight and Orlanna, at the end of July, will turn thirteen, they have found a common ground, a renewed sororal language.

Otherwise nothing is different since Howard said, "Changes," at the end of last summer. Rather, nothing yet has been altered. When this summer ends, the life Esme and Howard built over these last fifteen years will no longer exist, except in pictures and memories. Since the end of last summer, Howard has said, "I'm sorry. I never imagined I would want this. It has nothing to do with my love for you." For nearly a year, he has tried to expand, explain, rationalize, and summarize his undefined need to tear apart their world, but she can't make sense of any of it.

Last summer, the sky dazzled blue, pink wisteria bloomed, butterflies and bees darted among the flowers, and on weekends, the family raced in the lake, played Shark near the sandbar where the silt dropped into the deep, Howard so convincing that both girls yelled and flailed, headed straight for Esme, her open arms ready to save them. Lunches and dinners on the shore. Grand dinners at the cottage when Howard grilled steaks and uncorked bottles of thick red wine. There were nights when they finished two bottles just the two of them, and the next morning yelled to the girls, "Feed yourselves breakfast and go down to the lake. We'll meet you there later," and then they would screw in that unclear hungover way for hours. In early August, they had repainted the cottage. When the house was no longer a sad beige, but a sprightly light green, they debated whether the shade would hold up during the long pitiless winters.

Last summer, the day after Labor Day, they had returned to Buffalo, and the next morning began preparing for the new school year. The girls tried on their old school uniforms, prancing proudly in their cotton underwear in Orlanna's room. Aster's arms had become muscular from paddling after Esme when she swam her laps in the lake. And Orlanna had budding mounds she showed off. When Esme had sprouted at fourteen, a full year and a half older than Orlanna, it had been awkwardness and humiliation, a disgust with the way her mother's "friends" would comment about what was suddenly beneath Esme's blouses. When the girls were dressed again in their ratty summer shorts and T-shirts stained from dripping Bomb-Pops, they had helped Esme stow away what no longer fit and planned the next day's itinerary—uniform shop, sporting-goods store, dance shop, the Paper Barn out on the highway for school supplies. Later, the girls had washed faces, brushed teeth, donned nightgowns, read books, and bookmarked their places without their pre-summer bickering. Aster still reached for Esme, nuzzling against her mother's cheek, calling out, "Mommy, I love you," when Esme turned off the lamp. But Orlanna had yielded too, slinging her arms around Esme's neck and kissing her back. Turning twelve had inexplicably returned Orlanna to her cuddlier self, cooing into Esme's neck, saying, "I love you so much, Mommy." Esme had known this version of her older daughter would soon disappear in the push-pull of the next years, but right then, when the future was completely irrelevant, Esme had thanked the stars up in the sky that held off the coming world. It had been a glorious summer at the lake and her children loved their mother still. Everything was as imperfectly perfect as she could ever want.

The hallway was filled with family pictures: the promise of Howard's handsomeness becoming less theoretical; her own beauty settling over her cheekbones, illuminating her skin; the girls as smiling infants in paddle wings, then toddlers in sundresses. First-day-of-school pictures. Soccer pictures in which Aster looked ferocious, even at five. Orlanna's body lengthening over yearly ballet recitals. Pictures from the newly finished summer would end up on the walls: Howard and the girls splashing in the lake; Orlanna's birthday party dinner on the lawn, the candelabra flickering in the dark as if they had thrown a party for a noble Russian child; the homeless cat Aster named Friendless licking a plate of frosting with Aster's smile lighting up in the flash; she and Howard on their fourteenth wedding anniversary, underneath the flowering arch, posing for the girls who traded the camera back and forth. Howard had bent down to kiss her while the girls called out, "Smile now!" and Howard had whispered in her ear, "My bride still."

During the final weekends at the lake, their usual intimacy had fallen away. Esme had not taken the initiative, and Howard had been unfocused, elsewhere, and when they arrived back home, they had been exhausted from packing and driving and unpacking and feeding hungry, tired children. It was time they picked up where they had left off. In their bedroom, she had found Howard at the window, staring into their backyard, still dressed. She stopped in her tracks and heard him say, "It has absolutely nothing to do with you, but I can't be married anymore."

I heard the gunning rain over Howard's words. Words that must have struck Esme like bullets, the shrapnel sundering her heart, cracking open their life, revealing layers of unstable sediment, and yet, to me, his words evidenced a strength of character. He didn't say he had fallen in love with someone else, or discovered he was dying, or gay, only that he couldn't be married anymore. I thought it brave to cease living a particular life, to slam the brakes on the known, to want something else in its place. How strong his need must have been to so drastically change course. Ashby had not written him as a man eager to do damage, and I understood that as something Ashby herself might believe in—that there was a purity in searching for one's true life, no matter what might need discarding, the explicit, if unintentional, pain inflicted on others by such an act. Howard was much older than me, a father to two young girls, and still he was going to do what his spirit required.

I could change course without answering to anyone, without altering anyone's expectations, there was no one relying on me, and the thought that I could follow Howard's lead heated me up from the inside out. I rose from the couch and opened one of the vertical panes. Cold windy air rushed through the room and cleared out the warmth. Raindrops hit my face.

Howard had said to Esme he never imagined *this,* and I wondered how he had found the vitality hiding inside of him to create the life he needed to be living.

I needed some sign of my own internal life force and I dropped to the floor, did five push-ups, did five more, remembered when I could do fifty, did do fifty every morning. I hoisted myself back up and the couch sunk under my sudden weight. I picked up the book and continued on to the last page of the story.

On a snowy afternoon when they were dating, Howard had said to Esme, "Read me the names from the phone book in that mellifluous voice of yours." She found the directory in his kitchen and stretched her long legs out on his couch. "Abbott, Abelard, Acer," she began. At the start of the B's, Howard said, "If you're willing, I'd like to give you mine."

Now she avoids using the last name he gave her during their intimate wedding, no longer calls him Howard. To say either aloud makes her feel she has agreed to his decision. He calls her *love, darling, sweetheart* on the summer weekends, endearments devoid of all meaning, and when he says *Esme,* she can't imagine who that might be. When he plays games with their girls in the lake, she recoils from the knowledge that this is the last of *us, we, our family.*

In the cottage bedroom they share as if nothing has changed, she says, "Everything you do this summer will end up as memories the girls will examine microscopically. Filling in the blurred edges of what was happening precisely when those memories solidified into photographic truth." She says, "In the years to come, our daughters will try to work out the end of our marriage with the men who enter their lives, their bedrooms, their bodies."

"Please," Howard says, palming his ears. "Please don't paint any pictures." But she ignores him, wants him hurt. "To be clear, you are forming their suspicion of love, allowing the reality of being left and abandoned into their lives."

His eyes are blurry when he says, "There's no abandonment here. I'll always do right by the three of you. But I have to go before it's too late."

She's given up trying to figure out what he means. She does not know what would have kept them intact. She fears the coming search for something she will never discover. She hates that she will miss him forever.

The summer clouds skid through the sky and Esme knows that after Labor Day, Howard will not return home. He will go somewhere else, somewhere unknown. She wonders if he will ever appear for the girls' birthdays, or Thanksgiving, or Christmas, when wrapping paper and bows flower the carpet.

Sometimes against her wishes, her heart turns tender, and she nearly hopes Howard finds what he is after. She thinks it likely they may never see him again, that in order to move on he will need to forget he once had a hand in creating a world he didn't want. She thinks destiny will always win out over second-best, that it's an impossible burden on those left behind.

My own eyes were glassy when I reached the end. I thought Esme was right about destiny: how those compelled to find it will follow it anywhere. And I wondered how I might apply such a valorous philosophy myself. Howard's words made me understand that I no longer wanted to wish that I was living an alternative life, I wanted to be living it, no longer stuck in some state of suspension. I closed my eyes and tried to picture what my real life might look like, but all I saw were red spots behind my eyelids that crackled into fine lines that turned black. I thought then that I had never missed anyone as Esme knew she would miss Howard, and no one had ever missed me that way either. I asked myself—didn't I want to be missed? And then I asked myself the antecedent question—didn't I want to be loved? I believed that I did, but I did not grasp that to attain such, meant first finding a version of myself that I could love.

I gathered up my drink and *Other Small Spaces* and returned to my bedroom, where I stretched out with the book hanging over my head. More than once, I thought it looked like a guillotine.

In that way, I read "What We Learned," "Playing Detective," "The Good Italian Death," "The Fertilized House," "Orange Moon," "An Unexpected Conversion," and "Deep in the Valley," the one I first read when I was eleven.

It was eerie how I could relate to each story: the sugariness of childhood disappearing with a series of explosive frights; the youthful compulsion to discover the secrets of other family members, and the aftermath when those secrets are revealed; siblings provoking one another with dares that result in disaster; the adult children of a dead man left to contend with the mess he left behind in a life wrecked halfway through; even a woman's struggle with herself, with the tricks her mind plays, with the way her body betrays her, until she takes matters into her own hands. Every story resonated, opened the door to my early years, reminded me of my pointed hopes, forced me to consider where I was standing, how I had failed to leap big into the life I long desired, all those ancient and highly concentrated emotions flooding through me.

I was spent when I finished *Other Small Spaces.* From my bedroom windows, the streetlamps grinned whitely in the middle of rampant nature. The weather had dialed up again, the rain was approaching monsoon conditions, a tidal wave was washing over the street.

It was nearly eight, and I had planned to meet friends at a neighborhood bar, but I stood fixed in place, unable to go through the actions required to get myself cleaned up and dressed, thinking it would be base to introduce my regular life into what I was experiencing. The word *reverence* came to mind; what I thought I was feeling. I wanted to encourage the flow of such a rare emotion, feel its escalation within me, until there was an eruption, Pompeii, Vesuvius, Etna, the molten reverence prying open the constrictions that held me back, harnessed me, kept me chained up. I wanted to do what I rarely allowed myself to do: take a beat, revel in the unnatural sense of expansion that I had not felt since I created worlds for Henry the Squirrel to conquer with the words I plucked from the air, the only time in my life when I had truly shaped something from nothing.

I found a boxed pizza in the freezer, and turned on the oven, peeled the icy disc from its cardboard backing, thinking about shrinking spaces in which some of Ashby's characters felt most comfortable; her boy-named women; her recurring motif of water—in glasses, tubs, lakes, the ocean, an emptied pool; the search her characters undertook to find that juncture where they had turned away from happiness or watched as others stole it away. Her damaged people braved on, moved forward, recaptured their lives or started anew, took small steps or bigger leaps to find themselves in another state of being, even should that state be death. In her work, hopefulness accompanied even death. Evan and Karen, Nina and John, Robbie and Luke, Esme and Howard, Aster and Orlanna, the girl deep in the valley who knew she lived in a small box growing smaller still, and all the others I had read about, grew to know intimately, talked to me as I put away the bottle of scotch, happy for having not drunk more.

Ashby's stories were part of me by then, running through my veins, integrated into my soul, and my connection to her was so formidable that when I closed my eyes I *saw* myself writing those stories, felt that *Other Small Spaces* was mine.

I ate the pizza, and then I returned the book to my nightstand and looked at *Fictional Family Life* waiting to be read the next day. My heart felt large with possibility, and rumbling through me was something that nearly resembled joy. I expected that I would not easily glide into sleep, but I slept as deeply as if I were a child once again, certain of his own outstanding future.

Recording #3

On Sunday, I woke early, bursting with self-determination, and dropped to the floor. Five push-ups, then five more, then ten in one go; sweet pain I had forgotten about. Another ten and I stayed down for a while. Then, with disbelief, a final ten gutted out, barely, but I had proved something, whatever it was, to myself. The muscles in my arms seized, seismic quakes rolling up from brachialis to biceps to pectoralis major, triceps and deltoids quivering, guts rolling; tactile evidence of worthwhile accomplishment, the way my swim coaches had wanted us to feel after practices, the burn of exploit and achievement.

By five a.m., in clean sweatpants and sweatshirt, and with the coffee brewing, I surveyed *Fictional Family Life,* as I could not do the day before with Ashby's first collection.

The cover was divided into thirds. The top third was a blue-green globe with countries out of whack: Colombia next to Russia, Russia next to the Eastern Pacific Ocean, with the Galápagos Islands nearby, and Turkey on the other side.

The middle third was an intricate pen-and-ink drawing of a castle encircled by slender trees. There was grass and a pond and a white dog with faint yellow patches in the distance.

The bottom third was a street of identical suburban houses, one with a blue door.

I flipped the book over to another black and white photograph of Ashby. Gorgeous still, but less feral than she had been on the back of *Other Small Spaces.* A crown of curls, her smile full.

The dedication read: *Testify to the creation of lives and the requisite heroism in creating one's own,* and I felt something shift inside of me which I would not understand until much later.

The acknowledgment was enigmatic: *You know who you are—JA.* I did not know and wished I did.

The collection was also divided into three sections: "The Travels of Boys," "The Rx of Life," and "Familial Truths." Each contained six stories, the shortest ran thirty pages, the longest sixty.

With *Other Small Spaces,* I had moved past the trauma of

reading my mother's work, but on the verge of stepping forward into *Fictional Family Life,* I admit that had the sun been shining that second day of the holiday weekend, I might have interpreted it as a sign to limit my penance, to decide I had fulfilled it to the best of my ability. Instead, the rain was punishing, a testament to my mother's power.

I drank my coffee at the great-room windows and imagined the concrete squares of the sidewalk buckling, the street surrendering, the tar peeling back to reveal the shoring asphalt, sinkholes ripping open and caving in, my wall of windows shattering, submerging me right where I stood. I suddenly remembered my dream from the night before. It wasn't the old nightmare I was used to, death of a mother by a child wielding a two-by-four. Instead, I was wearing goggles and swimming through my neighborhood. The teenager who lives with his single father across the street was balanced on a yellow surfboard, paddling upstream, and tugging a drowning old couple behind him. I was treading water, looking up at the people gathered on rooftops digging for the courage to dive into the cascading surge. Someone yelled out, *Who's got the coordinate for Noah's ark?* and in the dream I had thought that figuring out the coordinates would be a good task for my squirrel.

I wondered for a moment what it might mean, but then I turned away from the outside world, refilled my cup, and assumed my position on the couch. It was time to begin.

I paged forward to the first section, "The Travels of Boys," and then to the first story, "Simon Tabor Introduces Himself."

When I was eleven, I believed I invented masturbation. Since then, in the early morning hours, I follow an exact routine: I briefly wake, pull my pud, traipse into my bathroom, turn the light on low, and pee. When I return, I push my dog back over to his side. Hercules snores a lot and sometimes I have to squeeze the wet black pad of his nose until he takes a big gulp and goes quiet. Then I crawl back onto my side of the bed and am gone, dreaming my fantastic lives. In these dreams, I am never who I am, a boy who lives a scrubbed truth, the subject of a medical file that reduces me to:

Patient Name: Simon Tabor
DOB: 1/28/1973
Hair/Eyes: Dark Brown/Dark Brown
Height/Weight: Short/Light
Diagnosis: Factor XI deficiency

In my dreams, I am ageless in a way that makes me understand that although I will soon be sixteen, I am not quite yet a man. In those other lives, I am called Deo or Abel or Icarus or Zed, and I speak Spanish, Russian, Turkish, and the watery babble of the great old tortoises. My chronology is all over the place: I live in this century or in the last, or in one way before that, raised exotically in Medellín, Moscow, Istanbul, or the Galápagos Islands. Depending on which dream I dream, my father is the former top lieutenant to the reigning drug lord of Medellín, or a fur-trapping Russian foreign minister, or a Turkish Ottoman pasha, or the man who discovered the Galápagos. My mothers are always tall and thin and beautiful and remind me of different kinds of full-blossomed flowers with tantalizing aromas. Whoever I may be in sleep, that boy wanders the globe and is intent on daring adventures.

To be clear, I know that I did not invent masturbation, a surprising fact I discovered when I read a book whose title currently escapes me, but in which the main character is so engaged. Regardless that human instinct guided me in a practice as old as the eons, the result left me unshakeable in my belief that I could invent, create, and manifest other realms, which has been a godsend, given the basic facts of my restricted life.

I felt excitement shoot through me: there would be stories wrapped inside other stories, wrapped inside other stories, wrapped inside other stories, an archaeological dig that would reveal new treasures as one dove deeper and deeper. I wondered what I would find at each level, what the beating center would look like.

The next story, "Simon Tabor Explains All," started like this:

I am diseased. I always do like saying it that way, as if I were a doctor in some West African village in a paint-peeled hospital curing some awful virus and have been inflicted after saving thousands with my amazing medical skills and ministrations, or as if I were patient zero who contracted some never-before-seen deadly flu, or, well, you understand what I'm doing here. But the truth is one false move can spell the end of my life. A splinter gone uncaught or deliberate tearings of the flesh. From the inconsequential to the major, nearly anything might set my blood free, and that is my disease. Everyone these days wants to be set free, and so do I, but not with my scarlet blood pooled around my cooling, bluing body.

Still unclear? Well, people today are sort of stupid, so I will spell it out: I am a hemophiliac. And I am the rarest kind, because not only isn't there any cure in general, no one has yet come up with a concentrate I could take, that would provide my body with what it's missing: factor XI. Apparently, XI is sneaky and wily, eluding the medical researchers. They have developed concentrates for hemophiliacs deficient in other factors, but if you're an XI, like me, you're out of luck. So I must guard my body's eight or so pints of blood that keep me alive, as one pinprick would cause spillage until I die. And until I have attained my own transcendence, I do not want that to happen.

Here are other basic facts of my life. I have been confined to my room since I was brought home from the hospital. Photographs show me as a handsome infant with almond-shaped eyes and a full head of black, corkscrewed curls. I had many visitors in those early days, as evidenced in Polaroids snapped by Judah, my father. I was two when pictures of people kissing and hugging me ceased to be recorded because the visitors had fallen away, something that still greatly disturbs my mother, Pearl, all these years later. What disturbs me more: there is not a single picture of me taking first steps out on the grass, or swinging on a swing at a park, or playing a game of dodgeball with neighborhood kids. Except for the trip from hospital to home, I have never been outside, and that has made my life simultaneously horrendous and incredible.

My domain is spacious and airy, the only room on the fourth floor of our enormous house, a thousand square feet belonging only to me. Up here, I experience firsthand all kinds of weather: the sun slanting across the room and catching at my eyes when I am reading on my bed; the heavenly feeling of being cloud-caught when the sky billows; the white noise of slapping rain, drops sometimes landing on my face when I am at my desk working away and a window is slightly ajar; fresh spring breezes that toss up from my mother's gardens the scent of sweet alyssum, and rustle my pillowcases, my notebooks, the journals to which I subscribe—artistic, political, and literary—and leave all over my room, stretched open like dancers in wide pliés to the pages I am currently reading.

A Turkish rug runs from my desk at the north-facing windows to the door, and the entire south wall is filled up with long shelves chock-full of books. Over the years, I have arranged my collection by publication date, which provided an interesting historical scope; alphabetically by authors' last names, which was dull; alphabetically by title, but so many titles began with *The* that I found it disconcerting to run my fingers over the spines and read *The, The, The, The, The, The,* which began to sound like *thugh*, as if I were a slow boy sounding out a difficult word. Currently my books are arranged in a crescendo of colors based on the covers. Books with red covers are grouped together, and books with blue covers are grouped together, and those with white covers, and green covers, and mustard-yellow covers, it goes on and on because books are wrapped up in more colors than you might realize. This visual coordination is very pleasing to my eye, and I put on the top shelf a violet gem of a book, slim and small, that glistens like a miniature stained-glass window behind which there might be some kind of treasure.

That violet book, called *The Summer of My Shimmerlessness,* is my favorite, although I have never read it. But as this summer might prove to be the summer of my own shimmerlessness, it is first on my list of "Books to Read." I turn sixteen soon, and from what my sisters have told me, and from what I have learned from reading, sixteen is monumental; one hill climbed, a new vista to see, and I want to climb that hill on my own two legs, see the vista that surrounds, breathe in fresh air. But, as always, in the wide-awake hours, I am forced to compress, down to nearly nothing, my expectations about what I desire.

Through the tall rectangular windows that reach the ceiling, I can gaze north, east, and west, and see rolling grass, soaring beeches and dwarfed willows, and the pond, lichen-encrusted, its water burred by the skin of algae the gardener forgets to scrape away, home to primordial koi. When Hercules is let out of my room to do his business, I hear him racing down the long winding staircase, his paws outstretched until he bangs through the doggy door. Then he is a blur of white fur against the blue-green grass, barking at the tall trees and small bushes, skidding to a stop to find me at the glass. He barks and barks, gets busy digging a hole, then trots off into the silvery beeches to find something: a lost pink ball, a desiccated beetle, a mouse fastened between his jaws and still squirming. Once he buries his find, he looks back up at me and bows, his little daily gift to his owner and master who loves him so much.

I have refused all the technological advances my parents offer up—television, phone, radio—and instead I rely on the written word and on my own imagination. Why should I torture myself by allowing in the outside world that I can never, will never, visit. I like imagining I live in very olden times, am Plato or Socrates or Marcus Aurelius, and have only my eyes to clue me in about what might be important and my brain to work through what I learn and observe. And I do intently observe from within my room all that unfolds out there, that spins in my head, that I experience in my dreams.

From my cloistered vantage point, I have spent many happy hours looking out over our oceanic backyard, to the speckled stone fence that surrounds our property, and then beyond, to a wide street with miniature houses, or at least that is how they appear to me. I have been told that those houses, much smaller than our palatial homestead, are of normal size, comfortable residences for families of four. I have never been able to assess that truth for myself, as, of course, I have never walked that street, or any street. My binoculars are well worn from all my investigating. Life out there is like watching a soap opera for the deaf. I track happiness sheltered between clasped hands, see the wounding anger that sparks from bodies when half of a couple stomps off and leaves the other behind. I have seen friendships dissolve with a pointed finger in a face, and love bloom with one glance. I am good at interpreting the source of pleasure, upset, the onset of veneration or lust. I notice emotions the way others notice the weather, which I have already said that I notice as well, along with birds. I am a birder par extraordinaire; all of my sightings written down in a notebook simply labled *Birds*.

However, when I stand at my windows with my binoculars pressed to my eyes and the street is empty, and remains empty for hours and hours, it is then I realize I am a prisoner, always dressed in one of the many pairs of pin-striped pajamas I own. When I am surrounded by that silence, when from down below my sisters, Veronica and Helena, are not engaged in a sisterly debate, and my mother is not calling out one thing or another, and my father is not yet home for the night, and when the birds have ceased shuffling between brown branches and tsking when they settle into their nests for the night, and the weather is doing whatever it does, I feel the fear haunting those who love me. *Beware! Beware!* I always hear everyone thinking, worried that I might suffer a fatal cut and my blood will flow unstaunched until I am emptied out. I will not lie—I worry too.

I assume that my creating other lives makes sense to you now, my dreams sending me to Medellín, Moscow, Istanbul, and the Galápagos Islands, places where I am someone who is free and adventurous. It's odd, because as many times as I have been Deo, Abel, Icarus, and Zed, at first, when I land in the same blank space, a tunnel of concrete, wearing my striped pajamas, I am not sure who or where I am. I dust myself off and head toward the white light beckoning in the distance. Sometimes I need only take three steps, sometimes four hundred, sometimes two thousand, until I step out into my new world and look down to see whether I am wearing huarache sandals, fur-lined boots, Turkish slippers, or flip-flops. Even when I say, "Oh, I'm in Colombia or Russia or Turkey or on an island in the Eastern Pacific Ocean," I need clues to recall my alternate life, clues thrown my way that I heed and roll into my being, until the diverse parts of myself are a united whole. Most of the time, at the start, I don't even remember my name.

My high school teacher, nut-sized Mr. Patel, a walnut of a man, once a medical school professor in Mumbai, reduced to teaching high school science in Rhome, came into my mind all at once, and I realized it was because of Kartar. Kartar and Mr. Patel shared the same lyrical intonations, the same nutmeg-hued skin. His son, Rajeev, had been in my class. From Mr. Patel, I learned the intricacies of systems I still have memorized alphabetically: cardiovascular, digestive, endocrine, immune, integumentary, musculoskeletal, nervous, respiratory, reproductive, and urinary; and about their systemic exceptions, diseases that arrested the body's mechanics. Mr. Patel lectured excitedly on hemophilia, called it "the royal disease." It was a physical science class, but he talked cheerfully about the stricken royal lineages of the Russians, the British, the Spaniards, the Germans. More than a few times, he uttered his calmly democratic statement: "Being royalty, with its power and riches and unfair advantages, also carries the possibility that your blood might be contaminated. A high birth will not save you, if your blood refuses natural containment within its earthly vessel."

So from Kartar to Mr. Patel, who buttered high school science with political theory, to Simon Tabor, a hemophiliac narrator suffering that inherited blood disorder where the body's natural clotting factor is absent. My mother would say nothing is random; coincidence does not exist, just the right time for forces to unite.

I reviewed the table of contents again. In "The Travels of Boys," the stories hinged on the first version of Simon Tabor, the hemophiliac trapped in his room, that began with "Simon Tabor Introduces Himself" and "Simon Tabor Explains All." In the next four stories, "Furia Returns," "Abel's New Game," "Icarus Dives," and "Zed's Scepter," the teenage hemophiliac was living as one of his imaginary boys in their exotic milieus.

I dove into the first one, "Furia Returns."

My bare feet echo until I am through that tunnel. Then I look around and there is the Museo de Antioquia, and the Uribe Palace of Culture, and so I know I am in the City of Eternal Spring, in Medellín, Colombia. *Policía*, guns tucked into their holsters, are guarding barricades, looking exhausted, their uniforms sweat-stained, and not at all snappy. It is a thankless job, policing the most dangerous city in the world, run by the infamous drug lord Pablo Escobar. As I walk past, I wonder how many of them are corrupt, are in Pablo's pockets, his cocaine still fresh up their noses. One cop waves at me, says, "*Paleto! Bienvenida a la ciudad!*" He's ironically welcoming me to the city, but I wonder why he's called me a country bumpkin. I look down and find I am wearing my huarache sandals, and loose linen pants, and when I finger my shirt, it is collarless. I realize I have a hat on my head, and pull off a *sombrero vueltiao* intricately woven in cream and black. The cop was right; I am in the clothes of a country boy, but I sense I do not come from the rural part. You see, there are always glitches in reality that I must work through.

I am still holding my hat in my hands when I suddenly find myself in an art gallery, and a man says to me, "Deo, *mi hijo,* explain to our illustrious guests the getup that you are wearing."

Oh, yes, right. In the City of Eternal Spring, where cocaine paves the streets, I am Deo Furia, and this man must be my father. My Spanish is rusty at first, but I know *hijo* means "son."

The guests are *Americanos,* a husband and a wife, who are stupid, or brave, to be in Medellín at this time.

"Well," I say, giving them the full force of my smile, "I am dressed like this because it reminds me of our peasant past. The sombrero, loosely translated as 'turned hat,' is a Colombian national symbol, handcrafted out of natural palm leaves using a traditional Zenu technique that can depict religious scenes or everyday activities like hunting and fishing. You need not be *religioso.* You need not be a hunter or fisherman, you need only love and respect the craftsmanship. This one, as you can see, is a geometric rendition. Stunning, is it not?"

I turn my eyes innocent and say, "*Padre,* you don't mean to sell my sombrero, do you? It is a rare one, made for me personally by the old man in the hill shack who creates hats only for those not born on the Ides of March." My father winks at me.

He is pleased because the *Americanos* have not moved from their spot in front of *A Woman Who Expects Too Much.* It is an enormous and expensive painting by the famous Colombian painter Gómez Días Muñoz, and *mi padre* would very much like them to purchase it. He is soft-shoe dancing, nearing the bulk of the painted woman in her frilled burnt-tangerine dress, pointing out what the artist was saying with the jeweled bracelets that encircle both of her wrists, her painted nails at the ends of small, childish fingers, the glove in her left hand, the clutch purse in her right. I think she looks like a human cake, with those three chins, the choker nestled against the bounty, her hair like meringue, a tangerine flower affixed behind her left ear. Her eyes are black currants, her brows arched, her lipsticked mouth tight. Ah, but she is all done up and ready for viewing, presenting herself, I think, to someone whose opinion she cares about and may not receive, unsure whether the frills, the long kimono-style sleeves, the sensual color of the dress suits her at all. She is a cake-topper, for sure.

"Deo," my father says, "allow Mrs. Warring to inspect your *sombrero vueltiao*."

I hand it over to the *Americana*, who smiles at me with her small white rodent teeth, the nostrils of her button nose flaring. She is elongated and flat as a board, spared of breasts, hips, any kind of saucy rear. It is hard to imagine that underneath their clothing, Mrs. Warring and *A Woman Who Expects Too Much* each have nipples, belly buttons, pussies, and haunches. The only thing they share in common: the prerogative of fortune.

The price of the painting is 361,000,000 COP, or $1 million. I am not sure how I know this because I do not remember seeing the price list for the art my father represents, but I know their images are in a binder on the shiny white desk at the front of the gallery, where a girl with a curtain of bright yellow hair sits with her legs crossed. Her gleaming thighs are sunlit-striped because of the iron bars over the skylight, installed to keep out potential marauders and thieves. But direct sun has found her face, giving her a halo and an angelic vibration, despite lips painted magenta. She nods at me, and I wave back.

"I will split the cost of shipping," my father says, and the *Americano* clucks while his wife strokes my hat between her pink palms, something salacious in the way she fingers the brim. The man paws his smooth coral chin for a while, until he catches from the side of his colorless eyes the slight nod of his wife. Then he says, "Yes. The Gómez Días Muñoz and the sombrero."

"*Lo que una decisión brillante*," my father says, and the tone in his voice opens the vault in my mind.

I know who my father is. He is Ernesto Furia, once Pablo Escobar's right-hand man, a step below the king, but with a golden crown of his own. Billions, hundreds of billions, perhaps trillions, who knows what my Colombian father has salted away in the false walls and hidden catacombs beneath our house in Envigado Finca, for I recall, too, that's where we live.

It's returning to me, the day the CNP, the *nacional policia*, scooped up my father and a few other high-ranking members of the Escobar crew, while Pablo escaped the clutches of the law, as he always manages to do. When I was allowed to visit my father in prison, he would say,

"*Mi hijo, cuando salga de la cárcel, quiero estar rodeado de belleza, por el art. No más crimen para mí.* And he's done that: he's an *abogado* turned cocaine trafficker turned gallery owner, surrounded by beauty every day now. Colombia is corrupt, violent, and bloody, but my father saw that its most important artists lacked representation by a person with a great eye, business acumen, endless connections, and cash, all of which Ernesto Furia has. Now he flogs their work until it gallops out into the world, on a personal mission to demonstrate that Colombia offers much more than drugs and bullets and all the *inocentes muertos*.

Hence Galeria de Furia, a purist's space with a not-for-sale-centerpiece: Gómez Días Muñoz's *We Pray for the Death of Pablo Escobar*. The single painting Ernesto says connects his past to a great day in the future, allows him to joke about previous pain. While my father works with the *Americanos* to document the transaction, I sidle up to the famous work and take it all in.

We Pray for the Death of Pablo Escobar is Muñoz's great painting of hope. In it, the infamous drug lord stands close to a blustery sky, surrounded by the red-clay rooftops of Medellín. On the red-tiled roof of a house in the foreground, his bare feet nearly dance the first steps of a *cumbia*. His white shirt is unbuttoned and bloodstained. Bullets have pierced his round belly, his neck, there is a direct shot through his forehead. The gun in his left hand is useless, his finger free of the trigger, the barrel aimed at the heavens, but his right hand still is outstretched, fending off the continuing barrage, as if he might prevent the mowing down that has already, in Muñoz's mind, happened. This painting, I remember, is my birthright. Ernesto Furia has sworn many times that never will Muñoz's masterpiece belong to anyone not a Furia, and I am the only Furia beyond him.

Ernesto pumps the man's hand, kisses the wife on the cheek, and when they walk out of the gallery, he leads me into his office. I see how his soul gleams white these days. From the closet, he retrieves a tan suede jacket. In those few seconds, when the door is ajar, I see stacks of *sombrero vueltiaos* on the shelves. This hat trick with the *Americanos*, it was not our first time—

Then Deo and Ernesto were on the Santa Helena highway in an old silver 911 Porsche Targa with the removable roof long gone, the wing mirrors too, bullet holes pocking the doors, racing the few wispy clouds moving fast through the blue sky. Soon they were entering the gates of a huge house monitored by an impressive number of closed-circuit cameras, calling out to Deo's mother, Adalina, who emerged like a goddess from the man-made lake, wishing her son congratulations on his last day of school, telling him his girlfriend called to wish him a happy sixteenth birthday.

In Colombia, I have a girlfriend named Isabel, a nice girl who goes to church on more than just her saint's day. At first, when her father saw that we liked each other, he refused to let Isabel out of his sight. But my father convinced him that he was completely reformed, a do-gooder now, and that Isabel had nothing to fear, no danger would be visited upon her, if she were allowed to date Ernesto Furia's son. Everything has worked out well. Isabel is gorgeous, and I am in love for the first time in my life.

Before I can say, "*Gracias, madre,*" a funny sound makes me look up. Two blue-green parrots are dancing on a nearby branch, their claws clicking on the wood, their beaks opening and closing, their high-pitched caws chirruping through the air, and I feel myself floating away.

The other three stories were just as enthralling. In frozen Moscow, Russian Abel breeds dogs free of bark and bite, but capable of furious meowing. Icarus can hold his breath for days, dives deep into the Eastern Pacific Ocean with no need for scuba gear, but loaded down with underwater cameras in order to photograph a colorful eel never before seen by man, brings it up to show his father, the man who discovered the Galápagos Islands. Zed, the son of a Turkish Ottoman pasha, reclaims his father's throne, rules the city from a palace overlooking the Bosporus Strait. In each, the relationships between those boys and their parents were tightly enmeshed, and all slightly off-kilter.

When I finished, I looked at the stories listed in the second section, "The Rx of Life," and from the titles it seemed that Ashby was going to widen the exposure, reveal the truth about the real Simon Tabor. Indeed, I would learn that Simon Tabor was not a hemophiliac at all, was not traipsing around the world in his dreams, but instead,

was a real boy confined to his room for a completely different reason. That widening exposure, those revelations, were immediate
when I began reading "An Afternoon at the Pool."

When the last bell of the school year rang on Friday, Simon Tabor
rode his bike home, parked it at the side of the house, snapped out
his bike pump, retrieved his old wading pool from the garage, and
inflated it until the dimmed dinosaurs in the plastic came back to life.
The family's backyard was spacious, bursting with flowers and a real
pool with deep water turned nearly white in the sun. If he wanted to,
Simon could have stripped down and gone for a swim, but that's not the
experience he was after.

There was a grassy verge close to the house, and there he set down
the blown-up pool. He unfurled the garden hose, turned on the spigot,
and waited for it to fill. When forced by his mother to water the
roses, Simon did not always remember to wind the hose back up, but
now he did, and stowed the contraption next to the brick steps that
led to the sheltered veranda.

He used his key to enter the house and locked the windowed patio
doors behind him. His dog came running and Simon leaned over,
petted the thick white fur. "Hey, Scooter, you good? You hungry?" In
the kitchen, he filled up the dog's bowl with kibble, gave him fresh
water, took a bottle of red Gatorade from the fridge, and left Scooter
munching away.

Simon climbed the wooden staircase to the second floor, hitting
each creak deliberately, his hand sliding up the rail. Usually, he took a
sharp right turn into his bedroom, the door to which he never left open,
but he had this morning, to show his mother he could be neat, an
organized human being. He went down the hall instead, past his
parents' bedroom, past the bedrooms formerly inhabited by his older
sisters, Phoebe and Rachel, to the very end where a thick rope hung
from the ceiling like something left over from an abandoned lynching.
He pulled the rope hard and released the hidden ladder to the attic.

Over the years, he had made many secret trips up there, always
hoping to find something more than the leftover rolls of pink insulation,
the trunk of old stock quotes that belonged to his father, the box of
costumes his sisters had worn for Halloween when they were children,

a brown tool chest filled with hammers and nails and the like that no one ever used. He opened the lid and pulled out a screwdriver.

At the far end of the attic, facing the street, was a diamond-shaped window not meant to be opened. Simon unscrewed the panes and stacked them on the floor. Then he dragged over his father's trunk, stepped up, and boosted himself out the window, onto the flat roof of his home. He took a long swallow of his Gatorade.

He had never seen the neighborhood from this height: desert plants instead of grassy lawns, front doors painted red, orange, yellow, and green. Their own door, which he could not see, was blue. In the late afternoon heat, trees were drooping in front yards and the houses looked sleepy.

He had only ever lived in this house, in dry, dusty Bakersfield. His parents and sisters had once lived an entirely different existence before he was born, in a place with snowy blue winters, where they made snowmen in the front yard and played games in front of the fireplace. For some reason, he was thinking of this when he walked across the roof and looked into the backyard. Shanks of sunlight sparked up from the shallow water in his old wading pool, and he remembered playing in it when he was little, Phoebe and Rachel sitting on the grass, dunking him again and again.

It felt good to be up here alone, above it all, where he could think quietly. What he had told his mother he needed to do. He kicked off his tennis shoes and curled his toes over the roof's edge. He drank down the rest of the Gatorade and left the bottle on the gravel. To be free and airborne suddenly seemed a wonderful thing to do at the onset of summer, and before giving it any more thought, Simon Tabor leaped out into the pure blue sky, experiencing seconds of marvel and awe before he plummeted down. Later, he would remember nothing but the way the water had sprung up like a waterfall in reverse, how the sun-warmed drops rained down on him. Then he lost consciousness.

Nathan Felt, the new neighbor from across the street, a man whose belongings had been unpacked the year before, but he had never been seen, watched Simon soaring through the air, and thought, maybe, though it couldn't be true, that kid could really fly. When he heard the splash, then the implosion when Simon struck the ground, he dialed

911, and ran across the street, through the Tabors' gate, into their backyard. Simon was half in and half out of the water, the plastic hissing with a leak, and he held Simon's hand until the ambulance slammed to the curb and burly men raced into the backyard with a red medical box and a gurney. They strapped Simon's neck into a brace, strapped him to the gurney, yelled out, "Desert Memorial," then took Simon away, and Nathan Felt waited out front for some member of the family to return.

It was both parents at once two hours later, driving their cars into the garage, the mother waving at Nathan as he rose from a boulder in their front yard.

"You're the new neighbor, well, not so new now," Renata Tabor said, placing a cake box on her car roof. "They had his favorite cake," Renata called across the garage to her husband.

When Nathan Felt walked into the garage, Renata was thinking he was handsome, the kind of man she wished her eldest daughter, Phoebe, would date. But Nathan Felt wasn't saying, "It's nice to meet you." Instead he was saying, "I'm so sorry. And I'm sorry, but I don't know your son's name——" and he continued on, tripping over the words he had considered how to say, about what he had witnessed—their son leaping off the roof. And what he had done—his immediate call for help. And the aftermath—that Simon had been unconscious when Nathan reached him, but he stayed with him and the EMTs had come quick. He was only part of the way through when Renata pressed her hands over her mouth to stopper her screams. Nathan Felt did not tell the Tabors how it sounded, the roar when their son struck the cement.

The streetlights were against them. Harry braked hard at the first red, then he sped up and caught yellows all the way, until they blew into emergency parking at the hospital. Renata was desperate, Harry wild-eyed, prepared for more violence in the emergency room, but when they ran in, it was quiet and empty, as if nothing bad ever happened in that long room filled with sick bays. The privacy drapes, green fabric on tracks, every one was pulled all the way back.

There was silence at first and Renata thought her hearing had been blown out by fear, but then she heard music, an old-fashioned transistor radio on the nurses' counter, tuned to the oldies station, and Renata recognized the Neil Young song, about a needle and the damage done, and she remembered being with Harry when they were young and unmarried, listening to that song while Harry's index finger inched down and he tried to find her perfect spot which back then he had not yet found, and Renata roared, "Off with the music," and the music was gone.

The emergency doctor on call appeared in front of them, pushing thinning blond hair back from his sunburned forehead. "Tabor," Harry said, and the doctor nodded. "He's alive, but several surgeries, to pin and plate together your son's shattered ankles, the mangled bones of which tore through the skin, to set his broken femurs, immobilize his unhinged clavicle, and his shoulders, which were wrenched from their sockets. We set his broken arm, too."

Late Friday night, when the anesthesia had worn off but Simon's eyes were still closed, the doctor who now had a name, Dr. Miner, had Simon moved into the hospital room so that when he woke, his parents would be with him.

The Tabors watched Simon from vinyl armchairs once the color of bright sunflowers, now faded and cracked. They watched as the nurses monitored Simon carefully with their adept efficiency. And while there were no guarantees, as Dr. Miner continued to tell them when he checked on his patient, flipped through the chart, rattled the IV linkages, and placed his long surgeon's fingers atop the chirruping equipment, Simon's brain was fully functioning. And the news, in general, seemed to be good: his brain had not swelled, and Dr. Miner thought it unlikely that it would swell in the hours to come, and the blood tests showed that Simon's system was free of alcohol and drugs.

"He is lucky not to have broken his neck, or his spine, that he will not be permanently damaged," Dr. Miner told them.

Amidst all of his *no guarantees,* Dr. Miner held out hope that Simon would eventually wake and be absolutely fine, "Once we release him, he will be housebound, room-stuck, months of healing ahead of him to mend what's been broken and split."

However, it was now Sunday morning and why Simon had lapsed into something beyond mere unconsciousness, lightly termed *a coma* by Doctor Miner, was unclear. Renata and Harry listened and nodded. They asked pertinent questions and received middling answers. At the end of every visit, the doctor pressed his hands to their shoulders and left the Tabors to sit quietly, to watch and wait, to absorb, yet again, their teenage son having, perhaps, done something to himself.

The other stories in "The Rx of Life" were narrated by Nathan Felt, the two EMTs, the two operating room nurses, Judith and Louise, and Dr. Miner. Every one of them was greatly and personally, and in some cases existentially, impacted by the broken boy asleep for such a long time at Desert Memorial. In those spearheaded by the doctor and nurses, Ashby somehow made the medical terminology read like poetry.

In the third section, "Familial Truth," the final six stories were narrated by Simon Tabor's parents, Renata and Harry, his sisters, Phoebe and Rachel, the part-time housekeeper, Consuela, and his dog, Scooter. Each debated whether Simon intended serious harm to himself or not, and through all those prismatic interpretations, the Tabor family's complex history uncoiled.

Harry had been a stockbroker who engaged in insider trading, and when he feared he would end up in jail, gutted, broiled, and eaten, he gave his ill-gotten gains to charities and packed up his family—then comprised of himself, his wife, and two daughters—and left Connecticut for Bakersfield, because it seemed that living in a city with stifled imagination would rein in his larcenous impulses. Now he was the guy who handed over insurance check payouts, the last best hope for people in the midst of terrible losses.

On the Friday Simon threw himself off the roof, the entire family was gathering to celebrate his sixteenth birthday. Phoebe, a lawyer, was driving in from Los Angeles, bringing with her a young man she described as her *paramour,* knowing that word would irk her mother, the paramour apparently some kind of prophet. Renata was hoping he was the kind of prophet who did not predict the future, but noticed the present. Rachel, working on her master's thesis at the University of Washington and waiting to hear where the Peace Corps was sending her, would, Renata knew, arrive with her strange vibrations all seemingly connected to Rachel's infatuation with Valentine, who was in her graduate program. It seemed possible to Renata that Rachel, who insisted on being called Rae, had not yet realized she was gay.

And at the quiet center of everything was Simon, the boy pale and waxy and still in his hospital bed.

"Bedside" began like this:

Renata holds her breath and waits for the chirrups, sweet as a baby bird calling out to its mother. There is the first one, then the second, the third, and on and on, an unwavering call Renata wants to believe is a sign from her own baby, calling out to his mother. These chirrups she has been hearing since Friday night are a sign of a sort, or at least a sign from the machines attached to him, aural proof of the steadiness, the durability, of Simon's fulsome heart. How silent he was, alert to nothing, when as a baby he woke to the slightest noise. His naps had required turning the house into a mausoleum. He could hear anything, everything, the neighbor's cat treading on leaves one house over, a quiet cough from a stranger out on the sidewalk taking an evening stroll, his sisters, before they left home, talking downstairs in the den about boys, when he was upstairs in his bedroom with the door closed. During this week that led up to she and Harry sitting here by his side, Renata had questioned his formerly remarkable hearing. "Simon," she found herself saying, then calling out more loudly, "Simon!" then yelling "SIMON!" because her son's hearing had become selective in that teenager way. There was so much before him, Renata had thought, but how would he get ahead if he refused to answer the simplest of inquiries? When Simon would eventually look up, he had said, "Mom, enough, I heard you. I need time to think." *Think about what?* Renata wanted to scream, but she had not, she had kept quiet. Now she wondered if she was to blame for this situation they found themselves in; the beckoning summer a misplaced joke, their world suddenly cold and sterile, their son, unmoving, silent, in his hospital bed.

Since Friday night, when her head is not bowed, Renata stares at Simon's black curls, heavy and lifeless on the pillow. Those curls, inherited from neither Renata's side of the family, nor from Harry's, made Simon appear to be running, even when he was still and focused, with an intensity that was stunning: comic books, stamp collections, five-thousand-piece puzzles, the histories of trains, the Southwest, the samurai of Japan, tae kwon do, a year spent writing haiku. Now, nearly every hour, Renata pulls one of his curls straight, then tugs a little too hard, hoping that a bit of pain will jostle loose whatever is clamped shut in Simon's brain. She imagines her son stuck inside a hole, a big boulder wedged atop, like the one in their front yard, where Nathan Felt had been sitting, waiting to deliver the news, and a mother's superhuman strength is needed to roll that boulder away, let in the light. She imagines, for some reason, parrots strutting back and forth across that boulder. Each time she pulls, she tells herself to expect nothing. But her heart folds up tighter when Simon's eyes do not open, when he does not move, reflexively at least, away from the pain. Still, it gives her succor, reminds her that she will always know his scalp intimately, though the days of washing his downy hair in the sink, and then in the tub, are long gone. That instantly recoiling curl shores up Renata's belief that Simon retains an essential vitality, a life force within, that he will prevail and emerge from this, and she feels her hope renewed. At least for a while. An hour later, when she springs free a different curl, tugs at it hard, she cycles again through fear-hope-fear, and bows her head.

Since Friday night, Harry has watched his wife pull on his son's curls. He does not understand what meaning the action has for her, or what effect Renata thinks it might have. He, too, has been drawn to physically connect with his son. Every so often, he places a sweaty palm on the sheet that covers Simon's left calf. The first time he did so, at five in the morning that dreadful first night in the hospital, Harry was startled to find that calf, remembered as matchstick thin, seemed overnight to have turned thicker, nearly muscular. Simon's failure to fill out had bothered Harry over the last couple of years—he himself had matured early in his own youth—but in that murky early morning hour, there was a new meatiness Harry was certain he would have noticed in late spring, when Simon took to wearing shorts to school. But he had not noticed any such change.

A nurse entered the room with trays of plastic-wrapped hospital food that she set down on the credenza. "In case you're hungry. You need to eat, keep up your own strength." Harry tried to thank her, but he was overcome by wracking coughs. Finally, he said, "Thank you, that's kind," and the sound of his voice, so thin and high, that voice from his boyhood, came as a surprise, how much he sounded like Simon. The nurse's smile was tender as she shut the door behind her.

Harry again placed his palm on Simon's left calf and it felt returned to the form he recalled, pliable and juvenile, and Harry was confused. Which thigh of Simon's was the real one? The thick or the thin? And he wondered if he had lost true contact with his son during the critical years, closed his eyes, and hoped that he had not.

I was spellbound and rapt, tearing through the pages, through the hours, all the while bringing the book closer and closer to my eyes, until I realized that whatever light there had been in the sky had disappeared behind the black clouds. I leapt up and turned on the lamps in the great room, saw my repeating reflection in the velvety black of my wall of windows.

I had only the epilogue left to read and I jumped into it immediately. The epilogue brought the book around to the start, returning to Simon Tabor as the hemophiliac who lived those other lives, traveled to faraway places.

Some may tussle with these disclosures, certain that these pages contain fabrications, and that I, Simon Tabor, am passing along deliberate mistruths to the naïve. Who can say what is true or what is false, when all of life filters through the personal. My own experience has taught me there is no golden ticket at birth; the richest life is stitched with thievery. Take what you need from everyone. Just do right by those stolen gifts. Exhaust all to ashes. If you are brave, you too may experience what I have experienced: a transformed life turned extraordinary, miraculous, and singular.

With that coda, *Fictional Family Life* concluded. When I looked up, I felt myself absent, not yet returned home. As I lived the existences of the hemophiliac Simon Tabor, and his imaginary alter egos, and learned the kaleidoscopic truth about the real Simon Tabor who had thrown himself off a roof, day had turned into night, and I did not remember when I last thought about food or drink, or my mother, or myself. I stood up and tried to rejigger back into my body.

It was four in the afternoon according to the microwave panel. Outside, the world was raw. The trees were stripped clean, branches trembling under the onslaught of water. The gutters were rivers.

Across the street, lights were on in the town houses and in the trim row houses. Shadows crisscrossed behind half-opened shutters and shades. No one walked on the sidewalk. Cars did not idle or drive slowly down the street searching for nonexistent parking spots. Perhaps my neighbors had listened to the same Weather Channel report yesterday. *Galoshes won't cut it, better be able to swim, stay home.*

The silence settled. But Simon Tabor's last words in his epilogue were pounding within me. It was nuts to heed the final command of a narrator who had pitched himself out into space, and then reimagined himself as a hemophiliac, as a way to somehow both distance himself from and understand his motivations, who had easily created a host of wild characters living lives he—they—wanted to experience. But there was so much power in the truths underlying *Fictional Family Life,* and I felt how those truths were arranging my thoughts, how Ashby's ultimate sentences presented a potential road map to my own future.

In my mind, I suddenly heard Johnny Cash singing in that gravelly voice deepened by hurt, perforated by longing, recorded maybe a year before he died. A line returned to me, Johnny's tumultuous voice digging deep—*If I could start again, a million miles away.* Perhaps I was wearing blinders, as horses do, or seeing what I wanted to see, or just confused, but Ashby's work was leading me toward the path I had long wanted to travel, showing me a way back to my past.

I called Lucky Star again. "Is this Kartar?" I said, recognizing his voice.

"Most certainly. The one and only."

"You delivered breakfast to me yesterday," I said, and reminded him of where I lived.

"No need to tell me, sir. You are the good man with the home that is comforting. Do you not ever visit the supermarket?" I heard shouting erupt behind him. The way Mr. Patel sounded when he yelled at Rajeev in the school parking lot. "A mixture," Rajeev said to me all those years ago, "of Hindi, Marathi, and some pidgin English words, all of it like guns firing when my father is pissed with me." I could translate the words shouted at Kartar without any problem.

"Apologies, sir. There is no need for supermarkets. None whatso-ever. What may I bring to you?"

I gave him my order and then he asked me something strange. "Sir, do you have any siblings?" I said that I had a younger brother.

"I have no sibling," Kartar said. "My mother says with great pleasure that she and the world can handle but a single one of me. You have a brother, so your mother must not say such a thing about you. I ask about your sibling because I could not feel him in your home. This brother of yours, is he the sheep?"

"The sheep?" I asked.

"Yes, sir, you know, the sheep, the one who lollygags around, always making trouble, never listening to his elders."

"You mean the black sheep," and for several awful moments I wanted to say, "Yes, yes, he is." But could Eric be defined as the Manning black sheep when he was rich as Croesus?

He had begun calling late that summer and engaging me in long conversations, which he had never done before; our previ-ous conversations had always been shorter and took place in his bedroom or mine, or out in the glen, when we both lived at home in Rhome, before I went off to college and he became who he was.

In our last one, just a few days before, he told me he was re-searching Dharamshala, where the Dalai Lama lived in a com-pound, a place of monasteries and stupas that Eric said were sacred monuments symbolizing enlightenment. Telling me that people stayed in Dharamshala for months on end, meditating, learning, making treks to all sorts of places imbued with healing properties. Telling me that people wrote letters to the Dalai Lama, hoping to be granted a private audience. And when I said, What's this all about? Eric said, I'm thinking I want a new life. I've done this one, and even though I've done really well, I'm not sure it's good for me. Don't most of us wish we could start over again? People say they would beg, borrow, and steal to change their lives. I just have the cash to do such a thing in my own way.

Then he was talking logistics, that the flight to Delhi took fifteen hours, and from there, he would make his way to Dharamshala. Though most visitors apparently took a thirteen-hour bus ride, the option of an overnight train from Delhi to a place called Chakki Bank intrigued him.

Like that movie we saw, he said, about brothers in India on a train, reuniting with each other and searching for their runaway mother. *The Darjeeling Limited*, I said, and I wondered if he wanted me to go with him, and I went through a rapid analysis of what it would be like to be in India with the younger brother I sometimes loved and mostly loathed because of his genius and his wealth and his besting a world I could never be part of. He did not feel the break in my thoughts, was talking then about how he'd take the overnight train from Delhi to the Pathankot small railhead gauge station, and from there take another train up the Kangra valley. I had no idea what a small railhead gauge station was.

Then Eric was saying, This is what the Internet guides say, and he read, "The ascending trip takes no less than six hours up through a beautiful valley and one should expect delays. At Kangra, you will make your way to the station for the final leg of your trip, a bus to McLeod Ganj in Dharamshala." Once there, I'll be on foot the rest of the time, he said.

I think now that Eric saw coming the crash that would send him to rehab, was already working out his plans before that Oregon detour, considering heading to India to stay a week, a month, or a year. I was skeptical and impressed and envious that the brightest among us have all the options in the world, could undergo such radical transformation, and that those of us without such gifts, who would most benefit from a completely different existence, would never have such a chance.

I could have said Eric was the black sheep and Kartar wouldn't have known the difference. Instead, I answered honestly.

"He's not a black sheep, just functions very differently than the rest of us."

And I felt a slow heat forming within me, about Eric's limitless choices and mine narrowed down to nothing.

"You do as well, sir. Perhaps just more quietly," Kartar said. "Sir, apologies, I am being summoned. I will see you within one hour, and I will pray that the rain has concluded by then. I look forward, sir."

I set out cash on the kitchen counter, flopped on the couch, stared at the ceiling, and thought again about Eric and the second life he was thinking of beginning, and about Simon Tabor and what he had done to create new lives for himself, and how, despite my moderate success at *Think Inc.*, I couldn't figure out how to get this first life of mine started much at all, a flickering flame already gone out. Then I slept until the doorbell rang.

"Good late afternoon, sir," Kartar said as he handed me my order. "Another long day of serious tumult." We both looked to the windows where we could see the jackhammering rain.

"Is it really raining as hard as I think it is?" I asked.

"I cannot know how hard you think it is raining, sir. But yes is what I say to you. I say yes because when I stood inside Lucky Star, I thought it was raining a certain kind of hard. Yet, when my uncle Gupta and I ran to the car to bring this delicious food to you, it was raining much harder than I believed when I was still inside."

I liked his explanation and I smiled at him and said, "Thanks for braving the weather again."

"My pleasure, sir. It is an interesting puzzle, is it not? How something like rain can be different depending on where you are standing when you are considering it. Much like life, I think."

I wondered if this kid was some kind of prodigal sage. In silence, we exchanged the chicken-scratched receipt for cash, and a tip he accepted this time without protest.

Then he said, "The principle applies to many things. I hope you do not find this strange, sir, but I have been meditating on your home since yesterday. To me, it is comforting, and yet when I paid you that compliment, I could see in your eyes that you were not sure if you agreed or disagreed. Sir, I will say it is like the rain. What matters is where one stands. From where I stand, this is a good home and you will do great things with your life in this place."

I stared at Kartar.

"Ah," he said, "I see you do not understand. My name, sir. Named as I am, I have the power to feel when I am in the presence of creation. Is that not what is going on here? You need not tell me, but I am certain that I am right. And I am sure you are wondering.

Lord of Creation is what my name means, sir. Thank you for the generous tipping. I must go. Uncle Gupta curses a great deal when he is kept waiting too long."

Kartar ran down the hallway. At the elevator, he turned back and waved. "Call anytime, sir. I enjoy our in-person conversations."

Kartar with his powerful, bestowed name had talked, I had listened, and he left a prophecy in his wake. Could the kid be right in some way? I wanted to run after him, flag him down on the sidewalk, ask him to detail his prophecy under Uncle Gupta's bright-red, all-encompassing umbrella. I stood rooted at the open door, my eyes sweeping around the great room, trying to sense the creation he felt in the space. Perhaps he was psychic or reincarnated, sensed vibrations or auras, saw colors specific to creativity, to artistic endeavor. Was my body surrounded by a field of light he had been able to read? I knew he was just a funny teenage boy who was good at delivery-door chat, but I couldn't help wondering whether the tale Kartar's mother had swirled around him might have left behind a residue of inexplicable special powers. It was hard to convince myself that it was all nonsense.

Since that day, a year ago minus twenty-four hours, I have often thought about Kartar and his prophesying abilities. How he sensed only the positive. Or perhaps it was that he could not see all the way to the end of my story, to the last page, the final words.

Recording #4

I watched the rain thrashing down from the breached heavens while I ate my Lucky Star hamburger and fries. The clouds in the sky were huge, as black and massive as rock formations. Across the way, the buildings were flat, one-dimensional. Despite the physicality of the rain, its vibrational force, there was a captured quality to everything. Underlying my thoughts was Kartar's prophecy. Rising toward the ceiling at the top of the bookshelves was my enormous stack of ninety-nine Henry the Squirrel books. I wondered whether my childhood stories were the reason Kartar sensed creation in my environs. I considered taking them down, looking through them for the first time since I abandoned the squirrel, but Kartar had said he felt he was in the presence of creativity, a creativity that was presently occurring, and those books were of the past.

Then I was standing in my bedroom, at my bureau, opening the top drawer, hurling to the floor balled-up socks and underwear, until I had emptied everything out.

There it was, at the back, in its shabby resting place. Ashby's secret manuscript, the copy I had made and stolen away. The reason for my penance.

But that penance was now complete: I had read her collections, and because of them, I had gained some greater self-knowledge and a potential guide to my future. There I stood, holding her huge secret in my hands, and I thought a novel named *Words of New Beginnings* surely contained additional truths about what I ought to do with my life.

Cash sang, *If I could start again,* and I wanted to be Howard after he made his decision to walk away from Esme. I wanted to be Simon Tabor finding ways to fly. I understood Peck Traynor now and wanted to live the outlaw life she had chosen.

I took Ashby's novel out into the great room, put it on the coffee table, straightened all of its edges. Then a thin book on the bottom of the bookshelves caught my eye. I walked over and freed it. *Creative Visualization* by Shakti Gawain. I had no recollection of purchasing that book, or of having read it. The tagline on its cover: "The Inspirational Best Seller That Has Led Thousands to the Fulfillment of

Their Desires Through the Art of Mental Energy and Affirmation." I opened to a random page and there was a grocery list in my handwriting: *OJ, TP, PT, milk, bread, PB&J, condoms.* I turned the list over. It was written on a receipt for a deli sandwich dated from the month and year I moved in here. The intervening years had not altered my trite needs. I felt utterly predictable, and then my breath dropped away. There was a wizened grief inside of me, and when an image came clear—a little boy at his white desk writing about a small gray squirrel's clever abilities in the face of trouble, stories that had made me feel I was unique—I understood I had been living with that grief for a very long time.

I wanted again to be that hopeful boy who did not yet know he lacked his own genius. I thought of Simon Tabor's directive in *Fictional Family Life* and felt again the strength I had experienced the whole of the day reading about him and the boys he created, a strength I had not felt in years, and I hung on to it right then, and forced it within me, sensed the way it altered the tide of my blood. I left *Creative Visualization* on my desk, poured myself a large vodka, sat down on the couch, and picked up the manuscript. I turned to the first page.

We were young, and some of us were beautiful, and others of us were brilliant, and a few of us were both—

I finished reading at five in the morning. For another hour I listened to the incessant rain and contemplated the book. It was sophisticated and complex, its skein of themes elegantly knitted together—about the nature of creation, hope, faith, community, the mandate to follow one's dreams, because to do otherwise meant certain death, an actual explosion of one's heart, or, and perhaps worse, the figurative explosion of one's being. I thought it was a huge book. Taut and tied together.

Why had she kept us all in the dark about what she was doing? Once she finished the book, why had she put it away? I looked again at the title page, at *Final Draft: August 10, 2007,* and tried to recall what was happening right then—I was off to college a few weeks later, Eric would drop out of school. But even those events, I thought, could not have prevented her from ushering her work out into the world. Nothing else I considered, like dissatisfaction with her creation, rang true. I was missing critical information, but I could not call to ask what had happened to her writing, to her career, to the book I had robbed.

And though I would have denied it then, I think what I thought was this: How dare she. She did not deserve her talent, barely utilized all of these last years. She did not deserve to have written this book that she had stowed away.

And I knew I had gotten it all wrong in Silicon Valley when I was forced to read "An Outlaw Life" and decided that learning Ashby had not wanted me somehow set me free. That knowledge had not set me free, not for a single day. I was still playing by the expected rules of behavior, still heeding the honorable code, permitting myself to be slotted in where others thought I belonged. It took reading all of Ashby's work to understand what true freedom could mean, what breaking through all the boundaries could do for a human being.

It took another thirty minutes for exhaustion to catch up with me, to stretch out on the couch, to reach the cliff of sleep. A last thought floated through my brain: *Words of New Beginnings* was the perfect title and I would not be able to use it.

I dreamt about the butterfly farm I went to when I was eight, a school field trip in a yellow school bus that left the parking lot in the predawn dark because the butterflies broke free of their prisons early in the day, if they broke free at all. My dream unfolded as it had in real life: at the farm, I covered my eyes after sighting the tightly wound pods—*chrysalides,* we had been taught—hanging from the rafters. My teacher said, "Look, look everyone, it's marvelous," as the guide pointed out the pods, until that moment immobile and defenseless, starting to move, a subtle crusade of pupae searching for a way out. I pressed my small fists into my eyes, deliberately missed the change on the rafted tier, the metamorphosis from pupa to imago—in class we had also learned those words—as the hatching butterflies fought for freedom and air and light. I refused to watch because I believed the butterflies were undergoing a sacred trans-formation that belonged to them alone, their secret. When I heard my classmates' excitement, I peered through my fingers, caught the butterflies just rising into the air, their wings working for the very first time. That transformation, from larvae to pupae to evanescent winged insects, was part of the natural cycle, and even so I had refused to be a witness as a child. In the dream, I was suddenly grown up and making a speech, though I saw no audience, just an endless expanse of blue water, clear as glass. My voice was strong and sure as I said, "Human transformation is something else entirely, mandating revolutionary activity that would wither under the eyes of an audience. We must take this step, use the keys handed over to alter our lives. I have my key, do you have yours?" Then a string of words flew across my eyes as if they were being typed on a screen—*morality, intention, responsibility, goodness, identity, desire, theft.*

When at last the dream fell away that Monday morning of the Columbus Day weekend, I felt a muted pain on my left side, inside of my ribs, close to my heart, that organ I once thought of as pure, or nearly so. I had done few things in my life that altered its original state, but making an illicit copy of Ashby's hidden book was the biggest one by far, then. I rubbed at the ache and found myself quietly repeating, *You will do what you need to do,* and then the pain subsided because I knew what that was.

Reading Ashby's work had clarified what I was too young to understand when my mother's fame stymied me completely, made me doubt myself, forced me to abandon Henry, the ramifications of that act, a slaughtering of my own passion, and the anger I had carried for too long. I needed to reignite myself. And there was Simon Tabor's advice for me to follow, precepts Ashby herself espoused in *Fictional Family Life.* I repeated the words by heart: *Take what you need from everyone. Just do right by those stolen gifts. Exhaust all to ashes. If you are brave, you too may experience what I, Simon Tabor, have experienced: a transformed life turned extraordinary, miraculous, and singular.*

I thought of those chrysalides I was supposed to have watched on that field trip. The tightly wrapped pupae struggling free from their homemade prisons, genetically prepared for the abbreviated life of a butterfly. The guide told us that the lucky ones who managed to avoid the predators inhabiting their fragile world would have a month to sip nectar, rest on the underside of a rock, effect their solitary goal, the laying of their eggs. Motivated creation. That is what I wanted for my life, and Kartar had prophesied that such would occur.

It seemed to me that Ashby's manuscript had remained hidden until I could find it, that my discovering it was intentional in a cosmic sort of way, the universe talking to me directly. Just as reading *Other Small Spaces* and *Fictional Family Life* made me feel those stories belonged to me, that somehow I had written them, or could have written them, my reading of Ashby's unseen novel rendered it visible, made it my own. The novel represented a chance for me to recapture my immense childhood dream, to make it arrant and real. The book, unused and clearly discarded, was what I wanted from the genius lost-and-found box.

I truly believed that had I not been forced to learn at such a young age that she held my treasured spot in our family, that she was famous, had won big awards, was still well known, sometimes recognized by strangers decades later, though she had only ever published those two books, a handful of other stories in magazines that made it into various *Best American Short Stories*, all of Ashby's words might have been mine. The very fact of her had usurped what-ever talent I might have possessed, had blown me apart.

She had noticed when I stopped writing my Henry stories, but when she asked, *What new adventure is he going to have?* I shrugged and refused to answer, and rather than interrogate me gently, a skill she had always used well and wisely until that very moment, she nodded and left me alone. Years later, when I intellectually under-stood she had not deliberately maimed me, it no longer mattered, the damage had been inflicted, and she was accountable.

But now I held in my hand a brilliant nine-hundred-page secret that could recast my entire life, serve as my own redemption.

I left a message with my editor at *Think Inc.* that I would be out for the week, finishing up interviews for my third-to-last article, though I had already written it.

I sat at my desk, under a pool of lamplight, the rain a rush and a roar against the windows, the world far in the distance, unrecalled beyond the thick curtain of clouds. For a while, I did nothing. Then I began to type Ashby's novel into my laptop, feeling all the while like the serious writer I had wanted to be.

On a whim, I altered the sex of a character, turned a man into a woman by adding an *i* to a name, making a *he* a *she*, a Bash into a Bashi, with all the attendant changes, because I could, and because I wanted to exert my own power over the work.

I typed past midnight, fell into bed, and when I woke a few hours later, I dropped to the floor for push-ups, made coffee, and picked up the phone to call Lucky Star with my breakfast order. Then I put the phone down.

What would Kartar notice if he was again standing at my door? I imagined him warning me, that fluted voice saying that this was not what he had meant at all, that my creative impulses were stolen and dark, already ransacking my soul, and there was little time for me to abandon my ways, scrub myself clean. I knew the diabolical truth, what I was intending to do, but I did not need someone else knowing it too.

I drank my coffee and toasted the heel of brown bread still in my fridge, and returned to my desk, to the manuscript that was already transforming into something else, regardless that I was typing her words.

It is hard to accurately explain how I managed to ambush the compunction with which I had been raised, my knowledge of right and wrong, the admonitions to never lie, cheat, or steal, how easily I threw my own morality aside. I wanted to usurp what belonged to her, felt that I had the right; she herself had lied to me all of my life. And although I knew, of course, who Joan Ashby was, that she was real, that I called her Mom in my regular life, not once did I consider her humanity, how my actions might affect her, did not once think back to Karen Sweet murdering Evan. I felt liberated from all normal constraints.

During the four days and nights it took me to type the whole novel, there were times I felt I was slogging up a muddy hill, carrying a loaded pack on my back, fighting a war of my own invention, a battle that featured revolutionary conversion and a desire for revenge, and very little guilt. It was not a no-man's-land, but I pretended otherwise, ducking and weaving, and marching relentlessly forward until I reached the last sentence, the last word, the last period, and typed *The End.*

When I finished, I sat there wondering how best to mask its origins. The psychological construct of *Words of New Beginnings* shared little with the various emotional psychologies the characters in her collections experienced; the nature of her work had altered and was no longer as instantly recognizable. I considered how she was famous for her short stories, was known as a writer married to the short narrative form, and she had never published a novel.

I went back to what I thought was a natural breakpoint in the book, and that's where I cut. I knew I might be doubling my risk of exposure, but I was making something new, companion books meant to be read sequentially. I named the first *Paradise of Artists*, the second *The Blissed-Out Retreat*, titles that came to me easily. It was impossible for them to bear my name, though I wished they could. I came up with a pseudonym that pleased me. I titled them and typed "by J. D. Henry" on each, and right then, the air pressure lifted. The rain had not ceased since I began reading Ashby's work, and now, seven days later, as I put the finishing touches on the books, the black clouds blew away.

Suddenly the sun was high in the sky, and I could hear horns blaring as drivers took to the flooded streets, tires crashing through rivers of water, imprecations stoppered for days let loose into chilly air that was a little less sodden.

I stood at my wall of windows and thought how the harms from the past inform the present; how old wishes are nailed to a person's endoskeleton, no matter that the bones have lengthened, solidified over the years; about the confluence of events in a life; the power of the written word.

Part III

WHAT IS THERE BETWEEN NEVER
AND EVER THAT LINKS THEM SO
INDIRECTLY AND SO INTIMATELY?

Clarice Lispector

kabhī nahīṁ aur sadev ke bhitar kya sambandh hai jo
inko itni ghanishtha aur paroksh roop se jorhta hai?

31

"Darling, could you fix my sweater for me?"

Joan looks away from the window to the old woman slumped down in her seat with a spine as liquid as water. Even now, decades after a romantic picnic in Central Park, she remembers Martin running a slow finger down her back, saying, "The spine is comprised of twenty-six bones, twenty-four separate vertebrae interspaced with cartilage, the spinal-cord nerves carrying electrical signals and sensory information, like touch, pressure, cold, warmth, and pain, from the brain to the skin, muscles, joints, and internal organs," and Joan wonders how this teeny old woman's spine still has the strength to accomplish all that.

"What do you need me to do?" Joan asks.

"If you could settle my sweater back where it should be, darling."

Joan weights down the wispy, hot pink shoulders, rolls the long sleeves up over the thin wrists.

"Thank—" the old woman begins to say, cut off by an announcement about the meals that will be served on the flight, a recitation of the movies that will play once the lunch service concludes.

"Oh, I've already seen all of those. What a shame. But how lovely, you and I can talk."

Joan sighs inwardly. In the past, she enjoyed the intimacies, on a train or a plane, when strangers revealed their secrets to her, the interesting material she sometimes gathered this way. But today, she is incurious about who the big Indian man is, or why this old woman is traveling on her own to Delhi. Today, because of Daniel, she does not want anyone else in her head.

"Please," Joan says. "I hope you won't be offended, but I don't want to talk at all. Perhaps the man on your other side?"

When the big man turns his head toward them, the air shifts with the invisible block he slides into place. That he has no intention of engaging is clear, and there is the hard look he sends Joan's way, but she feels impermeable, tucked into her corner of the row, the few inches of her own buffering space. She glances quickly at the old woman, wondering how she feels hemmed in by people who have no interest at all in her. Joan turns away, sees the faintest reflection of her own face in the window.

An hour since takeoff. An hour plus two since Joan entered the airport and lifted off from her own life. The plane has climbed, evened out, and is sailing along. Outside her window, the blue of the sky is hesitant, uncommitted. How far has she traveled in this hour? Has she crossed into a different time zone, or is she in the same hour and minute as those Mannings she left behind? She tries imagining Martin surprising himself, breaking away from his regular hospital and office routine, jumping naked into their lap pool in the bright light of day, his music blaring so loudly it can be heard in the glen, or riding his bike on the nearby picturesque path along the Potomac, embracing the wind his own body creates. Joan closes her eyes, but she can't picture him in either scenario. Even though he refuses to think so, would deny it if asked, they have long been in uncharted territory.

Last night, he'd said, "We've been lucky during our marriage. No event has come along that could have destroyed us. We can weather this."

"Weather this, like *we* weathered Eric?" she said.

"But he's okay now. We got through it."

"I got through it, Martin. Mostly on my own. And all of this, what Daniel has done, has destroyed only me."

"But I'm here, and I love you, and we're in this together." His voice was laced with need, that she affirm their marriage, its abundant healing properties, its ability to heal her, but she said only, at last, "Your love for me has no impact on this."

The window is cold when Joan touches it. Martin is angry that she has left on her own, that she didn't want him with her, but their son's theft has detonated her every past decision: whether to marry at all, bear that first child, and the one she knew came after, every choice, so thoughtfully considered and made, mucking up her own dreams. If she could travel back, she would cling to the nine admonitions set out in her notebook labeled *How to Do It*, forego love, marriage, children, eliminate everything right from the start. She would not forget a second time that there was no choice to be made, if she wanted to continue as the writer she was already proving to be. Martin would never think along such lines, could never imagine his life without Joan, without the boys, but it's her past that has been torched, her shimmering future that has expired, and their marriage, responsible for all of it, can't resurrect time past.

Joan straightens up. She should have asked Martin his plans over the forty-eight hours it will take her to reach Dharamshala, because now she imagines him leaving the airport, driving to Daniel's apartment, duking it out, frantic voicemails she hears when she reaches Delhi, about wounds and blood. From Martin, or from Daniel, or from a solemn-voiced nurse at a hospital. How would she feel if she learned they had taken each other down, were both dead? Not maimed, not left mute and motionless, fed through a tube, lungs inflating and deflating because of a machine, but dead, funerals and plots and gravestones and she wearing black. Her breath whistles out through her lips.

The sky has turned a rich pearlescent blue, like the color of heaven, like the sky over Devata when the sun shone after those ten days of rain. Endless blue atmosphere beyond the window, exquisite hours of her life lost to mothering, encouraging, caretaking, soothing, explaining, letting one know he was always in her thoughts, policing the brilliant one and his team of pale genius ghosts. Such irony that her choices have turned out to be the wrong ones.

When the drink-and-snack cart pulls up, Joan has to lean past the old woman again and again. "Apologies," she says, when she hands her credit card to the attendant, and when her credit card is returned, and when she is handed two small bottles, a plastic cup filled with ice, bags of peanuts and pretzels.

The sound of the ice cracking under the vodka is the first sound today that relaxes her. The lime wedges she requested are slivers, rinds only, the bits of fruit on the underside dried out. She should have purchased a third bottle. These miniatures contain so little volume and it could be hours before the cart comes her way again. She takes a long, cool sip, then sighs and shifts around in her seat.

"I'm Joan," she says to the old woman.

"Oh, how lovely, darling. I am so pleased that drink is refreshing you. I'm Vita Brodkey," and her name sounds like a mouthful to Joan.

She pats Joan's arm with a translucent hand. "Do you know, dear, that I am eighty-five years young? And now I am returning to the place where I was born. I want to be there when I die. I think it will give my life a soothing symmetry."

Vita's conversational opener leaves Joan floundering and Vita leaps into the gap.

"I was born in Udaipur. Some know it as the Pink City. My parents were British, my father some high-up in the Raj rule and all. And Udaipur was a storybook place to come up as a girl with parents at the top of the pyramid. The City Palace buildings. The old city with its winding streets. The temple towers. I attended a school set behind tall iron gates. Every afternoon, I ate lovely English cream teas. I went to countless parties. I wore ball gowns to galas. I spent my weekends at the club. I played tennis and watched cricket and sailed in small boats on the lakes. It was all so romantic. I don't know if they still call them the floating palaces, but that was what we called Jag Niwas and Jag Mandir. Because they *were* floating palaces. They had turrets and balconies and they floated on top of the lakes as if conjured from a beautiful dream. And then I was forced out of Eden, so to speak, forced to leave the only home I had ever known.

"I wish I could say it was for a scandalous reason, that I fell in love with a local Indian boy, brown and smooth and poor, but that wasn't it at all. Although the skin color was different, it was the same situation really, because I fell in love with the youngest son of a duke. Three older brothers meant Nigel had nothing of his own, as poor as any poor Indian boy in Udaipur, and Nigel would be left penniless, having to figure out how to make a living when he was educated to do nothing except to be literary and fun at parties. Nigel had no future, unless all three brothers died in some disaster that would eliminate them all in one go. And that wasn't going to happen. Nor was Nigel going to make a living, so his family had to find him a young woman with a serious inheritance, and I was not that young woman. I was not titled, and although my father had grown quite rich during our years there, my parents did not adhere to the tradition of bestowing an annuity on the groom or the deliverance of a dowry. Falling in love with Nigel let my parents know that my judgment was not to be trusted. If I were so pedestrian to choose a boy with a title but no future, then it was time they sent me abroad. So abroad I went. Finishing school in New York. Cotillions and debutante balls, where I met a nice young man from Boston, and married him, and to Boston I moved, where we had a very fine life together. Now that I am the age that I am, and have lived a life, I can tell you that I am not convinced the life I led with my husband was that much better than the life I would have led with Nigel. Inherited wealth is just that, and working for a living is just that, but that's neither here nor there, at least not anymore.

"In any case, Whitson and I had a beautiful boy who grew up for a while and then died when he was still quite young. Then Whitson died. And now I have been alone for more years than I was married, and we had a long marriage, longer than I was a mother. I stayed on in our house for all these years, alone most of the time. Sometimes I brought in young artists to stay in the empty rooms, and they were a delight, and taught me much, and I used to put out a cream tea on Sundays, and I popped bottles of bubbly on Tuesdays, and I liberally poured sherry on Thursdays, but now I have sold the house. The hardest thing I have had to do, other than giving up Nigel and burying my son. But I am lucky. Always lucky. Nigel never did make a living and he shot himself in the mouth with a hunting rifle, though I am certain it must have been an accident and not at all what was reported. And I have the years with my husband to remind me of what love might be. He was very smart when it came to investments and life insurance policies, insured himself to a high degree, but he also insured our son's life. Though, of course, we never expected to benefit. It is decades now since our son died, my husband ten years later. Back then a five-million-dollar life-insurance policy meant whatever it meant, and now it means so much more than that, so I am set. I gave up being Mrs. Whitson Tagamore, and returned to being Vita Brodkey, the name by which I was known in Udaipur. I expect to buy myself a beautiful place overlooking Lake Pichola, which is the lake I could see from my bedroom window as a child. I hear that Udaipur has changed much since I have been gone, but so have I, and perhaps we'll be perfect for one another.

"Darling," Vita Brodkey says, interrupting herself, "I hear the rattle of the cart. Another for you? I might have one myself."

Joan buys a third and fourth vodka for herself and insists on buying Vita's bottle of wine. Vita points out the wine she would like from the card in the seat pocket. On a trip from DC to Delhi, it is a Chardonnay from Long Island.

"You know, darling, since you're being so kind. Maybe two bottles?"

In Vita's hands, the undersized bottles look as large as magnums, and when Joan looks at Vita's face, her eyes are dancing. She is delighted.

Joan pours the vodkas into her cup and wonders how Vita's son died, hopes that her dead husband's financial acumen is real. She feels concern for Vita Brodkey, who is now engaged in some kind of ritual, the slow severing of the filaments of the bottle top, the slow pouring of the wine, the slow wafting of her speckled hand over the glass, trying to bring the wine's perfume up to her nose in this refrigerated plane. An ornate demonstration for a six-dollar bottle.

"Oh, absolutely lovely, darling," Vita Brodkey says, when she touches her glass to Joan's, then takes a delicate sip.

Beyond the small oval of Vita's face, Joan finds herself pinned by the eyes of the big man, who is watching them pour and taste. His stony face does not reveal what he thinks of their new companionship, and Joan lifts her glass in a toast, embarrassed when he turns away. Should she say something, offer to buy him bottles of whatever he might want from the cart if it returns? But then Vita is describing her plans when she is back in Udaipur. "I will begin to paint watercolors. Just little things. A way to paint the end of my days," and Joan swallows down the rest of her drink.

When lunch is served, Joan buys a fifth vodka, telling herself that the bottles are, indeed, small. Artists might have been trooping in and out of Vita's house since the death of her husband, but Joan thinks she has spent most of her time alone because Vita talks as if presented with the best gift in the world—the ear of someone interested. Her words are flowing freely, perhaps after being bottled up for a very long time. And everything Vita talks about entrances Joan, lifts her heart, serves as a stringent reminder that people love and lose, hopes are decimated, lives finished in an instant, and yet so much remains to be done, that life can go on. Vita regales Joan with more memories from her Udaipur childhood, her life as a young bride in the States, her early days of motherhood, the funerals she attended for son and husband.

The lunch trays are long gone when Vita finishes off her second bottle of wine. "I think, darling, that it's time for my nap. I hate to impose, but I have one of those special pillows just beneath my seat. Could you fetch it for me?"

Joan feels a sharp pang that Vita's wonderful stories are about to end, and she will be left alone for the hours remaining on this flight, with only her own story to consider.

"Do you want to stretch your legs first?" Joan asks. "Use the restroom? I need to do both."

Vita rubs Joan's arm. "I have the bladder of a blue whale, which has the biggest bladder of all the mammals. So I can stay right here," she says, which makes Joan smile.

It is a complex operation by which Joan is freed from her seat at the window. The big man rises unhappily, Vita Brodkey slowly sidesteps herself into the aisle, and then Joan is out, stiff from sitting so long.

At the back of the plane, the attendants on their jump seats are reading magazines, feeding themselves lunch from trays balanced on knees. She leans up against the porthole and stares out. Where in the world is the plane right now, and what lives are unfolding down on the ground too far away to see? Everything Joan once knew feels immensely distant. What if she could travel across the sky for the rest of her days, never landing, too far up to be touched by what has transpired in her life, set up perfectly in her little corner of space, with her face against the window? As she watches, the portholed sky gains an underwater density, a deep-diving blue. She should return to her seat because Vita is waiting for her. She has waited so long to not be needed at all, she never thought that being needed in the smallest of ways by a little old lady would make her feel there might be some point to it all. In and out of the bathroom, a request for bottles of water from an attendant unhappy to leave aside his magazine and his lunch and satisfy Joan's polite request. So nothing is perfect, Joan thinks. Even seven and a half miles above the earth, she is forced to deal with grumbling others.

She walks slowly back up the plane. Once she is again in her seat, Vita will nap, and Joan will be left in the silence she thought she had wanted at the start of the trip but now finds herself fearing.

Joan offers a bottle of water to the big man and is surprised when he takes it, surprised when he smiles and thanks her, and even more surprised when he says to Vita Brodkey, "If you'll permit me—" and then Vita Brodkey is dangling in the air like the weightless doll that she is, her head close to the ceiling, her feet hanging over the narrow void of navy-blue carpet in front of her seat. Just enough room for Joan to duck and reclaim her corner. "If you'll permit me—" the Indian man says again, and Joan hears Vita say, "Yes, how lovely," and Vita Brodkey descends through the air.

"Thank you, kind sir," Vita Brodkey says to the big man. But he has already recalled himself, his eyes glued to the front of the plane, the bottle of water resting in a hand as big as a mitt. Joan moves this way and that in her seat, trying to see what holds the big man's attention. She wonders if he is on the trail of a criminal or in search of a lost love, but all she sees are racks of heads, hair in a range of colors, bald spots, a cauliflower ear on a man lifting himself up, rearranging a pillow. It is impossible to identify the furtive or lovelorn from the backs of heads. She glances quickly at the big man, his stare unblinking, his eyes turned inward now. Maybe he's meditating, Joan thinks.

"Lean forward," she says quietly to Vita. The pillow, a beige canvas-covered square with a keyhole, fits around Vita's slender, mottled neck, suddenly poised as if on a chopping block, as if her head has already been relieved of its body.

"Is that comfortable?"

Vita nods, her eyes already closing, like a cat falling into a nap, and within a few minutes, Vita Brodkey, who is journeying to the place of her birth in order to die, is fast asleep.

Outside, the sky has changed again, gone from the deep-diving blue to a calm, solid wash of gray. By Joan's watch, there are nine hours to go before they land. Soon, shades are lowered and the cabin dark is cut by the movie flashing from the small screens above each seat, where people dressed in sherbet colors are running around on a lawn. All that extruding happiness makes Joan sad. She wonders how many others on board this flight have suffered at the hands of their children, who else wishes they could find themselves in some remembered place where they were once happy. She knows where her own happy place was—at her dining-room table in her East Village apartment, the pages she was writing multiplying. Then Joan is also asleep.

She is dreaming deeply. Great waves of water splashing up from somewhere far below, cool drops raining on her skin. When she peers down, she realizes she is standing over a crevasse, balancing on a tight-rope pulled taut between two enormous trees. She thinks, I must be very, very careful; then she feels a tug that excites the wire, and she's gripping her toes hard, hanging on, regaining her balance, feeling relief, but when she looks behind her, there is Daniel, kneeling, about to pluck the wire again, a deep laugh as he wraps his fingers around it, ready to make it ricochet like a sling.

She wakes to a man's voice saying, "This is your captain. The local time is nine thirty a.m., and the temperature is 36.67 degrees Celsius, 98 degrees Fahrenheit. For everyone aboard, you might be happy to know that Delhi appears to be in a cooling trend. It is one degree cooler today than it was yesterday."

Vita, too, is just waking up. The big man seems not to have moved at all.

Thirty minutes later, they have landed. When the plane comes to a stop and the seat-belt sign is turned off, the big man, whose linen suit has remained uncrushed, lifts Vita Brodkey out into the aisle, plows his body backward for a second time, and allows Joan to move out of their row until she stands in front of him. There is a delay in deplaning, they are told, and a groan rises up. It takes only a few minutes before the temperature in the plane rises, the air growing even more stale.

"How are you getting to Udaipur?" the big man asks Vita Brodkey.

"Aren't you a darling," Vita says. "A car is picking me up here, driving me there."

"That's nearly a ten-hour drive, madam," the big man says. Vita Brodkey nods happily. "Oh, yes, I know. I want to see the country one last time before I never leave Udaipur again."

The big man nods, as if what Vita Brodkey has said makes sense. It makes no sense to Joan.

Over Vita's head, the big man says to Joan, "And you? Where are you going?"

"The Delhi train station."

"Fine. You'll both follow me. I'll get you through baggage claim and customs," he says, snapping his fingers.

"Oh, marvelous," Vita says. Joan nods uncertainly. They shared a row of uncomfortable seats for fifteen hours, but he never said a word. He did not introduce himself when they first settled in, and he has not introduced himself amidst this hint of comradeship. Knowing his name would not alter his status as a stranger, but if he can do what he says he can do, she might as well accept his offer.

A breeze meanders through the cabin, too warm to refresh, but the doors have opened, and they are finally disembarking. "Stay close," the big man says.

At the gate, the big man catches a porter's eyes, nods, and a wheelchair appears in front of them, for Vita, who sits down happily. The big man leads the way, pushing Vita fast, and Joan slings her carryall around her body and hurries to keep up with his pace. He smacks his shoulder into a swinging door, and they are through, into a quiet back alley of the airport, and then into an open-air hangar, where the plane that brought them to Delhi sits like a stranded whale with its belly ripped open. Suitcases and bags and boxes fly through the air, tossed down the line of baggage handlers until they are loaded onto carts.

Three metallic gold suitcases topple out and Vita cries, "There is my suite of suitcases."

The big man yells, "Sunil," at one of the handlers, whose uniform is faded and grease-stained. Soon, Sunil has nestled Vita's bags around her wheelchair, like golden offerings to a queen. A few minutes later, Joan spots her black bag with its jaunty red ribbon. Next to Vita's aristocratic bags, it looks utilitarian, plebian.

"Everything retrieved?" the big man asks, and Joan feels like a child when she nods.

"Yes, darling, everything is retrieved," says Vita, and their group is off. The big man pushes Vita's wheelchair. Sunil pushes and pulls and hangs onto Vita's bags. Joan trots behind, pulling her rolling suitcase by the red ribbon, as if it were a dog on a leash forced unhappily to run.

The customs line is filled with people pleated between snaking black ropes. Outside, the line continues, fanning out in all directions. With the big man leading, Vita Brodkey and Joan are whisked through customs without being questioned, or presenting their passports, or hearing the click-click of the entrance stamp marking their arrival in Delhi. Joan wishes her passport would contain evidence of her trip here, of her escape, but without the big man's help, she might still be standing in that line several days from now.

Outside the main entrance, the air is heavy, humid, dirty, a yellow pall coating the scene. There are popcorn vendors, flower sellers, tandoori cooks, all those smells mixing together, along with the ripe aroma that hints of a zoo. Joan spies monkeys sitting in the sun, as if waiting for their ride, using the time to peel nuts.

Sunil marshals Vita's bags. The big man thunders out a long string of words. Sustained honking moments later. And then a driver in a car throws the upper half of his body out of the window, one hand waving and waving, his toothy smile bright, as he inches the car forward in the dense traffic.

"*Maim yaham hum*," the driver yells. "I'm here for you!"

Vita's little hands are waving excitedly. "*Namaste, namaste*, Abhay!"

"Vita, do you know that man in the car?" Joan asks.

"Of course I do, darling. That is Abhay, the great-grandson of my parents' chauffeur."

The golden suitcases are stored in the trunk. The big man lifts Vita Brodkey out of the wheelchair, places her gently in the backseat, and carefully shuts the door. Joan had not expected him to be so kind, out here in the open, in the crazy Delhi airport traffic.

Vita leans out of the window. "Here, darling," she calls to Joan. "Here is my card. Phone number and email. Call or write if you need me. You *will* be happy, I know it."

Joan leans in through the window and hugs the twin points of Vita's frail shoulders. When she steps back, the great-grandson of Vita Brodkey's parents' chauffeur twists around in his seat to kiss Vita's hand. The car crawls forward and Vita and Abhay call out, "*Namaste, namaste*," and Joan waves, until the big man says, "You're next. So follow me and keep up."

"Wait, please," Joan says. When he begins marching away, she grabs the sleeve of his linen suit. "Please, a moment."

Joan pokes her head through Vita's window again. "You made this trip so much better than I thought it would be. Thank you."

"Oh, darling, I know I did. You were a rough customer at first, but I believed you would come around. And wasn't I right? You told me nothing about yourself, but I know what you want, what you need. It's to be more like me, a woman following her heart. Like I said, call or write if you need me," and Vita Brodkey squeezes Joan's arm. "Last words of wisdom. Whoever you were as a child, she's your future."

"You!" the big man yells, as a sleek black car with diplomatic plates pulls up. "It will take an hour to get you to the train station. So let's go. Chop, chop."

In the diplomatic car, with her bags at her feet, the cacophonous sounds of Delhi disappear behind what must be bulletproof glass. When the driver leans on the horn, it is a distant honk, but he leans on that horn again and again, zigging and zagging each time the slightest space opens up. The streets are a messy jumble, filled with as many people as cars, and the driver uses a fast-slow combination through the traffic, jerking forward until he slams on the brakes. Joan loses count of the number of near collisions in just the first ten minutes.

An hour of this travel and Joan's stomach is turning over, her skin slick with sweat, her eyes dry and glued wide. The train station appears, and the driver yanks the car this way and that, until he pulls up to the curb.

"Buy your ticket inside at the window, not on the train," the big man says. He hands her a shiny business card. "For emergencies only."

Joan is left on the curb, clutching the red ribbon on her suitcase, her carryall hitting her square in the back, the big man's card in her palm. She looks down at the raised burgundy ink, at his very long name: *Sadayavarman Bimbisara Sundara Pandyan*, at his very long phone number: a string of digits nearly all zeroes. The information on the card explains nothing, but seems like proof, perhaps, of his exceptional importance. She turns the card over, another line of type in the raised burgundy ink: *Premiere International Facilitator.* She can't imagine the range of duties that title might encompass. When she looks up from the card, the black car, its driver, and all-knowing passenger have disappeared into the wild stampede of cars and taxis and mopeds and bicycles, and people sauntering up and down the street, wildlife wandering about.

A long, multicontinental trip during which Joan expected to fall apart has instead made her more resolute. The gloom, the fear, the bone-breaking sadness, none of it has dissipated. But there is a muddling because of Vita Brodkey and her story, her pearls of wisdom, her insight regarding Joan's future, and because of the big man who has delivered Joan to this next stage of her trip, leaving her with a brusque offer of emergency help. She does not feel quite as unmoored as she did when she first boarded the plane.

At the entrance to the Delhi train station, Joan sees the mob within, the madhouse that it is. There are men, young, middle-aged, and old, in black suits, or in typical Indian attire; teenage boys in low-slung jeans and oversized T-shirts, just like the kids in quiet Rhome, a town that is not even a suburb, is, in all respects, beyond anything ur-ban; older women in saris; younger women in business attire. At the indecisive border between the street and the station, she wraps the red ribbon around her wrist, feels her suitcase nipping at her heels, and charges into the remarkable human mass. Rocked and swayed by the press of rushing bodies, she wonders if the touch of so many will rub away her former identity, leave her earlier self exposed, shiny and new.

32

The Delhi train station has signs that demand NO SPITTING, and other signs that state WI-FI AVAILABLE, and cows wandering through, stopping every so often to look around, as if confused about where to meet their fellow travelers. Joan's purchase of a ticket for the overnight train to Chakki Bank involves loud admonishments that she failed to book a berth in advance, and then a poker spread of her options: an AC Chair car, an AC1 or AC2 sleeper.

"Not like the old days," the handsome young ticket seller says, calming down after his tirade. "Once, everything was all willy-nilly, everyone scrambling for spots on the trains. Now, seats and berths are reserved much in advance. But madam, you are lucky, because we always keep a few berths open for foreigners. I would suggest the AC1 sleeper for you."

Joan agrees to his suggestion though she doesn't understand the difference between AC1 and AC2. She buys her ticket, buys a dozen sealed bottles of water at the station shop, finds a small bench from which she watches the racketing, colorful crowd, listens to the jittering, laughing, high-decibel voices around her. As the hours tick by, she realizes she could wander Delhi a bit, at least around the station, but it seems too effortful to rise and make her way through the horde, to wander as lost as the cows on the platform.

When the train shudders into the station, Joan boards with the crowd. She winds her way through the carriages until she finds the AC1 sleeper car she purchased for the night. Despite what the ticket seller told her, she still expects to find people hanging out of the carriage doors, sitting cross-legged up on the metal roof; she has seen movies where such is the norm. Although no one clambers up to the roof as the train pulls away, no one seems to be settling into their assigned berths. There is a festive boisterousness in the corridors. The tea seller's cry of "*Chai, chai, garam chai*," supplies the refrain that fulcrums all the noises into a song nearly harmonious.

A steward knocks at her sleeper door when the train is thirty minutes out of Delhi. He tilts his head into the door. "Veg or non-veg?" "Veg, thank you," she says. An hour later, there is another rap on the door, and a different steward hands over a large vegetarian platter, its samplings piled high, but her appetite has vanished. It is the noise and the heat and the waiting all day and the fifteen-hour flight. She sets the tray down and leaves the relative calm of her personal enclosure, locking the door behind her. A human thicket loiters up and down the corridors as far as she can see, smokers puffing away, their heads out the windows, knots of people laughing or arguing in front of other sleeper cars whose doors are ajar. She follows the signs, through several carriages, across the open platforms, until she reaches the bathrooms. Inside, the air is fetid, flies buzz over the toilet. Joan stoppers her nose and unbuttons her jeans.

The night sky is solidly black, except for the white discus of moon she sees through the sleeper-car window. It reminds her of the picture she took in Cairo, of the pyramids lit up by a fingernail moon, when she was there for the international book tour for *Fictional Family Life*. A photograph accidentally great that she paid to have blown up and framed and now hangs on the wall next to all of those windows in Daniel's . . . She will not think about where that photo hangs.

She is on one of the flat mattresses hooked to the wall by a thin metal frame, the only thick sweater she brought a cushion beneath her. There is raucous chatter outside her door and the tea seller's *chai* perfumes his wake. The train moves smoothly through the country-side as stars pop into the sky, pinpricks of light. She sleeps fitfully, sometimes waking, instantly aware that this moon and these stars are hanging over India. Other times, her eyes flash open in the tinged dark hours, and she fears this trip she has sent herself on. She is awake at dawn, watching the bushes, trees, plains, and hills in the distance assume more natural forms. Then she changes into fresh linen trousers and a loose cotton shirt.

Ten hours after departing Delhi, Joan stands on the platform at the Chakki Bank station. She would like to be naked in a cool shower, her hair dripping wet, in a bathroom that smells nice, without flies diving at her thighs. Her lightweight clothes are already lashed to her skin, sweat trickles down her neck, beads her back, and it is just nine in the morning. Her black suitcase is dust-covered, the red ribbon somehow lost. At the far end of the platform is a beautifully maintained miniature dollhouse, a store, but the door is locked, she has already tried, and she wonders what time it opens. She would like a cup of coffee, something other than the granola bars she brought from home, which crumble like dirt in her mouth. Something to charge her back up in this overheated, somnolent, motionless place, something to affirm this particular choice she has made. She leans against a pole on the platform, under a wooden awning.

A trim man with a neat beard paces in front of the shuttered store, his stride jaunty and quick. He seems unaffected by the heat, his black uniform crisp and sharply pressed. He turns swiftly, and she can tell he has registered her presence.

"You are here for the *chhotey*?" he asks, when he reaches Joan.

"I'm not sure," Joan says. "Is that the Kangra Valley Railway?"

"*Haan, haan.* Yes, yes. So you will know in the future, *chhotey* is Hindi for *small,* which is what the Kangra train is. I welcome you here. So you know, I am the stationmaster. I can answer all of your questions."

The stationmaster links his arms behind his back, lifts his face to the low, heavy sun. The light churns up the black in his eyes, softens the cliffs of his face. There is an insistence in his silence when he turns his head to the empty tracks. He loves his *chhotey* train, Joan realizes, whose arrival she is apparently waiting for, wants her to ask questions about the Kangra Valley Railway. It is too early for a history lesson, but she should graciously give way, as she did with Vita Brodkey, as the big man did with her in Delhi.

"I would love to hear the history of your train," she says.

The stationmaster bows and says, "Since you have been kind enough to ask, I will tell you the story. Construction began in 1925, under British Colonial rule. In December of 1928, this train station was opened, for freight traffic only. In April of 1929, it became a passenger railway. But this dry citation of dates fails to tell the exciting and true story, how the Kangra valley tracks are an incomparable feat of engineering and their extreme importance to this region.

"Before there were any tracks or train, there was treacherous landscape with which to reckon. The mountain terrain was difficult. Torrential water from the monsoons and from the melting spring-time snows in the lower regions of the Dhauladhars flowed far below. Huge chunks of earth had to be detonated. The nineteenth-century construction engineers went to work building two tunnels through the mountains and nine hundred and ninety-three bridges across the water. And after all of that work, tracks had to be formulated for this terrain and laid down. Which they were.

"The Kangra Valley Railway remains an outstanding example of technological ensemble, and it illustrates a significant stage in human history. It was constructed in harmony with the beauty, serenity, and grandeur of the surroundings.

"Today, it is a heritage symbol of our region and it is responsible for the social, cultural, and economic creation and development of the settlement of the Kangra valley. More than ninety years after it was built, the track remains impeccably maintained. The stations are the elegant originals, as are the *chhotey* trains. Nothing about the railway is ordinary."

Joan wonders if the stationmaster will take a breath before launching into detailed descriptions of the first views Joan will see from those nine hundred and ninety-three bridges. Then the Kangra Valley Railway train sways into the station and shivers to a stop. The train is *chhotey* indeed. It is a tiny train, a toy train, a train meant to be played with by little boys who will upend it from its tracks, watch it fall over the steep precipice of an unused Ping-Pong table, and do it again and again until, in the midst of repeated wreckages, they are called for dinner.

"Please, I will help you," the stationmaster says. "The steps are narrow and it is easy to slip." He sets Joan's bags gently into the stair-well, then takes her left hand, and together they walk forward, as if they might start to dance, the stationmaster on the platform, Joan mounting the steel steps, until she is at the train door.

"Thank you," she says.

"*Eka acchi yatra hai.* Have a good trip."

The stationmaster does not care why Joan is here alone at Chakki Bank, or where she is headed. His second bow, deeper than the first, tells her, more than all his words have done, who he is, and what he wants from her, something simple and prized, that she enjoy and respect the train he loves dearly.

The gears mesh in a quiet gnarl. When the train slowly moves away from the station, the stationmaster doffs his cap, steps back, and flings his arms wide, not at Joan, who waves again as she passes him, but at his beloved leaving him behind. Right then, the train sends out the *choo-choo* of a toy.

Joan is astride a worn red leather seat in the shaky *chhotey* train throttling itself hard up the Kangra valley. There was no space or room to breathe outside of her sleeper car last night, but in this carriage, she can spread out. The passengers are few. There is a young mother and her two little girls, all dressed in Crayola-bright dresses, with long ribbons of hair, smooth as melted chocolate, trailing over their shoulders, the mother between her daughters, holding their hands. All three are looking out the windows. Two old men, their necks bent like swans, converse rapidly in what sounds to Joan like a high-pitched song, with a call and a refrain. And a woman, older even than Vita Brodkey, wears a cobalt-blue sari covered in crystals. When the sun strikes the crystals they dash rainbows against the roof of the carriage. The old woman keeps turning around, but her milky, cataracted eyes make it impossible to tell whether her smile is aimed at Joan, the voluble men, the bright mother and her girls, or reflects instead her happiness at being alive and aboard the Kangra Valley Railway.

Beyond the windows, the countryside is alien and lush. Below, steep gorges fall away, a perilous descent to a bottom out of sight. Ahead, in the distance, jagged mountains rear up like magnificent marbled statues, awesome and godlike. The land falls away and the train rattles across the first bridge. Nothing but unblemished blue sky all around.

Joan imagines her decades as wife and mother dropping thousands of feet to where the mountainous water flows. She need not settle for her old life, she could toss away her grave losses, say goodbye to a son, a husband, the life she once knew at home. Love was never critical to her, she could let it all go, and up on the bridge, it feels that easy.

Back on solid ground, the engine gathers rumbling power and streams forward. The momentum stirs Joan up, shakes questions loose in her mind, forces her to consider the implications in choosing to bring herself to India, headed to the very place where Eric now resides on some temporary basis, at the foothills of the Himalayas, in the state of Himachal Pradesh, North India.

Why isn't she on a train in some other equally distant place where, at the end of the line, she will find no one to whom she is related? Because Martin never wanted to come here, she thinks. And she did, always has, and now she is here, a conscious and unconscious return to her youngest self, making good on her girlhood promise when she read all those novels and short stories set in India. She sees herself at her desk in her parents' house, serious and thirteen, opening up her notebook labeled *Quotes I Like*. She remembers clicking the pen and writing down R. K. Narayan's words about being a writer in India: *The writer has only to look out the window to pick up a character and thereby a story.* She wonders if Narayan's words will prove true for her.

The train rockets through a pass of boulders and foliage and wind-stunted trees at angles, and Joan thinks there is nothing to do now about traveling forward, where one son is at her destination when she has left the other behind. She made Martin promise not to reveal her whereabouts to either. Eric won't know she's in Dharamshala until she decides to make herself known. Daniel does not know she has gone and that's the way she wants it. Martin knows where she is and, considering *she* doesn't really know where she is, that's sufficient, maybe even too much.

The trip up the Kangra valley takes several jostling hours. When the train comes to a halt, the young mother says to Joan, "This is your stop. Kangra Valley. Get off now." Joan grabs her suitcase and her carryall, and looks back before she steps off. That small feminine family, all bright colors and chocolate, are laughing at Joan from behind their hands.

Metal steps to packed ground, her rolling suitcase behind her, her carryall strapped across her back. The sign on the platform might be in Hindi, Joan can't tell, but people are yelling in English, "Kangra, Kangra. Bus. Taxi. Here, here," so she is where she is supposed to be, which seems astounding. But where Kangra is in relation to the rest of the world, or, more specifically, where it is in relation to Dharamshala is unclear, and what comes next for Joan seems indeterminate.

Several men are pedaling their rickshaws around the train stop and one man halts his in front of Joan. "Let me show you around, you can get off whenever you want." His voice has the sweet trill she already associates with India. His head nods gracefully while he speaks, and although Joan doesn't know what the nodding means, she knows it means something. The rickshaw driver's face glows, his black eyes sparkle with kindness, his black hair is thick and looks as soft as an animal's pelt.

"That's very kind of you. But don't I need to take a bus to Dharamshala?"

She lifts Eric's itinerary and it whisks in the slight breeze. The itinerary was never meant for Joan to figure out how to get where she is going, and no matter how often she read Eric's confusing margin notes on the *chhotey* train, she is not sure what combination of transportation— grabbing a bus or hailing a taxi or finding a rickshaw or walking—is required now that she has reached Kangra, in order to end up in Dharamshala.

"I think it says here that I'm supposed to take a bus eighteen kilometers to Dharamshala."

"I can take you there. I can tell you have traveled far. Better now to be outside in the fresh air. But so you know, it's McLeod Ganj you are wanting, not Dharamshala."

"Oh," says Joan. "Are you sure?"

"You do not know me, but you can trust me on this. Everyone coming here for the first time says they are wanting Dharamshala, but it is the hill station of McLeod Ganj that they are meaning. That is where the life you are seeking will unfold."

Joan looks down at Eric's itinerary and locates the name McLeod

Ganj, but there is no marginalia about McLeod Ganj versus Dharamshala.

"You're sure?" she asks.

"I am. Dharamshala is shorthand for the whole area."

"All right. So it's McLeod Ganj I want. Is it also eighteen kilometers from here?"

"Maybe four kilometers more. But a mere pittance along the earth comprised of so many miles. A total of thirteen miles or so, give or take. I cycle it many times a day."

He pats his thin thighs, stringy and sharp. When he flexes his calves, Joan sees the strip of his muscles, the lack of any fat.

"See. I am strong and the cycling is easy. Come. I am a good and harmless man who seeks only to be of service."

It is late afternoon, the sun is high and warm, birds are twittering in the trees lining the dusty road, and the rickshaw driver looks fine and respectable. She decides it is unlikely he will leave her for dead, and steps up into the purple carriage of the three-wheeled rickshaw, places her bags at her feet. The man turns around and smiles. "I am Natwar."

Just two days ago, Joan thought she might never smile again. But she has—at Vita Brodkey on the plane, at the stationmaster at Chakki Bank—and she thinks her younger self was right about wanting to come here, there is something particular about India that makes it easier for her to smile.

She smiles back at Natwar. "I'm Joan," she says.

"So good to meet you, Joan," Natwar says, gripping the handlebars of his bike, his legs starting to pump steadily, taking her and her bags and her sundered life away from the small train station and toward Dharamshala.

When Martin joined Men on Bikes, he researched bikes and tested bikes and talked about gears and weight and torque and handling, debating the merits of every single model, until Joan thought she might scream. And after taking his new sleek black bike for a test ride around their neighborhood, he returned saying, "It's kind of scary having your feet locked in. I keep thinking, what if I fall and my feet are attached, and what might have been just a tumble turns into something much worse because I'm falling with a bike attached to me?" Joan had thought that *locked-in feet* was an interesting metaphor for a long-term marriage. "I think you should be in control of the bike, not the other way around," she had said, and Martin agreed, swapping the locked-in pedals for flat ones. And then there were the cycling shoes Martin needed to purchase, each with its own merits and issues, and when Martin opted for the pair with double Velcro straps and a semiflexible sole, Joan watched him clip-clopping around the house, testing them out, and she said, "They're pretty snazzy," which they were.

She is recalling Martin's conundrums about his expensive bike and pedals and shoes because Natwar is wearing rubber sandals, his pedals are flat, and his bike is painted a cheery turquoise, but is clearly old, passed down perhaps through generations, and attached to the bike is Natwar's purple rickshaw that carries the weight of his human cargo. Natwar probably has never had a choice about the bike he might want to ride, or the footwear he might want to wear, or the pedals he might want to spin through the beautiful landscape.

Trees and flowers grow wild in pastures just off the road. Llamas are munching on grass. Kangri villagers and their children are industriously collecting firewood. Traveling thirteen miles or so in a rickshaw takes time, and it feels as if she and Natwar might well travel this way for hours and hours.

Suddenly Natwar rises up off his seat, cycling hard up a steeper road, bumpy and rock-strewn. At the top, he lets out his breath, and then they're moving fast on the flats until eventually a square opens up before them, as if they have stumbled onto a foreign movie set. Monks in crimson robes and nuns in saffron robes strolling everywhere, and people who must be locals, with their bamboo baskets, and others who are clearly foreigners, but at home in this unusual place, and tourists with short socks and sneakers and cameras slung around their necks.

Joan hears chanting, and the sound of lapping water, and singing bowls being struck, the pure sound of their gongs traveling through the air, across the square. In one of Eric's emails, he said the singing bowls emitted sine waves, and she wishes now she had bothered to find out what those are.

"Joan," Natwar calls over his shoulder. "This is McLeod Ganj. We will drive around until we find you suitable accommodation. No pressure because it takes time to look. Like life right? Lots of looking," and Natwar laughs a happy laugh.

He points out various hotels to Joan, bowed or topsy-turvy or built into the outcrops of rock. Joan shakes her head at each.

Natwar comes to a stop at one hotel. "Take a look," he says to her. "But I will say right now that I am not so sure about this place for you."

Joan steps out of the rickshaw and enters the hotel. When she returns, she is shaking her head. "You're right. Not the right one."

The second hotel she enters at Natwar's nod is too large and there is too much gold glinting on the railings, on the tabletops in the lobby, an elevator with a golden door. She might as well be in Las Vegas or Atlantic City.

Natwar shows her three other hotels, but none feels right.

"I'm sorry," Joan says, when she climbs back into the rickshaw for the fifth time.

"No worries, my friend. We will find that which is home for you. I can promise you that."

Natwar pedals back to the main square, past the monks and the nuns and the travelers and the tourists and the locals, past food stands where chefs are busy at their grills and flower sellers are stringing marigolds into necklaces. He takes another narrow dirt road and winds up another steep slope. Fifteen minutes later, he pulls up the drive that has led them to Hotel Gandhi's Paradise, its sign neat and demure, and places his sandaled feet into the dirt. "I am thinking that this one might be just right for you."

She feels like Goldilocks, walking across the sandy path and up the wooden stairs. The walls of the lobby are covered in loose panels of cloth, alternating strips of vibrant Indian red and the sunny yellow of those perky marigolds she saw in the hands of the flower sellers. To the left is a comfortable sitting area, and beyond the sitting area, an enormous window that looks onto a dense stand of trees, dark-brown and lighter-brown trunks, leaves in all shades of green. The place feels relaxed and comfortable and something smells good. Lit incense on a wooden table in the sitting area, its perfume subtle and soothing. A handsome young man, perhaps eighteen or nineteen, stands at the long, low teak reception desk, smiling at Joan.

"Hello," Joan says, "Do you have a room available?"

"Of course, madam. A lovely room. Would you like to see it?"

"No need," Joan says. "I'll be back in a minute."

She walks out of the hotel, down the dirt path she now notices is bordered by small white, yellow, and pink flowers, to Natwar on his bicycle with the rickshaw behind him.

"Yes," Natwar says. "Sometimes it is the sixth place that is the charm. It is what I always say."

Joan laughs and the freedom she hears within her own voice surprises her. She has not laughed since the night at the Sumners', the night before she discovered Daniel's theft, when Martin and Larry Sumner told stories about hospital politics, and she wonders whether it is today or yesterday in Rhome.

Natwar walks her bags into the lobby, and then the two of them are out in front of the hotel, beyond the stairs, and Joan says, "I forgot to ask how much for your good services."

"I never say a price. The client always decides."

At the Delhi train station, Joan exchanged dollars for a thick wad of rupees. The exchange rate on the board read 1 US dollar equaled 30.153 in rupees, so that means the dollar is worth more than the rupee, she thinks. Is that right? She fingers the pastel bills, Gandhi's face in her hands. The denominations are confusing and she has no idea if Natwar's trip should cost ten dollars or a hundred.

"Natwar, I would like to give you fifty American dollars, but I'm not sure what that looks like in your money."

"Thank you," he says, "I accept," and extracts several bills from her stack and counts them out to Joan. She realizes she might be hugely overpaying.

"One thousand five hundred and seven rupees is equal to fifty American dollars," Natwar says. He pockets the fare and then, surprisingly, he wraps Joan in his skinny brown arms.

"Blessings for you, my dear friend."

Joan closes her eyes and bows her head. Three people now have cared about her or done right by her since she left home: Vita Brodkey, the big man, and Natwar.

She is not aware when Natwar's arms release her, but when she opens her eyes, the rickshaw driver and his rickshaw are gone, a puff of dirt just settling back to the ground.

At the low reception desk, the young man says, "You are most welcome here at Hotel Gandhi's Paradise. We are so happy to have you. From where have you arrived?"

"The US," Joan says, and wonders if she should have said America. So she says, "America."

"I thought so. I am familiar with America from living there for two years. I have been back here for eight months," he says.

"Did you like it?"

"Yes, to some degree, but I returned home as soon as I could, wanting to be of aid to my grandparents who own this lovely multiperson abode. But I should not be so personal. My apologies. For how long will you grace us?"

"Three weeks, I think," and Joan sees his eyes beam with innocent pleasure.

"How excellent," and he holds up a key. "For your room. And just so you know, we are completely hooked in. Wi-Fi and cell service and all the small benefits of home."

He insists on carrying her suitcase and her carryall and Joan follows behind. He looks back and says, "We have many guests right now, but I had this sense that I ought to save our best room, and I am glad that I did."

She thinks he must say this to every traveler, about sensing their arrival, saving the best room just for them.

"A correction. I saved for you, though I only sensed you were coming, our very best pine suite."

Suite makes Joan think of Vita Brodkey's three gold suitcases. *Pine* she translates into *pining*, and she thinks that whatever kind of room this young man is going to give her, his best or his worst, somehow he knows she needs a place in which to pine over her losses.

At the end of the corridor, he keys the lock, opens the door, sets her bags inside, and steps out of the way.

"Breakfast will be outside your door every morning. I shall leave you now. But you can always ask me for anything. Call me up on the phone. Come find me. Yell from your door. Anything I can do for you, I will endeavor to do. I am Kartar and you have my word," he says, and Joan thinks how she once had a son whose word she would never have doubted.

It is indeed a *pine* suite. Pine bed frame, pine dresser, pine desk and chair, pine armchair, pine floors, and she laughs. A second laugh since arriving in Dharamshala, and when it sprints up a register, she knows she has kept herself sewn together for quite a long time and now the stitches are starting to tear.

Kartar called this cozy room a *suite*. It is a fraction of the size of the suites she and Martin have stayed in during their family vacations on island resorts, smaller than the rooms she was given as a young writer on her book tours, when she expected garrets. Still, it has all she needs. A thick double bed with an Indian-red coverlet. Sheer marigold-yellow curtains. A desk and chair. An armchair. An ample pine closet. A spacious bathroom with a deep tub set within a slatted pine box. Outlets ready for the adapters she remembered to take from Martin's drawer filled with such travel items.

She feels the need to settle in fast, to make this pine suite her own in an instant. Suitcase opened and clothes hung in the pine closet, folded into the pine drawers. Toiletries on the bathroom counter. Laptop, ream of paper, pens, pads pulled out of her carryall and set on the desk, then she dumps everything else in the bag onto the bed. A Butterfinger falls out, slipped in by Martin, an offering of a sort, and she rips it open, shoves half of it into her mouth, crunches away.

There is a small fridge under the counter in the bathroom, and she opens it hoping to find those little bottles of bliss—vodka, wine, whatever the alcoholic specialty might be of Dharamshala—those benefits of home the young man referenced, that she indulged in on the plane, but it is empty. She opens one of the bottles of water she bought at the Delhi train station, stashes the remaining six in the fridge, and the granola bars she is sick of. Chewing the last of the chocolate, Joan looks at the packaging, bright honey-orange wrapping, and thinks she has butterfingered her own life.

Suitcase and bag in the closet. Novels stacked on the nightstand, but they look wrong, and Joan realizes she has chosen to sleep on the side where Martin sleeps at home, next to the windowed wall. In Dharamshala, she will occupy the side that has never been hers.

She pulls the curtains all the way back, finds that the window is a sliding-glass door that leads out to a small balcony that overlooks the trees. In the reception area, she thought it was a stand of trees, but it is not, it is an entire forest. Joan doesn't recognize some of the trees, but she can identify the oaks and those that are some kind of pine, and she wonders if the pine furniture in her room came from the trees right beyond her balcony.

Then she looks beyond the forest, up and up, at the sky, and before she reaches the heavens, there are the Himalayas on high.

Her deep sigh needs no interpretation—she wants it to be decades ago, when she was still young, when all the choices were hers, before she birthed children, raised a thief, and a recovering addict here in Dharamshala on a quest, when her love for Martin was not so complicated, when her love for Martin had not existed. She believes the young man now—that this is his best room, a perfectly monastic space, safeguarded for a last-minute guest who requires a special cocoon for her broken heart.

She has been holding on, keeping herself upright for so many days, and then during the seven thousand five hundred miles of travel to Delhi, and Joan backs away from the balcony, finds herself flat on the bed, legs jackknifed to her chest, Martin's voice from deep in the past saying, "*Write and write, and just give me the moments when you want a break.*"

And she was foolish to believe him, because later he said, "*I've never been so happy,*" breaking his vow to her at the very beginning. So much blame to spread. Including her own. Her failure to demand her own needs, losing all of her years, sacrificing herself on the altar of motherhood to a son who saved himself from eternal extinction, to a son whose desperation she had missed. Had she followed her own course, she would have sent *Words* to Volkmann immediately, and if she had, there would have been no unguarded manuscript in a box in the garage for Daniel to find.

Now she is a woman who wants to be alone, a mother finished with that role, a writer unable to acknowledge the famed books are hers, unsure how to remember who she was. When she tries picturing herself writing *Words* for all of those years, she can't.

She wants only to leave everything behind, to transcend what has happened, the mistakes she has made. Every fiber of her hopes Dharamshala might be her imagined Devata where her characters came to stay, turning their backs on the outside world, rediscovering the truth of their childhood selves, finding the strength that had ebbed away, allowing their healing hearts to create.

Will this be her actual arcadia, her Devata rendered in three dimensions, where she finds the guidance she desperately needs about what her future might look like?

She needs clarifying golden words right now and wonders if they will fly down to her from the Himalayas, or perhaps one day float to her straight from the Dalai Lama's mouth, or if she will have to discover them for herself.

Just then she tastes salt. Salt from tears new and old and those formed so long ago they date back to childhood. In an instant, undammed, they are flowing, coming faster and faster and faster, sealing her eyes, cracking her skin, sinking her entirely.

33

There is ringing where Joan is, deep inside the ferocious jet lag, under the red coverlet that is over her head, her skull soldered to the pillow. The ringing keeps on, even when she sticks her head out, opens her eyes, sees her pine suite, feels her curdled pain. She can't figure out the sound, but it stops, and she thinks, *good,* and only when the ringing begins again does she realize someone's calling her cell phone, once, twice, who knows how many times.

Through thousands of layers of cotton, Joan hears a voice say, "It's Iger. Joan, it's Annabelle. Can you hear me? Are you there?"

"Yes. I'm here, absolutely exhausted. You got my email."

"There aren't enough words to express how sorry I am, to let you know we are mortified by what's happened, that we're taking every step to rectify it all."

"Did everything arrive?"

"Yes, the file with your novel, and the original book and the copyright registration you FedExed. I have in front of me the contract Daniel signed. His signature's illegible, but no one had any reason to question the author's signature. But it's my responsibility. I take full blame. I should have vetted the books, followed my instinct when they reminded me of your work, but for all these years, you've told me you weren't writing, so I never considered the books might actually belong to you."

"Book," Joan says.

"Book?

"Of course. Book. Two books now," Iger says.

"I should have sensed immediately that something was wrong because J. D. Henry—Daniel—wouldn't meet with me. He refused to provide photos and bios for the back flaps, said he was old-school, that the writing spoke for itself, that who he was and what he looked like would detract, but that he would send me the acknowledgments he wanted to use. It's so rare these days a writer doesn't want to be recognized, and I was thinking, how refreshing, Pynchon, Salinger, old Harper Lee, thinking it was time another writer came along who preferred mystery.

"Other things should have tipped me off too, like having to fight for the option to his next book because he really did not want to give it to me, talking about how he couldn't write on a deadline or with someone looking over his shoulder. And the fact that he only agreed to interviews he could do via email or on the phone. I thought maybe he was shy, or his face was somehow scarred. In the interviews he did give, he refused to reveal anything about himself personally, but he was incredibly erudite discussing the books. I thought he was a different breed of writer and I loved it. Never once was my radar turned on.

"I bought the books for an astronomical sum in a best-bid auction. It was fast, three days to read. It's no excuse, but I adored them, was elated we got them for the imprint. I hadn't intended to publish them as soon as I did, but they were ready to go, needed no editing, and now I understand why."

Iger pauses, and Joan knows she is waiting for her to acknowledge the compliment, but she doesn't.

"So. When one of my writers blew her schedule, I had a hole to fill. It won't make anything better, but the publicity and marketing campaigns have been very successful. Foreign rights sold in twenty countries so far, and they've been literary marvels since publication in March, colossal best sellers now in their fourth month."

From thousands of miles away, Joan hears Iger release her breath, through lips in her signature red no matter the late hour. She can picture Iger standing at her enormous mirrored desk, up on a high floor in her Manhattan office, a warrior marshaling the written dreams of others.

"Neil Silver, Daniel's agent, or rather former agent, is humiliated by all of this. He's doing all he can to be helpful. Forwarded second interview requests from *Vanity Fair*, *The New Yorker*, *O*, and NPR. Daniel refused their requests for interviews because they wanted to meet with him personally. It doesn't make sense now to put the books back together, but at some distant time, we can reveal you as the writer. If that's what we want to do. Or if sales flag. We don't have to make a decision now."

"Iger," Joan says. To stop her old friend—now her publisher—from doing what Iger does best, spinning words until she achieves her desired result.

"Iger, there can't be any interviews. I can't pretend to be J. D. Henry. I don't want to pretend to be J. D. Henry. I don't want to *lie*. Daniel's lie is what caused all of this. And I'm not ready to consider public ridicule and shame for him. Or for me."

"I get it. That's fine. We don't have to do anything now. Because the books are selling. I promise you, I'll make this right. I've got calls with your lawyers in the morning about everything that needs to be done. Rescinding the old contract between J. D. Henry and Annabelle Iger Books, drafting a new contract between you and AIB. I understand that your lawyer here in New York will claw back from Daniel the AIB advances he pocketed, and the West Coast lawyer is assuming the reins from Neil Silver for negotiating the film options."

There is too much information for Joan to process.

"Iger," Joan says. "I haven't hired any lawyers."

"You have. Or rather Martin has for you. He took care of all that while you were flying. Listen, try to let this all go if you can. We're making it right on this end. I'll call you again after I talk to them. How is India, by the way?"

It's her first full day in Dharamshala, and if Iger had said it was midnight in New York when she called, it's now one in the morning there, and in Rhome. She punches in their home number.

"I'm here and I'm safe, but I don't want lawyers. I wrote to Iger from the airport, and I just got off the phone with her," she says, when Martin picks up.

"You have to have lawyers, Joan. People to look out for your rights. Right now, both the agent and Iger are in precarious positions. You could sue the agent. You could sue Iger, the publishing house, her imprint, and you could sue Daniel. She has to do everything she can, and so does the agent, but you have to do the same thing. I've gotten everything going. I called our lawyer, who gave me the name of a New York lawyer, someone top in publishing, and she'll handle those aspects. I gave her your account details, told her to execute whatever legal steps she needed to take against Daniel. I know she's already contacted him, but I don't know anything more than that. And she gave me the name of a movie lawyer in Los Angeles, and that lawyer is up to speed. I know it's not everything you want, your name on the books, but at least you'll benefit as you should. Both of them are going to call you, not today, I guess, or not my today. It's nearly one thirty here. What time is it there?"

"Eleven. In the morning. I'm nine and a half hours ahead of you."

"Listen, try to enjoy being there if you can. I hope the weather's nice. I miss you already."

"It is nice weather," Joan says, crawling out of bed, pulling open the sheer curtains, confirming the truth of what she has just said.

"Martin—"

"Yes?"

"Thank you."

So Daniel knows that she knows. She wonders when she will hear from him, if he will send careful words arranged in a feeble defense, provide verbal reparation, a chest-beating apology, drown himself in a shower of mea culpas.

She remembers Kartar said breakfast would be outside of her door early each morning, and there is the tray with a covered bowl, a covered cup, a pale pink flower in a purple vase. She sets the tray down on the pine desk. The cooked lentils and barley tea are both cold, but the tray has been sitting out there for hours. She steps onto the balcony, feels the sun on her face, glad the two lawyers Martin hired for her are women. Men have messed up her life and now it's time for the women, herself included, to fix it.

Her reflection in the bathroom mirror is a shock. There is a leonine, savage cast to her eyes, something anarchic even, and inside, a ferocious desire to maul something, or someone, that fired up at Dulles the moment she sent the email to Iger, and only intensified during all the airborne miles, while riding the trains that brought her to this place.

She will let the lawyers Martin hired fight for her. She will let them go as far as they can. She will not be bested, even by a once-favored son. Whether she will expose Daniel as a filial thief and plagiarist is a much larger decision she is not yet prepared to make.

The severity of her expression does not alter while she brushes her teeth, washes her face, plaits her long black curls into a thick braid, thinking that if Daniel voluntarily returns the money, the bank account she opened when she was twenty-one will soon receive a mammoth deposit. Iger told her the amount of the book advance, seven figures for both. She tries to smile at herself in the mirror, to pretend she is part of the living world. Then she gives up and puts on lipstick, blushes her pale cheeks.

At the closet, she finds a fresh pair of linen pants, another loose top, the golden sandals gleaming with crystals she swore she would never wear until she made it to India. Slipping her feet into them, she thinks: *Now I am here.*

She is starving, the first vigorous hunger she has felt since she was at the limestone island, staring down at Daniel's Lewis Carroll quotes, those preposterous, infantile challenges. She retrieves a wad of rupees from her wallet, tucks them into her pocket along with her room key.

The pine suite door closes solidly behind her. Only now does Joan notice the expansive width of the hallway, the bright natural light streaming through large windows at either end, making the gold, copper, platinum, and clear crystals of her sandals pop and gleam. The stone floor is smooth under her soles. She has not been outside of the hotel since Natwar delivered her here yesterday afternoon. She is eager to feel Dharamshala air on her skin, the sustaining warmth of its sun, to see the wildflowers she saw along the dirt road when Natwar was biking so hard. She wants the sharp tang of coffee on her tongue, she wants something delicious to eat.

"Hello, missus. I hope you had a good night of sleeping," Kartar says, when she finds him at his post at the low teak reception desk.

"I did," Joan says. "Thank you. But please, you don't need to call me missus. If you could, just call me Ashby."

The simple act of claiming her original last name loosens one of the tight knots that has been lodged in her heart since she sat in the parking lot of the Tell-Tale Bookstore, her stolen work in her lap.

"Of course," he says, nodding. "I will endeavor to remember."

"Where shall I go for something to eat? I'm starving. I'm so sorry, by the time I brought in the lovely tray, everything had gone cold."

"No problem at all. Sleep is better than all the lentils and barley tea in the world." Then he is rummaging beneath the reception desk, and when he rises up, he hands her a thick guidebook.

"Take this with you so that you will always know where you are. Keep it as long as you are here. For now, you should head down the hill. After a while, you will come to the marketplace."

Hotel Gandhi's Paradise is a mile from the center of McLeod Ganj. The steep dirt road is rocky under her sparkly sandals. In the distance, Joan sees the multicolored prayer flags that Kartar said mark the beginning of the marketplace. There is no breeze, and the flags, raised on high sticks, hang down, as if taking noon naps. It seems she may never reach the marketplace, but then she is within it, walking past shops displaying Kashmiri scarves, harem pants, hand-knit woolens, prayer bells, tuning forks, singing bowls and mallets, glass jars of pickles and chutneys, jewelry presented to passersby on rough cloth or black velvet.

Along the main street, in front of the shops, are the food stalls she saw yesterday, their pungent offerings wafting into the air. There is the popcorn seller popping his corn, and the baker baking his Tibetan bread, and aproned chefs sporting white toques sautéing buckets of green vegetables, and other chefs doing other things to other kinds of ingredients. The delectable aromas harshened by the scent of frying red pepper. Joan considers dipping in, but it feels too soon, this is only her first outing, and Dr. Abram's admonitions are loud in her head. She has gone through too much to arrive here, on this street, in Dharamshala, in India. She does not want to be felled because she braved the fare at the stalls.

On Temple Road, she spots the Namgyal Café. The outdoor dining patio with its picnic-style tables is empty, though the air is warm, the sun centered in the sky. Inside, she is the only customer. A girl with a smooth brown face, a small nose, and stubby pigtails sprouting all over her head that makes Joan think of a sea anemone, waves her hand.

"Sit anywhere you want," she says. Joan takes a seat at a window table.

"Good timing," the girl tells Joan, bringing her a menu. "Our busy lunch hour is from one to three, so you're ahead of the huge crowd we always get. Just so you know, we have good omelets and our pancakes are breathtaking."

Joan didn't expect a café in Dharamshala to serve the same things as a coffee shop back home. In one of his emails, Eric had written Dharamshala was a melting pot of cuisines, dishes spiced with turmeric, Tibetan noodles, and something called momo that looked like dim sum. It is the first time Joan has thought of Eric since settling in at Hotel Gandhi's Paradise.

"What is the sweetest thing you serve?" Joan asks, surprised she is again craving sugar after Martin's Butterfinger yesterday. At home, she avoids sugar and fats. In her younger years, when she wrote every day, then wandered the streets of New York at night, she ate whatever she wanted, pizza, ice-cream cones, French fries, smelly cheeses and French breads, and when she took a break on weekend days and traversed Chinatown, she always ended up buying a box of almond cookies she ate one after the other on the walk home, and a fish fillet she wasn't sure how to prepare and ended up tossing out a few days later. Once she put *Words* into its box, she found herself obeying an incomprehensible, self-imposed code that resulted in an entire year during which she ate no meat, chicken, or fish, a year of giving up the flesh.

"Creamy banana cake," says the girl. "Made here every single day from scratch. It's pretty scrumptious."

Soon Joan is spooning the confection into her mouth, feeling the sugar hit her bloodstream, waking her up. She wants another piece, maybe three or four more, but she orders a latte instead, wonders if there is such a thing as Indian coffee. When the sea anemone girl delivers the cup, Joan looks at the design etched in the frothy milk. It is the face of a lion on the prowl for prey to snap up, jaw unhinged, sharp teeth on display.

She drinks it slowly, then pays her bill.

"Please come again soon," the anemone girl far from the sea says. "You're from America, right? I have so many questions to ask you."

"I'll come back, and you can ask me whatever you'd like," Joan tells her.

Joan window-shops through the marketplace until a large tent rises up in front of her. Kartar's guidebook says this is Tsug Lakhang, the complex that houses the Dalai Lama's residence, a temple, a monastery, a museum, a library, and archives. Eric probably wrote her and Martin about it, and Natwar must have driven past it and pointed. The white tent, she reads, is designed to shelter the devotees who congregate here daily. She looks up from the book and a woman is circling the main enclosure with a sick dog in her arms, apparently praying for its recovery. People are hunched like turtles in the open air, chests and knees on small patterned carpets lined up in a row. Joan hears them chanting.

Old and young—Dharamshalans, youthful backpackers, those wearing the look of the permanently transplanted—sit on benches under the shirred sun. There is a current running through everything, an intrinsic collectivity.

At the main entrance of the temple, two idols seated in meditation postures flank a large stone Buddha. According to the guidebook, the idols are Avalokitesvara, the bodhisattva of compassion, of whom the Dalai Lama is considered to be the current emanation, and Padmasambhava, the Indian yogi who introduced Buddhism to Tibet in the eighth century. The Buddha is Shakyamuni, the true Buddha, the Awakened Buddha.

> *Early in the young prince's life, he was profoundly troubled*
> *by the inherent human suffering he witnessed. As soon as*
> *he was able, he renounced his princely status and set off*
> *on a spiritual quest with a single purpose: to determine*
> *how such suffering might be overcome. He tried all*
> *manner of ascetic disciplines, but nothing, including self-*
> *mortification, had the ability to emancipate his mind*
> *and soul. He continued on his way, until he reached the*

*city of Gaya. There, exhausted from his journey, he sat
down under a Bodhi tree and began his usual meditation.
But something was different this time. The nature of his
meditation grew deeper, and deeper still. And then, suddenly, he attained what he had been seeking for so long:
an awakening, an enlightenment, an understanding about
the true nature of life and all things. From that day forth,
he traveled throughout the Indian subcontinent, sharing
what he had learned, tirelessly teaching people how to
unravel themselves from the suffering that life always
brings, how to unleash the great potential they carried
within.*

Joan would welcome an awakening, an enlightenment, the unleashing
of her own great potential here in Dharamshala.

She enters the temple. The first room is lit by small lamps, smells of
lamp oil and smoke. Writings and pictures cover the walls. The guidebook says these are the sacred hymns and mantras of Buddhism and
pictorial representations of its teachings. Did Eric read up on the history of Dharamshala, this temple, its adherents, the monks and nuns
who are in abundance, its pilgrims, before he arrived?

"Aren't you going to complete a *kora*?" a thin older woman says to
Joan in a crisp British accent. Her full-throated voice is jarring in the
silence where people are meditating and contemplating.

"Akora?"

"No, dear, not *akora*, but a *kora*. I've been watching you. Before
you take all of this in, it's best if you go back outside, down the path,
past the monks' quarters, which is the Namgyal Monastery, all the
way to the start of the trailhead. Then you circumambulate clockwise
and turn all the prayer wheels clockwise to send prayers out in all
directions."

"Does it matter that I'm not a Buddhist, that I don't believe?" Joan
asks.

"Everyone believes, even if they don't know it," the woman says.
"Do you believe in goodness?"

"Yes," Joan says.

"Do you believe in evil?"

"Yes."

"Do you believe we can make our way past our own suffering while we are in this world?"

Joan isn't sure about that, but isn't this why she's here?

"I hope that's true," Joan says.

"So make your first *kora*," the woman says.

There must be a question in Joan's eyes because the Englishwoman takes her hand, the way Fancy used to do with the boys, and leads Joan out of the anteroom, through the entrance, beneath the tent, down the path, past the monastery, to the very start of the trailhead.

Joan sees red and gold prayer wheels evenly fanned out all the way back up the path.

"That's the first one," the Englishwoman says. "Go over and turn it clockwise, only clockwise. It is literally an exercise in faith."

The prayer wheels are heavy. They do not turn easily. They require force of body and purpose of will, and after Joan turns the first prayer wheel clockwise, she and the Englishwoman walk to the next one, and the one after that, and the one after that, and on and on, and when they finish circumambulating around the entire temple complex, turning every one of the prayer wheels, Joan's arms ache and she is sweating. But the devastation, the desolation, the heartache, whatever she might call it, has shifted. The burden inside is still weighty, but there has been the slightest of movements.

At the temple entrance, the Englishwoman says, "I am Camille Nagy. You don't know anything, do you dear?"

"I don't," Joan says. "I've only been here since yesterday."

"Did you not study up?"

Joan shakes her head. "I had no time. But I will."

"I certainly hope so. There is much you can gain from being in this place, but you must know what you're doing."

Camille Nagy pats her neat flinty bun at her neck, flattens out the nonexistent wrinkles in her practical brown tweed skirt. She must be hot in those clothes, Joan thinks.

"If you plan on staying, perhaps we'll see one another again. I take Ela's meditation class every afternoon at two, right out in the Tsug

Lakhang courtyard, on the mountain side of the complex. It would be good for you to join in."

The older woman takes a few steps. "Wait," she says, though Joan has not moved from her spot.

"What is your name?"

It was easier to identify herself with Kartar, but with this woman it feels more like a declaration.

"Ashby," Joan eventually says. "Ashby."

Camille Nagy studies Joan with her coal black eyes, as beaded as a bird's.

"The first thing you need to figure out is exactly who you are, only then can you become who you want to be," and then Camille Nagy walks briskly away, in the manner of the spry and purposeful Englishwoman that she is.

Camille Nagy is right, Joan thinks, she does need to figure out exactly who she is, and then she is walking back into the monastery and climbing the temple staircase. At the top, a guard stops her.

"Before you enter this room, know that if you plan to circumambulate, you must do so in a clockwise direction."

Does everyone in India refer to walking as *circumambulation*, or does circumambulation mean the kind of walking one does only in places like this? Joan would like to know the answer to that, but at least she knows what she is to do.

The room is dim, years of layered paint peeling from the walls. Fifty or more monks are fluttering around, their red habits piped in blue. Their heads bald, their faces tranquil and composed, their mouths ascetic, even as they engage in animated debate. Not animated debate, Joan realizes, but animated prayer, their voices mingling and melding into a solid sound. She lets the voices wash over her, locates a single one, follows its elevation, its dips, until it disappears and is replaced by another.

An hour later, she is in the temple courtyard. People are sitting in a circle on red pillows, with their eyes closed, chanting away. This must be where the meditation class Camille Nagy attends is held, and there is Camille Nagy on a stack of red pillows, her body perfectly still, her stern mouth no longer stern, her lips turned up in a smile as she chants along with the others.

There are twelve different voices at twelve different registers, but somehow they come together, a unified sound, and when Joan feels she is intruding, seeing bared so many hearts, she walks on, to the back of the courtyard, until the chanting trickles away. Small pine trees in a row, and beyond them, the hills appear so close, a trick of vision, of perspective that encourages Joan to reach out her hands, to touch the toothy edges of the landscape, but reality is something different, and far away.

When the exhaustion of jet lag pulls at her, she makes her way back to the marketplace. The hotel provides its morning breakfast tray, but she did not ask whether there is a restaurant on-site, if she can order room service when she returns. She suspects not. She needs to be horizontal soon, on her comfortable bed, under the red coverlet, but if she wakes in the middle of the night, she will want something to eat. She sees a small store, its windows displaying children's toys, a tower of bottled water, an assortment of intricate kites. She buys a bag of potato chips, another Butterfinger bar, an icy Dr Pepper, which she has not drunk since she was a teenager, and starts up the hill to the hotel. She does not need to decide anything more about Daniel, not at this time. She does not need to consider when she should find Eric. She does not need to talk to Martin. She need only put one beautiful golden crystalled sandal in front of another, recall the creamy banana cake, the lion in the latte, the girl with her stubbed braids, the monks praying, the Buddha, Camille Nagy and the meditators, and everything else she has seen so far.

From the balcony of her pine suite, she watches the flaming sun impale itself on the Himalayas. Can prayers sent out in a single *kora* do the trick, correct the wrongs in one human life? Would her people in Devata believe in such a miracle? They might, Joan knows, but she's not there yet, for her the answer is still no.

34

She is in the tub nestled within its pine box, her cell phone on the ledge, when it rings. It is nine in the evening, Dharamshala time.

"Hi, Joan, this is Sherri Angell. I gather you know who I am. Your lawyer in Los Angeles dealing with the movie rights to the books."

"I do," Joan says. "Hello."

"Hi," and Sherri Angell gets down to business. "So the last two days have been very productive. We've got a final agreement, pending your approval. I've sent it to the email address Dr. Manning provided for you. It would be great if you could read it right away. If you're on board, then sign the signature page, and fax it back to me. I think we ought to lock this down right now. You're going to be very pleased."

"I will," Joan says. "Give me a couple of hours."

"Of course. Call me with any questions or issues."

In the fogged mirror, Joan's face is gauzy, her limbs wrapped in white steam. She looks like a ghost who may soon disappear for good.

Even at this hour, Kartar is still at the reception desk. "I have a favor to ask," Joan says to him, and explains what she needs.

"Of course, Ashby, with all of my pleasure. Come this way."

He leads her around the teak reception desk to a small alcove. Desk, computer, printer, fax machine. Next to a small stone Buddha, serene and contemplative, a stick of incense releases delicate smoky curls. He fills the printer tray with paper, shows Joan how to log onto her email, and the button she needs to press to print.

"I'll be out there. Just call when you require me for the faxing."

Soon she hears him on the telephone speaking in his native language, a musical lilt to his words, a songbird at work.

The printer is slow and the contract Sherri Angell has sent is long, and Joan sits in the cozy alcove listening to the shush of the pages. Then she begins to read.

The film options for both books total a million dollars, against a purchase price for each of three million, with more due Joan if the production budgets go over thirty-five million, forty, forty-five, sixty. She is entitled to five percent of any net profits.

She puts her hand to her forehead and stares at all of the figures, huge figures written out in words, in numbers with dollar signs between parentheses. Although the books do not carry her name, between the publishing and movie monies, she will be wealthy in her own right, and stands to become much more than that.

She balls up her right hand into a fist to stop its trembling before she can sign her name below the other signature, the signature of an international American movie star who, Angell told her, has started his own production company, wants these books to be his first major cinematic splash as a producer.

"I'm ready," Joan calls out quietly, and then Kartar is next to her, taking the slip of paper with the West Coast lawyer's information out of Joan's hand. Joan watches the stick of incense burn itself out, a last plume fading in the air.

Within moments, the fax machine whirs and delivers a confirmation page. The extraordinary contract she never could have imagined has been received on the other end.

Back in her room, there is a message on her phone. It is the East Coast lawyer, named Spellman, who says, "Hello, Ms. Ashby. Liz Spellman here. I'm calling to confirm that the funds from Daniel Manning have been transferred into your account, details supplied by Dr. Manning." Joan saves the message and the phone beeps in her hand. A text from Sherri Angell: "Thx. Got it. We're good to go."

Joan stands out on her balcony in the dark night, the lit stars looking close enough to swallow. Publishing advance, movie option money, Joan will have no need to ask for anything, not for her equity share of their renovated house, the land still in her name, Martin's successful practice, what they have in investments.

Is she really thinking about this?

About cutting ties, leaving the past behind, moving fully unencumbered into her future? Does she want to leave behind the man she does still love in some way, the good life that is theirs, the remnants of family, her position in the town where they are known and liked and admired? She would miss the grand architectural house, the lap pool in the bucolic glen, the Croatian limestone island in the kitchen, the shed hiding behind the weeping willow tree where she thought she would return to her writing.

Was her oft-desired flight from home, to India, her escape? Her son who went rogue and eviscerated his mother merely the excuse to do what she considered doing so many times? Well, his duplicity can't be designated as her excuse. But how convoluted it is: because of Daniel, and Martin's insistence on the lawyers, Joan can choose to live as she pleases, a life focused on her own work, if she desires, without any demands on her time, temporal roadblocks, emotional fastballs. She wonders if Martin understands that in helping her to negotiate this travesty, he has insured her freedom.

35

At dawn, Joan carries in the Hotel Gandhi's Paradise breakfast tray from outside her door. The flower is an orange lily in an orange vase. She sits at the desk and eats the delicious hot lentils, drinks the hot barley tea, considers Camille Nagy's instructions about educating herself.

She should find a bookstore down in the marketplace, spend some hours reading about where she is. Instead, she stretches out on the bed and thumbs through Kartar's guidebook. The entry about Bhagsu Falls intrigues. There is a temple nearby and a pool of natural spring water where one can take a "holy dip," before climbing to the top.

She did not bring a bathing suit or hiking boots, but in the pine closet are the sneakers she wears on the pressure walks Martin researches, when they drive to a starting point, sometimes an hour away, and take strenuous, speedy walks Joan finds bullet-pointed in a way she finds hard to interpret. The soles are thickly ribbed and should be sufficient for her to climb half a mountain.

By nine, she is outside the hotel on the dirt path, checking the hand-drawn map Kartar drew for her. Fields of flowers span both sides of the road that leads to the mountain she will climb to the falls. She climbs and climbs, passing a few cafés, shops selling tea and snacks and trinkets, and then, at the base of the mountain, a Shiva temple appears, caught in shade. Beyond, a lemon sun beckons.

She expected to find a lot of people preparing to ascend, but Joan is on her own. The trail is well marked, a gradual rise that grows steeper the farther she walks. There are straightaways and hairpin turns, and then the trail hugs the edge of the cliff. Far below, in the valley, there are black boulders and white boulders, huge as sun-drenched whales. The valley must be a riverbed, filling up when the rains come and the winter snow melts.

Unearthly silence, except for the quiet thresh of small insects she can't see at all and leave her alone. Her hair is damp from sweat, her legs sore, despite all her years of yoga. The air smells of crushed flowers.

A murmuring, then a thundering roar, and the Bhagsu Falls appear, powerful, picturesque, water gnashing against rocks, arching from its high point into a gorgeous aerial display. The sun folding into geysers sparks rainbows that remind her of the old lady in the blue sari on the *chhotey* who was still smiling when Joan disembarked.

She sits cross-legged on the ground for an hour, until her body is beating in time to the crashing falls. Then a second hour, fighting the jet lag she feels, amidst the deafening noise. Then a third hour, when the pounding reverberations of water against rock are humming through her, as if she, too, is a natural wonder, awake in a way that is wholly different and new.

Her muscles are tight from sitting on the ground for so long. She pushes herself up from the dirt, stretches her arms high, moves into the force of the sun, feels its tight grip.

She thinks that it is only her second day here, too soon to expect answers of any kind. She needs to engage in another *kora* or two, or ten, or twenty, perhaps give meditation a chance, sit on those red pillows and chant. Her people in Devata did not do that, but maybe she will.

She stares down the mountain, and begins the long walk back.

36

"Is this Vita Brodkey?"

"I know your voice. Such a lovely voice I thought, during our long trip together. How are you enjoying Dharamshala?"

This is Joan's seventh day in Dharamshala, and while the jet lag is mostly gone, each night, her dreams are terrible. She is a child breaking a window in her parents' house to escape their malevolent clutches. She is wearing a wedding gown and Martin is holding her hand, but instead of speaking her vows, black words big as ravens fly from her mouth, hang in the air, in the space between them, then start flapping their wings, sending the wedding guests running. She is newly pregnant with Daniel and taking a long knife to her belly. She is watching Eric leap into the darkness of space and does not pull him back. Horrendous dreams when she is in them, but so simplistic that no psychological interpretation is needed. She won't tell Vita her dreams, but Vita's advice, when she was in the car with Abhay at the wheel about to commence the ten-hour trip to Udaipur, has stayed in Joan's mind since that day. And it is nice to hear Vita's springy voice again.

"Everything is well here. How is Udaipur. Is it as you recall?"

"Nothing stays the same, of course. I was once young and beautiful, and now I am old and not nearly as beautiful, but I am staying at the Taj Lake Palace in the middle of Lake Pichola and it is gorgeous."

"The hotel is in the lake?"

"Right in the middle of the lake. It is a dream come true. I've taken some of the heritage walks offered by the hotel, to reacquaint myself with places from my childhood, and I have given in to my secret indulgence, sessions with the astrologer on the hotel's staff. Isn't that marvelous, an astrologer on staff! It seems only right to know what my future has in store for me."

Joan laughs. "And what have you learned, Vita?"

"Well, Biju says I am far from being done with love. A handsome man will sweep me off my feet. Love is waiting for me right around the corner."

"Love is around the corner in this life?"

"Yes, darling, in this life. Not the next. I asked Biju the same thing. What do I care about love in another realm? It's here-and-now love I'm interested in. Biju says her name means great, powerful, and awesome, and she never fools around with predictions of the heart or the wallet, that really she has nothing to do with any of it, she is just reading my life in my stars."

"Is the house where you grew up still there?"

"It is, darling, and someone has maintained it beautifully. I am meeting with an estate agent tomorrow who is going to take me around my wonderful old neighborhood. He says there may be an available house for me to rent, while he looks for a place I might buy. I must remember to ask Biju about that, if she can read my stars to tell me the address I should be watching for."

"Have you started painting your watercolors yet?"

"Not yet, soon though, I have promised myself that. But enough of me, tell me how you are spending your days."

"I have my breakfast at dawn here at the hotel, and then coffee midmorning at the Namgyal Café, a half-hour walk from where I'm staying, and the young waitress at the café, Lakshmi, asks me to explain how Boston differs from Dallas, Maine from Missouri, Los Angeles from Detroit, if cowboy boots are still in style, ripped jeans, the Japanese way of doing makeup. I didn't know there was such a thing as the Japanese way of doing makeup. She wants to know if she'll be seen as American if she dyes her hair pink or green. I can't figure out how she comes up with these various comparisons, or what she needs the information for, but I try my best, and the way she puts these ideas together is funny.

"And I've gathered my courage and eat dinners at the food stalls along Temple and Bhagsu Roads. The chefs nod and smile and hand me my order of momo. Scrumptious, as Lakshmi says. I've been to Bhagsu Falls twice, and to the Norbulingka Institute, and to Dalhousie. I've explored several temples, and the meditation rooms at the Dalai Lama's complex, watching the monks turning prayer wheels in that unhurried way they have. An exercise of faith I find impossible to grasp, even though I've done a few *koras* myself."

Vita does not know Joan's reason for being here in Dharamshala, and so Joan does not say that in these seven days, despite all that she has seen, it is a very slow process, this regaining of internal stability. Still, she finds herself breathing a little easier each morning in the buoyant air, and when Kartar says, "Good morning, Ashby," "Good afternoon, Ashby," "Good evening, Ashby," her name is beginning again to reflect something worthwhile.

"Sounds marvelous, darling. Please do not be insulted by what I say now. You sound like you believe you must prove what you've seen. That you're experiencing everything. But what you're experiencing is outside of yourself. Do you remember what I said to you—that you are meant to reclaim the young girl you were? I think you need a break from the sightseeing, or at least something more than sightseeing. You need to commune, not with nature at large, or the history of where you are, but with your own nature and your own history."

Before Joan can respond, Vita Brodkey says, "I do not need to know what ails you, but I know you came here to rediscover yourself and it is critical you do so. It would be a shame were you to return home without accomplishing that. . . . Oh darling, I must go. Biju has arrived for my third session. I do want to know what my next love will look like. Whitson was not very tall, and it would be nice if this one was. Call anytime!"

Vita is right. Joan has been alone, keeping to herself, walking everywhere, engaging only with Lakshmi at the café, with Kartar at the desk, nodding at those visiting the places she visits, but it is not the same as communing with herself. Indeed, her dreams are substantive evidence that she is avoiding that kind of communion.

She made one decision several days ago. She will not seek Eric out until she is ready.

Two decisions. Starting today, she will take a break from Iger's and Martin's phone calls. Her contract with AIB is now signed, so really, what is there to talk about with Iger, especially since Joan has taken off the table any discussion about Daniel's actions. And when she speaks with Martin, she finds herself gritting her teeth in response to his deliberately light and loving words. Last night, the words were not as deliberately light or loving. "When are you coming home?" She reminded him she planned to stay three weeks, but that her return ticket was open-ended, and she might not rush back. When he said, "Joan, nothing will get resolved with Daniel while you're so far away," she had needed to take a deep breath before saying, "Martin. I'm not interested right now in *resolving* anything with Daniel." For a long time, he was silent, transmitting over all the thousands of miles between them the cool current he meant for her to hear, the knowledge, too, that he was deliberately refraining from the fight he was yearning to start. He finally said, "Right. You're right. Stay as long as you need." From now on, she will no longer listen to their voicemails, she will send them travelogue emails of what she sees when she feels like it, but she will excise their voices, the way they insist on ushering in the faraway world.

Three decisions. Tomorrow she will go to that afternoon meditation class in the Dalai Lama's courtyard, and perhaps Camille Nagy will be there. How difficult it all is. She has what she has long wanted: an unfastened life. And she is starting to recapture the solitude and independence she forfeited with marriage and motherhood. She is free as a bird, beholden to neither person nor clock, coming and going as she wants, eating and drinking only when the urge strikes, not worrying about anyone's needs or desires or threats to their existence, but now that time is all hers, her mind no longer belongs to her alone, her heart pumps steadily, but when it thumps out of alignment, beats irregularly, she knows which hard beats belong to Daniel, which to Martin. Perhaps meditation will help.

Four decisions. She will give up expecting any apology from Daniel. His silence should tell her that he is aware the English language lacks sufficient words to explain his actions, that however she might have failed him, she did not deserve such devastation.

Five decisions. She will stop beating herself up for not yet contemplating the idea of writing. She is still a heartsick writer with stolen work, riven and given titles she hates. The fury has not cooled much. Perhaps the meditation can help with that too.

Six decisions. She will print out the letter she wrote to the Dalai

Lama at Dulles waiting for her plane to Delhi. She will ask Kartar if there is a special mailbox for letters written to him. She will ask if sending her letter to the Dalai Lama, with the hope that she might meet him, is like believing she can win the lottery.

Well, she has won a kind of lottery, hasn't she? But money doesn't solve everything: all the new dollars in her separate account won't alter the fact that Daniel has expunged so many years of her life, wiped out the motherhood she had never wanted but fully embraced, crushed the illusions she had about herself as a mother, and those dollars won't help her determine what her next steps ought to be, or return to her the grace she found writing all those words he stole.

The lottery she's thinking of, it's the spiritual one. How does she win that one?

37

In the courtyard of Tsug Lakhang, the Dalai Lama's complex, the red silk pillows are already set out, twelve of them in a circle, like numbers on a clock.

Three young men sporting weedy beards stand together, at pillows one, two, and three, hands deep in the pockets of their jeans, talking in whispers.

A young woman with cropped peroxided hair is trying to settle herself on the nine pillow. She is round as a ball, dressed in a white sort of muumuu, and the silk pillow disappears beneath her bulk.

A striking woman of indefinable age is behind the pillow at twelve. Her hair is an umber braid, thick as rope, a vermillion stripe down her middle part, a vermillion bindi between her eyebrows. She wears a green sari and radiates calm. She nods at Joan, puts her palms together, and bows. This must be the teacher, Joan thinks, and feels silly when she puts her own palms together and bows in return greeting.

Joan debates which pillow to choose and decides on the one at six. Turned away from the courtyard vista, she will give herself every chance to avoid distraction. Why does this feel so foreign to her, as if she is nearly a fraud? She has done yoga for years, thousands of classes that concluded with *Shavasna*, a silent pose that encourages the stilling of the mind. It doesn't last long, but for those five minutes in *Shavasna*, wasn't she meditating?

A hand on her shoulder. "You've come, Ashby," Camille Nagy says. "Good for you. I wondered if you would show up."

Camille is still wearing her Englishwoman's clothing, tweed slacks this time, in the same brown pattern as the skirt she was wearing when Joan met her, a cream blouse with a Peter Pan collar. She might be in her mid-sixties, but her clothing reminds Joan of the uniforms worn by private-school children.

"I'll sit next to you. I'll introduce you to Ela after," Camille Nagy says.

Her hair is in the tight bun Joan remembers. There is a funny incongruity between her buttoned-up appearance and her sweet "*Namaste*" to the teacher.

"*Namaste*," Ela says in return, sweeping Camille into an embrace, and Joan sees how the older woman stiffens, an Englishwoman through and through. Joan wonders if this is Camille's first time in Dharam-shala as well and somehow she figured out more quickly how to experience this place more deeply than Joan.

Camille bends down, removes her low-heeled practical shoes, and places them off to the side. She makes her way onto the seven pillow and closes her eyes.

A middle-aged couple arrives. They look to Joan like twins, their features so similar, white hair, sharp and straight, falling to their shoulders, prominent noses. It seems odd to her that their hands are locked together.

"*Namaste*," they call out to everyone, the man plopping himself down next to Joan, at five, his twin—partner, wife, or sister—at four.

The last to arrive is a couple in their thirties with a young boy, not more than eight. The child runs to Ela, throws his arms around her slim middle, hugs her tight, then jumps away like a baby frog, jumping and jumping until he lands, with his legs already crossed, on the pillow next to the teacher's. The parents take the pillows at ten and at eight, separated by the peroxided muumuu'd young woman.

Ela takes her own seat, the folds of her green sari spread out around her, a flower rising up from green grass, and strikes the gong, once, twice, three times, until the sound hangs in the air, binds them all together under its tonal embrace.

"*Moola Mantra*," Ela says, and everyone's eyes, except Joan's, snap closed, and the chanting begins immediately.

She tries to parse out the words. She hears: *om*.

She hears *sat* and *chit,* together—*sat chit*—then long words, then *sri*, then more long words, *sri* again, then more long words, and then *om* again.

Om is the start of the chant.

It goes *om sat chit*.

Then she figures out it goes *om sat chit ananda*, then all those long words, then *sri*, long words, *sri*, long words, back to *om*.

She will never learn the mantra simply by listening, the long words are convoluted, impossible to decipher.

She tries to keep her eyes closed, to chant what she has uncovered, but she stares around during the incomprehensible middle sections. Even the little boy who looks Midwestern milk-fed knows the chant by heart. She watches the words spill from his mouth perfectly, rapidly, as if he knew this language in the womb, as if he is one of her rare babies, a fetus imbued with instinctive knowledge of mantras that he carried beyond the canal and into childhood.

When the gong strikes again and everyone goes silent, Joan's eyes are closed.

She opens her eyes and looks around.

Everyone sits peacefully, relaxed, their eyes still closed, but not gripped tightly, as hers have been.

The chanting is over and Joan realizes the silent meditation has begun. She can do this part, she thinks. This shouldn't be too difficult.

Thoughts and images scud across her brain until she sees a brackish stream, her hand disappearing into the water, her fingers splayed, seeking the bottom. How far down must she go to touch the silky dirt. *Silky dirt*, she thinks. *Silt. The silt upon which she will build her new existence. Can you build on silt?* she wonders, she doesn't think so.

And then Daniel is in her mind, and the calm that was inching over her is gone. She feels the angry energy, recognizes it as a fight-or-flight response. She forces herself to stay on her red pillow, despite the urge to flee, sudden phantom itches attacking her arms, neck, head, the middle of her back, until all she wants to do is scratch and scratch.

This is what they call *monkey brain*, Joan knows. The disquieted mind that can't settle, hopping, jumping, leaping through fast-moving pictures, through rapid cycling thoughts, branching off into illogical tangents. Joan's thoughts are not going round and round, she is not stuck in an infinite loop, but she can't keep up with the way her mind is pulling off into every direction.

She tries again. Listens to her breathing, tries to become one with herself, but she is aware of Camille breathing next to her, and the man's deep breaths on her other side, and then she is thinking about them, the identical couple, wondering what their story really is—she can see them as twins separated at birth, adopted by two different families, finding each other at a bar, flirting and drinking and kissing, telling each other the stories of their lives, amazed that they are both adopted, pulling at the threads, discovering they were born in the same hospital on the same day, but they love each other, they say, when they are naked together, once more, on a bed in a cold room—

Then Joan tries again. Listens to her own breathing, tries to keep her mind blank, a perfect blank, just black behind her eyes, but shouldn't it be white?—

The gong sounds and she opens her eyes, hopes the silent meditation is finished. She has no sense of how much time has passed.

"For the benefit of our newest member, who would like to repeat the mantra we used today?" Ela says.

The heavy girl in the muumuu raises her hand and looks at Joan.

> *Om*
> *Sat Chit Ananda Parabrahma*
> *Purashothama Paramatma*
> *Sri Bhagavati Sametha*
> *Sri Bhagavate Namaha.*

Joan nods, as if now, at last, it makes sense. But, of course, it doesn't. Aside from *Om sat chit ananda*, the mantra flows right through her head. She knows she will never remember any more than those four words.

"I'll say each word of the mantra, and starting with Oliver, we'll go around the circle and each person translates."

"*Om*," says Ela.

"We are calling on the highest energy, of all there is," says Oliver, the young boy with skin pale as homogenized milk, an eight-year-old invoking the highest of powers, smiling so wide when he finishes, displaying every one of his milk teeth.

"*Sat.*"

"The formless," says Oliver's mother.

"*Chit.*"

"Consciousness of love," says muumuu girl.

"*Ananda.*"

"Pure love, bliss and joy," says Oliver's father, smiling at Joan.

"*Parabrahma.*"

"The supreme creator," says Camille Nagy, her eyes focused on Ela.

"*Purashothama.*"

The man of the identical couple pats Joan's knee and says, "Who has incarnated in human form to help guide mankind." She is relieved when his hand leaves her knee.

"*Paramatma.*"

"Who comes to me in my heart, and becomes my inner voice whenever I ask," says the woman of the identical couple. There is something Joan hears in her voice that sounds just the littlest bit dirty.

"*Sri Bhagavati.*"

"The divine mother, the power aspect of creation," says Young Man with Beard #1.

"*Sametha.*"

"Together within," says Young Man with Beard #2.

"*Sri Bhagavate.*"

"The father of creation which is unchangeable and permanent," says Young Man with Beard #3.

"*Namaha,*" says Ela. "I thank you and acknowledge this presence in my life. I ask for your guidance at all times." She pauses, looks from face to face, then says, "*Namaste.*"

"*Namaste,*" everyone calls back.

"Does anyone want to discuss their meditation practice? The peaks and potholes you may be finding?"

Young Man with Beard #2 says, "I can't seem to get past fifteen minutes when I'm meditating on my own."

Ela says, "Be grateful for those fifteen minutes. This is not a challenge of endurance. Be kind to yourself."

Young Man with Beard #2 nods and nods, wraps his arms around his skinny frame.

"See you all tomorrow," Ela says, and then everyone is standing, taking their pillows to a corner, stacking them up.

"Did you enjoy it?" Camille asks Joan.

"I think so," Joan lies. "I couldn't catch on to the mantra."

"If you keep coming, you will. You'll learn this one, and all the others."

"How many others?"

"I know two dozen now. Some teachers give handouts with the chants, but Ela doesn't. She believes the words must come to you from the air, not from a page."

Joan has believed the same thing, only her words, in the past, made it onto the page.

"You must come again. I am here every summer, from June through early September, and I've been practicing with Ela for years. It takes time, but this hour is specifically devoted to giving yourself that time. Come, Ela will join us, and we'll go for tea."

Joan would prefer not to spend the next hour discussing mantras, but Vita Brodkey would tell her that this is an experience she is meant to have.

"That would be lovely," Joan says, and when she slides her feet into her golden sandals, the crystals splashing in the sun, she is acutely aware of telling her second lie so immediately after what is meant to be a purifying act.

"Nice shoes," Camille Nagy says, stepping into her practical ones.

Ela, Camille Nagy, and Joan are at the Mcleodganj Teahouse, a canted house high up in the hill station, at a small table with three teapots, drinking Kashmir Kahwa tea from pretty white cups. When the server poured, he said, "This exquisite green tea has been used for generations to make the royal version of the Kashmiri Kahwa tea."

Joan wanted to ask if that meant they were not drinking the royal version, and if not, why not, and how the two differed, but she didn't.

"This is Ashby's first time in Dharamshala," Camille Nagy tells Ela.

"Welcome. What problem are you attempting to solve here?"

For a meditative woman, a teacher no less, Ela is very direct. And Camille, under the guise of refilling her teacup, pulls her chair closer to the table, closer to Joan, her head tilted slightly, to catch every one of Joan's words.

Joan is not certain what she wants to say. And suddenly she is wondering whether Daniel's theft of *Words* was a perverted way of turning his childhood dream real, and if so, hasn't she been proven right, that Martin was wrong, and she should have listened to her instincts— pushed Daniel to find out why he stopped writing about his squirrel. And she remembers her worry, so deep and real, that throwing Henry away would mark Daniel for life, had perhaps already marked him, that there was an enormity to his actions only Joan seemed able to see.

"A tough time with one of my children," Joan says to Ela and Camille.

"I am sorry," Ela says. "But you are lucky to have them no matter the issues. Camille knows this about me, but I will share it with you. I was once happily married, a love marriage, which was much rarer in those days than it is now, but I endured three miscarriages, in the first, second, and third trimesters, in that order, and then a still birth in the ninth month, and my husband left me for a woman who could hang on to what he planted in her belly. I was desperate for quite some time, and I came here from Bombay to seek answers and I never left. Two pilgrimage weeks turned into forty-five years. And it has been a far more fulfilling life than I ever expected to live. Please no condolences. It's all in the past."

The information Ela has just provided sends Joan spinning. Ela's been here in Dharamshala for forty-five years, after four tries at creating a baby? How old can Ela possibly be? She looks no older than Joan. Joan thought she and Ela were contemporaries and Camille was the older woman, but it might be Ela and Camille who are of the same generation. And Joan is simultaneously thinking, awfully, horribly, how she would have welcomed a miscarriage with the first one, how that would have obviated the second, but would Martin have turned sneaky, would she have had to become eagle-eyed, to ensure he didn't deliberately mess with their birth control that had failed just that once.

And she is thinking how she has long subscribed to the truth that many people can be parents, but most can never be writers.

And she's also thinking, given that she birthed two children whose existences she had acceded to, growing used to the idea, to them tucked up inside of her, that she can't imagine Ela's pain, the loss of so many potential wanted children, of losing a husband because her body refused to cooperate.

"And Ela knows this about me," Camille says. "Never married. Never wanted a husband. No children of my own, but I spend the school year teaching painting to severely handicapped children who belong to others, so I have my fill."

That Camille Nagy has never been married and has no children does not come as a surprise to Joan.

"What sort of children do you teach?" she asks.

"Children with developmental disabilities, traumatic brain injuries, autism, cerebral palsy, Down syndrome, fetal alcohol syndrome, Tourette's syndrome, any child with a cognitive or physical disability, and the easy ones, those who are merely blind or mute."

"What internal fortitude you must have for that incredible challenge," Joan says.

"The same as any woman. The same as you," Camille says. "Some can't easily hold a paintbrush or identify the colors that make them laugh or shriek, but every once in a while a child connects to their artistic nature, and it's a sight to behold, that sudden empowerment, a confidence they've never felt before, no matter how long it lasts, five minutes, an hour. But Dharamshala is my summer escape from it all, to study Kangra art, to improve my meditation practice, and to paint."

"Have you been painting a long time?" Joan asks.

"Yes, but long ago I abandoned my serious aspirations. Now I paint just for pleasure, another form of meditation."

"She is a very fine painter," Ela says to Joan, and turns to Camille. "Camille, you really should meditate about that, how to stop disparaging your own abilities."

Camille's face, always severe, lights up, a smile, a full smile, teeth and all. She is quite lovely when she smiles.

"I know, Ela, but one thing at a time. Can't become perfect too quickly."

Ela laughs and says, "Ashby, my friend Camille has just given us both very good advice. So if we're finished with tea, and you both are willing, would you join me for a walk to Dal Lake?"

When Joan nods, Camille smiles again, at Joan, "Good," she says. "It's only a mile and a half walk there."

They pick their way down the steep streets back to the main market-place, and then walk along a road Joan has not yet taken, until the thick deodars thin and reveal a path that leads to a yellowish-green lake.

In Kartar's guidebook, Joan read about Dal Lake, that it is sacred, and its source, somewhere very high up in the mountains, is sacred, and she expected the water to be clear, but it's not. She also expected to find a lot of people here, but she, Ela, and Camille Nagy are the only ones.

They follow Ela to the water's edge, until she stops and holds out her hands.

"Thank you for joining me. To celebrate my seventy-fifth birthday today on this earth, to celebrate Camille's return for another summer and our good friendship, and to celebrate your first meditation with us, Ashby. This is what I propose—"

"Seventy-five?" Joan says.

"Yes."

"My God, that's hard to believe."

"A life of reflection, of peace, is good for the skin. So are you game? Yes or no?"

"Game for what?" Camille says.

"Just yes or no," Ela says.

"Yes," Joan says.

"All right," Camille says.

And then Ela is unwinding herself from her green sari, and Camille is unbuttoning her blouse, and Joan is unbuttoning her linen pants, and off their clothes come, and Joan and Camille look to Ela, who unhooks her bra, steps out of her underpants, and Joan and Camille do the same, tossing everything away, and they are so beautiful, Joan thinks, the three of them shaded uniquely, faded gold, ecru, and cinnamon, their fifty-two-, sixty-five-, and seventy-five-year-old breasts still fine and firm, waists indented, hips slightly swelling, legs strong and useful, and they are naked on the shore of Dal Lake, running into the water, yelling at how icy it is, and Joan holds her breath and dives in.

38

In the middle of July, Joan sets out from Hotel Gandhi's Paradise. In her hand is Kartar's neatly drawn map, a squiggly line for the hill down to the marketplace, a long line for the marketplace itself, a big rectangle for the Dalai Lama's compound, and an X near the bottom of the paper where two roads collide.

"Right here, Ashby," Kartar said, pointing to the X on the paper. "This is where you go right. Then just twenty minutes more walking, and do you see here, this circle, that's when you will be where you are hoping to be."

Down the hill, through the marketplace, past the compound with its heavy traffic—two cars zooming by, three thin men pedaling their rickshaws, a young boy on a bicycle—then another twenty minutes.

Finally, here is the required right turn onto narrow Jogiwara Road, edged, as far as Joan can see, with flowers. Weeds have pushed up through the dirt, a straight line down the center, nature creating two lanes for the people who use it.

She passes a parade of yellow-robed monks heading back to their monastery, laughing and patting one another's backs. Ela's unlined face has taught Joan that ages here are hard to predict. Those monks, contemplative men looking young as children, might be so much older than they appear.

Families laden with rattan baskets are on the road too, on their way to the marketplace, the bazaars, the temples.

Soon, Joan is alone again on the road, and she walks and walks until at last she reaches Kartar's circle and the address written on the map.

The house on Jogiwara Road is an oasis, set back behind high lacy trees and low-slung latticed greenery. A cottage made of white bricks. A squared roof. Teak window frames. From where Joan stands, the extensive cottage gardens look like a natural version of the structured gardens and vegetable plots she and Fancy gardened into being, and Joan wonders if Martin is happy caretaking it all alone, his music turned up high, without her sitting nearby, reading a book, asking him to lower the volume.

She stares at the cottage, at the long stone path that leads from the road to the door. In the quiet warmth, Joan gathers herself, tries again to figure out what she might say, how to answer the questions certain to arise. She has been lucky that Eric has not sent any updates to his parents since her arrival here. She isn't sure she could have ignored his emails, or replied as if writing to him from the house in Rhome. He doesn't know she has been in Dharamshala for six weeks, but at least she has not had to lie, at least not yet.

A flock of tiny birds flies overhead, pale silver against the blue sky. There is time for her to turn around, to head back down the road, to return to her pine suite. She is considering doing just that, has made a quarter-turn in fact, thinking of walking in the front doors of Hotel Gandhi's Paradise, when the cottage door creaks open, the sound freezing her in place, knowing she is caught, that the moment is upon her. Eric is in the open doorway, in a halo of light, surprised too to find her standing at the bottom of his stone path, in Jogiwara Road.

When she last saw him in January, he was waving at her from under the awning of the Oregon rehab center, coherent, returned to life, getting hold of his demons, and she had waved from the back of the cab taking her to the airport. He was pale then, his black hair cut ragged and short, and now it falls past his shoulders, and he is brown, and dressed like a local in the long tunic and matching pants. His feet are bare. He is a young, handsome Buddha, a vision in white.

It takes him no time to adjust, to realize the woman staring at him is his mother, and then he is walking down the long path, his feet slapping against the stones. His body is loose, his joy obvious, bright-eyed and eager, radiating good spirits, a calm inner balance, and she remembers when she was caught up in the early writing of *Words*, late to pick up the boys, racing down the hill in the old station wagon where Daniel and Eric sat waiting for her on the school steps. Even when she had forgotten about them and was late, they ran to her. She can still feel her palms cradled around their young heads. Like a synchronized team, they pressed their foreheads into her abdomen, requiring instant tactile contact, the swoosh of her beating heart traveling down to meet theirs, sliding their hands around each of her thighs, like baby monkeys ready to scale a beloved tree.

She knows instantly that Daniel has not confessed his sin to his brother. Eric's radiant brown eyes reflect no sheltering secret. With his dark golden patina, his old recklessness has been smoothed away. The deep grooves between his eyes, the black circles he had just seven months ago are gone. He is alive and flourishing, standing on solid ground, without a trace of his time in Oregon. In her nightstand in Rhome are the notebooks Joan filled up each night after her days with him; pages splattered with the pain that leaked from his heart, that she saw streaked across his beautiful skin. She feels again the dichotomy that always did split her in two: aware that her son's anguish had pulled not only at her maternal instincts but also at the dense writerly threads that formed who she was, still tied her together.

She sees the new peace on Eric's face, feels the serenity that reaches to his core when he hugs her tight. He is lustrous in his composure, poised and graceful. He does not question his mother's sudden appearance outside his rented cottage here in Dharamshala, says only, "How wonderful that you've come. I was serious when I told you and Dad you ought to experience this place. I'm glad you're here. I hope you're going to stay for a good long while."

He wraps Joan's hand in his and leads her up the walk. "Did you know that *Dharamshala* is a Hindi word, derived from Sanskrit, and translates into spiritual dwelling, or sanctuary?" Eric doesn't need, or expect, Joan to reply.

He leads her into the cottage, into a large open room glazed by peaceful white light. The room is celestial, lightly anchored by bookshelves off to the right, a sunken white couch, a deep armchair in heavy white linen. Off to the left is the open kitchen, spices on the shelves, canisters of tea leaves, an orchid with snowy white petals dashed by drops red as blood. Running down the middle is a long wooden table, with its nicks oiled, that reminds her of her old writing table.

At the back of the cottage, French windows are ajar, and she sees the tousled backyard, ringed by tall, tapered trees.

Eric ushers Joan from room to room. His bedroom is simple. Whitewashed floors and furniture, a dark-blue rug, a neatly made bed with a white quilt and white pillows. A cloudy mirror hangs above a four-drawer bureau, reflecting the blue vase filled with bursting purple blooms, a type of flower Joan has never seen before.

The second bedroom is furnished similarly, just as simply, with dwarfed yellow sunflowers in a jade green column.

"It's all lovely," Joan says, the first words she has spoken.

"It is," Eric says. "You'll come stay here."

Joan smiles but says nothing. The seven years at home, with him and the others, day and night, are enough to last her a lifetime. She does not intend to move in with her son.

In the main room, while Eric fills up a kettle and sets it on the stove to boil, she inspects the bookshelves. Lots of books about the history of McLeod Ganj, the Kangra valley, the Kangra Fort, Dharamshala, British rule of the area in the nineteenth century, partition in 1947, the tribulations of the Tibetans, about the pictorial art of Kangra, Pahari painting, a book about the Maharaja Sansar Chand Museum, guidebooks for hiking and trekking in the Chambra valley, across the Dhauladhar range, over the Indrahar Pass, a slew of books about the Dalai Lama, and books written by the Dalai Lama, books about the prayer wheels, books about the Tibetan monasteries, the Sikh and Hindu temples in Rewalsar, slim volumes by Indian poets, and more.

There are no novels on the shelves, which she wouldn't expect, Eric was never a reader like Daniel, but there are also none of Eric's computer coding books, his dog-eared bibles that were cherished belongings not long ago.

Joan realizes she does not know what he has done with his apartment in New York, if he has rented it, or has a Solve employee staying there, or if it stands empty, his bed unmade, everything where it was, the liquor bottles, the pills, the various drugs, when he overdosed, was rushed to the hospital, then flown by private jet to Oregon.

The kettle whistles and Eric turns off the flame, opens a red tin can, measures loose tea leaves. He prepares the teapot with ceremony, swishing hot water inside, pouring it out, filling it to the top again, before he gently drops in the tea ball. Steam arcs out of the funnel, vanishes in the white light of the room. Joan wonders if he remembers the after-school tea parties Fancy prepared for them, the way he abhorred tea unless Fancy filled his cup mostly with milk, spooned in tablespoons of sugar, the cupcakes and Bundt cakes she made, saving a small bowl for each boy to lick with his fingers. She wonders if he remembers eating dirt, sticks, pebbles, all those baby aspirin.

The cottage is graceful, proportioned so nicely, a mix of no color and pale dreamy colors. It feels to Joan like a place of perpetual happiness. She can't imagine voices raised here, charging anger, disappointment, tragedy. A person intent on additional self-destruction would be discomfited by its calm, by the hope carried through the rooms on the slight breeze that travels through.

"Have you read all of these books?"

"A lot of them, but only a few are mine. They came with the place. The ones on Kangra and Pahari painting are really cool."

Really cool is the first connection between the Eric Joan knew and the one preparing a tea tray. She thinks of telling him about Camille Nagy, how for years she has studied the Kangra Valley School of Painting here. That an upright Englishwoman studies those paintings whose focal theme is largely erotic sentiment—*Shringar*—which Joan thinks Camille has probably lacked in her life. Camille has taken Joan to the Museum of Kangra Art to see some of those paintings. Lyrical and naturalistic, colors extracted from minerals and vegetables, and although they were painted more than four centuries ago, they have lost none of their enamel-like luster. Faces with porcelain delicacy, soft and refined, female charms on display, their bodies exceptionally beautiful. Standing in front of one such painting, Joan had said, "Our bodies were that lovely at Dal Lake," and Camille blushed and said, "Well, yours was." When Joan saw *Rama and Sita in the Forest*, painted in 1780, with the Kangra landscape of verdant greenery, trees, creepers, flowering plants on fields of hilled grass, brooks and rivulets and springs running through, Joan thought Devata looked exactly that way, the painting so similar to how she described her own arcadia in *Words*. Though they have grown close in these last weeks, sojourns to Kareri Lake, the Tattwani Hot Springs, the tea gardens in Chilgari and Dari, the daily meditation practice led by Ela that Joan has committed to attending three times a week, Camille still refuses to show Joan her own paintings using the Kangra techniques. Joan would like to share all of this with Eric, but it's not why she is here in his cottage with him, and she has been *here* in Dharamshala for far longer than he assumes.

Eric adds the teapot to a wooden tray, where porcelain teacups already rest. "We're ready," he says and she follows him out into the garden, an enclave surrounded by those tall, tapered trees, their leaves like lace, the perimeter lined with a variety of greens in all different shades, filled with haphazard beds from which spring all sorts of flowers, indigenous, Joan thinks, because she recognizes none of them, except for the blowsy, splashy rhododendrons in bright pink and red. There is a wooden bench, small chairs, and the sculptured trunk of a tree cut down long ago. A short distance away is a shallow pond, over which a wooden bridge leaps, snapdragons hovering at the edges. It is very much like the landscapes in the Kangra paintings, until she sees, near the pond, two white canvas slung-back chairs. This is where Eric has acquired his golden tan. She wonders if he has met a girl that he likes, if a young Dharamshalan woman arranges her own bared limbs on that second chair. She hopes so. It's time. After all, he turns twenty-two at the end of the month. She looks up and there is an immaculate view of the Himalayas, nearly within reach.

Eric sets the tray on the tree trunk and points to the small chairs, perfect for one of Fancy's tea parties. "They're very comfortable," he says, and the low height makes Joan feel she is emerging from the earth, that she is her very own flower, the way Ela seems to be when she arranges herself on a red silk pillow, her saris in abundant pastels around her.

Eric pulls the other chair closer to Joan, seats himself, lifts the teapot lid to check on the brewing. "I've grown to like tea, but it has to be strong. I hope that's okay."

She nods. "I like it dark too," she says.

He fills the two cups. "I have no sugar. I've given that up, given everything up. Absolutely nothing toxic since back then."

"I'm so glad," she says. "I don't need any sugar," although really she does, even just a few packets of the fake stuff.

The birds in the trees chitter, insects lightly buzz, a wisp of a breeze tickles the blades of grass. It is Edenic here, she thinks, sipping the pungent tea, rough with something soft at its base.

"Delicious," she says, and then the words fall away.

In the past, in their past, she would have filled up the empty space, spoken, inquired, felt responsible for their conversational interactions, and when she wasn't policing him, or yelling at him, then trying to encourage him to—well, who knows what she wanted to encourage him to do, or to be like. Perhaps more like Daniel, normal in some way, though Daniel has blown that concept away. But she had wished back then for Eric's normalcy, such a hard wish when his genius was so extraordinary. It had been like hoping a prima ballerina's legs were chopped off, or a sculptor's hands mangled, or a photographer's eyesight lost to an unprovoked acid attack, and when she was thinking those thoughts at the start of the seven-year cycle, she knew if her wish for Eric's normalcy were granted, she would be the one wielding the instrument of his death, directly responsible for the nuclear fallout. She had made that promise when she put her novel in the box, that he would not die on her watch, and not much later, that he would not die by her thoughts.

She lets the quiet grow around them, settles into it, into this nascent Joan, a runaway woman who is also, still, a mother to this son. She has worked hard since arriving in Dharamshala to banish *mother* from her thoughts, to not consider the sons that she birthed, to stay cushioned within the fantasy that she never gave anything up, never married Martin, never left New York, never experienced pregnancy and motherhood, or the sporadic friendships with the Pregnant Six, that she never stepped down from the heights of her powers, that she climbed from peak to peak, each one higher than the one before, and with each leap, from mountain to mountain, realizing more of her dreams, those she had dreamt about and those she had never thought to imagine, never relegating Joan Ashby to a closet, a drawer, a trash bin, a box in a garage.

When she looks at Eric, there is a bliss to him, not superimposed over his original nature, but altering his nature entirely, fundamentally.

This is another lesson for Joan to heed.

Vita would say, "It's all part of the reason why you're here."

Ela would say, "This awareness means you are concentrating well during your meditation practice."

Camille Nagy would say, "Don't get ahead of yourself. Pay attention."

At last, Eric tugs quietly at the silence. "Do you remember what I said I wanted to do when I go out of rehab?"

"I do remember," Joan says. "You said you wanted to sell Solve and take yourself to a sacred place where you could discover who you might truly be."

He looks pleased that she has recalled his words so easily, and exactly.

"So, I've accomplished two out of three so far. I'm here in this sacred place, and I sold Solve."

Then he tucks his bare feet up onto his knees, in a half-lotus position. This son, who eschewed athletics and exercise during his childhood, who spent his teenage years sitting at desks, at tables, on couches and floors, surrounded by his helping ghosts, developing his remarkable computer program, is as flexible as a pretzel.

Joan wants to ask him what the sale of his company means for him, wants to know when he plans to tell his father. She would have gotten a phone call or an email from Martin if he already knew about it. And she hasn't.

Martin will not be pleased by this news. He believes obligations and responsibilities are necessary to form a man, to make him good, to keep him solidly on his chosen road, the tenets of the navy vice-admiral at work. Long ago, Martin turned into a man of blacks and whites, who doesn't understand those are shades, not real colors, and can't understand people who know the right thing to do, and then do the wrong thing, inevitably hurting themselves, and others. He has no tolerance for what he views as self-imposed frailties. He sees Eric's sabbatical, his flight to Dharamshala, as a correctable error, a blip that Eric will soon right, get back to his ship, regain the helm, steer Solve into its limitless future.

Joan sees all at once that Martin's years of doctoring, the dreams and nightmares he claims to see when operating on his patients' eyes, have not shored up his own internal reserves. He is more vulnerable than she, has always been so, the way he wants only to consider the good in others, denies the existence of weakness, of trouble, of conflict, does not view life and its humans through the prism she can access so easily, the dark, the sickly ironic, the tragedies she once mined in her work. He has needed to believe that Eric would be all right, that a crisis was not truly upon them requiring his intervention. She knew though, and she was there: Joan, the most mothering of anti-mothers, has always been there, for both of her sons.

She wants to ask Eric so many questions, but then he says, "I'm practicing yoga every day. Like you always have."

She is here in India, the birthplace of yoga, and she has not sought out a class to take, and there must be dozens, has not, even in her pine suite, gone through the series of poses she knows by heart.

"It's been a while since I've done yoga," she says, wondering if Eric will find that strange, when its daily practice was her only enduring constant, a saving hour away from home, away from him and his cohorts, their equipment and meetings, her fears about what he, or the others, might be doing in secret.

"There's a yoga place that I like. We'll go together," is all he says.

This son of hers is remaking his life, proof that such can be undertaken, that she might do the same with her own. She has the opportunity right this moment to reconfigure their relationship, to leave behind the old labels and their usual roles, to enter a new way of being that has little to do with her past as his mother, with his past as her troubled, intractable, brilliant son to whom she has never felt especially close, whose absorption of every atom in her world was so intolerable.

She wonders what she ought to say to him, how much she ought to tell him, whether they need to clear the air, say all that has never been said, if she should confess everything.

What would she say?—*I am here in India because Daniel betrayed me; I'm sorry I loved him more than I loved you; I'm sorry he was so much easier to love than you were; I showed you my love when I sacrificed seven years of my life for you.*

Eric has changed, by choice, lit up from within, with the kind of self-reflective wisdom she thought his genius would refuse. She is different too, even in just six weeks, though her own ultimate path is still murky and unclear.

There is no need to tell Eric how long she has been here; with that light in his eyes, he might already know. Why not begin anew in this beautiful place, by allowing him to take the lead, to follow wherever he wants to take her, to cede her role as battle-ax, detective-mother, battalion chief.

"I want to tell you how I got here," Eric says.

She looks at him directly.

This might be the first time since his birth that their thinking is in sync.

He holds her eyes, which he never used to do, and says, "I started at the beginning with the Dalai Lama's book *The Art of Happiness*. What I should say is I came upon *The Art of Happiness* by accident or *The Art of Happiness* found me. Do you remember the bench we always sat on in Oregon, when there was a break between therapy groups?"

Joan nods.

"Well, the day you left, I went back to our bench and found *The Art of Happiness* underneath it. It was just there on the ground, and I picked it up and started reading it. And I couldn't stop reading it, and when I finished it, I researched it and learned it was the first book the Dalai Lama wrote. And somehow, through serendipity or luck, I had started at the beginning.

"Then I read his other books while I was at the center. *How to See Yourself as You Really Are*, *The Good Heart*, *The Wisdom of Forgiving*. I decided to skip *Advice on Dying*. Even though I was in rehab, I really hoped that's not where I would end up."

He looks at Joan to see if she's caught his small joke. She has and he grins.

"Then I read *Transforming the Mind*. The strange thing was that just before I ended up in Oregon, I was researching the Dalai Lama. Everything about where he lived, Dharamshala, if it was a place I should come to, and then I found those books.

"As soon as I began reading his teachings, I knew I had to change everything in my life, sell Solve as I told you I wanted to do, figure out how to dedicate my life to others in a meaningful way. That's why I came here, and why I started writing him letters as soon as I got here. I want help in making my intentions real.

"It's great you've come here now, because earlier this week, I got a reply. I'm going to be meeting him. I don't know when yet, but the letter said sometime in the next several months."

"So you're planning on staying here for at least that long?"

"Yes. But I might stay longer. Maybe forever. Would that be strange?"

Joan leans over and touches her hand to his cheek.

Did she last touch him in this intimate way the summer he went off to computer camp?

In Oregon, she'd kept her distance. Buying him the candy he wanted, new clothes from a local store, participating with him in the counselor-led meetings, participating in all the ways demanded of her, sitting with him on that bench while he talked, it seemed, about everything that had ever been in his mind since he was a child. She had been desperate for him to come through it, to have her fears assuaged about her own culpability. She had hugged him, and held his hand, but those touches, during those weeks they had been together, were still somehow removed from intimacy.

She realizes suddenly that Eric has ceased thinking of her as the enemy who wanted to hold him back, that he sees her now as a mother who wanted to save him. It is a stunning realization, and not anything she had imagined.

"How wonderful that you've got a response. And no, I don't think it would be strange if you wanted to stay here."

She won't say anything about having written her own letter to the Dalai Lama, that Kartar delivered her letter to the Office of His Holiness the Dalai Lama, into the hands of the Dalai Lama's secretary, where all letters addressed to him wind up. She does not want to blur the line, to say Daniel's name aloud in this garden, to take anything away from Eric, this new life he is creating.

"How many letters did you write before you heard back?"

"Eighteen. A girl I know, Amari, told me how hard it is to get a private audience with him, that he grants very few, and that even if granted, it might be four months or more before you actually meet with him. Amari said he gets hundreds of letters every day and the secretary reviews each case on its merits."

She wonders if Amari is the girl who uses the second canvas chair by the pond, then thinks she has sent only the one letter, and that if she is serious about trying to elicit the Dalai Lama's advice, she will have to write many more.

She is forming the words she wants to say to Eric, that she is relieved to find him so well, proud of his progress, gratified that he is alive, when for the second time, he taps into her thoughts.

"My past belongs to me, and yours belongs to you, and unless you need to talk about all that stuff between us, I'm fine if we don't. I've learned it's best to leave it behind, to keep moving ahead. I know you've been badly hurt. I just hope you don't blame yourself for me. I meant what I said in Oregon, it was all my own doing. You tried to stop me, I know that, but I wouldn't listen. I thought you wanted to keep me from my destiny. But that was never my destiny. This is.

"I know I can't snap my fingers to make it all okay for you, to wipe out all these last years, but this is a good place to find the solace you need."

He has turned into a young Buddha, replete with the wisdom, the truth, that Joan is trying to learn, that she thinks about in Ela's meditation class and when she is alone on her own. She should tell Eric he's not responsible for her being here, that she is here not because of what she suffered as a result of him or Solve or his troubles, but because of what his older brother has done.

Would Eric feel better or worse if he knew he was not the compelling reason behind this trip to Dharamshala? That his flagrancy with life and death did not send her in flight from home, traveling across the world, that life-and-death matters had not trumped betrayal? Would a fine parsing of the truth accomplish anything?

He has found insights into himself that she wants to protect. In so little time, in this garden for only a few hours, they are finding a new way of being together, perhaps a way of being together for the first time ever. She wants to keep this afternoon intact, enjoy its unexpected preciousness.

"I think it is a wonderful place for solace," is what Joan decides to say.

"I'm glad you agree," Eric says. "There is one thing we ought to talk about. What would you like me to call you?"

She knows instantly what he is asking, and is surprised. To both sons, she has only ever been *Mom*, or some rendition of that title. In

Rhome, everyone calls her Mrs. Manning or Joan, but here in Dharam-shala, those names have fallen away, she is never called anything other than Ashby. Never before has Eric cared about anyone's needs or wants, and the two of them have never been symbiotically entwined, as she thought she and Daniel were. And yet, Eric senses something so essential about her, about who she once was, who she became, who she is becoming again, and has thought to inquire. Somehow, he understands.

She is trying to figure out how to tell him she no longer wants to be called by that universal name, that she wants only to be known as herself, when Eric smiles.

"I've figured out a few things and that's one of them. Joan or Ashby?"

"Ashby," she says.

"Ashby it is." Then Eric says, "Why didn't you ever tell me you used to be a famous writer?"

39

Sirens are blaring beneath the salted rim of Joan's dream, an ominous whoop-whooping, and she is running through the Rhome house with its smooth mocking walls, the old nooks and cubbyholes and crannies gone, *Words of New Beginnings* tight to her chest, searching for a safe place to hide her manuscript. Violent pounding at the front doors and she freezes, knows the enemy will soon be upon her. She crests the surface and everything evaporates into an aqueous atmosphere.

She peers around her pine suite confused. The atmosphere in her room *is* aqueous, the air *is* misty, and there is clearly a billowy cloud floating up at the ceiling. The sheets are damp. A breeze blows through the room, riffling the curtains, scattering water on her skin.

It takes a few seconds before she realizes she left the windows open last night, the curtains pulled back, and the rowdy noise on the roof is rain. A loud thunderclap scares her upright. Then waves of water are hitting the windows, sending up huge swirls of foam. She's out of bed and looking at a world underwater. The rain quiets suddenly and Joan leans out into hot air so humid she could scoop up a chunk of it, roll it into a ball. Within seconds, she is soaked straight through.

The sky is cloaked in the darkness of night, but her watch on the nightstand says it's morning, nearly seven. Angry black clouds encase the far mountains, sit heavily upon the treetops of the forest. The bright-green leaves are bent into open palms, wide-mouthed bowls. The entire shape of the forest has altered to capture the hard splattering drops. There is a sweetness in the air, in the smell of the rain.

No one in Dharamshala seems to pay much attention to the actual calendar, but Joan knows it's the middle of August. The monsoon season, due in July and everyone said was late, seems suddenly to have arrived.

Joan pulls back from the window, strips off her soaked pajamas, and tosses them into the pine-slatted tub. Lakshmi, Kartar, Ela, and Camille have warned her that when the monsoons begin, the world turns upside down, sheets of water the only thing to see. More days with rain than without, and nothing ever fully dries out. That Dharamshala is the second wettest place in India. Joan forgot to ask what the first one is.

She did not pack for the monsoon season, although Eric had written her and Martin about it, telling them he was looking forward to a world washed clean. When she read that email back in Rhome, she had not thought of herself here. She does not have galoshes, or a slicker, not even an umbrella. She wonders whether, along the hill station's steep roads, men will spring up, hawking umbrellas, as they magically materialized on New York street corners when she lived there.

Dressed in dry slacks and a shirt, she brings in her morning tray from outside the door. Today's flower is a tall white aster in a thin red vase. She eats her lentils and drinks her barley tea at the desk, watches the forest bow to the onslaught.

Meditating three times a week with Ela and Camille, in the group whose membership frequently changes, has staved off the weight of her earliest days here, the strangling embrace of pain, the surprise she experienced daily about Daniel's failure to beg her forgiveness. But if the rains have arrived, and sightseeing will be a waterlogged experience, perhaps she should do what Ela and Camille say she needs to do: meditate every single day of the week.

The meditation has been helping. She has actually learned the *Moola* mantra by heart, and a second one as well, the *Hanuman* mantra, just four words in all—*Om Shri Hanuamte Namaha*—which translates easily as "Om and Salutations to Lord Hanuman." And although Joan does not know who Lord Hanuman is, Ela has explained that Hanuman invokes unbounded love, gives strength, grants success in devotional activities, and reveals the soul's power to triumph over adversities blocking the attainment of one's highest realizations. And sometimes it works; there are spans of two or three days when Joan is simply living this new Dharamshalan life. But the truth, never far away, can suddenly narrow her vision, reduce the world she's inhabiting to a dot, force her to question Daniel's reasons for shredding the fabric of her life, those answers still so elusive, and when she can see clearly again, she knows her recovery is like some sweet little newborn creature finding its legs.

In the last month, she and Eric have spent tranquil hours talking in his lovely backyard under the Himalayas, or exploring the archives, hearing lectures by the Dalai Lama's disciples. With Camille, she has visited shops and art museums, and taken trips to other sacred lakes farther afield, sometimes Ela joins them, sometimes not. On her own, Joan has met global travelers of every ilk: those who have left behind their grown children, disinclined to experience a new generational iteration of family life; those most interested in seeking out the newest thrill, the most exotic places; and those who spin her head when they speak of finding silence, opening their minds, connecting themselves to the great and the good on the pilgrimages they make to the shrines and temples in the mountains. Whenever she is in one of the local temples, she wonders what the great and the good means to her.

But she has been in this colorful setting long enough that her bearings are mostly gathered, and despite the brutality of the atrocious act that has given her what she wants, she has used her new laptop for nothing substantial.

If the rainy season is upon Dharamshala, and solitary hikes and walks and wandering through the sights can no longer hide what is coiled in the shadows, isn't this the time to start writing again, to hope that by returning to work she will puzzle through the disaster, figure out the future she wants?

The rain is solidly thrumming and Joan feels enveloped in the sacred space Eric talks about. She feels safe here in her pine room, her barley tea within reach, her laptop on her desk, now open, a clean screen before her, her fingers lingering over the keys. Where should she start? She is not a writer of nonfiction, or of autobiography, but should she write her own recent story to remove it from her mind, to shovel out the hurt still in her heart that manifests in her dreams? Or should she leave all of it behind: son, theft, the title *Words of New Beginnings*, and move on, move forward?

Before she can answer a single one of her questions, a golden light streams through the windows and blinds her. The sun has lit up her pine suite. The rain has stopped. The heavy fog has lifted. The sky is freshly washed. The peaks in the distance are bright and sharply defined in the sudden blue. The forest is soaked through, branches left askew, pulled back, a shy invitation to enter that clandestine place. Birds dart from treetops to branches, down to the forest floor, and back up again. She has no idea what kinds of birds these are, but they are nothing like the birds at home. At home, she can't identify any birds either, except for the blue jays and robins that alight in the gardens.

No morning bath today, the time without rain could be very brief. Face and teeth and lipstick and Joan is out the door, walking the hallway from her pine suite. In the lobby, she sees rain is falling again, but lightly, and here is Kartar handing her a bright-red umbrella.

"Thank you, Kartar."

"Of course, Ashby. Your first time experiencing the true miracle of water. It is the beginning of a whole new season."

The umbrella stem is long and solid as a walking stick, the unexpected words *Lucky Star* show through the material when she steps outside and opens the umbrella over her head. The clouds are high now, and finely wrought, and if she walks very fast down the steep hill to the marketplace, she might reach the dry environs of a bookstore before the next deluge drops from the sky. If the rain is here to stay, she would like some new books to read. She's not made much headway in those she brought from home. Since she learned to read, this might be the longest she has ever gone without being sucked up into other lives and worlds.

The ground, cracked and parched yesterday, is already a sea of mud. Her tennis shoes sink and slurp with each step she takes.

The exterior of the bookstore on Bhagsu Road is a faded lilac. A wooden board hanging at an angle must once have spelled out the name, the letters long bleached away. A chime tinkles gently when Joan walks into the quiet.

A young man is on a stool at the register, the spine of an open paperback crushed in his fine-boned hands. He is hunched over the book, his brown T-shirt caught in the vertical hollow of his slender chest. When he stands, the shirt spreads opens and Joan reads the green words emblazoned across it. BE THE BUDDHA. Serious directive or plea, who can tell? In her time here, she has seen that Dharamshala offers much, both to the trained and untrained questing for spiritual renewal and harmony, but very little deliberate irony. He releases his hold on the book and the tortured pages slowly relax, return to their home position, the front and back covers no longer perfectly aligned. He has cat eyes, irises like yellow quartz gemstones, and she is aware he is studying her. Then he smiles.

"Welcome. I'm Darpan. You can leave your umbrella in that corner. What can I do for you?"

"I'm just going to browse for a while and see what catches my eye."

"Yes, yes, of course. New fiction is in the second aisle, in both English and Hindi. And all the aisles are marked clearly. Let me know if I can help in any way."

The opaque drizzly light turns the tight aisles into bars of silver. The store's stock reaches the ceiling. She wanders slowly. There are glossy photography books of India's temples in full color, thick guides to each of India's states, books on farming, tea cultivation, flower growing, Indian wildlife, the birds of India, poetry books written by modern-day poets. There are geography books, political books, critical literary theory books in English, all of Shakespeare's plays, entire sets of Agatha Christie and P. G. Wodehouse, Icelandic, Finnish, and Swedish detective writers she recognizes because Martin has read many of them, fiction by India's major writers, in English and in Hindi, as Darpan said, books on Buddhism and Hinduism, a few on Sikhism, the collected sayings of the Buddha, of various Buddhas, of the Dalai Lama, and other philosophers who lived here thousands of years ago, books on art and sculpture, the making of traditional garb. How-to books on using Google, a computer, designing a Web site, learning acupressure and reflexology, becoming a personal trainer, a beekeeper, the fine art of antiquing.

She extracts whatever catches her eye until a tall pile rises from the floor in the fourth aisle. There is a low stool at the end of the row, and she brings it back to her stack, starts making her way through. She is deep into a collection of short stories by various Indian writers, reading one by a female writer, about a young girl who wins a writing competition and must learn what it means to give a story to the world, when Joan hears the door chime ring again, for the first time since she entered the shop, the sound of a friendly slap on the back, a few minutes of distant quiet whispering. Then a hand is holding a book in front of her eyes, and her heart jumps in surprise.

"This is the book for you. *Kalpit Parvarik Jivan*. Written by my most favorite writer."

Joan looks up at a man who might be forty or fifty or sixty; his face has the permanent browning of a pale man whose original skin has regretfully, but finally, adjusted itself to latitudes and longitudes for which it was never intended. There are carved lines around his eyes, caused by squinting into the sun, by smiling, or by both. Joan registers these facts in an instant, and then the book, thick and perfectly square, that he has said is the book for her, tumbles into her hands, and she is aware that her finger is bare, her platinum wedding band at home in her jewelry box.

"Will M," he says, and Joan has no idea what he has said.

Will M means Willem. Willem Ackerman is his name, a Dutchman long living on the subcontinent of India. A longtime photographer for *National Geographic*. A lifelong birder, a shorter-time widower, the father of two married daughters with children of their own, an erstwhile poet. This is the order in which he describes himself to Joan in the bookstore, and then he says, "And I am a consumptive reader, or should that be an all-consuming reader, or an uncontrollable reader, or a man whose reading is uncontrolled?"

Joan laughs. "I like them all. You can't go wrong with any of those choices. Well, maybe the consumptive reader. That might mean you're wasting away from consumption and doing so while you read. But that could be a nice way to go."

It is Willem's turn to laugh.

Joan looks at the book he has given her. The cover reminds her of the Kangra paintings, slopes of green grass, pastel flowers, but there is something of Chagall on the cover, in the shaggy dog on the ground and the boy floating up in the sky.

Inside, the pages are filled with sentences in beautiful Hindi script.

"So tell me about this book. You know I can't read a word of it."

"Join me for lunch at the café down the street and I'll tell you why it's an important book."

Willem has hazel eyes and unruly dark hair marbling into white, and when he shakes his head he is distinctly boyish. His face is craggy from a life spent outdoors, and his lashes are thick. He is long-limbed, broad-shouldered, and attractive. More than attractive, handsome, very handsome, and Joan thinks, why not, and says, "I'd enjoy that." Aside from the time she spends with Eric, she is either alone or in the company of Ela and Camille. When once her life was lived in the midst of the opposite sex, now it is primarily women. Willem might be a nice change of pace.

He orders them a Punjabi feast: lamb kheema, meat biryani, tandoori chicken, punj ratani dal made of five kinds of lentils, panjiri that has almonds, walnuts, pistachios, cashew nuts, dates, poppy and fennel seeds, in some kind of flour, puri bread deep-fried and puffy, naan bread served hot from the tandoor oven, three kinds of chutney.

She can't stop spooning more and more onto her plate, ripping off pieces of naan, dragging it through the bowl of spicy green chutney. It's as if she's been starving and only now realized it. She's embarrassed when Willem says to the waiter, "I think she'd like more of the good green stuff." Aside from her latte with Lakshmi at the Namgyal Café, she usually eats standing up at the stalls in the marketplace, in a hurry to make room for someone else. The last time she was in a restaurant with white-clothed tables was in Rhome, the night she told Martin about writing *Words*, her happy plans for her future.

"So what sort of poetry do you write?" she asks Willem.

"Two different kinds. Poems I write when I'm out waiting to photograph birds, and those I write alone with a bottle of wine. The first kind makes a sort of sense, the second nearly none at all. In either case, I do try not to write the gooey stuff." There is a foreign inflection to his English words that she likes quite a lot.

"Gooey stuff?"

"The sappy, the sentimental, the corny, the hackneyed."

She smiles and Willem looks at his watch. She wonders if he has somewhere to be, if he feels in over his head, if he had not quite anticipated how much she could eat. She wasn't aware either.

"So," Willem says. "It's nearly two. We are eating a fine lunch, I, at least, am enjoying the company. Could I persuade you to share a bottle of wine with me?"

Since the vodka on the flight to Delhi, when she toasted with Vita Brodkey, Joan hasn't had a drop.

"Absolutely," she says, and Willem nods to a man sitting on a stool at the back door. Then a bottle of red wine is on their table, and Willem has his Swiss Army set out, a small corkscrew pulling out the cork, and with one taste of the aromatic blood-red wine, Joan wonders how she has done without.

"That was Tikka Yashvir, the café owner," Willem says. "A fine and wonderful man. Once royalty when that mattered here. A former mayor of a nearby town. A close friend now, and he safeguards the cases of Montepulciano that I ship here. My own private stock that Yashvir keeps under lock and key, though he's always free to drink as he desires."

Kartar has told her that although Dharamshala is not dry, alcohol is hard to come by.

Willem fills their glasses, lifts his, and Joan lifts hers, and they touch, a small ting that rings out in the restaurant that has emptied of everyone but the two of them. He sets down his glass, and from his wallet he slides out a wrinkled, well-creased piece of paper, which he unfolds, and unfolds, and unfolds, and then smooths out, his palm running across a paragraph of typed words.

"May I read something to you?"

Joan nods. "Of course," she says, and sips again at her wine.

Willem shifts his chair back, switches his crossed knee, drinks from his glass, clears his throat, and begins to read.

The birds wing about noisily in the trees outside of my window, settle themselves down on branches. One flock is feathered in green and yellow bands, another reminds me of sailors on leave or of boys in varsity sweaters, their wings navy blue and wrapped in white stripes.

A lone bird with a bright white face and a red tufted cap slaps the glass where I stand and finds a thick branch to his liking midway up the maple. I wonder how birds agree on changing course when they swoop and turn, if they mate for life or are fickle, if some avian species mate permanently and others are Lotharios, as I would be in a heartbeat. I wonder what happens to a sick or injured baby bird, or to a baby bird that falls from its nest and is not easily found in the sinuous, vined tangle of jungle, or forest, or park. Do his parents send out a rescue party, or leave him be, to live out an abridged life, to die a natural death? So much of what I have learned from life, I have learned from birds. I love them so much. Their freedom, their songs, their clucking and cleaning, the way they own the sky. Sometimes I want to pop them all off, take a BB gun and shoot holes through their wings, see then how well they can fly. It seems unfair how life can be, stuck pining for what—for guts, for the soaring nature of bravery, for everything.

Willem looks at her when he finishes. She has not moved since he read the first sentence.

"That piece of writing spoke to me so intensely the first time I read it, and the thousands of times since. Of course, you recognize it."

Joan nods.

"When I found you in the bookstore, I knew who you were. Darpan knew who you were the moment you walked in. Darpan called me and said, 'Come now, immediately. You won't believe who is in the store browsing through books, sitting down with a whole bunch.' And when he told me, I came running.

"I can't tell you how many times I've read *Other Small Spaces* and *Fictional Family Life* over the years. Darpan is also a huge fan. Your books are in his store, or rather in his father's store."

It never crossed Joan's mind to check whether a small bookstore in Dharamshala carried her work.

Willem leans down to the photographer's bag under his chair and comes up holding the book he dropped into Joan's hands hours ago.

"*Kalpit Parvarik Jivan* is Hindi for *Fictional Family Life*. I knew you were Joan Ashby when I asked you to join me for lunch. You have been my most favorite writer of short stories for a very long time. I've taken both your collections with me when I hike up the Dhauladhars and spend nights in a tent on a rock ledge. Your words keep me company until the birds take again to the sky with the sun. Your stories have been all over India, and have spent huge chunks of time with me in the Pong Wetland.

"Considering I photograph birds as both my passion and my profession, you would think I couldn't imagine shooting a BB gun at any of those gorgeous creatures. But as free as I am, certainly compared to most people, I know I'll never experience what they do. The first time I read that paragraph, I felt I was Simon Tabor, a screwed-up teenager pretending to be a hemophiliac just for some relief from himself. I could see myself as him, trying to kill myself by flying off a roof, and failing, and sticking myself into a coma just to buy time, and dreaming about watching those birds giving me such tantalizing hope, then throwing me into utter despair.

"And hopefully this will not insult you, but you are more beautiful now, and trust me when I say that I know the young you. I used to stare at your pictures on the backs of your books, in articles I found about you, so much so that my wife, who was never a jealous woman, used to make fun of me, poke me in the chest when I picked up one of your books to reread. 'Oh,' she would say, 'you are nestling up to my competition again.'"

Joan feels faint, not because of a potential for romance, or sex, with Willem Ackerman, although she had been thinking about both before he pulled out that piece of paper, but because he sees her so vividly. Because to him she is still a vital writer, whose work he has returned to many times since her books were first published, because he has read her stories as a married man, father, widower, grandfather, birder, and photographer.

"I've always known you'd be fantastic, tremendous, and you are. And I always pictured you working at some great desk, putting such weird and wonderful stories together."

She wishes he were completely right, that not one day had passed in her life without setting down her own words, and not a single line since putting down the shallowest of roots in Dharamshala. There is a rapid pulsing at the base of her throat, and even as Joan thinks it, she knows what she believes is ridiculous, that her splintered soul is sewing itself back together, one loop of thread through the skin at a time, because Willem, and Darpan, have been profoundly touched by the truest part of herself.

It has been so long since anyone has viewed her through the correct lens, properly calibrated to her singular nature. The husband who says how much he loves her, completely unaware that she had written *Words* for nine years. The son who took her seriously as a writer, look at his actions, how that played out.

The Nirvanic feelings evaporate when her lungs viciously deflate, her fingers twisting into dying flowers, then turning to stone. She hopes the pain presages something good, that when it fades away, it will leave behind a hollowed-out Ashby, ready to be filled up by new words and work.

Willem's face is transforming into painterly cubist components. Despite the distortion, his eyes radiate. She sees kindness there, and a sort of love, love for the mind that strung together sentences that affected him so deeply. A strong arm is slung around her back, another strong arm wraps around her waist, and she is lifted down to the floor of the café, laid flat on her back, and Willem is yelling, "Yashvir, get water," and Willem pulls something out of his bag, and then plunges it into her thigh. The pain is outrageous and she screams.

"It's an EpiPen," he yells. "You're seriously allergic to something I fed you."

40

"You feeling okay now?" Joan nods at him from the café floor. She doesn't think it was a reaction to anything she ate, but to *Fictional Family Life* in Hindi, in a Dharamshala bookstore, in the hands of Willem Ackerman, hearing him read a paragraph of her own work written so long ago, before the choices she made affected the rest of her life.

"Why do you carry an EpiPen?" she asks as he helps her back into her chair.

"Because I'm usually far from civilization, and who knows when I might need a shot of adrenaline, or need to give one. You're really okay?" and Joan nods.

"Really," she says.

"I would hate to have killed you during our first meal. Let me walk you home. Buddhists, you know, can be a dangerous lot."

It is just before six when they are huddled under Kartar's red umbrella walking up the rocky-sloped road to Hotel Gandhi's Paradise. Willem is tall, but not as tall as Martin, and Joan finds it easy walking next to him, fully protected by the umbrella, sharing a bright patch of nylon. When she and Martin share an umbrella, she is left scurrying to reduce the space between the umbrella and the top of her head.

The rain is falling lazily, and when the clouds skid away, the early moon casts its silvery light over the road.

At Hotel Gandhi's Paradise, he insists on walking her up the stairs and into the lobby.

Kartar, as always, is at the low teak reception desk. Camille has been here, Ela too, but not Eric, and now she is walking into the hotel with Willem Ackerman, feeling scandalous for no good reason.

"Ashby, good evening," Kartar says, his voice rising half an octave as he bounces on the balls of his feet. "And I know you, good sir. Ashby, this is Mr. Willem Ackerman. I have never met you, but you are my hero, sir. Ashby, do you know who Mr. Willem Ackerman is? He is the photographer who has made famous the birds of the Kangra valley. Because of him, tourist trade to our region has increased. He is greatly responsible for the birding expeditions that have become an international attraction. And an all-around good guy. Never does he ask for a percentage, even though it is because of him that our locals are earning the serious kind of money." Kartar raises a hand and rushes into his hidden alcove, returns with a battered *National Geographic*.

"Do you think you might sign this for me? *To Kartar* would be sufficient, along with your name, of course, Mr. Willem Ackerman."

Willem laughs and signs the magazine for Kartar, who holds it carefully on his open palms, and says, "Excuse me, I must put this treasure safely away."

"So, now that I have his seal of approval, and you know who I am, how about coming with me to the Pong Wetland. Repayment for saving your life. It's really something to see, a huge sanctuary and reservoir nearly three hundred square miles, that attracts more than a million migratory birds. At least five hundred and fifty-five species of birds have been identified. For a long time, I was the only one out there. I've got a *National Geographic* commission and it would be fun to have company."

Why not, Joan thinks. "Sure. What do I need to bring?"

She is thinking a sweater in case it gets cold, shoes she might not care about throwing away afterward, a slicker and a rain hat of some sort. Tomorrow, she will buy what she needs in the marketplace, or at the Kotwali Bazaar farther down the road. When Willem rattles off items she doesn't expect, like several pairs of socks, changes of clothes, she wonders what she's agreed to, and learns, too late, that they will be out in the Pong Wetland Reservoir for three days, cooking their meals over a campfire, doing their business behind trees.

"You'll have your own tent and my assistant will be there as well.

He helps me in my work and he'll make our meals. All you need to bring is your good eyesight, your imagination, and your open heart. Nature will take it from there."

In her pine suite, stretched out on her bed, she thinks about engaging for three days in birding, something she's never thought about, with a man she does not know, has only just met, a stranger with whom she drank a bottle of good red wine, who used as a reference for his honesty and solidity, the copy of *Kalpit Parvarik Jivan*, which she inscribed to him at his request, his love of her work, her paragraph in his pocket, the ownership of camera lenses and binoculars that he showed her in the hotel lobby.

Suddenly, she is thinking about the old man she and Martin saw when they began taking their meandering neighborhood walks in late January, observing details they had missed somehow over the years—that certain streets were confusingly named Peachtree Street, Peach Drive, and Peaches Court; that three houses on one block had full-grown apple trees out front, thick trunks, twisted boughs, wizened apples in the snow that hung red and heavy months before—and the old man in the apartment addition over a two-car garage was always staring out from behind the panes.

Their walks shifted days and hours, but there he stood, dressed in a shirt and tie, his nose pressed to the glass, binoculars gripped in his fingers, ready to be raised to his eyes. Someone's father, perhaps with early-stage dementia, was what Joan thought the first time she spotted him and pointed him out to Martin. He seemed prepared to search for approaching enemy aircraft, but unless their local paper had failed to report it, small-town Rhome, in northern Virginia, was not under imminent attack.

Watching him from the street, Joan had remembered the phrase *ineluctably sad*, a phrase that made her sob when she was young and read it in a novel. In her own writing, she had never found a place where those words might belong, but the old man in the window with the binoculars, *he* struck her as ineluctably sad, and Joan found herself down on the sidewalk, her head to her knees, trying to catch her breath, which seemed suddenly to have disappeared. Martin, kneeling at her side, asked what was wrong, and she hadn't known. He had waited until she held out her hand, then lifted her to her feet, and they walked on, to the halfway mark of their walk, a lamplight at the end of a cul-de-sac piled high with snow.

On the way back, the old man was still in his place, looking out into the distance, unaware of the woman who had crumpled to the icy curb because of him, and Martin said, "You know, maybe he's an avid birdwatcher." Her chest was still tight, but she had smiled up at her husband, because even though it was winter and she didn't think it was true, it might have been, and his ability to find an innocent pastime for that lost old man had made her happy.

She is out of bed and researching Willem Ackerman on her computer. He is a giant in the world of nature photography and photojournalism. Five books of his photographs have been published by Taschen, a sixth by Abrams, a seventh by Rizzoli. He has given lectures at universities throughout Europe and in America about photographing birds. Should she feel guilty that she is going to be camping with Willem, that she finds him very attractive, that she, who missed out on the years of being girlish, giddy, and flirtatious, was instead the intense young writer, is feeling those very things now, that she has not talked to Martin on the phone in weeks, that her emails to him have not moved into serious territory, remain well-crafted travelogue stories?

Joan is waiting outside of Hotel Gandhi's Paradise at six two mornings later when Willem drives up in a bright orange jeep. The back of the jeep is piled high with equipment and rucksacks, but there is no assistant sitting in a seat.

"Jinpa's girlfriend came for a visit, and Jinpa, throwing out all manner of apologies, begged me to let him sit out this trip." This is what Joan learns at dawn.

"What could I do?" Willem says. "Love is love. Though I have met this girlfriend and I think Jinpa is in for a hard crash. She's much more worldly than he is, not from Dharamshala. I doubt the two of them will last beyond this week. But until she cuts him down, at least he'll have a good time."

What should Joan make of Jinpa's absence? Will she find herself rolling around with Willem in the dirt, zipped up together in a double sleeping bag? It is a very intriguing thought. When Willem starts the engine, she pulls closed the flimsy jeep door. What does it matter that she hasn't reclaimed her life yet? She is still a brave woman, with courage, she is here in India, sitting next to a world-famous photographer she's never heard of, but when Willem Ackerman turns the bright orange jeep around in front of Hotel Gandhi's Paradise, she is ridiculously nervous.

The jeep barrels down the road, past the Dalai Lama's complex, past the Namgyal Monastery, where Joan and Camille have made dozens of *koras* together. There goes Namgyal Monastery in the wing mirror on her side.

They fly past Kotwali Bazaar and Willem Ackerman is making pleasant conversation about the weather, telling Joan that, according to the weather reports, the late monsoon season is taking a breather. They will be lucky at the reserve.

"The formal name of the Pong Wetland is Maharana Pratap Sagar Sanctuary. Named after a patriot who lived in the sixteenth century," he says.

"A patriot of what?" Joan asks, and Willem looks over at her and grins.

"I never thought to find out. But I can tell you when it was created in 1974, it swallowed up homes, communities, fertile fields, people who had lived there since the dawn of time. They were all resettled away from the lake, or in Rajasthan's Thar Desert. Very tough on those affected. But it's a really beautiful place."

What has she gotten herself into, bouncing in a racing jeep with handsome Willem Ackerman, on a three-hour drive to some sanctuary to see birds?

She's here now and she might as well see where it all ends up. "Tell me more," she says, shifting in her seat to face him. And he does.

"Those are the Shivalik Hills, a primeval mountain range older than the Himalayas." All she can see from this distance are tall brown plains, and she wonders if her eyesight is starting to go.

"The Shivaliks turn green when the rainy season really gets going. See out there? That's the Dhauladhar range. The Kangra valley sits between the two. The Pong Wetland is just thirty kilometers from the foot of the Dhauladhar."

When Willem's geography lesson comes to an end, he presses a button and music mixes with the rushing wind. Shaking bangles and chanting falsetto voices—it sounds to Joan like an Indian pop tune stripped of its lyrics. Willem is quiet for the next couple of hours, intent on driving, and Joan thinks how nice it is to be in a car with a man who does not require the constant flow of conversation to signal that everything is all right.

Though her eyes are shut, Joan is not asleep when the jeep slows, then turns off the main road. She looks around, at the waterline far out in the distance, at the unpaved road that follows monsoon-carved bends. A pink stone building, six stories high, appears like an obelisk in the middle of nowhere. A balustrade encircles the roof. Large windows, like square spectacles attached to the stone, go from roof to ground.

Willem pulls the jeep up alongside the quirky building and cuts the engine. The sign at the front reads THE LODGE @ PONG. She laughs at how that @ sign spells futurity on the shore of a wetland of international ecological importance.

Willem looks up. "I know. Talk about confusing your guests. I've never figured out whether that's actually the name of the hotel, or the owner's attempt to advertise their Web site. When I've asked, no one seems to know.

"Listen," he says. "Without Jinpa, I didn't want you to be uncomfortable, so we won't be camping out. I booked us rooms here. There's a good restaurant on the roof, with a tremendous view of the reservoir. You can come with me while I work, as much or as little as you want. Or you can do anything at all that you desire."

She is so pleased by the existence of the lodge, so pleased she will be sleeping in a bed, in her own room, with her own bathroom, she hopes, and not in a tent on the ground, having to pee behind trees. She is grateful that Willem Ackerman has made such arrangements, has let her know she can do as she pleases. She smiles at him and thinks maybe it's time to try something completely different.

41

They have walked an hour out from the shoreline, across an arid plain dotted with shrines and temples left intact when the people were relocated and the land was flooded. Once the monsoon season arrives in earnest, the reservoir will fill up and submerge even these ancient structures, turn everything into an Indian Atlantis.

The lake, all greens, browns, and blues, is still a serious walk from where they are and it is busy there, over the water, where birds are congregating and socializing, the sun pebbled by shadows when the birds streak across the sky. She watches them floating on eddies of air, then diving, their watery world all flapping wings and screeches.

"Do you prefer them?"

Willem nods, and Joan likes that he understands her question.

"Because of the purity: the specifics of their life-spans, their migratory passages, their needs so basic, just sustenance and shelter."

"Do you think they experience emotions the way we do, like disappointment or loss?"

"Sure. Not so easy to identify, but love is apparent when they preen together or share food. Anger, when they wing slap, lunge, or outright attack. Happiness in the way they sometimes hum. Fear with the same fight-or-flight response we have. Even grief shows up when a bird is listless or drooping, or searching for a lost mate or a chick. Spend enough time with birds and you'll notice they mirror our human behaviors when we feel love or anger or any of the other emotions we experience with frequency."

Thirty minutes later, they reach the edge of the shrunken reservoir. Willem unfolds his collapsible tripod, readies his camera, lifts the binoculars to his eyes.

"They'll come soon," he says. And they do.

He is a beacon for the birds; they sail in gracefully and land, or dive-bomb the ground, but no matter how they arrive, they all wade into the shallow water, stand still, fetchingly turning their heads and opening their beaks, as if they know they are posing for their close-ups.

Willem shoots and shoots, switching lenses, removing the camera from the tripod, walking, stalking, or tiptoeing toward his subjects. Sometimes he ululates funny sounds, or sends out into the air low whistles. The birds circle and dart and allow Willem to do his work.

It is late afternoon when he packs up his photography equipment and they begin the long trek across the wrinkled reservoir floor to the far shoreline. It is strange walking on ground that will soon be under-water. Joan can feel the earth waiting to be fed by the monsoons, by snow that will fall in a few months, by the melting of that snow come next spring. She feels elementally attuned, miniature in the universe, nonessential to the ebb and flow of time. In this cratered landscape, with its sinkholes and its pecking flocks, she and Willem could be the last two people on the planet.

At the reservoir's border, a muddy fen rides the shoreline. Willem loads Joan down with his equipment, photography bag around her neck, tripod in her arms, and he lifts her up and over the black slop, his boots squelching in the muddy terrain, even though just behind them the land is dry and hard-packed. When he sets her down, she feels the tiniest bit of loss. It was lovely being in his arms.

The lodge seems deserted when they return, and Joan wonders if they are the only guests. The reception area is a barely decorated space, an elevated stone desk, a stone floor, a small chandelier hung on too short a rope from the ceiling. When she looks up at the wooden staircase, its hard angles seem like a solvable mathematical problem.

They climb the stairs together. On the fourth floor, Willem says, "Meet up on the roof in an hour or so?" Joan nods and walks up the next flight. She hears Willem walking down the corridor, the key in the lock of his door.

She pushes open the door to her room. Puritanical furnishings— two single beds covered in blue chenille blankets, a blue grosgrain rug on the floor—lit up in sunset gold from the windows someone has opened for her. She is used to the colors of India, the various shades of red and yellow, all banned from this room. It has the feel of an old boarding-school dormitory. She leaves her mud-caked shoes near the door. Standing at the windows, it is easier to recognize the bruised beauty of the wetland. Beyond the reservoir, the granite bulwark of the Dhauladhar range soars upward from its green base, peaks blanketed by an eternal glacial snow that Willem has told her will never melt.

She steps out of her grimy clothes. The bathroom is more luxurious than the room: large shower and tub, modern sink and toilet, a full-length mirror. She looks relaxed, the faint lines around her eyes erased, her cheeks flushed from the sun. In the shower, she is amazed by the dirt washing off her body, out of her hair, spinning down the drain. She stays under the water a long time, then twists her hair into a high knot and stretches out naked and damp on the bed. Her ass, thighs, and calves feel taut and sore from walking such a distance on uneven ground wearing inappropriate footgear; her thick-soled tennis shoes are not up to the task, she needs hiking boots like Willem has.

The golden-red sun is hovering above the peaks when she dresses in the Indian tunic she bought in the Kotwali Bazaar, slips on her golden crystal sandals. She unravels her hair from its knot, and it falls like a black river down her back. She contemplates her reflection, leaves it down when she feels the trigger of something unrestrained within.

Willem and Joan are not the only lodge guests, because this place is too remote for a casual drop-in meal, and there are other people already dining on the roof. A young Indian couple in traditional dress sits at one table, glowing like characters in a Bollywood movie, the air between them fraught with flirtation within preapproved limitations. Nearby, two old Indian women are watching over them, chaperones picking at their dinners. At another table, a middle-aged father and his teenage son are speaking French. There is an empty space between them, a missing wife and mother. The father wears a look of retained power, but he seems lost, and Joan wonders which is responsible, divorce or death. The boy might be fourteen or fifteen, his eyes revealing something painfully adult that makes him appear worn, older than his years. The others look over and nod when Willem and Joan sit down at a table. Despite where they all are, at the edge of a reservoir, on the roof of a lodge in the middle of nowhere, there is no easy informality, no introductions, no exchanging of stories about how or why each party is in this isolated place inhabited primarily by birds.

Willem has brought with him a bottle of his Montepulciano, which a server quickly uncorks. When he clinks his glass against hers, he says, "I've done this for a very long time, and I've learned firsthand that when I'm having a rough time in life, watching birds alters everything, provides the right perspective on the world."

Their second morning, an hour into their walk, Joan feels a thrill of recognition; she can identify a few of the birds she saw yesterday, recall their names. She is quick now to sight the binoculars where Willem points, to focus and find what he wants her to see, and it is still early in the day when he points out the Sarus cranes perched in the shallows.

He is good company, the way he provides just the right amount of educational information, before they again walk in silence. She watches as he scans the sky, the shallows, the mud, the small shipwrecked water in the middle of the deserted landscape. He has a list of birds he has been trying to sight over the years, to photograph for his own purposes, but today he is searching for buzzards, the subject of his next *National Geographic* piece.

"Are you aware we have a pack of flies following us?"

"My fault," he says, and pulls from his backpack packets of raw meat that he opens and heaves in all directions. "Maybe this will entice them."

They wait for hours, Willem on his knees, his eye at the camera that stands on the tripod, Joan on the ground, watching and waiting. It is peaceful sitting still in the midst of this preserve, listening to the blood sluicing through her veins, feeling the beat of her heart, the sunshine hot on her head, the way her eyes are fluttering closed on their own. Thoughts enter her mind and she lets them go, doesn't try to hang on. It is the best meditation she has yet experienced. Hours later, in their same places, not a single buzzard has come forth to claim the meat.

Up on the roof that night, a glass of Willem's wine in her hand, the sky is its own dark lake, a sea of dazzling stars high above, their twins reflected across the land, bouncing off the water in the distance. They eat and drink the good wine, which makes them loose and quick to laugh, but she's aware they skirt the personal, the facts about their individual lives, don't talk about those wishes strangers talk about, the ones kept at the back of the mind. Willem has not asked if she is married—he would not have learned that information from her books or from any of the articles once written about her—or why she is here on her own. She has not asked whether he has found romance again in the years since his wife died. He is a man of angles and contradictions, happy in solitude, talented at conviviality. He talks with directness, does not mince words, but there is an innate diplomacy to his speech, even when he speaks bluntly. Joan wonders if it is a Dutch thing to not inquire too closely about the lives of others.

At the fifth-floor landing, Willem brushes his lips against her cheek, the kiss as soft as she imagines a bird's feathers to be. She is disappointed when he continues down the next flight and disappears into his room at the end of the hall.

She'd left the windows in her room open, and the night air is warm and dry, the sky as impenetrable as she has ever seen it here in India. She thinks again about the pressure walks she and Martin started taking in March, distinct from their meandering neighborhood walks. After, Martin is always on a mission. He ignores their sweatiness, dispenses with their ritual kisses and caresses, instead he strips her, flips her over, and plunges in. Her hair in his fist, her head yanked back to the point just before pain, a forearm clasping her from shoulder to shoulder, hands gripping her ass, pulling her onto her knees, fingers wrapped tight around her throat, then driving back in—a fantasy she once enjoyed—but she never orgasms with him those times. The first time, it was the tenor that confused her, startled to be taken by her husband turned unfamiliar. That her pleasure was irrelevant to him had heated her blood in anger, until the air atomized. She had surrendered then, allowed him to press her head down into their pillows, aware he wanted her to dance at the end of his cock. That mental submission triggered the physical sensations, but still she had not come. When he finished, he had kissed the back of her neck and said, "I love you so much," and left her belly-flopped on their bed, shiny with their sweat and their liquids, shocked, a hint of bruise spreading across her jugular that would not bloom until the next day. Martin had turned back once more and when she smiled, she had not known whether her smile was real, whether she meant it. Over the surging shower water, she heard him whistling, a pleased taker of that which he wanted, demanding in a way that was new. After all their years together, new for him too, she had hoped. The sweat on her body remained moist, and Joan did not know what exactly she felt. The act had excited her. She and Martin still had the habitual lovemaking down pat. Once or twice, sometimes three times a week, year in and out, but the frenzied need they used to feel for each other, that had endured despite one baby, two babies, and life itself, had dissipated, then fallen away. Only when Martin headed into another part of the house had she moved, taken a bath, touched herself while imagining Martin holding her throat firmly, forcing her to arch and arch, he thrusting and thrusting. She had come in less than a minute.

Here at the Pong Wetland, in her scholastic bedroom on the fifth floor of the lodge, wishing perhaps Willem had swept her away, Joan tosses her clothes onto the other bed, and climbs naked under the chenille. For the first time since arriving in India, she replays that particular scene with Martin in her mind, substitutes Willem for Martin, shivers deeply when she lets go, and is asleep in an instant.

Late in the afternoon on the third day, Joan takes herself, and the small notebook in which she's recorded the names of birds she's seen, to the empty rooftop restaurant. Has this venture, these birds, taught her anything about her plan for the future, about herself? Is there something in her old life not yet fully extinguished, or in these pages of notes she has taken, in these fine days she has spent with the Dutchman, the trips to the reservoir, sitting at shrines, wandering through stone temples, tracking the birds, that she can use?

She scribbles away, surprised to find she's written *Vita, Camille, Ela, old woman in the blue sari on the train.*

Hesitant. That's what she feels. When she rolls the word around in her mouth, it is as hard as a marble, capable of choking her if it slid down her throat, and Joan knows she has arrived at a truth. But hesitant about what, specifically? To recommit herself to her work? She makes it a statement, says to herself, *I fear I will not be the writer I once was*, but the statement sounds false, like she is telling a lie. Is she hesitant because of what she may need to do in order to return to her writing? That thought squirms down into her heart and nudges itself into place, next to the knots formed by Daniel. However wonderful it might be, but a love affair with handsome Willem Ackerman is not going to resolve anything. What she needs to resolve is her own life. Should she take the theft of *Words of New Beginnings* as a sign to rebuild, or not to rebuild? She turns to a fresh page in her notebook. When Willem arrives on the roof, camera around his neck, carrying two glasses and a bottle of champagne, her pen is still poised in the air.

"A treat," he says, pulling out a chair with his boot, placing the glasses on the table. "The kitchen staff kept it cold for us since we arrived."

He pops the cork and pours and Joan is glad that he does not touch her glass with his, or make a toast. Their silence feels right, any words spoken a pretense about their ability to mold civilization. There is the snap of the bubbles and the sun gasps its last flares before it vanishes behind the mountains.

Willem fills her glass back up and says, "Joan Ashby, I think it's time I took you to bed."

42

Since returning with Willem Ackerman from the bird sanctuary and reservoir, Joan is at last writing. Her first evening back, she wrote a second letter to the Dalai Lama, and Kartar delivered it that night to His Holiness's secretary. The next morning, at eight, she sat down at her pine desk with her tea and her lentils, and opened the laptop to a blank page. Eight until one every day now, a firm schedule that buoys her each morning when she wakes.

There were egregious attempts: tortured pages about what brought her to Dharamshala, then tiny fictional stories that balled themselves up so tight no string she pulled could release them.

She aborted everything, and ceded at last, or perhaps finally, to the older women who refused to budge, standing firm as schoolmarms in her head. The illimitable Vita Brodkey, the stalwart Camille Nagy, the serene Ela, women who might have taken themselves to Joan's imagined Devata when they were in their twenties, and still lived there all these decades later, making their art, growing aged and wise, oracles handing down their earned nuggets about life, its vicissitudes, its joys.

Vita, Camille, Ela, and even the old lady in the sparkling blue sari on the *chhotey* train with her milky eyes and broad smile, have transfigured Joan, and her time here. No longer does she smell the rancid aroma of a son's betrayal, the rageful odors her own body gave off. Time itself has altered, is shaping itself into a resurgence and revival of her creative intelligence. She realized she wants what these women possess—the sensate truth that they are remarkable, even if the rest of the world barely spares them a glance. Each woman has a trumpeting call of *Here I am, listen and learn.* And Joan has been listening and she has been learning, taking up her own instrument again—the right words on the page—figuring out the way they ought to slide up against one another, or sing, or crash, filled with grace, with blood, with bravery.

She started fresh, warily constructing one sentence, then another, and then the one after that. It took a few days before she realized the stealthy steps were working. She felt like a burglar silently jimmying the lock and entering the house of her mind, of the minds of those older women, of all their individual dreams, hoping everyone's treasures would be out on display. Now, each morning, Joan keeps her steps light when she returns to the intriguing search, careful with the gems she is finding—the precious stones of miraculous and original lives lived, the semiprecious ones reflecting truths learned in the nick of time, the false gold of failures socked away in some cabinet in the farthest reaches of those houses, secret places no one wants to remember.

Joan pulls open the marigold curtains and returns to bed with her notebook and pen. It is early, hours before her writing day begins, and she wants to jot down everything in her head:

Paloma Rosen in downtown New York, in SoHo, in a vast windowed loft where the seventy-nine-year-old sculptor has birthed her sensuous minimalistic forms by chopping at marble and wood and twisting her chisels, hammers, mallets, and rasps. For the last fifty years, sliced free of life's normative strictures, Paloma Rosen has worked privately making her art, without need of outside approbation, never seeking an agent to represent her, a gallery to proclaim what she renders. Though she has no sign on the door, does not advertise, is not a grand dame of the art scene, serious collectors find her, her name whispered along, as the greatest sculptor of the century, a truth Paloma has always known, does not need to hear sung.

Her hands are arthritic from working her soulfully hard materials, the force required to carve into the hulking elements that the earth throws up—massive stones and exotic tree trunks transported on cargo ships and hoisted by pulleys through her windows. Knees bad from decades of kneeling as she carves, from climbing the double flights of steep stairs—a replica of the staircase at the Pong Wetland Lodge—six from pavement to home, five from pavement to studio, fifty internal steps between loft and studio, thirty-five steps from loft to roof

*deck and garden, all those stairs growing ever harder to manage. At this late
stage of her life, Paloma will take in a lodger, a Sherpa to run all her errands,
to traverse all those flights.*

*One young man will respond to her Wanted ad. He is Theo Tesh Park, a
name he has assumed, but why he needed a new name, or what he was named
at birth, is unclear. Also unclear is whether he's tall or short, broad or stringy,
handsome or plain.*

*When the heavy steel door to Paloma's loft swings open, his jaw will drop when,
in the middle distance of the huge place, he sees stone and wood behemoths: A
black stone goddess fresh from the earth. A single form rising from a narrow
point at its base, turning into a shield for a giant. Two incredibly long and
slender figures in white stone, nearly entwined, neither with any obvious human
features, but encased in love. Pale-pink wood carved into a sculpture of multiple
spirals, the insides painted a shocking red instantly making Theo Tesh Park
think of blood, of life and of death.*

*A mellifluous, husky, accent-tinged voice will bring Theo down to earth. "I am
Paloma Rosen," she will say, and Theo's spine will shiver when he looks down
at the tiny, beautiful old woman patiently waiting for his attention.*

"You're an artist," he will say.

*His statement will recommend him, and Paloma will hire him, and Theo
will prove himself trustworthy and competent, timely with the tasks Paloma
assigns him.*

*One morning, months into their arrangement, Paloma flicks on the switch
in her salle de bain and looks upon herself with fright, and remorse. Her long
white braids have unspooled in sleep, her eyes bloodshot, the blue of her pupils
bled down to some desiccated shade, her cheekbones cut into the skin, sharp as
blades, mouth gummy and dry. At this ripened age, she knows better: two of her
rye sours, or gin and tonics, every other night, after a good day's work. Once
she could drink with the best of them, but no longer, not in years, but Theo was
home last night, and exactly how many of those devastating drinks did they
imbibe? She feels how she will suffer all of this day.*

Suddenly, she will look away from her hands in the mirror plaiting the long, long platinum braids, braids she wore even when her hair was chocolate brown, the straight middle part to the nape, the gathered thickness divided in half, each half divided into thirds, then twined together and tied off with silver bands, plaits that reach her waist, and she will catch her own eyes.

She will know this headache of hers is not a bland hangover, that there was wildness last night, tamed wildness, of course, but she remembers Theo telling her about a drug-addled mother, a dead grandmother, a sister in the Mojave with other like-minded young people, thinking themselves old-fashioned hippies rather than failures. Or is that how Paloma interpreted what Theo told her last night, and he said he thought his sister was in a cult, or in something that seemed like a cult? Paloma might need clarification about that.

And Paloma will know she must have been cross-eyed drunk because she elicits others' stories while remaining private, and yet she must have told Theo a few of her own because Jean-Pierre Beson is in her head and, until this moment, she can't recall the last time she thought of that once and long-ago husband, of her former life, ancient now, in Paris.

Though the specifics are unclear, she will remember last night as one of revelations, timid at first, and although the air never cooled down, she is fairly certain she and Theo lit dozens of candles, and then their secrets were flying through all that beautiful flickering candlelight, whisked out of their mouths on the hot breeze that flowed in through the open windows.

There must have been an ungodly number of drinks because she will remember Theo pulling down a glass pitcher from the top shelf of a kitchen cabinet, and then he had armfuls of lemons and limes and blood oranges, taken from the large basket on the ten-foot-long marble island she herself hammered from an even larger piece, then chiseled, sanded, and polished, back in 1967, when she was twenty-nine and in her first full year in New York, living in the loft, owning the otherwise vacant building. Theo was slicing all that fruit, his big hands squeezing citrus halves in one tight squeeze, when she would have had to cut each into eighths to wring juice from the fruit. And she will remember pouring the dregs of rye from the dead bottle into the pitcher, then opening a fresh one and pouring forever, a stream of amber that went on and on, and the seltzer had sizzled, and the cubes had tinkled against the glass until the pitcher was brimming, and she will say, "Marcel Duchamp gave me this pitcher," bragging as she never did, and Theo will say, "Who's that?"

And there will be a song still on a loop in Paloma's head, the song Theo is embarrassed that he loves because it is played on the radio and Theo will not abide music played on the radio. A girl with a huge soaring voice singing *The stars, the moon, they have all been blown out . . . And in the dark, I can hear your heartbeat . . .* and Paloma will remember the singer's strange name—Florence and the Machine—and she will remember clapping her hands and yelling over the singer's voice, telling Theo to play the song again. And he had been like a puppy dog with a yummy bone clamped in his jaw, grinning his innocent grin, that precocious spirit of his making her laugh, both of them singing along. Theo's voice unexpectedly fine, knowing every word that trilled and thrilled. All Paloma could do was grab hold, here and there, of the words she recalled, acutely aware that the orchestral music and the starbursting voice of the singer were at odds with lyrics about a tumultuous love affair that blinded the singer, left her screaming aloud, until she found her lover's heartbeat, and knew she would stay in the darkness with him, or her, or whoever you was.

Later, when Paloma is downstairs in her studio, assessing the eight-foot hunk of soft butternut wood she plans to begin carving, Theo will sneak down the staircase, sit silently on a step, and she will be aware of him, wonder how long to give him to marshal the courage to say whatever he has come to say, to reveal the artifact she is aware she has forgotten in the hazy murk of rye and juices and seltzer and sugar.

Her relationship with Theo will fascinate her, but she will not have expected to feel this sense of commitment to him, and while it has taken her some time to adjust, the notion of caring for another in a pure way will not be, as she used to fear, awful. Until Theo, no one's needs or desires or expectations ever altered Paloma's intentions for her own life, or never for more than a few brief weeks or months, times consumed by lovers. It is not sexual attraction she feels for Theo, although he is a most beautiful specimen, and it is not romantic love, they are ages and worlds apart, but getting drunk together last night will be an indication of how they might speak to each other in the future, about the real things that propel them.

But right now, what she understands is that the love she feels for him is deep and protective, and wonders if this is this why the untouched butternut wood before her seems to hold two figures, one larger, revealing itself, one smaller, still shy. Although Theo is the tall one and she the small, the great maternal figure in the butternut speaks to her first.

Paloma does not pray, or not in some usual way, she is a Jew from Cairo, long divorced from a practicing French Catholic husband, and yet she will whisper words of hope, that the love she feels for Theo is not, mon Dieu, maternal. That would not work for her, not suit her at all. She has avoided all of that, was never a woman with those impulses, has had a tremendously creative and prosperous life because she never felt an iota of longing for a child of her own.

She will begin chiseling away the unnecessary bulk from the wood on the turntable. Her strength is not what it used to be, otherwise she would simply lean down and swing the turntable around until the other side of the untouched wood is before her. But this block must weigh close to a third of a ton, and she has only two choices: to call to Theo and have him move the turntable, or walk around to the other side of the wood. If she does either, she will have to admit she knows he is there, waiting for her to acknowledge his presence, to engage as he wants to engage.

She's not ready for whatever he needs to say to her, and so she will stare for a while at the wood until a wide ray of sunlight finds it, and her. Oui, there, just beyond the large rounded form, is the smaller one, peeking out, not quite ready to emerge, but its tentativeness is falling away. She will angle her head upwards to the deep-blue sky hanging beyond the huge windows. On the ledge, pigeons are cooing. She will want to smoke another clove cigarette, but she structures that vice as carefully as she works her materials, and she has an hour to go before she allows herself the second of her working day.

Since she is the one who has forgotten something important, something the two of them discussed during the drunken night, she will decide she might as well commence the communication that Theo wants. She can feel his intent to sit on the stair until either she, or he, begins.

She will say, "I hear you breathing up there, Theo. I am old, not deaf. If you want to say something to me, come down here, pull up a stool, and we can talk like the adults that we are. Oui?"

In an instant, Theo is on the studio floor, his bare feet kicking up dust, lifting one of the many stools in the studio, placing it close, swiveling to face her.

Paloma will not move, only stare at the bottom of the butternut wood, chiseled away. She thought it might be a flat base, but the wood is demanding there be no base at all, just the two forms freestanding, everything else carved away.

Then she will sigh, and swivel, and she and Theo will be face-to-face, just inches apart.

"Miss Rosen," Theo will say, and Paloma's heart will sink, for the lost artifact must be major.

He only calls her Miss Rosen when he is very nervous. Most of the time he does not use her name, neither first nor last. She knows he finds calling her Paloma challenging, as if he is not entitled to presume such closeness, and yet ils sont proches, the two of them spend more of their spare time with each other than with anyone else. He calls her Miss Rosen when he feels he has something to confess—when he runs the vacuum over some trinket that was sucked up into the hose and makes the machine smoke and splutter and die, when he borrows one of her old books and accidentally leaves it on the subway. These small things will never faze Paloma, but cause Theo grievous pain. She will wonder what happened in his young life to make him fear that such small mistakes would incur the ire of another, result in untoward fury he expects to be expended on him. More than once, she will have to say to him firmly, and as kindly as she can, that he is not to worry, that she knows he did not do whatever *it is on purpose, aware, when telling her of some misstep, how he seems to fear the slap of a hand, the punch of a fist.*

While he stares at her, and Paloma stares at the base of the wood, she will again wish she remembered more of the particulars of the family stories he told her last night, wonders if, within their coming conversation, and without inflicting too much insult, she might ask him to repeat what she cannot recall.

"Miss Rosen," he will say again. "I want to talk about the plans for the dinner party Saturday night. We sent out all those email invitations last night, and most everyone has confirmed."

Dinner party? Emails sent out in their drunken state? Screw her schedule, she thinks, and pulls the packet of cloves from her overalls, her hand slightly shaking when she lights it, breathing in deeply and exhaling a stream.

"Theo, please explain. Too much rye last night. I have no recollection of discussing, or agreeing to, a dinner party. I don't have dinner parties anymore, not in years. I cannot believe I would have agreed to such a thing."

"But you did," Theo will say, keeping his voice even. "You thought it was a great idea, then had me explain who everyone was before I added their name to the email invitation we sent. You even chose the evite we selected."

"Oh, mon Dieu, qu'est-ce que tu racontes? Je ne comprends pas. Un dîner? Non, c'est impossible. Je ne l'ai pas jeté un dîner pour un certain temps. Exactement qui ne nous invitons?"

When Theo does not respond, she will realize she has spoken to him entirely in French, and he has only picked up the basics in the several months he has lived with her, doing her bidding.

"The whole thing is impossible," she will say. "I was drunk."

"Maybe later, but not then, or at least you didn't seem drunk to me, just telling me about the dinner parties you used to throw."

A discussion of the dinner parties she used to throw is strong evidence; when she's had a little too much to drink, she tends to remember the past. Only then does she permit herself sentimentality, an essential release valve for how tightly controlled she is in her work, where sentiment is forbidden. Sober, the past has no place, only the future.

"How many people did we invite?"

"Besides you and me? Eighteen. You said, 'It's time we fill the space with laughter again, and music, and delicious food. It's time to have the dining-room table properly used, the chairs occupied by interesting people.' "

She will think first, what kind of language is besides you and me, *then she will think,* Yes, she could feasibly have spoken such words. *In the past, she regularly threw gorgeous, raucous dinner parties, but now she wants no such thing in her life. Theo, however, apparently does. And she apparently agreed.*

"When you interviewed me, you wanted to know if I could set the table for a formal dinner party. You haven't had me do that yet. And I can. I Googled how to do it, and printed out pictures of how everything should look on the table."

"D'accord. Return, Theo, to the beginning of it all. Whom did we invite?"

"I have the list," and he will unfold a wadded piece of paper pulled from the back pocket of his jeans, unfolding, and unfolding, and then smoothing it out, and then he will say, "Ready?"

"Non, mais read your list anyway."

Paloma will recognize most of the names, substantial people in the art world: curators at three New York City museums; gallery owners, three based in Chelsea, two out in refurbished sections of Brooklyn, all representing new and young artists on the ascent, and selling a ton of work; the second-in-command of a Los Angeles museum, which, according to an article she read in the New York Times, is enduring much squabbling among board members. Also on Theo's list will be three writers, for Art Forum, Frieze, and October, and a Parkett editor involved in artist monographs and catalogues raisonnés that Paloma has read with approval and pleasure. She personally knows two of the people on the list, the Floridian matriarch and patriarch who commissioned works from her in 1991. Physical giants, their raison d'être is the collecting of modern art—paintings, sculptures, video installations of people doing the same thing again and again. They own many thousands of pieces, lately keen on flashy sculptures, derivative works by a man who cares much about his looks and oversees an army of technicians. The family owns so much art they built their own museum, now open to the public, the surf not far in the distance. Paloma sculpted two pieces for them. The first, two stacked onyx cubes, each five feet square, with dicelike holes. The juxtaposition piece, in stark alabaster, was five squares and rectangles piled high, but much carved away from their centers, the dice holes writ large. She spent two weeks in Florida as their guest, left in peace in their three-story beach house. Eventually, the work was placed on a high dune, sea grass surrounding it, which could be seen through the back picture window, sand and sea and grass moving through the seasons, rising and falling, ever visible around and through the empty spaces.

Only three names will mean nothing to her, and Theo will explain that Mikhail Marovich is his friend, and he is bringing his wife, Vanessa, and a friend of theirs, about whom Theo knows nothing. This, Paloma will realize, is the first time Theo has invited any of his friends to the loft, though she has told him he is free to do so, as long as he does not permit them to disturb her, does not bring them down to the studio whether she is working or out.

What Paloma will want to know is how Theo knows these people, well enough to have their email addresses, familiar enough to invite them to a dinner party two nights hence at her loft. A dinner party on a Saturday evening in late August when most people who can afford to be gone from the hot city that never quiets are long gone, which includes all the names she recognizes.

She will wonder how her Theo—who works for veritable nickels, for a place to live and readily available food, for the educational course in the history of sculpture that she has set for him—crossed paths with any of them. In the normal course of his day working for her, never would he meet such people at the art stores, galleries, and museums she sends him to.

And how has he emailed them and received affirmative responses so quickly, every one of whom must have altered weekend plans to attend?

"Explain to me, Theo, how you know these people."

Looking down at the dusty cement floor, Theo will say, "Don't ask me to explain. But will you trust me?"

He will not lift his eyes to meet hers.

Paloma will think that if he had met them all at some arty shindig, he would have told her, but as far as she knows, Theo does not receive invitations to parties.

It is then she will wonder if these people are related to Theo's secretive nights out of the loft. Surely, the Floridians are not, but perhaps he has met the rest in a way that does not give him satisfaction or pleasure, that prevents him from telling her the truth, and yet he wants them to meet her.

This moment, Paloma Rosen will realize, is the moment, when she proves to both Theo and herself the love she has for him. An internal battle will wage inside of her. She will not want to be involved in any of this, not at all, and the forecast of unhappiness it will bring into her world.

After the wiry tension strings far out between them, she will finally say, "Oui, je vais tu faire confiance."

"Does confiance mean confidence?" Theo will ask. "That you have confidence in me, that you will go through with the dinner party you agreed to?"

They will stare at each other for a long moment, and Paloma Rosen will look back to the butternut wood and think there is so much to do to get the carving truly under way, and then, that a dinner party at this stage in her life, with such people coming to dine, specifically to meet her, is completely at odds with the philosophy by which she has worked as an artist. She does not need them, or want them, fears what might happen if she opens the door and lets them in. The Floridians are a different story, but Paloma rarely mixes with her collectors once her work is set in place.

She will return to Theo, to all of that longing in his face, his eyes wide and hopeful, and she will see that he wants this for her, and although she does not, she says what she knows she must say.

"Oui, Theo. For you, I will do it.

"Maintenant, did you water my grounding grass? Even from here, I can see it looks parched."

Joan pictures a long, rectangular concrete container, filled with aerated dirt, organic fertilizer, and grass, in the middle of Paloma's studio. Paloma Rosen's grounding grass, which is Theo's responsibility to water twice a day, with a hose that reaches from a deep, old-fashioned stone sink in the northwest corner. When she feels herself too lost in creation, or overly indulgent, Paloma eradicates those extreme impulses by kicking off her work boots and socks and stepping onto the grass, sinking into the loamy earth, the bottoms of her feet arched, then flat, against the soft grassy blades, until she feels rooted again.

Joan is far ahead of herself; she and Paloma are still in France, married to Jean-Pierre Beson. New York, in Paloma's life and in Joan's writing, is in the future. The old Duncan Hines factory that Paloma Rosen will buy and live in for decades is still churning out cake mixes that scent the neighborhood in vanilla, chocolate, strawberry. And Theo Tesh Park, whatever his original name may turn out to be, he has not yet even been born.

She looks down at the notes she has taken, at the poor sketches she has tried to draw of Paloma's remarkable sculptures, and realizes she is thinking of her own mother for the first time in years. Is it because Paloma speaks French—the language of Eleanor Ashby's rare warmth and kindness—or is it because Eleanor thoughtlessly became a mother knowing she felt not the slightest maternal instinct, while Paloma, who kept herself free from children, possesses, deep down, both the heart and the nature to provide that specific sort of sustenance, of care?

Joan shakes Eleanor Ashby from her head while she washes her face, brushes her teeth and her hair, pulls on a wrap over her pajamas, socks on her feet, and retrieves her morning tray from outside the door. Eleanor Ashby is gone by the time Joan places on her desk the day's flower, an orange vase holding an unopened yellow bud, drinks the hot tea, eats the steaming lentils that warm her up, powers up her laptop, and begins another workday.

At one, she takes a deep breath, leans back in her chair, and reads through what she has written.

The last time Paloma Rosen presided over a large dinner party she was twenty-nine and married, and living in a high-ceilinged apartment in the sixteenth arrondissement that received wonderful northern light and had immediate views of Boulogne Park and the Eiffel Tower. It was a long, cool place owned by her husband's family, and while Jean-Pierre was at the office, she painted in the deliberately unfur-nished room he called, without irony, *l'atelier de ma femme*. That last dinner party had been splendid: artists, writers, philosophers, and po-ets Paloma had known for years or a day. Although Jean-Pierre could not follow the corkscrewing conversations—"*Au-delà de mon métier*," as he said—he was a fine host in other ways, smiling and laughing and unstinting with the Besons' store of fine wine. Paloma had been a vision, all pale definitive beauty. Dressed exquisitely in a long-sleeved white gown, slashed open from clavicle to sternum, waves of glossy brown hair falling down her bare back. She was applauded as the *chef de cui-sine* at the end of the evening, which did not occur until the early hours of the new day. She and Jean-Pierre had fallen into bed when the light was breaking, made love, and did not wake again until the cocktail hour.

Not the next day, or even the next week, but the following season, early spring in Paris, she knew with certainty that both painting and marriage were too confining. In her studio that spring afternoon, Paloma stepped away from her canvas in progress and moved to the windows. Thunderclouds roofed the sky, the birch trees along the sidewalk, and the Eiffel, were shrouded in fog, and the park, spread out below in virgin green, was empty; no one strolling along the romantic promenades, not even the old man who led his crippled dog on a long walk in all kinds of weather.

She thought of how her husband of five years loved her, and was mostly competent in bed, and did not press the issue of their un-born children, and showered her with handmade jewelry soldered together with diamonds. But their years together had demonstrated there was something too angelic about Jean-Pierre, he lacked imagina-tive bad habits, could not fathom the internal propulsion that drove her. Paloma Rosen was made more sternly, and although Jean-Pierre would crumple, her defection wrenching his heart, she could not continue on if she wanted to live according to the precepts of her own personal faith, distant from any notion of religion.

Paloma considered the tangential selflessness of her disappearing act: Jean-Pierre would recover and be better off with a soft woman who wanted to become softer still, who wanted her belly to rise and her breasts to fill with milk, who would only ever use her hands for love and tenderness. Paloma understood what she had long known: she was not that soft woman, this sweet and tender life was not what she wanted, and painting was not her way forward.

By four, the thunderheads had released a slanting rain that hit the cobblestones hard, creased the tall windowpanes, and Paloma saw herself walking into the fog a free woman. Of course, there would be legalities, the divorce and all of that, but Jean-Pierre was an *avocat* and he could properly attend to the particulars, or instruct someone else to do so. At some point, she would have to sign documents severing their bond, but that could wait for future instructions she would leave at their bank, about how and where she could be reached, when she herself knew.

By five, her tubes of cadmium red, Prussian green, titanium white, lamp black, vermillion, marigold, and cerulean, and the thin and thick brushes made from hog bristles, red sable, and the hairs of other unfortunate animals, and the cans of thinner and turpentine, and her stained wooden palettes and knives were neatly packed away in boxes. She wrapped up in old sheets the blank canvases she had stretched herself and nailed into place on sturdy wooden frames. Against a wall, she set all of her finished work, made sure her name marked every piece. Perhaps one day these paintings, the last she would ever make, might be worth something, and she wanted Jean-Pierre to remember her fondly in the unfolding years, to possibly benefit from his tenuous connection to her, which would have faded by then.

Jean-Pierre was still at his office when Paloma placed the keys to their apartment on the tray atop the antique table in the blue foyer. She carried two bags: one of clothing that would see her on her travels, the second of her treasures—sketchpads and journals and a few favorite books. She debated the dramatics of leaving a note. To disappear without one was preferable, but Jean-Pierre, though he had the simple views of a man born into a well-to-do life, did not deserve that, he was good after all, and so Paloma set down her bags, and in his navy silk-walled study, she penned a few lines on his fine stationery, cribbed Jean-Pierre's name across a matching envelope, sealed the end of their marriage within, took the envelope back into the foyer, and left their relationship next to her keys.

The front door solemnly fell into its lock, protecting all she no longer cared about, was leaving behind. Out in the hallway, sepulchral light streamed through the tall framing windows at each end, and she saw that the angry rain had been tamed, a drizzle now, more mist than drops. Her heels clicked on the seafoam tiles as she walked the long corridor toward the lift.

She passed M. Alvien's door, where his wooden table with the indefatigable vase of dried flowers still stood just to the left, there the day Jean-Pierre carried her over the threshold of their own apartment, she in her wedding gown, a delicate, lacy confection that served up her breasts, something Marie Antoinette might have worn lounging at Versailles, and in the blue foyer of her new home, Jean-Pierre had unbuttoned every one of the hundred ivory satin buttons that trailed down her spine while she, out of character, stood docile as a lamb.

She reached the Montes' front door and there, on the wall, was a finger-painting made by Luc Monte during a morning spent with Paloma when he was seven. She saw Luc sometimes, swooping into the lift on his skateboard. He was a big boy now, nearly twelve, his nose too large for the under-face that spoke of his childhood, the shadow of distinct, distasteful hair emerging on his upper lip, and whatever artistic grain was once within him had disappeared. As far as she knew, the painting she was looking at was the only piece of art Luc Monte would ever create; she thought it unlikely he was destined for anything great.

No matter how hard and fast Paloma pressed the button, the lift was not rising, and she felt suspended, neither staying nor leaving, until, at last, it finally juddered to a stop on the seventh floor. For the first time in all her years living a married life in the lovely apartment with a husband who adored her, painting her pictures like a cossetted housewife whose art was viewed as merely a hobby, the filigreed door with its artisan-hammered metal leaves cut into her skin when she pulled it open. There was blood on her fingers, a cut across her palm. When she pulled the door shut and descended to the ground, her own blood sent her off, a crimson smear that told her this version of Paloma Rosen was already gone.

She headed to Gare de Lyon, the station from which she would travel by train to the first of several stops in other countries, on a quest to discover a material with which she wanted to work, an expressive material she could love over the long haul of the life she planned to create for herself. She wanted something tough and masculine, the kind of substance that required strength, that would decimate those who possessed no true bravery, some magical substance that once in her hands would make everyone forget the work had been done by a woman.

Joan's heart is beating hard when she looks away from the screen. She has been with Paloma Rosen as a child in Egypt, her art-school years in London, her time in Paris where she met Jean-Pierre, the whirlwind courtship, the wedding, the settling love, her world there in that arch, luxe environment, and now Paloma is leaving, has left, and there are endless avenues for Joan to consider as Paloma heads out into her new freedom.

Last night, Martin's latest email arrived and she declined to read it. This morning, she concentrated on her work, but the work is done, and her husband has something to say.

It still jolts Joan when she sees *joanmanning* as her email address. Here, she has not been Joan to anyone except Natwar briefly, and Willem Ackerman, and a Manning to no one. She has not been *Mom* or *Mother*. No matter the company she and Eric may be in, even among sojourners who mention the families they have left behind, the call of India louder than the call of home, he has never referenced their blood relation, has never faltered in calling her Ashby. Here she is only Ashby. The facts of her life—that she is someone's wife, has a husband, is a mother—are like old garments she removed one day and stored on a shelf in her suite's pine closet. Dressing again in those old clothes seems increasingly impossible.

Each time Martin sends her a message, she needs more and more time to reset her mind, to remember her other life unfolding without her, seventy-five hundred miles away. She can no longer picture Martin's face, not completely, or the routines of his days, in operating rooms, with patients, on his bike with Men on Bikes on the weekends, the order in which he pulls on his clothes when he dresses in the mornings, how he packs his suitcase for his surgical trips—it is all a white blank.

Lately, his messages, voice or word, carry a certain tone, a particular articulation, and she understands—he has shown steady patience, has allowed her to try to work through this travesty on her own, but he wants her back in their joint existence, has not agreed to her disappearing forever. She understands, but she bridles, rears up against his entreaties. She had evaded as long as she can, but it is time to read his email.

> I'm thinking of coming to Dharamshala. You've been there
> such a long time that I want to see what has kept you so intrigued.
> We could travel back home together afterwards. I am figuring out
> how to clear my surgical schedule and then will look into flights.

She is not ready to contemplate what her response might be. She has spent hours thinking about and then writing Paloma Rosen's escape from her old life, the way she chose to leave her husband, the future she envisions for herself. Has Joan already written the scene of her own leaving? Did it happen when she bought the ticket to Delhi, or went to Dr. Abrams for the shots, or when she and Martin were so quiet the night before she left, or when he drove her to the airport and they kissed, or when she boarded the plane, overcoming that first urge to turn back? Or has she not written that scene yet, has she not actually left him, has she not made up her mind? She closes her computer without writing a reply.

43

Joan bathes quickly and then she is dressed, a bright Indian tunic over the only pair of jeans she brought, her feet in the golden crystal sandals she intends to wear until it is too cold to do so, a light wrap in the bag on her arm.

She is hurrying down the mile-long hill from Hotel Gandhi's Paradise to the courtyard behind the Dalai Lama's compound, for Ela's meditation group at two, which she now attends daily.

She has known this day was coming, but she's been dreading when Camille leaves Dharamshala until next year, returns to her home on the outskirts of London, returns to her damaged children and the art-therapy lessons she gives them. It is the third of September, and Camille is flying tonight from Gaggal Airport in Kangra—the airport's existence fourteen kilometers southwest of Dharamshala a surprise to Joan—to Delhi, from Delhi to London Heathrow, then a train from London Heathrow to her terraced house at the end of a block in Twickenham, in southeast London, near the River Thames. She has shown pictures to Joan, springtime pictures of the front of her house: yellow daffodils in window boxes painted black, the window shutters painted white, a row of pink tulips on a small stretch of grass, ceramic ducks—that do not seem at all like Camille—marching along the path to Camille's pink front door. Behind her house, Camille has a glass addition that extends beyond her kitchen, where she meditates through the year until she returns to Dharamshala. She showed Joan pictures of that too.

Joan is the last one to arrive, to sit on the red silk pillows in her usual six position. Camille is in her regular place, at seven, and Joan squeezes her hand, then finds Ela at twelve, and smiles, and is shocked to see Eric sitting next to Ela, at eleven. She told Eric about Ela's group, but he meditates on his own in his backyard, or with the large group that gathers in the late afternoons at Tsug Lakhang, listening first to the Namgyal Monastery monks holding fierce, disciplined debates, until they fall silent, raise their hands and commence the meditation. But Eric is here, smiling at her, his ponytail, now nearly half the length of hers, thrown over one shoulder. In these months, Joan has kept separate Camille and Ela from Eric, and now they are all gathered together.

"*Namaste*," Ela says. "*Namaste*," everyone chimes in return.

"Our own Camille Nagy leaves us tonight, and so this is her last meditation in Dharamshala until next June. Before we begin today's mantra, which Camille will choose, I wanted to tell you a story about an Indian man named Chand who has a home nearby, but spends most of the year driving a taxicab in New York City.

"In New York, each day he passed a blind musician playing his violin on a street corner. And each day, Chand put a dollar into the case at the musician's feet. This went on for months, and then one day the blind musician was gone, and Chand debated what to do with his dollar. He put it in an envelope, and he did the same thing each day the blind musician was missing. Soon Chand had collected fifty dollar bills. When the musician reappeared playing his violin on the corner, Chand did not have the envelope with him. 'I have missed you and your playing, my friend,' Chand said to him, and learned the musician had been ill, but was better, and would be back to his regular schedule, playing on the corner each day. But the next day, the blind musician was gone again, and Chand continued to collect the dollar bills he would have otherwise given him. This went on for two years, until the envelope held seven hundred and eighty dollars. Chand added bills until there were a thousand, and then, when he knew the blind man was gone for good, he sent the money home, to Dharamshala, and asked his brother-in-law to donate it to the music school for the blind, with the request that it be used to buy instruments for musicians in need, which the brother-in-law did. Although Chand never saw the blind musician again, he has collected a dollar a day ever since, sending money back home to the music school. His donations have allowed the school to buy five violins, two cellos, and a flute, so far.

"This story carries the tenets by which we are intended to live, and underlies many of the mantras we chant. It is important to remember that the smallest gesture of kindness and generosity can have a huge effect, rippling the waters out from ourselves, allowing us to touch others in a wondrous way. Those of us who stand in the sun must share the light with others."

Ela takes a moment to sweep across each person's face, smiling all the while. Then she says, "Camille, which mantra will we chant today?"

"Ela, thank you for such an honor. And in the spirit of Chand, I have chosen the *Moola* mantra, in honor of my friend Ashby who has learned this mantra by heart, although her first time here she could not make heads or tails of it, and sweetly lied to me when she claimed to have enjoyed the experience. I knew she had no intention of coming back, but she did, and I am so glad for that."

Joan feels she's graduated from something important, or to something important, the way Ela, and Eric, and Camille are smiling at her, and those on the other red silk pillows, faces familiar and unfamiliar, smiling at her too. The tears she never used to shed, how much easier they come now, a few drops sliding down her cheeks, her hand in Camille's, and then Ela hits the gong, once, twice, three times, settling the group, knitting it together under that tonal embrace, and the chanting of the *Moola* begins.

After the chanting and the silent meditation, when the *namastes* have all been said, and the red pillows are stacked in the corner of the courtyard, Eric joins Joan and says to Camille, "I've heard a lot about you. I'm sorry we haven't met until today, and now you're leaving."

Camille says to Joan, "Is this the beautiful young man you've told me so much about?" and to Eric, "You're the lucky one chosen to meet with the Dalai Lama."

Eric nods. "It won't happen until next year, March maybe, or April, maybe even May. But time passes so quickly here."

When he has his personal audience with the Dalai Lama, Eric will be into his second year in Dharamshala, and Joan wonders if she will be here too, during those months, in a whole new year.

"I miss that a great deal when I'm back in London. Days are the same length wherever you are, but in a big city, sometimes they last forever.

"Ashby," Camille says. "I forget what you told me. How did you two meet?"

Joan knows she never told Camille any story about meeting Eric, as if he were a stranger she ran into at Namgyal Café, or up at Kareri Lake. For Joan, omission, while a sticky area, does not constitute an outright lie.

"I've known her my whole life," Eric says, which seems to answer the question to Camille's satisfaction.

After Eric waves goodbye and disappears around the side of the courtyard, Ela joins them, her blush-colored sari turning her into an elegant pale rose, her umber hair arranged on top of her head like flower petals. She hands Camille a package wrapped in pretty paper. "A small gift, to be opened when you're back in London on a day that's making you unhappy. Then a little Dharamshala to cheer you up."

Camille is softly crying and Ela is holding her close, and then Camille says, "Enough, I do this every year. Ashby, come with me," and Joan looks back at Ela, and Ela mouths, "See you tomorrow." Then Joan and Camille are at the bottom of the trailhead, below the monastery, performing a last *kora* together. Turning the heavy prayer wheels all these months has made the effort not quite effortless for Joan, but easier than it was at the beginning. Camille stampedes through the wheels, shucking them around, barely breathing hard at the end.

"Come to my cottage with me," Camille says when Joan joins her at the finish. "I have something to give you."

"I have something to give you, too," Joan says.

Camille's cottage is high up in the steep hills, near the teahouse where Joan and Camille and Ela first shared tea, before they ran naked into Dal Lake on Ela's seventy-fifth birthday. She has been here many times in these months, the backyard a postage stamp with the mountain rearing up right behind it, and each time Joan sees the cottage, she thinks of a sapphire that a jeweler damaged in the cutting. The whole house tilts, lists, really, to the left, and inside, the light has a cool blue glaze because the walls are all painted a cerulean blue paled down to its haunting jeweled base. She stole that color for the Parisian apartment Paloma Rosen has just left behind.

Joan stands at the front window and the whole of the marketplace is on view. At the Dalai Lama's compound, under its white tent, a broad crowd funnels into the courtyard to listen to the debating monks. The colorful prayer flags flutter in the late afternoon fall breeze.

From her bag, Joan takes out her own present to Camille, a shawl hand-woven by a woman named Pema who sits surrounded by skeins of wool at the back of her shop in the Kotwali Bazaar. The knitting woman reminded Joan of Carla, and the shop Carla used to own in Rhome, Craftables, just off Strada di Felicità, the last of the Pregnant Six to give up the lives they had led before motherhood.

"You didn't have to, but I'm so glad you did," Camille says, ripping off the paper, opening the box, carefully pulling out the shawl.

Joan had chosen carefully. Luxurious and oversized, in various grays lighter and darker than Camille's flint bun, with a vermilion stripe to remind her of Ela's own parted stripe and bindi.

"Absolutely perfect," Camille says, twirling around, ducking into her small bedroom to look at herself in the mirror. "I'll wear it constantly. Now, sit down, I'll make us some tea. There are a few things for us to talk about."

When their teacups are filled, and the teapot and a plate of Nakhatai cookies that Camille says she baked herself, "Eggless with cardamom," are on the table, Camille sets a bag on the floor near her chair.

"First, Eric is your son, yes?"

Joan was not expecting this. "Yes."

"And you have another son, don't you?"

"Yes."

And she remembers Daniel asking her questions the same way—was she a writer, did she have books published, was she writing anything then? And she remembers the answers she gave him: yes, yes, no. The third answer, the *no*, a lie. She had been writing *Words of New Beginnings*.

"And the other son, he's the reason you're here?"

Joan can't return to the discovery of her novel stolen and chopped into two, Daniel's identical Lewis Carroll acknowledgments at the back of J. D. Henry's books.

"Yes, and I thought about sharing—" and Camille cuts her off.

"Dharamshala is a place to figure things out, as I said to you when we first met. You don't need to tell me. If you had been ready to share with me, you would have, and you're still not ready. But I know how far you've come since you arrived. I've seen the pain, the confusion, the hurt and fear that riddled you, slowly starting to fall away, and that's really all that matters. When you're ready to tell me, we'll talk. It is the other side of the world, or it feels like it, but we're just a series of numbers away from each other. We can talk all we like.

"Drink your tea, Ashby, have another Nakhatai cookie. Good, aren't they? So the next thing," and Camille lifts the paper bag onto the table.

"The name Ashby was familiar, but I just never put anything together," and Camille extracts from the bag two books, in English, Joan's own *Other Small Spaces* and *Fictional Family Life*.

"Why didn't you mention *this* part of your life? I loved your books when they came out, bought the hardcovers, couldn't stop reading them, still have them at home. These I found at that bookstore at the end of Kotwali and bought them so you could sign them for me. Have you been to that bookstore?"

Camille is talking about Darpan's bookstore, where she met Willem Ackerman. "Not since August, the day of the first heavy rain."

"Well, you should visit it again because your books, in English and in Hindi, are stacked up in the window and above them is a sign that reads 'Dharamshala's Very Own Most Famous Writer.'"

"Holy Christ," Joan says.

"You meditate now, so maybe call to the goddess Durga, or Hanuman, or to the Divine in the *Moola*, or the Buddha."

And then Joan is laughing, and Camille is laughing, and they laugh until the laughter begins to turn, catching in their chests, their throats closing up, and Joan thinks how remarkable it is, the way laughter is so connected to pain. And then she and Camille are hugging a last time, and Camille is at the door, waving her shawl at Ashby—"You're Ashby to me, I can't imagine calling you Joan, and I really hope you're writing something new"—and Joan is waving back, unsure if she has nodded to Camille's last words, if she has acknowledged that she is writing something new, but she turns to negotiate the street because it is so steep, and with this laughing and crying, how easy it would be to fall, to trip over her golden crystal sandals, to roll all the way down to the bottom.

44

The Dalai Lama's compound is deserted when she passes it, the monks and the meditators have left behind chanting and silent meditation and are loud at the food stalls, keeping the chefs busy cooking their aromatic offerings. The sun is dropping from its height in the sky, the breeze kicking up when Joan reaches the end of Kotwali.

At the bookstore's window, she looks at the display Darpan has made of her collections, artistically arranged like five-petaled flowers. An English-language flower and a Hindi-language flower, every petal a stack of five books.

Darpan must have ordered these books specially. A small Dharamshala bookshop would not have on hand fifty copies of her collections, twenty-five in each language, initially published so long ago. The sign is something else: *Dharamshala's Very Own Most Famous Writer* in beautiful golden calligraphy, outlined a second time in silver, and a third time in black. The sign hangs across the entire window. It causes a crash of emotions inside of her.

The chime over the door tinkles when she walks in. There is Darpan, on his chair, mangling another thick paperback.

"Miss Ashby," he cries, and jumps up. "Did you see? Is it not marvelous? The books in the window, all I have left. I have sold one hundred in the last week!"

She is stunned, and her old agent, Volkmann, will be surprised when the royalty statements from Storr & Storr show the number of Joan's books purchased by a single store in a small village in India. The collections still sell surprisingly well and have long been a staple of colleges and universities and MFA programs, but she can see Volkmann scrunching up her face, saying to herself, "This can't be right."

"Willem has been gone since your trip to Pong Wetland, he's been all over, now following the birds in the Kullu valley, so I couldn't ask him to find you for me, and I don't know where you have been staying, but you're here now, and it is meant to be. Do you mind signing the copies in the window?"

"This is all such a surprise," Joan says. When Darpan's mouth turns doubtful, she says, "A great surprise. I love it," and she thinks she might actually love it. She wasn't sure on those steep hills down from Camille's. But she is now. She does love it. "I'd be happy to sign all the books you still have."

Darpan clears off the counter, pats his tall stool for Joan to use, brings the books to her in armfuls, and hands her a pen.

"So, Miss Ashby. Willem does not know this about me, but he is not the only writer, with his big articles and his little poems and his whatnots. I have my own desire to write, and I was wondering, if it was possible, if you had time, would you consider teaching me how to be a writer? And, if I am not getting too far ahead, *too far afield*, Willem always says, there are others here who fancy themselves writers. You could be our teacher, show all of us how to do it like you. You could become Dharamshala's first ever writing teacher."

Joan laughs. "I've never taught writing to anyone, Darpan." She can't teach them talent, but perhaps she can help them figure out how to put whatever talent they do have to good use. "But I might be willing to try."

"Wonderful, Miss Ashby, simply wonderful."

When she finishes signing the last book, her hand cramping from exhaustion, Darpan bows deeply. He straightens and says, "Miss Ashby. Don't believe Willem—" And she was wondering the same thing. She has not heard from Willem Ackerman since he dropped her at Hotel Gandhi's Paradise, a quick kiss on her cheek, and he was gone. She has wondered if the kiss marked the end of their new friendship because she declined his offer on the lodge roof that last night, to allow him to take her to bed. She is glad to know he left Dharamshala immediately, is off working, that there might still be a chance for them, though she has deliberately not considered the nature of that chance. At the very least, she would like their friendship to continue.

Darpan says, "Don't believe him because I am sure he told you that he has read your books so many more times than me, but I am like the tortoise, catching up to the hare."

That makes her laugh, and she says, "I don't know what to do with all of this flattery, Darpan."

"Miss Ashby, one can't flatter by telling the truth."

Joan agrees to return to the store on the third Saturday of September.

"It is the time I need to maximize the news that Dharamshala's very own most famous writer will be giving the first of many lessons in how to write as if the gods and goddesses have touched them too. Come at four. When you walk in, you will see how many of us want to be like you."

"Let's start with one lesson, Darpan, and perhaps leave out the gods and the goddesses," Joan suggests.

"Am I not the good salesman? One hundred copies already sold, Miss Ashby, only those copies in the window remain for selling, so everything is in good hands. Thank you for thrilling me today."

The sky is fighting against the onset of night, gripping the last rays of the descended sun, while Joan waits for the white-toqued chef to wrap her order of steamed spinach momo in wax paper, to drop it into a bag. She feels light on the ground, a little unsteady, dazed by the display of her work in Darpan's bookstore, from signing her name inside fifty books, from her apparent agreement to become an erstwhile writing teacher for anyone interested.

And she is thinking of Willem, glad to have learned he is not avoiding her, wondering when he will return to his Dharamshala house, a place she has not seen, thinking again, as she has at various times since that trip, of them entwined in a sleeping bag on the ground, wondering why she never imagines them in an actual bed.

Then she is beyond the marketplace, heading up the steep, rocky hill to Hotel Gandhi's Paradise, her mind leaping from Willem Ackerman to Paloma Rosen's love life. Thinking about how Paloma has never lived long-term with another in her loft, that when Paloma permits her preferred solitariness to be invaded, the lovers stay for a week, a month, six months, perhaps a year, a panoply of different kinds of love and physicality. How Paloma faces the mundane that always eventually worms its way into any relationship, regardless of the heated passion, the torrential lovemaking, or the calmer, more poetic love, but Paloma is never thrown off her own course, good at avoiding the feelings of others, does not engage unless she desires it.

How much fun to consider Paloma's lovers, their names, their personalities, the relationships they have or want to have with her. Paloma Rosen is, Joan knows, the kind of woman people want for their own, to possess entirely, no matter the cost.

She pictures a lover named Magnus, when Paloma is still in her thirties. A painter, Joan decides, of massive paintings that hang in museums throughout the world. She gives Magnus Willem's face, his physique, an accent, but not Willem's, and Magnus will have an incessant need to talk about the future course of their relationship, until Paloma says to him one night in bed, "*Arrêtes de parler!* Stop all your talking. Am I the woman, or are you?" and despite their year together, he will be gone three days after that, and Paloma will regret none of it, neither the interlude nor the hasty finale.

Perhaps Paloma has one serious lover per decade, Joan thinks.

In her forties, Samuel will show up at Paloma's door when his multivolume memoirs are racing through the literary world like a brush fire, scorching all named within, making his reputation and his fortune as a result. When Paloma reads his hundreds of thousands of words for the first time, she will learn he was married and divorced once, like her, but will not know he is newly married, a second time, claiming, when he shows up at her door, that she is meant to be his, leaving out the fact that he is not free. She will care not a whit about his marital status because in bed he is a dervish, but outside the covers, she will find he is too silent for her, the mere act of talking confounding him, and Paloma requires a sensational conversationalist. And though he writes like a demon, baring his entire life in his pages, in real life, he is far too meek, withers in the face of her strength. She will send poor Samuel away.

Joan is not surprised when she sees a woman twirling on a stool in Paloma's studio. She has a long Modigliani face, wan, suffering, and lovely. Lina will be stateless, Sultana-wealthy, ripe for all adventures, excellent at subterfuge, good company until her need for Paloma becomes relentless, jealous of Paloma's attention to the sculpture at hand. Joan imagines they meet at Paloma's fiftieth birthday party, and that night become lovers, a torrid week, or two, or three, but then Lina's black and unblinking eyes remind Paloma of a buzzard waiting to feast upon her desecrated flesh and bones, and clingy Lina must be sent on her way, sobbing about the unfairness of life, the mutilations to her soul from loving a selfish artist, a woman who prefers the coldness of stone to the warmth of Lina's lovely skin.

She sees Paloma in her sixties, still gorgeous, with those long white braids, her cheekbones and breasts still taut, and Joan imagines a Frenchwoman named Sabine, whose heart will be on her sleeve, eating up Paloma's working hours, keeping her in the warm bed that Sabine will call "our bed," though it is no such thing. Nestling Paloma against her own beautiful breasts, insisting on nuzzling way past Paloma's dawn schedule of rising, showering, Turkish coffee, studio. Wonderfully brutalizing love that enflames Paloma's most tender parts, until snap, the long hours of the day are wiped out in the craziness of consumptive sexual congress. Sabine has long legs that never end, balletic in bed, a female praying mantis, until Paloma shows her to the loft door and hands Sabine the small leather bag she brought when she arrived two months before.

In her seventies, Paloma will decide to become celibate, and will miss none of the blaze, the battles, the usurpation of her time, her heart, her emotions, by man or woman, regardless of how adept they are at the most intimate acts.

She will loathe the term "lovemaking." Will not abide calling it "sex." Always, in Paloma's mind, whether a mere coupling or a symphony of exquisiteness, it is *de se perdre en délire dans le corps d'un autre,* to lose oneself deliriously in the body of another.

At midnight, in the dark of her pine suite, Joan stares out into the Dharamshalan night, the moon lighting up the trees in the forest beyond her window. Unlike many of the birds she saw with Willem, whose names were unbeautiful—long-tailed shrike, large cuckooshrike, Himalayan bulbul—the trees in her forest glide off the tongue. The chirs are plush, their needles scented of smashed pine. The evergreen deodars have silvery-green leaves that capture even the weakest light. The Himalayan oak trees are rugged and tough. Soon, autumn will burnish the leaves that turn, will make the forest into a bonfire of colors, as she once wrote in a story in *Other Small Spaces*. All of Joan's ancient work is present these days in her mind, and she feels Paloma Rosen's clove-scented breath on her own skin.

Far in the distance, the moon turns the peaks, cliffs, and scarps of the Dhauladhars into abstract art, like a mammoth sculpture Paloma might carve.

Joan falls asleep thinking of Martin, whose email she has not yet responded to, and dreams of Willem lowering his camera, turning away from the flying birds, coming in close to kiss her, wondering if they will kiss well.

45

Since the night she left Darpan's bookstore, Joan has been working on *Paloma Rosen* at her desk from the moment she wakes until one, bath after, at meditation with Ela at two, sometimes spending an extra half hour with her, drinking masala chai at the tea seller's stall, and often writing again for an hour or more in the evening when she returns to her pine suite.

Tomorrow, in the late afternoon, she will show up at Darpan's bookstore and see what awaits her. She has been trying to write an outline for the class, simple instructions for beginning writers, but the page on her computer is still blank and she started hours ago.

When her cell phone rings, the caller is Eric. They have not seen each other since Camille's last meditation session before returning to England, but they have retained their comfortable ease with each other. They do not need to check in daily, do not mind when days pass without any connection, when they are together, it is loving, caring, good. In their last conversation, Eric said he was volunteering, but gave her no specifics, and said he was busy with other stuff too, and she thinks the other stuff he's busy with is the girl he mentioned in his backyard, when Joan first sought him out.

"Are you free on Sunday?" he says when she answers.

"Completely," although she writes on Sundays too. She wonders if she is going about this the wrong way—not saying a word to Eric about her daily writing schedule, about the book she is writing, this instinctive need of hers to keep it private until the work is completed, on the verge of entering the world. Lately, when she meditates in the group, she thinks about all the methods she employed over the years to keep everything separate—her work from family, writer separate from wife and mother. She has paid a steep price to hold on to herself, remaining silent during all those years of writing *Words*, the time she lost caring for Eric.

To discuss it all with him now, to lay herself bare, would require the whole story, complete truthfulness: a man who breached his promise about having no children; an unwanted child who made motherhood precious; an expected child who destroyed years of her life; a favorite son who shattered her dreams, stole what was closest to her heart; and then about her work—the published collections, the failure of *The Sympathetic Executioners*, the Rare Baby stories, the castle up in the sky where she wrote *Words of New Beginnings*, and now *Paloma Rosen*, who is fully Paloma, but embodies bits of Vita, Camille, Ela, and Joan, too.

There is too much to disclose, to explain, if she wants to provide Eric the full picture. And she would not feel right, not now, picking and choosing which pieces of the story to tell. She has frequently looked back through it all: what she always feared, what she tried desperately to prevent, happened anyway—the stirring and mixing and coalescing of motherhood and life and writing.

Here in Dharamshala, despite one child's near presence, Joan is returning to her own beginning, in solitude, writing away—does she want to alter the rhythm, the joy she is at last experiencing again? Her engrained instinct is to keep everything to herself, to keep the facets of her world separated. Like a port-wine birthmark staining the skin over her heart—even if she could remove the mark, laser it away somehow, it would leave behind an outline, a ghost of what was, of the past, of the life she was born into, of the child she became, of the adult who emerged from the ice and the flames.

Should she try nonetheless?

"I'll pick you up at ten," Eric says. "I've hired a car and a driver."

A hired car and driver costs little here, but it reminds Joan again how distant Eric is from the rest of the world. He's told her the particulars of Solve's sale, the figure tipping two billion. Investors and vested stock options paid out, and his share is fully half of that. He could fund the most eccentric dreams of an unlimited number of generations of his nonexistent heirs. He could buy deserted islands and develop them. He could take over ailing cities and fix them. He could right the economies of small failing countries. He could wipe out at least one disease. The marvels of what he could do with his money are infinite. Joan wonders what he will choose.

"We're going back into the past, Ashby," Eric says. "See you Sunday."

Joan looks at the blank screen. Despite what she's just been thinking about, she hopes Eric means the historical past, not the familial one, she really does not want to parse through her own past, and his, and Martin's and Daniel's. She shuts down her computer and closes the lid. She'll wing it tomorrow, no handouts, no lesson plan, she'll speak from the heart about what it means to be a writer, at any age, at any juncture in time. Anyway, she doubts Darpan's certainty that he will have a full house.

46

"Miss Ashby! Miss Ashby!" Darpan cries, pushing through the crowd spilling from his bookstore into the street.

"Come, come. I will lead you in. They are all here for you."

Joan tries counting the people on folding chairs in the entry, on the counter repurposed as a high bench, sitting on the floor, flattened against all of the walls, and all of the bookcases, in every aisle, perched at the edge of the window display.

Sixty, maybe more. It is hard to tell when there are so many and the bookshop is quaint and small. From the very old and stooped in colorful jackets to children who may not yet have learned to read. She sees her books in laps, in hands, under arms, balanced on top of heads. Those in the folding chairs, who must have arrived early to claim that preferred seating, are waving papers, clipped and stapled, typed and handwritten, some rolled up and used as drumsticks against their knees. Their stories, Joan thinks.

Was this how it used to be, when she gave readings in all those countries, across the States twice? Did masses show up to hear her read and talk?

She remembers the filled rooms, but perhaps she's forgotten those times when she read to only a few people, she at the podium, and those five or ten spread out in an auditorium meant for hundreds. Maybe she was lucky enough and never read to empty rooms.

So many memories: interviews with NPR, and Charlie Rose, with various newspapers and magazines, the interviews she gave to the reporter at the *Wall Street Journal* after her book tours, the long piece about her in the *New York Review of Books*, her talk at Barnard. She had been kind of a rock star then, hadn't she, without even being all that aware of it. And then took herself away, sheltered in Rhome, becoming what she had never wanted to be.

The crowd is noisy, everyone talking to one another, to Darpan, calling out to her, "Ashby, Ashby, we are here for you!"

It's ridiculous and marvelous and she thinks she should have told Eric about it, asked him to come, allowed him to see his mother, to see Ashby in a way he would not recognize, knows still so little about, and Kartar, and Willem, if he was back in town. She spots Lakshmi at the back, with her father, Hadi, and Pema, the woman who wove the shawl she gave Camille the day she went home, and she recognizes the food stall chef from whom she regularly orders momo, and waves at them, lets them know she's seen them, that she's touched they have come.

If *this* is what she experienced when she was young, how had she given up this reward for the long hours of shaping characters and stories, the sentences that brought them alive? Had she been too young to understand what she had been given back then? Is fame better in the later years? This is just a small bookstore in Dharamshala, but the pure adrenaline she's feeling reminds her that life is not yet at an end, that the powers of creation cannot been ravaged by time or events. Despite how she has been tested, despite being left with a conditional sense of her own being, she is still who she once was and is becoming again, a writer, and a woman as solid as Vita, Camille, and Ela. She knows this afternoon will keep her charged up through all the coming months of writing *Paloma Rosen*.

"Everyone quiet," Darpan yells to the crowd.

"Order, order!" he tries next, and when the decibel level fails to drop, Joan steps to the front.

"Hello, everyone," she says. "I'm Joan Ashby," immediately aware she has spoken her full name, perhaps for the first time since Natwar cycled her from the Kangra valley train stop to Hotel Gandhi's Paradise. And the room grows quiet, then still.

"Thank you all for coming, for choosing to be here. Darpan said he wanted to start a writing class, and asked if I would teach. There are so many of you today, perhaps it would be best if I talked a little about different kinds of writing: the fiction of short stories and novels; the true stories of histories, autobiographies, biographies, and memoirs; thrillers, crime sagas, and detective stories. Well, the list can go on and on."

She stays focused and precise, talks for thirty minutes and then closes. The audience has been rapt and she wants them to remain that way, does not want to be responsible for their losing interest, does not want to experience their losing interest in her. After today, she will be less of a mystery to them, and won't necessarily remain atop whatever pedestal they have placed her on.

"I'm happy to answer questions," she says.

Hands fly into the air. Joan is not completely sure they all know who she is, or have read her books, or will even read the copies in their hands that they previously purchased; her appearance at the bookstore might simply be a welcome break from the routines of their days. But no matter, she is having great fun, and even if the adulation is not specific to her, it still feels nice to be respected, made to feel special, to be looked at adoringly. And it's amusing watching Darpan hush those who presume to talk without being called on first. She wonders what they will ask her. She has vague recollections of banal questions thrown at her all those years ago, at the end of a reading. But surely here, in Dharamshala, a place threaded through with spirituality, the questions will have a different heft:

"Will you read my story?"

"Will you read my story?"

"Will you read my story?"

"You did not talk about writing about vampires and werewolves, why not?"

"Is it possible to write a good story in, say, three hours?"

"If I want to be a writer, do I have to read books?"

"Will you read my story?"

"What single piece of advice would you give?"

"Will you read my story?"

"Will you read my story and have your publisher publish it? It is very important to me."

It's nearly an hour before the questions peter out, an hour that severely taxes Joan's ability to deflect, in different ways, the dominant request, but she has made it through, and is still smiling.

When Darpan says, "If anyone bought a book Miss Ashby didn't already sign, she'll sign it now, but no pushing and no shoving," she leans over to him and, hoping she won't come to regret it, says, "Darpan, if you still want me to lead a writing class, then those with stories should leave them with you. It can't be a class this big, but I'll read them through and choose ten that show the most promise. We could start there."

"Brilliant, Miss Ashby," and Darpan gives out the new instructions, where to line up for the book signing, where to leave their stories, and just as Joan thinks it, Darpan yells, "Your stories better have your names and phone numbers, otherwise tough, you'll be out of luck, never part of Miss Ashby's most amazing writing class."

Christ, Joan thinks, it's true what Darpan said about himself; he is a sensational marketer, he could sell anything. She wonders how much he intends to charge. She does not want to be paid anything, but Darpan should make enough to hang a new sign out front. The bookstore could end up very busy after all this.

47

Other than Willem Ackerman's orange jeep, and the occasional jalopylike taxi with Camille when they explored places too far away for foot travel, Joan walks everywhere.

It feels odd to be in a shiny black Mercedes with fine leather seats, to realize that Martin drives this same make and model, bought last year, that could be parked this moment in his spot at Rhome General.

At the wheel is Vivek, whom Eric introduces as his right-hand man. Vivek, in jeans and a black leather jacket, is short and broad and his hair is buzzed down to his skull, but he has the ruddy, round face of a choirboy, his smile permanently attached.

Eric is as radiant as ever, and serene, but he's grinning, and they have barely cleared the Dalai Lama's compound when he says, "I have so much to tell you." She is thinking she has much to tell him too, has decided she will tell him about the wonderful afternoon in the bookstore Friday, about the writing class she has agreed to lead, about *Paloma Rosen*.

But then Eric says, "I've been volunteering at the Rogpa Daycare Center. Taking a page from your book. Maybe one day soon I'll want my own."

And Joan is taken aback, that page from her book isn't one she had wanted to heed. Despite his agelessness, in spirit, in outlook, in the wisdom he has acquired, Eric is still so young chronologically. She wants to say she does not believe the experience of having a child is necessary to live a great or good or happy life, can cause the opposite. She would soften the declaration with a lie, that she would never change having him and his brother, and tell him a new truth, that she really does love him.

"And working at Rogpa gave me a lot of ideas. They cater only to little children, but I'm aiming higher. Amari has helped me research what's worked in the past in Dharamshala, when it comes to charitable good works, and what hasn't. And I've decided to open a center focused on providing children aged five to eighteen with specific kinds of extracurricular education: arts, like photography, music, and dance, different kinds of sciences, like astronomy, even computer coding, if there's interest. This coming week, we're looking at spaces we won't outgrow in a couple of years. I've hired an Indian lawyer in McLeod Ganj and he's set up a nonprofit for me called Good Manning Works, and the center will be called Good Manning. What do you think?"

Joan takes a moment to collect herself, looking at Eric's face, so eager to hear what she has to say. Her own news can wait. It's not far in the past when he ignored her completely, when he would not have cared what she thought.

"It's a huge undertaking, but I shouldn't be surprised. You started Solve at thirteen, why not an educational center at twenty-two. That's not much older than some of your potential students," Joan says. "Does that feel okay with you?"

"It's weird, I know. But my life experience is completely different from theirs, and, in most ways, I feel so much older than I am."

"Will you run it?"

"Yes, and Amari will come on board, and there's a place for Vivek, too," he says, putting a hand on Vivek's shoulder.

"Space first, and if there's no appropriate space, then we'll build exactly what I see in my mind. I've looked at land and an architect from Mumbai is coming week after next, a friend of Amari's father. I've been talking with him on the phone."

"So, Dharamshala is going to be home for you."

"Yes. It already is. In a way Rhome never felt like home to me. I hope that doesn't upset you."

Joan shakes her head. She understands exactly what he means.

"And Amari? So are you dating each other?" she asks.

"More than that. But you already figured that out."

One son is nearly dead to her, this son she is getting to know in a different way. Is Eric telling her she will suddenly become a mother-in-law? Motherhood, she still mostly wants in the distance, and now, mother-in-law-hood, a young woman possibly wanting to bond with her? The thought is much to contemplate.

"She's great, you'll love her. She's been working at the Tibetan Institute for the last three years."

"The Tibetan Institute of Performing Arts? I've been there. Camille and I saw a troupe rehearsing something called a *lhamo* opera, a masked dance drama, it was explained to the audience. Thrilling and bizarre, even if we couldn't understand what any of it meant, or what it signified. Our fault, I'm sure."

She wants him to know she will do whatever is required for Amari to feel included.

The mission statement on the front door of the institute articulated its goal in pretty script: *To share Tibet's cultural heritage with international audiences.*

"Is Amari Tibetan?"

"No, Indian. From Mumbai. She thinks she was born into the wrong life, like I do. What her family wants for her, she doesn't want for herself."

She is not hurt by Eric's statement. She understands it. Joan was born into the wrong family, Martin felt he had the wrong father, and she wonders how many people in the world feel that way, if Daniel felt that way, and if he did, does he still?

How does she ask Eric if Amari knows about Solve, his money, his time in Oregon?

"Have you and Amari talked a lot about your lives?"

"She knows everything. Dropping out of school, my company, my rehab in Oregon, the money I've made."

"Has she told her parents about you?" Joan knows little about Indian castes and how they work, or about arranged marriages, and wonders what trials might be ahead for the young couple.

"They aren't that happy that I'm American, but they like that I live here, and that I've run my own business, and that I'm starting something real. That I'm not one of the backpackers or hippies who come wandering through, never wanting to go home."

Vivek calls back to them. "We've gone twenty-seven miles, just ten to go."

A good time, Joan thinks, to move away from young love.

"What a wonderful way to invest your money, in the lives and futures of others. You should be proud. I am. Have you told your father about the sale? About your plans for the center?"

"I'll know when it's the right time to tell him about everything," he says, which tells Joan that Martin still knows nothing about the sale of Solve, or that their second son is never returning to Rhome, or that he is in love and it seems to be very real. It strikes Joan again how rarely she and Eric mention Martin.

They are in a part of the Kangra valley Joan passed through on the way to the Pong Wetland with Willem.

"I forgot to tell you. Daniel wrote me a few days ago, said he bought himself a year's membership at some yoga studio near him. Maybe I'll turn around his way of thinking after all. If I can turn Daniel around, maybe I can do the same for Dad."

Joan doesn't want to picture Daniel in a yoga class, standing on an unfurled mat, preparing to assume one of the poses she did for so many years, those poses restoring her sanity in those hours she was away from Eric, his minions, the house. She doesn't want to feel this agonizing pinch at her heart.

After all these months in India, meditating on everything, she is no closer to understanding how her eldest son's thinking went so awry, does not know if he has processed the message she intended to send by her flight.

This is the first time Eric has spoken of Daniel to her, and she wonders if her Buddha-like son either knows more than he's letting on, or intuits something profound. Unless he asks her directly, Joan has nothing to say on the subject.

"One mile," Vivek calls out.

"You haven't told me where we're going," Joan says.

"Masrur. But that's all I'm going to say."

Vivek refuses to join them. "Have this time on your own," he says. "I'll stay with the car." And then Joan and Eric are walking on a dirt path, and the wind begins to whistle, and then the air hushes, and they round a bend, and there, in front of them, is a massive temple painstakingly carved out of rock, out of a single stone, on the edge of a large pond reflecting the temple's myriad surfaces and planes in the autumnal sun, and Joan inhales deeply.

"It was carved in the eighth century," Eric says. "It's actually fifteen temples. The central temple right in front of us is carved inside too, and there are seven temples on either side, but they're carved only on the outside. They call it the Masrur Rock Cut Temple, and the Himalayan Pyramid, and some call it a wonder of the world."

Stone.

Everything is carved from stone.

The temple fronts, facades, courtyard, outer doors, even the pond that was built to reflect the temple to the sky, to the heavens.

It is extraordinary to look at, and Joan touches Eric's sleeve, and he nods.

She steps away from him, enters the temple on her own, runs her hands over the hewn rock.

People carved this temple, with their hands, with small tools, like those Paloma will use.

Joan wonders how many people it took, how many decades, or centuries, to conceive this vision, make it come true. How many people died during the building, a construction possibly from hell, and if it wasn't, how long before this contemplative and peaceful place was finished, opened to people eager for a sacred temple in which to pray.

She passes a large family, Tibetan by the cuts of their faces, their melodic intonations, and she leaves them behind, walks deeper inside.

The farther she goes, the cooling air takes on a mineral scent, the keenness of the born earth. She reaches the inner sanctum sanctorum, a room of rock, its walls sheared, but not made perfectly smooth, and she is completely alone. In front of deity idols she knows so little about, will never fully absorb, she kneels on the stone, feels how quickly it warms under her palms.

She puts her hands together in *namaste* and closes her eyes.

She thinks of Paloma Rosen, her flight to destiny, the materials she intends to make her own. Joan has researched so many, what a sculptor might choose, and for Paloma it will be stones and woods, loving most working in marble—a verb and a noun of pre-Greek origin: *to flash, sparkle, and gleam, glassy, crystal-like rock, shining stone.*

They are similar, she and Paloma, carving away in materials that are equally intractable, hard to chisel. By amputating her past and working in stone, in marble, Paloma Rosen will hurtle herself into her future. And Joan, what is she doing precisely? Working in words, trying to hurtle herself into her future, undecided about whether, or how extensive, an amputation of her own life is required. She has not yet had any response to the two letters she has written to the Dalai Lama, a third one written and delivered by Kartar to His Holiness's secretary just this morning. Each letter Joan has written to the Dalai Lama has expanded her story. Today's included how welcomed she felt by the crowd in Darpan's bookstore.

She is kneeling in this stone temple, thinking how hard stone is, how it endures for eternity, and when she rises, she knows she is not prepared to leave this remarkable Indian world, not ready to step back into the small world of Rhome, to be with Martin, to answer the question of Daniel.

Just beyond the carved front doors of the temple, Joan steps out into the sunshine, and stops. Eric is next to the pond, a young woman by his side, her hand in his own. The girl is a lovely sapling tree, her hair up in a simple twist, loose pieces falling around her face like soft twigs. They are taken up with each other, and Joan studies them from a distance. They do not seem like two young twentysomethings in love for the first time. There is a maturity between them, a thoughtfulness that love has not blinded. The way their hands are clasped together, how Eric touches her cheek, how the young woman puts her hand on the back of his head, Joan sees they fit together. And it has little to do with how pleasing they are to the eye.

She would like to say to them take life slowly, don't rush into making babies, but life here is different, slower and faster, deeper than the modern world allows. They will figure out on their own the tribulations, enjoy every sweetness.

Their bodies curve toward each other in a way that is beyond lust. They want the same life, consummately attuned to each other already. There will be no internal negotiations for either of them, no broken vows, no thoughts of what must be done to keep alive a love that was never expected. They will be helpmates for life.

She walks slowly toward them and when she is ten feet away, she coughs lightly. They look up in unison, both smiling happily at her, and Eric says, "Mom, this is Amari."

48

It was Eric's only slip, calling her Mom when he introduced her to Amari. The rest of the afternoon, it was Ashby as always, and Joan was surprised by the twinges of something, of sadness, maybe of loss, when he did so. Lovely Amari, twenty-five to Eric's twenty-two. Both of them shadowed by who they were in the lives they previously lived, so young to already carry such histories, Joan had thought, then remembered she had been the same, a life lived in full by the time she was twenty-five. Martin's and Daniel's lives were free of that delirious leap from childhood to special existence. Did the normality of their own passages explain certain things? Was this why Martin had overstepped her boundaries so often in the past, failed to respect her authorial privacy, wanting to be inside her head, wanting what she could not, would not, give him, an explanation about how her brain worked? Was this why Daniel had stolen *Words*, to jump the divide, breach the gap between himself and his mother and younger brother? Should she have recognized he would deem his own accomplishments commonplace, lacking the rarity he so desperately desired, was it all there in that competitiveness he had shown early on? Using Joan's own work to trounce her, to beat her soundly at whatever game was in his mind, might have seemed like fair play to him. But Daniel was not a child when he made his decision, he was an adult who knew what he was doing.

The sun is thirty minutes from rising, the birds in the forest are still sleeping, and these thoughts are too titanic for her barley tea, her hot lentils, the day's sprig of fuchsia petals in a celadon vase. Hotel Gandhi's Paradise trays are never without their surprising flowers, even though it is the second week of November. Thanksgiving in Rhome is just ten days away. She has not heard back from Martin, no response to her last email weeks ago that said simply, *Please do not come.*

On her pine desk are the ten stories she winnowed from all those left on Darpan's counter. She had been wrong: the crowd, or most of them, knew who she was. Forty stories were left for her to read, many with personal notes identifying which story of hers was their favorite and what it had meant to them. She is still astonished by the geographic and temporal distance her work has traveled, humbled by the power they found in her words. Early on, she gave up trying to figure out if she was reading a story written by a female or male, the Indian names not making it easy, and decided not to worry about an evenly divided class, read only to find truths in the work. She moves quickly over the ten she has chosen, reads again their opening lines:

The girl looked in the mirror one day and realized she was no longer small, but grown.

Navin picked up his younger brother where he sat playing with blocks on the ground, threw him over his shoulder, and took him for a walk. They lived in fresh air, and the boy did not get enough.

I, Rati, do not want to marry the boy my father has selected. He is shorter than me, with the body of a baboon, the eyes of an owl.

Prasad was very, very old and he had a story to tell his family that would alter the way they saw the world.

Feni's name meant sweet but she wasn't.

Iti and Ibha were sick of praying to Buddha.

My mother chants when she wakes up, when she prepares lunch and dinner, when she is alone in her bed. The father I never knew, I think he's in her chants.

Qasam is going to storm out of this fucking valley and get somewhere good.

Wimal hid in the fort and knew she was going to die. She could hear the man sliding back the thing of his gun, the bullet dropping wherever it needed to go.

Het, Haan, and Omu have been friends since they were children. They played games together and slept in each other's beds, and used each other's mothers for love when their own wouldn't do, or was dead.

She puts the stories aside, feels she has chosen well. *Paloma Rosen* awaits. Since Joan's trip to Masrur with Eric, she and Paloma have been in picturesque Italian towns, a side-trip to Croatia, where they toured a stonecutters' school and Paloma briefly considered renting a weathered stone house overlooking the harbor, but decided against it, kept to her plan.

Theo Tesh Park is in Joan's mind all at once, suddenly fully developed, wanting the chance to start to tell his own tale. Perhaps thinking of Eric and Daniel has made Theo Tesh Park so insistent right this minute, or maybe the stories she has chosen for Darpan's writing class set him loose. Whatever the reason, she clears off her pine desk, leaves only the barley tea, flips through her notebook remembering all the things she thought and wrote about weeks ago, then, fingers on the laptop keys, she lets Theo take over.

Theo Tesh Park is not his real name. The name he wore in his turbulent boyhood, through the losses of his teen years, is embossed on an old Sears card hidden in his wallet, used once when he was ten and his mother had disappeared again on another drugged bender, and his grandmother, his sobo Chiyo, did not drive, and Poppy, his older sister by three years could not drive, and he had in his closet only ripped jeans and T-shirts he had outgrown, and school was starting the next day. He had taken the local bus by himself to the store, already figuring out he would need to do everything in his life on his own. Trashing the Sears card would eliminate the last shred of evidence that once he was called Emilio Inari Andramuño, but it resists when he tries, a talisman against his past.

Despite all the changes he has made in his life, he still thinks of himself as a boy from Steinbeck land, living nearly as hard as some of his characters. In high school, when his English teacher saw him reading Steinbeck's books, she had said, *Good for you, Emilio. You'll find that the prose is supple and muscular, that he has extraordinary empathy for ordinary people, those who have been marginalized and dispossessed.* He didn't know then that Mrs. Abbott saw *him* as one of the marginalized and dispossessed, and even when he did, he kept reading Steinbeck, and Salinas was still the salad bowl of the world, with its farms of strawberries, tomatoes, spinach, broccoli, cauliflower, and celery, manned by small and sweaty men and women and children, he nearly the same brown shade as them, but they were even more downtrodden, because at least Theo stayed in one place year-round. But that didn't alter the truth that Mrs. Abbott was right, about his own general marginalization and dispossession, even in his own home, such as it was, blast any amen to that. The place that had been home for a long time was a rotting bungalow in poorest Hebbron Heights, but the faintest of memories remained in his head, of his early years, maybe until he was five, when his father was still around, and he, and Poppy, and their father, and their mother, and Sobo Chiyo all lived in the rich section of Salinas, in a splendid house he sort of remembered.

Three years ago, on his nineteenth birthday, he was inside the Salinas Amtrak Station, counting his bucks. He wanted Amtrak, but could only afford to cross the country Greyhound-slow. With the ticket clutched in his hand, he focused upon the amorphous plans for his future, let go right then of the notion of familial resurrection. His sobo Chiyo was dead, he had written off his stringy, strung-out mother, unzipping men's pants before he'd even hightailed it out of the bungalow, all for whatever crystal she might be handed in some teensy plastic bag, and he had given up hope by then that Poppy would reappear.

His sister had skipped out of his life one day, telling him she was heading to the Pacific Ocean with a few friends for a day at the beach. The Pacific was just eight miles from home, though neither of them had been, not once in their lives, but Poppy didn't find the ocean, or she had never intended to make her way to the beach, instead she sent him a single postcard that said: *EIA—I'm hanging with a group in the great Mojave, off I-40. They're gonna turn the desert into an agricultural oasis, and you know I've got a great green thumb.* He knew no such thing about her, had never seen her raise a thing, and when he Google-mapped

Mojave and I-40, there wasn't a house or a gas station or a restaurant in any direction for hundreds of miles, just sprawling desert with a complete lack of access to water, and he'd wondered what the hell she was doing. Salinas was a town more than 99 percent dry land, its water calculated at a mere 0.16 percent, but the Mojave was a place even drier and more inhospitable. He didn't understand whether that had been her plan all along, or whether she'd gotten herself caught up in something, sometimes those sorts of things happened to Poppy.

He wrote to the PO box she'd written on her postcard, telling her to get away from whoever those people might be, because they had to be loony living out there in the desert, told her to save her money and be prepared to hop a bus when he figured out where he was going. Back then, he was only thinking about leaving. He's never heard from his sister again, but every month he writes another letter and sends it off, like she might be some kind of wise ghost who can hear what's buried in his chest.

He left Salinas at 1:15 in the morning, saw California, Arizona, New Mexico, Oklahoma, Missouri, Illinois, Indiana, Ohio, and Pennsylvania rolling past his worn seat. The people who sat next to him through California and Arizona slept or sang or smelled, those who got on in New Mexico wanted to talk about aliens they'd met. When the bus reloaded in Tulsa, Oklahoma, close to midnight that second day, a kindly black woman with a picnic basket full of fried chicken took the empty aisle seat next to him and shared the chicken she had flattened and battered and crisped, a succulent breast, a drumstick, then another one, passed from her basket to his hand and into his mouth, and she told him her entire family tree, reaching back eight generations, regaling him with stories that were funny or sad or bittersweet, filled with great moral lessons he never expected, finishing one and saying, "So if you liked that one, let me tell you about this one," until she said goodbye to him at 8:30 a.m. in Lebanon, Missouri, there to welcome the birth of a second cousin's fifth baby. He slept alone through the rest of Missouri and Illinois, but in Terre Haute, Indiana, a nice girl got on, headed back to college in Indianapolis, after a weekend at home with a family he imagined as 3000 percent normal. "We always spend this weekend, right after the New Year, talking about what we want the year to bring to us as a family, and to each of us individually." He had not ever heard anything so lovely.

Still, no matter what he was forced to hear, or respond to, the smiles he had to give, or the grimaces, asking this one or that to please stop talking to him because he just wasn't interested, except for Gladys of the chicken and the biblical tales, and the college girl because listening to her family life was like eating cotton candy, he figured out his new name. Plucked right from the air, with three parts like his old one, but these three parts he had chosen himself, and they sounded good together when he whispered them aloud, incapable of identifying him as any one thing. When he stepped down from the bus near the tip of Manhattan, on Wall Street, he was Theo Tesh Park.

He's done every kind of shitty job to get by since landing here—dishwasher, dog walker, market-shelf stocker, a waiter in a bunch of diners owned by big, back-slapping Greek brothers, as a secret, non-union super's assistant in rundown buildings up in Harlem and out in Red Hook. He's manned, from midnight until seven, twenty-four-hours-a-day-three-hundred-sixty-five-days-a-year shops that sell tobacco and crap. He's learned the really upscale neighborhoods of Manhattan, the ones with wealthy people in every apartment, trawling through and pushing away the weak nuts muttering to themselves before dawn, gathering up all the plastic and glass himself, stuff he's turned in for nickels and dimes at the posh grocery stores nearby. Then he learned there was a far easier way to make money. But in any case, before then, he proved to himself he could survive, and this year's resolution was to find a place he could call home.

Fifteen interviews to find that place—people thinking they were interviewing him, he knowing it was the other way around. Then the sixteenth place, with all those endless stairs that he now races down and up several times every day, six double flights to the enormous loft on the top floor.

That afternoon, when he stepped across the transom into the huge loft, his jaw dropped when he caught sight of the stone and wood be-hemoths in the vast middle distance. One in black stone, hovering just above the floor, made him think of some kind of encroaching goddess newly emerged from the depths. A second form, in green stone, rose up from a narrow point, seeming incapable of maintaining its balance, and yet it did, holding a shield for a giant, an off-center hole drilled straight through. The third sculpture made him think of lovers, two incredibly long, slender figures in white stone, nearly entwined, one slashed from top to bottom by a thin, narrow recessed rectangle, the other with a hollowed oval where a face would have gone, neither with any obvious human features, but he felt love surrounding them, from the spaces between them, and from where they nearly, but did not quite, touch. The last sculpture was the tallest, would learn later was the wood of a pear tree, the color flesh-tone pink, carved into multiple spirals, like the inner workings of sea shells, or the geometrics of the body, the insides painted a shocking red that instantly made him think of blood, of life and of death.

He saw the sculptures first, before noticing anything else in the loft, had wanted to run to them, to feel their vibrant angles and curves, to follow the lines of the goddess, put his hand through the shield's hole, the lover's oval, run his fingers down the scooped-out rectangle of the other lover, to touch the cold of all those stones, the warmth, he imagined, of the smooth pink wood. The sculptures— *The Bones of Dido 1967*, *Hercules 1970*, *Gasping Fish 1973*, and *Silence 1976*—stood six, eight, ten, and eleven feet tall, carved by Paloma Rosen early in her career. He didn't know their names then, or that she had decided never to part with them despite magnificent offers to sell.

He had stared, floating in some distant galaxy, until a mellifluous, husky voice, tinged with an accent, brought him down to earth.

"I am Paloma Rosen," the voice said, and Theo Tesh Park's spine shivered when he looked down and found a tiny beautiful old woman patiently waiting for his attention.

"Welcome, Monsieur Park," she said, and led him into the loft's living-room area. He sat all the way back on the biggest, deepest couch he had ever seen, his long legs and big feet sticking straight out, jeans pooling around his knees, galumphing tennis shoes horizontal, six inches up from the floor. She had watched him silently as he rearranged himself, until his feet were flat on the white wood planks.

"You're an artist," he said, embarrassed by the hunger he heard in his voice.

She said nothing, leaned in closer, her stare so direct, appraising, evaluating, weighing him up for a very long time. He felt she was receiving him within herself, like a cookie, a grape popped whole.

"I am indeed," she had finally said. "Are you?"

Was he what? An artist?

The way she was looking at him, he thought she had to know he was not much of anything, was certainly no artist, unless there was something artistic about figuring out how to get by, the cons and short shrifts to get what he needed, to keep himself afloat, dressed, and fed, with someplace to lay his head at night.

"I'm not any kind of artist," he said.

"You have lovely black eyes, unusual, without a speck of any other hue, no green, no hazel, no dashes of silver or gold, no occlusions. You may not be an artist, but you remind me of someone I was once close to, and he was an artist. But never mind all of that. *Sans importance. Hors de propos.* You and I are sitting here to discuss whether you might be the person I am seeking, the person I need at this time. Let us see how it goes."

Among all the English, she tossed in musical words Theo could not understand, that he realized were actually words in a foreign language, that were as foreign as he felt on her enormous couch in her unbelievable home with those extraordinary sculptures within view. He relaxed a little when he realized she was foreign, in maybe more ways than one, maybe even more than he.

She was forthright and unsentimental, explaining to him why she had decided to give up her happy solitary existence, to take in a lodger now, some young person to replace the burnt-out lightbulbs, sweep away the decorative cobwebs, kill the spiders that spun them, fetch the basic groceries, make trips way uptown to Spanish Harlem, where prices were cheaper and lug back the staples, wait out the cycles at the one Laundromat in the neighborhood so that her work overalls and shirts, and her scrubbing cloths, with the right amount of softener for polishing her mammoth stone forms, were done right. The washing machine and dryer in the loft were not to be used for anything related to her work, but could be used to wash anything else. She would need him to sweep her studio and not touch anything, clean and sharpen her array of sculpting tools as requested, stropping them with a leather strap. Did he know how to strop with a leather strap? Could he use a whetstone to sharpen the kitchen knives to an inch of their lives? Could he make a mind-bending tuna fish salad, one that included pickle juice and capers and the thinnest chopped pieces of a single jalapeno? Was he capable of setting a lovely table for a formal dinner party? Did he know about all the forks, knives, spoons, glasses, and plates that accompanied such a formal party? Could he turn a cloth napkin into a swan, a turtle, a bow tie? Did he have issues with doing housework, find it beneath him, or consider it woman's work? Could he wash windows, mop floors, wash the stove, clean the oven, clean out the refrigerator, set fresh contact paper in the kitchen cabinets, scented paper in her bureau drawers?— pointing then to some large space behind the opaque floor-to-ceiling screens he was familiar with; his sobo Chiyo had a small Shoji screen at the foot of her bed, as if that whisper-thin rice could withstand the wrath that sometimes blew through the bungalow.

Did he know how to clean showers, sinks, toilets? Did he understand that the blue toilet-bowl cleanser had to be scrubbed with a brush, not left to do the work on its own, which it could not, and would only leave unsightly stains if not immediately attacked? Could he unscrew the grids over the air vents, rid them of all the dust clods that built up so supremely it was like seeing penicillin growing, without any need for a microscope?

Could he do all she needed to him to do, whatever her requests, however mundane, peculiar or illogical, in exchange for room and board and a monthly stipend? When she told him how much she would pay him to live in the loft, to do what she asked him to do, it was a fortune she was offering. He would have lived there and done everything she wanted for free.

"If you prove yourself, if perhaps you're interested, if I think it feels right, if you feel right to me, I might train you to become my assistant, an artist's assistant, teach you everything that you need to know, should know, about the world of creation. Which might actually help you create your own life. Of course, if I decide to spend the time training you in that way, and you prove yourself talented at such work, I would pay you an additional daily rate. But I will not pay you for the education you must undergo."

Theo listened spellbound to this world she was painting for him, a world he had never known existed, that he might actually be part of one day, and he wanted her to keep talking about it all, what she thought he might do in this remarkable place, in his own life, even when she came to an abrupt stop and was waiting for him to speak.

In that long, tensile silence, he stared into her blue, blue eyes, ocean blue, ice blue, a frozen blue, the kind of blue that relaxed the marrow in his spine, a blue so strong it nearly erased the wrinkles lining her face. It wasn't like *that*; she *was* beautiful, but old. Maybe even older than his sobo Chiyo, who cowered and ran to her plain room with her Shoji screen and her Butsudan shrine whenever his mother was back on the drugs, a brown bear on a rampage, blaming everyone, Sobo Chiyo particularly, for how things had turned out. And Sobo Chiyo doing her best to care for Theo when he was Emilio Inari Andramuño, and for Poppy, before Poppy disappeared into the desert, until she died, and Theo left home for good.

On her deathbed, in her fossilized voice, in the Japanese she always spoke, his sobo said to him: *I love you, but attend to what I say. You are a child of a weak woman, and I hate to say that about my own, but she has never had the strength to do right by herself, and she's never done right by you or your sister. I will die knowing I failed her, that she failed herself. But if you make good, when you make good, I'll know that too, and I'll rest easy in my grave.*

Sobo Chiyo was buried now in Salinas, in the special hallowed ground in Yamato Cemetery intended especially for the Japanese, which she was, 100 percent. The way his mother was, but not Poppy or him entirely. Theo believed that his sobo had rested easier these past three years, somehow knowing he had gotten himself away, and he was positive that the woman whose name meant *eternal, a thousand generations*, was finally truly at peace since Paloma came into his life.

That afternoon, answering the odd questions asked of him in the strange interview, Theo Tesh Park knew Paloma Rosen was the kind of person not made twice, no one else like her existing in the world, and when she said, "Do you have any questions for me?" he couldn't believe he had the courage, the daring, to ask if she had any children.

"My artistic nature, the force of my needs to accomplish my work, the way my life works in service to that, would not have mixed harmoniously with motherhood. Early on, I knew I did not want a life of bobbing and weaving between art and family, they fighting for my attention, me always being torn between the two, unable to acknowledge the truth in my blood, that no matter my ability to love, creation of art would always win out. For me, marriage, family life, motherhood were not sacred, art itself was then, still is, the great sacred thing, and from my earliest memories, I have always been devoted to it. So, perhaps more of an explanation than you expected, but *non,* no children for me."

He had been so glad to learn there were no children lucky enough to have her as a mother, and thought his own mother should have made such a choice, not had the children she was incapable of caring for, had failed to love beyond all else. Of course, had his mother been smart, he would not exist, and despite all the hardships, Theo wanted to be alive, perched on the edge of Paloma Rosen's huge sofa, thinking that maybe the best mothers were those who hadn't birthed their own, didn't know some young man was that minute choosing the role for her.

He had said yes to everything. Yes to being her errand boy, yes to all the mundane or peculiar or illogical tasks she said would be his to accomplish *avec empressement,* and when he must have looked confused, she said, *with alacrity,* a word he knew was English, but had no idea of its meaning. "Promptly," she had said next, and he had nodded and said, "I can do that, I promise." Yes to all the learning she said he would have to tackle in order to earn the potential of one day, perhaps, becoming her assistant, though he had not a clue what she meant by any of that. New places had opened up in Salinas before he left, galleries bringing suave monied people from Los Angeles and San Francisco, who bought the paintings that hung on walls. Theo had seen those buildings undergoing gut renovations, then the shiny floors, the white walls, cool folk trooping in and out of glass doors in a slinky dance, all of them, men and women, utterly gorgeous. He had walked past and wondered about the canvases he saw, what it all meant, but he had never gone in, had never felt such a place was meant for him.

Paloma Rosen had been staring at him, waiting for him to answer her question about whether he was willing to be schooled by her, to engage himself in a course of education, and he said, "You're the first real artist I've ever met. So I wouldn't know what you would want me to do, as your assistant, I mean, but I'll do whatever I should."

Her laugh was true and real, deep-throated, manly really, and she had said to him, "Good, but we shall not worry about any of that now. *Mais,* time will tell."

Though he had seen her at the front door, had followed her to the couch, when she stood up right then, at what he thought was the end of the interview, he had been shocked by her size. There was such power and force within her, the extreme magnetism that caught him, that he could see snaring so many others, but she was little, small, at least a foot shorter than he, with the long thick braids of a child, but pure white, swinging against her waist, and when he expected to see delicate hands, because there was something delicate about her, a serious elegance, she held up one hand, beckoning him to follow her deeper into the loft, when he thought she was going to show him the door, and that hand was outsized, the thick fingers bare, not a ring of any sort, the knuckles shaped like wizened marbles, nails very short, nearly, he thought, cut down to the quick, though she did not seem to him a nail-biting kind of person. That she might make someone else bite *their* nails, that he could see.

He had followed her across the entire loft that seemed to stretch out forever, past the ten bookshelves standing on their own, with comfortable chairs and lamps set about like orphans, passing the enormous windows, one by one, each maybe ten feet long and four times his height, and he was nearly six and a half feet tall.

When they reached a far corner of the loft, she opened a door to a bedroom, and walked in, and then opened another door.

"Don't be scared," she said. "Come in and take a look," and the bedroom was like being in heaven, all white and windowed and large, its walls filled with art, and he took many more steps forward, and peered around her to see into the white bathroom, that was old-fashioned in a way that the loft was not.

She had stepped back then, and measured him from his feet to the top of his head, and said, "I think you're too tall to use the bath as a bath, *je suis désolée,* but you can rehang the showerhead so it's higher up," and he saw she was right, the water would just graze his ribs.

When he looked back at her, the flats of her palms were flying over the neat comforter laid across the king-sized bed in this room he prayed might become his. Thick fingers smoothing out every stray wrinkle, and she had stopped and looked up at him, said, "I am so sorry, Monsieur Park," and his heart had roller-coastered into his stomach. "I should have asked you this first, because it's a requisite— are you good with tools?"

He was very good with tools, had fixed the family bungalow in Salinas, the fraying electrical cords, the frenzied plumbing, the door hinges that refused to stay put, the doors that never properly closed, the washing machine that bucked at will. He had not been able to do anything about the house itself, but he had kept it running, kept his sobo and his mother and his sister sheltered under a roof that never once sprung a leak. None of the people he had lived with in New York owned tools, wouldn't know what to do with them even if they had, but he did.

"I can do anything," he said to Paloma Rosen. "I can put a tool chest together with all the right stuff." He didn't have the money to stock a proper tool chest, but he would figure it out.

"*N'êtes-vous pas doux*," Paloma Rosen had said to him, and he said, "I'm sorry, but I don't know what that means." She had laughed again, but he could tell that her laughter was with him, not against him.

"It is French for *aren't you sweet*. And, *oui*, you are *très* sweet. Do not worry. I own every tool you might possibly need. One last thing— if you do not like the art I have put on the walls, you must tell me. *Maintenant*, follow me."

It was so new to him, how someone could be both warm and briskly dismissive; he was used to only warmth from his sobo and his lost sister, cold from his mother.

Then he was again sitting on the huge couch and Paloma Rosen was in front of him, a beautiful old lady with mannish hands sitting on a tree trunk that only now he noticed. Its girth so big he imagined the way the tree must have been, so old, living forever, tucked away in a forest no one had ever been able to find.

"*Alors qu'est-ce que vous en pensez?* Sorry. So what do you think, Monsieur Park?" she said. "I assume this is a palace compared to what you're used to."

She hadn't known, still did not know, the half of it. He had never set foot in any place like Paloma Rosen's loft, and that he would have a large bedroom of his own, his own bath. . . . The Salinas house was mean and small, and he had slept for years on a dingy pull-out couch in the canted living room. In New York, he had agreed to romantic entanglements that did him no good, just for a roof over his head, in Manhattan, in Brooklyn, in Queens, small places well cared-for, but sometimes cockroach-ridden, and when his quasi-roommates told him what they paid, he couldn't understand the fortunes they spent. Three years sharing the beds' of others, doing whatever they asked of him in all of those other ways. But then he had found Paloma Rosen's wanted ad hanging from a lamppost: *Artist offering room and board in exchange for errands and housekeeping. SoHo. Only serious applicants able to live-in need apply. Please, my days are very busy, I have no time to waste with perverts.*

It had seemed like a joke, but he had written to the email on the notice, and received a confirming email setting the interview. Even when Theo was on the subway coming from the depths of Brooklyn, getting off too early and making his way uptown, to a six-story building on a narrow cobbled side street named Wooster, with two businesses on the ground floor, a coffee place and a flower shop with blooms of every kind and color in metal containers on the sidewalk, it seemed like a joke, that the chance to live in the building, in the neighborhood, for free, for odd jobs, couldn't possibly be real. But he had taken the chance, had run up all those stairs, neatened the topknot he had worn since he was twelve, and knocked, and then it seemed that the gig was his, if he wanted it. And he did.

He willingly, eagerly, does all that Paloma asks of him, will continue to do all that she asks, and he is studying hard, reading the books she has given him, and visiting the museums and galleries she puts on his to-do list, taking notes about what he reads and his impressions of the exhibits he visits, wanting to understand art, to understand Paloma Rosen, who she is and what she sculpts, to be able to speak her special language.

They get along very well, he thinks, as long as he leaves her alone, does not bother her when she disappears down into the studio for her thirteen-hour days, unless she calls to him, and then he comes running.

Paloma Rosen chose him, Theo Tesh Park, and everything changed. He has wondered, these months, if she knows he chose her, too, as the recipient of his goodness, of the love nearly dried up in his heart.

Joan exhales. The daily writing of *Paloma Rosen* is mending her own heart, allowing love to run through it again, at least for the work, for Paloma and Theo, for Eric, too, for Vita, Camille, and Ela, and the others she has come to know here, her talks with Lakshmi at Namgyal Café, and the stern face of her father, Hadi, the café's chef-owner, who lights up when Joan requests that he surprise her with whatever he would like to cook, wants her to eat. Joan's heart is mending just as Paloma Rosen will mend Theo's heart. Theo Tesh Park will love her, and Paloma Rosen will love him back, against her will, until she gives in, tosses away the precepts by which she has lived her life.

Paloma doesn't yet know that Theo has chosen her to mother him, and then Joan is thinking about Camille, who did not want children, but provides art therapy to children so difficult it must be hard to find the love, and yet she does; and about Ela, who wanted children but could not bear the fruit, and now her children are those who sit around her on the red silk pillows, guided in meditative practice, learning the lessons she gently imparts; and about Vita, who lost a child before his twenty-first birthday. And how Vita and Camille and Ela, all childless, continue to mother Joan in their distinct ways, even when she bristled with Vita, refused, at first, Camille's overture. And aside from her own explicit motherhood, Joan is about to become another kind of mother this Saturday afternoon, nurturing ten Dharamshalans who want to crack open their shells, emerge with wings that might flutter, allow them to fly on the words they arrange.

All the ways in which women become mothers of some sort. Is motherhood inescapably entwined in female life, a story every woman ends up telling, whether or not she sought or desired that bond; her nourishment, her caretaking, her love, needed by someone standing before her, hands held out, heart demanding succor, commanding her not to look away, but to dig deep, give of herself unstintingly, offer up everything she can?

49

After her post-work bath, Joan stands naked at the open windows in her pine suite, the solemn chill of impending weather on her hot, damp skin. The chirs are still green in the forest, but the oak leaves are already burnished, a carpet of gold and red on the forest floor. She'd packed light for three weeks in India, but at the last minute she tossed in a pair of boots, a pair of jeans, and a black cashmere sweater, her workhorse attire since the weather has dramatically cooled. In her sixth month, she is no longer prevaricating about the fact that she is living in Dharamshala. And because that is true, and because winter will arrive soon, she will need to buy suitable clothing. She's been through all the shops in the marketplaces and bazaars, bought several Indian tunics she wore when it was warm, but nothing for a cold and snowy Dharamshalan winter. Her linen pants and shirts are too light now, and her golden sandals with their luminous crystals have been put away, in the pine closet since late October.

She dresses in her warm clothes—her new uniform—gathers up the ten stories and her own notebook and races out of the hotel and down the hill. She will miss the final outdoor meditation with Ela in the courtyard today. Starting tomorrow, meditation will be held in the banquet room of a teahouse on the edge of sacred Dal Lake. Then Joan is through the marketplace, at the end of Kotwali, at Darpan's bookstore.

A sign on the door, in silver italics, reads: *Closed for Writers' Class Until 5 pm.* The chime tinkles when she walks in. Darpan has prepared. A long table is in the open space between the counter and the first row of bookshelves. Twelve folding chairs, a pad of paper and pen at each place, in the middle, a pitcher of water, glasses, plates of cookies that have the misshapen look of homemade.

"Miss Ashby, welcome, welcome."

"Everything looks perfect, Darpan. So nice of you to think of water and cookies."

"I am very excited and when I'm excited I eat, eat, eat," Darpan says. Joan thinks that can't be true. He's wearing a white T-shirt with DHARMA OR BUST in gold across his concave chest, and she could count his ribs beneath the thin material if she tried.

"So, this is your place, at the head of the table," and Joan feels like Ela, at the top of the clock. She has sidestepped the conversation with Darpan, about whether the class will meet just this once, or once a week for a month, or more. She does not intend to leave Dharamshala, but there is such freedom in being again a writer at work, a woman at liberty, and she had said to him, "Let's gauge everyone's actual interest, see if they're willing to do the hard work, before making specific plans," and he had agreed.

And then the chime over the door is ringing madly, neophyte writers swarming in, calling out "*Namaste*, Ashby. *Namaste*, Darpan," handing wrinkled rupees to Darpan, thanking him for the pads and the pens, scuffling over which seat they want, the cookies on the plate disappearing rapidly, and Joan is surprised to find that the teenager with the anemone braids who serves her the roaring lion lattes at the Namgyal Café, who asks her all about America, is among them. One of the stories she selected was written by a Lakshmi, but it's not an uncommon name.

"Hello to you all," Darpan says. "Welcome to the best writing class in the world. And now our illustrious teacher will take over."

Joan smiles at each of them, the way Ela does, then says, "Let's start with everyone giving their name and briefly explaining your reason for wanting to take this class. Lakshmi, you can lead us off."

"I'm Lakshmi, and I want to take this class to become as smart as Ashby." Not what Joan had in mind, but it's a start, and when she realizes Lakshmi wrote about Rati, the girl whose father has selected a husband for her, she wonders if it's true, if Hadi is already arranging a marriage for his daughter, with a short boy who has the body of a baboon, the eyes of an owl, if this accounts for all of Lakshmi's questions about life in America. That she is preparing for her own escape.

"I am Hoshi," the old man next to Lakshmi says. He is taller than most Dharamshalans, with a full head of white hair, deeply etched wrinkles over his entire face, like a glass well cracked, but the pieces still, somehow, intact. "I have always been a writer in private, and before

I die I want others to read my stories." He had written about Navin picking up his younger brother to take him out into the fresh air.

Next to Hoshi is a heavyset, middle-aged woman, in a bright-yellow sari, with a thick and pilling sweater over her shoulders, the vermilion stripe down the part in her hair.

"Edhitha," she says. "I am a wife and a mother and I am tired of being told I make up too many stories and so I thought I might as well do it for real. Prove to them I am not a liar, but a storyteller." Her story was about Feni, whose name means sweet, but she isn't.

Next to Edhitha is the youngest member of the class. "I am Qadir. I am twelve. I am happiest when I am writing, considering the nature of the universe." He wrote about Qasam wanting to storm out of the valley and get to somewhere good, the only writer who had used a swear word in his work. He reminds Joan of Daniel, the intelligent young eyes that stare without blinking, the early need to ponder the big questions in life. Joan wonders if his parents are aware of his intelligence, his command of expletives.

"My name is Onir," says the next young man. He is handsome, with long sideburns, and a neat, well-trimmed beard. "I am only twenty-three, but I like to tell stories as if I am an old man and have already lived my entire life." His story was about old Prasad with a story to tell his family that would alter the way they saw the world.

"I'm Taj. I was raised a strict Buddhist, but have broken away." Joan thought he was the same age as Onir, homely where Onir was handsome, balding where Onir had an abundance of hair. Taj had written about Iti and Ibha, who were sick of praying to Buddha.

"I'm Jalaf. It is a great honor to meet you Ashby, to be sharing a table with you. I am quite overcome," and there are tears in her wide brown eyes, and Joan says, "I'm so pleased you're here. Would you like to say anything else?" but Jalaf can't talk, just waves her hand at Joan, then at the woman next to her. Jalaf's story was about the girl who sees herself in the mirror and realizes she is all grown up. Joan thinks Jalaf is in her early thirties, but she has no bindi between her eyebrows, no vermilion stripe down her part, no rings on her fingers, or in her lobes. Is she unmarried, alone, lonely? The story had struck Joan that way, that the narrator was lonely and sad, and in real life, it seems Jalaf might be indistinguishable from her narrator.

Next to Jalaf is a woman nearer in age to old Hoshi than to anyone else. Early seventies perhaps, and immaculately put together. Rouge and lipstick and brown eye shadow, the heavy coats of mascara turning her eyelashes into thick spider legs, her hair pulled up high, dressed as if she lives in New York or in Paris, structured jacket, skirt, high heels. Unusual attire for the valley. She plays with the gold earrings she wears, a nervous tic maybe, Joan thinks.

"I am Medh. Bombay-born. Brought here as a young bride. I have maintained journals my entire life, my stories a blend of fact and fiction." Her story, about a woman who thinks her mother's constant chants contain the father she never knew, had been evocative and touching.

"Zafar. Forty. I was a monk in my early years. Fell in love and left the temple. Now I love my wife, drink beer, watch action movies, read rip-roaring stories. Guns and mayhem, that kind of thing." He is strapping and bald. His brown leather jacket zipped all the way up to his chin. From peaceable monk to mayhem seems like a long climb, or fall, Joan isn't sure which. He had written about the girl hiding in the fort and knowing she was going to die. If Zafar aims to write action stories, he will need to learn the parts of a gun, like actions, stocks, and barrels, how bullets slide into chambers.

It is a teenage boy's turn, the same age, Joan thinks, as Lakshmi. There is a stillness in his face, his eyes look sleepy, but take everything in. "I am Tanvi. I am in my final year of high school. Last year my mother died and now it's just me and my sister and my father. I think this class will help me feel better." Tanvi had written about boyhood friends who played games together and relied on each other's mothers for maternal love.

Joan always took the opposite approach with her work, even in her earliest stories, never writing about her own life. But nearly all these stories, with the exception, she hopes, of Zafar, intrigued by guns and death, the work seems to mirror the writers' realities and Joan wonders how best to help them dive in, delve more deeply, how much of her instruction will require therapeutic intervention versus the indefinable aspects of writing.

Darpan speaks last. "I will work hard on my stories," is all he says.

As she leads them in a discussion about how the class will work, what it means to workshop a story, the revisions they will be required to do, their potential goals for themselves, she realizes this will not be a onetime class.

For the next two hours and forty-five minutes, Joan watches Lakshmi, Hoshi, Edhitha, Qadir, Oni, Taj, Jalaf, Medh, Zafar, Tanvi, and Darpan start to break out of their shells, find common ground with one another, always looking to her, for guidance, for illustration, for explication, as their serious faces grow lighter, smiles opening wide, white teeth flashing the private desires they carry within, that she will see them through to the other side, where their hopes might match their dreams. She isn't sure most of their dreams revolve around writing, but it doesn't really matter. She is heeding the call of these people standing—well, sitting—before her, with their hands held out, their hearts demanding succor, commanding her not to look away, but to dig deep, give of herself unstintingly, offer up everything she can.

When the clock shows it's already five, Darpan says, "Thank you for a most wonderful first class, Ashby. Everyone knows what they must do this week. You must work hard on your stories and be brave, like Ashby says. On Monday, I will have behind the counter copies of everyone's stories, so make sure you come and get your packets. Anyone who doesn't will be tossed out of the best writing class ever." And just like that, Joan is running a writing class, with a taskmaster she need not beckon or call.

There are hugs and bows and handshakes, and then the writers scatter away. Darpan bows to Joan and says, "Maybe we should consider more than one class a week? Start a second class?"

"I can only handle one, Darpan. I'm busy with other work."

Darpan's eyes light up. "One never asks a writer about her work, and so I will not, except to say, if it is true what I am thinking, then I am most delighted in every way."

Joan smiles. "Don't let your thoughts run away. Or let them run away, but to your own story, which I'm interested in reading, since you didn't turn one in."

"I will make you proud, Ashby. Don't you worry about that."

Then Joan is out the bookstore door, sighted for home, and that's what she hears in her head: *home.* It has such a different connotation now. *Home* no longer means the soaring house, the gardens and vegetable plots, the red maples, the elms, the Cleveland pear trees, the weeping willow, the shed she and Fancy built themselves that she imagined turning into her writing office. It no longer means the long lap pool in the glen, or the knoll, or the four acres of land. *Home* is no longer Rhome, and Joan might as well directly acknowledge such truths to Martin, who may not be part of *home* anymore either.

Home is now her pine suite, with its red coverlet bed, and her laptop on her pine desk, and the forest outside of her windows, the marigold curtains creating a frame.

Home is Ela's meditation class each afternoon, it is Darpan and the bookstore, Kartar at the front desk, her friendship with Willem, if he ever returns. It is Eric, and will be Amari. It is her calls to Vita in Udaipur every two weeks, talking to Joan from the house Vita has bought on Lake Pichola, and her weekly Sunday calls with Camille, after Camille meditates and wants to catch up.

Home is *Paloma Rosen*, the book that is tangibly and seductively flowering. It is Theo Tesh Park finding a true home with Paloma.

Joan is nearly up the hill, nearly at the hotel, when she imagines *Paloma Rosen* published. She stops in her tracks and realizes readers of her famous collections will believe *Paloma Rosen* is her first novel, that the critics and reviewers will waste time conjecturing what has taken Ashby so long to publish again. Iger sent her an email last week telling her that *Paradise of Artists* and *The Blissed-Out Retreat* are still on various bestseller lists, asking again if it might be time to correct the wrong, to clarify that she is the writer, not the ignoble J. D. Henry. It still feels like an impossible decision to make, and she has been so happy lately, she does not want the fury that accompanies such thoughts, having to chant *"Om Dum Durgayei Namaha"* over and over again: *Om and Salutations to that feminine energy which protects from all manner of negative influences.*

Perhaps she'll agree to acknowledge her authorship of the books if they're nominated for some kind of prize, then Joan is up the hotel's wooden stairs, and Kartar is at his post, at the low teak counter, calling out "Ashby, happy late afternoon. A letter for you from the illustrious Willem Ackerman, hand-delivered just an hour ago by himself, and also a large package," which he lifts onto the counter. "From USA. Rhome, Virginia, it says."

He hands her Willem's letter, and says, "I will carry the box to your suite," and they walk down the long hall, and she opens her door, and Kartar places the box on her bed.

"May I do something else for you this fine afternoon?"

Kartar has never once failed to make good on his promises, and looking at the box on her bed, at the letter in her hand, Joan knows what she needs.

"Any chance of another nice bottle of white wine?"

"I will endeavor to do my best. If I can find more than one, Ashby?"

"More than one, yes. More than two, yes. Up to five, if that makes the job easier." She wonders if she should simply ask if he can find her a case. She reaches for her bag, for her wallet, says, "How much shall I give you?"

"Later Ashby, later. Let me see first if I can perform what I am promising."

It's not easy getting wine here, but Kartar has proven himself a steady supplier. Along with his earlier deployments on her behalf, he gifted her a heavy-duty corkscrew wrapped up in Indian red cloth. Now that Willem Ackerman is back, Joan could ask for a bottle or two of the rich red wine from his cache, but she ought to read first what he has to say.

"I'll endeavor to return promptly," Kartar says, and shuts the pine door behind him.

Martin has sent this package from home, which used to be her home—is still hers, she emends—though it doesn't feel true anymore. Dharamshala has become her home, and whatever exists beyond Dharamshala is a story someone else wrote long ago. She looks at the package on the bed, and then at the letter in her hand, and knows which one interests her most.

50

The envelope contains a single piece of paper, thin as tissue, folded into thirds, and something heavier and square, a photograph. Of Joan. Joan captured secretly by Willem Ackerman's eye and lens, under a dome of blue sky, on the roof of the lodge at the Pong Wetland, looking into the distance, her notebook open to a clean page on the table, her pen in midair. She remembers that moment, when she knew she needed to resolve her own life, find a new iteration of herself. Up on that roof that late afternoon, she hadn't yet shed her old self, the amorphous body that had carried her along, she had not yet fully hurled herself into the feast of the future, was not yet ready to saunter or gallop, was still just crawling. But she looks beautiful sitting there, balanced on the knifepoint of resolution, and she is pleased Willem took this picture of her. Other pictures have been taken, of the places she's seen, of Eric's cottage, of Eric and Amari, of Eric and her, of Ela and Camille, and the three of them sitting on the red silk pillows, their heads tipped together, at Darpan's bookstore surrounded by people, but not a picture of her alone, in India. Willem Ackerman has caught the steel of her core, the tenderness with which she was binding herself together in those days. She unfolds his letter.

I am back from my professional travels and the months away allowed me to find my bravery and acknowledge that I fell in love with you the moment I read your words a long time ago, and saw your pictures on the back of those book covers. Perhaps my wife was right to be jealous, the way I returned to your stories again and again. I took this picture of you at the sanctuary, one of dozens I took without you being aware. When I printed this picture, these were my thoughts: Joan Ashby is ready to find herself again, and she is ready to experience a true

and rare love. Even here in this land outside of time, the com-
plications of life follow us, and I promise that I will not be
such a complication, but know that I have missed you and my
offer of that true and rare love will stand for all time.

She feels again like that giddy girl she never was, the way she felt
with Willem in his orange jeep, the way she felt with him during every
second of those three days, imagining something more between them,
then saying no to his offer. And what she thinks next surprises her: she
never tested Martin's love, never learned how he would have reacted if
she had said all those years ago, "We agreed on no children," and held
him to his vow. They were equally complicit, in turning conditional
the pure love they once had.

A quiet rapping on the door of her pine suite—Kartar with three
bottles of good French Chardonnay, two wineglasses, and a bucket of
ice, all set out on one of the breakfast trays. An unexpected fresh flower
for the end of day, a stalk with tremulous scarlet petals in a marigold
vase—the colors of India—and French wine in Dharamshala. Two
wineglasses because Kartar harbors hopes that Willem Ackerman will
sweep Joan off her feet, that true love will be found at Hotel Gandhi's
Paradise, and if Kartar knew what was written in Willem's letter, his
romantic nature would zoom into overdrive.

Joan has learned that Kartar's time in the United States altered
him in only one way—he became an Americanized romantic. At
twenty, he holds all those notions near. When he told Joan about the
movies he watched when he lived there, he said, "Oh, Ashby, how
much I loved those rom-coms. I learned so much about the broken
hearts of people when they make mistakes in matters of love, how one
must travel that long road to reach the heart that fits your own." He
was surprised when she gently explained that rom-com stood for romantic comedy, and he was not meant to take such movies seriously.

When he has placed the bottles, glasses, and ice bucket on the
dresser, Joan asks how much she owes, and he shakes his head.

"Kartar, if you do not take what is owed to you, I won't be able to
ask you for anything else."

"All right Ashby, I will do it your way. My father would say one
must accept what one is rightfully owed."

"Your father is right," Joan says, and presses on him rupees for the wine and a large tip, as she always does, which he slips into his pocket. She kisses his cheek, sees him blush, and then he is out in the hall, and she barely hears the lock click closed. Two bottles into the bathroom fridge, the cork of the third pulled out. Joan fills a glass with the warm wine, scoops ice from the bucket, plunks in a few cubes.

She reads Willem's letter a second, third, and fourth time, then puts it aside, her heart beating a wondrous and strange little tune.

Kartar's corkscrew slices through the thick tape wound around the box from Martin. She pulls back the flaps, lifts out each item, places it down on the quilt.

Here is a thick letter from her husband sealed up in an envelope.

Here are three supersized bags of red licorice vines, which make her smile.

Here is a newly purchased tube of her lipstick, still in its box, the make and color exactly what she has used for years, a shimmery sort of blush shade. She is nearly out of the one she brought, and she feels a warm rush inside, that Martin would know what she puts on her lips, would think she may be running out.

Next a layer of clothing. She never thought to ask Martin to send her a few things, but he has: her white hat, gloves, scarf, and down jacket, three sweaters, including her favorite one the color of a blued icicle, a pair of her heavy-duty boots, wool trousers and jeans, a plastic bag with bras and underwear, two pairs of her warm pajamas, and her comfortable old sweatpants she wore on cold nights when they nestled together in bed watching a movie. This box seems to say he understands she doesn't yet have any answers to his questions, that he is giving her all the time she needs.

At the bottom are several novels with Iger's publishing imprint stamped on the spines, along with a handwritten note from Iger to Martin.

Martin,
I never realized how good a man you are. With Joan
stomping through Nirvana, my thinking about you has

altered completely. Sorry for doubting you all of these years.
I wanted her to write, not bake bread and babies and backseat
her own work. Apologies for the unkind thoughts I had about
you in the past. I hope you won't mind sending on these
books. She might be in need of reading material, beyond
what the Buddhists suggest.
     Xoxo,
     Iger

Martin would not have liked learning Iger blamed him, for Joan's
lack of output, for taking her to Rhome, for making her the mother of
two sons, and Joan knows that he deliberately included Iger's note to
remind her of his good qualities, that he thinks she may have forgotten.
She thinks about calling him to apologize for Iger's words, but Iger's not
entirely wrong, and Martin would interpret such a call as an invitation
to come here, or a tacit acknowledgment that she is ready to return
home, and neither is accurate. Paloma Rosen would not call Jean-Pierre
Beson, would never doubt her decision, imagine it in any way a mistake.
Joan hasn't yet made a mistake, and she doesn't want Martin to bank
on something she is not sure she can or wants to deliver.

The last thing in the box, tucked into a corner, is another box, small
and compact, filled with bubble wrap that machine-gun pops when she
tries to uncover what's hidden inside. It is like something belonging to
a spy, a secret decoder, or a minuscule bomb that will blow her up if
she makes jarring moves or moves too fast. She knows it's for the
computer, she thinks it's called a memory stick.

She opens Martin's letter:

Dear Joan,
     I miss you. I hope these months have allowed you to solve
what you needed to solve, but please, it's time for you to come
home, to return to our life. I never agreed—

It goes on for eight pages, but she only needs Martin's opening
salvo—the confused mix of caring followed by demand—to know that
the rest of his words will be at odds with the box he has sent her, the

warm clothes contained within. This is how it's been, she realizes, conditional love all the way through, despite giving him what he wanted right from the start. It's Martin's love that has been conditional, it's why he did not notice, or care, when she stopped writing, or when she began writing again, wrote *Words of New Beginnings* over nine long years, the reason *why* she wrote *Words*, with its story about an arcadia, her Devata, or why he left her to do the dirty work, policing Eric all on her own. His life has taken no detours, has not been delayed at all, moved forward as he wanted, every step exactly as he arranged. There is no need to read every word of his letter this moment; she will, later, from start to finish, and figure out exactly the stand she will take, but right now she wants only to know why she has been sent this memory stick that came wrapped in its own box. She moves her index finger down through all the pages looking for an explanation, but Martin does not mention it at all.

She strips out of her jeans and pulls on the old sweatpants. She lifts the blue sweater to her face, inhales her perfume long twined into the weave, scented with their past. And suddenly she is pining, as she did in this room at the start of her life here. But pining for what she and Martin had, at the very beginning, and the good and sweet times they have shared these marital years, and it catches her hard.

She trades her workhouse black cashmere sweater for the blue and her stare shifts from Willem's photograph of her, to his letter, to the mysterious black device. She carefully inserts it into the slot on the side of the computer and an icon pops up on the screen. She clicks it twice, and when it opens, there is an audio file simply labeled: *For Joan Ashby*.

Months ago, she tossed into her suitcase the miniature speaker Martin gave her, along with the laptop. She's never had any reason to use it and it's sitting in the top drawer of her pine bureau. She retrieves it and finds the small hole on the laptop, plugs it in.

In the instant before she presses the button, she thinks how her world is this moment fantastic, that she will lament no longer, that life is too short for anything else, that she has all she needs, all that she requires—the orchestration of her days and her nights, her writing, her meditation, her explorations, her new friendships, her new class of writers, her blessings, whatever sins she may choose. So many of her people in her stories sinned, though never before has Joan considered their actions this way. But weren't they all sinning—big and little sins, some thunderous, some small as a white squeaking mouse. And she, Joan Ashby, in her own life, she has not sinned nearly enough. Except in her thoughts, the anger and impatience she felt toward husband and children, in her selfish desire to get back to her own life, subject only to her own needs. But outright sin, no, there's been none of that; she rejected Willem's offer on the roof of the lodge when no one would ever have known had she spent that night, and all the following nights, and days, with him in bed. But that's not the kind of sin she means, and she wonders when and how she decided it was sinful to heed her own destiny.

Then she presses Play.

51

It is Columbus Day weekend, a weekend of symmetry for me. I am looking out my wall of windows, sitting in my favorite armchair that you found for me when I bought this apartment. The chair is covered in some kind of soft fabric that makes me think of a blue lake, and I wish I were on the banks of that lake right now. Instead, I have a digital recorder in my hand, as weightless as my steps in the wrong direction, heeding my every word, the various inflections in my voice.

I have debated what to call this recounting. I considered "Testament," but my brain reconfigures that into Last Will and Testament, which makes me think of death, and although I deserve severe punishment, I hope even you might think death extreme. I considered "Explanation," but that implies there is one, and no configuration of reasons or rationales exists to justify my actions. I have decided to call it "Recordings," since I am doing just that—recording to confess, to elucidate, and, I guess, to soothe in some way. No matter what, I will have told my story. Such a roundabout way to arrive at a story worth telling: I never expected deceit and deception would figure in its creation.

When you left for India, a departure without warning, or at least without any warning to me, I thought only that you had taken Eric up on his offer to visit him there. I know now that you left because of me and what I had done. I remain thankful that your maternal instincts kept you from revealing my treachery to the wider world, that knowledge of my actions has been limited to Annabelle Iger and the lawyers. I did everything asked of me to put the debacle legally right, to allow you to recapture your stolen work: I signed declarations and quit-claim documents and wire-transferred the ill-gotten funds out of my account and into yours.

If it helps, know that I have suffered mightily for my transgression:

my original life has vanished and my very brief pseudonymous existence has gone up in smoke. I brought these consequences on myself and I expect no sympathy. I also do not expect your forgiveness to come easily, or perhaps at all. I can put myself in your place now, and it is impossible for me to imagine forgiving someone who absconded with my life's work, my own heart, but I hope you will try.

I thought reading *Other Small Spaces* and *Fictional Family Life* would sink me, instead they set me free. Of course, I used that freedom in the wrong way, but I honestly thought J. D. Henry was my way out, my way forward, my future, and that he could do what I never could do, never could be. It has been surreal to be him, even if for such a short time, to have tasted what you experienced early in your life.

I've considered how best to start, and I think it is like this:

I, Daniel Manning, am the commoner in a family renowned for its brilliance: mother, father, much younger brother, all masters of their particular universes.

Daniel's voice rocketing around her pine suite in Hotel Gandhi's Paradise, the Play button she stabs again to silence him. There is a bitter taste in her mouth and the mauled bubble wrap on the bed looks ominous, the kind of thing, in great quantities, one might use to wrap up a lifeless body.

Joan drags the pine armchair to the window, curls up inside of it, and looks out at a small corner of her unbelievable world. Weighty clouds hide the distant mountain peaks. Overhead, the sky is unblemished, the deep green forest sparkling beneath a spirited moon. She drinks down the wine.

Hearing his voice is a shock and she does not want to hear it again, to listen to more of his words. Her finger hesitates over the button, but then she presses it firmly, his voice emerging so sure, so steady.

Looking back, you should have been my natural first reader—we talked about the big books I was reading—but in the beginning I did not seek you out. Maybe it was deliberate, an unconscious choice not to hand my work over to another writer, though I did not know—or thought I did not know—that you were a writer until I was in seventh grade. It was to Dad I went, at least in the beginning.

When I came back home from Silicon Valley, my tail between my legs, never once did you say, "I told you so," and I thank you for that. I never told you that after I moved to DC and was trying to figure out what to do next, I looked for someone who could decipher the map of my life, give me the directions that would deliver me out of the wilderness. I found Dr. Vidal.

"What brings you here?" he asked me. I had recently finished reading *Myra Breckinridge*, and so I asked, "Are you related to Gore Vidal?" Dr. Vidal opened his notebook and uncapped his pen. "If there was a family relation, how do you think that would affect our work together?" "I don't know," I said. "No way, I guess. But it would be an interesting fact." He made note of that.

A few minutes into our second session everything heated inside of me tumbled from my mouth into the cold air of his office. Vidal pressed on. "We ought to further explore your boyhood memories, your resistance to analyzing such key events in your life." I said, "I'm not being resistant. Haven't we been talking about those memories for the last fifty minutes?" "I think it would be more accurate to say that we have been talking about not talking about those memories for the last fifty minutes," and then Vidal rose from his chair to signal the end of our time. I walked home that day, an hour on foot, and when I reached my street, I knew Vidal was right.

He hit me hard in our third session. "Let's discuss how you think your mother contributed to the wrong turn you took in your life." I chewed up time. Crossed to his window, stared at the old linden trees planted straight as a picket fence down the wide avenue. Filled cups of water and drank them down. Finally reoccupied the beige corduroy chair designated for the messed-up and the lost. Across the floor, Vidal sat in his own chair, a kingly black leather, and waited. I stared at him, felt my resistance locking me down. He raised a trim black eyebrow. I sighed. "So when I was a kid and started to write stories, I didn't know my mother was a writer. And once I learned she was, I lost what was my mine, lost all of my drive."

Vidal lifted that eyebrow again. I could see he recognized the wrong turn I had taken as a boy, and that he was not going to hand over the coordinates so I could alter my direction, attain my proper course. I would have to find those coordinates on my own.

"Would you say you felt envy? Jealousy? Competition?" I shook my head at those freighted words. "She's my mother," I said. "Of course not. Look at how she turned my stories into books. Encouraged me to keep writing." Vidal cocked his head. "All true. But you're a smart guy, Daniel, so let's see if we can't skip to the meat. You read serious books early on, so you knew writers existed, and you didn't feel threatened by them. Is that accurate?"

"Accurate," I said.

"Since you believed you were the writer in the family, do you think it's possible you have unresolved emotions toward your mother?"

"No," I said, but I knew that *No* was not clean.

Vidal twisted his mouth. "Do you think you found it difficult that your mother already held that honor? Holds that honor still, and the admiration that comes along with that kind of talent, it would be hard for anyone to process. Certainly a child with similar aspirations would have a tough time. Do you think that's possible?"

"Do you know who my mother is?" I asked. I had never told him your name.

"You're deflecting," Vidal responded. "Avoiding identifying fundamental truths about who you really are. Don't you want to acknowledge the past, unmask yourself, possibly return to writing which you say you are keen to do, even if that means following in your mother's footsteps?"

I had nothing to say to any of that—

Joan stops the recording again to catch her breath, refill her glass. She hadn't known Daniel had taken himself to a psychologist. Apparently therapy failed to uncover how he lost the plot of his life, a state of confusion he never disclosed to her. She was wrong in thinking he told her everything. She thinks of when he was a little boy, how she was a mother cat and he the kitten; with Eric, she was a guard dog caring for a baby hawk; with the theft of her work, she turned into a lioness.

She watches the Dhauladhars use their power to shuck off the hovering clouds, and the early faint stars are up there, lives and deaths charted in the sky. She inhales, sips, touches the button that brings Daniel back into her life.

In my childhood, when I marched around my bedroom with a new story in my hand, a pencil stuck between my lips, imagining myself a famous writer, I was too young to understand that if I followed through, if I truly had talent, and luck, my stories might be read by others, beyond mother and father, and baby brother, if I promised him lollipops after. And then, suddenly, millions of people were reading *Paradise of Artists* and *The Blissed-Out Retreat,* to which I had appended my name, or rather J. D. Henry's name. And yet who was I, and what had I actually achieved? A pseudonymous personage, a burglar of the glorious words put together by another—

Joan listens to the story of a reader's spellbound weekend during which childhood hurts are revisited, the small hurts looming enormous when endured by a child, the way they slithered deep inside and fed off the warmth of tissue and blood and a child's flawed desperation, the need that time never abates, to become that hero the child imagined he was, to make himself known and worthy of recognition. What's missing, Joan thinks, is any awareness by Daniel that the seeds for such elevation were within him the whole time.

She is saddened, horrified, flattered, unwillingly fascinated by how articulate he is in analyzing her work, describing the ways he was moved, the application of her stories to his own life. And the beautiful modulation of his voice holds her when he reads excerpts of her work in the way she intended her stories to be absorbed. There are so many revelations in his artistic confession—what she did wrong, what he did wrong—all underscored by the low tone of arrogance, the artfulness she realizes is not new, she heard it every time they spoke from the moment that must date from his theft of her work.

My tremulous defense today might be that I confused who was the reader and who was the writer when I submerged myself in Ashby's published words, tasted her unpublished words on my tongue, in-haled it all until I floated on a sea of infinite creation. In important ways, it's true, but such a defense would not hold up in a court of law, and I won't condescend by arguing I was in some mental state that diminished my capacity to know right from wrong, or caused me to be unaware of what I was doing, the actions I was taking. I am not minimizing what I did, but I feel it important to explain that my actions were based in hard truths, at least in my own truths, in my own reality.

It might be easy to deem me a fraud, a consummate con man, a thief of the work I thought abandoned, and that I believed I was bringing into the light. I think such facile labeling underestimates critical points, points I determined when I stood at my wall of win-dows and thought how the harms from the past inform the present; how old wishes are nailed to a person's endoskeleton, no matter that the bones have lengthened, solidified over the years; about the confluence of events in a life; the power of the written word.

This suffering with which Daniel has so closely aligned himself, he will have to let it go, leap into the depth of the world, stop playing it safe, take risks that belong to him alone. He wanted the Devata she created in *Words*, the one she has found here in Dharamshala, but he must make his own, in a terrain that suits him. Paradise belongs only to the creator. Joan lifts herself out of the pine armchair, feeling older than she ever has, and pours herself a third glass of wine.

I have been narrating my story all of this Columbus Day weekend. Three days so different than last year, no biblical storm and rains, just a blue sky and white clouds. It has been difficult hearing myself explain my actions, but at least I have done something. An attempt to rectify the wrong. Whether you have listened to my entire story, and will find a way to forgive, I have no way of knowing.

I admit to some mild satisfaction as well. A narrative structure has evolved from my wrongdoing. By virtue of my reprehensible actions, the attempted assumption of an unearned life, the theft of words written by another, I have created a substantive piece of work all my own.

The sun is slipping away on this third and final day of the holiday weekend. I've been watching its path, noting its weakening light, and it strikes me for the first time that recording my story is not at all the same thing as writing fiction from scratch. Again, I have reined myself in, failed to take that great leap into the life I once wanted, and who knows, despite all that has happened, maybe I still do.

No doubt I have time until you send me some sign regarding my fate as your son. Perhaps I ought to use the coming days, weeks, or months judiciously, start at the beginning again, and write this—my story—for real.

Then there is silence. The recording is finished.

He's right, Joan thinks—there is a manifest talent in the framing of his tale, the cohesions that bind it together. It might even be a story she would write, as fiction, call it *Words of New Beginnings*; that good title still belongs to her, waiting only to be unpacked.

Did Daniel say he was sorry?

Her head is filled up with hours of his words, but Joan is certain that particular one was missing.

She looks up into the Indian sky, at the faraway stars dressed up in their prehistoric white, the past informing the present.

She will write a fourth letter to the Dalai Lama, have Kartar deliver it to His Holiness's secretary in the morning. There on her nightstand is the basket filled with Hotel Gandhi's Paradise stationery, and she places a stack on her desk. She will use the full force of her own words, include the new depths of her story, the additional facts she has gleaned from her son's tale. She must set everything out as accurately as she can, as honestly as she is able, by hand. He hasn't responded to her three previous letters, but perhaps he will, to this one.

Joan pauses. She realizes it is not to the Dalai Lama she needs to write, but to Daniel. She never tested Martin's love, but she will test his. She opens her laptop and begins:

> Daniel—
> *If my lessons to you during all your formative years failed to take, I can't teach you anything at this late date, and I should not*

expect to hear you say the word "sorry," but your recorded voice,
the excuses you have made for yourself, will not do. You tried to
eat me up, but you must find another way to assuage this hunger
of yours, a different form of satiation. The books are mine, a
wedge between us that must be removed, so that you can begin
to find the life meant for you.

The nature of your crime is more important than the punishment,
but the punishment cannot be avoided. You must purify yourself,
come clean, own up to what you have done, tell the truth—not to
me, for I know the truth.

It is primal, what you need to do, but it is the only way you
can scale your limited horizon, see beyond it. This isn't a story
you need to write, it's a story you need to finish. You still have the
potential for a long, good, and fulfilling life, but you must have the
strength to do what's right, acknowledge your theft publicly,
atone for the sins of J. D. Henry; only then will you be through
to the other side. And I promise, if you make it there, I will be
waiting. Still your mother. Still a mother who loves her son.

She reads it over several times, satisfied with what she has written. She attaches the letter to an email, types in Daniel's email address, writes in the subject line: "It Is Up To You," and looks at the computer's clock.

It's three in the morning in Dharamshala, only five thirty in the evening in DC. She will wait to send off her letter when it is the dead of night there, when Daniel will likely be sleeping. In three hours, there will be soft footfalls in the hallway outside her pine suite, Kartar placing her morning tray at the door. She's drunk nearly the entire bottle of good French Chardonnay, and she could use some strong barley tea, a bowl of steaming lentils.

Joan sits up straight in her chair at her pine desk.

In Daniel's recording, isn't there a delivery boy named Kartar with an apparent ability to forecast the future, who intrigued, and then frightened, him? A boy who worked at a place called Lucky Star? Joan has a Kartar, and although he has never forecast her future, he knew she needed a special place in which to pine, and was the first to call her Ashby, and offered her a guidebook she still uses daily, and drew the map that took her to Eric's cottage, and lent her an umbrella stamped *Lucky Star*, and extolled Willem Ackerman's character, which sent her on the journey to the bird sanctuary, and has hand-delivered the three letters she has written to the Dalai Lama, and is it possible that she and Daniel have shared the same Kartar, that this young Indian man has figured in both of their lives in subtle but immeasurable ways?

52

Joan sleeps deep inside a dream. Martin and Daniel are at the edge of a vast snowfield, cross-country skis racked against their shoulders, and Daniel has shaved his brown curls clear off his skull, turning him monkish. Father and son are debating which path to take across the untouched infinite white, and she watches them set off. There is a cottage in the distance, mountains rising behind it, and Joan knows it belongs to her. Instantly, she is inside, and finds the white walls entirely covered in words. Someone she doesn't recognize passes by and says, "Wonderful story," and Joan reaches out a fingertip and finds she can smudge everything away, leave nothing behind.

The prophetic dream stays with her even when she wakes. She's been asleep only a few hours, but the world outside her window has altered completely, the forest blanketed in unexpected snow, the tree limbs and boughs already heavy under the sudden white weight that glistens and gleams. In the distance, the snowy mountains are lit up by the November sun rising over Dharamshala, thin and brittle and bright.

She brings in her tray. A snowy white flower in a white vase, as if Kartar knew what weather would happen today. It is only two in the morning in London, and Camille will be sleeping, but Joan sends her an email Camille will understand. "I'm ready to tell you about what brought me to Dharamshala." She looks at the stick Daniel sent her, filled with his memories, thinks of tossing it out into the snowy forest, imagines it sinking beneath the layers, lost forever, then leaves it next to her laptop, next to *Paloma Rosen* deep inside.

While the pine-slatted tub fills with hot water, Joan drinks her barley tea and eats every last lentil, finds what she's looking for in Kartar's guidebook, and makes notes.

It is odd to be in the bath hours earlier than usual, hours before her writing for the day is finished, but she soaks for a long while, and then dresses in the warm clothes and sturdy boots Martin sent her in the care package.

From her pine closet, she pulls out the backpack she has not used since her trip with Willem to the Pong Wetland. The notes she made from Kartar's guidebook, bottles of water, bags of dried apricots and sunflower seeds, two apples, a set of warm pajamas, extra socks, fresh T-shirt and underwear, toothbrush and toothpaste, face soap, moisturizer, lipstick, a roll of toilet paper, identification, a stack of rupees, Willem's letter to her, and the photograph he took, her notebook and pen, all go in.

It is eight now. There is no time difference between Dharamshala and Udaipur, and she hopes Vita Brodkey will be awake. A single ring, and Vita is saying, "Hello."

"Vita, it's Joan. How are you?"

"Darling, I am simply marvelous. Alive for another day. And like I promised, I am painting away like an old, happy nut. I decided that my idea of painting small watercolors was nonsense, I need huge canvases, ten feet tall, to capture all that I am. Who knows, perhaps I'll paint only a few before my demise, but I have ten of them leaning against the walls in my second guest room. Enough of me, a call this early feels important. So darling, tell me everything."

It would take too long to tell Vita Brodkey everything, but Joan tells Vita her immediate plans, and Vita says, "How wonderful, darling. I knew you would get there, and really, I'm as proud as if you were my own. We need to talk about you coming to Udaipur for a while. Winter is the best time here, the desert heat is gone, just a lovely tropical climate. So different than real winter in Dharamshala. So think about it and call as soon as you're back. Have a marvelous time, and remember, I will not tell you to be safe, safety is for fools, but remember everything, because that's what I'll want to hear."

Joan says, "I will and I will," and then Vita is gone.

She looks at the email to Daniel on her computer screen, her letter attached, hits Send, and there it goes, Daniel's own future flying to him in Washington, DC, from India. He might still be up, it's only going on eleven there, but it won't matter if he reads it, she will be gone.

Joan grabs her backpack, leaves her pine suite behind, finds Kartar already at the low teak reception desk, musky incense lit on the table in the sitting area. "Good morning, Ashby. You are up and out early."

When she sees his bright and open face, she thinks how Kartar is not an uncommon Indian name, just as Lucky Star is not an uncommon name for a diner—she Googled it this morning and found twenty diners and bistros named exactly that—so it is most likely a bizarre coincidence. Still, she considers asking if he lived in DC during his two years in America, and if so, whether Lucky Star is his family's diner, and if it is, whether he worked there on weekends, and if he did, whether he delivered meals to a young man named Daniel Manning, and if he delivered such meals, whether he prophesied about the creativity he felt taking place in Daniel's apartment. She nearly says something, but decides to retain the mystery, to keep close the mystical connections she wholeheartedly believes in these days.

"Kartar, I think I know where I'm going, but I want to be sure. Can you draw me a map to Triund? And then the location of the Rest House, and then from the Rest House to Illaqa?"

"Of course, Ashby," and Kartar pulls out a large unlined pad and begins sketching.

"It's nine kilometers from the center of McLeod Ganj, but only eight from here. You'll take one of the oldest routes used by the Gaddi shepherds of the Chambra and Kangra valleys.

"Now here," he says, writing *KARTAR AND ASHBY* at the bottom of the paper, "is Hotel Gandhi's Paradise."

Then he draws a long line upward and says, "You'll walk up this road, and it turns into a path, but keep going and going until you reach Triund," and he makes an *X* to mark the spot, "from which you will see all of Kangra.

"Now here," and he draws a box past Triund, "this is the Shri Kunal Pathri Devi temple. Make sure you go there.

"Then here," and he draws a house with a chimney, "this is the Rest House.

"And here," he says, drawing another windy path that seems to go uphill gently, "this is Illaqa, where the monks spend the summers in meditation and prayer."

Then he draws a mountain with a mouth, and says, "This is Lahesh Cave, where you'll go deep inside and see the snow-fed waterfall."

She takes his detailed map and folds it up, slides it into the pocket of her down coat. "Thank you for this, Kartar."

"How long will you be gone, Ashby?"

"Two days, maybe three."

Kartar smiles and nods and does not look worried at all by her plans. Perhaps this journey is not as foolhardy as she already thinks it might be, and for that she is glad. She is eager to be above it all, up on Triund, to see the Kangra valley in the snow, the temple, Illaqa, the cave, the waterfall. She did the calculation back in her room: eight kilometers is just under five miles, just five miles uphill to Triund.

"Shall I give Mr. Willem Ackerman any message should he come by again, or phone?" Kartar asks.

"I'll find him as soon as I'm back."

"Very good. Have a wonderful time, Ashby. *Namaste.*"

"*Namaste*, Kartar," and then Joan is out the hotel's front doors, and down the steps, into an exalting cold, snow coating the ground, a floating snowfall falling from above, but no wind at all. The sun's thready light plays hide-and-seek between the clouds.

The climb will be steep, but she has taken so many hikes since her earliest days here that neither the angle nor the distance is of any concern. She is warmly dressed, sweater and jacket and hat and gloves and scarf, her pack a comfortable, easy weight against her spine, still strong and upright.

She thinks of Vita Brodkey making a full circle of her life. She thinks of Camille always returning to this place for a revival of her life force and spirit. She thinks of Ela finding her purpose here, after the life she had expected to live was torn from her. She thinks of how Paloma Rosen would never back away from her destiny, would only march inexorably forward.

Joan starts up the hill in a silence made pure by the delicate white flakes, large and light and lacy, and her own certainty. It takes an hour before the hotel is out of sight, lost somewhere far below, where pastures of flowers will hide beneath the snow until springtime. She inhales the second, minute, hour, day, month, the cold, the hill, the snowflakes on her face, her fate.

Two hours later, there is a looped bend in the road, a brief upward turn that will set her climbing toward the tree line. She can see that the easier grade of the hill will soon give way, turn precipitous. She is all alone, but she has no fear, only hope that she will see the snowbirds Willem Ackerman has mentioned, perhaps even the musk deer, but not the black bears; she hopes they have gone into hibernation. She imagines the rainbows in Illaqa's snow-fed waterfall, wonders how fast its waters run. She's walking and thinking of the way Paloma Rosen might walk, then she's thinking of Paloma Rosen walking slowly from her Wooster Street loft to Chinatown on a hot summer morning, and when Joan sees a huge boulder up ahead, just off the main path, she heads for it, drops her pack, fishes out her notebook and pen. She won't maintain her daily writing schedule on *Paloma Rosen* over the next few days, and she needs to get down exactly what she's seeing in her mind, what she's hearing. She settles down on the boulder, rips out pages from the back of the notebook black with words, turns to a fresh page, and begins to work.

53

It feels like a long walk from home to Chinatown this morning. When she must be clear-headed and sharp, her dreams have left her jumbled. She feels herself buckling down into the concrete, the weight of the steaming summer heat pressing down on her head, though it is still early, and a Saturday, and Chinatown is mostly sleepy and quiet.

Foot after foot, heading downtown, then east, her left knee sticking, her right knee catching, but she's going to make it all the way to Haiyang Best, the best seafood market in Chinatown, the only seafood market she has frequented since landing on the shores of Manhattan.

Her heart is rattling a bit behind her breastbone, and her breath has narrowed to strange wheezes at the back of her throat, but on she marches in her crisp white Converse sneakers, her boy-sized dungarees, a shirt of white cotton eyelet that she likes very much. Dangling from her ears are hammered gold Indian earrings, three tiers of concentric circles like she herself once carved out of pear tree wood, the earrings purchased in Udaipur when she traveled there alone for her fifty-second birthday, and ended up having a lovely affair. She feels fetching today, dressed in something other than her workaday attire, the first time, perhaps, since the winter day she interviewed Theo. Je me sens sexy? she asks herself. Non, she does not exactly feel sexy, well, perhaps there is a soupçon of sexiness still in her bones, in her sculptured face, and this morning, in her queenly bathroom mirror, she felt her old beauty was wearing very well.

And though she may be huffing and puffing, and likely needs both knees replaced, something that will never happen—she will not expire on an operating table—she feels a power today in her soul. That it might have anything to do with Theo's dinner party, she refuses to consider. The phrase "our dinner party," wends around uncomfortably in her head. Her agreement to participate merely a gesture of kindness to someone she cares about in some way or another.

Straight down Wooster until she reaches Grand, and veers to the left. It always is much farther than she imagines, the north-south blocks very long, and several west-east blocks, and now, when she has the fish store in sight, a few more steps and she will be within the cool confines of Haiyang Best, there is a small stumble, not a trip, but she feels the concrete coming at her all of a sudden, and then she is on a chair in Haiyang Best, Young Wong on bended knees, looking up at her.

Her first thought is that he looks nothing like his father Chang or his grandfather Hai, extraordinarily handsome Chinese men she used to flirt with, when both she, and they, were younger. Chang is rarely in the store anymore; he runs the transportation part of the business and is down at the docks, and Hai, when Paloma has seen the old man, he grabs her hand and kisses the back of it, and they exchange brief greetings, for they have known each other in the most basic of ways for half a century. When the old man is in the store, Paloma finds it great fun to watch him hanging out the front door gazing at the young pretty women who walk by, checking out their behinds, sometimes calling out, "You're a beauty," then listening to the titter of those young women's laughs.

But it is Young Wong in the store this morning, which is how Paloma Rosen thinks of him, and with whom she has not developed any kind of relationship. There were times after leaving Haiyang Best, after all that happy flirtation, when she pondered about Chang and Hai on her walk home, but Young Wong, not once has she thought of him when she is again out the door, purchases in hand. When Chang introduced Young Wong to her perhaps a year or two ago, he said, "This is my son, the third generation of Wong men to care for Haiyang Best," and she wondered how the son felt, being the third generation of caretakers, but not droll, or quick with the compliments, and not at all handsome, critical genes lost in the generational transition.

Now, sitting in the red plastic chair, looking at Young Wong on his knees, Paloma has a chance to observe his face up close, to study it under the color of exhaustion, or heat prostration, to use her age for her own purposes, while she catches her breath, and he asks if she is okay, can he get anything for her, does she need medicine of some sort, should he call an ambulance? Long moments pass during which Paloma shakes her head once, twice, three, four times—non, non, non, non—giving her the opportunity to see that Young Wong is not as ugly as she thought, that he has a fascinating sort of beauty, a face Picasso might have painted, all bulging eyes and skewed lips, unlined skin and crystal-clear warm brown eyes. The minutes inure to Young Wong's benefit, for eventually Paloma thinks, But he's beautiful, and how have I not seen this before, when I have come to buy fish? It is a face worth sculpting. He looks as if he might be a few years older than Theo Tesh Park, the physique though, is short and narrow, while Theo is tall and still thin, but shoulder-broad.

"Miss Paloma Rosen," Young Wong says to her, no longer appearing like a Cubist rendition of himself, "Please tell me, what can I do for you?"

"Water first," Paloma Rosen says. "Fish after."

In Haiyang Best, Young Wong—Da Wong—trails after Paloma, one arm outstretched in case he must steady her, the palm of the other crossed over his apron, over his heart underneath, still beating hard from the tough old puo puo's near collapse. She drank down two glasses of cold water and her color returned, her cheeks no longer concave, but slowly reinflating, softly wrinkled silk being pulled taut. He wouldn't mind touching that skin, seeing if he can transfer its texture to paint when Sunday comes and he's free of fish, free of this place. Her blue eagle-eyed stare is back, her mouth the exotic color of the bold fuchsia flower he once tried to paint from a picture off the Internet, but he should not leave her alone for a minute. If she collapses again and dies, it cannot be here in Haiyang Best. And so Da follows behind while she roams his aisles, such majesty in her walk, those blue eyes so smart when she flicks her head in his direction to make sure he is in pursuit, a clicking that he hears coming from her and thinks might be her brain actually working away.

He wonders what she would think if she knew there were times she was the subject of Wong family dinners, Yéyé' Hai and his fùqīn, discussing seriously the nature of a country in which a woman like Miss Paloma Rosen was alone. Despite their cluck-clucking, when he was young, Da heard in their voices respect, affection, pleasure in the way her name rolled oddly on their tongues, their desire to say Miss Paloma Rosen over and over again. When he grew older and still they were talking about her, he realized their tones reflected the intimidation she made each man feel, for they thought her a strong woman, nearly a siren calling to Da's forebears to desire something beyond their own tight world. Of course, neither had moved beyond their tight world, and neither knew much about Miss Rosen at all, except for what they imagined in their own heads, just as he, Da, does not know anything about her. But with her in the shop, the time they just spent together, with worried Da on his knees, those dinners when she was the topic are on his mind, how she was such a luminous curiosity to Yéyé' and Fùqīn.

"That loup de mer, Young Wong," Miss Rosen says, pointing to a huge black sea bass, laid out on ice with his cohorts, its eyes glassy——all-seeing or no-seeing, is what Da wonders perpetually, constantly, day after day.

"It is twenty pounds," Da Wong says. "Cleaned, but not gutted."

"Parfait," says Miss Rosen. "I like to eviscerate myself."

It is only the true chefs who gut their own fish, and sometimes even they instruct Da to have it done for them. Da looks down at the old woman's hands, thick-fingered and resting lightly on top of the glass case, and wonders how well she yields a knife. It does not seem to Da that she has the requisite flexibility or delicate touch to do the job right. But it is what she wants and he knows from the stories told about her at the dinner table that one does not question Miss Rosen.

Da nods at his cousin Bai, who works alongside Da perpetually, constantly, day after day, chattering in Da's ear all manner of naughty things when the shop is empty of customers, naughty things Da can't stop thinking about, unsure if he is interested in them or not, naughty things falling out of Bai's mouth even when Da says, "Bai, despite your name, you are no person of purity." Bai lifts the hefty bass off the ice, begins wrapping it in thick white paper, using too little tape as always, until Da throws him a sharp look, and Bai returns it with a shoulder shrug, then rips an overly long strip through the teeth of the holder.

Without Da being aware, Miss Rosen has moved deeper into the store, to another case, this one open to the air. He hurries after her and slips behind the case she stands before, staring down into the mound of prawns piled high. The tiger shrimp of the sea, is how Da thinks of them. Brown and orange shells, skinny feelers, and those angry black eyes moving around ever so slightly. The air and the ice doing them in.

"When did those arrive?" she wants to know.

"Two hours ago," Da says.

Paloma nods her head. "Ten pounds, merci. And your cod?"

"Follow me," Da says, slipping back into the aisle, gently grasping her elbow, steering her way.

"Très bon," she says, looking at the cod laid out in a perfect, synchronous row. "That display speaks to me, Young Wong, as if the fish were marching forward into battle, or are the stakes of an iridescent picket fence. I'll take eight, petites, s'il vous plaît."

The only customer, Da thinks, to ever notice how he has arranged any fish in any of the twenty cases in the store.

Da nods again at Bai, and says, "Eight, Bai," and then in rapid Mandarin, "Nǐ tīng shuōguò ba?"

Bai says under his breath, "I heard that cousin, I'm not an idiot," and Da shrugs his shoulders.

"Et enfin, anchovies," Miss Rosen says.

Da speaks no French, only fish, and leads her to the case with the anchovies.

"Ten pounds, merci. Eviscerated and descaled."

Bai, following along, is crestfallen, so much work to do on ten pounds of anchovies.

When Bai does not move quickly, Da says to him, "Xiànzài zuò tā, zuò tā kuài, nǐ lǎnduò de hùnhun." *Do it now, and do it fast, you lazy bum.*

"And now, *deux boîtes de caviar*," and Da indicates she should continue down the aisle, to the double-stacked and refrigerated display at the end which showcases Haiyang Best's assortment of roes from different kinds of pregnant fish.

Opened silvered tins front each case. The roe cling to each other, froth over the edges, interesting formations Da always thinks, as if someone has carved those roe into sculptures. The exemplar tins are Da's doing, to allow customers to see the panoply of roe the store sells. "Let them examine the color of the eggs, their size, large, or medium, or small. Let the customers imagine the skin of those eggs cracking easily or sharply between their teeth, the explosion of smokiness or saltiness assailing the senses. Allow them a taste, if they ask," Da had said to Yéyé' and Fùqīn, until Grandfather and Father were convinced, said he could do it his way.

Roe, Da will still eat.

"Ikura, Tobiko, Masago, Kazunoko, or Tarako?" Da asks, mentioning the types most frequently purchased.

"Quelle est la différence?" Miss Rosen asks.

Hearing the word *difference*, even in French, is enough for Da to understand what Miss Rosen wants to know. But he stops for a moment. Usually, he rattles off the ten types of roe they sell, but there is something about Miss Rosen, beyond what his father and grandfather used to say about her, that makes Da throw out his summary speech, want to give her the personal touch.

He opens the case and leans down to the top tray, places a finger next to the Ikura, talks with more volume than he usually would, so she can hear him through the glass—who knows if she might be deaf. "See how big these eggs are. So red-orange. Looking soft to bite into. This is Ikura, big salmon roe.

"But these tins here," he says, pointing to a quartet of display tins all sprung open, the roe making Da think of miraculous clouds hugging one another in the sky, absolutely impossible to touch—how has he not seen this in

all his days working at Haiyang Best? He should be painting tins of opened roe.
His heart is pounding happily from his discovery, but he continues on without
missing a beat.

"*These, Miss Rosen, are varieties of Tobiko, flying fish roe. Teeny-teeny eggs.*
Its untouched color is red-orange, like salmon, but Tobiko is often colored. Squid
ink turns the eggs black. Yuzu turns them nearly yellow."

"*Gorgeous, Young Wong,*" *Miss Rosen says.*

"*And if you look over here,*" *Da says, watching as Paloma follows his finger*
to the other side of the case. "*This is Masago, smelt roe. Do you see how the*
eggs are even smaller than the Tobiko?" *and he is gratified when the old woman*
vigorously nods.

From this vantage point, when she is facing Da through two panes of dis-
play glass, she does not look old at all, just gorgeous and refracted, lit up from
within by a thousand-watt bulb. He rarely sees faces in his daily world that he
would like to paint, but he would like to paint Miss Rosen's. Preferably just her
face and neck, perhaps the hollow of her throat, but the rest of her lost in
blackness, the kind of blackness Diego Velázquez used so well, an icon of Da's
that sometimes, when he feels brave, he tries to copy, with abysmal results. But
Da would try again with Miss Rosen as his subject.

"*And these tins here. This is Kazunoko. Herring roe. See how it is a single*
cohesive mass, as if it is an intact piece of fish? It is not, but it has a firm, rubbery
texture, and its natural color ranges from pink to yellow.

"*And this one is called Tarako. Alaskan pollock roe that people eat salted*
and grilled."

This is the best Da can do, and Miss Rosen, all five feet two inches of her,
stretches back up and says, "*Merci, Young Wong. I have learned so much in such*
a short time. Mais, je crois que le caviar vert est très beau."

Da raises his head over the counter and looks at Miss Rosen.

"*Ah, oui, yes, I think I want the green caviar, like a colony of delicate*
vegetation attached to an undersea rock. The color is so beautiful, so lush."

"*That is one version of our Tobiko, flying fish roe, the eggs quite small, but its coloring, the reason it is green, is because it has been mixed with the Japanese horseradish, wasabi."*

"Oui? Vraiment? I do love sushi and wasabi. So does that mean the caviar is good and spicy? Might knock people out with surprise when they spoon a bit into their mouths. Make them gasp and fall over and die?"

Da twists his lips together. Is Miss Rosen planning on buying his wasabi Tobiko and then adding some kind of poison to it, killing anyone who eats it? If the tin is found in her bin, with Haiyang Best's seal on it, the store, the company, the Wong family, will be in serious trouble. She cannot be saying what she means.

"Yes, it is spicy. The Japanese horseradish will surprise them, and, I guess, it might knock people out if they aren't expecting the bite."

"That is what I want then. Two tins. I want to surprise people with a taste they don't expect. See them flying to the floor."

So Miss Rosen only wants a taste sensation for her guests, Da can appreciate that. He pulls two of the wasabi Tobiko tins from the case and takes them to Bai's workstation.

When Bai has finished gutting and descaling the anchovies, and wrapping and taping and packing the rest of Paloma Rosen's selections, bagging it all in ice, and Paloma has counted out from her small change purse a series of large bills that pay for her expensive order, Da says, "Miss Rosen, I will have someone walk you home, carry the heavy bags for you."

"Not someone," the old woman says. "You, Young Wong. You can walk me home, carry my bags, bring that fish and Tobiko up all of my stairs."

Da sighs and reaches behind for his apron strings.

Haiyang Best is kept iced like a freezer and by four each morning, Da Wong is inside, shivering in the dark, preparing for the new business day, waiting for the deliveries, deliberately not turning on any of the lights, wanting to feel the pain of his life. Quality and assurance, these are the words by which Da lives his quotidian fishy life, able, when asked, to spout the store's history—

blah, blah, here for fifty years, certain to be here for another hundred, blah, blah—having given it so many times to tourists who come around, all low-rent journalistic interest without purpose.

Da is startled by the heat when he steps outside into the morning, with Paloma Rosen's bags of fish looped around his wrists. He eats his lunch and takes his short breaks in the backroom in which it is impossible to warm up, to have a creative thought, or any thought at all. And when Da locks up, always the last to leave, Bai skipping out hours earlier as usual, it is late, nearly midnight, and since the summer began, the sun is always long gone, the rancid heat of the day just barely reduced, day again returned to night.

"Very hot," Da says to Paloma Rosen.

"No different than every single day this month," she says. "Where have you been?"

Always inside the fish market. He has forgotten how the rest of the world lives during a steamy Manhattan summer, the way even in Chinatown people slow down, cease zipping around one another, more decorous about not catching elbows or ankles, the lot of them sagging and damp, sweat beads on foreheads, unsightly circles spreading under armpits, tracking down shirt backs. It is a heat fugue Da is joining, everyone together in some version of hell, and yet he feels freed, unexpected joy and relief spreading through his icy insides, warming his fingers, his face, his toes.

"Look," he says, "the asphalt is bubbling," and Paloma Rosen stops dead on the sidewalk, looks at the street where the potholes, re-tarred again and again, each layer a shiny, stretchy black, are indeed bubbling.

"I have not yet been able to figure out how to make stone appear to bubble like that," she says, a sentence whose meaning Da cannot fathom.

"Young Wong," she says, "do you have a camera on you? Can you take a picture for me?"

Da Wong wonders if she is light-headed again, for it must be obvious to her that he, a fishmonger, hanging onto her fish, is not a photographer on the sly, a camera on a leather strap around his neck.

"I have no camera, Miss Rosen."

"A phone. Do you have a phone? You must have a phone with a camera, all the phones today have such things attached. Even I have a phone that has a camera, but I left it at home."

Da Wong does have a cell phone in his shirt pocket and when he is not sure what to do with the heavy bags in his hands, Paloma shakes her head, and says, "Don't be a dummy, give them to me," and then he is standing over the bubbling tar, taking a picture, and another, and another.

"And one from a little farther away," Paloma calls out.

Da backs up and shoots again and again.

"Now one from directly above, up as close as you can get."

A car is barreling down Grand, and Da watches Paloma Rosen step out into the street and put up a palm, "Arrêtez-toi, idiot," she yells loudly, and there is the screeching of car brakes, the driver leaning out of his window, yelling, "What the hell, lady?"

Da kneels down on the hot, dirty macadam and takes a picture of the stirring tar over the cavity that leads to who knows where, or how far down.

When he and Miss Rosen are back on the sidewalk, the man in the car lays on his horn again as he passes, jabbing his middle finger in their direction as if his finger were a gun and he could shoot them both with a bullet, shoot them dead where they stand.

Paloma returns the bags to Da. "When we get home, I'll give you my email address and you can send them to me."

Da Wong will send her the pictures of the pothole, for what purpose he does not know, but he can use them himself, to try and capture the movement of something prehistoric underneath an old irregular street, try to make it come out right in paint. Miss Rosen has, for the short-term, returned Da to the land of those who are broiling, but living.

They move slowly down Grand Street. Da Wong would not have thought Miss Rosen a window-shopper, but she is dawdling past the store selling Chinese fans, halting in front of the Chinese apothecary, its window stocked with glass canisters filled with teas and medicinal herbs. Inside, along one wall, are hundreds of mahogany drawers all the way up to the ceiling, the Chinese pharmacist busy scooping out leaves, petals, black pellets, weighing, and bagging, and consulting with his patient, a stooped Chinese man holding the hand of a woman who might be his daughter. Young and old are sitting silently on chairs waiting their turns.

"Young Wong, amazing isn't it? There are no labels on any of those drawers and yet he moves with such certainty, such directness, knowing exactly what to retrieve and from where. You have the same directness when you move about in your store."

Da Wong is surprised again by this second compliment, that Miss Rosen would have noticed that he knows his stock intimately. Although he refuses to call himself such, his father insists that it is a great honor to be a third-generation seafood specialist, wishes Da would wear the special white apron Fùqīn had embroidered with the honorific in red. Da will wear only a plain apron, unadorned, does not want to proclaim to his insulated world a title that makes him feel small, that he is not in his right skin, when, to his family, such should make him strong and powerful. He is rebelling these days, eating no fish, has not in more than a year. He may have to sell the fruits of the sea, he may live his life surrounded by their eyeballs, their mottled or rainbow skin, may have to care for them like his children, and clean and devein them, but he does not have to make himself one with them. Now he keeps his own innards free, no more fish sliding down his gullet.

They are nearly past the windows of the Double Crispy Bakery when Miss Rosen stops and says, "Let's go in here."

The bakery is filled with its homemade sweet and savory offerings and ready-made delights. Plastic containers of their good almond cookies are piled high on the counter. Inside the cases are endless trays of tiger-skin cheesecakes, melon-puff pastry cakes, snow skin moon cakes, Macau-style egg tarts, fluffy pumpkin buns, all manner of creamy desserts, then the seaweed buns, the pork floss buns, everything so colorful and ripe, including a tray of desserts *that confuses Da's mind, looking like American hamburgers with some strange pink blob on top, or like ripe breasts with nipples, like he has seen in Bai's dirty magazines, either way he tries to see those particular desserts makes his stomach roll. He looks away fast, finds his eyes taking in all manner of Swiss rolls packed up in tight plastic, orange sponge, and chocolate tapioca, butter sponge, strawberry, peach, mocha, and Da Wong is suddenly ravenous.*

"Almond cookies might be a nice touch," Miss Rosen says, and Da Wong hopes she is talking to herself.

The exchange happens quickly—a bag with eight containers of almond cookies slides up Da Wong's arm, knocking against a bag filled with fish, a piece of Tiger Skin Cheesecake is placed in his mouth, which he opens automatically, like a hungry child, Miss Rosen's curiously thick fingers barely missing his teeth.

He reaches up to hold the cake steady as he bites it in half, fish banging against his cheeks.

"Say nothing," Paloma Rosen says. "My treat. Un petit merci for carrying my goods home."

Da Wong could not speak if he wanted to, his mouth crammed with such sweetness. He could eat everything in the bakery and still not find himself stuffed.

To the woman behind the counter who is handing Miss Rosen her change, Miss Rosen says, "Madame, s'il vous plaît, please also two of those Swiss rolls, strawberry tapioca and orange sponge, and two of those split balls, whatever they may be . . . Oui, oui, the flashy magenta one, and that one, quelle est la couleur? Would you say it is chartreuse?" Da knows Miss Rosen has seen him staring at those pastries.

The counter woman gives Paloma a disgusted look. "We are not fancy here. Only simple colors. Pink, red, yellow, green."

"Then one of the pink ones and one of the green ones. Merci," Paloma says, the tone of her voice not rising a beat, as if the fifty-dollar bill she handed over for the almond cookies and the rest has not been thanked with rudeness. Da

Wong is embarrassed by such treatment. He does not like what he does for a living, but never would he treat a paying customer in such a way.

The woman tallies Paloma's additional bakery goods, extravagantly yanks bill after bill out of the pile of change, hands Paloma a single dollar. "Good day to you," the bakery woman says, and huffs past a red curtain to the back.

Back on the sidewalk, Paloma says, "Some people get up on the wrong side of the bed all of the time. Nothing one can do about that. Ici," she says, and removes the bag of almond cookies from Da Wong's wrist. "I'll carry the pastries home, but they are all for you. Well, not the almond cookies, but the rest."

"It's not necessary, Miss Rosen," Da Wong says, wondering how to lick his fingers clean of the tiger-skin cheesecake without looking gauche, or like a beggar, or knocking himself again in the face with her fish.

"Young Wong, because I am old, I get my way, and as a result, I am in charge of determining what is necessary. D'accord?"

Da stares at her.

"How is it that at my age I find myself all at once consorting with people who speak no French? Somewhere along the line I have made some kind of cosmic mistake. What I said was, 'Okay?' So you and I, Young Wong, are we okay?"

"We are very okay, Miss Rosen."

"Très bien. That means 'very good.' Now, what do we have here?" and Da Wong is catching on. She doesn't expect him to respond to her casual comments. Her casual comments are intended to put him at ease, to feel that a young fishmonger walking a beautiful old lady home with forty pounds of fish on his wrists on a hot August day is nothing unusual. He wonders if his father and grandfather ever provided door-to-door service for customers. He nearly hopes he is breaking new ground here, or shattering some taboo, fraternizing with the clients, doing something father and grandfather might have quite liked to have done for Miss Rosen, providing such personal care which Haiyang Best does not need to do, the way the fish flies out the door, on the backs of people, in their bags, in ice-filled crates shoved through the open doors of vans. There

is a handsome chef with a restaurant in Harlem who comes down twice a week, spends an hour and no more, selecting exactly what he wants. Tight skull, dark-brown skin, dressed in interesting clothes. In winter, he wears brightly colored socks that Da thinks of as Mr. Marcus's happy socks.

As they pass the GoodLuckJade/Crystals store, its jades and crystals jumbled together, Miss Rosen says, "I've often wondered if such things work," and Da Wong thinks of his special crystals, his large piece of deep-green jade, all set out on a clean cloth on his windowsill, how he picks them up one at a time and puts each to his forehead, rubs it between his fingers, feels its warmth, its vibrations, tries to believe completely, and yet nothing ever changes.

He wants to say, "No, they do not work at all," but then he and Miss Rosen are in front of the vegetable market, a great cornucopia spilling onto tables and into bushels. Durian fruits hold a position of importance on their own raised shelf, looking tough and unassailable, the way Da Wong thinks they should look, smelly beasts he abhors and the rest of his family adores, so stinky they must be eaten with a shuttered nose.

Da Wong dislikes them and everything else in the world that appears one way but is really another, except when it comes to his painting, then he likes things to be hidden, known only to him. Or at least he keeps the work itself hidden from others. Sometimes he paints layers and layers and layers, trying to figure out what should happen next and having no idea of which way to go; other times, he knows exactly what he is after. Still, regardless of whether the work comes easy or hard, even when he is alone in his small room with the easel he found tossed away in a Dumpster on Great Jones Street, and the canvases that he buys one by one because they are costly, and his brushes, and paints, his ideas swirling like sparklers in his head, he feels himself avoiding the truths of himself.

Past 精, with its limp yellow chickens hanging from hooks in the window, Chef Uk at the counter mixing up a vat of the day's marinade, its tables empty at this hour, and Lendy Electric, the only place on the street not open until noon.

Cars race down the cobblestone streets as they cross Elizabeth, Mott, Mulberry. The WELCOME TO CHINATOWN sign hanging over the street looks sad to Da Wong, its lights turned off, the letters barely visible in the slanted morning sun. Past narrow Centre Market Street, known, on the flip side, as Baxter, and then Chinatown recedes as they step forward into Little Italy. Da Wong did not to think to ask Miss Rosen where she lives. Despite the weight of the fish and the heat, and his stomach churning from the pastry sugar, now that he is free, he hopes it is a long walk.

When did he last leave the shop, or Chinatown, for that matter? Was it last year, perhaps back in December? He cannot remember. How pathetic that he has no memory of leaving the confines of his world, when such an unusual action should be a firecracker event, the colors of all that exploding gunpowder created by his own people emblazoned on his brain. How hard could it be to remember when he last escaped from a life circumscribed to a single building. He lives over Haiyang Best, on the third floor, and the rest of his family lives two floors above him. Since childhood, he has always felt separate, removed, an outsider among his clan. Even the way his family's names fit each of them, and his does not, tells the story of his life. Yéyé's name, Hai, means coming from the sea, and he started Haiyang Best, Fùqīn's name is Chang, which means thriving, and the store thrived under his guidance, his mǔqīn's name is Lì húa, which means beautiful pear blossom, and his younger sister's name, Jinjing, means gold mirror, both of which fit mother and sister perfectly. Only Da's name does not suit. It means accomplishing, but what he is accomplishing in his life he could not say. Even when da is used as a word, it does not apply to Da. It means big, large, loud, strong, heavy, huge, and he is the opposite, small and quiet, only his heart is big, large, loud, strong, heavy, and huge, and it weighs him down.

Sometimes he thinks he is no different from a lobster caught in a cage under the waves. He has wondered whether the lobsters are aware of their imprisonment, the vast seafloor suddenly out of their reach, if they have a false sense of security, are unclear about what their sudden caged existence means.

He carries no such delusion. He knows he is caged, imprisoned, and with each year that passes, the lock is a little more rusted, until one day it will be impossible to break. Since his twenty-first birthday, five years ago, he has commenced a slow-moving battle with his parents, fought in his quiet way.

Mǔqīn and Fùqīn remain upset about his tendency to keep to himself. Politely extending them all the venerations they are due, he bows to them, and says that as long as he must work in the family business, he must be afforded some privacy. It is a concept that bites at the way he was raised, what his family expects from him. It took a dozen tries to explain to his parents what he was asking of them, the sacrifice he understood they would be making so that he might find some little happiness.

"American ways have altered our once-good boy," his mǔqīn had said in Mandarin.

And Da could not explain that being American had nothing to do with it. After all, how American could he be when he never leaves Chinatown?

He is Da, which is his only explanation. He is not like his parents, or his sister Jinjing, or his cousin Bai, or Bai's younger sisters and brother and parents, who live on the top floor of the Haiyang Best building. Da's and Bai's fathers are brothers, two years apart, but they look so nearly alike they call themselves the Wong twins, arms thrown across each other's shoulders and happy laughter when the two of them are rocking the scotch.

Da does not share the same excitable Wong temperament, their love of being together all hours of the day and night, eating together and working together and watching American movies dubbed in Mandarin they buy from the bootleggers on Canal. In a big mass, they all take part in the Chinese New Year proceedings, eleven Wongs all together, his family of four, Bai's family of six, and Yéyé' Hai.

When Da realized he would have to take what he wanted, that his parents would not simply give in, he started showing up for dinner only on Sunday nights, and he endures so much grumbling and mumbling and declarations that Da must not really be a Wong when he enters his family's home. Always he shakes his head, says, "What you are saying is not true. I am a Wong through and through," though really he would give anything not to be. All through those dinners, all the reminders that Da is the eldest Wong son of the eldest Wong brother, the only son in this wing of the Wong family, and he has obligations.

"In not too long," his father says, "Haiyang Best will be yours to run on behalf of us all. Running it until your own son has come of age to take over from you." It is, to Da, an intolerable jail sentence.

Da's sister smiles when his parents discuss his failings, as if he were not at the table hearing it all. Seven years younger than Da, Jinjing is as Americanized as a nineteen-year-old Chinese girl can be who lives at home and is not allowed to date. Bright and reflective, a perfect embodiment of her name, pleased to have all the parental attention, saying that she will take over from Da, run Haiyang Best if he does not want to, pinching Da under the table whenever she puts herself forth as a better heir, a painful twist to his upper thigh that he cannot decipher, whether it means she is kidding or not.

He would step aside happily if his parents allowed Jinjing to take his place, if he could go off to a place like Paris, live in a small room like his own, but higher up, an artist's garret. Paint and parks and pretty people, maybe then he would uncover himself. But Jinjing will never run Haiyang Best. She is a daughter first of all, and second-born, and their parents have other plans in mind for his sister.

His thoughts have catapulted him far away, and he returns to the sunny sidewalk, walking next to Miss Rosen, whose step is suddenly springing. She has such a nice voice, Da thinks, deep and musical, with that French lilt to her words, and she is saying, "I'm going to salt-roast the sea bass I purchased from you, Young Wong. A bed of Kosher salt in the pan, then after I have cleaned the fish, I shall stuff it with Herbs de Provence—" and Da decides to join the conversation. Already it is the most interesting thing he has heard in a long while.

"How do you prepare such herbs?" he asks.

"Très facile. Rosemary, fennel seed, savory, thyme, basil, marjoram, pars-ley, oregano, tarragon, bay leaves, and my own dried lavender flowers. All stuffed right up in there. Then I make the salt crust to seal in the moisture and gently steam the fish in its own juices. A plaster of two egg whites for every cup of Kosher salt. Some people use only water, which is ridiculous. It is the egg whites that bind the salt most effectively, like making un papier mâché, as children do in school. The crust becomes solid when baked, sealing in la loup de mer entièrement."

"That sounds like it would be enjoyable to make," Da says, thinking of his hands in such a mixture, up to his wrists, even if the goal was a coating for hateful fish.

At Lafayette, Paloma makes a right and Da follows suit.

"Oui. Très délicieux. It is very impressive and looks very complicated, mais, un, deux, trois, easy as pie."

"What will you do with the other fish?" Da asks.

"With the cod, a pâté. Your fine anchovies marinated. Your spicy green flying fish roe served with crunchy potato latkes made from scratch. So much more, but we can talk recipes another day."

He likes that she has referred to them having another day together, and follows her marching up wide Lafayette until it narrows, comes to a halt at Spring Street.

"So, Young Wong, while we're waiting to cross, tell me one true thing about yourself. Anything at all. But preferably something you don't tell most people."

He is unused to anyone inquiring about his interior life, but still he can answer immediately. *"I would be less stoic,"* he says, and when he releases that hidden assertion into the thick hot air, the queerest feeling comes over him, a coolness from within, instantly lowering the temperature of his overheated, sweating body. His heavy heart weighing a few ounces lighter.

Cars trying to beat the changing light screech to a stop halfway into the crosswalk. Paloma says, *"Très intéressant. S'il vous plaît expliquer. Explain in more detail, if you would."*

He waits until they have reached the other side, and then looks down at the top of Miss Rosen's white head, just as she looks up. For the first time since she arrived at Haiyang Best, he allows her eyes to capture his.

"I am exhausted from living a life that makes me want to complain day and night, and saying so very little about it. I am locked up inside. There is much I want to do, but I need to escape first, find my way, find the place that I belong."

When she nods slowly, thoughtfully, Da is filled with hope that she might have the answer he needs.

"What are you doing at eight tonight, Young Wong?"

"Selling fish. We do not close until ten."

She begins walking again, and he keeps pace.

"Can someone replace you? That other one, the stingy hoarder of tape, the one scowling over my anchovies?"

"My cousin Bai? I cannot trust him to close up properly."

"You feel locked up inside, so maybe this is the exact step you must take, to walk out the door."

Will he free himself by simply having Bai lock up the store? He ponders as they continue down Spring, crossing Crosby, Broadway, Mercer, Green, until she makes a quick left onto Wooster and continues to the middle of the block.

"We are home," Paloma Rosen says, standing in front of a great steel door flanked on either side by an eight-table coffee place and a florist.

"Miss Rosen, I've been thinking over your advice, and I don't understand."

"You will, Young Wong. You are to have your cousin lock up tonight because you are invited to a dinner party. Here, at my home. I might as well have one guest of my own and I have chosen you. Now, let's go, up the stairs. There's someone I'd like you to meet. I think you might have much in common."

Joan does not know where Da Wong has come from. She did not expect to find a young Chinese fishmonger who yearns to be a painter in *Paloma Rosen*, but he exists now, along with his dirty-minded cousin,

Bai, and the history of the fish market she has named Haiyang Best. But she saw Paloma Rosen on a steamy summer morning on an expedition for the procurement of seafood, shopping for the ingredients of a fine meal she has no interest in preparing.

She is, as Joan thought she might be, a sensational chef. She cadged Paloma's recipes from dishes Martin experimented with when he took up cooking as one of his new interests, preparing dinners for the two of them from the start of the year until she escaped from Rhome.

Joan thinks how Paloma's unwilling need to do right by Theo Tesh Park brings into her extravagant force field another young man who desperately desires clarity in his life, but does not yet know it is Paloma he requires. And Paloma Rosen, becoming a reluctant surrogate mother to Theo Tesh Park, will become more than a mentor to Da Wong, another mother of sorts, the one who will show him how to break free and discover his own new horizon. And Da Wong will see his future opening up when, after climbing the six double flights of stairs, he steps into Paloma's loft, and then is led down the fifty steps to her studio, to see the new sculpture she has only begun carving. Within the untouched grain of the butternut wood, Da will instantly see the mother and child that Paloma sees, and Da will believe himself that child, Paloma the maternal, sheltering being, though Paloma imagines it herself and Theo. Da will look around the studio and feel he is home, the way Theo feels in Paloma's presence. And Da can imagine painting his canvases in a far corner, out of the way, nearly out of sight. *If only*—he will think.

Joan reads over all she has written and wonders what will happen between Theo and Da—a friendship, a brotherhood of sorts, a love relationship, a fight for supremacy in the affections of Paloma Rosen? She's not sure, but their journeys will be utterly altered by the old artist who will help them find a place in their souls where they will always be home.

And Paloma Rosen? Her life too will alter in countless ways when she fully opens her heart to Theo Tesh Park and Da Wong, a massive renaissance in this late stage of her life that she never intended, desired, or imagined, but will learn to embrace.

She understands now why she had been researching Mandarin

words and rude sentences, Chinese names and their meanings, types of fish and caviars and Chinese desserts, the Chinese symbol for the restaurant with the scrawny yellow chickens hanging in the window, the way the streets are laid out down there, her own recollections of wandering through Chinatown when she was a young writer and done for the day working on the stories in *Other Small Spaces* and *Fictional Family Life*, making notes of everything in the back of the notebook. It had made no sense to her over the last week in her pine suite, but it's so obvious now.

There was always going to be a Da Wong. Just like there was always going be a Theo Tesh Park, and a Paloma Rosen. And a new Joan Ashby, freed from her story that had contained the tragedy she knew it required—the arc of calamity and catastrophe and misfortune and heartbreak. Her own Devata here in Dharamshala resurrecting her from the past, the whole of it making her so much more than she ever anticipated.

She looks at her watch, two hours have disappeared in a heartbeat, and suddenly she is freezing, and practically soldered to the boulder, and her body creaks when she stands, but then she's jumping up and down in the snow, warming up her limbs, getting the blood flowing, relieved when she can wriggle her toes.

She slips her notebook and pen into her pack, slides the pack onto her shoulders, and she is climbing again, up and up and up, past thick deodars and oak trees, their branches woven together, intricately entwined from years of buffeting by strong winds.

The heavens have the snow on a switch, heavy snowfall that tapers off, then begins again, over and over and over. She climbs for another hour, then a second, then a third, wondering when she'll reach the top, telling herself to be patient, that she's on the right path, will arrive soon enough. At last only a few gentle flakes are falling, and then the snow ceases entirely.

She pushes herself up the steepest slope yet, seven hours away from Hotel Gandhi's Paradise, drops her pack to the ground, and stares out. Kartar and his guidebook were right about Triund Hill.

She is at the peak, surrounded by majestic, spellbinding views, the expansive Kangra valley below, all those layered houses in the villages, and the vast energy running through the atmosphere, caused by the massive Dhauladhars, hits her like lightning. This is what it feels like to be home in the world.

She inhales deeply. She has shed all constraints and expectations, and she knows, as hard as it was, she did the right thing with Daniel. If some form of motherhood is part of every woman's story, she has given one she birthed and grew from scratch a chance to find his way back. The decision she made wasn't for her or for Daniel, not really or not only, but for those women who desired children and failed, for those who lost children to deaths nearly impossible to withstand, for those who tried their best and couldn't make stick all the good lessons, for those caring for the damaged children who belong to others, and for those mothers and children who are lost to one another, left alone, and starving for love, wishing for the sweet snap that might make everything all right again. It was within her power to do right, and she did. The rest is up to Daniel.

Meanwhile, she has *Paloma Rosen* to complete, and writing students to teach, and a son whose accomplishments with Good Manning she would like to see, perhaps be a part of, and Amari to get to know, and she wants to meditate again with Camille and Ela in the Dalai Lama's courtyard, and she wants the three of them to run naked many more times into Dal Lake, into all the sacred lakes in Dharamshala, into all the sacred lakes in the whole of the Kangra valley.

She thought she needed clarifying golden words straight from the Dalai Lama's mouth, she thought she was waiting for him to respond to one of her letters, but the answers she has been seeking, she has discovered them herself. She has a marriage to end, a Dharamshala cottage to find now that Hotel Gandhi's Paradise has served its high purpose, a home where she can live and write, a potential love to explore.

Snow begins sifting down, but a thin ray of sunshine has escaped, lighting up the clouds above and the valley below in waves of soft molten gold, pewter, and crystal. It's growing late and a little colder, and she should make her way to the Rest House. She pulls out Kartar's map, but, of course, it's not drawn to scale, and she isn't sure if the place she will stay for the night might be right around the next stand of trees, or much farther than that, and then she hears, on the breeze that has suddenly sprung up, "Joan Ashby, Joan Ashby," and in the distance, beyond the top of Triund Hill, is Willem Ackerman, waving his arms, pinwheeling the snow.

"Kartar called me," he yells out, running toward her, covering the distance between them rapidly, growing larger with each bounding leap.

He looks wonderful to her, grizzled and handsome and fully at home in these surroundings.

"What are you doing here?" she asks, when he reaches her.

"Waiting for you."

"But I'm on a pilgrimage."

"I know. Kartar thought you might be. But why not let someone walk with you, beside you?"

"I don't know. I thought a pilgrimage was meant to be done alone."

"Well, you're wrong. You don't need to do it alone. But what took you so long? I expected you hours ago."

The snow is a curtain dropping from the heavens, falling down all around them, huge flakes dancing in the narrowing space between them, and Willem is reaching out his hand to take hers, but before she holds out her own, before she takes the next step forward, Joan says, "There are so many lost souls in the world, and I had to stop for a while, to write about another lost boy who is about to be found, saved by a woman who never imagined herself a mother."

LITERATURE MAGAZINE
Fall Issue

(RE)INTRODUCING JOAN ASHBY

Although Joan Ashby declined to discuss with us her twenty-eight-year absence from the world of literature, she is breaking her lengthy silence in a major way.

Working from a cottage in an Indian valley beneath the Himalayas, she has embarked on the next act of her writing life. Ashby's long-awaited first novel, *Paloma Rosen*, will be released next year in January. Her second novel, *Words of New Beginnings*, will follow in late December. Two novels in a single year from this exceptional writer reclaiming her voice.

Thus, this is the perfect time for those unfamiliar with her work to read her collections, and for those who are already familiar to read her again. Then brace yourselves, as we at *Literature Magazine* are bracing ourselves, for what will come.

Acknowledgments

Joan Ashby might not thank anyone, but with heartfelt gratitude I thank my wonderful connector, Pam Bernstein Friedman, my stellar agent, Erica Spellman Silverman, and my terrific editor and publisher, Amy Einhorn.

Deepest thanks also to:

Everyone at Flatiron Books, especially associate editor Caroline Bleeke and vice president/director of sub-rights Kerry Nordling;

And at The Borough Press, Harper Collins UK, which acquired the first foreign rights to this book, especially Suzie Dooré; publishing director; Kate Elton, publisher; and Charlotte Cray, associate editor.

And to:

Sherri Ziff, great friend and best critical reader, willing to read everything, wanting to read anything.

Atienne Benitez DeConcillis and Ginger Buccino Mahon, whose friendships mean so much to me.

Michael Stewart, for being the good man that you are, and the dearest of friends.

David Smith, for all that we share in our strong and generous friendship.

Tikka Yashvir Chand, a lovely and kind man, who informed one of the characters.

Dr. D. P. Singh, for the Hindi translations.

James Lloyd Davis and MaryAnne Kolton, early and enthusiastic readers, so generous of heart, time, and spirit.

And to:

Herbert and Annette Wolas, all-around fantastic parents, loving, supportive, and fearless, who have always said, "We can handle whatever you write."

My sisters, Collette and Claudine, and their families, the Rasmussens and the Shivas, who have happily followed my writing life.

Eli and Ava, my bonus children, thank you for being in my life and allowing me to be in yours.

David and Anita Dickes, my FIL and MIL, who cheer me on.

Ming Wolas, Pearl Wolas, and Henry Wolas Dickes, who spent and spend much time sitting quietly while I work, watching the sentences come and go.

And to:

Michael Dickes, my brilliant husband, who illuminates all that he creates, makes his own words sing, his own images fly, who adores nearly all of the words that I write. A short story brought us together, and how lucky we are that those particular words spelled true love. NC, NL, ND, ND.

And to every bookseller and every reader of this book, my most enormous thanks to you.

Recommend

The
Resurrection
of
Joan Ashby

for your next book club!

Reading Group Guide available at:
www.readinggroupgold.com